# PROLOGUE

All but two were gone. The plush green canopy of summer had long since succumbed to the shorter days and the cold, ravaging winds of December. Now there were just two red leaves clinging to the young isolated maples, which grasped for light and life against the high shade of the pine grove. It was these same pines that would carry death to the young, unguarded woodland. The leaves, the trees, the creatures, the community of the forest, even the grove itself, would falter and fail against the rush of the implacable foe. Fire had come to take them all.

The two leaves played upon a growing breeze as distant flames inhaled the clean breath of the wilderness. They had danced before on many a wind, and high on their branch, they would dance just once again. They had not known fire, only the peace and beauty of creation. And now it was upon them.

At first the burn moved as a thin bright line inching slowly across the forest floor. The leaves, still damp from the morning's mist, matted the ground and smoldered before igniting. Their smoke moved ahead of the flame as both crept slowly up the ridge toward the grove. In their wake, a pristine wood, once warmed by autumn's color, now lay wasted and cold in the black monotones of a charred earth and the singed bases of the trees.

Then the fire quickened as it pressed itself into a dry bed of needles. Fueled by the volatility of resins, fed by unceasing gusts of air, it loosed new fury upon the hapless pines. It leapt from root to crown, from limb to limb, from tree to tree, until all that was once ever green was left dark and lifeless. The trees dissolved in the hot, swirling light, exploding almost instantaneously, one behind the other.

The leaves now played on a different wind, on the upward drafts of a heated thermal. They jumped and bent with each spike of the approaching flame, barely dodging the touch of fire. When the flame withdrew, they pulled against the tether of their stalks and then rose again to avoid the surging blaze.

It was a moment of time before one leaf broke free and lifted skyward, only to meet the glowing ash, then burn. The second dipped against the flame and was gone. So it was for every living thing.

The young Shawnee stood in disbelief as the wind suddenly shifted. He had set the fire as he was told by his elders.

"Burn the leaves and thickets that we might move the buffalo and elk toward our winter camp. The spring will bring back the young shoots and tall grass for more to graze next year."

And so he did. With his torch of gathered pine knots, he spread a line of fire a thousand yards across the width of the long valley. The fire would move along the banks of the narrow stream, riding the soft wind at its back. It would not want to climb the steep hills with their rocky cliffs and talus. Neither would the herds climb to seek other meadows. They would move with the stream. They would stay with the sweet water and thick grasses until the flames bid them run.

Then, where the stream met the great river, the buffalo, the elk, the deer and all the beasts of the valley would cross into the waiting spears of his hungry people. His family would not know the cruelty of winter this year, for he was giving them life with his fire, which would race until it tired at the edge of the waters. It was the perfect plan, except in this world where the Shawnee lived with the whims of nature and where nature had contempt for the plans of man.

Flames eased across gentle hillocks, urged by a slow, unbroken breeze, and small herds scattered before a low blaze that steadily swept the vale. But as the mid-day sun warmed the land, the wind revealed its betrayal. With sudden ferocity, it turned into the faces

# When Green Leaves Fall

Jack A. Robey

outskirts press

When Green Leaves Fall

v3.0

This is a work of fiction. Names, characters, businesses, places, events, locales, and incidents are either the products of the author's imagination or used in a fictitious manner. Any resemblance to actual persons, living or dead, or actual events is purely coincidental.

The opinions expressed in this manuscript are solely the opinions of the author and do not represent the opinions or thoughts of the publisher. The author has represented and warranted full ownership and/or legal right to publish all the materials in this book.



Outskirts Press, Inc.
http://www.outskirtspress.com

ISBN: 978-1-9772-0704-3



PRINTED IN THE UNITED STATES OF AMERICA

*For Diane*
*and in Memory of*
*Bill and Juanita Robey*

of the young Shawnee and his kindled fire and threw them both toward the fortified walls of the mountain.

The youth moved quickly up the hill and into a shaded wood, where a thickening haze now hugged the ground. The swiftness of his feet whirled the smoke up and away behind him, but despite his speed, he could not be free of it. Tree after tree, hill after hill, he pushed through the forest ever upwards with a fading hope that he might flank the fire before it trapped him against the distant seam of rocks.

The conflagration found momentum on the steep sides of the ridge, and threatened to overtake the wary young warrior. He knew well the danger. He could hear the snapping of a distant blaze. He could almost feel the warmth of its light. There was one escape, only one diminutive chance for survival. He must race the fire up the mountain through the pine grove, ascend the crags and hide in the shallow pools of the rocky dome. One chance...race the fire through the pine grove.

He ran. The Shawnee ran with the strong legs of youth and the fearful mind of a child. He had little time, though the blaze was not yet upon him. The mountain was steep, and he would lose precious minutes sliding among the leaves and stones. He did not know a way through the crag and would need every moment, every measure of strength and energy to scale the steep cliff.

No man could outrun the fire once it touched the pines, so his life was wagered against his speed through the open hardwood forest. He must quickly make time. He must clear the pines before the fire reached the edge of the grove. There, it would rage into the high crowns of the trees with such intensity that stone would seem to melt beneath his feet. The air would give no sustenance to his body, and huge incendiary balls of flame would rain upon the mountaintop far ahead of his approach. The consequence of failure was death, slow and torturous, and the utter horror of it impelled him to press far beyond his human limitation. He understood. The savage force would surely yield merciless destruction to whatever dared defy it and to any who might flee its terror. Nature intended no exceptions. He ran. He ran.

The Shawnee was not afraid to die. He was a warrior, a hunter, a survivor of a most primitive way. He had faced death on many occasions and was assured of his place in the hereafter. But death? Not by fire, not now. He had reason to live.

He passed almost effortlessly through the oaks and poplars and chestnuts of the lower forest. The ground was firm and the grade moderate. He was used to running long distances, especially in the spring when men conducted raids against their enemies to the north. The sky above him remained clear and for a brief moment, he forgot the menace that was crackling at his heels. He paused at a brook and pressed his face to the water, sipping and splashing to dampen his long black hair and naked chest.

As he turned to look back into the valley, he saw new signs of the smoke that moved in advance of the fire. He tried to leap the brook, but fell on the slippery rocks. He tried to rise, only to fall again in the soft mud of the bank. It was a nightmare come alive, as his attempts to move were thwarted by the simplest of obstacles. Finally, he gathered himself and was again vaulting toward the pine grove.

The Shawnee found no relief. Saplings choked his way through an endless thicket of small trunks and needles. Even his eyes could not penetrate the dense pine barrier, but his legs nevertheless powered forward into the grabbing, gouging web of limbs. The smoke was now heavy and his lungs nearly burst for the want of air. He gave little notice to the throbbing ache in his legs and feet or to the burn of his sweat as it coated the wounds of a hundred briars and jutting branches. His flesh was torn, his spirit faltering, but he ran.

It was not long before he heard the deafening quake of the canopy fire. The pines were ablaze. Fifty yards...He would be clear. Twenty-five yards...He could not breathe. Ten yards...The heat blistered the skin of his back.

Strange though, his mind began to give comfort from the pain. His movement was steady and his thoughts were elsewhere. What would become of his family or of the beautiful child he was to marry in the spring? He pictured them, and then, only her. He saw her dark eyes and shining black hair. He remembered her as they would chase through the meadow. She was agile, graceful. He thought of her laughter, her tears, the softness of her sun-browned skin. He thought of the children they would have, of the days growing old with her, of his caring for her and her love for him. He could not die. He could not burn. He must find his way through the crag.

With the fire closing in, he had lost his opportunity to climb the wall of rock before him. He had no time to think, but only to react using his training as a hunter. He veered to the right along the base of the cliff and sprinted with his final burst of power along a well-worn deer trail. Both the trail and the Shawnee warrior disappeared among the boulders that climbed to the dome above.

He had nothing left. The flames of the crown fire were carried by ash over the precipice and began to ignite the thin grasses of an upland field. He desperately crawled across the fiery grounds toward the pools that lay as mere depressions in the granite bedrock. The rainwater trapped within could save him. The massive dome of rock would not burn.

The Shawnee tried to stand to continue his race to the safety of the stone. But his legs failed him and he fell back to the ground in despair. He could no longer sweat against the sweltering heat and he could not cry for his lost future. The running and the fire had siphoned the last of the water from his limp body.

Suddenly, he could feel the hard, cool surface of rock beneath him, and through his stinging eyes, he could make out the silhouette of an oak tree, a massive white oak that stood defiant against the daunting smoke and flame. And there were others beyond, arboreal giants rising up from the lee of the mountain, trees with the girth of a chieftain's lodge and with immense, ungainly limbs grasping at the graying sky. There, by the oak, would be the pools, and there, in the distant shadow of the big and towering timbers, a healing brook might flow.

But he lay still upon the rock and was now blind to all, except the memory of a Shawnee girl.

---

# CHAPTER 1

It was hot, uncommonly hot. A fierce sun broke upon the morning, and by midday, even the shadows had wilted. Those who could now sought their usual shelter, only to find false refuge. Porch rockers and paper fans, shady groves and sweet spring water, even damp towels cooled with the melting remnants of block ice proved unavailing. It was simply too hot, much too hot for remedy.

Morgan Darrow had all but conceded that point when he found some measure of relief in the narrow gorge just south of town. A low stream lapped the base of a long curving cliff, while the dirt lane he was travelling and adjacent train tracks crowded the steep rail cut on the opposing side. The natural effect of such a canyon was, of course, wind. Air pressed through the gap with a surging velocity, lifting dust devils from the road and tossing dry leaves into the stream. Warm as it was, the breeze still whisked the sweat from his neck and face, and he was grateful.

Morgan looked to the sun with disbelief and to the high ridge beside him. Far above the gorge, a second wall of cliffs jutted beyond the tree tops. It was baffling why he had never before noticed the feature, especially being so close to home. In the heat that enveloped him, he thought about the Shawnee warrior who once raced to such a precipice with fire at his feet and smoke in his lungs. Whether true or not, the old tale had lingered in these mountains, and every boy grew up scanning the crests and wondering if this crag or that bluff just might be the place, known by tradition as the Shawnee Scarp. Someday, when the weather was again merciful, he might climb to find the answer. Though, for now, it seemed a most unlikely quest.

Morgan heard the gurgles and could almost smell the purity of the brook. It was difficult to resist the refreshing cool that hovered over the gentle flow, and as he neared the water's edge, he gladly acquiesced. He loosed the knots that bound his boots, rolled off his socks and hurriedly plunged his legs shin deep onto the cold, sandy bottom. His toes curled, and he sighed with a sudden sense of deliverance.

An unexpected drought had settled on the hills and threatened to steal the last days of an otherwise perfect spring. The stream, as usual, was an early casualty. It ran shallow, and the once steady roar of rushing water was now reduced to a quiet burble. But there was enough water to give some movement to the brook, and the mere sound of it soothed Morgan like a lullaby. He stretched back on the leafy bank, his feet still in the stream, and he listened to that quiet song of nature until his mind was adrift in the flow.

There must have been dreams in the short peace that followed, but if so, they were forever lost to a startling clap and the subsequent explosion of droplets that pelted the boy and 20 feet of the ground around him. Morgan reeled from the splash just in time to glimpse a second boulder plummeting through the air. It hit flat against the surface of the brook and after soaking its intended target, settled harmlessly on the murky bottom. Yanking his bare feet from the water, Morgan gasped and shook off the cold spray that now dripped from his face and shirt.

"Hey there! Seems to me you're all wet," cried a familiar voice.

Morgan turned to find Dewey Baughman standing over him, no shirt, no shoes, his trousers rolled above his knees. The skin under his left eye was purple and puffy. His nose was disfigured and swollen. With the back of one hand, he unconsciously dabbed at a flux of sniffles, while with the front of the other, he wiped the glistening sheet of perspiration from his forehead.

Unkempt and uncomfortable, Dewey was more mired in misery than even he would confide. The dust from a long walk up the road collected on his belly, brow and cheeks, and as the sweat moved down his body, it left white tell-tale lines against his skin. He was big for a boy of 17, and big men, regardless of their age, were not meant to endure such weather.

Morgan responded rather tersely, "I could have done without the shock. A simple 'hello' would have sufficed, don't you think? Why don't you grow up?"

"To tell ya the truth, such a notion never crossed my mind," Dewey answered, completed unaffected by Morgan's tone. "What's to be gained by growin' up?"

"Well, Dewey, if you haven't figured that answer by now, I reckon there's no chance of me convincing you to change your ways." Morgan pointed to the broken nose and black eye. "Though, by looking at you, it seems like others have tried. How did that happen?"

"A little scuffle at the pool hall."

"The pool hall? I thought you weren't allowed in there."

"Some days I am, some days I ain't. It depends on whether or not they're servin' them damn wood hicks."

"Well, now you know why you should stay out of the place. There's a lot of trouble in that part of town, especially when the crews come off the mountain. Did you win your fight?"

"Some fight. This big fella pushes a little fella, and the little fella hauls off and punches me."

Morgan leaned over to inspect the eye. "He landed a good one, I'd say. Did you hit him back?"

"Nope. With my face throbbin' so and me feelin' all that spinnin' and blur, I didn't think much on gettin' even. I just hauled ass out of there."

"Dewey, as long as we've been friends, I've never known you to run away from a battle. Next time, maybe you should. I don't recall you ever having won one."

"Don't tell your Ma 'bout this, Morgan. Ya know how she hates fightin'. I wouldn't want her thinkin' poorly of me."

"Sure, whatever you say, but good luck hiding that shiner. It's going to last awhile."

Dewey fingered the recent distortions of his face. "Does it look that bad?"

"Pretty bad."

"Damn," he said. "I'll never hear the end of this one." His eyes showed genuine concern, but only for a moment when he stepped from the shadows into the broiling rays of the sun. "Lordy, it's hot out here!" he whined, moving the conversation to something more relevant. "I've damn near stripped down to nothin' and I still can't cool off. I swear it's 110 degrees even in the shade."

Morgan laughed unsympathetically. "It feels a bit more tolerable after people sneak up and soak you while you're napping. Thanks a lot, by the way."

"Don't mention it." Dewey waded into the brook. "Oooo...that is nice. Yes, sir...real, real nice! Jesus, Morgan, in all your days, can ya recollect a more deplorable run of the temperature? I've been cookin' out here for hours, and I swear this sun ain't gonna quit workin' on us until we're all chicken fried up and sweatin' out gravy. Oh, yeah, I'm really likin' this water. Too bad it ain't deeper."

Dewey watched with satisfaction as his friend was forced to use an already damp shirt to dry his face. "I nailed ya but good this time. You're wetter than trout spit. Hell no, I ain't gonna grow up! And just what would ya do if I did? There's no fun without a few shenanigans. Your life has too little excitement as it is."

Morgan wanted to ignore the barb. He knew that Dewey was anticipating his response, and he struggled to withhold comment in the spirit of their lifelong competition of wits. Despite his intial reaction, he was neither surprised nor annoyed by the sudden intrusion to his privacy. In fact, he rather enjoyed the refreshing effects of the water and was certainly grateful for the companionship. That being said, he knew better than to acknowledge such antics or be baited into reprisals. Dewey simply enjoyed a good war of words and pranks too much to ever lose one, and Morgan's only true means to a victory was in disregarding the enemy altogether.

"What's that? The cat's got your tongue? Come on, Morgan, ya gotta say somethin' back at me. Your mind is burnin' with a fiery retort. I just know it. I can smell the smoke."

Dewey prodded, but Morgan resisted, at least until that moment when the smothering heat and the incessant noise of the goading combined to shatter his will. At that point, he had lost the battle.

"Dewey Baughman, you can scare the peace from a Sunday morning prayer! Did you know that? Why do I bother with someone so intent on driving me to insanity? To you, the pleasures of sin are but blessings from God. You curse and complain and connive, and still, no one has the heart to condemn you. No one, except me, that is...me, probably your only real friend. I just don't get it. Frankly speaking, I don't have the slightest idea on what it takes to bridle the devil that's in you, and that fact doesn't bode well for your future."

Dewey grinned as he offered his rebuttal, "Devil, huh. Hey, I'm not the only one who sleeps durin' them prayers."

Morgan scowled, "Just what in the world are you talking about now?"

"Call it what ya will, but that preacher goes on and on and on with his prayin'. I'll give ya odds that half the congregation dozes off every Sunday. I just happened to be the only one that dropped a hymnal on Mrs. Barrett's toes. Frankly, if the woman hadn't screamed, people would've paid me no mind at all, and the prayer would've gone on another ten or 15 minutes. I think I did folks a kindly favor, and yes, now that ya mention it, I do feel right good 'bout it. Christ, it is...so hot...out here!"

Morgan was astounded. He asked again, "What are you talking about?"

"Church, that's what! Beatrice Barrett and our long-winded parson. You know."

"Yeah, I know. I forgot all about your escapades in church last week. Believe me, I now regret saying anything."

"Then, I reckon I'll accept your apology," Dewey said smugly.

"My apology! Who started all this nonsense? Who got who wet?" Morgan shook his head in disbelief at Dewey's customary twist of reality. There was no point in saying more.

Dewey had always been Morgan's best friend. He had a habit of showing up when he was not needed and most of the time when he was. He would talk Morgan's ear off, curse with the devil and complain like a caged, hungry bear. Still, his heart was warm and his way, despite a generous amount of imperfection, was gentle and easy to abide.

"Ya gotta agree, that was one damn fine splash. I angled it right into ya.... not an easy throw from where I was standin'," boasted Dewey.

"Yeah, real fine."

The boys eventually settled on the bank of the stream, their feet dangling in the cool, wet shallows. From time to time, they would reach down with cupped hands to taste of the brook or rinse their faces of the gathering beads of sweat. There were no words between them, just similar thoughts about their simple life in the mountains, about the future and where the fates would lead them. Such were the moments that made them brothers. Even at such a young untested age, they were men enough to know that the quiet understanding between them was always the true cord that had thus far bound them together.

"What a life," muttered Dewey, feeling the heat finally dissipating from his body.

"Yes, it has its moments, and this sure seems to be one of them," Morgan agreed. He was again almost to the point of dozing. "What have you been thinking about?"

"I don't know. Not much. Quite a lot. I don't know. My mind keeps jumpin' from one thing to another. Mostly, I'm just lovin' this cool feelin' around my toes. Why do ya ask? Ya got somethin' on your mind?"

"I think I'm bored. Don't you ever get bored?"

"Well, we can find somethin' else to do, if ya want."

"No, I mean I'm bored with everything. I'm not unhappy, mind you, but I want more out of this life and don't have a clue what it is or where to find it. You know what I mean."

"No, not really."

Understanding Dewey as he did, Morgan was not particularly surprised by the response. "We're different in that way. There's no fire anymore, and I've been thinking I need to rekindle one before too long. A home in the hills is not the place for everyone, I suppose, and I'm considering moving on once school is done."

"That's a hell of a thing to say. You love these mountains."

"And that's the whole problem. I don't want to go, but..."

"There's no 'but'. It's just the heat talkin'. This weather can cook a man's brains."

Morgan knew that Dewey Baughman would never leave the small world he had always known. He would remain content with whatever the people and nature around him chose to share. He would feel little anticipation and even less disappointment so nestled in the shadows of the Alleghenies, and for him, the path to happiness was just a short walk around a very familiar corner. Morgan envied him that. His own trail was much more obscure.

"Life isn't as simple as you try to make it out, Dewey. Sooner or later, you're going to face some tough decisions, just like me."

"Yeah, but I ain't gonna worry 'bout 'em just like you. The older ya get, the more ya fret. You're worse than all them damn sissies up at the school house, swoonin' and whinin' over every little thing. Jesus!"

"That's not fair, and you know it." Morgan now tired of the conversation, especially the cursing. "For the love of God, Dewey, why do you always take the Lord's name in vain and insist on slipping that one four-letter word into every utterance? Seriously, it's begun to worry me. Your language gets worse every time we're together."

Dewey considered the question. He had heard it on numerous occasions, and after what he had just said, he knew that Morgan deserved a thoughtful answer, if not an apology. Unfortunately, he was not accustomed to offering either one.

"What word exactly?"

"You know full well what word."

"Ya mean 'damn'?"

"It's not at all becoming. You are better than that."

"No, I keep tellin' ya I'm not better than that. I am who I am, and I like my words just fine."

The air was boiling around him and Dewey's eyes burned with sweat. Right as it was, Morgan's sermon seemed as annoying as the temperature. Dewey struggled to reposition and suddenly slapped at the brook with the flat of his hand. Water sprayed in all directions.

"It's much too hot for your lectures, Morgan. I swear 'cause it's fun, and I reckon it's fun only 'cause it aggravates you so. That's my way of keepin' you in your place. Now, enough of this talkin', there's too much hot air as it is."

"I'll stop the lectures when you stop the cursing."

"It's a deal," Dewey said, extending a hand to seal the pledge. He placed his shirt in the stream, and then, applied it to the back of his neck. "Whew! Just when the hell will we see some relief from all this heat?"

"Ah, Dewey! You just promised me, and there you go again."

"What, 'hell'? 'Hell' ain't no cuss word. It's a place, sure enough."

"Not the way you use it."

"Damn, Morgan, you are sure in a foul mood today, and I know just why. Ya wanna know why? 'Cause it's hotter than hell out here. There! I got it right this time. I hope you're happy." Dewey nodded and smiled with satisfaction, indicating that he had made his final point in the matter. Before Morgan could reply, he shifted his attention. "Hey, I just got me an idea. It's a ways yet to the river, but let's go swimmin'!"

Morgan laughed at the futility so common to his discourse with Dewey Baughman. "You are hopeless. Do you know that? And I'm giving a great deal of credit more than you actually deserve."

He lifted himself from the edge of the water and began restringing the top laces of his boot. He tipped the boot while smacking its leather side, and a small pebble dislodged and fell to the ground. He did the same for the other, then, looked up at his friend. "Swimming? That sounds pretty good to me, and a little more water might just clean up that filthy mouth of yours."

"Not likely."

By way of the road, it was another two dusty miles to Avery's pool, a natural swimming hole at a sharp bend in the Charity River. The river ran deep most of the year along that particular stretch, and the hole sometimes reached eight to ten feet to a sandy bottom, even during the dry months of summer. On the outer turn of the bend, a ragged cliff towered high above the pool. The ages had carved an array of steps and ledges across its face, giving purchase to those daring souls who would leap or dive into the dark green water.

Anchored on the opposing bank, a large sycamore stretched 70 feet or more over the middle of the Charity, where it could drink freely of both the river and the ample sunlight. To this tree was fastened a long, thick hemp rope, heavily knotted near its base to form a crude seat for a swing. Some time or another, an intrepid lad had shimmied 40 feet up that wide trunk to secure the rope, and throughout the season, scores would trust his work as they released their grip to plummet into the chilling depths. It was the perfect swing, the perfect swimming hole, the perfect river for two young men seeking refuge from the relentless heat.

Dewey was melting with every step. "Listen, Morgan, I can't see me walkin' another whole mile to that river. What ya think 'bout crossin' ol' man Avery's pasture and makin' up some time?"

"That works for me," Morgan replied. He had his fill of argument for the day and was pleased to finally hear something on which both could agree.

The boys left the road through a part in the high weeds and walked up a narrow game trail toward the pasture. A cottontail led the way for much of the distance, then raced off into the deep grass as the two reached the rail fence of Mr. Avery's field. Vultures soared above them, but all else in nature seemed safely tucked in holes and shadows, well beyond the reach of the raging sun.

With a single bound, Morgan cleared the top rail and continued on, while Dewey climbed over and managed to attach himself by means of a long chestnut splinter hooked deep in the crotch of his pants. He crashed forward dragging a portion of the fence behind him. The rail, the splinter and a swatch of faded gray fabric tumbled to the ground as the boy stumbled in a vain attempt to maintain his balance. A covey of grasshoppers flew for their lives as he rolled hard onto the field. When he again stood, it was as a scarecrow coated in the straw now clinging to his sweat.

Morgan looked over his shoulder, but moved steadily into the field. "Are you all right?" he asked, still walking.

"Yeah...yeah, no harm done. Let's keep goin'." Dewey lumbered closely behind him, probing curiously at the gaping hole of his trousers.

It was still a fair distance to Avery's pool, but after crossing the ridge by way of their shortcut, the boys finally left the pasture and slipped into a large stand of trees. They found themselves perched above the cliff. Hot, fatigued and ready for a good swim, they contemplated jumping simply to avoid the treacherous hike to the base. But the height of the cliff was formidable. They hesitated, each waiting for the other to make a decision.

"Let's do it," Morgan said, finally breaking the deadlock.

"Ya think?"

"It's the quickest way that I know of."

Dewey, of course, was hoping for a different, less daring kind of decision. "Ya mean jump? From right here? I was thinkin' of gettin' a bit lower. If I hit the river at this height, there ain't gonna be any water left to swim in. I'm goin' to that ledge down yonder."

"Suit yourself. I think I'll try it from here. We've done it before."

"What, clothes and all?"

"Look at us. We're dripping already. That river certainly won't make us any wetter."

Morgan braced himself for the long leap over the edge, careful not to look too closely lest he lose his nerve. He closed his eyes tightly and waited for his courage to peak. It never did. He was dissuaded in the split of a second by the sounds of an enormous splash and the subsequent violent thrashing of water. He peered over the ledge, but from his vantage point could only see the froth and ripples of the action below. Dewey had either jumped or fallen, but either way, something was clearly wrong.

"Dewey!" he yelled loudly. "Dewey, answer me!"

There was no response from his friend, but a high-pitched scream suddenly rose up from the river and left him faint against a sudden rush of fear. His knees buckled, and he steadied himself to avoid tumbling down the rocks.

The screams continued, and in response to their alarm, Morgan scrambled along the side of the cliff to where he might better see, and without forethought, he sprang from the nearest outcropping into the black pool below. He surfaced amidst a ring of foam and bubbles, expecting to find his friend seriously injured or drowned, but was relieved to see Dewey standing chest-deep in the pool, choking up what he would later describe as half the Charity River from his lungs.

"Hey, are you all right?" Morgan asked, treading water.

"I am, but I ain't too sure 'bout her."

He was attempting to focus on a young woman flailing desperately from her position near the bank. As he wiped the wetness from his eyes and regained his composure, Dewey could recognize Sadie Buck cowering in the shallows.

"Get away. Go away!" she screamed repeatedly. "Get away!" Silver sprays of water cast violently in every direction.

At first Dewey assumed a snake had intruded on the pool. Perhaps a bee or horsefly was harassing her. Maybe worse. He could not imagine. As he moved to her aid, her hysteria became frenzied, and he finally halted in utter bewilderment. He could not begin to understand her fright until he realized that he, himself, was the threat. He suddenly knew why and stood motionless as he affixed his stare upon a solitary figure on the shore.

Auralee Buck was beautiful in her own way. She was Sadie's older sister by one year and at 17 had developed into the better part of womanhood. Her tall and powerful build, her well-curved torso, her rosy, rounded cheeks, and her brilliant red hair had had their effect on Dewey many times. She had always been one of the smartest girls in school, and with the advantage of her size and full figure, she wielded a confidence and attitude that made the boys tremble. He had often thought of her in that very special way that drives young men beyond all reason. He had longed for her and yet never had the courage to say a tender word.

Auralee now stood naked before him, baring all the blessings that God had bestowed upon her body. Dewey ignored the continued screams of the younger sister and aimed his complete attention at the shore. He would not allow shame to interrupt his gaze, and he committed to memory every turn and indentation of her ivory form, her large breasts still wet from the river, her legs pink from the cold.

"Damn", he whispered. He could only stare, and for that long moment, the girl would not walk away.

Morgan ignored the rivulets that flowed freely down his face and neck. He was drenched, but felt nothing of the water. His muscular chest heaved with each full breath. He had not seen Auralee, and he no longer heard the cries for privacy so dramatically demanded by Sadie Buck. He was drawn to a third girl, who stood calmly in a shadowy recess of the pool and watched him as he moved ever closer. Her hair fell damp across her shoulders, and black mud adorned much of her youthful face. Waist deep in the water, the softness of her skin and the perfect substance of her young breasts were revealed to any who would see. But Morgan would only view the azure of her eyes, eyes that shimmered like the afternoon sun glancing and dancing across the ripples of the river.

Neither spoke. Their eyes, not their lips, expressed the soulful message of their newly awakened hearts.

Sunday mornings could never be the same. Morgan awoke when the dawn's first beam of light probed the gap of his curtains and settled on the goose down pillow by his head. He was groggy from a lack of sleep, the image of the girl at the river still playing on his mind.

He dressed and staggered down the narrow staircase on his way to the kitchen. Annie Darrow was already at work preparing breakfast.

"Good morning, son," she said quietly. "How about fetching some cooking wood for your mother? I'm running short."

Morgan nodded sleepily and moved toward the back door without a word.

"Wait, Morgan. Come and give me a big hug first."

He placed his arm around his mother's shoulder as she swept back a wave of his hair and kissed his forehead.

"You look so tired."

"I'm all right, Ma."

He pushed the warped screen door that led to a small porch, then grabbed an axe and a log of seasoned oak from the wood bin. In no time at all, he reduced the piece to a small pile of one-inch kindling.

Morgan's mother was the strongest of women, God-fearing, hard-working, family-loving. She seemed to live only for the happiness of her children and for the selfless support of her husband, who year after year did less and less to warrant her loyalty. Lawson Darrow was a good provider for the material needs of his family, but it was Annie who provided the love, the discipline, the touch and care so necessary to every child. And it was Annie who had earned the eternal adoration of her eldest son.

Morgan often wondered about his parents. Their past was always a mystery to him. It was a secret, the kind where some details are disclosed while others, the more telling ones, remain carefully guarded. He wondered why his father drank so heavily, as if to kill some chronic, incurable pain. He wondered why his mother seemed so melancholy when she reminisced in the privacy of her garden or in the quiet comfort of her small maple rocker. His parents shared lost days and forgotten dreams. That much had been evident since he was a child. But as a young man, he now felt the depth of their disappointment in one another, and he wondered if they would ever see beyond the past to find their peace together.

As the saw filer at the Watoga Lumber Company, Lawson held a critical position maintaining the jagged cutting teeth of the huge bandsaws. The quality of his work defined the efficiency of the mill, and consequently, he was better compensated than most employed in the industry. He was a fair man, much of the time. Though not religious, he was never one to deny others their own way. When Annie insisted that the children be raised in a godly home, Lawson allowed her the freedom to manage the spiritual training as she saw fit. He tried hard to conduct himself properly for the benefit of his children, but whiskey had stolen so much of the man that Annie once loved. At times he was vulgar and violent, angry at things less transparent than the wind. At times, he was simply gone. While he never brought harm to them, too often his family was made to feel the fear and resentment of his wrath.

Annie spoke to Morgan, "Is Jacob up yet? He's a hard one to stir."

"I'm not sure, Ma. He was still asleep when I got up. That boy may seem glued to the bed, but when his feet do hit the floor, he's running over me like a holy terror. I tried not to wake him."

Morgan shared a large pine bed with his brother. Jake was six years old, 11 years younger than Morgan, but had already become the shadow that followed Morgan's every step. He was one of those special gifts of life that came to Annie later than she would have wanted, but he remained her unbridled joy.

She pleaded with her son, "Please, run up and rouse your brother and sister. Breakfast is almost ready, and I haven't heard so much as a rustle."

When Jacob and his sister, Cora, finally made it to the kitchen, their father already had downed his customary feast of eggs, country ham and hash browns. Using his last large bite of buttermilk pancakes, he sopped the remaining blend of yolk and potatoes. It was the Sunday breakfast, Morgan's favorite, but the boy had little appetite and was satisfied with a simple piece of toast sweetened by his mother's black raspberry preserves.

Lawson took a last sip of his coffee. "We don't sleep all day in this house. If you want breakfast, you'll rise at a decent hour. Do you understand?"

Cora and Jake dropped their heads in obedience to their father. They responded in unison, "Yes, Daddy."

"Make sure you do, because there will be no meal for you this morning. It's disrespectful coming late to the table, and I'll not have it… from any of you! I will have respect."

Annie tried to intercede. "Lawson, the children were not given a time for breakfast. Today is Sunday. We always let them sleep…."

"Don't counter me, Annie! Someone around here needs to teach them about manners."

"Yes, they do, and hopefully by example."

Lawson saw the stern expression on Annie's face and wisely gave up the argument. He grunted in anger and stormed from the kitchen.

Morgan rose slowly from the table and opened the ice box, where a bottle of milk sat cool against the block. He poured two glasses for his siblings as Annie handed the children their breakfast. She said softly, "Your father didn't understand. Now, say your blessing and eat before it all gets cold."

The First Methodist Church of Devlin. It was a strange name considering there never was, nor ever would be, a second or third. It was a rather substantial structure for a country church, but simple in design. Local stones selected from the rapids of the Charity River and timbers milled in town blended well against the nature of the surrounding hills. Six large gothic windows, each glazed with colored panes, lined both sides of the sanctuary. Two more windows straddled the twin front doors that opened into the vestibule. The inner walls and ceiling were faced with tin, pressed and painted to resemble a master work of molded plaster. Along the chair rail that encircled the room, a delicate floral pattern of olive green, and rose and lilac weaved subtle color throughout.

Still, it was a humble church. Almost everything, including its furnishings, was built by the hands of those who came to worship, with the exception of the front windows. These were adorned with magnificent stained glass mosaics commissioned in New York, one of the Christ at prayer in Gethsemane, the other of Adam and Eve huddled in their shame at Eden. They were a prized gift from Charles Austin Devlin, in honor of his son's 13th birthday, and meant as a cultural contribution to the mill town he had established eight years before from his corporate office in Pittsburgh. A brass plaque below each panel displayed his name, as did one of the oak pews, in recognition of his single visit to Sunday services.

Nestled among green fields and stately elms on a knoll above the edge of town, the church lifted its steeple high above all, except the mountains and the rolling clouds. Its bell rang pure and rode easily on the country air, surpassed only by an occasional crack of summer thunder or the frequent howl of a steam whistle.

Of course, there were other churches, Baptist and Catholic ones on Market Street and a small Brethren congregation that met at the Moose Lodge on Sunday mornings. The Presbyterians made their presence a few miles down the valley, but for the most part, First Methodist stood as the spiritual icon of Devlin. At one time the Baptists seemed to contend for this honor, as their attendance swelled and the construction of a new brick wing was considered, but the 'hell-fire and damnation' and the "double thy tithe" sermons of the new minister came once too often. Predictably, many of the citizens migrated back to the Methodists for a kindlier reading of the Bible. And all were welcome. Every faithful child of God, and even his less so righteous neighbor, was welcome.

The paddock in front of First Methodist Church was an indication of a changing era. A single motor car now parked on grounds once reserved for an array of horses, buggies and farm wagons, and loosely aligned in a long, curving row, the diverse conveyances displayed a technological harmony that would not survive the decade. The unexpected change toward a horseless society would simply come too fast.

Morgan never understood why, or even how, his father happened to afford the only other motor car in Devlin. It was a rather classy and expensive vehicle, a 1905 Model F Ford, and even the town's more wealthy residents could not claim such a luxury as their own. Perhaps they had no need for it. Morgan suspected that the Ford was payment for the sale of Lawson's family property on the Gauley. The estate was a good piece of bottomland, and some retiring lawyer out of Charleston was anxious to have it for his dabbling in agriculture. The new farmer, obviously, had no need of a vehicle that was stymied by the muddy wallows so prevalent on the highway, and Lawson Darrow had no love for the land. It was a poor trade, Morgan always thought, considering the heavy splatter and cakes of dirt that forever coated the car's fenders and spoked wheels.

Morgan stopped at the front of the church and reminded Jacob to hold the door for his mother and sister. Then he parked his father's Ford on the damp grass of the field and looked to the white cross atop the country steeple. The bell had ceased its ringing. He was late.

While the piano sounded out a prelude to worship, Morgan took his seat next to Cora. He scanned the sanctuary and noticed Dewey fidgeting on the wooden pew to his right. He nodded a greeting to his friend, but Dewey rightfully kept his focus toward the altar, toward his minister, and of course, toward Auralee Buck, who sat just two rows away. She was devout, poised, and, to Dewey Baughman's ogling eyes, incomparably alluring.

Cora nudged Morgan with her elbow, but he ignored her. She nudged again. "Stop that, Cora," he said softly.

She leaned toward his ear and whispered, "Have you ever met Sarah Dabney?"

"No. Sh-sh-sh!" It was an abrupt response, audible to some who turned their heads with an eye of disapproval. He smiled sheepishly in silent apology.

Morgan had forgotten the sanctity of the place. For the moment, he was savoring what little he recalled about the unknown girl at the swimming hole. No one, nothing, had ever settled so heavily on his mind. He had hoped to see her at the service, considering she was a friend of the Buck sisters, but such hope was perhaps just foolish expectation. She likely attended some other church, or maybe none. She may even practice another religion altogether. Who was she? He was desperate to know. What did she really look like, where did she come from, how did she feel about him? There were no answers for such questions. He and Dewey had left the river so fast that he had learned nothing about her, and now, his heart was clamoring for a mere sign that the girl was even real.

Of course, he might ask Auralee or Sadie, that is, if he could ever talk to them again following the incident at the pool. Surprising the girls like he did, they must think him rather perverse. No, it was difficult enough just coming to church and facing them from across the room. In his embarrassment, what could he possibly say?

Cora was not deterred by his lack of interest. "I'll have to introduce you. You will like her. She's sitting next to Sadie." But Morgan was not listening.

Dewey Baughman continued to fidget. It was unusual for him to be anxious for a church service, but in this case, he knew Auralee was a faithful member of First Methodist. She had aroused his emotions to such a stupor that for the past 20 hours he could not eat, sleep, move, curse or otherwise function normally. Church made him even more desperate, forcing him to wrestle with the options of repentance or lust.

As the congregation stood and sang the opening hymn, he only hummed the verses because of his fixation with Auralee's swaying body. Her back was straight and her head high as she voiced each familiar stanza. Her hips rocked with the steady cadence struck firmly against the keys of the piano. Dewey's mind drifted during the prayers as he envisioned her standing alone on the bank of the Charity. He was thankful that he had seen her so completely exposed, and yet, ashamed that he was in God's house feeling no remorse at all for the passion that vision now conjured. It was Sunday, which gave him some provocation to temper his thoughts, but for Dewey, temptation was the master of conscience. He wanted Auralee and felt he would do just about anything to be with her.

Dewey ventured a prayer of his own, "Lord, I think I'm in love with Auralee Buck. I never really seen who she was until now, not really, and what I seen yesterday and what's been in my heart ever since is grabbin' at me and tearin' me up inside. I reckon I need your help. I guess I'd give up just 'bout anything if I could...well, if you could... persuade her to like me."

Dewey remembered Morgan's lecture regarding his inappropriate language. "I can stop my cursin' if ya want. I'll stop my complainin'. You just tell me which one. Please, Lord...please... I feel this is right serious between me and Auralee. I thank you. Amen."

It was a silent prayer, and when Dewey opened his eyes and looked up at the cross beyond the altar, he felt he had just undergone a spiritual transformation. He would try hard to keep his covenant with God, and he knew as sure as faith builds confidence, that in a short time, he would have his precious Auralee.

Morgan took no notice of the young woman next to Sadie. When the service concluded, he moved quickly toward the open doors of the church. He firmly shook the pastor's hand, commending him on the meaningful sermon that he unfortunately never heard, then, hurried back to the motor car. His mind had never been so clouded. He was vulnerable to a deep and wonderful emotion that he could not hide from those who knew him well, and he was not yet ready to share the intimacy of his feelings. In his father's Model F Ford, he would be alone with his thoughts.

Morgan was not sure what he had become, but he knew he had changed. Without a word, with only a look, the girl had transformed his every desire, his every dream. She appeared in his every thought and was the center of his every plan. Yet, he did not know her. He did not know her name or voice, where she lived or how she came to be by the river bank, drenched, her face disguised with mud. The pool was an eternity away, and so was this girl he loved but did not know.

Cora startled him, "Morgan, come out of there. I'd like to introduce you to my new friend, Sarah Dabney."

Morgan was reluctant as he slipped from the black leather seat and his solitude, but gracious as he extended his hand in fellowship.

At first, his eyes were cast down, a habit of boyish bashfulness, but he slowly raised them to receive an unexpected gift of the girl's bright and embracing smile. He saw the blush of her wind-blown cheeks, the slight upward turn of her nose. He saw her silky hair, a dusty yellow of harvest wheat, flirting with the gentle breeze. And he saw the sparkling blue of her eyes.

Morgan returned the smile as he pressed her delicate hand into his palm. With the breath of his sigh, he spoke her name, "Sarah."

# CHAPTER 2

Lowe Yancy and Black Jack Clark moved painfully slow in the evening's dim light, assembling what would be a poor semblance of a camp. Usually, they would take the time to set a proper tent, or at least, stretch an overhead tarp. They would clear the sticks and rocks from the site, lay out their cots and bedrolls, then feed, brush and hobble their pack animals. Usually, they would dig a fire pit and fill it full with orange glowing coals in preparation for a late, satisfying supper. And usually, before the day was done, they would clean and service their equipment, review their drawings and calculations, and talk quietly about the state of the world or the endless wonders of the southern Appalachians. Usually.

Camp had become a routine matter for the men. They conducted it with acute precision, being well-versed from their years of experience. But today had been one of those especially difficult trials, long and hot and fraught with needless errors. It had been a day where every effort was taxed by either bad luck or carelessness. As a result, neither man had any notion of keeping with the evening protocol. Camp would be where their heads first touched the ground.

After weeks of hauling equipment and urging a reluctant horse over logs and streams, hills and ledges, the men were not at all surprised to find that they had stumbled into the middle of nowhere. Of course, they had been there before. It had always been a remote and elusive place over the years, a mystical place with ever changing scenery, a place that would occasionally appear to them, but only when their ability and resolve to push harder or farther waned to near nothingness.

This time it appeared as an upland meadow, full of the offerings of spring, of wild flowers and succulent green grasses, of calling birds and sweet fragrances floating on a breeze. The ponds that swelled the lazy creek screamed with the songs of peepers. There was the infrequent splash of a trout or otter, leaping out or slipping in, that rippled the still surface of the water and swayed the rushes where a heron held its stoic pose.

The meadow was a shared domain, but the dams and pointed stumps and crisscrosses of barkless trunks, each too large to move, gave testimony to the gnawing orange incisors that had whittled back the forest's edge. It was the beaver's home, engineered by instinct and constructed by persistence. It became the refuge of many a woodland creature, and the men, too worn to set their own camp, sensed their welcome as well.

Come morning, spring beauties and lupine would paint the ground with hues of snow and sky, and other flowers, such as trout lilies and blue violets, May apples and red columbines, would drip with dew. Robins would flock across the loose soil probing for breakfast, and cardinals would flutter from willow branch to maple limb and back again. In the morning, everything would sing anew. Everything. Lowe Yancy and Black Jack Clark were counting on it.

Perhaps it was best that evening hid most of what the meadow offered. Beauty deserves delight, and the men were no longer capable of such feeling. So very tired, they would gladly accept any plot of earth as a proper bed on which to rest, but here, here in the middle of nowhere, they were granted the cool air and clear water and soft, flat ground needed to restore their exhausted bodies. It was a kind place, and for that, they were at least thankful.

"You gonna want yo supper, Mr. Yancy?" Black Jack asked, moving sluggishly after tending to the horse. "It be my night to cook. We ain't had us a bite since noon. You gotta be starvin'."

"No, I'm not hungry. Make it easy on yourself."

"You think, maybe, we should set up de tent?"

Lowe looked at the sky and saw crisp detail in the face of the rising moon. "No, it's a clear night. Frankly, I'm done in, Jack. I'm calling it a day."

"Yessa, I reckon dat de one thing left to do. I gots to throw some water on my face, but I'll be settlin' in just a bit. I done run out o' steam."

Lowe had barely enough energy to speak. "Once I'm down, I'm dead until morning. You sleep well, my friend." With that being said, he fell upon a musty, wrinkled tarp and gathered it like a satin sheet around his shoulders. He murmured in the comfort.

"How about some coffee? Some jerky? Mr. Yancy, you ought eat somethin'," Black Jack insisted.

"No, nothing for me, but you do what you want, Mr. Clark."

There was no need for formality between the two men, but Black Jack had gotten into the habit years ago, and Lowe, unable to fully break him of it, mimicked his method.

"You gonna sleep like dat, clothes and boots and all? No blanket neither?" Black Jack spoke in a motherly tone.

Lowe had almost nodded off. He sighed, "I'll never know the difference. You sure have a mess of questions for a beat up, tired old boy. You must've been surveying a different line than the one I ran today."

"I is beat, sure enough, too played out to even recollect how to rest. Hmm.... Still, it don't seem right, you sleepin' with dem boots."

The grass rustled as Black Jack positioned his bedroll against the empty pack saddle. He knelt down, his dark face daubed in moon glow, and he spoke as if only to himself. He knew that Lowe would understand, despite the man's coolness to most things religious.

Lowe had never learned to follow or to accept another's charity, and, consequently, never acknowledged any debt for his deliverance. But for Black Jack, it was different and all so simple. Only those who knew the course should lead the course, and others should wisely remain close behind. It was the mantra that guided his walk through life. He was a man of deep faith, and his God knew well the way from dismal to sublime. God had crossed that very ground before and had led him, had led both of them, to the serenity and safety of the meadow. Of this, Black Jack was certain. He now whispered his few humble words of gratitude.

"Hey, you put in a good word for me," Lowe interrupted, not meaning to be disrespectful.

"I always do, but you know'd dat all along. Every time me and de Lord gets to talkin', we hear you listenin'."

Lowe yawned. "You hear me listening? Maybe the two of you just talk too loud."

"Maybe so. Nothin' softer dan his whisper, nothin' louder dan his roar. Jesus know just how to say it, and he know just what to say, to dem who takes de time to listen." Not meaning to proselytize, Black Jack grabbed the extra blanket he had rolled for a pillow and laid it over his weary friend. "Yessa, I be sleepin' well. You do de same."

Lowe was out of words or even thoughts. Instead, his body sank into the cushion of grass, and his mind slipped far beyond the mountains and meadows that had been his life. He would never know exactly where.

Some enervation was certainly predictable, but neither Lowe nor Black Jack could have anticipated such utter fatigue come end of day. It had somehow become an all too common condition, and both were slow in recovery. There should have been four on the crew, maybe more, but that was a mistake in judgment they knew they would have to accept and forget. The remaining term of the contract was brief, and considering the unforeseen delays of a lingering winter, they had had too little time to recruit assistance, especially trained surveyors. They pulled what additional resources they could from within themselves, pushed their will and bodies to the brink, and worked from dawn to dusk until the job was done and done well.

The survey was now complete. The boundary was marked. It had been a successful effort that kept them moving across the umbra of the mountains for the better part of six weeks. They had crossed far into "the Big Timber," so labeled by the loggers who were yet to travel there. To most, the place was known only by an occasional yield of enormous round logs pilfered from its edge, but those who sought fortune in the value of trees imagined correctly the vast spoils that were situated just beyond that edge. Soon Lowe and Black Jack would present their maps and findings, and they would report seeing hundreds of millions of board feet of prime hardwood ready for harvest. They could inform the company of a terrain suitable for the construction of rail lines, of wide flats for the stockpiling of timber or installation of lumber camps. Many would be required to clear such an extensive tract.

The Big Timber. It was rich land they had seen stretching across the numerous slopes and basins, a land blessed with sound, mature timber, with ample water and wildlife, and beauty beyond description. The survey report, unfortunately, would change much of that, at least for the generations of men and women who would come in the aftermath of the cut to settle these once hidden hills of West Virginia. It would never again be the forest the men had witnessed. It could not return as ageless and pure. They felt the loss, even before the first saw ripped across the first tree. But the company would be satisfied with their work and would eventually reap wealth beyond decency. As far as their contract was concerned, that was all that really mattered.

The lure of good money demands prudent action to get it, and harsh competition from mill companies and timber speculators as far away as Roanoke, Cincinnati or Pittsburgh dictated the need for a formal survey. Most companies preferred to purchase only the timber rights to a property, having no real interest in the ground beneath the trees. But some landowners showed even less interest and took what money they could for title of their acreage, just to be free of the mountains once and for all. Local mills were prolific, rising almost overnight on the flats of every river and tributary. Some disappeared just as quickly, as the timber was lifted from the land and the edge of the old growth forest retreated into the more inaccessible headwaters and highlands. Supply was ever dwindling, and the cost of dirt beneath the Big Timber was but a small obstacle to those who would have its trees.

There were an estimated 48,000 acres at stake, not including the uncharted properties claimed on some of the upper plateaus, and the Watoga Lumber Company would not risk a major loss due to land disputes and legal manipulations. Old records, generated years earlier by a series of meets and bounds surveys, were sketchy and, to a large extent, nonexistent. Courts were crowded with claims and counterclaims supported by such records. The survey was a necessary expense for the protection of timber rights.

Similarly, Lowe and Black Jack had to look to their own interests, knowing their work was only part of the company's current undertaking. More jobs were to be awarded, and other crews might be asked to finish the task of setting boundaries. It was hard but lucrative labor, and the men pressed themselves relentlessly to ensure an extension of their contract.

Perhaps it was the rising humidity of spring or the yellow clouds of pollen that choked their sight and breath, or their extra winter weight not yet burned by the bustle of the new season, or the 40-plus years that each man reluctantly counted unto himself. Maybe it was the steep terrains and the swift currents they were forced to cross, or the simple fact that the work was more demanding than a couple men and a horse should attempt. Regardless of reason, the men sprawled without fire or supper or further comment onto their tarps, and both fell immediately into a deep renewing sleep. The fate of the wilderness, the profit of the company, the promise of personal gain, these were of no consequence. They were just too tired to care.

Lowell Yancy first tried his hand at surveying when he was a 12-year-old boy. He never gave up the trade in favor of other work, and except for a couple seasons while he finished his eighth and final year of school, he found little else to occupy his time. Nothing was more satisfying than surveying. The fact that his work provided a reasonable and almost steady income was not important. What was important was Lowe's freedom to explore one of the last frontiers of the East. Surveying was an excuse to pursue his and every other man's fancy. It was a means to travel where others had not gone before, to hunt and fish and walk and breathe in the fresh, unspoiled havens of nature. He loved that. He loved trees and animals and the wildness of the forest. And he eagerly learned of these from the same men who taught him the use of the chain and compass and the calculations of the survey. Much of what he had become as a man was a living tribute to the times he spent with his father and uncle plotting their course through the deep wood. His life was committed to knowing and continuing their passions. They were his heroes, now passed to another world.

Lowe was 42. He had considered that his life may be more than half over, but if he felt regret, it certainly had nothing to do with an occupation that ushered him time and again into the heart of God's country. He never knew his mother, who died bringing him life, and he only once came to love a woman, to really love a woman, one who tenderly enriched that life far beyond any alluring touch of the wilderness. But she, too, had left him. He missed them both, having been cheated of his time with them. If he actually felt regret, it was for the too few moments he was given to fully appreciate the people and places he loved so dearly.

John Lewis Clark had long ago accepted the name of Black Jack. He was the friend and partner, and in many ways, the teacher of Lowe Yancy. A son of slaves who toiled in the rice plantations of South Carolina, he in some ways had suffered a tougher life than his parents as he struggled to find his rightful place in a world that did not want him. He had not lived their bondage, but then again, they never felt the constant humiliation and defeat of a young black man wanting desperately to succeed against the prevalent storms of racism and distrust. Promised a brighter future, he was denied the path that might lead him to it. Of course, he would never consider such foolish comparison. Unlike his mother and father, he was at least free to try and fail.

Black Jack learned the trade mostly from those who hired him for cheap, difficult labor. He studied their actions. He mimicked their ways. He posed questions until he knew their business well.

As the great plantations of the South divided into smaller farms, new boundaries were to be formed, and his jobs often took him into the swamps among the snakes and alligators of the southern lowlands. From the black waters he learned to be fearless, from his white bosses he learned his craft, from the heat and grueling work he learned to be strong and from his mother, a woman who taught herself numbers and words despite the serious prohibition against slave education, he learned to use his mind. And he married well at an unusually early age, but lost his beloved Hettie shortly thereafter to a sudden strike of the fever.

They were a good team, Lowell Yancy and John Clark. They first met on a crew assembled by Lowe's uncle some 25 years earlier and never once felt provocation to part. When Lowe chose to venture on his own, he was quick to hire Black Jack as the best survey man in the mountains. The bond grew strong between the men, and they shared everything from their meager assets to their strictest confidences.

John Clark was six years older and two inches taller than Lowell, and it was he who, in good humor, looked down at his youthful protégé and floated the name "Low." The handle received universal acceptance, with minor modification, and from then on, Lowell Yancy answered to a new name. It was the start of a banter that only friends can sustain, and Lowe was quick to retaliate with a descriptive moniker of his own. John Clark became "Black Jack," partly for the darkness of his skin, but mostly in cynical response to his strong Christian aversion to gambling. They both accepted their new identities with pride. It was a sign of their bond, a privilege of their companionship, the undeclared right of one friend to rename another.

Morning came late, but still too early for the men buried in the dark comfort of their tarps. It was well after eight before the sun bore down on them with enough heat to stir them from slumber. Before rising, Lowe stared blankly into the cloudless sky, struggling to recall why he lay contorted on a damp ground, fully clothed, with no camp, no smoldering fire and, most importantly, no coffee simmering in a scorched-bottom pot. He reluctantly rolled from his shallow depression in the grass, evaluating his pain with each slow turn of his body. The aches were normal, many but normal, and they would work themselves out as the hours unfolded.

Black Jack laughed as his friend took his first awkward steps into the new day, limping and moaning and scratching himself just about anywhere his hands could reach. He presented the horse a feed bag of grain, released its hobbles, and patted its rump as he passed toward the beaver pond.

"Mornin', Blu." That was all Lowe would say. Without hesitation, he stepped waist deep into the water and stood there.

"What you fixin' to do?" Black Jack asked, not anticipating a reply. "I expect dat water be cold, or can't you even feel it yet? You might at least take off dem boots."

"Too late for that. Mr. Clark, never in all my born days have I known a man to worry so about another man's boots. First, I'm not allowed to sleep in them, and, now, I can't even get them wet."

"You does only what you want and only when you wants to do it. Dat's an undeniable fact. So, go on. Dat soggy leather ain't puttin' dem blisters on my feet. Go on with you! Wear yo Sunday shoes in de bath, if it make you happy."

"Why that's ridiculous. These are just old boots."

"Dey yo only boots and de best you got."

Lowe grumbled, "If you're so hell bent on being my mother hen, stop pecking so early and put on some coffee.

"Goodness, you is some kind o' surly, and dat ain't no way to start a day."

"Aww, don't you have some job to do?"

"You my job. When de Lord made you my brother, he gave me dat one tough assignment, and believe you me, dis mornin' duty always been de hardest. Yessa, I best put some fire under dat pot o' coffee. When de sun rises, it just ain't yo time for shinin'."

Lowe took a long breath, and without bending, let his body fall into the deepest part of the pond. He sprawled in a dead man's float for as long as his lungs would allow, then rose like a leviathan when his senses finally registered the icy temperature of the water.

"Holy Jesus, that is cold!" he cried out, almost breathless.

"Mr. Yancy, I's more dan curious as to why dat come a surprise. Good thing yo heart still pumpin', 'cause I got me some real doubt about yo brain," Black Jack said mockingly.

Lowe ignored him, rubbing his arms to counter the numbing of his skin. He looked over at the beaver lodge, a distinct domed mound of sticks in the far center of the pond. "Those little rodents must run a fire under there to keep warm, because this is one cold, cold place." Then, he tried to coax Black Jack. "But it's really not so bad once you're used to it. Honestly, Jack, it's flat out invigorating. Come and join me. If the water doesn't kill you outright, it'll certainly destroy anything that's growing on you!"

"No, thank you, I's keepin' all dat ice water just as far from my privates as possible. Froze up plumbin' might never get fixed."

"Ah, my friend, you have lost your sense of adventure."

As if he had not learned from his first emersion, Lowe dove flat-bellied back into the pond, swam as best he could against the weight of his trousers and boots, and then sloshed and shivered as he climbed the bank and crossed the meadow grass. "Whew!" he exclaimed. He shivered again as he removed his shirt and turned to face the sun.

"I was fixin' to fry up some fish," Black Jack said. "Dat is, 'til you scared every one back down de stream. Still, it be my turn to cook, so I'll try to rustle up a little somethin'."

"Take your time, Mr. Clark. Really, take a bath if you want to. It's been said that cleanliness is next to godliness, and I couldn't help but notice how your religion of late has appeared a little weak, if you know what I mean."

"Mr. Yancy, you just suffer all dis soil and stink and anythin' else you think be crawlin' on me, but suffer it, mind you, while you fetches wood for my cook fire. I ain't no beaver to jump in such water, but I's sure hungry enough to eat a few trees. Go on now, so's I can start us a breakfast."

When the meal ended Lowe gathered the frying pan, the metal plates and utensils, and washed them in the stream with the clean ash of his fire. He set them next to the coals to dry and laid back down on his tarp. "I could snooze here all day. That was a good meal, Jack. You're a right fine cook. I'm only sorry that I won't do so well by you when I fix the supper tonight. Of course, you could take my turn if you want."

"Nice try, but yo cookin' ain't so bad," Black Jack responded. "Least wise, I ain't died from no poisonin' yet. I s'pose we best put things together before too long and make our way out o' here. Don't you think?"

"Actually, I'm of a mind to set a real camp. Maybe take some time to fish. It's a good place. The survey's not due for another week, and I could use the rest. We could try some exploring."

"Explorin'? What we been doin' all dis time!" Black Jack was dumbfounded by the suggestion. He was not the least bit inclined to take a single step more than necessary. But the resting and the fishing - he liked the idea. "Lord knows I's weary, like dis old horse we been loadin'. Blu's got him some good grazin' here abouts, and I surely could use me some time to go ober yo maps and calculations. De weather seem likely to hold up for us, dat is if storms don't brew in all dis heat. Nah, I don't hanker for no explorin', but I be glad to unload dem packs and settle in a while."

The tent and camp went up in short order, and before long the men had dropped hook and line into the beaver ponds. It was almost too simple, nearly unsporting. The bass and bluegill were so accommodating that most of what were caught were summarily released back to the frigid pools. Only the largest were kept as a steady exchange continued between creel and pond. But the brook trout proved elusive, and the men became all the more charged. They switched to fly rods and reveled in the combat as fish after fish teased and took to the lure.

Black Jack's face was all grin as he flipped his rod and let the fly touch lightly on the water. "Mr. Yancy, we dead and done gone to heaven!"

"Nope, it cannot be so, Mr. Clark. I haven't bought my ticket for heaven, unless, just maybe, you've arranged for someone to open the big gate for me. You seem to know all the right people, after all."

"No, every man is to buy his own ticket. I keeps tryin' to tell you dat. Say, how many you caught so far?" As usual, the fishing had become a contest.

"About the same as you. I'll tell you what, whoever snags the next good one wins the match. Fair enough?"

"Why sure, Lowe, I gots to give a man his fightin' chance. Seein' how poorly you count when you tallyin' yo fish, de 'next good one' seem de only sure way to declare me a winner. But dat fish gotta be a nice pound or better. You agree?"

"Yeah, I agree, and it has to be a trout. You agree?"

"I do. Now, commence yo fishin'."

Lowe was never the angler that his partner was, and this particular competition was essentially all but over with Black Jack well in the lead. Both men, of course, knew the count, but Lowe was known to hedge his numbers on occasion in hopes of stealing the coveted bragging rights. Cheating or not, he rarely won the contest.

"Hold on! Another be comin' to dinner! Hold on, you fat little fish you. You is about to make old Black Jack a very proud man."

A huge trout suddenly crashed into the air, having already consumed Black Jack's bait. The fish thrashed for minutes against the man's skillful play of the line and gave one last, futile lurch before being netted. Black Jack, grinning as before, held his trophy high in the air before the eyes of God and Lowell Yancy.

"Now ain't dat a beauty. Thank you, Lord!" he shouted. "Thank you, Jesus! You does provide in my time o' need." Black Jack had retained his right to boast.

Slumped shoulders and a glowering expression revealed Lowe's frustration with yet another loss. He cast time and again, but from then on, his lure floated without response on the still surface of the pond.

"I give up!" he grumbled in disgust. "You've got all the luck. They're not biting anymore, at least not for me." Black Jack started to reply, but Lowe cut him off, "Yeah... yeah, I know. Call it what you will, I still say it's luck."

"What you mean, 'you give up'? You says to me, 'one fish,' and I catch dat fish. To anyone else, dat mean you lose. When de race be over and yo horse come in last, it be too late to say, 'I give up.' You say to de champion, 'I lose.' You say, 'Congratulations, yo pony run de good race and whipped mine right soundly. So I be happy for you, Mr. Clark, 'cause you is now de champion.' Dat what you say."

"Don't push it. There are other ponds, other days. We'll test these waters again."

"Amen to dat."

Lowe grabbed the creel and began to clean the fish against a large, flattened stone. "You know, Jack, I'm thinking about a brief change of scenery. I've got a hankering to check out those cliffs up yonder." He pointed his fillet knife toward a narrow gap. Beyond was a distant outcropping that capped a high ridge, barely visible in the haze. "You want to go?"

"Is you serious?" Black Jack squinted to better focus on the cliffs. "Dose rocks? Way out dere? Well, it ain't high on my list o' things to do right now. Frankly, dat be a good deal farther dan it look." He wondered about his friend's state of mind, considering their exhausted physical condition only the night before. "You seem a might unsettled, Lowe. I's near dead from walking dese hills, and you picks up some crazy notion about more climbin' for just de fun of it. You been runnin' hard on yo self over a month now. What's got its hold on you?"

"Nothing."

"Well, somethin' sure been tuggin' yo rope. You a different man dan you was when we started out. Maybe you just tired. Is dat it? You tired, Lowe?"

"You're a sly old dog, Jack. You always catch the scent of trouble before anyone else. That's a handy talent, I suppose. I don't know what's bothering me for sure. Now that we've finished the survey, I'm not so anxious to get back into town. You know how it gets sometimes. I need some good quiet time to sort it all out."

"Well, dis here a right proper place for dat kind o' thinkin'."

"I reckon I'm just turning into one of them moody fellows I never had much use for. God help me, there's nothing worse than a whiney man."

"Ah, you be fine in a day or so." Black Jack knew Lowell Yancy as a man who never tired of the forest, but sensed a deeper reason for his need to be there. He pulled a battered old watch from the short pocket of his vest and sprung open the cover. "Half past noon. You need be gone already if you is set on reachin' dem cliffs."

"Are you coming along?"

"No, you go. I never told you, Lowe, but when I lost my Hettie, with no warnin' and no mercy, dem blue peaks was callin' to me. I had questions. Dey had answers. Mine was a troubled soul, and dem hills give me back de want and strength to live. Best you go alone dis time to find yo's. No offense meant, o' course."

"None taken."

Lowe walked over to the edge of the pond and lifted a six foot piece of sapling. It was straight, strong and skinned white by the gnawing teeth of the beaver. He placed it across his knee and pulled hard. The pole showed only a hint of bending. It had balance. It felt right.

"Not a bad little walking stick," he said, as he laid the pole across the ground, "and just long enough to keep those rattlesnakes honest." Content with his find, he went on to collect a full canteen and his holstered revolver.

Lowe looked one last time toward the long, rocky ridge, as if this was to be his final chance to reconsider the climb. His goal was more than a fair distance away, and while he had no intention of abandoning his plan, he could not help but wish that the cliffs were closer. He bagged some fried biscuits left over from breakfast and a few cuts of salt ham. In afterthought, he rolled a blanket and strung it over his shoulder.

"I expect to be back by dark, Mr. Clark. If not, I'll manage up on the mountain until morning. Save me some of that fish." He lingered momentarily trying to remember anything forgotten, but nothing tangible came to mind. Still, something was pulling at a heartstring, something to do with his friend.

"Black Jack, why in the world didn't you...? Oh, never mind. It's not important." He started slowly out of camp, but returned after only 20 paces. "Tell me something, Jack, before I go. I've often wondered why you never remarried after Hettie died."

Black Jack smiled, both stunned by and grateful for the interest. He now knew what was troubling his friend, and it really had nothing to do with his question.

"Well, I tell you dis much, for Hettie and for me, it were all true...every day of our short life together. Every feelin', every word, it were all true. I still love her, as much dis moment as when I first seen her standin' before dat preacher. Lordy, Lowe, she were one magnificent woman, my Hettie. I just keeps on lovin' and thinkin' on her. Dere ain't room in de human heart for two such women, so I stays with what I got. I always been most happy to leave it dat way."

"Don't you get lonely? Don't you miss the feel of a good woman next to you?"

"Yessa, I do, but a strong, warm mem'ry can be a fine companion at such times. My wife, she don't leave me, and dat's a fact. And besides, Mr. Yancy, dere ain't many o' my people to be found in dese parts. Findin' another like Hettie be right tough, even for such a smart and handsome fella like me. Listen, you best move on. I be lookin' for you come nightfall."

Lowe was nearly out of sight and out of breath when he looked back to see John Clark cleaning and filleting the rest of the morning's catch. The man was at peace, always at peace, and Lowe envied the gentle, positive spirit that allowed him to embrace each turn of life as a prize. Lowe's legs were heavy and his will to explore waned with each uphill stride, but thinking about Black Jack, he felt strangely obliged to withhold complaint. He climbed quietly out of the valley and into the gap, stubbornly facing the challenge he had placed upon himself.

Lowe looked and listened in vain as he paused briefly at the base of the mountain. Life appeared suspended in the dead calm of the afternoon, but he knew better than to believe it. He was aware of the sweet springs that seeped below the rocks, of young shoots that pushed away from their seeds beneath the soil. Somewhere a wary fawn was nestled behind a thicket, and beyond the high ceiling of green leaves, the unspoiled air moved in light gusts across the blue sky. He knew of these things, neither seen nor heard, and each in its own way was very much alive. They were buried treasures, and like a pirate combing a familiar shore, he always took the time to rediscover the unfathomable wealth. He was never fooled by the afternoon calm. The woods may rest, but there was always life on the mountain, always some hidden jewel just waiting to be found.

Lowe was reluctant but continued on his journey, acutely aware that every crashing, crunching footstep was an effrontery to nature's repose. He disliked being the one to disturb the peace, but it was a fleeting concern at best. He soon quickened his pace toward the summit. His muscles, now stretched and rejuvenated from their morning stiffness, claimed the energy of his soaring spirit and moved him with an ease he had not known since youth. He bounded up the hillside. With one hand on the walking stick and the other grasping for saplings, he pushed and pulled himself steadily upward, foregoing rest lest he lose whatever force or magic propelled him to the top. His body was free of pain and his mind uncluttered. Only the mountains could give him this. Black Jack was right. Such a place would have answers.

But Lowe had not yet reached the top, and the mountain had many other things to show...darker things. When he paused for a taste of water trickling from a moss-covered ledge, the euphoria and momentum of his boyish bounce both ceased with an abrupt and rude reminder of his true age. His leg threatened to lock into a million cramps, and he threw himself on the damp ground to message his tightening calf. But the pain took him anyway, and he writhed in its grip, desperate to find the one position that might offer relief. Intense agony proved words useless, and Lowe twisted into the bed of brown leaves, groaning, his teeth gnashing. In seconds, it was over. He lay contorted, frozen against an uplifted root, absolutely still so as to not provoke another attack.

"Oh, dear God, I hate that," he said aloud, cautious about triggering another cramp. He pulled the plug from his canteen and drank some water. Thinking he needed salt as well, he ate some of the ham and biscuits. His leg eventually relaxed, and he was able to slowly rise to his feet.

Somehow the mountain changed through all of this. Lowe did not see it at first, his eyes and purpose having been focused on the cliffs ahead. But as he brushed himself off, he noticed black soot coating his clothes and hands. He turned to find the source, and immediately saw evidence of a great and ancient fire that had ravaged the forest, scarring and charring as far he could see. On the uphill side of the oldest and widest trunks, a blackened hollow gave testimony to the mass of burning sticks and leaves once collected there. Where it could, bark stretched across the wounds, but could not conceal the irreparable damage.

"The fire...it must have been intense," he uttered to himself. "Yet, the trees still stand like nothing ever happened. That was a long time ago, maybe even a hundred years or more, but they're still here. Mmm...mm." He was amazed at the resiliency of some things, but his body was no longer one of them. He moved on, this time limping toward the cliffs.

The mountain steepened as he neared the long wall of rock, and it became increasingly difficult to keep his footing. A thick hedge of laurel proved even more the obstacle, forcing him to sidestep the hill for 200 yards until he reached a wide bed of talus. The pile of fallen boulders was certainly a pleasing sight. He could ascend the giant slabs like a stairway right to the base of the precipice.

From the bottom of the talus slope, Lowe observed the small gap below him and searched for his camp among the beaver ponds. He could barely discern the wispy line of smoke rising from the vale. No doubt Black Jack was settled next to the fire preparing the survey report. He should be with him. After all, there was work to be done.

A breeze stirred, and not long thereafter, a fickle wind whipped and whistled with uneven surges across the exposed ridge. Lowe looked to the west and the changing weather. The high cliff shielded his view, but a dark column of clouds still peaked from beyond its ledge. He felt little concern. If a storm was approaching, it would likely pass to the north, as many storms did. They met less resistance slipping along the valleys. In any case, he had come too far to turn back. His leg was sore, but he kept climbing the boulders.

The escarpment seemed impregnable. Almost 60 feet in many places, it was an ancient volcanic intrusion that ran the full length of the mountain. Maybe, in his younger days, he might have attempted to scale it, but at this point in his life the notion never occurred to him. Of course, there was no way that he would be denied the top. The forces of nature and his own physical limitations had always been an inadequate match against his will. He traversed the cliff's base hoping to find a natural break that would lead him up.

Lowe kept his eyes on the troubled high horizon, hoping without faith the clouds would amount to nothing. But the harsh rumbles resonating from beyond the cliffs were portents of an angry sky, and it became clearer as he climbed that there was real danger ahead of him. The sun became blotted, and he stood alone in the path of a rising tempest.

The sky was now purple and green with turmoil, and the air grew cold against the film of sweat that lined his body. The wind intensified, and for a few long minutes, the swirling gusts jostled every tree from crown to root. But as suddenly as they started, the gales stopped in an instant, and the mountain was again seized by a deafening silence. Everything waited. Everything braced. Everything trembled in its place, including Lowe Yancy.

For the first time in his life, the man felt small and insignificant. He was an intruder on this ground, and all of nature now watched to see how the storm would deal with his trespass. And for the first time, he felt unwelcome by the wilderness he had always known. The clouds churned violently as they positioned themselves above the unsheltered land, and Lowe huddled against the rock. In the fragile quiet, he waited.

Suddenly, just over the ridge, the sky tore and the sizzle and crack of lightning shook the earth. It echoed repeatedly from the distant hills. The brief moments that followed seemed endless. A single splat of water caught Lowe on the cheek, but before long, a steady pelting of rain and hail would sting and soak his tough, weathered skin. The wind recommenced, as well, and the trees soon bowed and twisted like prairie grass.

A second bolt of lightning slapped the ground harmlessly, while another ripped through the length of a nearby cherry tree. Smoke and splinters shot from its trunk. Gravel and sticks rattled down from the cliff, as the mountain seemed to heave and shudder in the throes of nature. Lowe looked for a haven in the face of solid stone, but finding nothing that would afford him better protection, he remained exposed on the spot where he stood. He crouched ever lower and tucked his head under his arms. Helpless against the violence of the storm, he countered his growing fear with a misplaced reliance on his ever-shrinking luck.

The lightning fell like spears, one by one missing their mark. There was a tingle on his neck and the hair lifted from his flesh. His eyes were blinded by a close burst of light that hurled him into the air toward a solitary boulder. He never heard the sound. He never felt the force that cast him down the hill.

Momentarily stunned, Lowe cowered and trembled at the power now launched against him. He finally gathered himself and crawled to the far side of the huge boulder, which jutted over the steep slope below. A cave-like depression gave the man his refuge, and he curled his muscular body like the frightened and punished child he had become. Trees fell uprooted in the driving wind. Branches and leaves dropped like the rain around him. He hid for an eternity with his fears, awaiting the sun that would not return. The storm passed into night.

It was too late for a fire, and the damp wool of Lowe's blanket seemed adequate against the evening air. He would remain in the shelter of the overhang, where he was at least dry and not altogether uncomfortable. He peered out at the stars, now close and sparkling against the ink of the sky, and he watched the fading flashes of the storm as it pounded against some unknown, far-away place. Lowe would take the summit, somehow, come morning.

Sleeplessness is a garden for many thoughts, but most of what grows in the span of night is despair. The storm had bared him open, made him see for himself that all which once seemed solid in his life had never really been more than sand. The strength of his youth was eroding with the days. His body could not last forever, and someone, some being greater than him, would decide on a whim the moment of his final breath. While he had fought the grasp of death before, for some reason his own mortality now laid heavy and real upon his soul. Suddenly, he was no less frail than others who had already succumbed to death's grip, and he knew that, in time, he too would be taken from this world he loved. There was a certain bitterness and anger that swept over him. He was not prepared to leave, not now, not ever.

If life was to be but borrowed time, Lowe wondered how he came to squander the loan. After all, what was he but a roamer satisfied with a meager living and a few sets of clothes? His family was gone. He had friends, but not many, having spent most of his years tromping across the remote spaces of the region. And what had he done for others? Nothing. What had he done for himself? Not much more. When other men sought love and family, Lowell Yancy shied away. He was too wary of responsibility or confinement, or, perhaps, too afraid of disappointment and pain.

There was a woman though, some years earlier. She was one worth cherishing, but in the end, her life belonged to another. She had had no right to want Lowe, nor he to desire her, and knowing that, they broke from the one deep love that might have abraded his fears. She left him, simply vanished, and like a fire-scarred tree, he stood alone with the hole she burnt to the center of his being. Time could hide the wound but never heal it. The years might break him, but they could never alter his image of her, so lovely and loving. She remained deeply embossed upon his memory, and the fantasy that once was his life would last until his final breath.

Lowe rolled to reposition himself. His hip ached from the lumpy ground, his calf twitched with a new threat of cramps and his mind was dizzy from the ceaseless spin of worries and regrets. He was beyond tired and far from sleep. The night stretched mercilessly.

While it seemed like dawn might never arrive, it did so only to find Lowe finally slumbering in peace upon a dry bed of leaves. Not fully awakened, he crawled groggy and disoriented from beneath the boulder into a morning cloud that hugged the mountain. The gray cliff above him was nearly invisible beyond the dense curtain of mist.

Lowe gathered his scant belongings and, without hesitation or breakfast, trudged up the slope and along the base of the precipice. It took him the better part of two hours to find a small break in the wall, where a steep trail climbed like a winding chute to the summit. He took it slow and easy, careful of the slippery rocks and the menacing twinges to his leg.

The fog became heavier the higher he climbed, and when he reached the top, he could not see 10 feet into the drifting white veil of vapor. It was both strange and beautiful. Again, there was stillness and quiet. He was not disappointed as he listened and looked for what he knew would be nothing.

Lowe walked blindly into the cloud and across the unknown. The grassy plateau was broken by a scattering of stunted trees, which, one after another, arose from the fog to block his approach. Misshaped by ice and wind, fire and drought, they were all the more grotesque probing from the murk, their spindly arms reaching for the only man who dared pass their way. He stepped around them, only to find more, hundreds of macabre forms that stood like demons among the smokes of hell. The wind had twisted the branches into hideous contortions, and warty round galls bulged from the forks of their trunks. As though cursed, every crown had been swept sideways into an awkward, lasting pose. They pointed the way ahead and beckoned Lowe to come forth until he eventually vanished in their midst.

It was an eerie place, foreboding and forsaken. He sensed some sinister force drawing him farther and farther into obscurity, but pressed on, thrilled with the hope of new discovery. Still, he walked cautiously and reached to his side to finger the grip of his holstered revolver. If he was not alone, at least he was ready for what may lurk in the thick surrounding gray.

Lowe continued slowly, carefully choosing his every step over the rocks and sticks that lay hidden in the deep thatch of the grass. He passed beyond the disfigured trees and reached a stone swath that now cut cleanly through the high meadow and across the ridge. It was like the pavement of a Roman via, pitted and worn, settled and cracked by the centuries. Isolated boulders stood to its side like statues lining a great avenue, left in their place to break or melt against the march of a million seasons.

He followed that swath until it widened beyond his sight in every direction. No longer any hint of forest, there was only rock, and there was no color, except the pale, irregular patches of yellow and green lichens that formed scabs across the weathered surface. Small puddles of water pocked the stone, and larger pools were etched into shallow, lifeless ponds. There seemed to be no end to the massive dome spreading beyond the cliffs to the far unseen edges of the mountain.

Lowe stopped to rest when he came to the trunk of a large tree, obviously toppled a day earlier by the powerful winds. Its green leaves were still fresh, not wilted, and they clung securely to the branches. He sat there, opened his pack and began to eat. The fog, he hoped, would lift.

There was no evidence of other tall trees on the rock formation, and there was no explanation as to how this particular one could have gained its footing on so desolate a ground. Lowe's curiosity led him along the length toward what he thought would be the exposed roots. But after 40 feet, the wood curved gradually upwards back into the cloud where it connected to the bole of a behemoth, and very much erect, white oak tree. Lowe went breathless with surprise. What he thought was a trunk was but a mere branch, the outstretched arm of a giant.

As best he could measure, the bole spanned 15 feet, even wider at its base. He could not begin to calculate its vast circumference, and instead, sized the tree by the seconds it took him to pace from drip line to stem. He guessed at the canopy width, maybe 110 feet, if his stride was at all accurate. Through the shielding of the mist, he could not see the top. He could not see the end of the long stout branches that whorled around the center and drooped under their own weight to the stone-hard ground. He could not see the round, outreaching form of its crown, but he knew without question that his find had surpassed the extraordinary.

He placed his hands against the rough, white bark and stood there, trying to feel the energy, the aura, maybe even the wisdom, that must surely emanate from such an old and venerable piece of creation.

"My Lord, my Lord, what have you done?" he whispered. Never in his years of discovery had he seen such a wonder. He found comfort there. He felt safe in the shadow of something that could so long and so grandly endure. It was a timeless work, a living object of perfection. It was, to him, the true evidence of the omnipotent God. He had needed such a sign, and he felt powerless to remove his hands.

The moments went by uncounted, and it was not until the cloud thinned briefly that he became impelled to move. There was more, and he raced across the rock and through the lifting fog to find it. He stopped short of a second cliff that dropped into a cottony white abyss. Lowe squinted against the now growing glare.

Piercing the clouds were tips of other massive crowns, with huge limbs and branches that loomed above the hidden glen. They grabbed the fog like a bather grasping at a towel, trying to conceal the secrets of her body. It was a virgin wilderness, never seen, never touched and never spoiled. It had to be. He had never witnessed such trees, and he wanted desperately to see more. But, for the time being, those secrets would remain closely guarded. The forest had dissolved in yet another rising tide of the silvery morning mist.

The sound of two gunshots bounced somewhat muted across the surrounding hills. The point of origin could have been anywhere, but Lowe knew in an instant who fired the signal. He drew his revolver and placed two rounds of his own in the sky. Black Jack would know he was safe.

Reluctant to leave, he nonetheless retraced his steps past the white oak and across the dome to the trail descending the escarpment. In a few hours, he had made his way back through the small gap and over the valley into camp, where Black Jack was fishing.

"Hear my shots?" Black Jack asked, not diverting his attention from the pond.

"Yup, sure did. Hear mine?"

"O' course, I wouldn't still be down here doin' dis if I hadn't, now would I? Dat storm look to be mighty mean last night. How'd you fare?"

"Good enough. How about you?"

"It never hit down dis way. No rain. No nothin'. Never in all my years has I seen anythin' like it. It just hangs up on dat mountain, den slides on down de ridge. Dere were a whole lot o' lightnin' and noise. You had me worried."

"I'd have to say I worried myself some, but, all things considered, it was a right nice walk in the woods."

Black Jack reeled in his fishing line and strolled over to where Lowe had seated himself near the fire.

"Catch anything?" Lowe asked, as he presented his friend with a mug of coffee. Black Jack responded by pulling two plump trout from the creel.

Lowe laughed. "I should've known. You're so lucky. As easy as you snag trout, I'll bet you could hook a minnow using boots for bait."

Black Jack ignored the taunt. "Well, Mr. Yancy, I hope you found yo answers up on dat mountain."

Rubbing one hand across his unshaven jaw, Lowe pondered before speaking. He pulled his hat back from his brow and felt a cool air brush against the exposed band of sweat.

“There’s a lot on that mountain, but not answers. Not for me. Not this time.” He swallowed the last of his coffee and gazed back at the line of rock that capped the distant peak. “On the other hand, Mr. Clark, I may be getting closer to figuring out the questions. And when they come to me...well, I’ll know just where to go to set things right.”

# CHAPTER 3

The town of Devlin was not a large community, but it seemed like the hub of all civilization against the uninhabited frontier of the mountains. West Virginia had remained largely undetected as America reached westward far beyond its border. Its forests, with the exception of those nestled in the arable river bottoms, often avoided exploitation.

When the Civil War ceased, there was a need for resources to rebuild a broken and expanding nation, and there were new industrial technologies, especially the railroad, which opened the region for immeasurable harvests of timber and coal and oil. By the turn of the century, Devlin was one of many infant villages that circled that forgotten frontier. Just nine years later, it was a small but thriving town, anchored to the economy of trees.

Devlin could boast about its modern advantages. Apart from what the lumber company owned or managed, it had four churches, two barbershops, a couple of law offices, a firehouse and a bank. There was a rather grand hotel, modest in size but ornately constructed by the C&O Railroad. It served the important guests who came to fish the river's teeming stock of bass and trout, to hunt the bountiful game of the nearby high country or to simply enjoy the more lavish culinary experience of the continental dining room.

The town had boarding houses and rooms, some of them nicer than others, to further accommodate the weekly influx of railroaders and loggers. It boasted a small theater that presented occasional local and visiting performances, and it would not be too long before silent moving pictures, already a rage in the cities, would fill the seats every Friday and Saturday night.

The Loyal Order of Moose, known as the 'Lodge', owned one of two brick buildings in town. The second was the community's administrative center and Town Hall. There was even talk of telephone boxes being installed in some facilities, but until that would happen, the Western Union office would stay busy with a constant exchange of telegrams between Devlin and the other world.

And the town was not without its endearing oddities. There were only two food establishments, owned separately by cousins. One was known as Whitman's Café, the other as Whitman's Restaurant. Joe Hanson's gas pump and mechanic's garage was next to Johannson's Livery and Feed Store, and H.H Castle's Hardware Store was, in fact, part hardware, part millinery, and part produce.

Confined on a slight hill above the main rail line and the Charity River, these buildings and others straddled a wide dusty avenue, often cluttered almost to the point of impasse by people and horses, wagons and an occasional motor car. The avenue was officially and appropriately designated Market Street. While Devlin included the customary grid of residential side roads and alleys, Market Street claimed nearly all of the town's commercial business. It was given a speed limit, concrete curbs, wooden sidewalks, and 12 attractive gas lamps, evenly spaced over the three essential blocks. It was the only road in and out of town, and it could be an arduous journey when the rains changed dust into mud. Most travelers simply chose the train.

On the outskirts, on the far side of the tracks, there were saloons, but only two since Devlin enjoyed a reputation for public decency. Still, one saloon was renowned for the fairness of its gaming tables and the other for the fairness of prostitutes who occupied the upper floors. The saloons were the shame of the town, though many a respectable leader, never claiming to have indulged in such base amusements, nevertheless argued for their fiscal and social necessity. Such concerns brought tax revenues, and they managed the misdirected vim of those who came to escape, if only for a day or a night, the backbreaking isolation of the logging fields. In their place beyond the tracks, the saloons had their purpose.

Nearby was the laundry, an unusual blend of functions that included a beer bar and a side room with pool tables and dart boards, five cents a game. Proper women never entered because of the beer, and family men were equally reluctant because of the laundry. Needless to say, the laundry was cooperatively owned and staffed by men, Irish boys who had tired of their hard life in the lumber camps. Like so many businesses, it prospered from the steady patronage of bachelor wood hicks, the young men who worked the mountain and returned desperate for clean clothes and not-so-clean entertainment. The laundry was the scene of many a brawl, provoked by a clash of over-nurtured egos or underlying bigotries between persons of different race or culture, all hungering for the same security and respect. The Irish learned quickly how to quell a mean fight or rid themselves of a sour disposition, and angry men often found themselves moving airborne through a side door to the alley.

Civic pride rested in the Devlin School, which was thoughtfully positioned next to a wooded park on the flat meadow atop Briar Mountain. Most small communities would educate their children through the eighth grade, sending the brighter students to distant cities or larger towns for higher learning. But Devlin wanted better for its children. It offered 12 years of education for those who would continue, partly because the mill subsidized the county for the privilege of better schooling. Mostly, however, it was due to the presence of a learned, talented, and respected principal who demanded that every child be given the best opportunity for academic accomplishment. Popular for miles around, the school attracted to Devlin the best of workers seeking the best of life for their families.

The Watoga Lumber Company was, of course, the keystone of the town. While it did not own each and every property, it did provide most of the jobs, capital and commerce. The future of the lumbermen was tied to the fortune of the company. Labor was a privilege, and work associated with the mill was gratefully received and conducted. In turn, the company did what it could to make the town a proper place to live while not sacrificing its quest for the ultimate profit.

It constructed comfortable, rentable houses for its workers, houses that speckled the entire eastern face of Briar Mountain, lasting houses framed and sided with a durable chestnut board and batten. These were homes of similar appearance, some larger, some not, some painted, some not, but all with common design. All had shady porches to fend against the humid summer heat and steep pitched roofs to divert the weighty winter snow. All had wooden shingles, wooden fences, wooden walkways and wooden privies. All had kitchens warmed by wood stoves, cool shallow root cellars and a middling space for front yard flowers and backyard vegetables. The company drilled wells. It erected water towers and piped water directly into their buildings. It ran wire and brought electric lighting, generated by the mill and available until the daily 10 o'clock blackout when the plant reduced its power.

The Watoga Lumber Company hired the only doctors in town and the only dentist. It built the only hospital, a white, one story building heated with steam radiators from the underground pipes and boilers of the mill. For one day a week, every week, it operated a meat shop that, in the absence of adequate refrigeration, was forced to butcher at night and sell every cut by the following afternoon. There was also a harness shop, a forge and even an icehouse, with its deep underground basin packed tight with northern ice brought to town each winter by rail. And it owned the C. A. Devlin Supply Company, best known as the 'company store,' the largest building in town.

Their hard leather soles clattered over the wooden walk as Lowe and Black Jack hurried toward the mill office. Lowe held in one hand a tube of survey maps and, in the other, a worn leather portfolio filled with relevant data and reports. Black Jack carried a duffle bag slung over his shoulder.

"Are you sure you don't want to come with me? You belong there," Lowe asked for a third time.

"We talked on dis before, didn't we, Lowe? If you's set on losin' de next job, all right den, I'll come along. I appreciates yo feelin's, but dis ain't de time nor place to press a point on dem dat holds yo future. Right now, we needs our work to live, and de problems o' black folk, dis old boy in particular, be better cogitated some other day. You go in dat office and finds us some more work, and stop all dis frettin' about me."

"But, Jack, if we're going to be partners...."

"Lordy, you stubborn! Dis be a troubled world, but it always been dat way. You can't spin it different just 'cause you want to, and dere's no sense in bitin' de hands dat feed just 'cause we ain't so partial to all dey dishin' out. You hear me?"

"I hear. So, what will you do while I'm at the meeting?"

"I's hungry. I aim to drop dese here rags at de laundry, den test dat daily special at Whitman's. Pot roast, accordin' to de sign. But I can wait."

"No, don't wait for me. I had a big breakfast, and it's still a bit early."

"Suit yo self, but you meet me back at dat pool room, and I be glad to spot you a game or two.

"That sounds like a good plan. I'll meet you there, probably in a couple hours."

"But don't you dally none. By de time you gets dere, I likely be finishin' dat second beer."

Two beers were his limit. Black Jack felt that more robbed him of his senses, made him susceptible to the common temptations and left him wobbly, witless and drowsy. But two beers, fresh from the tap, in a cool glass, the head foaming and lapping over the rim -- that was just harmless indulgence. He was already on his way when Lowe yelled back to him.

"Mr. Clark, you watch out at that pool hall. Some rough characters hang out there, and you know all too well how they love to give you an excuse to whoop up on them!"

Black Jack had avoided many fights over the years, but in those times when avoidance was not an option, he was usually the one left standing. He was all bone and muscle, the muscle being the stronger of the two, and he never left a fight once it started.

"Right, Mr. Yancy, I understands yo worries. Now, you think seriously on mine. Make good with dose reports."

The men parted company on the edge of Market Street, and Lowe traveled the full length of town and then some before reaching the mill. He never liked presenting the reports and wished that his partner could be with him in support.

Management at the mill consisted of some highly trained professionals, who often seemed skeptical of the efforts of people with Lowe's limited formal education. The top men were knowledgeable and capable enough. They were diligent at their business, and he respected that. But over years of dealing with such men, he had grown to expect a certain condescending demeanor. He resented the fact that, in their arrogance, they did not even try to recognize the extent of his own vast training and experience. He loathed their lofty airs, their academic credentials, their fancy suits, their extravagant offices and mansions, their precise way of articulating what they mean to say. While these may have been the accepted standards of success, Lowe wanted no part of such success for himself. It required too much show and not enough of the real man behind the achievement. Perhaps there was envy, but if so, it remained unknown to him. He so rarely desired more than what he already possessed. No, it was not envy. He reached for the brass handle and opened the heavy door.

"Yes, sir, may I assist you?" A clerk rose from his desk to greet him.

Lowe removed his hat. "I'm supposed to be meeting with an engineer by the name of...of, uh...." Lowe fumbled in the side pocket of his suit for a business card, and after a few awkward moments, retrieved it. It was soiled and wrinkled and ripped.

"Oh yes, here it is. I'm here to see a Mr. Irwin Dabney." He nervously slipped the card back into his pocket and then tightened his tie. His starched collar drew up close and scratched at his neck.

"I assume you must be Mr. Yancy? Mr. Dabney and the others are expecting you. Conference room. Third door on the right."

"'Others,' you say?"

"Yes, sir, it is my understanding that your meeting includes not only the project engineer but Mr. Devlin and his son, as well. They arrived from Pittsburgh only yesterday, so you may not have been informed."

A cold sweat formed beneath his clothes, and Lowe hoped that his anxiety was not also evident on his face. Few had met the owner of the company, and Lowe could only guess why he would choose to attend such a routine meeting. It was an opportunity for sure, if not for some future reward, then for some immediate disaster. He rubbed his finger over a temple, testing for sweat.

"Third door?" he asked.

"Yes, on the right."

The conference room was not as opulent as the corporate offices in Pennsylvania, but Lowe was nonetheless affected by the richness of the space. The town had few rooms like it, and it seemed out of place in the bustle of a lumber mill. Walnut wainscoting paneled three of the walls. A Persian rug warmed the center of an already beautiful parquet floor. There was a stone mantel above the fireplace and polished brass on the sconces that lined the walls, but these were merely for effect since everything was heated and lighted by the power of the plant. A large enclosed bookcase and a long, oval table, both of striped maple veneer, dominated the furnishings. Ten leather chairs surrounded the table, which had as its centerpiece a half-filled decanter of scotch whiskey, a water pitcher and several glasses, all of heavy crystal.

Lowe noted these things in a glance as he entered the room, but what caught his attention was the one non-paneled wall, which was totally covered by a mural celebrating the mill and its founder. He paused for a second to study it before joining the others already gathered at the table.

"Lowell Yancy, I presume. I'm Irwin Dabney, engineer for the next phase." The men shook hands. "And this is Mr. Charles Devlin, who I am sure requires no introduction, and his son, Austin."

Lowe greeted each man in turn, his grip so firm that both subtly massaged their knuckles as they moved to take their seats. He complimented the owner. "Mr. Devlin, it's a pleasure to finally meet you. Sir, I couldn't help but notice the painting on the wall. I think it shows a very good likeness of you."

"The painting?" Charles Devlin asked, feigning not to understand. There were five works of art situated about the room, but only one had been dedicated to Charles A. Devlin. "Oh, yes, you refer to the mural. Actually, it appears more like a caricature to me. I certainly have had better portraits done, but would agree that this local artist does a fair job. I was rather surprised. Do you care much for art?"

"I like what little I've seen of it."

"Of course. You no doubt get sparse quality time to roam the galleries. I am sure you are a very busy man, with so much of your activity being conducted in the wilds. I almost envy you that."

"It is a good life, sir, and it suits me."

"Well, I understand from Mr. Dabney that you are an excellent surveyor, based on previous jobs you have done for the company, and that you are ready to report on our lands just west of here."

"Yes, sir, and I believe I have a favorable report."

"Good...ah... um...please forgive my poor memory, your name again is what?"

"Yancy, Lowell Yancy."

"Mr. Yancy, I was told you have a partner, a colored fellow, who helped you with the survey. Have you had him long? You know, it is funny. Most of the Negroes that have worked for me over the years would have never taken to an occupation like yours. Your man must be special. Does he assist with all of your projects?"

Lowe wondered if he was being tested or taunted, but either way, he felt his jaw clinch as he strained in non-response. It was fortuitous when the owner's son unwittingly salvaged the situation.

"Father, please, let us move on to business. I have an engagement with Sarah this evening, and I have asked her to meet me here. I have about 20 minutes. If you want me to see something, by all means let the man show it."

Charles Devlin would not tolerate insolence in any person,

except his son, who regularly displayed it like a badge of power and confidence. The young man's rudeness was pardoned without so much as a word.

"Feel free to lay out your papers on the table, Yancy. Can I offer you a whiskey?" Devlin poured one drink and handed it to his son, and then poured another for himself.

Lowe responded, "No whiskey, thank you. I would appreciate some water, if you wouldn't mind." Devlin looked incredulous, almost offended. It was a very expensive scotch.

"How about you, Irwin, can I pour you a glass?"

"Yes, thanks, I'll join Mr. Yancy in some water. Is there any way I can help you with your report, Lowell?"

Lowe stopped shuffling his papers long enough to look Irwin Dabney square in the eyes. He had appreciated the courteous gesture and now liked the sincerity revealed in the man's expression. Dabney was a true gentleman. That was evident. An apology, at least a silent one, might be in order.

"No, but I thank you just the same. I believe I'm ready."

Lowe took his time explaining his findings and figures and answering all the questions put to him. He described the terrain in detail, pointing to the notes on his plat, and he identified all creeks and bogs, cliffs and other obstacles that he thought might hamper access to the tract. He had conducted numerous samplings in the forest to form an opinion of its timber potential and determined as best he could that there was well over three hundred million board feet of prime hardwood available, just on the small portion he had surveyed. In his mind, the numbers were astonishing. Charles Devlin seemed less impressed.

"What were the primary species you encountered?" Devlin asked.

"It's all in the report, but there is a tremendous growth of oaks, a rather even mix including the white, red, black, and chestnut oaks, and some outstanding groves of yellow poplar and sugar maple. Some slopes seemed heavy with chestnut and some had pure stands of white pine. It was not so different than other woodlands here abouts. We saw beech, red maple, basswood, ash, cherry, birch. What was really significant was not the diversity, but the size of individual trees, most diameters measuring three to four feet."

"Frankly, from my standpoint, it is all significant." The owner was blunt. "You do not seem to quantify your statements, Mr. Yancy. I was expecting better information."

The project engineer interrupted to defend the report, "Charles, Mr. Yancy was not tasked to provide solid yield projections, but to identify property lines and give us reasonable description of the land and standing timber. We will have additional appraisals as we begin each phase of the harvest."

"Oh, I see." Devlin looked at Lowe in the trappings of his gray Sunday suit, but refused to recognize the man as anything more than a backwoods lout. "And how do you actually identify the property lines, Mr. Yancy? Did you blaze my trees with a slash of your tomahawk, or do we follow a more sophisticated process nowadays?" The man's humor was unintentionally impertinent, as he compared Lowe's efforts with the primitive pioneer methods of claiming lands and marking boundaries.

Lowe was insulted, but he still smiled. Before he could answer, Austin Devlin slid back his chair and rose to his feet. He commanded, "Hold the thought, Yancy! I will be right back." Then he left.

Lowe did as instructed, and the men refilled their glasses in the brief interim. They could hear a muttered conversation played out in the hallway. Austin's voice was muffled, but the clerk's response was audible enough to define their entire discourse.

"I've not heard from her, sir.... No, sir, not a word.... I assure you, Mr. Devlin, I have no way of knowing that, but I will inform you the minute the lady arrives."

Footsteps could be heard returning to the conference room, and when Austin reached the door, he ended his conversation with the final words, "See that you do. I hate being made to wait, by anyone." No one questioned him as he returned to his seat.

"Go on, Mr. Yancy, the boundary," said Irwin Dabney, anxious to resume the report.

Lowe held up a four-by-four-inch metal tag embossed with the words 'Watoga Lumber Co.' He described the positioning of the plates. "One of these was placed every 500 feet, tacked to a tree at least 24 inches in diameter. Steel spikes and rock cairns mark the corners, as prescribed by our contract."

While Lowe continued speaking, Charles Devlin donned his eyeglasses to stare at the mural on the far side of the room. He looked at the rendering of the lumber mill, at wide logs being drawn from the pond and up the long jack-slip toward the band saw. It was clear he was no longer interested.

"Tell me, Mr. Yancy, are you familiar with the local term, 'the Big Timber'?"

"Yes, I believe I am. It refers to the old growth forests off to our west. The trees there are reportedly larger than generally found in these parts."

"Do you believe, Mr. Yancy, that this tract encompasses the Big Timber, or at least a portion of it?"

"I suppose so, sir. The growth I witnessed was, like I said, as much as four feet in diameter, three feet on the average."

"No, that may be good wood, but the Big Timber is twice that, three times the size of the trees you describe. Does our land include forests of that magnitude?"

Lowe's mind could not help but drift back to the high plateau and the clouds that had once consumed it. He thought of the great white oak, larger than any tree or any living thing he had ever before witnessed. He thought of the small valley beyond the cliffs and the virgin giants that rose out of its mist. And he knew, there was no way he could surrender them to this man.

Devlin continued, "That's what I want, Mr. Yancy. That is what we are looking for, and that is what I'll have. I want you and Mr. Dabney here to get me the Big Timber. Now, you tell me, do I already have it?"

Lowe chose his words carefully, "Well, I didn't see such timber on the ground I was surveying. Of course, you have further boundary work to be done, and the Big Timber may yet be there. I just can't say."

Dabney interjected some rational thought, "Charles, perhaps

you hold too much stock in this notion of the Big Timber. It's mere folklore, from what I have been able to ascertain. It started years ago with the legend of an Indian boy...."

"Yes, yes, I know. The boy found trees so great and strong that even fire could not harm them. But, I tell you, Irwin, I think there's more to this. There's a fortune out there. If we do not have it now, I want us to have it later. You work on that. Call it the next phase if you have to, buy more land or cutting rights, but find me the Big Timber."

A knock interrupted the discussion, and the door was opened just wide enough to allow the clerk to show his face. "I'm sorry for intruding, but your visitor has arrived, Mr. Devlin."

"Well, that's enough of this nonsense for me, gentlemen. I have an engagement and shall not keep her waiting, as she has done to me," said Austin.

The clerk stood by the door as though waiting to be dismissed. "Shall I escort her to the room, sir?"

It was Dabney who responded, "Yes, if you would, please ask Sarah to step in for a moment."

"Never mind that," countered Austin, as he tidied himself on the way toward the door. "I am sorry, Irwin, but Sarah and I really must be going. I have a reservation, you know, and we are late as it is. This has been enlightening, so please don't stop on my account."

Irwin Dabney was provoked, but refused to show any sign of indignation. Still, despite Austin's father, he had no intention of ignoring the young man's haughtiness.

"You forget yourself, sir, or perhaps you did not understand me. Your reservation will wait another minute or two. Austin, I want to see my daughter." He nodded to the clerk. "Please, show her in."

Sarah Dabney bounded through the door with obvious excitement at seeing her father. Her mother had passed away years ago, and Irwin Dabney lived from then on to be everything she needed. Father, mother, teacher and friend, he was by her side and in her heart as they made their way together through the years of her childhood. She adored her father, and the embrace she gave him almost made him buckle from want of breath.

"Daddy, you've been meeting long enough. Let these poor people go home."

"We'll be done soon, don't you worry. I understand you have dinner plans with Mr. Devlin."

"Yes, at the hotel dining room. You should join us. You should all join us, right, Austin?" Austin Devlin rolled his eyes, but dared not speak, still feeling chastised by the girl's father.

Dabney spoke for him, "No, dear, but thanks. You two have fun. You don't need us old timers around watching Austin spoil you. Besides, we have a few other things to accomplish. But before you go, let me introduce you to someone. This is Mr. Lowell Yancy. Mr. Yancy knows more about this area than any man alive. I'm certain of it. According to rumor, he is somewhat of a modern mountain man."

The girl curtsied lightly. She seemed honestly impressed and wanted to hear more about the mountain man. Lowe was intrigued himself, never before being so described.

Sarah liked him in an instant. Just seeing the man, with his straight, strong frame, his face and hands weathered from his time and toils deep in the forest, his eyes highlighted by the wrinkles of his smile, she knew there would be wonderful stories. She loved an adventure, and Lowe Yancy could, no doubt, tell of many.

Lowe bowed to meet her curtsy. "Your father exaggerates a bit, miss, but it is a true pleasure to meet you."

"Well, then, we shall surely see each other again. I look forward to it."

"Come on, Sarah!" Austin's patience finally gave out. He took the girl by the arm and escorted her from the room.

The train rolled down from the camps and the loggers came with it. Good men for the most part, many slipped off the left side of the flatcar and headed up the hill straight for home and family. Others exited on the right and raced as a horde for an unholy night, somewhere on the far side of the tracks.

Many hurried to the shops along Market Street, before the five o'clock closings, or to a barber, a doctor, or an old friend patiently waiting in some restful nook of the town. They took their letters for mailing, their boots for mending, their tools for repairing, and their dirty clothes for cleaning. What they could not or would not do for themselves, they hired out. And when the business was done, they would then look for their pleasures.

Everyone bathed, or at least should have. It was the weekly regimen, the unspoken requirement for re-entry into civilization. Everyone bathed. They shaved. They combed hair and brushed teeth, and those that had them put on clean shirts or suits as they underwent the transformation. The backwoods stench that had marked their arrival was soon lost to a fragrance of talc and bay rum cologne. For a day or so, they paraded like fresh scrubbed puppies, free of dirt and bugs and itch and now ready for play.

Black Jack waited patiently in line with his duffle bag slumped at his feet. When the Irishman yelled, "All right lads, who'll be next," the line moved and Black Jack pushed the bag another measly foot forward. He stared straight ahead, trying not to think of the cool, cheap beer flowing from the small bar in the game room beside him. Worse, the bay rum was not so effective in a place where pile after pile of soiled clothes had been laid upon the laundry counter. The wait was frustrating, the smell offensive, but Black Jack was too much the gentleman to complain, even to himself.

Of course, others were more than willing to do that for him, but the gray-haired man handling each foul load of laundry found it easy to ignore their whines, just like he ignored the stink of their garments. Every filthy pile was another pot of gold, and his work, despite the pervading wafts, was far and away easier than that of a logger.

People may have looked with surprise, or even disdain, but no one was so perturbed as to voice an opinion when John "Black Jack" Clark entered the pool room. He may have been a curiosity of color in the crowd of white, weather-burned faces, but in the pool room, he was considered just another overworked hick in search of a good time.

For a black man, the town was a collection of both welcoming and forbidden places. Black Jack learned early in his life which was which, and right or wrong, it was his peaceful nature that led him to where he would be most freely accepted. The laundry was such a place. He went to the bar, got his beer, and pulled up a stool to watch the games.

There were four billiard tables in the large, square room, and each of them was crowded with players and spectators, many just waiting their turn to challenge. At the table closest to Black Jack, a young man, tall, heavyset and unwieldy, pressed as best he could through a group that blocked his way.

"Hey! I'm tryin' to make a shot here," he said, pleading and pointing to the cue ball with the tip of his stick. Many of the men moved back, but one chose not to hear.

"Excuse me, sir," the boy asked again, more aggravated. This time the person shifted slightly, but not near enough to allow the shot. He was a huge man, a fat and powerful man, with carelessly cropped red hair and a long untrimmed mustache.

The boy reiterated, "Pardon me, mister," but was again ignored. Forced to lean awkwardly across the table, he lined up his angle as best he could and slowly drew back the cue.

The young man had developed a rather decent eye for the game, and he was confident in his aim and ability to bank the striped ball into the side pocket. So confident, in fact, he even called the shot, but the person behind him decided it should be otherwise. As the cue thrust forward, the big man jogged the boy's elbow, forcing the stick to dip. It struck at the base of the ball instead of the center, lifting and bouncing it with a loud thump. The shot missed the intended pocket while the stick scraped hard across the soft green felt.

The man laughed hard, as did some of the onlookers, and he held his own pool stick high over his head as a sign of coup. The boy, angered and embarrassed, failed to see the humor and pushed without effect to move the man back.

"Come on, there ain't no need for that! You're messin' with my game," the boy complained.

"That I am," replied the big man. He laughed all the more. "What's your problem, boy? Can't ya take a joke?"

"I didn't think it was funny."

"Everyone else sure did." The big man looked around to verify his support.

"Well, everyone else didn't miss their shot."

"What's one shot, unless you're playin' for stakes? How much ya got ridin' on this game?"

"Nothin', I was just practicin'."

"Huh? With all these fellas waitin' for a table, you're out here just practicin'! Well, I tell ya what, I'll play ya for fifty cents."

"No."

"One dollar. You look like ya know what you're doin'. Come on, boy, a dollar is a heap a coin."

"No, thanks, not interested."

"Too steep for ya? Ok, then. We'll settle on a two-bit game. You rack and brake. Here's the cue ball and here's my money." The man picked the white ball up from the table and handed it to the youth. Then, he slapped a quarter onto the felt.

"Listen, I ain't interested. Play against someone else, will ya? You can have this table when I've run the rest of these balls."

"Well, if you're not interested in playin' me, then, I reckon it's only right ya give up the table now, so the real men can make some real money. Why don't ya move on, sonny?"

"Mister, I ain't leavin."

The man was not accustomed to argument. His size alone generally discouraged it. "Sure ya are. You're goin' all right, if I have to show ya the quick way out!"

He drew his fingers down along the tips of his mustache, wiping droplets of beer that were clinging to it. He laid his glass on the table and started toward the youth.

Then, the brogue of the gray-haired Irishman rang clear across the room, and everything seemed to freeze in its place. "You wouldn't be startin' up somethin' now, would ya, sir? We'll have no shenanigans, if ya don't mind. These are friendly games for friendly people, and I want no man to be hurt pursuin' his fun."

"Mind your own business, Irish."

"Now that, you see, was not so friendly. Would ya care to restate it?"

"I said, 'Mind your damn business.'"

The Irishman's expression became stern. "I believe it is ma business. You see, these are ma tables, the lad is ma friend, and I don't mind tellin' ya...."

He looked over at the boy, who stood awkwardly braced for battle, his legs bent and his fists rolled close to his chin. On his face were just enough whiskers to tint his rounded jaw, and like a child wearing a brother's hand-me-down, his naked toes peaked beneath the edge of his oversized britches. Part man and part youth, he was stout and brave and defiant, but he was clearly no fighter, at least not the kind who might actually prevail.

The Irishman finished his sentence, "...and I don't mind tellin' ya, as big as he is right now, he'll never be a suitable match for the likes a you."

"Fine, then you run him out of here before I do."

The Irishman walked over to the table and said calmly, "It's a good idea. Dewey, me boy, you don't belong in here today. We're a bit too busy. You know our agreement. You can play when it's slow or if ya have your nickel for the game, like all the others. And ya know darn well you don't have the money. So, come on, lad, be on your way. I'll see you another day."

The boy resisted at first, but passed into the crowd without rebuttal. He paused for some reason when he spotted Black Jack. He understood being asked to leave under the circumstances, but could not fathom why certain people, people like Black Jack Clark, had been allowed through the door in the first place.

"Go on, Dewey, before there's a problem." The Irishman nudged him.

"All right, I'm goin'," Dewey grumbled, and then smiled at the Irishman as he delivered his parting statement, "but ya owe me a beer for leavin' so peaceably."

"Ah, lad, ya know better than that. You buy your own beers here, and I'd rather ya buy them when ya put another year or two under your belt. You've got your blarney, sure enough, but you're not a true Irishman, ya know. You have to watch your consumption, or it'll ruin ya."

The room again erupted into laughter as the tensions momentarily eased.

The fat man was content watching Dewey walk out the door. He placed his enormous hand on the Irishman's shoulder. "That's tellin' him, Irish. The last thing we need is that chubby little bastard hoggin' our pool tables. We've been walkin' through enough weeds back at camp, and sure don't want them under foot when we're here in town. It's good ya sent him packin'!"

The small man swatted the huge hand away, like a fly. "They're *my* tables," he said quietly. He drew close, so close that the big man could feel his breath as he spoke. "Funny, isn't it? The boy didn't call you names, and ya must be twice his size and age. You are trouble, sir, and it's best you leave us as well."

The fat man reeled in shock and contempt. "Huh? Why ya scrawny little leprechaun! No one kicks me out. I ain't some stupid boy that ya can soft talk away, and you're not man enough to put me where I don't want to be!"

Two more men walked out from the laundry, both of them bigger than their Irish friend. They stood ready, almost anxious, for what might happen next, but their compatriot waved them back. He was cool and focused, confident in the power of his words.

"Saints forgive me. Now we have a problem. You've upset me countrymen, and it'll be the devil gettin' them to settle again. So please, sir, would ya leave us before things get bad?"

"I ain't goin' nowhere, and you and your friends can go straight to hell!"

"Dear me, I had hoped to avoid all this. Perhaps you would prefer to talk to Shawn. He's a bit more experienced with customer complaints, and I've made such a shamble of this one." The Irishman twisted his head and shouted over his shoulder, all the while keeping his eyes on the red-haired man. "Shawn! Shawn, put on your jacket and step out for a moment. A gentleman asks to see you."

"I don't wanna see no one. Just leave me be, if you know what's good for ya!" exclaimed the big man.

In an instant, another Irishman had joined the three, all of them together not the size of their adversary.

"Why, ya fool, he's smaller than you!" The big man began to laugh so hard he almost dropped his guard, but expecting a rush, he quickly sobered himself.

"Aye, but he's powerful and he carries a lot weight in this town. Besides, it's not Shawn himself that should be your concern."

"What? You gonna tell me ya got a whole army of little people back there?"

"Enough of this. Show him, Shawn." The fourth Irishman pulled back the lapel of his tweed coat and revealed a silver shield of authority. "Mister, meet Shawn Harrigan, *Constable* Shawn Harrigan." The policeman rested his hand on the top of a holstered pistol to make sure there could be no misunderstanding.

The Irishman continued, "You can see, sir, Shawn comes prepared. He's never been one for takin' chances. Now, if you'd kindly remove your wet glass from me table and leave, I would be so obliged. Would that be satisfactory with you, Shawn, or do ya prefer to make an arrest?"

The constable said nothing. He just observed as the fat man screamed and blew out of the room like a rumbling storm.

"You're a bunch of nothin', the lot of ya! If I see any of you tater eaters or that stupid kid again, I swear I'll take ya down so hard you'll wish you were dead!" The door slammed shut and the situation was over.

A group of men wasted no time stepping up to Dewey's table. One gathered the balls and racked them into a tight triangle, while another positioned the cue ball for the break. Then, they each tossed a dollar's ante onto the green felt.

The room was back to normal, smoky, noisy and stale, and Black Jack, still on his stool, was ready for that second beer.

Lowe was mentally worn as he turned down the sidewalk onto Market Street. It had been a long meeting, but all and all, it was a good one. Unfortunately, Mr. Charles A. Devlin did not seem too impressed, but in that regard, the feeling was mutual. Lowe cared little for the man, but assumed that was the general consensus of those who had met him, at least in similar circumstances. Devlin was predictably pompous, and his hunger for wealth at the expense of the forest was more than alarming. And frankly, as a father, he was as profound a failure as his son was a pretentious cad. They were rich in plunder but poor in character. Their brief acquaintance had shown Lowe that much.

But the other man, Irwin Dabney, was a pleasant and respectable sort, and he was the one who awarded the contracts. Lowe was both relieved and grateful when Dabney mentioned there would be more work for the survey team, immediate work that would take him and his partner back to the marvels of the Big Timber.

The walkway was crowded. One by one, establishments were closing for the evening, and everyone scrambled to complete their business before the weekend. It seemed like people were coming at him from every direction, and Lowe stopped and started, twisted and turned, trying to make his way across the town. It was easier to traverse a briar patch, he thought.

Finally, there was only one obstacle between him and an open corridor through the chaos. He quickened his pace to overtake a young man and a wiggling little boy gleefully saddled on his shoulders. Lowe sidestepped into the street and prepared to pass, but the boy prodded his carrier and the two lunged ahead, the child yelping with delight.

"Go, Morgan! He almost got past us on the left. Hurry! He's gainin' ground!"

"Jake, this isn't a race."

"Yah-huh, is too! And that man's gonna win it if you don't go fast!"

Morgan tried to accommodate the boy's wishes, but every attempt at fast impressed a more serious need for slow. "Jake, move your hands. I can't see. Come on, let go, you're pulling my hair!" he shouted.

The child repositioned his hands, but in seconds, they were right back to tugging at the ears or nose or anything else that might secure his grip. Then, there came the inevitable "clunk," followed by the rhythmic creaking of a low-hung shingle. The boy held his head and slumped.

When Lowe reached the pair just seconds later, Morgan was already looking at the red knot rising from young Jacob's forehead. Lowe steadied the swaying sign and then squatted to check the extent of damage for himself.

"Are you all right, young fellow? You were moving pretty fast up there."

The boy tried to get some sense of his injury from the stranger. "I hit my head."

"Yes, you did. I saw that."

"Is it bleedin' bad?" Jacob asked, and gingerly dabbed his fingers over the bruise for a sign of blood.

Lowe tried to put him at ease. "No, it isn't bleeding at all, but I'm sure it smarts. I've busted my own noggin a few times over the years. That was quite a race we had. Looks like you're the winner."

"Yup, Morgan's a good ol' horse when he wants to be," the boy said, "but he don't watch where he's goin' half the time."

It was a line he had stolen from his mother. He had wanted to cry at first, but the whole conversation was distracting, and his justification for tears was somehow lost in the words. Still, an opportunity for attention was not to be dismissed. He feigned a sniffle.

"Sorry about that, little brother. He'll be fine, mister. He's got more knots than a sassafras tree. Isn't that right, Jake?"

"I need some ice, Morgan. Are you sure it ain't bleedin'?" If there had to be pain, he could at least hope for blood. He sniffled again.

"Nope, no bleeding. Do you want me to take you home so Ma can fix you up?"

"Ice!" His voice wavered with the best piteous moan he could muster. "I...I... I need... some ice."

"But there isn't...." Lowe interrupted Morgan with a wink, and then, offered his own suggestion for a remedy. He pointed to the 'open' sign still displayed in Castle's shop window.

"If you fellows don't mind my intrusion, I think this store is still open. They might have a shave of ice for us. Maybe a stick of candy would be the proper medicine for a nasty bump like this one. What do you think?"

"It's not worth the bother. Really, he's fine. Jake, here, can be a bit dramatic with the right audience," replied Morgan.

"Don't you say that! I could use some o' that medicine," argued the boy. He immediately sent Lowe fetching.

By the time Lowe returned, another young man had joined the pair, and the lump on Jake's head was little more than a memory. It was just as well, since the small piece of ice had all but melted in his hand. He offered the candy to Jake, but was careful to not interrupt the ongoing conversation. Lowe sat down next to the child, and beneath the shaded awning of the shop, they quietly licked on lemon sticks.

"So, he kicked you out...even though you didn't start it?" Morgan asked his friend, incredulously.

"Yeah, but that's okay. If he hadn't, I would've pounded that big tub of lard somethin' fierce."

"Oh, stop it, Dewey. The only fight you were ever close to winning was with Jake, and I'm almost certain he won that one."

Dewey smiled at the boy. "Sure, but Jake's the toughest little man in town. I didn't expect to win." He reached over and squeezed Jake's toes. The boy smiled back. "So, Morgan, what ya doin' tomorrow?"

"No plans."

"That's good. There's a load of saw logs comin' off the mountain, and they say it's one worth seein'. Some of the biggest cuts yet, one timber to a flat car. I heard some of them pieces had to be left in the woods while they figured out how to best move 'em. There was even talk of splittin' 'em just to lighten' up the weight for skiddin'. They gotta be huge. You wanna go?"

"Mind if I bring Jake?"

"Nah, bring whoever ya like." Another thought came to Dewey. "Hey, I'll bet them logs will set purdy high out of that mill pond. They probably won't roll much either. It might be a good time to try our luck walkin' the pond."

"You think? Some plans are best when not carried out."

"Not this one. We've figured on this one since we was 10, and right now might just be our last good opportunity. Let's do it."

Dewey and Morgan had always talked about sneaking into the mill pond to practice their log rolling. Ever since they were boys, they had imagined themselves walking from one embankment to the other, stepping across the slippery timbers that floated side by side or end to end. Growing up, they had relished the stories of the river rats who could balance on the wet, spinning wood while breaking up a jam or sorting a partially submerged raft of logs. These were once important people, back when logs were driven to the mill by way of the river during the spring melts. They kept things moving. They turned snags off the beach and cleared them from the eddies and rocks. They made the best of the swollen flows and kept the timber afloat until it was recaptured downstream at the mill.

Of course, they often were maimed or killed by those flows, but to the boys seeking their adventure, that fact made it all the more worth their doing, made it glorious and inviting. It was a piece from an era lost to the coming of the railroad, and Morgan and Dewey wanted to hone their skill while there were still a few old timers who could appreciate and critique their method. The pond was the place, and the time, if there was ever to be a time, had to be soon. They would not be young forever.

"I don't know, Dewey, it's a crazy idea. It always has been," Morgan said.

"That's true. But admit it, you still wanna give it a shot, don't ya?"

"Part of me does. The smarter part of me doesn't. When were you going to try it?"

"I was thinkin' 'bout Sunday. We can't get near that pond tomorrow, but come Sunday.... Well, there ain't no one at the mill on Sunday. We could meet there, say at four?"

"We'll see. I'll have to let you know."

Lowe stood up and offered the candy. "Pardon me, gentlemen, did you say there's going to be a shipment of big logs?" he asked Dewey.

Dewey had no qualms about accepting a treat from the stranger. He reached into the paper wrapping to find a peppermint stick. "Thanks, I don't mind if I do. Yeah, tomorrow. I heard they were bringin' out the largest trees yet. Apparently, there was a small pocket of 'em hidden up some back hollow. I guess there ain't too many of 'em left nowadays."

Lowe agreed, "Not many at all. The native groves are pretty much gone, and those that aren't will be taken soon enough. Well, I might have to witness that load for myself."

"Then ya ought to come, mister. It should be downright educational."

Dewey turned back to his friend and realized quickly that Morgan's attention was now focused elsewhere. He followed Morgan's stare. "Well, look you there, Morgan. That's her! She's the yellow haired girl from Avery's pool."

"I can see her plain enough," Morgan said flatly.

"Wow, she's some kind of pretty, all dressed up like she is."

"I reckon she's always pretty," Morgan responded under his breath.

"I wonder who that fella is that's courtin' her. Can't say I've ever seen his face around here before, can you?"

Morgan said nothing.

Lowe watched the couple move along the opposite side of the street toward the hotel, and he instantly recognized them both. "The girl's name is Sarah Dabney," he said, "and the boy...his name is Austin, Austin Devlin."

"Ya don't suppose that's *the* Austin Devlin, do ya, mister? The owner of the mill?" Dewey asked, showing his surprise.

"Well, I don't reckon he owns it yet, but that's him in the flesh, the heir to a lumber empire. You know, it seems a strange coincidence that I met them both for the first time only a few minutes ago."

"So, how well do you know this Devlin?" asked Dewey.

"Like I said, I don't, but it doesn't take long to size up the quality of a person. I can tell you, boys, that young lady can do a whole lot better than young Mr. Devlin. If I was 25 years younger, I wouldn't be standing here watching. I'd be racing over there just to get in line for the day she cuts him lose."

"Aah, I got me a girl," Dewey said proudly, "but this Sarah sure is a looker, a little too much so for the likes of us, I'd say."

Morgan was still without words. He could not hear them. He could not speak them. He was drowning in the depths of his own envy. He so wanted to be that man, if only to walk by Sarah's side, but with every step taken toward the hotel door, she moved another whole mile beyond his future. His silence was revealing, at least to Lowe Yancy, who knew Morgan's kind of pain all too well.

Lowe picked up his case and nodded his goodbye to Dewey. "You fellows have yourselves a good evening and be careful around that mill pond." He waved to Jake, still seated and now sticky with sugar, and then he patted Morgan on the back. "Don't give up, son. Let the girl see who you really are. She'll know the right man when she meets him, and I promise you, it will never be the likes of Austin Devlin."

# CHAPTER 4

The dusk was gray and silent, and Morgan strained to hear some sound, any sound, from the fading forest around him, but there was nothing except a faint crunch of gravel shifting beneath Dewey Baughman's nervous feet.

"Come on, let's go," Dewey pleaded, anxiously teetering back and forth on his heels. "It's near dark already and we still got us a mile or more to go."

"Wait," Morgan replied in a low airy tone. "Wait and listen."

Dewey froze in place and cupped his ears for what seemed an eternity of boredom. Twenty seconds passed.

"All right, I've waited. I don't hear nothin'."

"Exactly."

"Exactly what? I can't hear a blessed thing and neither can you. Quit foolin' around and let's get out of here!"

Morgan was deaf to his friend's entreaties. His speech fell into a soft, disturbing monotone, and his gaze locked on the black void of a distant hollow.

"They say these hills have been haunted for centuries by the ancient Shawnee. They say that the Indians cry from their spirit world for their lives lived and lost in the greenwood, that the mountain air carries far the sound of their wailing to those who would stand and listen alone in the wilderness. A great nation now gone. A once invincible people now gone. But they say the Shawnee are still here among us, waiting in the cover of night's gloom and watching on high until the forest might again attain its purity, until it is rightfully returned to them as their eternal place. Stay quiet, Dewey, we might hear their moans."

Morgan had chosen his words well. From the corner of his eye, he could see that Dewey was uncomfortably captured in the thought. The two were still, as they again listened to detect the mysteries of another cool, spring evening. But the woods were strangely vacant, and Morgan's words were the only sounds of both the living and the dead.

There are none so old as to be fearless of the dark, but a man must never reveal his doubts. Dewey believed this, though he was nearly overcome by those doubts. They were growing by the minute. They deepened with every darkening shadow and with each evocative word that battered his wall of reason. The silence in itself was eerie, but Morgan's voice now conjuring devils in the befalling night was more than he could take. With his feet implanted, he searched with every sense to detect those who were no longer of his world. As Morgan spoke, Dewey kept his vigil. Though he could not find them, the spirits might well be there.

Morgan Darrow could not create ghosts, as hard as he tried. He closed his eyes, extended his arms and hands, and held his breath like a medium waiting to be possessed. "And you know, they say, that in these very mountains, a Shawnee warrior once died a most horrible...."

Dewey exploded in an outburst of nerves. "Well, hoo-ray for *they*!" He preferred to appear more cynical than cowardly and was relieved to find that the noise of his own voice was an antidote for fright. With that in mind, he kept talking, "I'll say one thing for ya, Morgan, you're sure eloquent when ya wanna be, but save that damn nonsense for the women folk, will ya? I ain't particularly interested in hearin' your talk just now. We need to keep a move on. Besides, who the hell are *they* with all them opinions? I don't suppose you or anyone else can rightly say!"

It was a good little tirade, and Morgan was quite satisfied. There was nothing like a spooky story to enliven the dead of night. He had set out after Dewey's imagination, and he caught it. The master of mischief was rarely duped, but now, he fell unaware like a princess to a spell. It was petty retribution, but long overdue, and Morgan took pleasure in the effect. He watched with delight as Dewey squirmed and knew there was no benefit to disclosing the truth.

Dewey repeated himself, "Yeah, save them stories for the girls. They don't work on me. I don't care 'bout your Indians, and frankly, them spirits don't hold much interest neither. Whoever *they* are, I wouldn't give two nickels and a damn for what *they* say!"

But Morgan knew better and decided to continue his initial tact. "Sh-sh-sh. Seriously, Dewey, do you hear that?" He posed the question as they stood absolutely still by the side of the road, far from the noise of Devlin and the Charity River. "Really, can you hear it?"

"Hear what? I still don't get nothin'."

"If you listen closely, and I mean really closely, I believe you'll detect something. On nights like this, you're bound to hear it."

Dewey tried again, but to no avail. "What? What the hell am I listenin' for? There ain't a livin' thing out there!"

"Sh-sh-sh. The sounds of the forest don't always belong to the living."

"So, ya think some spook is out here tryin' to talk to us. I think you're crazy."

"Well, I've heard people say it's just the air... not the wind that hisses across the grassy field or through the needled branches of the cedars, mind you, but the air itself as it drifts slow and free in the peace of the night. It's so quiet it almost screams inside your head. Still, that's not what we sense this evening."

"That's not what *you* sense. There ain't nothin' in these woods to hear but the dead calm, and even that's quieter than a turkey buzzard at a thousand feet. I ain't sensin' nothin'."

"Dead calm. I couldn't find the words, but you sure did. Spirits must have other places to haunt besides old buildings and cemeteries. Why not here? Dewey, why not now?"

Dewey was still fearful, but now, he was also intrigued. Goosebumps formed across his nape as a shiver climbed to the tip of his spine, yet he mustered his courage for one last try. He listened, and this time he heard.

"Yeah, yeah, I can hear it! It's like a breath, like someone breathin' slowly into my ear. Almost nothin', but still, there's a little somethin' there. I can't make it out."

"That's it. Maybe like a whisper, a very faint whisper, from someone or someplace far and unseen. You know, it could be the Shawnee speaking to us from the dead calm, if you believe in that sort of thing."

Dewey considered for a moment. The concept of a ghost actually talking to him was one he was not willing to grasp, especially on so very dark an evening. "Well, I don't believe in it, not one bit," he said, now shaking.

The ruse had played out perfectly, and Morgan was content to bring the discourse to a more rational conclusion. "No, I guess I don't either, if I have to be honest. Yet, I do know these hills seem haunted in a way. I feel it every time I hear a screech owl calling through the dark, or mourning doves cooing at first light, or when trees creak without even a hint of breeze. Sometimes I feel it when I hear a steam whistle echoing through the valleys long before I see a train or hear its wheels rumbling on the rails. And it seems like I'm always alone when I feel it. Do you know what I mean?"

"Maybe so. Maybe so, but what I know for sure is that you have scared the bajeebers out of me, and ya meant to do it. I'm impressed. But it's gettin' dark. Let's move on."

"Wait a minute, Dewey. Try it again with me, just one more time."

They began to listen in earnest for the sound of air, the whisper of a ghost, the peace of night, but a barred owl, as if prompted, hooted from a tree high on the ridge above them. Another responded from the opposing mountain, and seconds later, yet another signaled from the distant valley. Both boys were momentarily startled, and Dewey began to concentrate all the more on the shadows.

"I got me a real case of the willies, and I ain't likin' it. But, Lordy, I have to give ya due credit. How did ya manage that thing with the owls? It was great."

Morgan had turned to begin his walk toward home, while Dewey stood fast, contemplating his own question and waiting for a reply.

"Tell me, how did ya do that?" He repeated the question louder, and then, realized that his friend had slipped down the road, far beyond his sight. There was a brief pang of terror. "Morgan!" he yelled. "Morgan?"

From the pitch of the new night came the answer, "Not me, the Shawnee."

The steam whistle blew a defining series of mournful tones as the train approached the final bend into Devlin. Everyone, both at the mill and in the town, was aware that Engine No. 2 was home, and with it, another bounty of logs sectioned from the magnificent trees of a once great and untouched wilderness.

The train had hugged the Charity River for miles, but finally veered away when it reached the back edge of the millworks. It crept ever slowly, passing each feature of the site in turn, from drying yard to engine shop, from power house to mill, as though orienting the raw timber to the facilities and processes soon to be involved in its transformation.

The lumberyard, itself, spread over 18 acres, laden with endless pallets of boards and posts and lath of varied dimensions. Stacks stood side by side, many 30 feet high, along hundreds of yards of track-lined docks and aisles. Here were the new boards, each precisely stowed to dry straight and true, given adequate time and some gentle stirring of the mountain air.

There was spruce and pine, oak and ash, maple and poplar, chestnut and cherry, and numerous other woods, the essence of a forest sacrificed for the building of a young and growing nation. The yard teemed with the sight and smell of fresh cut lumber. Yet, more was not enough. The trains kept coming and going, always moving the rich resources of a hidden, virgin land.

No. 2 was a Shay engine, designed specifically by lumbermen to haul the huge burden of timber from remote seams and ridges of the high Appalachians. Its size was small and light relative to other locomotives, and the unique gearing of its wheels gave it critical traction against the severity of the hills. Where other engines might flounder against the pull of a steep grade or pitch on a radical turn, the Shay would prevail.

The train left the yard and slipped past the switch with a rhythmic click and clunk as its wheels labored down the siding toward the millpond. It stopped in the shadow of a low water tower to quench the thirst of its large, cylindrical boiler. Then, with a hiss of steam and a clang of flatcars jolting against their couplings, it began to move again.

It passed the machine shop, alive with the sound of hammers and torches salvaging the chassis of an old rusted caboose. It passed the foundry, capable of manufacturing all that was iron, every part, every tool, every welded rod or plate. It came to the planing mill, where planks were smoothed and shaped into flooring, molding, and other specialty pieces, and then to the dry kilns, their brick compartments full with racks of green lumber being heat-seasoned against the ruinous effects of rot and warp. And there were warehouses and sheds and more lumber docks, as No. 2 kept easing toward the pond.

The red brick walls of the powerhouse and adjoining boiler room were mottled with dark stains of oil and soot. Still, they were the only splash of color amidst the weathered grays of wood and corrugated metal so prevalent on other structures. Four smoke stacks loomed 110 feet above these buildings, lifting high and away the hot, white plumes generated by their furnaces.

The boilers were the heart of the mill, and they pumped feverishly, nourished by an endless supply of scraps from the lumber operation. Fire formed the steam; steam built the pressure; pressure moved the pistons; pistons drove the shafts; shafts turned the belts; and belts, leather belts, powered the saws and generated the electricity for lighting and machinery. Steam-borne energy. It was the lifeblood of the industry, the town and the people, collectively known as Devlin.

When a band saw turned, so did the wheels of an entire operation. Throughout the millworks, a multitude of men and a maze of conveyors, running upward and downward, overhead and underneath, all worked as one to move a steady yield of finished products, the lumber, the pulpwood, the chips and dust.

The train rolled another 260 feet along the entire length of the saw mill, before finally coming to rest at the side of the pond. There was an occasional vent of steam, but the engine was seemingly noiseless against the loud clatter and wheezing of the mill machinery. High in the loft, two eight-foot band saws screeched as they ripped board after board from the mother logs.

The mill pond, only an acre in size, was already crowded with floating and submerged timber, and the bull chain made little difference as it continually snagged the wet logs and conveyed them up the jack-slip to the waiting blades. As long as the Shays were running their windy course down the mountain, the small pond would never run short of material. There was always another load, another section of forest that would soon plunge heavily into the black oily water.

The scent of honeysuckle sweetened the air as a light breeze lifted the fragrance from a vine covered fence. Young Jacob Darrow and his brother lay head to head in the short grass beneath a spreading walnut tree. They peered at the branching silhouette above them.

"I don't know the answer to that question, Jake. I suppose someone thought the tree was worth saving. Maybe they're just waiting for it to grow bigger before they cut it. Of course, it does tend to dress up this view of the mill, and it certainly provides a lot of fruit."

Morgan reached along the ground and picked up the half-eaten hull of a year-old walnut. "The squirrels sure like them. I guess we all do." He tossed the hull into the air, and Jacob rolled to avoid its fall. "Oops! That wasn't such a good throw, was it, Jake? I darn near hit you."

"It was good all right. You were aimin' right at me, but I was ready for you this time!"

Jacob grabbed a handful of grass and threw it to the wind, which carried it straight into Morgan's face. He ripped another handful of turf, roots and all, from the ground.

Morgan surrendered. "Okay! You win, little brother. You win."

They both settled back against the land and watched the branches sway in the air. They were waiting for the far away whistle of Number 2.

"Do you think the logs will be two times bigger than this walnut trunk?" Jacob asked.

"Much more."

"Will they be four times bigger?"

"I think even more."

"Six times. Ten times. How much?"

"I don't know, but the word is that this is the biggest of them all. It's supposed to be at least eleven feet wide, Jake. That's huge. It's so huge that they can carry only one log on each flat car and they need five cars to bring in the entire tree. It's hard to imagine, isn't it?"

"What kind is it?"

"I was told a white oak, likely three to four hundred years old."

"But, Morgan, why? Why do they cut 'em down? I've never seen such a tree, and they're gonna be gone, all of 'em. I don't want 'em to kill the big trees."

"Sometimes I don't either, Jake, but that's how we have to live. And the trees do grow back." Morgan moved his hands to cradle the back of his head against the firmness of the ground. "Maybe, if we pray real hard, God might let us live to be 400 years old, like in the days of Noah. We could watch the big trees grow from seed. What do you think?"

"I don't think so. It all makes me sad. I don't want 'em to cut the big trees, and I don't want 'em to take this nice walnut. Do you reckon they will?"

"Like I said, I just don't know."

The steam whistle blew, and the long-anticipated train began its crawl through the millworks. Jacob sprang to his feet.

"Now, Morgan, let's go! We can't miss the splash."

"I'm right behind you. In fact, I'm going to beat you this time!"

The race to the millpond was on, and in less than a minute, Jacob was declared the usual winner against the long athletic legs of his older brother. While the train crept to a stop, others also began to congregate around the edge of the pond. Lines of men pressed through the doors of the mill buildings, and families scurried from their hillside homes toward the coming spectacle. The jack-slip carried nothing to the saws, which like all the other machinery, was now idle and abandoned.

Eleven feet, four inches in diameter, 16 feet long, the first gargantuan log dwarfed both the engine and the 10 men who had gathered to roll the huge timber into the millpond. At first everyone stood well clear, as one worker applied the tip of a long pole to release the clasps of the anchor chains. One by one the chains slipped loose and rattled across the railcar floor before dropping in a heap to the ground. The heavy log remained in place.

The men then positioned themselves behind it, and in unison they attempted to turn it with the leverage of their peaveys. On the count of three, they grunted and pushed, but the barbed poles were useless against the log, to the little surprise of the onlookers and crew. The trunk refused to budge, and the workmen backed away without a second attempt. In 10 minutes, a steam loader was pulled to a parallel track, and with its long steel arm, began coaxing the massive timber toward the wooden ramp that lined the bank.

The railcar rocked and creaked under the shifting weight, and the ground quaked as the log finally rolled and crushed onto the surface of the ramp. When it bounded into the pond, a great wall of water shot forth with fury over the small sea of logs, and a geyser of spray lifted high, settling like a heavy summer rain. Then, the log disappeared into the blackness of the water, only to rise again like an angry whale, spouting mist and scattering all that lay before it.

Those who witnessed kept their silence while the mound of water rushed to every curve of the pond, lifting effortlessly the vast tonnage of wood within. The swell inundated the banks and then rolled back upon itself in the middle. Only when the waves transformed to ripples did the crowd cheer with nervous excitement. The same response followed as each section of the ancient oak submerged, resurged and settled.

"Was that incredible or what!" Dewey Baughman had barely reached the site in time, but what he saw astounded him. He tugged on a wild lock of Jacob's hair. "That was somethin', wasn't it, Jake?"

Jacob answered, "It was scary, but I liked it!"

"Yeah, pretty powerful stuff. I liked it, too."

Morgan welcomed his friend with a half salute. "So, where have you been, Dewey? We were looking for you."

"I've been out tryin' to spot Auralee. She was gonna be here, but I ain't seen her. You haven't seen her, have ya?"

"No, I sure haven't, but then again, I haven't been looking for her. It's a big crowd."

Dewey scanned the mass of people as they began to disperse toward the mill and town. "It beats me how I missed her. I'm right certain she was comin'." He switched the subject, still perusing the crowd. "Hey, Morgan, I guess tomorrow's your big day, huh?"

"Big day? Well, if you're talking about my birthday, I guess so. I'm surprised you even remembered."

"Oh, I didn't remember nothin'. Jake told me. I guess that means you're gonna duck out of our pond walk."

"I haven't yet decided what I'm going to do," Morgan replied.

"Well, ya need to do this. Frankly, ya need to try a few other manly things, if ya know what I mean. It's high time. You're pushin' past 17. If ya put such matters off, the next thing ya know, nature won't be there to help ya along." Dewey raised his eyebrows up and down with sinful suggestion. He grinned.

"Be careful with that kind of talk, Dewey." Morgan gave a cautionary glance in the direction of young Jacob.

"Listen, if the boy was older, he'd be the first to agree with me. It's time to put a little hair on that chest and find yourself a woman. Why just last night, Auralee and I...."

"Dewey, that's enough! I don't want Jake to hear your sordid details."

"Okay, you're right, of course. I'm sorry." Dewey continued anyway, but lowered his voice as he cupped his hands over Jacob's ears. "And they are sordid, believe you me. If I'd only known from the start just how good the manly pleasures would be, I'd have made damn sure I was born with a beard and ready for action. I don't know why we have to wait so many years for the good stuff. A design problem, I reckon. Yeah, if I'd only known...From day one, when that midwife first smacked my tiny pink bottom, this little baby would've spent his first breath on earth askin' if she were already spoken for. It's that good."

"It is, huh."

Morgan would not believe a single word. He recognized Dewey's claims of amorous endeavor as being wishful thinking, but also knew that it was just a matter of time before his friend could convey some unembellished truth in the same regard. Dewey's lascivious desire for Auralee Buck had vanquished the last of his patience, and he was beyond ready for the inevitable surrender of his virtue. Morgan knew a lie when he heard one, but chose to let this one stand.

"I declare, Dewey," said Morgan. "It's best to keep some things personal, but as long as we've been friends, that's one lesson that never managed to take hold. I suspect there's a whole lot more to being a man than knowing the manly pleasures. You keep on this way and you're likely to find out."

"Just what are ya gettin' at?"

"It's real simple. Stupid and careless doesn't make the man, despite what some fellows do and most ladies think. I really like Auralee, but you need to make sure you know what you're getting yourself into. Loving the wrong woman can be as dangerous as walking this pond. You think on that. Those big logs should not be tested, and we're stupid and careless just considering the idea. I'm not sure what to call us if we actually try it."

"Listen, you're gonna do it. Somebody's got to. We've been

talkin' 'bout this so long I feel like I've strolled across that pond in my sleep. And with them new timbers takin' up half the space, it should be easier than Christ's walk on the water. You'll be fine, trust me. I'll be here to save ya, just in case you're not as nimble as ya appear to be."

"Wait just a minute! I thought the plan all these years was for us to cross together."

"It was, but I changed my mind 'bout that. It wouldn't be safe. I weigh too much. I'd sink them logs, and then, where would you be? Plus, I'm already a man, remember?" Dewey grinned again.

"So, in other words, you don't have one argument that makes a lick of sense, but I'm supposed to risk everything for some child's folly."

"That 'bout sums it up. What ya say?"

Morgan was afraid to give the matter more serious thought. Doing so would stop him from facing his challenge, and he really wanted to try. "You know, Dewey, I think I could make it, and I'll do it on one condition."

"And that is?"

"That is you come with me, like we always intended. And I mean all the way over that pond, or under, as the case will probably be. Your company will be my birthday present. It's all I want."

Dewey grimaced. "Hell, I never gave ya no present before. Why start now? If I was to land in that pond, I'd soon be with yer Shawnee Indians hauntin' these mountains. I ain't ready for that. Thank ya, anyway."

"I'll take that as a firm 'yes' and meet you here at 4:00, just like we planned."

Dewey continued to offer a litany of reasons why he should not walk the logs as he and Morgan started back across the field toward the walnut tree. Never really capitulating, he nonetheless abandoned all arguments at seeing Auralee Buck and Sarah Dabney emerging from the shade. Auralee waved to him. He was encouraged to hurry.

"Hey, it's Auralee! I knew she'd make it." Dewey shouted to his girl with a show of boyish excitement. "And it looks like she's got some company."

Morgan also saw the girls, but Sarah was not waving. Her hands were folded in front of her, and when she spied Morgan moving toward her, she spun in place and looked back into the canopy of the walnut. In his mind there could be only one reason, and he felt the sharp sting of her disinterest.

"I guess they're waiting for you, Dewey."

"Yeah, I reckon she loves me. I weren't too sure the first time I saw her, when she was all wet and naked at that swimmin' hole." He looked around sheepishly and was relieved that young Jacob did not hear the comment. "But, thank the Lord, she's come around to my way of thinkin' real quick like."

"You are lucky... about Auralee, I mean. I've known you forever, and I've never seen you care for anything or anyone quite so much," Morgan said.

"Hell, yes, I'm lucky. Let's go catch up to 'em. I need to talk to her."

"No, you go on." Morgan looked down at the ground and scuffed the toe of his shoe through the dirt. "Just be here tomorrow on time, and don't wear those heavy boots of yours. They'll drown you and me both when I have to pull you from the water."

Morgan laughed, mostly to hide his truer feelings. Then, he looked again at the girls across the field. He saw Dewey racing toward them and wished he had gone as well.

The millpond was in no way inviting, especially to someone accustomed to swimming in the clean, clear pools of the Charity River. The pond was a dead basin filled with every type of refuse the lumber mill might discard. In some angles of light, a rainbow of oils would cling to the surface. In others, the only color was a deep amber-black of tannins leached from the soaking timber.

A stale yellow froth bubbled out of nothingness where the wind lapped water against the bank, and in the leeward shallows, there was dark clarity only until a gust of air moved the froth as a drifting mat of waste. Sawdust, bark and shavings, blown paper, tossed bottles and cans, there was such utter pollution that the pond required draining and dredging every year. Sometimes more.

"Tell me again why I'm gettin' ready to do this?" Dewey was gathering his courage.

Morgan looked across an almost solid deck of floating logs. "Well, you were right. I always wanted to walk these logs. I can hardly see the water from the timber. Today's the right day, if we're ever going to try it."

"Uh-huh, somehow, it don't feel so right to me. I know why *yer* goin'. You could never resist a dare. Ya love any physical challenge, and most of all, you're absolutely crazy. But, Morgan, the Lord knows I'm a lot smarter than you and not near as athletic. So, please, answer my question, why am I doin' it?"

"I can't say. You showed up, and that's enough for me. I'll go it alone from here. In fact, I'd prefer having you on dry land in case something goes wrong." Morgan smiled at Dewey and shook his hand. "Happy birthday?"

"Ah...sure, happy birthday, Morgan. I guess I forgot ya again, but I'll be there if ya need me."

"I know that."

Morgan knew that his only chance to cross the pond was to move fast, taking short, rapid steps. If he depended too long on any single footing, the log might roll and plunge him dangerously against the other timbers or into the septic water. He focused on that simple strategy... step quickly...step high...don't let them turn. Don't let the logs turn!

He broke his grip on Dewey's hand and leapt down the ramp to the closest timber. He jumped from wood to wood, like a squirrel frolicking among branches. His mind was barely ahead of his feet. There was no time to plot a course. He could feel the smaller logs give way under his weight and learned at once to rely on the more massive cuttings that floated higher above the surface. Still, he sometimes slipped on the wet, loosened bark or stumbled on a raised knot, but his strong legs and stronger determination kept him balanced.

He could not pause even for a moment to look for an end. He

focused in the split of a second on the nearest step, then on the next, and the next, and the next. The pond had no end.

"Morgan! Morgan!"

Morgan seemed to recognize Dewey's voice, but his mind and body were moving too fast to comprehend what was occurring behind him. Not even Dewey's brief cry for help or the sound of a man crashing hard upon the water would break his pace. But the scream that followed, the unexpected, horrifying scream of a young child, shot through his consciousness and crippled his movement.

"Jake!" He turned, trying to keep upright on the log, striving to keep his feet stepping quick, stepping high, while he scanned the far bank. Dewey was gone. Jacob jumped wildly on the edge of the ramp. Unable to swim, his brother was much too close, much too vulnerable against the deep danger of the pond.

"Jake! Dewey!" Morgan wanted to tell his brother to stay safely back. He wanted to call to his friend, to make sure he was unharmed, but all he could manage were names. "Jake! Dewey! Jesus, no!" The logs parted suddenly and his feet could no longer find the next step. He plunged into the blackness, into the absolute blackness beneath the logs.

A simple way in, there was simply no way out. He twisted beneath the surface of the water and lost direction. There was no light, and in his blindness, he began swimming downward until the growing pressure and the coldness of the muddy bottom made him realize his deathly error. Encumbered by his trousers and boots, Morgan kicked frantically, hopelessly, to find the surface, but found, instead, an impenetrable ceiling of wood. Sliding hand over hand across the roughness of the bark, he dared not lose touch, lest he again become lost.

He pressed desperately against the logs, and with each push, sank back into the deep. He pried the narrow space between two timbers, but had not the strength to separate them. Kicking, all the while kicking, he then moved laterally along the base of the logs in search of light, some faint glow that would lead him to air. But the darkness was complete.

Morgan's lungs prepared to burst, and as the bubbles of life sifted from his lips, he felt weak and warm and still. His fingers slipped from the wood above and he drifted slowly downward. Only now was there light.

There was no pain as the peavey tore through his shirt and pierced the skin of his back. There was no pain as a strong hand reached through the water to grasp his hair and pull his limp body to the surface. Morgan's lifeless frame was hauled across the curvature of one of the large oak sections and dragged to the shallow edge of the pond. The same strong hand lifted him to the bank and began to press firmly against the small of his back.

"Push! I see the water comin' from his mouth. Push!" Dewey was white with terror, with disbelief, helplessness and guilt, as he saw his friend slumped in a posture of death. He knelt beside Morgan's pale body. "Push, mister. Damn it, Morgan, breathe! Don't leave me livin' with this. Ya can't quit me now." He struggled to see clearly through the mist that filled his eyes.

Jacob watched, and sensing Dewey's fear, wept quietly at the thought that his brother may be forever gone. A lonely emptiness washed over him, and he drew close.

"Is he gone, Dewey? Is Morgan dead? Is he drowned?"

Jacob was much too young to learn of death. The tears trailed across the pink of his cheeks and fell as droplets on his brother's ashen face. He lifted Morgan's head even as water continued to pump from the lungs. His tiny fingers caressed Morgan's jaw and opened wide the mouth, so that more water might leave the body and make way for life. It was all he could give.

Another voice responded, "No, son, I think he's coming around." Morgan's upper body suddenly lurched as his lungs began to voluntarily give up the water. With each expulsion came a short, desperate gasp for air. "Good. Good! He's breathing again. Keep coughing it up, boy. You're going to be just fine."

In relief, Dewey and Jacob both threw themselves upon Morgan's back, perhaps to hear the renewed movement of blood and breath, perhaps just to be near the one they almost lost.

“Easy, now, he’s still got a lot of pond water inside him.” The boys reluctantly pulled away. The stranger ceased his massage and nodded in satisfaction as Morgan’s eyes regained their awareness.

“The light. Thank God for light.” Morgan spoke between the coughs in a weak, hoarse voice, “Who are you? What happened? Dewey, Jake, are they all right? What happened to Dewey?” He coughed again.

“I’m fine, Morgan. Now I am. I tried to follow ya across them logs and fell on my ass at the very first step. I’m sorry I messed ya up. Damn near killed ya.”

“You said you wouldn’t use that word, Dewey.”

“I know. It ain’t the right word for a time like this. I’m thankful, Morgan, flat out thankful. I don’t know what else to say, except I’m sorry.”

“Jake, you all right?” Morgan put his arm up, beckoning Jacob to come nearer.

Jacob was hesitant, as though he was looking at a ghost, but he gradually edged forward to take Morgan’s outreached hand. “I’m all right. I’m scared. You really scared me.”

“I sure didn’t mean to, but you don’t need to be scared anymore. I won’t even tell Ma you came down to the pond. It will be another one of our secrets.”

The stranger interjected, “Be glad he did come down to the pond. When your friend here fell in, the boy’s scream got my attention. When you slipped under the logs, he ran across them to show me where you were. He’s brave. He’s a real hero, this little one.”

Morgan yanked his brother to his side and held him. “I’m proud of you, Jake. I owe you my life. I’m very proud.” Then, he looked to the stranger. “I feel like I know you. I’m sorry, though, I don’t even know your name.”

“Lowe Yancy. You don’t recall, but we met yesterday in town. Jake won the race, remember?”

“Yes, I do remember. Well, you saved me, sir. I can never repay you.” Morgan coughed hard to remove more of the water.

“No need. I darn near stabbed you to death with that peavey.

You'll feel it tomorrow, I'm sure. It's best you get to the hospital or home to put a poultice on it. Your chest and throat are going to hurt for a few days, too. Yeah, boy, you were the biggest fish I ever hooked. When Jake showed me the spot, I pushed the logs apart just enough to see your final bubbles. I knew you were almost gone, so I tried to find you with the hook. It hit a bit hard. Hope you're okay."

"Mr. Yancy, thanks. Thank you for everything. I wish I could give or do...."

"You know, maybe there is something you could do, but only if you want to. In a week, I'll be leading a survey crew up through the mountains. It's beautiful beyond belief out there, and I could use the help of a couple strong, young men. If you're interested and your parents allow you to be gone for a few weeks, I encourage you to take the job. I'll pay you well."

Lowe Yancy continued to paint a picture of remote country where virgin timber adorned green mountain slopes. He talked wages and duties and described the pleasures and ordeals of life in the far away lumber camps.

"Trust me, boys. It is hard work, long days, but you'll never feel better when the sun goes down. Give it some thought and let me know once you've recovered from all this."

Dewey spoke quickly, "I'm in, and don't ya worry none 'bout Morgan. He's in, too. He'll follow me anywhere."

Lowe looked at Morgan's soaked and exhausted appearance. He chuckled. "Yeah, I can see that. Just let me know, boys. I'll be leaving Monday week."

Dewey and Jacob braced Morgan's arm as they moved across the field toward the walnut tree and the dirt road beyond. It would be a slow walk to home.

The cry of a red tail resonated high above the valley, and Dewey wondered if the others had heard it. There was still that question about the Shawnee spirits, but at least his friend was not among them.

# CHAPTER 5

Morgan was distressed at what he heard as he ascended the steps to the porch. His mind responded quickly, and he turned to his friend and brother who were trailing behind him.

"Dewey, how about taking Jacob over to your place to try some of your Ma's cookies? Could you do that?"

"Huh? What cookies?" Dewey responded, startled and confused by the unusual request.

With a brief begging glance, Morgan tried in vain to communicate his sense of urgency. "You know, those really sweet cookies, the sugar ones." He addressed his brother, "Go with him, Jake. Mrs. Baughman's a fine baker. You loved that peach pie of hers, and I'll bet her cookies are even better. Bring me back one, will you?"

Morgan's voice was trembling and hoarse, bearing evidence of his anxiety and sense of alarm. But cloaked in innocence, Jacob focused on the cookies. He responded immediately, "I'd like some. Can I come to your house, Dewey?"

"Huh?" Dewey repeated himself, dumbfounded by Morgan's strange behavior.

"Please, Dewey, something's happening here, something serious. Take little Jake and go."

"Ah, yeah...sure. My Ma would love to see ya, Jake. Let's run over to my place and see what goodies we can find."

Jacob did not hesitate at the offer, and the two boys disappeared around the corner of the house before Morgan cautiously opened the cottage door. The argument from inside the kitchen was loud and threatening, and Morgan listened only to determine if he should intrude. He entered the parlor undetected and sat quietly on the edge of a small piano stool. There he waited. There he worried for the future of his family.

"Yes, you will, and you'll bring it now! Don't make me tell you again." Lawson Darrow spoke harshly, but could not intimidate his wife.

"Don't do this, Lawson. I baked it for Morgan's birthday. The children will be back soon, and I thought we could celebrate together. It's a special day."

"I work myself to the bone for this family. Is it too much to ask that I be given first consideration once in a while? I only asked you for a piece. You'd think I was trying to steal a national treasure. Get the cake! Now! I need to go to the Lodge, and I can't wait any longer for your kids to come home."

"They are our kids, Lawson, both yours and mine. You don't know what you're saying. You don't want to be like this."

"Annie, get me that cake this instant, or I swear you'll regret defying me."

Lawson picked up a rifle that was leaning against the corner cupboard. He lifted it to his shoulder, placed his finger on the trigger, and aimed it at the face of his wife. The woman did not flinch.

Morgan made his presence known, "Pa, put it down! Put the gun down."

"Stay out of this, boy. Get out of here! Your Ma and I have some things we're discussing. Just get!"

Annie was strangely calm. "It's okay, Morgan. Do as your father says. He's not going to hurt me. He's just had a couple too many drinks and is a little confused."

"Shut up! Don't judge me, Annie. You are always judging me, and now you're going to start doing what I say, whether you like it or not. I said 'Get me that cake!'"

Lawson lowered the rifle momentarily, as he turned and scowled at his son. "And you, didn't I tell you to get the hell out of my house. Respect me or feel the brunt of my fist. Your choice, boy."

Morgan had to muster his diminished strength to merely stand.

Minutes ago, he had survived drowning, and now he shook with exhaustion and shivered in clothes still damp with pond water. He reacted using the little power left within him.

"You are not my father. My father doesn't treat his wife that way. You're a sad, tortured man, Pa. You're not my father, not while the whiskey speaks for you."

"Get out!" Lawson dropped the rifle on the kitchen table and brandished his fist toward Morgan. "Maybe it's high time I taught you a lesson, as well."

Morgan showed fire in his eyes, though his body was weak. "You're not going to hit me, Pa, not on this or any other night. Go to your Lodge. Go drink with your friends, but leave us alone."

Lawson tightened his fist and moved in anger toward his son, all the while trapped in Morgan's piercing glare. He raised his arm to strike, but Morgan stood defiant. He held the fist close to Morgan's jaw, but hesitated long enough, just long enough to lose his want of violence.

Lawson's arms slumped to his side, and he walked silently toward the door. He knew he could never hurt his child. Ashamed, he left.

"Ma, he could have killed you. I've never seen him this upset. He's half-crazy. We should lock the door. I should get the constable."

Annie crossed the room and accepted a long hug from her son. "No, the gun wasn't even loaded. I knew that. Forgive him, Morgan. Your father loves us, but he fights a demon that we can't understand and he can't destroy. I pray hard for him. He so badly needs our prayers."

"But he was ready to pull that trigger."

"No, Morgan, that rifle is his gift to you, to show you how much he really cares. He's waited weeks for this night, for your birthday, just to watch your expression when he gave you the gun. He loves hunting with you, and he has wanted you to have your own deer rifle ever since you could walk. I wouldn't let him. I'd say every year, 'Wait until my Morgan grows up'. Well, you are grown, son, and your father and I are very proud of what you have become. He'll be sober tomorrow, and he won't remember a thing he's said or done. We need to forgive him, to be strong for him."

Morgan pondered Annie's words as he picked up the rifle from the table. He examined it closely. "It's beautiful. Just look at the curly grain on this stock...walnut...remarkable...Winchester Model 1905...a .32 caliber...a 10-shot magazine. Pa bought this for me?"

"Yes, for you. He loves you very much."

"Sometimes I wonder, Ma. Sometimes, like tonight, I want to..." Morgan left the thought unfinished. He was fatigued and suddenly overwhelmed with compassion for his father. "He's sick, isn't he, Ma? He's lost in a way. I guess I should go and fetch him home."

"He will find his own way. For now, it's best we let him be."

"Well, tomorrow he'll be sober. So tomorrow, maybe he can show me the gun. And Ma, you serve him first, okay? The cake, I mean. Serve him a big piece of my cake."

"I will, son. Your father will like that."

They spoke no more of the incident, and Annie moved purposely to other topics. "Why are your clothes so wet, Morgan? You look like you're coming down with something."

"You always think I'm getting ill, Ma. I'm not. I just fell in some water doing something stupid."

"By stupid, I suppose you mean you were walking those logs at the mill pond."

"Yes, ma'am, but how did you guess?"

"Sometimes, mothers just know things. You finally yielded to that reckless temptation of yours. Ah, Morgan, you promised me that you wouldn't."

"I did promise, but that was years ago when I was a boy. I'm a little more capable now."

"Before hearing this, I would have thought so, but the child you once were never broke a promise to his mother or tried such a foolhardy stunt. I'm not sure I like the idea of my little boy growing up. I can't watch over you anymore, not like I want to."

"At this point, you shouldn't need to. I'm sorry to trouble you so."

Annie's expression exposed her frustration and anger, but it was not with Morgan. "What troubles me is the Watoga Lumber Company," she said. "That filthy mill pond may yet kill some innocent child. It's a public nuisance, and it needs a fence. It's high time I go to complain."

"That won't do any good, and it really isn't necessary. Maybe Devlin needs some smarter boys. I know I'm not one of them."

"You are smart enough to not make the same mistake twice. So, I guess all I now have to worry about is little Jake."

Morgan did not want Annie to know that Jacob had been near the pond, or for that matter, that he himself had almost died beneath the floating timbers. He hoped that she would not probe further.

"Actually, Ma, I doubt Jake will ever try what I did. I'm sure he knows all too well how dangerous that pond can be. I've taught him the best way I know."

"By example?"

Morgan's failure to reply was answer enough, but Annie already suspected there was more to the story. She could see that her son was weary and knew that the truth would surface in time. It always did, if not from the mouth of Morgan, then from Jacob or Cora. She could afford to be patient and was willing, this time, to forego a mother's rightful reproach.

Again, she deliberately changed the subject. "Have you asked anyone to the dance next Saturday? It's only a week away, you know. A gentleman should give a girl some notice."

"No, not yet. I really don't know anyone."

"That's nonsense, Morgan. Every girl in town would love to accompany you. Stop being so bashful. How about the Buck girl... Auralee?"

"No, she's with Dewey now. At least, he hopes so."

"Well, I'll bet her sister would enjoy the dance. I always thought she had the loveliest red hair, and Cora has even told me that the girl is rather sweet on you."

"Yeah, she's pretty. Actually, Sadie may be the last person who would want to be with me." He recalled her embarrassment and screams from the edge of Avery's pool. "No, I can't think of anyone. Maybe I'll just stay home."

"Morgan, you will not stay home. Even your sister has a young fellow taking her to the dance, and I want you there, too. Believe it or not, your father asked me to go, and despite his behavior tonight, he'll be ready to take me. He's a fine dancer and a romantic man with a fiddle. I want my family with me. All of my family."

Morgan looked at his mother. For the first time, he saw lines in her once soft face. There were strands of gray from her temple to her loosely tied bun of chestnut hair. Her long dress was frayed where it dragged the floor, faded where her food-stained apron failed to shield it from the sun. She was weary from the labors of life, worn from the demands of motherhood and marriage. She asked little for herself, and Morgan knew he could not deny her now.

"All right, maybe I'll just go it alone."

"Hey, I know! What about Cora's new friend? She has just recently come to town and probably hasn't met too many of the young people yet. Why don't you ask her? She should love to go. Her name is Sally, Susan, uh.... Oh, my! What in the world is her name?"

"Sarah. Her name is Sarah."

"Yes, that's it. Now, she would be just perfect. You should ask Sarah."

"Ma, a man has to wait in line for a girl like Sarah Dabney. I'll find someone. Don't worry. I'll find someone, but you have to promise me a dance."

Annie glowed. Creases radiated from the corners of her eyes. The lines of an aging face deepened, but she was still beautiful.

Morgan Darrow learned the important aspects of shopping from his father: know what you want, know what it's worth, know where to get it, then get it and go. For the most part, the boy was able and well-practiced, often buying what the family needed in his parents' stead. Yet, the company store was extraordinary in its diversity. Every time he walked through its door, a host of distractions blurred his focus, and he found himself lingering and fingering through a myriad of unnecessary goods and equipment.

Casks of nails, cans of paint, bins of seed, and the like crowded the center aisles. Tools and hardware of all descriptions hung from the racks or rested on deep shelves and drawers along the walls. The drug counter was stocked with bottles, boxes and cans containing every known patent remedy and local potion or tonic. By the register were jars of licorice strings, gumdrops, horehound and other candies. Bottles of Coca-Cola and root beer bobbed in a wash tub chilled with spring water and irregular chunks of ice.

One room was laden with the latest fashions of hats and garments, home wares, blankets, bolts of fabric, canned foods, jewelry and notions of every sort. There were clothes and toys for children, especially at holidays, and there were home decorations, furniture and furnishings for the complete house.

Even appliances, such as sewing machines, stoves and ice boxes, could be purchased from the floor or specially ordered and later delivered by train. Under roof on the back lot were bulk supplies of animal feed, building materials, coal and kerosene. The company store had everything that Morgan might possibly require -- everything, and that in itself was a problem.

A small bell jingled as he entered. This time, he paused only to scan the large open rooms he had seen a thousand times before, then reluctantly moved on toward the loft and men's clothing. The sales floor was utterly congested with an overstocking of merchandise, but nothing appeared different, except the five empty chairs facing the coal stove. The white-haired men who regularly filled them had moved outside with the warmer weather and were now trading their tall tales from a long wobbly bench on the store's front dock. Their former place by the stove was the only uncluttered space.

Morgan stood alone in the doorway and sighed, "Lordy, how I hate buying clothes."

"What's that you say, Mr. Darrow?" a voice called out, hidden behind the counter.

"Oh, hello, Mr. Blackman. I didn't see you back there. I suppose I was talking to myself."

Sam Blackman was a stout, middle-aged store clerk and manager, always anxious to help a customer and forever searching for an opportunity to banter. He stood up slowly. The waist of his trousers hung low on his large round belly, and from habit, he tugged on his brown suspenders to pull them up.

"You know, son, I tried talking to myself once. I recall it to be a most perspicacious conversation. So, what can I help you with today?"

"Well, for starters, maybe a definition." Morgan stuttered as he slowly sounded out the word, "Perspa...presta...What was it, 'prespitatious'?"

"No, I said, 'perspicacious.' Honestly, Mr. Darrow, aren't they teaching you boys anything up at that school? *Perspicacious*, it means I'm sharp as a tack, perceptive, insightful. As a result, I'm a rather engaging conversationalist when I talk to myself. Everything I say to me is completely understood and utterly inspiring. Anything else you need?"

"Nothing really, except maybe a shirt. Thanks, by the way, for the lesson."

"Here at the Supply Company, there's never a charge for education, and everything else is just downright cheap. We'll find you that shirt. You know, I can always tell when there's going to be a dance in town. All you young folk have been sprucing up this week. If you don't mind me asking, who are you going with?"

"I wish I knew, but I guess I'm going, with or without some girl on my arm. Ma says it's important to her that I be there. So, I'll be there."

"Well, from past experience, and I mean a very distant past, I would say you best hurry up. The pretty gals are probably already taken, and you're likely to end up with some warty little thing that spent four long years just trying to master the fifth grade."

"Yeah, I appreciate all the encouragement," said Morgan sarcastically. "That's no way to talk to your favorite customer, now is it?"

"You're my favorite now, huh? I reckon you're right about that. You've been a steady visitor to this store for 10 years or more, by my recollection, and I expect your babies will be shopping here in years to come. I only hope they don't have warts like their mother!"

Morgan appreciated Sam Blackman's jocularity. Above all else, it was his humor and genuine fondness for people that ingratiated him with the customers. Sam never had a troubled day or an unkind word, from the standpoint of those who crossed the threshold and jingled the bell above the door. Whether or not they were spending their fortune or killing their time, every person in the store was his favorite.

"Listen, young fellow, this town is full of pretty women. You go up those stairs to your left and find yourself a new shirt, or a tie, or maybe a little bottle of sweet cologne. Do this and the girls will come running to you. It's a guarantee of Sam K. Blackman and the C. A. Devlin Supply Company. If you need some help, just holler. I'll be down under this counter restocking a few things. You enjoy that dance."

"Thanks, Mr. Blackman. I'll give it my best shot."

Morgan looked up at a wide balcony, the area designated for men's clothing, and then ambled to the staircase. He hesitated before climbing, his attention drawn as always to a large upright cabinet stocked full with shotguns and rifles, fancy pistols and shiny knives. The gun rack was missing one particular piece, perhaps the very one he was given on his birthday.

In that moment he thought well of his father, who had chosen for him the perfect gift, the hunting rifle, and of his mother, who reminded him that truly perfect gifts were really much more simple to impart. Love and respect, they suffer no cost, no limit of supply, and they are ever more precious than the material offerings. Still, he prized that rifle and was grateful to the man who provided it.

Morgan was overwhelmed by the untidy stacks of shirts and

trousers piled high upon the tables. He browsed the different styles, looking for anything suitable. Finally, he settled on a tumbled pile of cottons, their sizes, colors and patterns all in disarray, having been picked over by the rush of young men preparing for the upcoming dance. Of course, color or pattern was of little concern. Morgan preferred white, the plainer the better. Common as it was, white was easy and always acceptable, and he needed easy when it came to selecting clothes. But size? It was the one factor that always seemed to change. He languished for minutes, simply thumbing through the shirts.

Even from his place behind the counter, Sam Blackman could look up across the room and see Morgan Darrow lost in his dilemma. Most of the boys who visited that week faced the same problem, and the clerk knew that it was just a matter of time before he was summoned. He was half way up the stairs when the door creaked and the tiny bell chimed.

"Good day, Mr. Blackman. My daughter and I may need some help picking out a nice dress. Are you as proficient with women's clothing as you are with hardware?"

The clerk toddled down the steps. "Not hardly, but I do know what *pretty* is, if you require a second opinion."

He addressed the man's daughter directly, "It's nice to see you again, miss. You can trust that I am not the one who decides our line of ladies' fashion. Consequently, I'm sure we'll have something you like."

Morgan continued to agonize over the shirts and consciously ignored the conversation below, but something he overheard soon captured his attention. A warm wave of emotion rolled through his body and spirit. He strained to look over the heaps of clothes to the floor below him, but could see nothing except the white tin ceiling of the store.

Sam Blackman spoke again, "Mr. Dabney, I'll be right here if you require assistance. Tell your daughter to use the back closet if she wants to try on her selection. Just pull the cord for a light."

"Thank you kindly, Sam."

Morgan heard correctly, "Mr. Dabney." He moved closer to the balcony rail, careful to not be seen. She was there. Sarah was there, in the same store. He picked up some shirts and pretended to examine them, all the while stealing quick glimpses of the fair-haired girl below. She was so very beautiful, so captivating that he could not resist watching her every move across the floor. He tossed the shirts on a pile and stepped back another foot from the rail, his eyes locked on Sarah.

Morgan watched as the girl slipped a brown skirt from the rack and tried to match it with several different blouses. For the longest time, she held a beige blouse close against her body as she peered into a long oval mirror. One hand lifted the material to her shoulders while the other flattened it upon her midsection, pulling it taught against the curve of her breasts. She twisted to different angles watching what the mirror might reveal. Content, she took these clothes and a separate dress of indigo to the closet. Morgan waited.

Sarah returned donning the blue dress and again positioned herself in front of the mirror. She swayed and swirled, observing the hem as it whisked lightly above the floor. Then she freed her hair, which had been loosely gathered in the back, and pulled it aside to her left shoulder. The soft yellow tresses shone like gold against the deep color of the bodice.

Morgan looked on intently. He liked the dress. He liked the delicate ruffles that edged her neckline and wrists. He liked how her camisole peeked through the sheer fabric and the comely way she danced before the mirror. But even more, he liked the way a few loose strands of hair graced the exposed white of her neck and curled across the soft indentation just beneath the lobe of her ear. Here, her ivory skin would surely melt against the moist, warm touch of a kiss...his kiss. He sighed at the thought of it.

Morgan tried to redirect his attention, embarrassed by the boldness of his thoughts. But he was beguiled. What he watched, he wanted. His eyes and his heart hungered for more. As Sarah disappeared into the dressing closet, he fully expected her to emerge wearing the brown skirt. Instead, the clothes were draped over her arm, and she walked directly to the counter. The indigo dress had been left behind.

He felt a sudden, overwhelming urge to confront her. He needed to read in the expression of her face some acknowledgment of their moment at Avery's pool. Perhaps she would not share his memory of that day, or worse, she might look to him with cold indifference when he again peered into those eyes.

It was difficult to give up the anonymity provided by the loft, and Morgan was more than wary of what might follow when he came into Sarah's presence. Nevertheless, he snatched the nearest shirt from the table, descended the stairs and moved bravely toward the counter. Even his fingertips felt the beat of his heart. He had to face her. He had to know for certain, though she may forever turn away. He would take the risk.

Mr. Blackman watched Morgan approach with a wine-colored shirt that would fit a man over twice his size. He understood and said nothing. He just winked and continued his attention to Sarah.

"Some of our male customers have made it clear that I lack the necessary flair of the haberdasher. I draw greater criticism from the ladies. I accept their opinions, of course, being content to just know what I like when I see it. That being said, you have selected a beautiful skirt and blouse, Ms. Dabney. I expect you'll be turning a few heads come Saturday. I assume you're attending the big dance."

"Yes, and thank you, Mr. Blackman. You are very kind. You do have so many wonderful things in the store."

"Will you be going with a special beau?"

Sarah hesitated before she answered, "I suppose he's been my special beau for as long as I can remember."

Morgan felt his heart sink beneath his feet. His disappointment must have carried like a siren, for Sam Blackman noticed it instantly and lost that twinkle in his eye as he continued to help the girl. An awkward quiet in the room threatened to expose him, and Morgan spoke out of impulse to end it.

"I liked the blue," he said.

Sarah spun around and smiled in recognition. "Did you? I rather liked it myself, but I think this color better suits me."

Morgan tried to again look into her eyes, but could not do so without revealing through his own eyes the anguish that consumed him. He looked down instead.

"No, I prefer the blue. It's your hair. The dress is right with your hair." He wished he could touch her, feel the softness of her hair, hold her delicate hand in his. He looked up slowly. It took courage to face her.

"Please, pardon my manners. I'm Morgan Darrow."

Sarah giggled. "I know that, silly. We met at the church, at the river. Don't you remember? I know all about you from your sister and Sadie. I'm Sarah, Sarah Dabney."

Morgan saw no virtue or benefit in lying, but if Sarah did not share his affection, he could not allow her the truth. He had considered the possibility of another man in her life, but the reality had hit swift and hard. He wanted to hide just how weak he had become.

"Of course, I remember. You just look different today for some reason. I don't know why I didn't recognize you from the start."

Sarah asked, "Will you be coming to the dance, Morgan?"

"For a little while, perhaps."

"Wonderful. Do you like to dance?"

"Ah, I suppose, but I'm not very good."

"I'll bet you are. In fact, I heard Sadie say you were a fine dancer. Maybe someday you will dance with me."

Morgan forced a smile to the corners of his mouth. "Sadie? I don't believe I've ever danced with Sadie. I'm really not very good. But someday...maybe."

Sarah had hoped for an earlier opportunity than just "someday," but sensed that Morgan was uncomfortable with the conversation. She wondered why, like she had wondered so many things about him since their first meeting at Avery's pool.

She turned back to Mr. Blackman. "I'll pay scrip for the clothes.

Daddy says our account is going to bust wide open soon." She handed him a printed note marked *C.A. Devlin Supply Company. Valued for Trade and Service Only. $10.*

Mr. Blackman neatly folded the skirt and blouse, and packaged them separately in brown wrapping paper. He handed the packages to Sarah.

"There you go, miss. Come back and see me again soon."

"I will, and thank you." Sarah began to open the door, but hesitated. "Mr. Darrow, I will not forget your promise of a dance, and I love the shirt you're buying. I hope you intend to wear it on Saturday."

Morgan spread the oversized red shirt, now loosely wadded in his hands. He replied almost sheepishly, "Oh, actually, I was looking for a white one, and...well...a much smaller one might be in order."

Sarah smiled. They took one long last glance at each other before she pulled the door behind her. Again, the little bell jingled.

Dewey Baughman was a poor dancer and the last person to ever realize it. He loved to dance. To the bounce of a 12-string banjo, he would throw his arms to the clouds, kick up his legs and howl like a hound, but he never seemed to move from the spot where he started. He could go that way for hours, and at the end of the evening, he generally ignored exhaustion and pleaded for more.

Tonight was different. Tonight he was with Auralee, and every song was supposed to be a graceful, romantic waltz. When they were not, he simply pulled her close and stepped to a cadence of his choosing. Auralee did not seem to mind. They danced for a complete hour before the band rested and the orange sun settled in the sky.

"Thank God," Auralee uttered under her breath, truly grateful for the break.

"The band'll be back soon enough. Come on, Auralee, let me rustle us up some punch, and we can drink it out there under the trees."

"Dewey, I'd love something to drink, but it's awful dark in that grove. Some animal might come and get me. I think we should stay put, right here."

Dewey was surprised by the girl's sudden apprehension. She was not such a person to show fear of the night.

"But you're missin' the point, darlin'. Some animal truly wants to get ya, and he will get ya, if ya just give him the chance! Let's go under the trees, just until the music starts."

Auralee spoke sternly, "I believe, Dewey Baughman, it is you who may be missing the point. There's only one animal I need to worry about, and it's at least persistent if not dangerous. No, my love, we are not going out there under the trees, and if you're smart, that will be the end of it."

"Okay, don't be angry with me. I want whatever you want. Wait right here and I'll get the punch. And don't be mixin' with any of them other fellas while I'm gone!"

He was reluctant to leave her alone, but started across the dance floor to the far side of the pavilion. Auralee leaned upon a low stone wall. She shook her head and rolled her eyes as she watched Dewey mope and lumber through the crowd.

Sadie came up and sat next to her sister. "Having a good time? What happened to Dewey?"

Auralee's mind was elsewhere. "That boy is always hungry," she thought aloud.

"Well, there are some wonderful deserts on the table. He won't have any trouble finding food around here."

"No, I mean he's always hungry for something else, like me, for example. He wears me out when I fight him, and he wears me out when I don't. You know what I mean."

"Oh, my!" Sadie was at a loss for words. She blushed, even though she knew how deep the romance had already become between her sister and Dewey Baughman. It was more information than she was prepared to hear.

"Where's your fellow?" Auralee asked.

"I don't know. He's over with some of the boys, probably stealing a chew of their tobacco. I'm not impressed. That's an ugly habit. I wish the music would kick up again." She scanned the pavilion, hoping to find another person for a dance. "You know, I heard from Cora that Morgan's coming alone tonight. I wish he would hurry."

"Why? You have a man."

"Well, just for the evening. I don't aim to keep him, in any case, and I'm sure he'd allow me a dance or two with Morgan while he's away with that tobacco. I doubt he'll even know. Frankly, Auralee, I don't rightly care."

"Sadie, what's got you so suddenly interested in Morgan Darrow? You hardly noticed him all this time."

"I guess it's Sarah. She said she thought he was about as handsome a man she had ever seen, and that just made me look a bit closer. He really is, you know. I don't know why I couldn't see it before."

"Sure, he's nice enough looking, but I like my big man, Dewey. You can keep your Morgan."

Sadie lifted herself away from the wall. "I intend to do just that."

The music resumed lively, and the colored paper lanterns that lined the pavilion swayed with the motion of the dancers. Lawson Darrow led his wife to the center of the floor. He took her by the waist with his right hand and clutched her fingers firmly with his left.

"Ready?"

Annie beamed. "Very ready."

Lawson counted aloud, "And one, two, three. One, two, three...."

The two lifted their feet and bounded in unison across the floor. Both smiled and laughed through the turns and swirls that carried them from one side of the room to the other. In dance, they were inseparable, in every step, together. Annie wanted the music to play forever. Lawson felt he could never tire.

It was not until the band rested again that Annie began to worry about Morgan. She had not seen him, and the night was passing quickly by.

"Lawson, should I be concerned about Morgan? He hasn't arrived yet."

"I don't think so. This park is a long way up the mountain, and he's probably just taking his time enjoying the stars. You know him as well as I do. Besides, he walks the same road every day to school and sure isn't about to get lost now. He'll be here soon."

"Could you, maybe, go to the school to see if he's coming? I'm still a little worried."

"Annie, you hate to see your little boy grow up, don't you? He's fine, I tell you, but if it puts you at ease, I'll fetch him. Now try not to dance until I get back. It won't do for you to wear out ahead of me." Lawson kissed his wife on the forehead and disappeared into the dark of Briar Mountain.

A half-hour went by before Morgan finally appeared. He stood near the top of a short set of stairs and watched others lark in the cool evening air. He shivered in the whiff of a breeze.

"I know one sure way to warm you up." Sadie Buck tugged upon his sleeve, then caressed down his arm until her hand met his. "Come and dance with me. That'll do the trick."

Before he could protest, Sadie had pulled him into the crowd, and they joined the rhythmic flow of the dancers. Morgan's ability was rough, at best, but Sadie redeemed him by taking the lead or sounding out the music's cadence. She relished the time spent in his arms and cared very little about the movement of his feet. To tune after tune they danced, until the girl spotted her escort finally returning to the pavilion.

"Now, Morgan, don't you wander too far away from me. We'll try this again before the night's over."

"I expect you'll soon be busy with another, Sadie, but thanks for the dance. This was nice."

They parted company, and Morgan walked to where his mother was standing pensively by the wall.

"Oh, Morgan, there you are. You've been missing a great party. Did your father find you?"

"Why, no, was he looking for me?"

"I sent him long ago. I can't understand where he could be. I hope he's not...well, I hope he hasn't found a bottle somewhere out there."

"Me, too. But stop worrying, Ma. I'll see what he's up to. If he's into the whiskey again, I'll come get you, and we'll just have to take him home."

Morgan had moved only a short distance away when a familiar voice addressed him, "Are you leaving so soon, Mr. Darrow? I'm still awaiting my dance. You do keep promises, don't you?"

Sarah was a vision that would only appear in the best of his dreams. She looked fresh and vibrant with expectation. "Sadie was right," she said. "I've been watching you with her. You dance quite well. I don't mean to be presumptuous, but...."

Morgan interjected, "Sarah, the blue one...you are wearing the blue dress." He was flustered with admiration. "You look so...so...." The words, not the feelings, were difficult for him. "Sarah, you look beautiful."

"I wanted to be beautiful tonight, especially tonight. You convinced me that the indigo might just draw the attention of a certain young man, so I went back to the store. I'm glad you like it." She slipped her finger under his tie and lifted it lightly from his shirt. "And you, sir, you look quite dapper in red. Much better than white, I'd say." She smiled approvingly.

Morgan was too old to be so callow, but he seemed blind to her advances and deaf to the subtlety of her remarks. He probed cautiously, "I thought you were here with someone."

"I am, and I would like to introduce you to him if he ever returns. He told me he wanted to leave soon, but I've stayed rather hidden in this corner, hoping to see you before we left. Tomorrow, we'll be returning to Charleston."

It was not the response Morgan was seeking, and rising hope again melted as he first thought about the special man in Sarah's life, and then, about her going away. Just when the spark seemed to kindle his confidence, it was washed cold with a reminder that she might be lost to him, that he was not worthy of her true affections. He wanted to crawl to some place deep within himself where his emotion and pride could not be further wounded, but not finding such a place, he shielded himself with a false air of indifference.

"Oh, Charleston. I'm sure you've been looking forward to getting back home."

"No, not at all. I really like it here."

"You do? Well, that's interesting. I would've thought you preferred the city over some stick town like Devlin. I figured a woman like you would want to settle down in a place like Pittsburgh or New York, where there are opportunities and people more of your kind."

"Of my kind?" Sarah took exception to the comment. "The people in Devlin are my kind, at least most of them. Someday, you might know me well enough to understand that."

Morgan kept his guard up and did not react. "Personally, I've been thinking that I need to get away. Maybe head west. Maybe out to Oregon or Minnesota. I've learned a good deal about saw filing from my Pa. It's a trade I could take just about anywhere. A lot of people from these parts have gone west for lumbering jobs. I was thinking I should go."

"I'm disappointed to hear that. We need our men here in West Virginia. You seem so suited. I wish you would stay with us."

The conversation became awkward as Sarah awaited her dance, and Morgan, in protection of his feelings, tried all the more to avoid it. He wanted to be with her, but his mind refused to allow his heart to further commit to a failing cause.

"Well, I wish us both the best wherever we go. If you'll excuse me, I'm on an errand to find my father right now. About the dance, I'm sorry, Sarah, but perhaps another time?"

"Of course," the girl said graciously, not really understanding. She would have danced a thousand dances with him, if only he would ask.

He softened for a final moment. "Will you be back? I mean... anytime soon?" Morgan queried.

"I don't know, but I certainly hope so."

"I hope so, too." Morgan felt overwhelmed with regret and struggled with every word. He decided it best to simply walk away. "It's always nice seeing you, Sarah. You do look beautiful."

The girl stood in splendor at the edge of the room, and Morgan watched her longingly with stolen glances as he resumed the search for his father. His efforts were in vain. He saw an acquaintance with every turn of his head, and his progress through the crowd was hampered by a steady flow of greetings and small talk. Frustrated by this, he was strangely relieved when he happened upon Lowe Yancy.

"Evening, Mr. Yancy. I didn't expect to see you tonight."

"Frankly, I didn't expect to be here, but it's a right nice party. I'm glad I made it. How are you?"

"All right, I guess." His discouragement showed in the words. Lowe recognized the sign.

"So, was that your special gal you were talking to?"

"Which one?"

"Good point. I forgot how it was for you young fellows."

"I didn't mean it that way. I don't really have a girl." Morgan was anxious to switch the subject. "Well, if you've come to dance, I wish you'd ask my Ma. She's been standing over there waiting for Pa so long that I'm starting to feel sorry for her. You haven't seen him, have you?"

"I don't reckon I've ever met your father. We've never crossed paths that I know of." Lowe stretched his neck for a glimpse of Morgan's mother. "Which one of those pretty ladies is your Ma? There are several over there."

"Oh, that's right. In a town like Devlin, I naturally assume that everyone knows everyone else."

Morgan pointed to a brown-haired woman standing alone and lovely, like a school girl waiting to be noticed. Her hands were folded behind her back as she swayed ever so slightly with the tempo of the music.

"Do you see her?" He pointed again. "Right over there."

Lowe had aging eyes, but could see the woman clearly. It was evident that the years had not stolen her youthfulness. On a second look, he found something very familiar about her, but passed it off as just heredity and the obvious resemblance to her son. Morgan's smile, his strength and athleticism, even his passion for life, were somehow conveyed by the woman at a glance, and Lowe was not at all surprised that a boy of his quality would proudly claim her as his mother.

Still, there was irony in her likeness to another. The vision of one woman had stalked him both day and night for years, and now, in the dim colored light of the lanterns, she seemed suddenly resurrected and real. It was an uncanny trick of the mind, a callous duping of the heart, and too much the coincidence to be fate. Yet, when he looked again, she was no longer the girl never forgotten. She was just a fine lady he had never before met.

"Yes, I can see her. You certainly favor her."

"That's a good thing, I suppose," Morgan quipped.

Lowe laughed. "I mean no offense to your father, but I expect that is a good thing."

"Come meet her," Morgan urged. "Get her to dance, will you?"

Lowe watched Annie intently as he responded. "Regretfully, I'm a bumbling excuse for a dancer, and I'm afraid I'd embarrass the poor woman just by asking. Besides, it wouldn't appear proper. You do understand, of course. Right now, I need to head on back to Black Jack, but I look forward to meeting your folks at some future opportunity. Your mother is a very handsome lady." And with that said, he shook the boy's hand and left.

Morgan scanned the room for another view of Sarah, but being unsuccessful, he reluctantly proceeded in his search for his father. He was not gone long before the music ceased and a man's voice began to call loudly from the corner of the pavilion, his words slurred but still distinguishable.

"People...hey, people! Listen up, my friends...uh...since our musicians are off somewhere's...getting refreshed...with a good snort or two, I'd imagine...uh... I'd like to try my hand at playing... a little song for you." He grabbed a fiddle left on a chair by the front edge of the stage. "I don't suppose Jimmy will mind me testing out this here instrument...uh...for just one little song, do you?" He cried blindly to the crowd, "How about it, Jim? Can I play her?"

A man in the back of the pavilion responded, "Yeah, play the thing. Do whatever knocks your socks off!"

"Thanks, Jimmy. I think...I think I will. This is for my beautiful and beloved darling...who I surely admire. You all know her. She's about as perfect a woman...as God ever made and the best partner a man could hope for. You probably think she deserves a lot better than me, and I am right now...I am right now at a loss for argument."

Another voice rang out, "Get on with it, Darrow! Play us the song!"

"All right then...well, this is for you...my darling Annie."

It was clear that Lawson had found his whiskey, and many doubted that he was sober enough to play. His legs seemed unstable, and at one point he almost tumbled to the floor. Some looked to Annie, expecting a rightful sign of humiliation, but Annie knew Lawson's ability with a fiddle. It had been too many years ago, and she now anxiously awaited the return of that lost passion he once had shared with her. She felt anticipation, not shame.

But Morgan was mortified. "Oh, dear God!" he exclaimed, as he pressed his way toward his father to hurry him back to the privacy of their home. He stopped short when Lawson rose up and swept the bow across the thin bridge of the Appalachian fiddle.

Sweet tones began to lift mournfully into the country night as the whining of his strings bore a slow, unknown melody. The sound was rich and pure, and it drifted like a balm over the near valleys and hills. It soothed every broken heart. It warmed every cold heart, all in the same tender progression of his notes. No one thought of the whiskey.

The fiddler's tears rolled freely upon the instrument and glided on its sound into the very soul of Devlin. When he was through, when his last note faded with the final echo across the mountain, when he had captured all who would hear, he staggered among the speechless people, then the applauding people, and presented his hand to Annie. Lawson said simply, "Forgive me."

Annie took her husband by the arm, and they began to step again as one, this time more slowly down the road toward home.

Some minutes passed before the band struck a new waltz, and Dewey was the first to arrive on the floor, with his Auralee, of course, tightly in tow. Morgan saw his friend for the first time that evening, and noticed with envy as Dewey swept the girl into the air before settling into another hour of dancing. Some leaves clung to the back of her skirt. It was clear they were happy.

He turned and looked again for Sarah, but she was gone. Another man had taken her away, so far away from him and Briar Mountain and the little town below. He cursed his foolish pride. Sarah was gone, and he had given her absolutely nothing to remember.

# CHAPTER 6

The trail up Jasper Hollow was gradual but well-worn by the feet of old Noggin, Silas Monk's mule and companion of 11 years. Once a week the pair would journey four miles down the hollow into Devlin for provisions, and their constant passage cut deep into the moist loam along Jasper Creek. The path etched even further with each wash of summer storms and with the secret traffic of men who came for Silas' superb corn liquor.

Impassable to wheeled vehicles, the trail ensured the old man's relative seclusion from the world. But sometimes the world came to him. By horse or by foot, people traveled to hear the countless stories of the rare and rugged man who had known the Charity River Valley as a lonely virgin wilderness. He was the vestige of a fading age, a proud patriot in what he called the War for Southern Liberation. He was a brave woodsman who explored and trapped and settled where others had not been. In every sense of the word, they came to taste the spirit of the ancient man of the mountain, the renowned distiller who could mix magic with his cauldron and corn.

Noggin walked lazily among the exposed rocks and roots, but was sure-footed on his way to home. He strode through a dense, gnarled thicket of laurel before leaving the shadow of the woods, and slowly entered his paddock next to the small barn and cabin. Innocence and buttercups grew in the sunlit edges and framed the field in faint hues of blue and yellow. It was a pretty place, a bit weathered and worked, but welcoming as it nestled at the crease of the mountain by the cool shade of hemlocks.

Eleven years. They had ridden together for 11 long years. It had been almost that long since Silas lost his Emma to the cancer, and the new mule served as a rather fair and immediate replacement. There can be no misunderstanding, he loved Emma dearly, but both wife and mule put upon him a yoke of obligation that lay heavy against his roving ways. Both required considerable attention, and Silas supplied an endless shower of accolades and gifts and service to keep them content. While Emma held her husband stifling close to home, Noggin strained his patience with a proclivity to wander into many a dismal situation. When Emma died, Silas left his home on the outskirts of Devlin, loaded up the young mule, and returned to a pioneer life on Jasper Creek.

"I wish she'd taken this blind, bastard mule with 'er! God rest 'er soul," Silas grunted as he pulled a 50-pound bag of corn off the animal's back. "This time I found 'im belly deep in the edge o' the mill pond soakin' like a ruttin' hog in mud. He thinks it's hot outside? Jist wait until I load 'im down in August. It took me right near an hour to find 'im and almost as long to coax 'is ass out o' that mud bath. Damn, bastard mule... thinks he's royalty."

Silas suddenly became aware of visitors. "Well, howdy, boys!" he exclaimed. "I hope ya ain't been waitin' long."

Lawson Darrow responded, "Maybe you should sell him. A lot of folk could use a strong mule in these parts. He'd bring you some good money."

"Nah, that ain't happenin'. Would be like tradin' family. I may shoot 'im, but I'll ne'er sell."

Noggin bent his neck far to the side and peered at the old man with one large brown eye. The raving had gone on incessantly for four miles, and now was the right time, apparently, for the mule to put an end to it. His head reared up, and he sneezed a wet insult upon his forever ranting companion.

Silas ignored the spray and loosened another bag of grain from the packsaddle. Then, he stroked the long, lathered neck of his mule.

"Yeah, I hear ya, feller. It ain't easy gittin' old, is it? And it ain't so pleasurable puttin' up with the likes o' me day in and day out. I know I been tough to live with, but truth is, I cain't git along without ya."

He returned his attention to the guests, who had walked the long trail and arrived at the cabin only minutes earlier. "Sorry, boys, Noggin's a might shy o' the social graces."

"'Noggin'. That's a peculiar name. Just how did he come by it?" asked Lawson.

"Emma. I jist called 'im 'Mule' until ma Emma riled me one day with one of 'er dadblasted commands."

"And I suppose you don't like being told what to do." Lawson could relate from his own experience.

"That's exactly right. I told that woman I was a headin' out fer a couple two or three days o' huntin', and ya know what she says to me? She says, 'Silas Monk, ya ain't goin' nowheres.' She says, 'Winter is a comin' and chores need a doin', and ya ain't goin' nowheres.'"

"And did they?"

"Did they what?

"Did they need doing? The chores, I mean."

"Well, sure! Thar was a bit o' corn left to pick, some taters still in the ground. But I'd a got around to all that in due time. Emma was right partial to 'er own way and didn't hold with no contrary opinion. She demanded I git out the house and jump to it. Her partin' words o' the day was 'Work before whimsy is the way o' the wise. Why don't ya use yer noggin fer a change?' she says."

Silas was flustered, as if the entire incident had only occurred the previous day. "Mm...mm...oh, that woman. If I heared 'er advice once, I heared it a thousand times. 'Work before whimsy's the way o' the wise. Use yer noggin.' Truth be told, fellers, that were a real fine suggestion, one of 'er best. So, I jist saddled the mule and headed on out fer the hills. He's been Noggin e'er since."

Silas scratched behind the mule's long, pointed ears. "Yup, this here is ol' Noggin, the damnedest, most cantankerous animal to walk on four legs. Say! I'm forgettin' my own manners. Ya must be plum dried out after walkin' so fer. What can I git ya boys today? Need a sample?"

"I was hoping you'd ask," Lawson responded.

"All right then, water, whiskey or cider? What's yer pleasure? "

Lawson had not traveled so far for the mere taste of water. "I've had a real hankering for some of your whiskey, myself. Never did cotton much to cider."

"Whiskey it is! How 'bout you, Lowe?"

"Well, maybe I'll try a sip of the same. It's still early," said Lowe Yancy.

Silas searched for a brown ceramic jug. There were several about the yard, but none were filled. "Ah, horse apples! These is empties, every dadburn one of 'em!" he exclaimed. "But don't lose yer hope. Hold on and I'll fetch us a new jar from inside."

He entered his cabin, and the men outside were entertained almost instantly by a run of colorful expletives. He finished with, "Cain't find nothin'! Not a blame thing! Even my hogs won't squat in filth this deep. But me? I jist heap up more o' the mud and shit and keep a callin' it 'home.'"

A bottle shattered upon the wooden floor. Another sailed through the open window, landing half way into the paddock. Silas stomped out of the cabin empty handed, red faced, and ready for battle.

"This place's got more clutter than green woods in a twister. Fifty bottles under foot and not a galldern one of 'em is holdin' a drop! It's Emma, I tell ya. She ne'er approved o' no still, and it would be jist like 'er to come back from the grave to dispose o' my product. Thar's no end to a woman's tamperin' with the things o' men, and my Emma was the queen o' such mischief. And it appears she's still mighty good at it! Sorry, fellers, I stashed 10 jugs or more here 'bouts, but jist where seems to escape me. I swear that woman keeps stealin' my memory, as well as my liquor."

"You can't blame your wife for your old age, and it's only the old age that toys with your memory. Emma was a good old gal, and you know it. We can help you look if you want," Lowe said, in a kindly rebuke.

"Hell, what do *you* know 'bout such things? All them women

are good ol' gals when ya ain't married to 'em. Boy, don't ya preach none to me 'bout wives until ya git one o' yer own! It were Emma, all right. I know 'er ways."

"Maybe it was the mule. Have you thought of that?"

The notion was ludicrous, but nevertheless, Silas stopped in his tracks, pretending to consider it. "Nah, he wouldn't dare." The old man walked around the cabin, crossed the yard, and entered a root cellar half buried in the bank. He came back with four dusty jugs of his premier corn liquor.

"Here it is!" he shouted. "It finally come to me, and, o' course, it all makes perfect sense that I'd stow my finest in that thar cellar." Then he added, "I been findin' lately that this ol' brain's the most unreliable tool in my shed. Too bad, 'cause every other piece I got is nigh on busted or rusty. Sorry, Emma. My mistake."

Silas continued the conversation as he repositioned an old rocker closer to the men. It was his outdoor chair, rickety and cracked from the passing of the years. He had always referred to it as a wild rocker, like a feral cat that never spent a day under roof and was forced to fend alone against the wiles of nature. Maybe for that reason, no one but he attempted to sit in it. Every morning, as he first stepped from his porch and scanned the extent of his property, he seemed surprised that the chair was still there, just as he had left it the day before, as if chairs could come and go at will. When he sat, it was clear to Lowe and Lawson that the rocker and the old man had found real comfort in each other.

"So, where ya been, Lowe? I ain't seen hide or hair o' ya in months. I knew ya wasn't dead 'cause nothin' can kill a critter like you, but I was beginnin' to think ya no longer took to my cookin'."

"Mr. Monk, I believe no one could like your whiskey better than I do, unless, of course, it's Lawson here." Lawson nodded in agreement. Lowe continued, "But I tend to sample in moderation nowadays. This kind of juice can take a man down if he isn't mindful of its punch. Regardless of that, it wouldn't hurt me one bit if you were to move your still, and yourself, a little closer to town. It takes a full day just to come visit, and at your age, someone needs to look in on you from time to time."

"Look in on me? Ya mean look after me, and I'll shoot the poor bastard that tries. I went through all that with Emma. Ya still ain't told me where ya been!"

"Well, Silas, I've been traveling a good deal, running a survey along the New River for some mining outfits. It's kept me out of the area for quite a while."

He watched Lawson reach quickly for a tin cup. Silas poured the whiskey, and his hand shook until it spilled the precious contents over the metal rim.

"Why don't you fellers roll up a log and take yerself a seat. We'll spin a yarn or two, and if ya don't mind, I'll git ya back up after a while to help mix a new pot o' mash," the old man said. "It were a real surprise seein' the two of ya hoofin' up my trail. I ne'er figured ya fer friends."

"Yeah, it's a long story," Lawson said.

"Sonny, don't make it too long. At my age, it's all borrowed time."

"I reckon it's borrowed time for everyone. Don't you think?" Lowe corrected the man.

"Yup, so it is, so it is. Go on with yer story, Lawson. I'm curious. It don't seem like you boys have much in common. I'm tryin' to picture ya as partners, but I jist ain't seein' it."

The truth shall not wait, nor shall it suffer the opinion of fools. It was a philosophy that Silas endorsed throughout his life, but he was especially keen to it now that he had attained his elder stature. He enjoyed exercising his new freedom of expression, a right he claimed through his considerable accumulation of years. In old age, his every thought seemed to leak through his lips and his every whisper rushed out roaring like a raging flood. It was all beyond his control, but what needed saying was said directly, simply and without remorse or hesitation. It was a more honest time of life, and he made the best of it.

"Go on. I'm all ears," he said.

"Well, Lowe and I grew up on the Gauley. I got married young and ran head on into life. Lowe drifted into the mountains, and that's about the size of it."

"When did ya hook up?"

"Just yesterday, believe it or not. Lowe came knocking on my door, looking for Morgan. The boy got into some trouble down at the mill pond, and Lowe had to pull him out. He was checking to see if Morgan had recovered. My wife and the kids were away, and when I opened the door, I was shocked, to say the least. Before that, it had been about twenty-five, maybe thirty years. Wouldn't you say, Lowe?"

"Maybe longer."

Silas inquired, "Yer boy all right?"

"Yeah, he's tough. Anyway, I was about out of good drink at home. We had enough for a couple shots, but it was a long, dry night after that. I mentioned my need to come see you, and, well, the rest you know. Here we are."

Lowe looked closely at Lawson while he talked. They were never really friends, just neighbors who shared the same hidden hollow in the mountains. Their houses had been a few miles apart, and every experience beyond childhood had separated them even further. Lawson had his wife and children and home and trade, and all the expected lifetime successes. Lowe had nothing really, and he was too late for Lawson's kind of living, no matter how much he may have wanted it.

Frankly, it was amazing that Lawson could even recognize him at all. A wide brim hat, some gray hair and stubble, a bit more weight and a bit less memory, all made for a fine disguise. But somehow, Lawson knew him instantly. It troubled Lowe. He had no recall for faces, except maybe one face, and hers was a vivid image freshly embossed with every drift of his mind.

Without leaving his chair, Silas began to refill the cups. "And yer wife, how's she gittin' along?"

Lawson gulped the whiskey and held out the metal cup for more. He swallowed that as well, then, finally replied, "Silas, you are a true artist in your craft. I've never sampled finer." There was no answer to the old man's question, and Lowe was left to wonder why.

The success of the still was not only in the well-measured ingredients, the grist and sugar and yeast, but in the water that percolated from a limestone shelf deep beneath the ground. It surfaced as an artesian spring bubbling through the large cracks of a nearby boulder and then flooded a natural stone basin before falling freely to the passing creek.

Silas believed that morning was the proper time for making good whiskey, when the dew and fog were at their best and somehow blended into the recipe like seasoning. By dawn, his fire would already be raging under the large iron cauldron, and soon thereafter, alcohol-rich vapors would rise into the copper swan neck, an inverted funnel-like dome for capturing the steam. As vapors filled the copper neck, they would press into the condensing coil, or worm. They would cool and then trickle clear into a white oak barrel.

"Some folks like it straight from the worm. But let me tell ya, it ain't fit to drink until it sleeps in them barrels three or four years. Gives it color. Gives it character."

"I doubt either of us would argue about that, Silas. Have you got a few bottles we might take back with us?" Lowe Yancy asked.

"I got some three year. That's what yer drinkin' now."

"Good. I'll need a couple gallons to carry us through the next project."

"And I'll need twice that!" Lawson interjected.

Lowe admired Silas Monk. As a boy, he had listened closely to his stories of the past, as they were told to Lowe's father and uncle. He had watched intently as a younger Silas displayed his cunning against the trials of the mountain. Now, in the absence of family, an older Silas was alone and vulnerable, and Lowe felt called to look after his aging friend from a respectful distance. A thought suddenly came to him.

"You know, Silas, Lawson's comment about selling that mule

has given me an idea. Why don't you and Noggin join me on my survey of the Big Timber country? I could use your knowledge of the land, and we might even find some time for a little hunting and fishing."

"Hell, I'm too damn old to stomp around them hills again. It's been too long. When did ya say yer leavin'?"

"I didn't, but we're hauling out tomorrow on the morning train. We'll hit Camp 7 and pack out from there for the Big Timber. Of course, only you know if you're up to it. I've got some young fellows who could probably benefit from some of your experience along the way. One of them is Lawson's boy. He's strapping strong and might even carry you up a hill or two, if you need it. What say you? I'll even pay for the service of the mule. Come with us, Mr. Monk, and it'll be like yesterday."

Silas leaned over to pour Lawson another cup of liquor. "Ya goin', too?" he inquired in a gravelly voice.

"Thanks. Good stuff," Lawson said, as the whiskey drained smoothly down his throat. "I wish I could go. But no, I've got a job that won't keep."

The old man rose awkwardly from the rocker and hobbled over to Noggin. He stood quietly for a few moments as he tickled the animal's wet, gray nose.

"We'd sure hate to miss the opportunity, wouldn't we, ol' friend? Ain't likely to git back to that country unless we join up. Well, Lowe, if you can bear an ornery ol' man and a lazy, worthless sham fer a pack mule, then I reckon we be headin' to the Big Timber along with ya. And I promise ya, hill or no hill, no one need carry me. My legs do their own walkin'. My hands do their own chores."

When the men finished their drinks, Lawson and Lowe put jugs of whiskey in the canvas packs carried for that purpose. Lawson kept one out for the long walk home and began to lead the way down the path. Hiking along the creek, they marveled at the coincidence of their reunion and their common affection for old Silas, but Lowe found little else in the discourse, or the man, that was of honest interest. Still, he attended politely as the alcohol seemed to do more and more of Lawson's talking. A half mile and a quarter bottle later, Lowe Yancy suddenly became the man's very best of friends.

"Lowell, I'm not sure how the years slipped by without our trails ever crossing before now, but it's been way too long. Having both stayed in these parts, one might conclude that you've been avoiding my company."

"Or you mine. A lot can happen to keep people apart, Lawson. Sometimes it's best to leave things as they are. You can't always go back," Lowe said, feeling uncomfortable about striking a new friendship.

"We're not going to let that happen, are we? Whiskey's best when it's poured two cups at a time, one for the fellow you're looking at. Have a swig, will you? I hate to drink alone."

Lowe waived off the bottle, as he had done several times previously. Lawson gulped a shot, then, took some deep breaths and rubbed hard on the bridge of his nose to counter a predictable onset of blurred vision. Nothing seemed to help.

"You know, Yancy, when you and my boy get back from that survey, we'll do this again. Or, better yet, I'll have my woman prepare your favorite meal. You'll all be ready for some home cooking by then. If you tell me what you want, I'll have her fix it just the way you like it. Bring the whole crew along!"

"Well, that's certainly generous, but you best check with your wife. I wouldn't want to impose on her. A big supper can be a lot of work for a woman."

"Why, that's nonsense! She isn't that busy, and besides, she has to cook for me and the children anyhow. What's a few more mouths? Believe me, she's beholden to you for pulling her boy from that mill pond, and she'd be downright insulted if you refused the invitation. You have to come."

Lowe was reluctant to commit. He let the subject end without further comment, and Lawson's attention drifted with another taste of whiskey.

"I don't know what gets into that boy's mind. Imagine him

thinking he couldn't kill himself crossing the pond like he did. He's just plain stupid," said Lawson.

"I guess we're now talking about Morgan? You know, a boy can do stupid things and not be stupid. I think you're being harsh."

"You don't know him. He's just like his mother and getting more so every minute. There's too much opinion flowing through my home these days, and the two of them are set to drive me crazy with it. Throw in a few more antics like that log walking, and they'll get me there. You should hear how she defends him. I'm not about to take it."

"Oh? You don't hold with their way of thinking?"

"It's *my* home. When they're out there working to pay for it, they can have their damn opinions."

"I reckon you have a point, but frankly, I was quite taken by young Morgan. He's sharp minded, strong, polite, someone to be proud of."

"That's kind of you to say. And you're right, the boy isn't all bad. He's got his value. I'll pass the compliment on to his mother. She can be hell on me as a wife, but sure has a proper touch with those children of hers."

"So, your wife isn't all bad either. I was beginning to wonder."

"The verdict's still out on that one."

Lawson returned the jug to his lips, but did not drink. Instead, he reset the cork and then abruptly stopped in the middle of the trail. In an instant, he appeared sober.

"Yeah, I'm glad you see the good in Morgan. He's grown too fast, and I was never able to keep up with all the change in his life. Annie kept him to herself for the most part, though we've had our times. We used to like to hunt and fish, especially to hunt, and the boy seemed only in the house long enough to sleep. He loves the outdoors. I can't say I always treated him right, and lately, I can't say I even know him, but he's been my pride."

Lawson turned to face Lowe, man to man, eye to eye. "I need you to watch out for him. He's handy, but he knows just about enough to get into some serious trouble. You risked your life once to save my son, and I would ask that you do it again if need be. Morgan and I have some things to work out, things I can't talk about, but I need him back. Do you understand?"

Lowe could not fully understand, but he did recognize a degree of sadness and regret in Lawson's voice. He wanted to be reassuring. "I'll treat him like my own, and I can promise that I'll bring him back to you in one piece." He hesitated before saying more. "Lawson, I just have to ask, do you ever tell him how you feel?"

"How I feel?"

"You know, that you are proud of him."

Lawson again raised the jug, but this time, he removed the cork with his teeth and took a long swallow before answering. Whiskey seeped from the corner of his mouth into the short hairs of his beard. He wiped it with the back of his hand.

"No, no, I guess I don't. His mother dotes, not me."

The men continued their walk in silence, except for the tramp of their moving feet and the trill of a wood thrush high in the green-leafed canopy.

Morgan and Dewey stood on the banks of the Charity where its deep channel skirted the adjacent rail yard. Dawn had lingered for an hour before a white sun peaked over the eastern mountains and bathed the valley floor with its light. Then, and only then, did the warmth of a new morning loosen the clinging veil of fog from the water's surface. Despite the maddening whir and clang of mill machinery, the river would not awaken. It flowed at peace beneath the silver mist.

"It looks like I feel," Dewey muttered, as he stifled another yawn. "What a sleepy little river."

"Yeah, especially along this stretch. Pretty though, this time of day."

Morgan rubbed his puffy eyes. He leaned down to pick up a thin rock, then, whipped it low to skim across the flat water. He counted 12 skips, each shorter and much more rapid than the one prior, and he watched as the ripples began to overlap each other. They were altogether gone when a single blare of No. 2's steam whistle pierced the morning air. The boys shuttered at the noise.

"Men, let's get a move on! This is our ride." A man's voice hailed them from beyond the tracks.

"Big Timber, here we come!" cried Morgan, jumping to the summons.

Dewey lacked verve. He patted his bulging stomach, arched his back, slowly stretched his arms far above his head and yawned yet again. Finally, he slogged toward the sound of a second whistle.

They were off, each for their own purpose, on a new adventure in an old and very special place. In the Big Timber, nature had so little experience in dealing with men, and she might be harsh to those unfamiliar with her ways. The boys would be strangers there, intruding on her sanctuary, interrupting her timeless world, and both Morgan and Dewey wondered just how she would come to greet them. Dewey was nervous. Morgan was charged with anticipation.

Anxious to stow his animals and equipment, Lowe Yancy offered only a succinct welcome to his crew. "Morning, boys, let's get it loaded. We can talk later."

"Boss, ya want us to throw all of this on board? Everythin'?" asked Dewey, trying to be certain of the man's instructions.

"No, leave my instruments right where they are. We don't 'throw' instruments. And let Black Jack handle Blu. The horse is used to him."

"What 'bout these food crates?"

"Crates? What's in them?"

"Looks like vegetables mostly. There's potato sacks, some flour and other stuff, as well."

"Oh, yeah, that has to be for the camp. We'll load it, too. Put it on after Black Jack and Silas finish with the animals."

A tall, wiry man, his skin brown from heredity and furrowed from time, immediately maneuvered his long fingers around the bridle of the horse. He tugged and led the animal up a planked ramp into the rear section of the flatcar.

Lowe addressed the crew, "Black Jack, once you're done attending to Blu, don't forget his apple. It might settle him for the trip. Boys, you put these packs and camp supplies forward in the car. Tie down anything that can roll. And leave my survey instruments and essentials until I get back. I won't be long."

"Where's he off to?" Dewey uttered to Morgan after he climbed awkwardly into the front of the car. Morgan shrugged a sign of uncertainty. Dewey spoke again, this time with unexpected impatience, "Well, don't just stand there! It ain't gonna move on its own. Toss that stuff up here, and let's get on with it!"

His friend raised no argument, though his compliance meant doing all the carrying and lifting by himself. It was a rare moment when Dewey Baughman showed enthusiasm for labor, and Morgan thought it only best to encourage such spirit, considering the amount of work ahead of them. He heaved the hay bales first, then some sacks of feed and a number of heavy canvas bundles and leather bags. In addition to these, he moved bedrolls, individual packs of clothes, loops of rope and surveyor chains, a holstered pistol and two rifles in leather scabbards.

After grabbing the last remaining items, two ceramic jugs, Morgan looked with disgust at Dewey's handling of the equipment. "Nice job. A real nice job," he said sarcastically. "I'm not sure I'm ready to trust you with these." He returned the jugs to a safe position on the ground.

Dewey had dropped each piece haphazardly on the rough, wooden floor, making little effort toward plan or order. However, one strategic row of grain bags stretched six feet along the left edge of the car. On this, he fell prostrate. He squirmed and rolled until his back molded the pliable bags around the curves of his large body. "There now, that was easy." He folded his hands comfortably over his chest. "Wake me, Morgan, when the boss has another job for us."

It would not take long. Lowe Yancy arrived as Black Jack was securing boards along the horse's flanks, which he hoped would stabilize him during the unsettling ride into the hills.

"Good idea," said Lowe. "Jack, when you're done, Silas may need you at the millpond. I'll start loading the instruments."

"No, I has plenty to do right here. You send dat young fella dat's weighin' down dose feed bags." Black Jack pointed to Dewey, who looked far too comfortable in his repose. "From what I seen, he and old Noggin is just a couple o' patches cut off de same rag cloth. I ain't sure dey gonna hold up when our knees be down in dat mountain dirt."

"They'll be just fine once we're under way." Lowe defended the boy, but still accepted Black Jack's advice. "Dewey!" he yelled.

"Huh? Who, me?" Dewey had not heard a word, but the raised level of Lowe's voice brought him instantly to attention.

"The mule."

"Yes, boss, the mule. What 'bout the mule?"

"You need to fetch him for us. He's over in the millpond and apparently not too anxious to leave it. Do what you need to do, but we got to have him soon. Try the rope. As I recall, you didn't fare so well the last time you were over there."

Lowe and Morgan snickered, but the boy refused to acknowledge the attempt at humor. "I'll give it a shot, boss."

Dewey grunted as he left his makeshift bed, and again, as he leaned over to steal an apple from the top of Black Jack's unsealed basket. Forgetting his rope, he sauntered toward the pond and the sound of an old man grousing.

"Ya four-legged demon! If ya git that pack wet, I'll shoot ya where ya stand and leave yer damned carcass floatin' in the water." Silas Monk could not believe the audacity of his mule. He continued to curse as Dewey stood empathetic and waiting, hearing every vile complaint issued to the animal. "Please, ya good fer nothin', mean minded, mangy tail mule. Please! We got us a train to catch."

There was something Dewey instantly liked about this frustrated old man, and he laughed to himself as Silas slipped back and forth from rage to desperate plea. Finally, he interrupted, "Are you Mr. Monk?"

"That I am, son. Ya Lawson Darrow's boy?"

"No, sir, they call me Dewey. I'm workin' the survey with Mr. Yancy." The boy gave the old man a hardy handshake.

"So am I, I reckon. So's this damn mule, if I can e'er git 'im out of the water. Feller, if ya got a notion, now would be a right good time to speak yer mind. Otherwise, go git me one o' them guns up yonder in the train car."

"I might have me one idea that could work, somethin' I learned from my friend, Morgan. Ya see, the more I rant and cuss, the more pleasure he takes just ignorin' me, which, of course, drives me right on up the wall. I do get even from time to time, and he breaks down now and then. That's when I hear the lectures 'bout morals and such. Frankly, mister, I like to cuss. Cussin' keeps me steady. But sometimes it's just not properly appreciated by others. Point is, all that rantin' and ravin' and cursin' doesn't move Morgan Darrow one little bit. He just gets all stubborn and religious on me. I suspect we have a similar problem here, and maybe a little sugar would be the better coercion. What's your animal's name?"

"Noggin."

"Noggin? What kind of name is that?"

"It ain't important, boy."

"Hmm...Noggin."

Dewey spoke in a secretive tone, as though the mule should not be allowed to hear. "Mr. Monk, why don't ya head up to the train, while I have me a talk with this brute? I think we'll be 'long shortly."

"Yer in way o'er yer head, young feller. This here mule ain't like no other. The only thing to move the likes o' Noggin is that thar Shay engine. Hook 'im to the tail o' the train, and we'll drag 'is sorry ass up that mountain and right on into camp."

"I'd like to try it my way, if it's just the same to you."

"Sweet talkin' a mule. I declare, boy! Well, I warned ya. Do as ya will." Silas shook his head, but nevertheless, walked away toward the tracks.

Dewey squatted at the edge of the pond. The mule stood indifferent, like the wet logs that surrounded him.

"You should know, Mr. Noggin, that Mr. Blu was given a big, juicy apple when he stepped onto that flatcar. I saw me a whole basket of sweet fruit just ready to eat. There's also a great deal of hay and other goodies for the trip. I ain't believin' for a minute that you're willin' to leave it all to some horse."

He pulled out his apple, showed it to the mule and then bit deeply into the moist red skin. The crunch was as audible as he could make it, and the juice dribbled to the tip of his chin.

"Well, ya know where they're at if ya want 'em. I gotta go." He moved slowly up the bank, eating his apple as loudly as possible.

Dewey resisted a temptation to look back until he was again nestled on the grain bags, but was not at all surprised to see that Noggin had followed only a short distance behind him. Without lead, the mule climbed the ramp and took its place at the rear of the car.

Dewey pretended to sleep, and he was smug as he mimicked the earlier words of his boss, "And, Black Jack, once you're done attendin' to Mr. Noggin, don't ya forget his apple. He earned it."

The black man grinned, conceding the boy's accomplishment, and reached into the basket for the promised treat.

Silas Monk spoke the thoughts of all, "Well, I'll be damned."

The Shay engine inched along the side rail through the gray shadow of the lumber mill. When it emerged into the light, both Morgan and Dewey were standing in the open car. They looked beyond the mill at the community that clung to the slopes of Briar Mountain. It was their home, and they were leaving it. They had never done that before.

Dewey strained his eyes searching in vain for Auralee. Perhaps she was waving, crying, professing her love for him from some unseen perch far across the valley. Perhaps not. There was no sign of her. He returned to his bed of grain and pouted.

Morgan watched, as well, but through a blind stare that only looked deep into his memories. The river, the church, the store, the park, they were all about Sarah now. They had no other meaning to him, just Sarah Dabney and the brief wonderful moments he had known in her presence. Every feature of her beauty, every word she had spoken, every dream she haunted, every hope she instilled, were recalled and submitted to the lasting reminiscence of his heart. Sarah was gone from Devlin, and his memories of her might have to endure a lifetime.

The train climbed without hurry far into the steep, rolling countryside. There was little to hinder its progress, except the occasional switchbacks and the frequent unevenness of the narrow tracks. The flatcars, near empty on their journey up the grade, swayed back and forth and bumped hard against the joints of the metal rails. Still, for the men and animals that accompanied Lowe Yancy, the ride and rhythmic sound of the wheels below seemed soothing. Dewey slept. Morgan pondered what might lie ahead.

As the short train wound across creeks and ravines and through acres of clearing, Morgan was struck by the endless carnage of skid trails and abandoned slash. He saw huge stumps, some wider than the height of men, dominate a terrain where once great trees stood as invincible guardians of paradise. It was a disturbing sight for one who so loved the beauty and vitality of the natural forest. Mourning this now denuded garden, he could barely comprehend the necessity of its destruction. He could find no solace, despite the dense young growth already emanating from the scars. He could offer no justification, even acknowledging the vast need for timber and the good in the men that were there to cut it. Looking across this defenseless, vanquished land, Morgan felt ashamed for being a part of it all. He and his kind were but plunderers, who stole too much from the wonder of a once grand and virgin wilderness.

The only road into Camp 7 was railroad, and the journey from Devlin took a long two hours, even on the best of days. Halfway to this destination, the crew was stirred from their rest when the train banked against a cool north face. The side wind that had pursued them up the mountain suddenly ceased, and from the engine's panting stack, a rain of cinders now drifted steadily back upon them.

Dewey's position subjected him to the worst of the dry, black deluge, and he was compelled to relinquish his seat of comfort. The clutter of equipment left few alternatives for relocation. He could sit among the animals or next to the black stranger on the far side of the car.

He chose poorly. All eyes watched in disappointment as Dewey wobbled across the ever-shifting deck, passing Black Jack on his way toward the mule. But before he could settle, Lowe Yancy rose and spoke sharply, "Dewey, not there! No one sits there."

"Sir?" Dewey questioned. "The cinders. They're blowin' in my eyes."

"Not there. You can take my place, if you have to." Lowe pointed to an open space barely visible among the bundles. He moved toward Black Jack and laid his hand upon the man's bony shoulder. "Some things refuse to change, my friend. You'd do well to forget it."

"Dat sure enough true. Maybe dey ain't meant to change, but I keep livin' for dat day just de same. You is always standin' with me, Lowe, and dat be de one thing dis man won't forget."

Prejudice had run rampant over generations like a foul air that permeates a city, an air not chosen but breathed so much that the stench goes unnoticed by the bustling crowds. Wariness and abuse on both sides of racial and ethnic lines kept the strings of discord taut, and unity among people of different looks, and faiths, and customs, and languages was a rare and tenuous expectation. It would take friendships to prove that common bonds were stronger than petty differences, but few were being forged.

For a man of color, there were scant white friends. Black Jack counted himself fortunate, considering his long and loyal companionship with Lowe Yancy. And he held no malice for young Dewey Baughman. The boy just breathed the same air that blew everywhere across the land. He knew no difference. He felt no wrong as he passed by the black man to sit among the beasts.

The train was only a quarter of a mile from camp as it chugged slowly past a neat row of shanty cars, lining a side track on a long terrace just below the railroad cut. The cars served as movable housing, and the chimney pipes still smoldered from the morning coffee of men long since returned to the forest. Beyond the cars was a small cantonment of makeshift huts and tents. Clean clothes hung from the guy lines, dripping wet from an early wash or the ever-lingering dew.

Morgan observed some women gathered around a long table. They were ironing and folding the bright whites of work shirts and undergarments. Through their gestures, he could almost hear their rebuke of one who had scuffed carelessly by, kicking yellow dust into the air. Farther away, another woman beat the grime from a small blanket with a stick, while yet another chased frantically after a toddler, hell bent on escape. There was a squeezebox and a pair of large, worn boots on a fireside bench, an upended spittoon riddled with bullet holes and a deck of cards half scattered across the ground. The things of men were evident, but nary a man. Only the women could be seen.

"Is this it, Camp 7?" Morgan inquired loudly above the rumble of the train.

Lowe answered just as loudly, "No, just around the bend. They call this Slip Town. It's the Italian camp."

"Slip Town?"

"Yeah, Slip Town, on account it slips down the tracks every time a new section opens. At least, that's what one fellow told me."

"It's not very crowded."

"Of course not, they're up in the hills cutting skid trails and road grades for the loggers. It's rough work opening this country. They're pretty tough boys."

"And those women?"

"Wives. Whores. I don't know."

Morgan offered a polite wave as the train passed the women, but he was purposely ignored.

Lowe pointed to the shanties. "I'd be happier than a bunny in briars if they'd stick us in a few of these cars for the night. Loggers are known to knock walls down with their bunkhouse snoring. These boxes make for right cozy little cabins, as I recall. I stayed in one once. It had a decent mattress. You can open a window or light up a fire in the stove. Really, they give all the creature comforts of home."

Dewey yawned as he mumbled a response, "Creature? Which ones exactly, the chiggers, the bed bugs or the rats?"

"Oh, that just depends on who was bunking the night before. I reckon it could be all three, or even a hundred others you haven't mentioned."

Dewey laughed nervously. "I hope you're kiddin'. So, where do these people eat? There ain't nothin' but tents."

"That's a bit of a sore subject in these parts. The men take their meals with the loggers. Some of them even sleep at the bunkhouse, though it's overcrowded enough at camp to move most of them down here. Unfortunately, loggers hate to be crowded and foreigners don't like to be pushed. It can be quite a show. There's no love lost between them, that's for certain. We'll tread a little lightly today, boys, until we find out just who likes who."

"But we're still leavin' in the mornin', aren't we, boss?" asked Dewey, his face now flushed with consternation.

"That's the plan. First light."

"Good. I'll be ready. I ain't much for fightin' nowadays, and that goes for just 'bout any kind of varmint."

Morgan added, "He's now a lover, you know. He's finally got himself a gal and can't afford to mess up that baby face of his with fisticuffs."

"Yeah, so I understand."

West Virginia could hardly deny the wave of immigration that swept onto the shores of America. National growth and industrial development demanded labor, hard labor, to extract the rich reserves of wood and coal. As their grandfathers before them, immigrants ventured their meager fortunes in the quest for a greater share of hope and future. They crossed an ocean with Old World ways to build New World aspirations. Austrian, English, Hungarian, Irish, Italian, Welsh, it did not matter. They took to pick and shovel to build roads and tracks, shafts and tunnels. Some became miners, loggers, lumbermen and carpenters, some even grocers, bankers or lawyers, but most notably, many were the men who prepared the way through a difficult wilderness. Theirs were the rails and trails on which would flow a raging stream of timber and stone.

Needed but not welcome, they were foreigners. Their white skin and similar ways afforded some degree of tolerance, but to many, they were a pestilence that could invade and destroy the livelihood of a people already struggling against the grasp of poverty. As the Shawnee once resisted the piercing advance of European culture, so it was for many a white man who wanted only to preserve the simple life he knew. The ethnicity of the nation, its most profound accomplishment and resource, was a scourge to those defiant of a changing way and time. Most would learn acceptance, but some would bring the stinging lashes of hate and distrust to bear against those they could not understand.

Segregation was thin protection against acts of prejudice. Immigrants, especially those not fluent in English, congregated in the far corners of a town or in the isolation of a backwoods camp. In separation, they found a fragile peace, but their progeny, not themselves, would come to know the promised freedom from fear and tyranny.

The train engine had almost come to rest under the water tower's long spout, and Morgan jumped easily from the slow-moving flatcar. Dewey and Lowe had already dropped the side rails and slid the ramp toward him. He lowered it to the ground while Black Jack readied the animals for off-loading. All the while, Silas Monk stood apart from them and searched for his bearing among the high cliffs that capped the distant elevations.

"Boss, what do we do for food around here?" Dewey queried. "I'm half-starved!"

Lowe laughed. Dewey seemed to talk a lot about food. "It takes a great mind to stay so focused on one thing, Mr. Baughman. I envy you that. First of all, we tote this equipment and feed over to the back room behind that mule barn." Lowe motioned to a stable by an empty corral. "Then, we take all the camp supplies to the rear door of the kitchen and hopefully earn us a little favor with the staff. I expect Cookie might conjure up a little something for us. What do you say, Mr. Monk? Do you think these wood hicks might spare some food?"

There was no answer from the old soldier, only a curious gaze toward the eastern hills. Silas pointed to some far away peaks, their features indiscernible to his aging vision. His arm reached out as if to bring the mountains closer, or somehow clearer, and his hand quivered as it strained to locate some vague promontory or vale. He said nothing. He just pointed. His lips trembled and wetness coated the squint of his eyes. Then, he dropped his arm, wiped his face with the length of his sleeve and began to look again.

"Silas?" Lowe asked. Again, there was no answer. "Mr. Monk, are you feeling poorly? Mr. Monk!"

Silas broke suddenly from his stupor and blurted a gruff response, "O' course not, I'm fit as a Dixie fiddle! You young folk fret too much o'er the likes o' me. If I want to look around, I'll look around. Worry 'bout that equipment, and let's git on with this here job!"

He selected a bulky package and heaved it across one shoulder. His back was conditioned for such work, but the nimble legs that once moved a young Rebel and trapper had long since lost their vigor to time. Silas took short, careful steps down the ramp and moved his load to the stable. He returned repeatedly, each time for a heavier piece and another futile scan for the places of his past. Age might hamper. It could muddle, but it would not break the indefatigable spirit of the man.

It was half past noon when Cookie greeted the crew in the mess hall. He was quick to offer them a meal, but insistent that they wash before coming to the table. Their skin was ashen with the gray tint of cinders.

"Just like being home, huh, Jack?" Lowe said. "I could've sworn I just heard my mother telling me to wash my face."

Black Jack rejoined, "Dat old civilization sure keeps on houndin' us, don't it, Mr. Yancy? We is always comin' and goin', and it be dere all de time sayin' what we needs to do. De sooner you wash, de sooner you eat. Yessa, dat sounds a lot like my Mama."

The men moved to a long porch fronting the hall and found a row of wash basins filled with clean water. A single bar of lye soap and a tattered but neatly folded towel lay next to one of the basins. Lowe finished scrubbing his hands and splashed water on his soot-covered face.

"Enjoy this, boys, it may be the last soap you see for a few weeks. Black Jack, toss me that towel when you're done with it." His friend gladly obliged. "How about you, Dewey? Are you ready for the towel?" Lowe goaded, still sensitive about Dewey's treatment of Black Jack on the rail car.

Dewey looked over at the brown-skinned man and shook his head. "No thanks, boss. I'll air dry." He then dabbed his hands on the back of his trousers and prepared for his long-awaited dinner.

The hungry crew relished an assortment of breakfast and supper leftovers. The cook stayed with them, hungry himself for the latest news from Devlin and the world beyond. While they talked, he hauled a basket of potatoes from the pantry and began to peel.

"Lowe, did you bring me anything besides news?" Cookie asked, still concentrating on his potatoes.

"Of course, some of Silas' best."

The old man blushed faintly as Lowe continued, "But I don't know. Whiskey, no matter how good it is, it's a serious contraband around these logging camps. A great cook is a rare find. If you lose your job, Silas and I will have to answer to a mighty ill-tempered lot. A more prudent soul would keep the bottle to himself."

Lowe may have sounded serious, but Cookie knew better. "Lowe, I'm a secretive, selfish man. Trust me, what I value I do well to hide, especially a good drink in a dry camp like this one. I've got no hankering to give up fine corn liquor to these timber wolves. So, you hand it over and don't concern yourself."

"Fine, then. I'll sneak you a jug this evening, and we're much obliged for the meal."

When Lowe Yancy backed away from the table, the others took

a final sip or bite, then followed him. Dewey lifted his leg over the bench, but clumsily caught his big foot on the edge and brought the long seat crashing to the floor.

The sound startled Cookie, and the resulting slip of his paring knife left a thin bead of blood across his thumb. It was the blood that brought to his memory a warning he intended to share earlier.

"Hey, you best be careful tonight. We have some boys in camp that move just about wherever and however they please. They've had themselves a time with that poor Italian group. It's a bitter bunch of roughnecks, could easily be a deadly bunch. From what I see, Black Jack and these young fellows with you...well, they may be prime for trouble."

"And just where is the superintendent through all of this?" Lowe asked.

"Afraid, I guess. He takes his supper elsewhere to avoid what would be a mean fight. I can't blame him much for that. They could kill him in any real scuffle, and he's not about to give them that chance. They're right good loggers, from what I'm told, and that may make them a bit more tolerable in the minds of management."

"I can't believe the others tolerate a bully in the ranks."

"Well, someone has to be the first to stand. I guess no one really wants to be knocked down."

"Yeah, I know how that works, but what about the county sheriff?"

"There's been no law broken, least wise not yet, or not that I'm aware of. Just a few teeth and some pride. But the day of reckoning is coming on fast. Make sure you're not part of it."

"Well, thanks, Cookie. We'll keep an eye open."

Cookie's warning chafed the nerves of Morgan and Dewey, who had anticipated some conflict with nature but not with men. Lowe sensed a growing uneasiness in their expressions and felt obliged to console them. It was a fatherly task, and he had little experience in nurturing. He looked directly at Morgan and answered the question that neither boy had posed.

"Hey, this isn't anything for us to worry about, and if it is, we'll deal with it. You understand?" Lowe strained to recall an appropriate adage or story or sage morsel of advice so adeptly offered by his own elders in such times. He came up with a lesson that his father called "the journey," and he recited it as best he could remember.

"The fact is, boys, we just walk on the same old road. Sometimes it's muddy and sometimes it's paved. There are lots of hills and bends, short cuts and long detours. There's a magnificent view at one turn and a senseless horror at the next. But it's just one road, so you have to keep walking it. And you go on all the way to the journey's end, where you rest with the memories of your travel, both good and bad, and with a rightful pride for having come so far. Do you know what I'm trying to say?"

The boys struggled for a moment to grasp Lowe's message. They looked to Silas and Black Jack for some special insight, which, of course, was not forthcoming. Silas eyed the empty sky, shaking his head. Black Jack stared at the ground. While they were strangely uplifted by Lowe's words, in truth, they did not have the slightest notion of his meaning.

Dewey braved a response, "Mr. Yancy, I can't honestly say that I'm gettin' it. It's a cozy thought though."

"Well, let me explain it another way. It's proper to fear something that can harm you, but in doing so, you still have to stand tall. You have to face some monsters from time to time. It's just part of that journey. Now, does that make it clearer?"

The boys were mute, and Lowe sighed in frustration. "Oh, never mind. I just thought it would help if I.... Well, never mind."

"You done yer best, boss. And I think we understand now, don't we, Morgan? Morgan!"

"Huh?" Morgan's mind seemed elsewhere, and Dewey gladly gave his friend a thump on the head to help him refocus.

"Pay attention! We gotta face monsters."

"Huh?"

Dewey thumped him again. "And we gotta stand tall."

"Huh? And quit thumping me!" Morgan protested.

"Well, then, listen up! The boss says we gotta face monsters and stand tall and walk on a road and have rightful pride and a lot of other good things. And you're not even hearin' it."

"Huh?" Morgan threw his arms around the top of head to avoid an imminent third assault.

Silas and Black Jack began to laugh, mostly at Lowe Yancy, who was impervious to the boys' obvious effort to tease. The boys laughed, too, and in short order, Lowe was in the thick of it. He could take a joke. In fact, he welcomed this one.

"You sure had me, fellows. I reckon I'm not much on philosophy or advice," Lowe said, being self-effacing.

"Nah, ya talked real fine," Silas countered. "But them boys is addled, that's all. It ain't yer fault."

They all laughed some more, but behind the merriment, there was still trepidation. His words may have been lost to them, but Lowe's confidence was warmly reassuring. For the remainder of the day, the crew cleaved to each other and to their leader's every direction, and as the weary loggers finally returned, the boys watched for trouble behind every corner of the camp.

The call to mess was sounded by a flourish of hammer strikes against a long, dangling section of steel plate. The metallic clang could be heard a mile away, but Cookie feverishly beat the dinner summons until files of men were seen scampering across the camp yard. Some raced to the wash house, others to the water basins upon the porch, but all arrived clean for supper. Cookie's rule: Enter unclean, exit unfed. No one would risk an offense to the cook, including the bullies who pressed their way to the head of the line over the silent objection of their fellows.

The quality of the cooking was evidenced long before mealtime by a host of delectable aromas, which escaped through the kitchen's open windows to torture the waiting, weary and hungry men. When Cookie finally signaled to his assistant that the doors should be opened, a voracious horde rushed to take their seats.

They swarmed around three lengthy rows of tables, then quickly settled like bees to a hive. The noise of conversation deadened as the loggers eyed the steaming platters and serving bowls and the queue of Italian men moving quietly to their place near the back of the room.

A short, skinny man, his black hair gleaming with pomade, rose from the bench and saluted. "Come now, brothers, let's show some respect for the road builders, our hard-working friends from over the ocean." He clapped his hands, but no one joined him. Everyone knew his intention. "Ciao, amigos! Bon journo, ya damned bunch o' garlic munchers! Ya interlopers! Ya got no jobs of yer own, so ya come out here to steal the bread from our hungry mouths. Why don't you sons o' bitches just get back on them ships, go back home and leave us poor boys be?"

The Italians ignored him, as did most of the other men assembled in the room. They had witnessed the spectacle on too many occasions. The man was a ruffian, a loud mouth that would not be quelled, and any attempt to quiet him was a sure invitation to trouble.

Suddenly, a huge hand grabbed him by the seat of his trousers and yanked him back to the bench. A second hand, deformed and devoid of both pinky and ring fingers, swept across his head to tousle his neat, wet hair.

"Mind yourself, Leon. Some of these fellas seem to enjoy this foreign trash. The way you talk, ya might hurt someone's feelin's. Ya may even get someone really fightin' mad. Now how would that be, right before the blessin' of all this good food? Besides, you're making a fool of yourself. Italians don't understand 'amigo.' It's a Mex word. Do ya see any of them big sombreros hangin' on that wall? Of course not. Ya need to settle down and give a man some peace."

"Sure, Farley, it wouldn't do to upset somebody," Leon complied, fearful of Farley Ochs' unpredictable temper and embarrassed by the mock scolding. The others listened, but stayed safe in their haven of silence. Those who understood pretended not to hear.

The last group to enter the mess hall was Lowe Yancy's survey crew. They hooked their hats on the few remaining pegs that lined the wall, then looked for space at the tables. As they waited to be seated, a solemn voice was raised above the steady murmur.

"Gentlemen, it is time to give thanks." Calm filled the room. Heads bowed. The man prayed fast.

"Dear Lord, we thank Thee for the generous blessings of Thine earth, for the bounty of food that nourishes us, the bounty of nature that sustains us and the endless bounty of divine love that guides and protects us on our passing through a darkened wilderness. Though we are unworthy, we humbly accept Thy gifts and are most grateful. Amen."

"Amen." The word resonated in a chorus of masculine voices.

The clamor and scramble for food that customarily followed an evening grace seemed suspended as the loggers came to realize, one by one, that visitors were in their midst. They were especially attentive to the lone black man who peered boldly across the room at their astonished white faces.

"Easy, Leon, it's just a nigger. Ya see one, ya seen them all." Inciting words, they were again loud and for all to hear. But Farley risked no additional comment and hushed as Cookie approached the five men at the door.

"Black Jack, I mean no offense, but you may want to eat back in the kitchen. I've got a couple chairs in there. It would sure help to keep the peace."

"Mister, dat be just fine with me. Show me de way."

Lowe Yancy was angered. He always was at times like this and intentionally cast a cold, resentful glare in the direction of Farley Ochs. He was tempted to react further, but resisted, and passively followed Black Jack across the room. The others took seats among the strangers.

It was high misfortune that Morgan, Dewey and Silas became separated. They sat one at each of the three tables, crammed between loggers already wrestling for larger portions of the meal. Neighborly men heartily welcomed Morgan and Silas, and squeezed uncomfortably to accommodate the new comers. The old Confederate was slow to situate himself, but wasted little time tossing tales about wars and wonders, wildcats and women. Some knew him, others knew of him, and he reveled in the swelling glow of celebrity.

"And thar I was, me and all them brave Virginians, preparin' to march a long open mile across that field, smack into the mouths o' them Yankee guns. Don't mind tellin' ya, fellers, when General Pickett signaled the advance, I near pissed my trousers. Truth be told, I'd a dug me a hidin' hole right thar on the spot if them other Rebs didn't pop straight up and start to movin'. We was packed so tight in formation, my feet ne'er touched the ground fer the first three, four hundred yards. Though I still had me a mind to do it, it were too late then to commence to shovelin'."

Silas pointed to a water pitcher, and one of his listeners quickly poured him a drink. The old man gulped. He waited, then he burped.

"Pardon me fer that. I been tryin' all my life to master the technique, but I still cain't talk and swallow at the same time. Where was I? Oh, yeah. Well, many a fine boy didn't walk back when that charge foundered. And I doubt I'd be a talkin' to ya now, if it weren't fer a Yankee saber that missed its mark and clipped my suspenders clean as a paper cut. My britches dropped straight to my boots, and I fell flat to that ground jist as hard as if a Minnie ball slapped me upside the forehead. I bounced back, sure 'nough, and tried my damnedest to git o'er that fence, but it jist weren't gonna happen. Ya cain't raise a leg with britches hobblin' yer ankles. By the time I was near to managin' it, our boys were makin' tracks back the other way. So I raised my musket fer one last shot, and before lead cleared the muzzle, I stood bare assed in a deep blue sea o' Yankee trouble. And, brothers, that's exactly how I run. I tossed that weapon, got hold o' them britches, and moved my bare ass out o' thar. It weren't pretty. It weren't pretty at all."

Silas guzzled the remainder of his glass of water and belched yet again. "Sorry," he blurted, in a reflexive offering of apology. "Strange, I ne'er since been afraid fer dyin', but, by golly, I known some fearful nightmares 'bout showin' fer duty without them trousers. I tell ya, thar's jist no dignity in war."

Silas ingested a fork-full of potatoes and peas to indicate the end of his story, and a roar of approval lifted from the table. It was incentive for another tale. Thus, he would sample a few morsels from his plate and still spin the yarns of a well-spent life. He ate little, but there was nourishment enough in the captivation of new found friends.

Dewey walked almost completely around the table before he spotted a vacant seat next to a most colossal man. Rolled sleeves uncovered the scarred and rippled muscles of his forearms, but most of the man's strength was buried beneath the bulging fat of his round torso. His face was pitted. Some said it was from the small pox when he was a child. Others said a sheriff in Kansas took him down with a lucky, distant blast of his shotgun. The truth was that he did hard time in a Texas quarry, and the razor-like slivers that flew from his sledge cut him every day for at least three years. No one knew his crime, but they all knew his proclivity for evil.

All other characteristics aside, it was the claw hand that most would associate with Farley Ochs. He never missed his fingers in regards to common function, but the freakish appendage proved time and again to be a valuable tool for intimidation. He was once a brakeman with the Pennsylvania Railway, until a fateful day when he carelessly looked away during the coupling of two boxcars. His large hand crushed into bloody bits when the steel locked in place, and it was said that Farley never cried out or even wrenched with pain. He wrapped the stub in another man's sweat-stained shirt and simply walked away.

Farley gave little regard to the figure coming up behind him and aggressively shoveled oversized bites of fried steak into his mouth. White gravy coated his thick, russet mustache, which curled with unruly twists to hide the relative smallness of his mouth. A waft from his unwashed body nearly turned Dewey away before he could take his place. But when Dewey reached his seat, the man seemed to know exactly when and how to move. He slid his rotund body across the bench to block the boy's way.

Momentarily stunned, Dewey stepped cautiously toward the

space on the man's other side, but the logger again shifted his position.

"What ya think you're doin'!" Farley demanded.

"Just lookin' for a seat. This is the only spot left."

"Well, you won't find it here. I'm in this seat. Try those foreigners over there, or maybe ya could eat in the kitchen with that nigger friend of yours. Go on."

Farley thrived on confrontation. Dewey did not. He felt small, maybe for the first time in his life. Small, angry, confused, humiliated, he burned with so many emotions that he froze with inaction. Yet, he knew too well that this was the inevitable test of his mettle. He had to respond decisively, consequences notwithstanding.

The fat man scowled as Dewey addressed him, "Look, I don't want no trouble, but if you…."

"If I what? Say it, boy! Threaten me, why don't you, while I'm havin' a peaceful dinner. Let's see how far this flies." He held up his mutilated hand and grinned like the devil he was when the boy reeled back in a moment of revulsion.

Dewey prepared to challenge, but before another word could spill from his lips, Cookie walked out of the kitchen with a reserve plate of hot rolls and placed them on the table.

"Dewey, sit down there and start eating before this food gets cold, or worse, yet, before it's all gone," Cookie said.

"Yes, sir," responded the boy. He was glad for the interruption.

Dewey quivered with relief as he seated himself next to the fat man and loaded a plate with food. For the time being, Farley kept his thoughts and eyes to himself, as did the hungry young man, who was careful not to brush so much as a breath against his tormentor. He had hoped that the matter was forgotten and began to devour the feast before him.

Another from across the table grinned as he spoke, "I missed your name, fella. What was it again, Dewey?"

"That's right," the boy mumbled a reply, his mouth now filled with food.

"I had me a dog named Dewey, a mangy but good-tempered

mutt. Say, how 'bout fetchin' me some of that coffee over yonder. Would you do that for me, Dewey?"

A fireplace and two wood stoves were required to heat the mess hall in the cold of winter, but during summer, one stove remained fired to warm an ever-ready pot of coffee. Dewey looked over his shoulder, saw the pot and answered, "Sure, I'll be glad to."

The man was still grinning. "Yeah, fetch it, Dewey. Go fetch!"

The boy did not recognize the insult. When he left the table, Farley winked at his accomplice, took the boy's plate and scraped the food onto his own. Dewey's outrage was evident the moment he returned to find both his meal and place gone.

"Mister, I don't know what I did to put such a burr on your hiney, but I've had enough of your tauntin'. I'm hungry and I want to eat."

"Hey, just look at that dish. Ya already finished." The big man pointed to an empty plate now pushed to the center of the table.

"Damned if that's so!" Dewey stepped over the bench in an attempt to force his way to the seat, but stumbled and fumbled the hot coffee onto Farley's lap.

The man squealed, "What the hell! You don't listen, do ya?"

A huge elbow moved with astonishing speed and caught the boy in the center of his stomach. Dewey gasped and fell breathless to his knees. He moaned, then staggered to his feet. The bully arrogantly returned to his meal, while his victim recovered and positioned to pounce. Dewey plunged hard against the man's broad shoulders as Farley rose slowly to face his young quarry. The boy lifted his arms to shield against the coming punch, but a powerful fist passed easily through his guard and left him bloodied and buckled on the floor.

Again, Dewey gained his footing and pressed toward the giant foe, who grabbed him by the wrists and violently threw him down. His head caught the edge of the table, and Dewey crumpled.

With a raised hand and a cold, black stare, Farley Ochs challenged the stunned onlookers. He branded them as cowards, but expected little else. Only fools would oppose him, and loggers were not such fools. Overconfident, emboldened, he could not foresee that one that would spring from the crowd undetected and undeterred.

With deceptive power, Black Jack brought the huge man down using one strategic shot to the groin, and as Farley buckled, a bony knee lifted high against his chin and sent him sprawling with pain. But, in an instant, two others hurried to revenge their downed companion. As they passed, Leon Hopper dragged a knife deep against Black Jack's rib and then stepped away to watch him bleed.

"Well, nigger, maybe ya ain't so different. Yer blood does run red."

Black Jack held his side long enough to feel the pulse of blood dampening his shirt. He was moving against his assailants when Lowell Yancy embraced him from behind. Lowe whispered urgently to his ear, "Back away from this, Jack. Back away. You're hurt. You can't win this one."

But Leon beckoned, brandishing the point of his knife. "Don't listen to him, Mr. Black Jack." He spoke the name with contempt. "I don't think I'm quite finished with ya, yet. I need to teach ya about yer place in this world, and it sure as hell ain't here. It ain't nowhere in these parts."

Surprisingly, Black Jack responded in a soft patient tone, and all were quiet as they strained to hear. "My place in dis world? Mister, my place ain't in dis world. Not really. I walked many a year with Jesus, and today, he and me might just go on home."

He felt the blood racing through the wound. Calm braced his spirit, while a weakness began to subdue his flesh. But he intended to have his say, even if it was to be with dying words.

"Yessa, snakes like you been circlin' around me for most my time, and I waited long for dis day when I could say I ain't scared o' you. I ain't scared 'cause I know my place ain't in dis world. Today, Jesus give me peace and says to me, 'Come on home, Jack. It's okay'. Mister, I's proud and willin' to oblige him against yo ugly hate. Yo hate cuts us all, not just dis black skin, but dese poor white folk who speak deir own native tongue, and dis young fella, who just wants a meal like every soul dat sits a table.

"My Pap called me John Lewis Clark, and dat de name I take with me, if you and de Lord decide it be my time for leavin'. But

'Black Jack?' Now, dat's a name Mr. Lowe Yancy give to me. He my brother. Dis old man, dese young boys, dey my brothers, and dey all calls me Black Jack. It don't matter none dat dey white. You see, I don't hate white, 'cause it ain't de color dat taints a man. It be de hate itself. And, mister, hate's got one powerful hold on you. So, you ain't my brother, and you best call me Mr. Clark.

"I'll hush now so you can get on with yo killin', if you is still of a mind to do it. John Lewis Clark and old Black Jack, dey ain't runnin' from no snakes."

Lowe Yancy yanked Black Jack clear from the two charging men and barely missed being flayed by a swing of Leon's long knife. He stood firm as the other assailant turned and swung wildly with a fist. Lowe blocked the strike with his opened hand, and with a powerful grip, he twisted the man's wrist so hard that the bone snapped. The man retreated in pain, and then, maddened beyond reason, he rushed back, driving his head and the full weight of his body into Lowe's midsection. They tumbled violently. As Lowe faltered from the impact, Leon sprung heavy on his chest, forcing the air from his lungs. They battled, gouging and punching at close quarters, until the knife again was brought to bear, this time against the soft tissue under the curve of Lowe's gaping jaw. He froze in defeat. Any movement would be his last.

"Nigger lovers," the thug cursed. He hurled insults and slaps at Lowe Yancy as he lay defenseless under the point of Leon Hopper's knife. Leon enjoyed pressing the blade so as to lightly pierce the skin, but Lowe would not yield his pride. He stoically withstood the torture. The two men intensified their abuse, and for a moment, it appeared that Lowe would cry out. But he denied them, he defied them, and they struck harder and harder, again and again.

Suddenly, a slender figure darted with near mythical speed and, with a low dive, launched the unsuspecting men from their victim. They crashed in a tangle of benches and bodies. The knife slashed harmlessly against the air until a swift kick crushed Leon's hand, freeing the weapon and sending it spinning across the room. As the men wrestled for control of their attacker, he wiggled from their grips and leapt away. The thug, now tiring, tried to stand, but a harsh jolt to his temple sent him back to the floor.

Leon retaliated with deathly fury. He jabbed wildly and flailed in desperation against his quicker adversary, but to no avail. A single blow to his unprotected jaw sent him coiling in agony. Exhausted, he rolled to his hands and knees and was finished.

Morgan stood tall. He massaged his aching knuckles and heaved for air while keeping a moment's vigil. There would be no reprisals. The fighting was done.

Silas stormed through the mess hall door and fired a warning round with a revolver he had retrieved from the mule barn. Splinters trickled from the pinewood ceiling and settled without effect on the injured men below.

"Stop this, all o' ya! I've skinned a few varmints in my day, and right now, I'm fixin' to shoot the first polecat that so much as wiggles 'is nose!" He pulled back the hammer of his pistol, and soon more wood dust sifted downward.

"Silas, put that thing down!" Lowe Yancy called out, while Morgan helped him to his feet. "The fight is over. It's been over."

Not convinced, the old man cautiously moved closer to where he could better see the three bullies, now curled in anguish on the floor. They groaned as they coddled their breaks and bruises.

"O'er?"

"Yes, over."

"Oh. Well, I'll be damned. I missed another one! Did we win?"

"I reckon so, except Black Jack. He took a nasty cut."

Silas saw the wet, ruddy stain on Black Jack's hand and clothes, and he rushed to attend his fallen comrade. He stuffed the muzzle of his gun deep into the pocket of his trousers and pushed onlookers out of the way.

"Let me take a look at this," he said, kneeling. He ripped the shirt away from Black Jack's ribs and probed the seeping wound. "Does it hurt ya much?"

Black Jack writhed. "Yessa, when ya pushes on it like dat."

"Stop bein' such a baby and set still!" Silas tore a square from

Black Jack's shirt and pressed it against his side. "This'll stop yer leakin'. I'll need to sew ya up, Jack, but I reckon we'll have ya with us a l'il longer. You can git on home to Jesus some other day."

Morgan cradled Dewey's head and applied a cool, damp cloth to the swelling jaw. The half-conscious youth was muttering about the one thing he loved more than food.

"Hey, you're not Auralee," he said, after his vision had cleared.

"No, I'm not. Sorry to disappoint you."

"Yeah? Well, ya did. Where am I? What in the world's happened here?"

"We're still at the lumber camp, where you just put up a real good battle with that heavy fellow. That's what happened here. But, of course, you lost. For some reason, you decided to attack the biggest, meanest person in the room, and he didn't much cotton to it. Go figure."

Dewey looked over at Farley and the others, who were receiving rather cursory care from Cookie and the loggers. He strained to remember, but there was no recollection of the fight. He then spotted Black Jack, wincing in pain as Silas nursed the open wound.

"Dear Jesus, what did they do to him?"

"He's the one, Dewey. He shot clear out of nowhere and put that fat man down so hard he's still not up. That other boy there, he snuck up to Black Jack and ripped him wide open with a knife. Black Jack, of all people, he's the one that saved you."

The camp superintendent worked through the supper hour compiling time sheets and timber yields. When news of the latest scuffle reached his office, he instinctively grabbed his shotgun and raced without forethought in search of Farley Ochs. He never imagined finding the brute groveling for help from the underside of a collapsed dining table, and the sight cheered him immeasurably. His biggest problems, three troublemakers, were now despondent, disgraced and wallowing in their own sweat and blood. His job had just become easy.

Without compassion for their suffering, without even the pretense of investigation, he summarily dismissed the men from his service and ordered them locked under guard until the arrival of the county sheriff. There was not a word or thought of protest from others who gathered and watched.

Shoulder pats and handshakes, praise and congratulations, offers of assistance -- these were the laurels of respect and admiration tossed to each member of the survey crew. Many a white hand reached down to encourage the wounded black hero, and many a phrase or expression conveyed heartfelt remorse or gratitude. For the men of Camp 7, John Lewis Clark helped lift the burden of their prejudice, and at least for a while, they were brothers.

Morgan accepted the accolades with humility, Lowe with indifference and Silas with delight. But Dewey ignored them altogether as he waited next to Black Jack's weakened body. When the litter came, he slid his arms under the man and gently transferred him to the canvas. Then, he gripped the wooden handles and asked, "Who will help me?"

The last of the evening was spent in recovery, but before nightfall, the battered crew was again assembled by the tracks, waiting for the last run of Shea Engine No. 2. This time, they were sending Black Jack back to Devlin. Silas could patch the worst of wounds, but Camp 7 was not the place for mending.

"Morgan, why don't you go along and see Mr. Clark to the doctor. You can help him get settled at the guest house and then catch up to us in a day or two," Lowe Yancy ordered.

Dewey objected, "No, boss, I'll be takin' him, if it's just the same to you. I got me a nice firm bed and a Ma who bakes the finest cookies in the state. Just ask Morgan. Black Jack will be at home until he's fit for work. We'll see he gets all the care he needs."

"Son, your Ma doesn't need a boarder, especially one that's...."

"That's what? Bleedin'?" Both men knew what Lowe intended to say, but Dewey refused to hear it. "Ma wasn't never like me, Mr. Yancy. She'll want a boarder, when I tell her what he's done."

"Just the same, Dewey, he's best off in his own surroundings. So are you, and frankly, so is your Ma. The folks at the guest house like Jack. Trust me, they'll look after him."

Dewey was not convinced, and he decided that the decision would be better made at the far end of the tracks. With Morgan on one side, he lifted the litter onto a flatcar, which was partially loaded with broken machinery being sent for repair. The boy placed a second blanket around Black Jack to ensure against the cool of the summer night.

"I'm sorry they ain't towin' a caboose on this run, Mr. Clark, but we'll make do." He removed his brown brimmed hat and rested it on Black Jack's uncovered head. He pulled it low to the brow, just above the man's tired eyes. "There ya go. Maybe that'll keep them cinders away."

The train, heavy with logs, crept down the mountain toward Slip Town and beyond. Morgan watched it until the trailing smoke disappeared in the dusk. He felt different somehow, more free, more proud, more confident, more prepared for what may lie ahead. Life, after all, was just a journey. It was just a walk on the same old road, and on this day, he had traveled so very far.

# CHAPTER 7

Morgan's head tossed and turned away from the mysterious light that was penetrating his heavy eyelids. The brilliant beam seemed determined to follow his every move and eventually forced him to abandon the comfort of his sleep to discover its source. He struggled to see clearly, but could not. He strained to lift himself off the thin mattress of his bunk, but was curiously powerless against the apparition that stood safely masked behind the glare.

He squinted to shield himself, but another glint burst upon him. His sight instantly turned to white. The light flickered and darted through his irises, in and out, on and off, until his body suddenly convulsed against the flashing effect. Then, at once, it ceased.

Morgan closed his eyes and began to rub them, but the whiteness continued to glow like a million twinkling stars, which faded ever so slowly as he again peered across the room. The ghostly figure was faint, too faint to discern, but the source of the light became sharply clear. It was a golden ring, of all things, and the same sunbeam that brushed it to a rich luster now painted color and warmth on the pale hand that wore it.

It took only the slightest motion of the specter's delicate finger to guide the light back into Morgan's face. He was blinded to all but the hand and the ring, until the phantom floated gracefully toward him through the raining rays of the dawn.

It seemed to be a woman, her flowing flaxen hair haloed in the same brightness that pierced the sheer fabric of her gown. She had perfect form and motion. She passed before him like a scent of flowers borne on a warm, dry breeze. He breathed deeply and watched. He knew her smell. He knew her face.

"Sarah? What are you doing here?"

"I belong here, silly. Where else would your wife be at the break of such a fine day? I thought you would never awaken."

"My wife?" Morgan asked in a groggy state of confusion.

"Sh-sh-sh." She quieted him and placed her tiny hand with the ring upon his lips. Her other hand pulled the loosely tied strings of her nightgown, precariously clinging to a single shoulder.

Morgan kissed the ring, and with his own hand, he drew her now naked body to him. He began to touch her, to gently caress and explore her hidden secrets and pleasures...first, her hair, then her cheeks, her slender neck, the softness of her flawless breasts, the downy smoothness of her belly and the curve of her small, rounded hips.

But the light, it was still there, and it now lingered to distraction. It became hot, until it again bleached his vision and stole all sensation from his touch. It was a blinding spike of light, a vexing stab of light, and Morgan finally jerked to avoid it. His damp skin parted from the woman's as he broke away from their locked embrace. Sarah dissolved into the radiance of the morning.

"Wake up! I already let you boys sleep to a shameless hour. Wake up before I decide to throw away your breakfast!" Cookie moved from the doorway, and sunlight flooded across the bunkhouse. "Come on, fellows, you've got a long day ahead of you. Get up now!"

"Have mercy, Cookie. What time is it?" Lowe Yancy questioned with a yawn.

"Eight o'clock. That's the hour and the day's half shot."

Lowe rolled out of his bed and attempted to stretch. "God, I'm sore," he complained.

"I'm not surprised. You put on a good show last night, which is why I let you sleep."

"Thanks. I suppose I should rouse young Morgan." He looked at the large lump under the covers of a distant bunk. "I imagine he's hurting quite a bit himself."

Pain is the one true mentor of a man, an infallible teacher that guides and guards him through the gambles of life. Its lessons are real and lasting, and they entail no reiteration. Whether it is the ache of a bruised and broken flesh, the anguish of a hopeless spirit or the torment of a heart, pain sets an indelible mark upon his memory.

Morgan awakened to Lowe's nudge and to an agony comprised of all such pain. The exhilaration and the exhaustion of battle had weighed heavily and left him both weary and restless through the night. Oblivious to the musty smells and the chorus of snores that had permeated the room, he laid sleepless, hour after hour, thought after thought.

The predawn activity of the bunkhouse had been anything but quiet, as men scrambled clumsily for clothes and boots and raced in the darkness toward the aroma of breakfast coffee. Despite the noise and his restlessness, Morgan could not muster the will or energy to lift himself from the softness of his pillow. As the last of the lumbermen filtered out through a creaking door, the new silence overcame him like an opiate. He fell deep into a welcomed, undisturbed slumber and deeper still into the fervor of his fantasy.

His dream had been alive with the touch and smell and taste of Sarah, who simply disappeared with an untimely prod and the call of an all too familiar voice. For a moment more, he lay despondent trying to savor the brief affair, but the details of his passion vanished with her.

Morgan groaned with his first effort to move. "I'm trying, Mr. Yancy," he said, "but it's not going to be easy. I may need a whole pot of coffee and another week of sleep to be much use to you. You go on without me." He was half hoping that Lowe would agree and drew the cover of his bedroll back over his head.

"Forget it, boy. We'll be hobbling through the hills together, and I'm going to need you to hold *me* up. That's why I brought you along. Besides, it's a good day for a walk. Come on, up and at 'em!"

Morgan winced at the thought of walking. In fact, any movement seemed an unreasonable course of action. His young muscles may have been limber, but they were not immune to soreness. He stirred again with a long reach for his trousers that were slung across the end rail of his bunk. His swollen fingers and aching muscles would not bend, and sharp jolts shot through his body. The trousers still on the rail, he fell back and resettled into the warm, soft cushion of his bed. For Morgan, pain had taught its lessons well.

Lowe Yancy would have cringed at the deplorable condition of his crew had he himself not been so fatigued. Instead, he laughed at seeing the pitiful remains of the small group assembled in the corral.

His partner and most knowledgeable man, John Lewis Clark, was laid up in Devlin with a serious knife wound. Dewey Baughman was home, as well, recuperating from injuries of his own. Morgan was an almost tireless worker but nearly debilitated by aches and pains, and Silas, his teamster, his scout, his friend, was 73 years young and nearly blind. Even Noggin, the mule, was not ready, at least in spirit, and rudely showed his customary disdain for the upcoming journey. He hid in the far shadow of the barn, his feet planted in defiance and his soiled gray rump turned in refusal toward the others. But then there was Blu, known as "True Blu" or "Good Ole Blu' by the men who had come to depend on him. Blu alone was raring for travel.

Lowe patted the animal. "Well, one out of seven's not so bad! Mister, looks like you'll be leading this outfit today, and believe me, it is going to be an effort just to keep up. How about taking it especially slow and easy?" He stroked the coarse, reddish hair along Blu's withers, and with a gentle tug on his bit, he and the pack horse moved side by side across the dust and debris of Camp 7.

Morgan followed at a close distance, massaging his hand and scuffing his leaden feet through the dirt. He could hear Silas's voice berating the stubborn mule, still holding fast to its place in the stable, but there was no need to stop and wait. He knew the old man would catch up in Noggin's own good time.

Their passage was easy at first, and, with the exception of an occasional complaint from Silas, it was rather peaceful. The Italians had done their work well. A new rail bed was ready for the opening of additional timber tracts, and its gentle grade was a clear corridor through the otherwise impenetrable forest.

One man following another, the party moved slowly between endless steel rails. The men, like the boys they once were, stretched their strides or hopped to keep their footing on the narrow ties, evenly spaced beneath the tracks. It was a game each played unaware of the other, and a mile slipped behind them before a word was even spoken.

Before long, they had caught up to the loggers. They could hear the whiz and bang of saws and axes, the cries of warning and the eventual crack and crash of trees tumbling to the earth. They could hear the sounds of wide-spread activity, but a thick, green hedge of rhododendron, a natural wind break some 20 feet in height and 20 yards in depth, blocked any real view of it. It was just as well. In the mind of each surveyor, the savage consumption of the woods beyond was a bitter foretelling of the forest's ultimate fate.

Farther up the track, large landings had already been cleared for the ongoing deposit of fresh cut logs. Deeply worn paths ended at each site, where a steady flow of mule teams dragged in a mounting supply of timber. Muleskinners affectionately coaxed each animal by name as chains of logs were skidded down the trails to the landing. From the side of the track to the far edge of the clearing, stacks of timber were piled high while awaiting transfer to the mill. Soon, a steam loader mounted on a flat car would ascend the rails and begin to deport these beginnings of a rich woodland harvest. So much was being taken so fast. Again, it was the foretelling of fate.

The whole idea bothered Morgan, who struggled to justify the destruction of God's nature against the material needs of society. There was in trees a certain dignity, a stateliness that few men would achieve. They had history. They had purpose. They endured the harsh assaults of years, sometimes of centuries, and all the while they would give back to the air and soil and flowing waters, give back to the elements that nourished them. They should not have to give more, especially to men, who would grab the essence of the forest and send it away to those who would never comprehend the greater depth of its offering.

These logs on the landings had been stripped of every limb and leaf and dragged from every niche of the mountain. Scoured and gouged, they would soon be transfigured into fresh lumber stacked high at the Devlin yard. They would become rough framing or polished floors, sculpted panels or crafted furnishings for some distant urban center. Trees, in Morgan's mind, deserved better. The mountain deserved better than to be burgled of its clothing and jewels and left to persist bare and beaten against the throes of nature.

Maybe it was the idealism of his youth that lifted his love of the living tree so high, so far beyond than the mercenary values of its lumber. Maybe it was his inexperience with life in general. He had no livelihood, no dependents. He had no needs that demanded his loyalty to the industry. In his youth, he could afford a nobility of thought. But the men who worked tirelessly beyond the hedge of rhododendron, they had families and requirements that bound them to their occupation. They were compelled by survival to think in more pecuniary terms, and to them, the great trees, beautiful as they were rising majestically from the forest floor, must still be taken down. It was an irreproachable choice. Like the starving hunter who sights his prey and looks into the wide brown eyes of the deer, many were the loggers who found displeasure in their fateful swing of the axe.

His weariness, the cadence of his stride, the even placement of the ties, all worked to entrance Morgan as he walked quietly with his thoughts. His mind set a relaxed pace, and he lost cognizance of the time passed or the distance ahead. It took a rude and sudden slap from Noggin's tail to bring him back to consciousness.

Morgan unwittingly bumped into the animal's hind quarters, and the insulted Noggin bucked in surprise. Instinctively, the boy leapt backward to avoid a deadly blow from an iron-shoed hoof. Catching his heel against the edge of the rail, he took an ungainly roll down the short embankment of the bed. He got up quickly, startled but unhurt.

Silas steadied his mule. "Whoa, Noggin! Easy, Noggin. Ain't nothin here to hurt ya. It's jist ol' Morgan back thar." The mule brayed and twitched to show his uncertainty.

"Morgan, you okay?" asked Lowe.

"I think so."

"What in God's name are you doing, son?"

"Sorry, Mr. Yancy, I wasn't paying much attention. My mind was wandering a bit. I just walked into him."

"I'll say it was wandering. Noggin's a big animal, and most folk would find him a target hard to miss. You have to be more careful. He can kick and kick to kill."

"Hell, that ain't the worst o' it," said Silas, who struggled unsuccessfully to stifle his laughter. "I once heared of a cowpoke from out thar in Texas. I believe it were Mobettie, Texas. Yes, sir, that's the place. Well, the place really don't matter none, do it? It were an ol' camp fer buffalo skinners, cattle drivers and such, a nasty, dirty li'l hole of a town. Well, I guess that ain't got no particular importance neither.

"Anyway, I hears this feller weren't too good at roundup and resorted to some mean ways to move them cows along. He'd whoop a li'l, fire off 'is pistol, crack a whip, do everythin' normal, but nothin'seemed to motivate them animals -- nothin' except walkin' behind and ticklin' 'em with the tip of a big ol' bowie knife. Now, once he got 'em to movin', he'd jist run with 'em, makin' sure they wouldn't stop. Them bovine weren't much fer bein' stuck with no knife, but what could they do? They moved right on, I tell ya."

Lowe and Morgan listened and waited to hear exactly where Silas would take the story. Silas did not know for certain himself, but he was willing to continue as long as he held his audience.

"Well, that boy was bound to cross the wrong animal sometime or another, and sure 'nough he did. He pressed up against an old Longhorn bull with 'is goods a swayin' back and forth and hangin' nigh to the ground. When that bull caught glimpse o' the knife, he naturally got a disturbin' impression and a powerful inclination to protect what was near and dear. He took off wild-like with the cowpoke followin' close on 'is tail. But jist as the feller were ready to stick 'is blade, the bull pulled up short and the whole man, all but the boots, plum disappeared through the back door o' the beast. True story, as I live and breathe!"

"Why, Silas Monk, you never told a longer lie in your entire life. And, frankly, that's your most disgusting attempt, yet," Lowe complained.

"Nevertheless, I stand by every word."

"Did the cowboy live?" Morgan asked, not so much believing, but wanting to hear more from the depths of Silas' imagination.

"Well, son, what ya think happened? O' course, he didn't live. Thar ain't no one before or e'er since survived such a tragedy. I reckon it were li'l consolation fer them left mournin' a good partner, but I was told thar weren't no long sufferin' on the part o' that cowpoke. He died in the instant, most assuredly from a hideous case o' sudden embarrassment. O' course, that poor bull still felt a might discomforted, though even its pain must've surely passed before too long."

Silas paused for Morgan to give his story due consideration. "Ya likely figured by now that thar's a message in all this, one pertainin' to yer collision with ma mule." He waited for the inevitable question.

Lowe supplied it, anxious to move on. "I'll bite. What, pray tell, is the lesson?"

"The lesson? Why that's simple, Mr. Yancy. I'll tell ya the lesson. If ya don't want to be the 'butt' of an old codger's joke, jist keep yer damn face off 'is ass!" The old man slapped his knees and let out a roar of laughter.

"Oh, dear Lord." Lowe looked to Morgan and shook his head. Still, he laughed. "Here's the real lesson, son, watch where you walk. It's dangerous enough out here without being reckless. And, also, try not to give Mr. Monk too much incentive for telling his yarns. He's way overstocked, and he won't stop until he's told us every one of them."

"Yes, sir, I'll try to be more careful."

"Good man. Now let's head out."

The crew continued another half mile to where the railroad abruptly terminated at the edge of a natural sink. The depression was wet with seep water and bogs, but still proved a better course for construction of tracks. Here, the Italians were laboring to install a log tram that could temporarily carry the trains over the mire. The heavy timbers would essentially float over the wet ground, but would be long enough and strong enough to support a locomotive and its trailers, at least until a more stable bed or trestle could be engineered.

Covered in muck and sweat, the laborers stopped to watch as the surveyors approached. At some point, they recognized the threesome, and a loud cheer greeted the men, followed by a score of handshakes and friendly phrases in an unknown tongue. One Italian swung his fist through the air, flexed his arm to show the sinew, beat his chest and then pointed to Morgan. The boy was honored.

But the glory was short-lived as the workers returned to their tasks and the crew proceeded into the bog. Each step through the peat pulled at their boots and threatened to trip them with wet grasping suction. At one point, Lowe's knees collapsed under him, as his feet stuck and his body lurched forward. He arose with some difficulty, half drenched and brown with mud, but continued the slow progress across the sink as though nothing happened.

The bog was just wide enough to prove exhausting, and the men were glad to finally sit on the dry land beyond.

"That was somethin'," Silas said. "I think it done stretched my legs another two or three inches." He rubbed hard against his skinny thighs and calves.

"We've been through worse in this line of business," Lowe responded, "but I can't recall feeling so worn out."

He pulled off his leather boots and socks and drained the muddy water as best he could. Morgan and Silas did the same. Then, they each found a log or patch of level ground on which to rest. Lowe used the opportunity to talk about the task before them.

"This really shouldn't be too tough a job. We're only verifying a couple lines set by an old 1779 metes and bounds survey, and three miles of that seems to follow the course of Pennywhistle Creek. The trick, of course, is in finding the first corner, which is nothing but a chestnut tree.

"Thar sure won't be no chestnut tree after all this time!" Silas exclaimed. "I reckon we had us a long walk in a swamp fer nothin'. Ya might say our dinner rabbit jist disappeared down 'is hole, and we'll be headin' home hungry."

"I don't give up so fast. No doubt there's little left of that tree, but the records also describe a big square boulder nearby. Now I ask you, with such description marking our spot, how can we possibly not find it among the million other rocks that line the creeks in these parts?"

"Ya ain't serious. That's what ya got? Even if ya ain't given up, I reckon maybe ya should."

"We'll find it all right. It's what we're paid to do, and one way or another we always manage. Anyway, all this is part of a new tract just purchased by the Watoga Company, which should end up being about 7,000 acres. It's mostly hardwoods, and some really large ones from what I understand. I do believe that Mr. Charles Devlin intends to buy up all of West Virginia before he's through. It would be nice if we could keep just a tree or two for ourselves."

Silas found reason to grouse, "Folks nowadays got too much money fer their own good, and when they git to spendin' and buyin' up things, they ain't satisfied until they purdy much ruin it fer the rest o' us fellers. Give me jist a piece o' that money and I'll save them big trees, if only to spite yer Mr. Charley Devlin."

Lowe watched Silas' face turn pink with anger. He always could gauge the depth of the man's ire by his shade of red. It was an impish impulse that caused him to stir the old man further.

"Silas, I always figured you for a man of great means, and now you tell me you don't have any money?"

"Sure I have money, but it ain't the kind we're talkin' 'bout jist now."

"I don't believe I've ever seen you spend so much as a nickel, and that still of yours has run just about day and night for as long as we've known each other. Mind you, I'm not saying you're a skin flint that kept the first penny he ever earned, but if you ask me, you should start putting that vast wealth to some good use. Buy up a few of those trees, and let's make a park for folks to enjoy. Or, better yet, get a hold of an acre or two, and we'll build a cabin for Morgan and that little gal he's been pining over."

Lowe waited for Silas to ignite, but instead was surprised by his calm, didactic response. "If you youngsters wouldn't squander every red cent ya earned, ya'd have yer park and a lot o' other good things in time. Quit lookin' fer us old timers to bail ya out. Money can git a might scarce, but it ain't nothin' but good sense to hold out some coin fer another day. If ya cain't be thankful, at least be smart when the good Lord throws somethin' extra yer way."

It was a good response, another lesson, and Lowe was reminded that his old friend was a lot more than tall tales and temper.

"Well, Silas, if you happen to change your mind, let us know when you're ready to dig up that treasure of yours. Morgan and I will drop by with a wagon and spades."

"I seen right off what yer tryin' to feed me, Mr. Yancy, and I ain't gonna bite. Never ya mind 'bout my money. I know jist where it's hidin', and come any day now, I'll be commencin' to spend it on a long line o' loose women and loud saloons. I was fixin' to invite ya along, to share it with ya, but ya been messin' with me. So, I reckon I'll scare up some new friends, maybe Black Jack and that boy, Dewey. I already like them fellers a heap more than e'er liked you."

"Now, there's no need to get so hurtful. You've never been one to waste yourself on wild living, and you know I'm the best friend you've got, short of the mule. Forgive me, so we can move on with this survey." Lowe extended his hand.

Silas replied smugly, "It's too late fer all that. I'm gittin' new friends, I tell ya, and I'd rather kiss the damn mule than shake that hand o' yers." Still, he grasped Lowe's hand. "Come on, Morgan! Let's find the man 'is corner, if only to shut 'im up."

Morgan was still focused on the topic of big trees, and as the crew steadily wove a way through the forest, he caught only glimpses of small cliffs high on the mountain.

"Do you think there's any chance we can make it as far as the Shawnee Scarp?" he asked.

"Huh? Where did you hear about the Shawnee Scarp?" Lowe replied with surprise.

"I thought everyone had heard of it. It's somewhere here abouts in the Big Timber, isn't it? I was hoping you and Silas might have a better idea as to where."

Lowe knew more than he wanted to disclose. "For me, the scarp is just myth. There's no such place on the maps. So, to answer your question, I doubt we'll make it that far. But who knows? Some stories bear out in time. You heard about the Indian boy, I suppose?"

"Yeah, he raced up the cliffs to escape some huge fire and died on the rocks by a grove of giant trees."

"That's the legend, according to most folks. Some swear he never actually perished in the fire."

"Yeah, I was told that, too. The mountain felt compassion for the boy, after he outraced the flames and scaled the cliff. It let him heal in the cover of its forest."

Lowe scoffed, "For some reason, everything has to have a heart in an Indian tale, the rocks, the sun, the river, the earth. Mountains don't feel, Morgan. They just are."

Morgan kept recalling the story as he had heard it. "After all these years, no other person has been allowed to approach those woods, and the Shawnee Scarp still stands somewhere like a fortress keeping the secret of the mountain. They say 'Dead men tell no tales.' Isn't that right? Well, that Indian sure didn't talk, so he must've died up there. That must be why the place remains a mystery, even today. It's a sound basis for legend."

"Well, you believe what you want. No one ever knows for sure when it comes to folklore. Indian legend is more often nonsense than history."

Silas joined the discussion, "Ain't a single word o' it true, as fer as I'm concerned. I been all across these here hills, and I ne'er seen a tree like in them stories. I ain't sayin' thars no big'ns, but them that are out thar jist ain't the giants ya been talkin' 'bout."

"It's a legend, Silas. It might be true. It might not, but wouldn't you like to see them if they really did exist?" asked Lowe. "There must be some place your feet never traveled."

"Well, ya make a decent point. I reckon thar could be a crest or two I ain't passed o'er as yet. Ya ne'er know what the woods'll hide."

Each of the three men looked up to see the near and distant cliffs that lined the peaks. Their treasure could be almost anywhere.

Morgan confided to the older men, "I know I sound strange, but big trees seem to call to me. I can't help but marvel every time I'm near one. It won't be long before men like Mr. Devlin cut through the last of the Big Timber, and I seriously doubt the future will ever be patient enough to allow its return. The old growth, the virgin woods, will be nothing but another tall tale in the years to come. I'd really like to get up there and find that place before something or someone comes along and destroys it all."

Silas responded with his usual cynicism, "And somethin' or someone sure 'nough will come. They always do. The land has a mighty poor grip on its wonders, and it don't take much to wrest 'em free and haul 'em all away. I'm with ya, son. It ain't gonna be no time at all before them trees is gone, and gone fer good."

Lowe listened, and all the while was warmed by his growing bond with these men. He might have walked a thousand miles for just a glimpse of such a forest, and his companions, an old soldier and a young philosopher, would surely have begged to join the quest. In truth, he had seen what they now only imagined, and he could guide them on their way to that very special place. He could make true the myth. He could make real their dream.

The task of surveying the boundary along Pennywhistle Creek would not be as easy as Lowe anticipated. Heavy flows of previous years clogged the stream with branches and boulders, and the folded layers of bedrock created deep holes and sharp ledges just beneath the glare of the water's surface. The men tethered their pack animals while they spread out and scouted the rocky wash.

It took hours to find their starting point. According to the original deed of almost 130 years prior, the boundary was said to corner at the "great chestnut, six feet wide, blazed by a 'diamond-X,' three and one half rods west of a large square rock centered upon the creek." A hand drawn illustration of the blaze was included in the records.

After a frustrating search, the crew finally came upon an enormous boulder that blocked the center of the stream. It was similar to the many others they had seen anchored in the Pennywhistle, but by size alone, it was different enough to warrant closer attention. Lowe looked in all directions.

"Hmm, this may well be our large square rock. See any chestnuts with a blaze?"

Silas and Morgan both scanned the banks from where they stood. They spotted chestnut trees, but none of a size to fit the ancient description.

"Don't bother looking for a living trunk," Lowe added. "I think if we find anything out here, it'll just be a remnant. The tree may be down, but chestnuts tend to linger for years, even on the ground. So look down low. Look for saplings grown from the mother log if you don't see signs of a snag."

The search was unyielding as the men inspected every bush and tree within throwing distance of the boulder. They ended their effort and had regrouped by the creek when Silas recognized a shallow indentation about 35 feet from the center of the rock. On the uphill side was a leaf-covered mound of dirt, radically eroded by time but still showing the earlier uprooting of a tree.

"Thar's yer chestnut!" he shouted, with the excitement of discovery. "The wind snatched 'er right down to the ground, pulled the roots and dropped 'er crown. It were years ago, I'd say, seein' it's all gone but the hole."

"I think you're right," said Lowe. "Good eyes. I missed it altogether, standing darn near right on top of it."

There was nothing left of the tree. Decay had taken it cleanly, but a cluster of chestnut sprouts in the indentation and the evidence of wind throw was conclusive in Lowe's mind. He would use the center of the depression as his benchmark for the survey.

It was late in the day, and Lowe looked at the tired expression of his men. "I'm sure you fellows want to move on, but I'm beat, and we can't really accomplish much more today. Let's set up camp and start us a fire and supper before dusk settles in. Any argument?"

There was none. Silas and Morgan set out at once to unpack the equipment, and before long, a fire was crackling on the bank of the Pennywhistle.

The men settled quickly after their meal, anxious for some sleep. Silas scoured the skillet and bean pan with creek sand, while Morgan gathered as much firewood as the remaining daylight would allow. Lowe tended to the animals and his instruments, readying them for an early morning start. When they finished, Silas and Morgan crawled into their bedrolls, unaffected by the hard ground beneath them.

"I'll turn in after a bit," Lowe said. "I'll try to be quiet, but just looking at the two of you, I don't suppose I could wake you if I tried." With a jug of whiskey cradled under his arm, he carefully maneuvered across the rocks in the creek and climbed onto the massive boulder.

"What's he doing?" Morgan whispered to Silas.

"What he's done every night fer the past 20 years. He's jist lettin' 'is mind work o'er a few things."

"Is he all right?"

"Sure, son, he's fine. As time goes by, the weight o' livin' jist gits a might heavier. A man's gotta find the best way to lighten the load. That's all he's doin', tryin' to find 'is way."

"You mean he's praying."

"Yeah, I reckon. In a fashion he is a prayin', and I ne'er knew a man better deservin' of an answer. Fer some folks, sleep brings dreams, but fer others, it's an angry swarm o' demons. Mr. Yancy's on that rock findin' strength to face them demons. They'll be comin' at 'em the very second he closes 'is eyes. Fer sure, Lowe Yancy's known some restless nights. Let's settle and let 'im have what li'l peace thar is."

Through the twilight, Morgan watched the staid silhouette upon the rock. There was no motion except an occasional lift of the jug, and even that was infrequent. Whatever fight he had ahead of him, it was clear that Lowe did not need whiskey for an ally. Perhaps the old man was just wrong about his friend. Perhaps Lowe Yancy needed nothing because he feared nothing. He was in every way strong and self-reliant. He was in every way what Morgan had always hoped to be. How could there be demons?

A match flared, a lantern glowed, but both illuminated the man on the rock for only a few stretched moments. It was a curious use of the light. When it was extinguished, Lowe blended with the coming darkness, and Morgan drifted into an unencumbered sleep.

The workday began early the following morning, and each of the men was refreshed and ready. Lowe was taken back as he first peered through the sight of the transit and saw white hands pulling against the survey chain. For the first time in a quarter century, Black Jack was not with him, and he felt a certain melancholy in the absence of his friend.

Black Jack may well have been the better of the two men regarding the application of their trade. The man's sharp eyes, his strength, his skill with the compass, his knowledge of the woods and his attention to detail made him particularly adept at his work. But his inability to write, at least legibly, restrained him. Lowe managed the instruments, and Lowe kept the maps and records required for such a business.

Black Jack preferred, instead, to be the head chainman, the man who moved forward through the brush, hacking a line of sight for the compass reading. It was his job to pull the steel measuring tape, or chain, and to report back precise readings. More importantly, he reviewed Lowe's notes and drawings, and with a sharp application of memory, he often corrected critical entries at the end of the day.

It was painstaking work, but Black Jack would never relinquish his chosen role, not to Lowe or anyone else who offered to share in his labor. But now, Morgan would have to perform in his place. The boy would do well.

"It's quite simple," Lowe instructed, maybe leaving out a few details that might discourage his young protégé. "I read off the compass, and you position yourself and the chain as I instruct you. You pull the chain tight along the horizontal plane and give me the reading. Like I said, 'quite simple.'"

"And what do I do if something's in my way, like a big tree or a boulder?"

"Well, you bust through or pick it up and move it. Of course, if that doesn't work, we'll shoot at right angles around it. You'll learn as we go."

Pennywhistle Creek did not hurry in its course through the rocky valley. It just meandered, except where the boulders and ledges forced a heavier rush of water. The sun burned hot when unhampered by the woodland canopy, and Morgan was wetted more by his sweat than the splash of the stream. Still, as far as summer work goes, it was the right place to be.

His boots remained damp from crossing the bog a day earlier, and there was no point in trying to protect them from further damage. Out of habit, he rolled up the legs of his trousers, then, tromped with his chain to the center of the stream. He pulled the chain. He read the measurements. He even cut a number of nuisance limbs that were making an otherwise easy passage difficult. Large rocks and long logs, drenching pools and fitful shallows, nothing of the kind would hinder his effort. Black Jack would be proud of him.

Morgan watched intently as his boss signaled to move left, right, forward or backward. He was a quick learner. He absorbed everything Lowe said to him, and within hours, Lowe was introducing him to the operation of the compass and to the specialized system of recording. Three days later, their bearings had led them from the banks of Pennywhistle Creek to the more trying slopes of the mountain.

Traversing the stream valley was anything but simple, but it seemed so, relative to the steep climbs they now faced while marking the uppermost line of the boundary. Sweat pumped from Morgan faster than he could replenish it. With a hatchet in one hand and a cluster of chain pins in the other, he made slow progress chopping a narrow alley through the dense thicket of mountain laurel. Beads of salt and wetness seeped through the pores of his brow and stung as they flooded his bleary eyes. His shirt, his britches, even the linings of his hat and boots, were saturated with the water of his thirsty body. The clothes hung heavy and caught the rigid branches, which tore mercilessly at his fabric and skin.

He longed for the pools of Pennywhistle Creek. Once obstacles, numbingly cold and treacherous, they now would be a welcomed salvation from the summer heat and humidity.

"All right, let's take a reading!" Lowe called out, after repositioning his transit and tripod.

Morgan dropped the hatchet immediately, grateful for any respite from such work. He wiped his face with a soaked sleeve and then awaited further orders.

"Sorry," continued Lowe, "but we need to pull the chain again. I don't trust this distance. Do you want a break?" Even the shade was blistering, and Lowe endured the same punishment as his small crew. He wanted to press on, but was careful not to overwork them. "Take some time if you need it, Morgan. Grab some water."

"No, I'm okay. I'll be right up."

It was only 20 yards across the slope of the hill to the tripod, but the heat and thick vegetation made it seem much longer. Morgan's pride would not let him show his growing fatigue, so he forced himself to move quickly across the pointy snags and uneven ground.

Lowe held one end of the chain over a long pin, which had been pressed into the ground to indicate the last point of measurement. Morgan dragged the other end along a line determined by the compass. When an arm gesture from his boss signaled that he was off the bearing, Morgan corrected the error by moving a couple feet to the left.

"It looks good from here. What do you have?"

Morgan drew the chain taught. "Uh, it appears to be 68 feet... uh, 68 feet, maybe four and three tenths inches."

"What? Check again!"

Morgan reexamined the chain. "Yeah, that looks about right."

Lowe Yancy laughed heartily, so heartily, in fact, that a pair of quail flushed from their cover and a trio of squirrels scampered wildly for the safety of the limbs aloft. The mule brayed and the horse neighed, as if joining Lowe's merriment. It all seemed strange.

"My Lord, I've awakened the entire universe!" Lowe shouted, and then, attempted from afar to explain what he found to be so amusing.

"Morgan, when we get back to town, I intend to buy you spectacles. The whole chain is only 66 feet, remember? I want to be a little accurate in these measurements, in case Mr. C. O. Devlin really wants all this land he's paying for. Let's try it again."

The pack animals continued hollering in their own manner, and Lowe looked over his shoulder to see Silas at his limit trying to calm them. Something was clearly not right. He motioned for Morgan and then disappeared to the far side of a knoll.

By the time the boy reached the ruckus, Silas and Lowe had already backed away. Silas was lifting himself from the rocky ground, rubbing a new pain in the small of his back and cursing the ill temperament of his mule. Noggin continued to react, but not to his master. He ears folded back from his head. His thick neck jerked. His hooves gleamed silver as he bucked with fear and fury.

Lowe yelled, "Silas, get yourself out there before he kicks your head in!"

"Damn that mule! Ya ain't gotta tell me twice."

The old man did exactly what his friend and common sense told him to do. He ran for his life, as fast as his spindly legs would carry him. Once over the knoll, he fell to the earth, beaten and breathless, but far and free of the mule's inexplicable hysteria.

Lowe and Morgan again attempted to quell the frantic animals, but managed little more than to prevent stampede. The reins slashed through the air like whips, as the men reached time and again for control. Morgan finally found his grip, only to have it wrenched away by a sharp flinch of Noggin's huge head. Lowe had even less success.

Silas's heart pulsed heavily, and he could have heard the perspiration pumping through his pores if not for the loud, desperate cries of his partners. They commanded, they consoled, but the animals refused to be pacified.

"Let 'em be, boys! Ya ain't gonna calm 'em nohow," he yelled. The advice went unheeded.

Nothing within his power would help the situation. Silas understood that, though he was tempted, at least, to sneak to the top of the hill and shoot the mule. Considering the absence of a gun, he rightfully decided against that idea and chose instead to remain comfortably behind until the commotion subsided. He nestled against a leaning trunk, rubbed and rested his eyes from the stinging drizzle of sweat and sought mercy from a devilishly hot and stagnant air. It was not long before a single stir of warm breeze eventually hissed through the canopy, and when it did, an odd, new sound became audible with the swaying of the trees.

The old man peered over the tops of the laurel to a branched maple rising high above him. There, curled in a ball of black shining fur was a cub nestled between two limbs. Wonder and fear overtook him simultaneously. He crawled to his feet and scanned as best he could through the green wall of forest. He braced in expectation, ready to either flee or flop to the dubious safety of the ground. It all depended on the mood of a charging, angry mother.

He cried out, "Bear! Yancy, bear! She's a big'n and she's pissed. Git the guns!" Then he looked to the knoll, and seeing no one, began his retreat toward the refuge of his companions.

The mule and horse now raged in terror. The closeness of the woods had caged them with an unseen predator. They smelled the danger, but could neither turn back nor run forward in escape without trampling the men desperately trying to control them. The animals heaved and bucked with frenzy. Bags and equipment were flung with each twist and arch of their backs.

Noggin jolted with alarm and threw himself into the side of Blu, who reared his head violently against the mule, sending it on a thundering crash into the underbrush. The horse, too, lost his footing against the shallow, rocky soil, and tumbled into the laurel. His panic was contagious as he tangled deep in the entrapment of limbs, his legs kicking wildly at the empty sky.

"What's going on!" Morgan shrieked, as he crawled to higher ground away from the terrified pack animals. Lowe had no time to answer. He dove and whirled to the far side of a tree, narrowly avoiding a kick from his horse.

"Bear! Cain't ya hear me? We got us a bear! Open up yer ears and git them dad-blasted guns!"

This time they could hear Silas. They could hear the horror in his voice. They needed their rifles, but the weapons were packed on the mule. Noggin, now on his feet, shied away as Lowe tried in vain to approach.

With not a second to waste, Lowe left the animals in their misery, and stumbled as he dashed along Silas' path to the sound of now indiscernible screams.

Suddenly, the screams stopped, and a shiver of fear rolled like a wave through his body. The ferocious roar of a great black bear loomed above all other noise, and for a brief moment, crushed Lowe's resolve to go a single step further. But Silas was over that knoll, alone at the mercy of a deadly beast. Lowe continued his race up the hill, afraid of what stood beyond.

Even the bear was silent when Lowe came into view. The man froze in disbelief at the brutish creature that prodded and tossed his friend like a toy. The old man vanished under the thick black coat, then, reappeared as the 510-pound animal rose to sniff and nudge her defenseless prey.

At least Silas was alive. With his head tucked tightly between his belly and knees, he guarded his face and vital organs from the bear's probing snout. He was a rock, without sound, without movement. To be anything else would be death.

Lowe yelled. He waived his arms in a hopeless effort to intimidate the animal, but the bear ignored him as though he were a common songbird. He grabbed a stone and threw it hard, and she roared again, this time out of pain and anger. She turned momentarily to face him down, but maintained her hold against Silas' curled body. Lowe backed away. He dared not intervene lest she destroy them both with a powerful swipe of her stiletto claws.

Then the sow heard the whine of her cub high and safe in its sanctuary. She sniffed the air and lifted away from her quarry. Her enormous head rocked back and forth before she rose up awkwardly onto her powerful hind legs. Her huge paws darted. Her mouth snarled, brandishing pink teeth stained by berries and blood.

Another roar from the mother, another whimper from the cub, the two bears nuzzled at the base of the maple and soon were gone into the green cover of home.

Silas remained folded in a locked grip of his own arms, until Lowe finally convinced him that the assailant was gone. Even then, he stretched out slowly and stiffly while he self-examined the seriousness of his wounds. Lowe helped him struggle to his feet, and all three men gaped at the extent of Silas' injury. There was none. They stood bound with disbelief until Silas broke the spell.

"Thank the good Lord fer deliverance! I didn't reckon on nothin' except bein' a pile o' blood and guts. Boy, I ain't even bleedin'. I'll be damned."

"You're all right. I can't believe she let you go like that," said Morgan. He wondered how a man of Silas' years could survive such an attack, much less stand and talk about it like some commonplace occurrence.

Lowe chimed in, trying to ease the tension, "He's all bone and bad odor, Morgan. Even a bear is particular about her food. I'm sure glad she didn't haul the old man's carcass down this mountain. We'd have both died in the heat trying to fetch him back."

Silas protested, "The hell ya say. I s'pose I should be honored you'd even take the time to come lookin'."

"To be honest, Mr. Monk, I haven't been that rattled since I don't know when. I'll tell you this much, I was stupid to not keep a rifle ready. If anything had actually happened to you..."

"If somethin' was to happen to me, I hope ya'd have sense 'nough to avenge my demise upon that damned mule. He knew all along what he were doin' and weren't 'bout to give up no rifle fer my sake."

"You're alive anyway. You're with us and in one piece. We'll thank the bear for that."

"Jist be glad it weren't no mountain lion. I seen a lion take a calf down once, drag it through a fence and across a field before I could even squeeze off a shot. Them cats are keen killers, but black bears jist wanna be left alone. Old mama knew 'er baby was fine up that tree, but she still needed to press 'er point. I reckon I was too close to 'er youngin' to be ignored. Now, if I was to touch 'er cub, she'd a ripped my throat from my neck and kicked my head clear o'er to Nicholas County. Yeah, be glad it weren't no cat. If a cat cain't eat ya, it'll still tear ya to pieces jist fer the fun o' it. It's a fearsome critter, I tell ya."

Lowe looked at Morgan, who seemed more disturbed by the attack than the old man who had faced it.

"Don't worry, Morgan, the bear is long gone, and there hasn't been a mountain lion out here in years. They were all hunted off," he said.

"Sure," argued Silas, "if ya choose to believe them so-called experts. They ain't ne'er in their life been standin' this deep in the woods, so they cain't know much."

"Silas, I think the boy's done in, and whether you agree or not, I think we've all had enough for one day. The danger's gone. Let's let it rest. We'll get these animals squared away, and then, we'll do the same."

"Yer right, o' course. No need to fret, son. It's all jist a piece o' history now. Thar were no harm done, and ya got yerself a right good story fer yer grandbabies."

Understandably, camp came early, after the men tended their animals and collected the equipment widely strewn across the knoll.

It was nothing short of miraculous that Silas could have survived such a bear attack. Both his flesh and mettle were unbroken. His body had escaped unscathed, except for a few bruises and scratches, and his spirit had somehow remained undaunted. Morgan was amazed. He was astounded by the extent of the man's courage and even more so by his luck.

Lowe broke sticks across his knee and set them precisely over the smoke of the kindling until a proper fire raged. Then, he attended to Noggin and Blu, feeding and stroking and talking with a low voice in hopes that he might calm the unnerved animals. It took longer than he expected, and when he returned to the fireside, he was pleased to find Silas serving up a meal.

With their bedrolls spread under a canvas lean-to, their bellies filled with biscuits and beans, and their minds still racing with the bear, the men became consumed by the leaping colors and rhythmic snaps of the campfire. Morgan was first to breach their silence.

"Life is too fragile, isn't it? It's just too uncertain. I thought I'd live forever, but it seems like anything can come along and take you down...anything, at any time. You know, just in the past few days, we've battled bears and bullies. I've drowned and nearly passed away from this ungodly heat. I don't know why all this is happening to me now."

Neither of the men responded right away. They were watching the fire, sorting through their own issues and reflections. It took some time to actually hear what the boy was saying. The quiet lingered awhile before Lowe felt ready to remark.

"Yup...anything, at any time. That's a fact, Morgan, but it's the experiences in life, not the years, that count. Maybe these things happened because you dared venture a little farther just to find something new, or because you chanced your own well-being for the good of some friends. Living is worth some risks. In fact, it isn't living without them." Lowe smiled, and the lines of his weathered face deepened to show the trials of his years. "The truth is, today is just our training for tomorrow. It never really gets any easier."

Morgan was hoping for encouragement, but was satisfied with

honesty. "Well, if this is the training, I'm not sure I'm ever going to want the job that comes later."

"Oh, I think you'll take the job, son. You've walked a thread the last few weeks and handled yourself well when most men couldn't cope. Good men like you always take the job. For now, just count your blessings, because no one can count the days. Isn't that right, Silas?"

"He's right, boy. I ain't sure which, but yer either charmed like a rabbit with six feet or cursed like a demon forced to sit through Sunday school. Either way, yer a survivor, and good things'll come of it. Mark my words, good things'll come, if they ain't here already. Give 'er time."

Morgan nodded, as if to say "thanks", not only for their words but for the way they cared. Even across their generations, he could feel a growing attachment, much like the tie he had formed as a child with Dewey Baughman. He could not explain it, but he was willing to die for such a friend. And these men, and Black Jack, too, they were but strangers when they chanced their own deaths to save two ingenuous youths. Friendships come slow to a man, and yet, Morgan could claim many. Perhaps Silas was right. He already possessed the good things.

He looked closely at the stone faces of his companions as they again fell silent to the spell of the flames. He sensed in them a melancholy, a loneliness. After all, they had no one in this life but themselves, and on so many a black evening, they must have longed for more.

"Mr. Yancy, can I ask you a personal question?"

"You can ask. I don't promise my answer."

"Well, sir, I was wondering...do you believe in God?"

"Do I what?"

Lowe was taken back by the inquiry. He considered what might have prompted it and recognized the immense burden the boy now shouldered. The currents of life were flowing swiftly, moving him toward the dangerous deep and far from the safe, carefree shallows of his past. He naturally grasped for an anchor, which, in this case, was an untried and unseasoned conviction in a greater power. Lowe wished that he could help, but the question was perhaps too intimate, too difficult for a response. He waited, and then, he finally spoke with his eyes still locked to the glow of the fire.

"I used to. And I don't know if you can ever really stop believing, but it's a struggle for me sometimes. Lately, God and I haven't seen eye to eye. If he's out there, I hope he's still trying to make things better for folks. A lot of fools depend on him. I know that much."

Morgan's faith proved weak and faltering, but he was hoping that Lowe could somehow prop it. The reply was disappointing.

"I believe," he said emphatically, having to convince himself. "I believe real strong, and everything we've been through isn't going to change the way I feel."

"I hope that it doesn't. A good test should make you stronger."

"Like I said, Mr. Yancy, I was just wondering. I thank you for bringing me out here. Both of you, thanks a lot. I think I'll call it an evening and turn in."

No one really said "good night." Silas winked at the boy as he moved past him toward the lean-to, and Lowe just lifted his stick as he poked it at the fire.

"He's a fine boy, ain't he?" Silas said, after Morgan had vanished into the comfort of his bedroll.

"Yup."

"Hard worker. Damn hard worker."

"Yeah, he is."

"Glad he come along."

"Me, too."

"He looks up to ya, ya know."

"I did not know. He must be a smart boy, too," Lowe said, trying to interject some humor.

"Tarnation, Lowe! I'm tryin' to tell ya somethin'."

Silas looked into the lean-to to be sure that Morgan was sleeping. He drew closer to his friend and lowered his voice.

"He looks up to ya, and that puts the burden square on yer shoulders. Ya shouldn't be tellin' 'im things like "believers are fools".

He knows better, but ya don't set a youngin' against the teachin' of 'is folks. It ain't right. Yer place with yer Maker is yer concern, but that boy's place is still the business of 'is Ma and Pa."

"He's man enough to think for himself."

"And boy 'nough to still have 'im a hero. If yer gonna be a hero, Lowe, be a good'n."

"I hear you, Mr. Monk. I'll try to be more careful."

Silas was not completely satisfied. "Yer right, o' course, I reckon he's a heap more man than boy. But Morgan don't need to hear 'bout no woman problems neither. He'll have plenty of 'is own fer too long."

"So, what are you trying to say?"

"I'm jist sayin' that every night around this fire ya start moonin' fer that woman. The boy don't need to see it, and...well, it ain't nothin' he ought to hear."

"I had no intention to talk to him about her. It's private."

"Maybe not, but that boy looks up to ya fer some reason, and he knows when yer hurtin'. At some point, he'll wanna be told why, and I'm right sure 'is folks don't want ya sharin' all them shameful truths o' yer life."

Lowe objected, "There's nothing shameful about it."

"Some would argue," Silas said flatly.

Lowe was in no mood for this particular discussion. It had always been a little one-sided in the past, and the words of his old friend were becoming as monotonous as they were intrusive. Still, Silas had his opinions and felt obliged to share them. While there may have been an element of truth, the message was now just rain on the sand. It passed right through him, doing nothing more but to dampen his resolve.

Crippled by a dream with no chance of fulfillment, by desire left wanting for requital, Lowe had to realize that it was long since time to let them both go. But he would not. Despite the urging of his best of friends, he held fast to his only turn at genuine love.

"All these years, I've been faithful. I've been...."

"Faithful? Hell, ya act like you was married to 'er. Was ya e'er married?"

"You know that I wasn't, but I reckon it depends on what you mean by 'married'. If you're talking about some showy church wedding, I guess I've never taken the step. I would have, if she was willing to be free of her past. But if you're talking about the promise, the one a man only makes to a woman when he knows she holds his heart and soul forever deep against her own, then yes, I have been married. I am still married."

"Lowe Yancy, yer a fool. This'll git ya nowhere."

"Probably so. You can't always control who, or how, or when you love. But if it's right and if it's real, you recognize it for what it is, and if you're smart, you pursue it to the end. There might never be a second chance."

"Well, if that's the case, why didn't ya hold on to 'er? She belonged to ya. I'd sure as hell ne'er let 'er go."

"Silas, she didn't belong to me. You know that. She was a married woman. She had a child."

"So, she belonged to another man. Ya don't see nothin' wrong with that?"

"She belonged to no man, neither to her husband nor to me. If it were just a man standing between us, I would have taken her long ago and never looked back. But she belonged to that child, and the child had a right to be with his natural father."

"Rights, huh. Ya had no right stakin' claim to another man's woman, and that's why yer bein' punished so. It aint no wonder ya cain't sleep, when yer conscience keeps tappin' against yer soul."

Lowe swallowed hard. His throat was dry from argument. "He left her, Silas. He left her without so much as a word for over a year, and it wasn't the first time. I'd say we did have a right. She's the one, the only one for me, and knowing just that, I'll take what I've got over any life with another."

"Son, stop to think. She set ya out on 'er line to jist flutter in the wind, and she likely don't care no more, even if she remembers ya."

Lowe pondered that possibility. "If her heart's changed, then everything about us was a lie, everything we said, or did, or wanted to do. We broke some serious rules in our love for each other.

If she's moved on, if it is all a lie, then I'm a man without honor, without future, and without hope. I just can't believe that a feeling so strong could ever really die. She must still care."

Morgan listened. He never really slept, but lay quiet and attentive to the conversation around the fire. He knew it was wrong, but still strained to hear each and every word softly spoken in the confidence of two friends. His mind was awake with conflict between righteous judgment and earthly compassion.

There was no question that adultery was sinful. His mother had taught him well the meaning of the Commandments. But in the dark truth about Lowe Yancy, there was something curiously acceptable. Whatever happened between this man and the woman he loved, his conscience had declared him free of guilt. His passion seemed warm and decent, his fidelity, everlasting. He was respectful. He was understanding and patient as he waited forever for her return. Strangely, their bond seemed built on some divine foundation, and Lowe was blessed with an unshakable devotion by the very God he now chose to deny.

But it could not be so, not in Morgan's world. He thought of his mother, of her soothing voice reading the scriptures and posing the prayers. She would never approve. She could never accept the way Lowe Yancy conducted his life, and, perhaps, she was right.

Suddenly, he felt the cold wave of anxiety overtake him. He must find Sarah. There may never be another chance. If she married some other man, how could he.... Morgan refused to finish the thought.

Lowe rose to his feet quickly, signifying the end of discussion. He grabbed the kerosene lantern and his saddlebag, and like every night before, slipped into the solitude of night. He pulled from the bag a leather packet, and from that packet, a tattered yellowed letter. He began to read the single page:

*I regret I again must postpone our meeting, and I know not when I shall next have opportunity to see you. My life seems intent on stealing the few precious moments that I might share, and I am saddened knowing how much our separation must hurt you. Please forgive me. Please try to understand.*

*My son grows like trumpet vine through a garden. He climbs on everything and races at the mere sound of an opened door. I can scarcely keep up with him.*

*My husband, for the first time in so long, has renewed his interest in our relationship. He once set me adrift through his indifference, and now, I suppose he sees that I am floating away. He wants me back, Lowe. He wants to change for the good of our family.*

*How can I not give him this chance? Though my heart may break for want of you, I must see this through - for the child's sake, if no other.*

*Know that my love for you is enduring, so pure that it casts the sin of our passion from my conscience. Yet, this same conscience will not allow me to abandon them.*

*So I must leave you, and I must hurt you as I hurt myself, until such time that God is merciful and again brings me into the warmth of your arms.*

*You are my heart's desire. Always.*

The letter cut as deeply at this reading as it did the first and hundredth time he saw it. And the man, strong as he was in mind and body, could not help but weep, as his loss again became all too real. He could live with the pain only so long, and the letter laid his emotions bare and begging to be dealt with. He placed the lantern on the ground and looked high into the dancing shadows of the trees.

"If my love is sin, then why did you bring her to me? Why was it all so honest and tender in the short days we had together? God, are you there? Were you ever there? This is not punishment, but torment. I cannot abandon them, not the memories, not these feelings. You know me, you know this heart, and while I may never again hold her close, only you can understand why, after all this time, I can never let her go. Are you there?"

Lowe began to fold the letter, careful of the worn and fragile creases. He placed it in the satchel and drew out another letter, equally damaged and discolored from the frequent handling. There was no postmark.

He sniffed hard against the pressure of his sinuses and wiped the tears that felt peculiar slipping from his puffy, clouded eyes. He had forgotten how to cry. He gathered himself and began to read again.

Silas grunted as he strained to move his stiff, throbbing joints away from the fire. The heat felt good against the evening chill, and he had been sitting much too long enjoying the healing warmth. He cautiously tested each step as he hobbled through some brush toward the dim lamplight and Lowe Yancy.

Lowe noticed him and quickly stuffed the leather packet among his belongings. As the old man approached him, he turned aside to conceal the frailty of his reddened eyes.

"Too late! I already seen ya. I cain't understand why ya keep beaten on yerself fer a woman. Yer too young to lay stagnant in the water. Thar's too many frogs in this here pond to croak o'er jist one."

"Silas, we've been over this ground. I know it's hard for you."

"Ya hear me out, Lowe. Yer like a son to me. Yer all I got to treat as family, and it's clearer than April rainwater that I ain't gonna be around to pick up yer pieces much longer. So I gotta try while thar's time, and yer jist gonna have to listen. I ne'er know'd no other way than to lay it down as I see it, so don't git all uppity when I come to speak my mind."

Silas had said it many times, but he spoke from the heart and always deserved one more hearing. The old man took on a serious tone.

"I could teach ya a thing or two 'bout women folk, but you and every other young buck got all the answers. I gotta good mind to talk to this gal myself, jist to tell 'er what a woebegone wreck ya become. Even if she know'd how ya felt, a good woman ain't gonna have nothin' to do with such a sad case o' the walkin' misery. I reckon she's a decent sort though, 'cause ya wouldn't take up with no woman lest she be a proper one. But knowin' that, I cain't figure why ya stepped out without so much as a partin' wave. She deserved to know yer feelin's. She had a right to see how much ya hurt, how much ya cared, even if it be a sorry truth. And you, ya deserved better than to spend yer life waitin' fer a miracle. Pride, boy! Too much o' it always jumps to bite ya, and to me, ya seem purdy much chewed up after all these years."

Silas paused for a moment to reconsider his position. "When yer fightin' against yerself, yer bound to git hurt, and we all need some help in patchin' up them wounds. Jist remember, me and Black Jack, and even the good Lord Almighty, is always gonna be close. I want ya to know that." Then, he added, "I'm sorry to brow beat ya, son. Guess thar's nothin' else to say."

Lowe was humbled. "I think it's all been said," he replied. "No one, and no father, could have said it any better."

Silas threw his arm down to feign disgust and moved back to the comfort of the campfire. He knew the man would disregard his every word on the subject. Lowe always did.

# CHAPTER 8

The summer of 1909 passed far too quickly, taking with it the few remnants of Morgan's childhood. He had slipped beyond his youthful innocence to face some of the striking blows that chisel upon the spirit and character of every man. The hot, dusty weeks of summer had sculpted him much more than the previous 17 years of his life.

Morgan began to see himself as one of those leather-faced woodsmen who draw a meager subsistence but great passion from the forest. His work on the survey crew introduced him to a wilderness far more beautiful and wild, more vast and remote, than he ever imagined possible. He had come to be respected by the men of Camp 7, the loggers, knot bumpers, gandy dancers, teamsters, grab-drivers, smithies, cookees and every other worker that would proudly bear so descriptive a title. Their measure of a man was not just the power in his arms or his diligence on the job, but the integrity of his thoughts, the flow of his humor and the charity of his heart. In Morgan's case, there was one additional criterion against which few others were even called to be tested. He had a resolve to press forward when fear judiciously screamed for retreat. Morgan had shown them courage.

Such men judge critically the true quality of another, and they had declared Morgan worthy, worthy to endure their hardship as they hacked and sawed against the edge of nature, worthy to share their common love of the very forest they would fell on behalf of the Watoga Lumber Company. In their acceptance, Morgan was deemed a man, and he would not look back for some time to recall the fantasy and joy of his boyhood days.

As excited and certain as he now was about a future in the mountains, Morgan was tortured by his timidity in the pursuit of Sarah Dabney. The days of August seemed to evaporate in their heat, and the opportunity to know the girl had vanished before he could express anything more than a casual greeting. He had remained largely mute in her presence, signaling an indifference that fell far from the truth. He had watched her intently, admiring her every move and aspect, and knew there could be no other woman in his life, no greater desire than to simply be with her. But now she was gone. As a boy he could seek some folly that might allow him to forget, but as a man, he was forced to acknowledge the silent pledge he made to himself and to Sarah. Somehow, someday, he would find both the girl and the words to proclaim the yearning in his heart.

The summer had taught him much about himself, and he dwelled on these thoughts as he rinsed his razor in the porcelain wash bowl and grabbed a towel to wipe the remaining shaving cream from his face. He placed an arm in the white cotton shirt that his mother had pressed for him the night before. Annie never left a wrinkle, and this day, extra starch held the fine creases and pleats of his sleeves. It was the first day of his final year of school, and his mother made certain he would begin it well.

"Let's go, Jake! You don't want to be late on your first day," Morgan yelled.

"Comin'!"

Jacob had such enthusiasm for school that he virtually rode on air as he descended the stairs. He landed with a loud thump that quaked across the pinewood floors and jostled the few wall hangings that adorned the small house. He darted through the room to the kitchen to give his mother a warm hug, then, vaulted back to meet Morgan and Cora, who were already waiting on the porch. The rusty spring of the door moaned as he threw it open, and Jacob was well on his way through the yard before it retracted, pulling the door with a slam.

"Whoa! Hold on there! I've got your lunch," Morgan hollered.

"Oh, yeah," Jacob replied, as he came to an abrupt stop, "I can't forget that!"

He was embarrassed that his excitement had allowed him to overlook such an important detail. After all, he was now officially grown up. He was finally going to school. He walked back to his brother mustering the composure required of such a newly matured gentleman, but was all the while burning with a child's desire to run and jump and yell.

Morgan opened the round lid of a tin pail and began to announce the contents, "Listen up, Jake. I made you a ham sandwich, gave you an apple and some of Ma's cookies. Now, if you can't eat it all, come find me, and I'll be more than happy to help you out."

Jacob grunted, "Not likely." He snatched the handle of the pail and resumed his accelerated pace. "I'll see you at school!" he cried back to them, liking the sound of the words. Before they could respond, the boy had disappeared among the high weeds of the neighboring garden.

Morgan and Cora carried similar lunches as they followed Jacob down the steps of the porch. They paused briefly in the yard, while Cora tried to determine which of the dusty trails ahead would be least devastating to her morning fresh appearance. Morgan understood the dilemma.

"You look really nice, Cora, and you don't need a bunch of dirt and sticky hitchhikers all over that dress. Would you mind if we followed the road up to the school? It's a bit longer than the path, but I think we have the time. I'd like to show everyone just how pretty my little sister is today."

It was the right thing to say. Cora beamed with pride and appreciation of her brother's thoughtfulness. She looked down at her dress, touched her hair and then cuddled against his arm as they began to amble up the country road.

The Devlin School crowned a ridge that loomed high above the town of the same name. It was reached by a single narrow lane that weaved among a hundred hillside houses as it switched back and forth to the mountaintop. Beyond the school, the road continued to a nearby water tower, but ended thereafter in an area of green lawns and dark stately trees, known simply as 'the park.'

The school was built on a large isolated flat, which allowed considerable space for play. Its ball field, often congested by the scurry of little feet during weekday recess, was a favorite gathering spot for Sunday baseball games and weekend picnics.

The building itself was a white, single story structure, with four large classrooms separated by a narrow hallway. At its front was a low tower that housed a cast iron bell, lusterless in both appearance and sound but, nevertheless, effective.

The westernmost door at the end of the hallway was perhaps the most heavily used, as it led to the playing field and a bank of five wooden privies, three for the girls, two for the boys. Through the door at the other end was a splendid view across the meanders of the Charity River toward long, blue ranges, which faded sequentially along the eastern horizon. The small town and mill seemed dwarfed in the distance below.

There, on top of Briar Mountain, high and away from the mill machinery and the rumblings of a railroad, the air was sweet and quiet and conducive to the molding of young minds. It was there that Arthur Tutwiler dedicated his life to the service of others.

In many ways, Tutwiler was the Devlin School. For 10 years and 10 dollars more a month, he was principal, teacher and custodian, with all the rewards and challenges therein. He ordered the books, taught the lessons, disciplined the children and guided the three youthful teachers assigned to assist with younger students. He arrived every winter morning to fire the stoves, and he departed each spring evening, after having swept the endless dust that indiscriminately settled through the large open windows. Well versed in all things academic and cultural, impassioned by his mission, he existed for the betterment of his pupils and personally mentored every student over the age of 13.

Principal Tutwiler was a tall, wiry man, whose erect stature and poise reflected the perfection of his character and earned him the respect of an entire community. He walked and spoke with deliberate caution, as though evaluating every action before committing it to others. He was strict, yet also giving. His regard for his students was genuine, and so was his disappointment in those who would fall short of their potential from a mere lack of personal effort.

The principal pulled a gold watch from his pocket and noted the time. “Ladies, I suppose you should make your way to the rooms. The children will be here anytime, and we need to be ready.”

The young teachers moved quickly to their appointed stations with a slight feeling of trepidation. Principal Tutwiler felt it himself, as he removed his coat from the back of his chair and walked slowly to the closet beneath the belfry.

He checked his watch again. It was 7:25. Then, he reached high through a dark hole of the closet ceiling and pulled hard on the end of a long, suspended rope. The clang of the bell ripped through the silence as the sun sliced the last of a morning fog. He cinched his necktie and opened wide the door.

Sixty-eight children passed in a single file, each with a quick bow or curtsy, a brief handshake or a simple “Good morning, Mr. Tutwiler.” Morgan and Cora were at the end of the line.

“Well, Mr. Darrow, I trust you had an adventurous summer. It’s good that you made it back to school in one piece. I heard some rumors.”

Morgan extended his hand. “Yes, sir, it was good summer, but believe me, there were a few moments.”

“Really? Perhaps we shall hear about those moments.”

“Oh, I don’t know about that, sir,” Morgan replied with some sense of alarm. Mr. Tutwiler graciously waved him through the doorway.

“And you, Miss Darrow, I hope you intend to be one of my best students again.”

“I’m going to try, sir.”

“You always do, young lady. It is so nice to see you again.”

Cora was delighted to find her old seat vacant as she entered the classroom. She looked around at Morgan and her many playmates of summer. For her, it was a very good day.

The joy of first day seemed to wane rapidly for some, however, as reality took the form of school work and thinking. By afternoon, Morgan had fallen to daydreams, and Dewey, already disrupted by his preoccupation with Auralee, was never one for sitting or studying. Following a short break, the room was filled with a low murmur of voices, a flurry of giggles, the rustling of paper and the rattle of desk chairs scooting and rocking across the wooden floor. It was a reaction anticipated by Principal Tutwiler, who knew well the ways and needs of children. He decided that it was time to sharpen their attentiveness.

"I would like each of you to cease what you are doing and give me your complete attention." He waited with a stern expression while the commotion in the room subsided.

Dewey felt a sudden faintness, and a cold sweat began to form across his forehead. "A quiz? It's only the first day, for cryin' out loud," he grumbled, half under his breath.

Mr. Tutwiler seemed to read minds and responded without expression, "No, this is not a quiz, but that, of course, may come later. It is best you stay prepared for such eventuality. As students, I expect each of you to study hard, pay attention to what is said in class and be *settled* so that others may think without your hindering. Always stay prepared, mind you, and you will have little worries in this class."

He looked into the eyes of his students. They were focused solely on their teacher. "Good! Very good. For now, I need you to note the following dates set aside for special projects." A sigh of relief could be heard throughout the room.

"I believe most of you are aware of our annual fall cleanup day. For those who are not, this is a time when the older students come to help with the maintenance of our school building and grounds, while the younger children tour the mill and railroad facilities. I've scheduled the workday for Friday, Sept. 21, and everyone should consider their participation as mandatory. Your parents have already offered their consent. We have many tasks, and each of you will be expected to do your part, as I am sure you will."

Most of the students were accustomed to physical work, having regular chores at home. Many were obligated, even during adolescence, to maintain part-time jobs to supplement their limited family income. And for some, workdays were a welcome relief to the drudgery of study.

"I will tell you that you should wear clothes that you are not afraid to soil and bring gloves. I shall post a list of projects in the coming days. Also, in appreciation of your involvement, I have arranged for lunch to be kindly provided by your mothers and the Women's Circle at First Methodist Church. So, mark that date. Any questions?"

"Can't ya give us a clue what we gotta do?" a voice called from the back of the room.

"Who's speaking?" asked Mr. Tutwiler. "Oh, Mr. Vernelli, please remember to raise your hand before commenting in class. Thank you." Mr. Tutwiler went on to answer the question, "I have not yet completed the list, but can say that one project will be particularly difficult and will require the assistance of some of you boys. I am looking for a few courageous volunteers."

"But what's the project, sir?" the same voice inquired.

"Mr. Vernelli, please...the hand."

"Oh, yeah. Sorry, Mr. Tutwiler." The boy's arm shot high above his head, and he again blurted the question before the teacher could officially recognize him. Appreciating the enthusiasm, Mr. Tutwiler ignored the breach.

"I think it might be best that I first find my volunteers. I will inform you later as to what will be involved. So, how about it? Are there any brave and trusting young men in this classroom?"

The hands of every boy and three of the girls were instantly lifted in the air.

Mr. Tutwiler smiled and said, "Well, thank you all. I am afraid this job will not be properly suited for young women, but ladies, I greatly appreciate your interest. Trust me. There will be other work for you. Mr. Darrow, Mr. Baughman, Mr. Smith and Mr. Vernelli, I would like you to help me with a little job up in the attic, and if you can stay just a few minutes after school, I will explain the details at the end of class today. Will that be all right?"

Proud to be among the select few, each of the boys replied, "Yes, sir!"

"Now, the second date involves your first homework assignment. We will be focusing a lot on our creative writing this fall, and I want to begin by seeing how each of you respond to the art of poetry. In my hat are pieces of paper that list different styles and subjects of poetry. I would like you to come up one at a time, select a slip and read your selection to the class. I will record the type of poem you have chosen. Are there any questions?"

Auralee Buck raised her hand.

"Yes, Miss Buck."

"What if we don't care for our selection? Can we trade our slips?"

"No. Let's see how we do with our luck of the draw. Everyone will write their poem according to their selection. Other questions?"

There were none, and Mr. Tutwiler finished with his instructions, "Excellent. The due date will be Oct. 8. You will be expected to recite your work before the entire class, so I hope you will give this assignment due diligence. Please come forward."

Several of the girls, seated toward the front of the class, rose obediently from their chairs and formed a short line near the desk. Other girls followed, and Mr. Tutwiler recorded their choices as they read the words hand-printed on the slips. The boys were much more reluctant and aired their displeasure with a collective groan, which was promptly quieted by a sharp glance over the rim of the teacher's reading glasses. They complied without further comment, and when they were through, the teacher summarized the list of selections.

"...Pastoral...Miss Buck, Sonnet...Mr. Weller, Romanticism...Mr. Darrow, and Mr. Baughman, it appears you will write us a limerick. How appropriate! I do look forward to that."

"Ah, Da--!" muttered Dewey. He mentally bit his lip to avoid blurting what for so long had been his chosen piece of profanity.

School was not the proper place, and Mr. Tutwiler was not a person to tolerate a boy's natural iniquity. Dewey had no idea what a limerick was, but it could not be good. No poetry was good. But then again, any punishment decreed by Mr. Tutwiler would certainly be worse, as personal experience would indicate. Dewey was relieved that he had caught his blunder in time, and even more relieved that his teacher did not look up.

"I mean, sir, what exactly is a limerick?"

"I suppose that is what you will be learning, Mr. Baughman. Do not worry. Poetry has never been proven lethal, and frankly, you may have fun with this particular choice. Limerick, any topic...Mr. Baughman."

Principal Tutwiler looked at the pocket watch that he had set as a reminder on the corner of his desk. "3:56. I suppose it is time to ring the closing bell. Class, I thank you for your excellent inquiries and responses today. I believe each of you actually became smarter over the summer. I am proud of you. Now, do not forget your homework assignments. I look forward to seeing each of you bright and early tomorrow morning."

The room was beginning to empty when he remembered his four volunteers, who now gathered impatiently at the side of his chair. "Oh, yes, gentlemen. Thank you for staying."

"So, what is this secret project, Mr. Tutwiler?" Morgan asked.

The principal looked at the boys almost apologetically. He paused to carefully consider his words, but could not find a more suitable way to say it.

"Bats. We are going after bats."

Dewey and Morgan stood at the side of the school and stared wide-eyed with dread at the broken louvers that vented the attic. They could not help wondering how many of the grotesque little creatures may have flown through such a gaping hole. Whatever the number, the bats were likely now dangling in mass from the long, dark rafters.

"It could be awful hot up there. Don't ya think, Morgan? I hate workin' in the heat, especially in them real tight places."

"It's actually a rather cool day. Face it, Dewey, you just hate work in general."

"Well, that's absolutely not true!" Dewey protested. "I only hate the work I've had to do so far. Given time, and prob'ly lots of it, I'll no doubt come across a job that suits my particular charm and talent. But I gotta tell ya, Morgan, it ain't gonna be this one."

"I can't argue with that," Morgan agreed, still watching the louvers.

Dewey began to rave, "I hate bats. I mean I really hate 'em. They're as ugly as sin and carry all kinds of vermin and disease. And they spread the same damned afflictions as them crazy foxes and coons. You know, Vernon Leitz got bit by one a couple years back, and before he up and died in a pool of his own spittle, he totally lost his mind. That's the God's truth. Those bats up there'll drop right off that ceiling and stick in our hair. You just watch. They'll get all tangled and have to scratch their way free, and that, my friend, is when they start suckin' the lifeblood out of us. I'm tellin' ya, I hate bats and I'm not doin' this. No way."

"Leitz died of a bite from his own dog," Morgan replied, setting the record straight. "You complain about mosquitoes, too, and you should be downright grateful that the bats are out there night after night just doing their job. Now, we have to do ours. There's no ducking it. We gave our word."

"I'll bet ya a silver dollar that dog was first bit by them bats, and that's what really killed ol' Vernon Leitz. His murderers are just waitin' for us to climb into that attic, and that'll be the end of two more fine fellas. I don't know 'bout you, but I ain't ready to give up the ghost." Dewey pointed to the vent. His finger shook with genuine nervousness.

"You don't have a silver dollar, or even a copper penny, for that matter. You might as well stop working yourself into such frenzy. We're going up there, Dewey, and that's all there is to it. Auralee would have a fit if she only knew what a coward you can be."

Dewey cringed. "Now, that's not fightin' fair! I ain't no coward, and I ain't no shirker neither. I'll do what I gotta do, but Morgan, sometimes I could just smack ya upside the head for gettin' me into these things."

"I didn't make you raise your hand, *Mr. Volunteer*."

"No, but I didn't raise my hand until I saw yours go up first! I really wish we didn't have to do this. I'd prefer leaches or rattle snakes or wolf spiders, anything to bats."

"Well, it's a small consolation, but these brown bats are not vampires. They don't suck blood. Come on, there's nothing to fear. They've been in your own house and virtually every building in Devlin at some point or another."

"I know all that, but this time I'll be crawlin' around in their space, and they may have an attitude regardin' intruders. This could be one very hostile reception."

Morgan chuckled at Dewey's uneasiness, but thought he had presented a reasonable argument in the end. There was no way to convince his friend about the merit of bats, especially at a time when his own fears brought doubt to the subject.

Mr. Tutwiler approached. "Well, boys, I suppose you heard that Horace Smith has broken his leg and will not be joining us for the adventure."

"Wow...that's too bad, but where's Vernelli?" Dewey asked without compassion.

"Mr. Vernelli asked to be excused from this project. He explained that he was a bit concerned about handling the animals and might be of better use doing other work. So, it appears it will be just the three of us today. Are you ready to get started?"

Morgan nodded, and Dewey gave his friend a cold, threatening look. "Morgan, if the bats don't get you, I'll bite ya myself. Yes, Mr. Tutwiler, I reckon we're as ready as we'll ever be."

The boys used the top of their ladder to force open the attic hatch, which was positioned high in the ceiling at one end of the school hallway. They then braced the ladder against the edge of a dark and ominous opening.

"Allow me to go first, gentlemen, if you would," Mr. Tutwiler proposed.

There was certainly no disagreement. Dewey held the base of the wooden ladder, while his teacher and friend disappeared into the blackness above.

At Mr. Tutwiler's suggestion, each of the three men was dressed in a long-sleeved, heavy flannel shirt. The thicker fabric was for extra protection, though it offered little. They wore brimmed hats and leather gloves for the same purpose and carried coal oil lanterns to illuminate the work area. The steep pitch of the school roof allowed them to stand comfortably in the middle of the attic, but they would need to crawl and reach blindly for their quarry in the dark angles of the building. The clothes would be their only shield against bites or scratches, and even the principal had doubts that his plan was infallible.

"Aren't you coming up?" Morgan shouted down to Dewey.

"Well, who's gonna hold the ladder if I'm up there?"

"We don't need anyone to hold the ladder. You've got to see this!"

"I'm not at all sure I want to."

Dewey buttoned the top of his shirt and pulled his collar tight to his neck. He then tucked his pant legs into the top of his boots, hoping to ensure that the wily "vampires" could not find their way into any piece of his clothing. He seemed to take forever climbing the 12 rungs of the ladder.

"My God, what's that?" he inquired, peering in dim light through the cobwebs.

A whitish gray matter was amassed in heaps across the attic floor. One of the piles stood four inches high and stretched along the entire length of a rafter.

"Guano...uh, bat dung," answered Arthur Tutwiler. "I suppose we will need to clean this up before we deal with the culprits that made the mess." He called down to some of the other boys and asked them to send up some coal scoops and extra ash cans. "Guano is quite valuable for the manufacture of gunpowder. It contains potassium nitrate. We might want to save some of it for experimentation this winter."

As repugnant as the job appeared to be, Dewey decided to make the best of it. He slid his scoop along the floor, gathered a full paddle of the guano, and dumped it hard into a can. At once, the bucket seemed to explode with a fine and most foul powder, sending each of the three men scrambling for the bottom of the ladder. They were gasping for air.

"Dewey, for Heaven's sake, go easy!" Morgan pleaded.

Dewey, covered with dust, was franticly sweeping it off of his sleeves and hat as he choked and coughed in disgust. He could only nod to show his agreement.

After a few minutes, the attic air settled and the trio again ascended, this time with scarves pulled snug around their faces. Within a half-hour, they had sufficiently removed the guano without further mishap.

Mr. Tutwiler lifted his lantern high toward the ceiling, just over the site of one of the dung piles. "We can pretty much tell where the bats are roosting by the accumulation of guano. Look here."

The boys came close to examine the beam. Along its edge were scores of small, furry brown animals, so densely colonized that they resembled a fine pelt in the lantern's faint glow.

"Wow," Morgan uttered, in a succinct expression of wonder.

Dewey stood a short distance back and looked cautiously over his friend's shoulder. They both started and leaped away, when one bat momentarily stretched his black webbed wing to establish a better hold on the rafter.

"What do we do now?" Morgan inquired, astounded by the sight before him.

Dewey responded, as though he were stating the obvious, "We gotta get 'em out of here. We're gonna kill 'em."

Clunk. A bat fell dead upon the floor. Clunk. Clunk. Two more dropped with simple taps from a pointer stick that the boy had commandeered from a classroom below.

"Dewey, stop! You don't need to do that. We're not here to kill them!" Morgan exclaimed in horror.

Clunk. "Ah, hell, I missed!" A fourth bat dropped to the floor and began crawling for the safety of the darkness. Dewey raised his stick to strike again, but a leather glove quickly covered the hapless animal.

"That's quite enough," Mr. Tutwiler said quietly. "I think, if we carefully grab them one at a time, we might avoid exciting the whole colony."

The principal reached up with his other gloved hand and gently pried one of the creatures from its place on the rafter. The bat was so light and lifeless that he was uncertain as to whether he had actually retrieved it. He tenderly laid both animals in the base of an ash can and replaced the lid.

"You see, that is all it takes, a little care and a gentle touch."

"I thought ya meant to kill 'em!" Dewey blurted out. He sounded disappointed.

"Only if it becomes necessary, and that would be quite a shame. We can release them all by the river, after the vent is screened and patched. It is better that way. Do you not agree, Mr. Baughman?"

Though ever so reluctantly, Dewey grimaced and nodded his acceptance.

So it began. One passive creature after another was placed in the ash cans until both Dewey and Morgan had lost all apprehension for their work. Fear fades with familiarity, and the repetitive handling of the tiny, ghastly monsters yielded a new respect for what had fast become just fuzzy, fragile, helpless little beings. The boys continued their task without so much as a scratch, until they had removed over 200 bats from the attic.

Pleased with themselves, they hurried through the school door to watch a pony cart, loaded with ash cans, make its way down Briar Mountain toward the river.

"There they go. I hope they stay down there this time," said Dewey.

"I just hope someone gets those louvers fixed," Morgan replied. "But, really, it wasn't so bad a job after all."

"Nah, not so bad, but blast my hide for volunteerin'. One thing's for sure, you can raise your own hand if ya like, but for now on, mine ain't leavin' my pockets."

The older boys were organized into crews for the maintenance of the building and yard, while the older girls were assigned to receive the food as it arrived from the church. It was their job to organize the noon picnic, and they wasted little time setting the meal in the shelter of the nearby park.

When the iron bell tolled the welcomed call to dinner, Morgan and Dewey walked as heroes into the grove, where they were flooded with questions from their young admirers. By Dewey's account, they had thwarted ghoulish attacks from the most dreadful of beastly devils.

"Oh, it wasn't that way at all," Morgan responded time and again to the many inquiries. "They're just innocent little animals... not too pretty, mind you, but not at all dangerous."

Dewey painted a different picture. The children wanted horror, so he gave them horror. He told of huge vampire bats clinging to his trousers, crawling up his legs and torso and ever closer to his throat and jugular vein. As fast as he could remove them, others swarmed to take their place. He explained that only the heavy clothes and a steady disregard for his own safety allowed him to persist in his task. Few others, if any, could have withstood such an ordeal. Somehow, Morgan Darrow and Arthur Tutwiler were lost in the lengthy telling of the lie.

But all children love a storyteller, and Dewey kept them spellbound until the meal was served. Auralee smiled at her man approvingly, and he beamed with pride. He delighted in the attention, especially hers.

Morgan moved away toward a long table constructed in the shade of the tall trees. Draped with cotton sheets, the table was laden with every sort of food that could be picked from September gardens or prepared in a late summer heat. There was fried chicken stacked high on platters and smoked meats sliced thin for sandwiches. There was sweet corn, the cobs already dripping with hand-churned butter and salt, and salads and slaws, ripe red tomatoes, lettuce and succulent squashes. There were deviled and pickled eggs, pickled cucumbers, pickled pig's feet...pickled everything. There was sourdough and wheat bread, biscuits and jellies, and applesauce laced heavily with cinnamon.

The desserts were at the far end of the table: melons and peaches, pound cakes and cookies, fruit pies and tarts. There was even fresh lemonade, squeezed from a whole bushel of yellow lemons and mixed with fresh spring water and white crystalline sugar. It was all right there, all the treats a student could want and all lovingly provided by mothers and the altruistic women of First Methodist Church.

The feast went on noisily as the children filled their plates and began to gorge their stomachs, but it would not be long until the inevitable interruption. A loud scream pierced the air.

"Get it off. Get it off! Somebody, help me! Get it off of me!"

Morgan recognized the scream in an instant. He had heard it before at the swimming hole, and for some reason, he knew exactly what now struck terror in the heart of Sadie Buck. He raced through a crowd of fleeing children to find Sadie violently kicking her leg and swatting at the hem of her skirt.

"I'll get him, Sadie. Just hold still."

"It's on my leg! It's crawling up my leg! Get it off of me!"

Without thinking, Morgan whipped the girl's loose skirt and petticoat above her knees. A small bat was frantically screeching and moving up her stocking across the side of her thigh, trying desperately to avoid her futile attempts to dislodge it.

"Be calm, Sadie! I can get it."

With those words, Morgan enclosed the frightened animal in the palm of his hand and rapidly carried it to the edge of the grove, where he laid it safely in the hole of a tree. He returned to Sadie, who was in her chair still trembling and sobbing with fear. Her head was down against her freckled, white hands and her long red hair concealed sodden eyes from the children who gathered closely around her.

"Please, everyone, leave her alone. Let's give Sadie some privacy. I can take care of her."

Morgan knelt down beside the girl and placed a comforting hand over her fingers. They were wet with tears.

"It's all right now. Hush. The bat's gone and you'll be fine. You'll be just fine." His voice was soft and reassuring. "Sadie, I didn't mean to take such liberties. There was a panic, and I...I...I didn't think for a second about your dress or leg. I swear to you, I would never have...."

"Morgan, it's okay. I thank you for what you did. Thank you so much."

He lifted her head and looked deep into her sad and swollen eyes. "Really, it's all over now. Don't think any more about it."

She fell into his arms and wept.

It was time to finish up the day's chores, and Morgan had to run to catch Dewey Baughman. His friend was already on his way to the schoolhouse, as though anxious to find more work. Morgan would not believe it. He recognized an escape when he saw one.

"Dewey, hold up there!"

The boy skulked at the corner of the building. He was conspicuously quiet when Morgan finally overtook him.

"Okay, what did you do?" Morgan demanded an accounting.

"I ain't done nothin'!"

"Oh, yes, you did! How did that bat find its way onto Sadie Buck?"

"I didn't do nothin'."

"You said that already. You are so guilty, Dewey! You scared that poor girl almost half to death."

"I swear, Morgan, I sure didn't mean to. It weren't a prank, if that's what you're thinkin'. I had the bat sittin' in a Mason jar next to me and Auralee. Sadie was four or five feet across from us. I was gonna show it after lunch - Ya know, so the kids could come up and see one nice and close. I reckon somebody kicked the jar when I wasn't lookin'. Yeah, that's it. That's all it was. Still, maybe I should apologize. What ya think?"

"Are you sorry?"

"Well, a little. It was kind of funny until she started that cryin'. I sure hate it when they cry."

"You know, Dewey, considering your feelings for Auralee, Sadie's likely to be family someday. You better start being nice to her."

"You are absolutely right. I'll apologize. Even though it were no fault of my own, it's the least I can do." Dewey snickered at his next thought. "The way ya had your arms all wrapped around that girl, I'd say you're well on your *own* way to bein' in the family. We'll be brothers."

"Brothers-in-law. You are such a half-wit! Don't set any plans around me and Sadie Buck. She was just upset about the bat, and that is all!"

Dewey laughed. "Sure, brother, whatever ya say."

"Poetry," Morgan uttered, "what *is* the point? Just some pretty words that only make a lick of sense to the fools that write them."

Morgan was frustrated, like most of his classmates who let the final hour get too near. Tomorrow, the assignment was due. Today, he was no closer to composing a love poem than he was to owning the entire Watoga Lumber Mill. He was one of three students who drew that particular topic, "Romanticism," but, of course, the other two just happened to be girls. The assignment should be easy for girls, he thought. It was debasing for him.

There was a certain amount of reading required, and the boy had arduously perused the works of Burns and Keats in preparation. Annie owned two compilations of their verse, and she was excited to share her favorite excerpts with her son. Morgan remained unimpressed by what he heard, or more importantly, uninspired, but he kindly withheld any comment for his mother's sake. He wondered why she, and others like her, could be so moved by such a manipulative crafting of the language. He knew he was different in that regard. Obviously, he was too weak in heart for poetry. He was too poor in soul to appreciate the spiritual depth of the art.

Still, Morgan knew about love. He knew the helpless, hopeless feeling of a passion that he might never share. He knew how love was all consuming, how it stole sleep from night and dreams from sleep, and how it rendered all things once important as mere trivia. He knew love penetrated the total being and was, at the same time, both wonderful and horrible. It was a power of the inner self that seemed endless and beyond control.

A million words had been scratched across the face of the paper, but only a few resembled a poem. Morgan read them again, then again and again.

*My love for you is like skies of blue –*
*Unclouded spans, forever true.*
*The raging storm may come your way,*
*But blue, my blue, will shine that day.*

"Dear God, what am I doing!" he exclaimed, half cursing, half praying for some word or phrase he could eventually call poetry. His frustration was exhausting, and he laid his head upon the table with a hope that rest might yield results.

As he drifted to the edge of consciousness, Morgan felt the girl's intimate presence once again. He could look into Sarah's eyes. He could see her long hair as it deftly concealed the perfect features and alluring expression of her face. In her, he found his happiness. For her, he felt both the calm of contentment and a deep, unsettling ardor, all made vivid in a single passing of a thought.

"Morgan! Morgan, Mama wants you! Mama wants to know when you're gonna burn that big brush pile in the garden. Can I help you do it, Morgan? Do you hear me, Morgan?" Jacob suddenly burst through the door of the room, instantly waking his brother from his all too brief reverie.

"Yeah, I hear you just fine, Jake. I guess now is as good a time as any for a fire." He crumpled the scribbled piece of paper, and threw both it and his writing pen to a half-filled basket on the floor. "Grab that basket, Jake. I've got more to burn than just brush."

Most of the material gathered for the burn was from trees stripped during recent storms. Some were the briars and other garden invaders not worthy of the mulch pit. All of it seemed too green to fire.

"This stuff will never burn without a little help. How about getting me the can of coal oil from the shed?" asked Morgan. Jacob was always anxious to assist his brother, especially with a fire, and returned with the heavy can, its fuel splashing from its nozzle.

"Be careful with that, Jake. Kerosene can be dangerous if you get it on you, and it will kill every living plant it touches. You're splashing it all over the yard."

"Can I wet down the pile this time? You always get to do it."

"I suppose, but you have to be careful, very, very careful. Okay?"

"Okay, Morgan."

Jacob began to douse the pile, as Morgan struck a match and lighted the end of a worn-out broom. The young boy knew to back away when his brother applied the impromptu torch to the oil-soaked debris. The sticks ignited rapidly but without explosion, and Jacob raced to find other objects to heap on the fire.

The smoke first billowed black from the oil, then, white from steam generated by the wet plants. Jacob delighted in both the flame and the immense column that lifted high above the mountain before dissipating into a clouded sky.

"It's not burning very well over here. I'm gonna give it some more oil," Jacob called out. Before Morgan could stop him, he dumped the remaining contents of the can. He thrilled when the flame spiked high above the pile.

"Jake, that's the best way I know to blow yourself up. Now, leave the fire alone!"

Jacob immediately complied with his brother's wishes and disappeared into the shed. He hurried back to Morgan, this time holding a baseball and two gloves.

"Let's play catch until the sticks stop burnin'," said the boy, already bored with the dwindling bonfire.

"Well, that's a good idea. Toss me one of those gloves."

Jacob examined the mitts. Both were cracked, more from dry rot than overuse, and the lacing of one was so frayed and detached that the fingers flopped apart as Jacob punched his fist against the shallow leather pocket. This glove, of course, would be Morgan's. The young boy kept the other, its webbing intact, and he stood for a moment working the discolored ball into the deep brown depression. When the glove was ready, the boy was ready. He threw a fast ball that ended with a loud thwack, the kind of crisp sound only a baseball can make as it slaps the perfect center of the mitt.

"Good one, Jake! A real steamer."

"That's just my warm-up pitch. Watch this!"

Thwack. It was another great toss, and from then on, Jacob supplied the rest of the conversation, "Okay, don't throw so hard... toss me some high ones...let me be the pitcher and you catch and call strikes...don't give me any more grounders...let's pretend we're in a big game, and it's all tied up." Jacob directed and Morgan happily obliged, until the fire was finally reduced to a few failing embers twinkling in the dusk.

The brothers retired to their room. Morgan took new pen and paper, and when Jacob slept, he wrote without hindrance or hesitation of thought. His very first poem was to Sarah.

Mr. Tutwiler called the morning roll, then stood tall behind his desk to see the nervous faces of his students. Only two circumstances ever elicited such a widespread sense of dread, and if not a test, then it must be the chosen time for poetry and recitations. While he was sympathetic to their plight, the teacher greeted his students with a long admonishment.

"Good morning. I am very pleased to see so many here today. In the past, I have been consistently amazed that more of my pupils fall absent on this particular occasion than any other day of the school year. I am not sure of the correlation, but am quite certain that poetry, in itself, is not a valid cause of illness. Nor is public speaking, for that matter. This year everyone seems prepared, and I am appreciative of both your attendance and your diligence.

"To those who have struggled to compose their poem, I need not say to you that you should respect the effort and achievement of your fellows. You each know the difficulties endured in trying to formulate an exact message, to discover the perfect word or phrase, the right rhymes and rhythms. You have, by now, learned that poetry is a journey into your very soul, that a good poem is not simply spewed from your mind, but drawn slowly from the depth of your being. Your emotions, your fears, your memories, your hopes, your joys, your disappointments, all often unknown to you, merge together into a creative power, and it is that power that presents to you a unique gift of phrasing for the conveyance of profound, inner thought. A poem illuminates what is most important to the poet in but a brief window of time. You did not write your poems. You experienced them. Regardless of whether we understand your meaning, your poem and your journey have been significant – very significant to you.

"To say the least, it is a challenging endeavor for anyone to reach their deepest feelings and then present them to others. I applaud you, each of you, for allowing yourself to be so exposed. Today, I will not be judging your work, but your effort. Everyone who stands and delivers a poem to this class will receive the highest possible mark.

"Now, to those younger students who have not been asked to compose a poem, your moment will be here soon enough. I expect no less than your full attention and encouragement for every one of our distinguished bards."

With those words, Arthur Tutwiler set the tone and eased much of the tension felt by his older students. One by one they walked to the front of the room, and holding a page marked with only their best cursive script, they presented their poems. There were verses of love, patriotism, religious fervor, nature and war. There were sonnets and limericks and one or two styles never before witnessed by Mr. Tutwiler. One piece was carefully written in French, and after its reading, was loosely interpreted by the teacher, himself. He was quite impressed. With humor and sadness, fantasy and realism, questions and answers, the poems were as varied as the personalities presenting them.

Dewey lumbered to the front of the room and glanced down at Auralee with a mischievous glint in his eye. He then turned his attention to the class.

"The title of my poem is *The Young Maid from the Mill*, dedicated, of course, to a certain fine lady who shall remain nameless at this time." He winked at Auralee. "I like to think of it as a love poem, even though it's officially called a lim'rick. I was told to write a lim'rick, so that's what I got. We'll just consider the thing a lim'rick first and a love poem second. That way I get my grade and maybe a little somethin' extra."

A few of the boys snickered, and Dewey immediately clarified his statement, "Extra credit, ya morons!"

"That will do, Mr. Baughman. Proceed with your recital," said Mr. Tutwiler.

"Yes, sir, I was just gonna say that my hours of study in the matter have shown me that good poetry can actually be both. Say, there is credit for writin' 'em both. Is that not correct?"

He looked to his teacher, hoping to see some special acknowledgment of his additional effort. The man could not be duped.

"It is only one poem, Mr. Baughman. Perhaps, you could go on and share it with us."

"Yes, sir, I can do that."

Dewey pressed the paper close to his face and refused to look up until his recitation was complete:

*About the young maid from the mill,*
*Who was blessed with a look that could kill,*
*I encountered what seems the girl of my dreams,*
*But she is ignoring me still.*

*About the young maid from the mill,*
*To see her presents such a thrill!*
*Soon comes the day I'll steal her away*
*To a little white church on the hill.*

*About the young maid from the mill,*
*I think she would rather have Bill.*
*My gosh! That is sad. I wish that I had*
*Fallen for sweet, chubby Jill."*

The poem continued for five more stanzas, depleting Dewey's bank of rhyming words. He was most gratified by his classmates' rousing approval. He bowed to their laughter and applause and apologized with some minimal measure of sincerity to his friends, Jill, Bill, Phil and Gil, for the liberties taken in the use of their names.

For some reason, Morgan Darrow was next to the last to be called, and the long wait had seemed interminable. He had hoped to be done with his reading quickly, and despite the mistakes others may have made in their presentations, he knew he would soon be looking the fool. His throat and lips became strangely dry. His hand shook noticeably as he tried to retrieve the sheet of paper, pressed the night before between the bound pages of his composition book. He did not relish this opportunity to share his innermost thoughts, but nevertheless, rose from his desk and took his position facing the class.

Like Dewey, he tried to avoid looking at his audience, but was betrayed by his eyes as they unintentionally glanced at Sadie seated on the front row. Hearing Morgan's name, she had adjusted her posture to a princess pose and pulled a lock of wavy, red hair from her face. She wanted Morgan to notice her, and without trying, he did. He offered her his smile, which she gladly returned, causing him a visible flush of embarrassment. He fumbled into his presentation.

"I guess I was told to write a love poem. Ah, I mean a poem of Romanticism. Believe me, it wasn't my choice, but I suppose you could say it was just my bad luck of the draw." He paused to take a deep breath. "And I never did come up with a suitable title, which I now think I should have. In my experience with this assignment, I often found that the title was the only thing that made any real sense. Oh, I'm sorry, Mr. Tutwiler."

"That's quite all right. Not all creative writing is good writing."

"Thank you, sir. Having said all that...ah...ah...I hope, when I'm through with this poem, that you who are forced to listen to it will not be wishing for that title. It's rather short, so just bear with me."

Morgan's voice cracked under the strain of nervousness, and he asked the class to pardon him as he poured a cup of water from a pitcher on Mr. Tutwiler's large oak desk.

He was still flushed when the teacher interjected, “Mr. Darrow, please forgive this interruption. It appears I need to leave the room for a few moments, and I would not want to miss hearing your poem. Stay where you are. I will be right back.”

The time that Mr. Tutwiler was away seemed like eternity. Morgan stood awkwardly at the front of the room trying to avoid eye contact with everyone and trying even harder to ignore the quiet taunts being made by Dewey and his friends. He was about to return to his desk when the principal re-entered the room.

“Class, we have the honor of welcoming a new student today. She’s in her 12th year and comes to us from the City of Charleston. Her family has just moved to Devlin, where her father will be the new project engineer responsible for extending the rail spurs into the Big Timber country. I am pleased to introduce you to Miss Sarah Dabney.”

Mr. Tutwiler momentarily stepped back into the hall, leaving Sarah alone in the doorway. Her eyes fixed on the first thing she saw, the only other person standing in the room.

“Good morning”, she said, looking directly at Morgan.

An uproar of individual greetings from the class muted Morgan’s airy response, “Good morning, Miss Sarah Dabney.”

Morgan watched Sarah as she weaved her way through a maze of desks and well-wishers, seeking an empty seat on the far side of the class. He would have watched even longer, if not for the beckoning of Mr. Tutwiler. The clamor subsided, and Morgan Darrow was encouraged to begin. Mostly from memory, he delivered his words slowly and clearly.

*A song in my heart plays softly and slow*
*For no one to hear, save me, my love.*
*A poem in my soul of dreams long ago*
*For none to endear, save me, my love.*

*The gray mist of morning, the blue autumn skies,*
*The red cast of sunset, a moon on its rise,*

*These were my treasures 'til I looked in your eyes.*
*Maybe someday, perhaps somehow,*
*We might share them, my love.*

*A strength in my arms waits restless and wanting*
*To hold you, to show you, that you are my love.*

There was silence in the room. Mr. Tutwiler walked slowly up to Morgan and accepted the written copy of the poem. As he had done with each of the other submittals, he briefly glanced over the page to appraise the more technical applications of the language.

"Yes, that certainly does qualify as a love poem. Well done, Mr. Darrow. I believe you must be a true romantic, despite your declared aversion for such verse. Yes, well done."

The class applauded as Morgan returned to his desk, still diverting his eyes in nervous humility. As the teacher called for the last poem to be read, Dewey leaned over and murmured, "Nice job, Morgan. That sweet poem of yours could almost make me wanna kiss ya. By the way, look over there at Sadie. Ya brought some tears. I said it before and I'll say it again, you're gonna be one heck of a brother-in-law for me and my Auralee."

Morgan slowly raised his head to find Sadie dabbing a lace handkerchief against her milk-white cheek. He was surprised, if not gratified, that a poem, his poem, could have such an effect on a woman. He tried to see Sarah's reaction, as well, but she faced forward, disclosing to him only a thin blue bow twined with soft strands of light-yellow hair. He gazed in admiration, if only at the beauty of her hair, but suddenly dropped his stare when she turned ever so slightly to steal another glimpse of that handsome boy, the one from Avery's pool.

When school ended for the day, Morgan lingered awhile on the lane, hoping Sarah might pass his way. He could hear her voice in conversation with Cora, Auralee and Sadie, and knew they would soon overtake him from the sound of their rapid steps shuffling down the gravel road.

Cora called to him, "Morgan, wait up! I didn't get to tell you how much I liked your poem."

"Thanks, Cora. It was just a poem."

"No, it wasn't just a poem," Sadie spoke defiantly. "It was a declaration. It was more than I could have ever hoped for." She threw her arms around Morgan and held him tightly. Her face was nestled against his chest. She raised her hands over the back of his neck, pulled herself up and placed a light kiss upon his lips. "And I loved it, Morgan. Thank you for thinking of me. Thank you for writing it."

"But I... I didn't write...." Morgan could not finish his sentence. Sadie again pressed hard against him, and as she did, Cora and Auralee, and Sarah Dabney, gave her the private moment she wanted.

"Sadie, please, you don't understand."

The girl refused to hear him. Morgan gently drew away from her embrace to watch the others disappear into the deep green of the mountain. His heart left with them.

This time, Sarah would not look back.

# CHAPTER 9

It was autumn. It was a time of early reds, when the dogwood and the gum, the creeper and the sumac, each splashed their crimson against the lingering green of the forest. It was a time of fragile white frosts dissolving with the first glint of a new day's light, of geese flying south between the orange hues of sunsets and pumpkin fields. It was the season of yellow harvests being stuffed into high lofts or low cellars and of brown nuts sinking into a rich, black earth, now softened by welcomed rains. Autumn. It was the time of color and coolness, when the land yawned before its inevitable winter sleep and men braced for the coming of the cold.

Morgan loved the fall. He loved the uncertainty of the season. He loved how crisp blue skies of one day became ominous storms the next and how afternoon warmth chilled within minutes into frigid night. Fall meant change, sudden change, and for Morgan Darrow change usually brought fervor and hope. He embraced the autumn with anticipation.

"Ma, those logs make for pretty shaky shelves, don't you think? I'm afraid you're going to knock everything over if you're not careful. Why don't you let me bring out the table for you?"

Annie looked through the billowing smoke and rising steam of her kettle. She steadily pushed a long, angled paddle around the edges and across the center of the huge copper pot, then repeated the motion, making sure none of the contents would stick and burn against the hot metal. A steaming mash of chopped apples and frothy sweet cider, the hot mixture bubbled and splattered, but fell harmlessly back into the pot. She kept stirring, around and across, around and across, around and across.

Behind her were bags of sugar, jars of molasses and metal pails once filled with peeled minced fruit. There were bowls of ground cinnamon and tins of cloves, nutmeg and other "secret" spices that made her apple butter the favorite choice of friends and family. Each of the ingredients rested precariously upon the wobbly ends of five upturned logs. At Morgan's urging, she looked to reexamine their stability.

"No, honey, the logs are fine. They're sturdy and I'm being real careful."

"But wouldn't it be easier to just use a table or even a plank?"

"A plank. Now there's an idea, but never mind that now. This arrangement is more than adequate."

Annie's kettle fire was always situated near a ready supply of firewood, and the larger logs at the edge of the stack were easily rolled into position for makeshift tables. It was a practice that had always worked well in the past, and she saw no advantage in changing it now.

Looking across the yard with some expectation of seeing her daughter, she added, "However, if you really want to be of some assistance, you could find your sister for me. It's her turn on the paddle, and I said I'd call for her when I was ready for a break."

"I'll take over for a spell, if you want."

"That's okay. Cora enjoys being a part of this, and she'll much prefer the kettle over her other chores. It's always fun to do something different. Fetch her for me, will you, Morgan?"

"Sure, Ma, I'll find her," he said, "and maybe I'll see if Jake needs a hand getting up those walnuts."

Coals hissed, and Annie saw brown spatter leaping from the boiling pot. She reacted quickly and kicked some of the brighter embers away from the bottom.

"Actually, that would be helpful. He doesn't seem to be making much progress, even though piles of nuts are springing up all over the place. I think he's playing one of his games. Regardless, none of the walnuts seem to be making it to the stone, and I'm going to need them quickly if we're going to have a dessert for tonight's social. As soon as Cora takes over here, I'll get started with my baking. If you want to be nice to someone, try helping your sister. She'll need to rest her arms after a bit."

"I can do that," Morgan replied.

Annie peered at the empty sky and exhaled heavily. She mumbled, "Oh, I'll never get all this done. I suppose I can use the chopped nuts from last year, if I have to."

"What's that, Ma?"

"Nothing. Just talking to myself. See what you can do to move Jacob along, and I'll be most grateful."

Annie made use of a worn-out millstone that lay flat next to the backyard shed. Abandoned to weeds for most of the year, the stone was perfect for shucking walnuts. She would place several nuts on its hard surface, and with strikes of a large wooden mallet, she could quickly crumble each soft brown husk, one at a time, until only the tough inner shells remained.

She often let these shells dry before using the same mallet to crack them open, exposing the sweet meat within. With the sharpened point of a knitting needle, she spent hours picking and prying until her canning jars were teeming. There were other, faster ways to clean walnuts, but Annie's efforts were never about speed. She savored her labor like one enjoying the finest of wines, and her success was in the product gained, not the time lost. Stored high in the pantry away from the appetites of her children, free from bits of broken shell, her walnuts were always ready for baking day.

Young Jacob had wanted to try his hand at shucking, ever since Morgan showed him how to use the mallet, but Annie thought the better of it. It was a messy job, to say the least, and Jacob's idea of cleaning walnuts was to smash every husk and shell and fruit into an indiscernible pulp. The boy understandably saw such work as great fun, and he pressed until his mother finally acquiesced, still against her better judgment. Her concerns would prove valid as the morning progressed.

Morgan thought aloud as he and Annie watched the boy at play, "You know, Ma, that brother of mine has always been part squirrel, the way he scampers about. Now he's even collecting nuts. Look at him. He's into everything."

His mother smiled knowingly. "Yes, Morgan, and he reminds me of another little 'squirrel' who sadly has grown too old for toys and games."

"Don't worry. I still have my fun from time to time. You talk like I'm a doddering old man. Next thing to happen, you'll be booting me out of the house so Jake can have his growing room."

"If he's anything like you, he will certainly need the space. But you know better than that. This house is your home, and that upstairs room will be your bedroom for as long as you choose to live here. Still, I suspect you'll be venturing out on your own before too long. I truly dread the day."

Annie returned her attention to the apple butter. "Go on now and see if you can find Cora."

Gingerly stepping between the walnuts and some larger Osage oranges that littered the yard, Morgan headed toward the house in search of his sister. He stopped before he reached the porch, seeing his brother crawling through the grass, his bare legs protruding from his hand-me-down knickers.

"Jake, you're going to wear out those trousers, sliding around like that."

"You already wore 'em out, Morgan. That's why Mama gave 'em to me to wear."

It was an accurate observation, and Morgan marveled at the acumen of a six-year-old boy. "Oh, I suppose you're right about that. Now that you mention it, they do look familiar. I'm surprised they're not in a rag bag by now."

"Tell that to Mama. They ought to be."

Jacob stood up and pointed to some recent holes, one on the knee and the other on the inside seam of a pocket. He tugged on the pocket and a dozen acorns dropped from the base of his knickers.

"Gosh, what are you doing with all of these nuts?" Morgan asked, now curious and momentarily forgetting about Cora.

"Mama told me it was my job to get 'em so I can chuck 'em. But I don't wanna chuck all of 'em. I'm gonna need most of 'em for later."

"*Shuck*, Jake. The word is *shuck*. And we don't *shuck* acorns. We *shuck* walnuts." He tried to be instructive by sounding out the beginning. "Sh-sh-shuck. Sh-shuck. Now you say it."

"Chuck. Ch-chuck."

"No, that's not quite right. 'Chuck' means you intend to throw them. It's sh-shuck."

Jacob had trouble forming the word, but he tried again and again, "Ch-chuck...Chuck...Ch-ch-chuck."

"That's pretty close. Some things are just a little harder to say. We'll keep working on it," said Morgan, as he playfully tweaked his brother's nose.

Morgan observed neat piles of walnuts, Osage oranges and a couple metal buckets filled with acorns and hickory nuts. Each pile, each bucket, indicated thorough sorting by Jacob's busy little hands.

"So, Jake, what exactly is your job? Ma doesn't collect all of these. She only keeps the walnuts. I don't think she'll want any of the others."

Jacob became defiant. "Well, she said I should help by pickin' up, and that's just what I'm doin'!"

"I see," responded Morgan, who remained skeptical. No one bothered with acorns or hickories anymore, except maybe a passing squirrel, or deer or turkey. Jacob was clearly up to something. He usually was.

"Besides, I got plans." The boy was hesitant to divulge his mission, and the mystery in his voice drew Morgan's curiosity.

"Plans? What sort of plans?" Morgan probed.

"I better not say," Jacob answered, trying to maintain the advantage of secrecy.

Morgan knew the mind of his brother and could immediately recognize the stir of imagination. As was often the case, he would join in the fantasy, taking whatever acting role was assigned to him by his brother's vivid creativity.

"Uh-huh, you can't really trust me, can you? After all, I may be a spy or enemy agent. That's it. You think I'm a spy for that army now camped across the valley. Well, maybe I am and maybe I'm not, but either way, your secret is out. You're smart to gather ammunition while there's still time. That is what you're doing, isn't it? Gathering ammunition?"

Morgan looked up at an old tree house, clinging to the red oak on the corner of the lot. "You know, I used to have to defend that fort not so long ago. I could join forces with you if you want. My men are itching for a good battle."

Jacob listened, pleased that Morgan was willing to play, but was cautious not to speak. Perhaps he had said too much already. He was tempted to accept the offer, but could trust no one, especially Morgan, who had battled against him on so many similar occasions. His older brother possibly may not be all that he said he was. He was known to trick, and Jacob knew he could not chance such a potential enemy being armed with the arsenal of bullets and bombs that now lay scattered across the ground. Perhaps, if he remained mute, Morgan might move on, unaware of his strategies.

But Jacob would soon be ready for war, regardless of the enemy. He was not yet sure who would dare oppose him, but his imagination had time to conjure the worst of antagonists. After all, the meaner the villain, the more glorious the victory. His young brain would leave no detail undecided, even the horrifying armaments, the villainous scowls and the scarred, deformed faces of his cruel advancing foe. His mind painted a grim picture of a superior force marching against his tiny fortress, drums beating, dust swirling, light reflecting from the shine of sabers and bayonets and soldiers howling for vengeance and blood. His blood. He looked past Morgan toward the humble wood structure nestled in the wide notch of the tree.

The tree house, another hand-me-down from the childhood of his brother, had seen a great amount of use during the summer, mostly peaceful, but as the leaves began to thin around its walls, the fort suddenly seemed vulnerable against attack. Much could be done to save it. Nuts, everywhere beneath the trees, were the weapons of his fantasy, the gifts of a changing season. He would gather them and wait.

It was like an Indian summer, when the Shawnee prowled the settlements during a respite from foul weather to take food, livestock, blankets and other necessities against the freezing cold. Fall offered opportunity even for adversaries. Wary settlers had to be prepared. It was a time when prudent men readied against invasion and when brave men stoically awaited their glory. It was the time for battles and boys.

Jacob's ordnance had always been strong. He could depend on both a good right throwing arm and his powerful slingshot, once fashioned by Morgan, himself. And now, autumn provided the necessary ammunition for a proper fight. He must stay busy stocking his fortress with the tools of his war.

"You go on, Morgan. I got me some things to do."

"Tell you what," said Morgan, "if you run inside and tell Cora that Ma is ready for her, I'll start shucking some of these walnuts for you. Ma needs them for her baking."

Jacob was in no way anxious to give up any part of his collection, but looking across the yard to the numerous piles, he felt assured that a few missing bullets would not affect the outcome of the war. Besides, as entertaining as it surely would be, shucking could always be done, and perhaps should only be done, on a less significant day.

"Sure," he said, after brief consideration. He effortlessly lifted himself from the ground. The knees of his britches held a mosaic of leaves and grass over large wet circles of green and black stain. He swiped his hand across his legs to clean them.

"Cora!" he shouted, "Cora, Mama wants you! Cora, Mama wants you to come outside!"

Morgan put his hand over Jacob's small mouth. "Hey, anyone can shout. Now go inside and tell her like I asked you to do."

Jacob wiggled until he was free of Morgan's grip, and he bounded toward the front door of the cottage. The sudden slam of the back door told both boys that their sister had already heard the message.

"Too late," Jacob cried, then, pointed to the nuts still dispersed over the yard. "Okay, you can pick up what you need for the stone, but don't take any from my piles. They go right to the fort."

Morgan slipped back into the fantasy. He spoke somberly, "How much time, Jake, before there's an attack? For my men's sake, I need to be ready."

The boy's body went rigid, and a stern, troubled look came to his face. "Don't know for sure. But they're comin'. They're out there and they're comin' on fast."

The intensity in his young eyes and voice made the scene all too real, even for Morgan. Both boys shuddered with a twinge of fear as they attended to their tasks and envisioned the malevolent horde that soon would gather at their gates.

Annie baked. Morgan cleaned walnuts for over an hour, taking turns with Cora stirring the apple butter. All the while, Jacob moved tirelessly up and down the ladder of his tree house, taking load after load of nuts, until his field of battle was finally clear.

Dewey Baughman strained under his own weight as he lumbered up the steep trail toward the Darrow cabin. He puffed loudly.

"Come on, Dewey. We need to get you in shape. The Big Timber's still out there waiting for us, and you'll never get to see it if you can't handle a little hill like this one." Lowe Yancy prodded, and at the same time, he motioned for Black Jack to hurry.

"I reckon all dat good eatin' and fine lovin' packs de weight on a body," replied Black Jack. "De Christian in me say we should help a young brother up dis long and wearisome grade."

"It's the very least we should do," Lowe agreed.

The two men simultaneously grasped the seat of Dewey's trousers, and with complete indifference to the graphic expletives of his protest, they ushered him straight up the hill.

"What the...hey, what ya think you're doin'! Stop that! I'm goin'. Come on, let go of me. Hey, I'm goin'!"

They stopped only when a walnut bounced sideways across their path. Another, flying at a high speed behind them, could only be heard as it crashed into the underbrush. When a couple more skipped by, seemingly from nowhere, they looked up and around and through the scraggly pines that lined the trail.

"Just where the hell are they comin' from!" Dewey exclaimed, not seeing any walnut trees looming above.

"Danged if I know," said Black Jack, looking high at the needled branches. Another nut hit the ground. He picked it up. "Unless dey be pine cones, which I is rather certain dey ain't."

Lowe crossed his arms over his head for protection and moved cautiously up the hill to where he had a clear view of the house. The others followed while the walnuts continued to fall all around them.

"Well, I declare. I think those boys up yonder are gunning for us," said Lowe.

Black Jack disagreed, "Nah, dat ain't so, Mr. Yancy. Dey's just tryin' to knock dem nuts out o' dose trees. Best I can tell, dey ain't even seen us."

Lowe grabbed Dewey by the shoulders, swung him around, and pretended to use his large body as a shield. "You don't mind, do you? Morgan's aim looks to be pretty good."

"It's better than good!" Dewey exclaimed, after a walnut whizzed past his head and smashed into the rocks behind him. "Hell, yes, I mind! He almost got me with that one. You find your own cover!"

"That's exactly what I was doing."

"Well, damn it all, find yourself some other place to hide!" shouted Dewey, who was still catching his breath and not at all receptive to further taunting.

"Just where would you suggest?" The nuts were hitting the ground like hailstones.

"'Bout a hundred yards back down this mountain ought to do it, or we could charge and give 'em some of their own medicine."

It was time for action. Dewey had to believe that this was no accident. The walnuts were a dare, clearly a dare, and he could never resist such a challenge, especially one issued by Morgan Darrow. He picked up a walnut and threw it back toward the tree house. The nut cracked loudly as it exploded against the wooden walls. Startled, Morgan looked down the hill just in time to see Dewey winding up for a second throw. Behind him were the others, the vanguard of Jacob's imaginary invasion.

"To the fort, Jake! Run for your life. I'm right behind you!" Morgan shouted with a pretense of panic, and the boy scrambled into the safety of the tree house before another nut could fall. But Morgan moved more slowly, and an acorn caught him smartly as he contorted to pass through the fort's narrow entrance. "Hey, watch that! This is supposed to be a friendly war."

Several more acorns suddenly pelted the wall. "You fellows might want to consider your surrender now, or forever wish you had!" Morgan yelled both to his friends and to the invisible army that was rushing into formation. A walnut slammed like a rock on a fat limb just above their heads. "By the sound of it, General, I don't reckon they're too keen on my idea of surrender. What do you think?"

"No, I don't reckon they are. And I don't want 'em to be. We haven't even started to fight, yet," Jake responded, showing his displeasure with Morgan's suggestion of an early capitulation.

Morgan cried out to the enemy once again, "Okay, you vermin, you band of snakes, I have warned you! You're up against the great General Jake and the best supplied army in the world, and we're not apt to show mercy."

The tree house was filled from wall to wall with nuts, piled so deep that Morgan lost sight of his shoes as his feet struggled to find their place.

"General, the battle could get right messy before we're through," Morgan said, feeling the wet of walnut juice on his socks.

Jacob stayed in character. "Fightin' ain't meant to be easy. This is war."

The enemy carelessly continued their advance upon the fort, unaware that they had come within the sight and range of young Jacob Darrow. At first, he sniped at them using his slingshot with acorn bullets. His aim was precise, and Dewey howled from the momentary sting of his wound. But they kept coming.

"Pour it into 'em!" Jacob commanded.

"Yes, sir, but I almost feel sorry for such a brave and dying foe. We have the fort, the best of weapons, and all of the ammunition." The boy simply glared at his brother. "Yeah, I know," said Morgan, "this is war."

It was, in fact, an unfair war. Of all the combatants, only Jacob actually intended to strike a living target, and he achieved more success than his 'enemies' originally thought possible. The others, throwing for mere effect, were wholly satisfied by the sound of their varied projectiles battering the sides of the tiny structure. Still, they were outright delighted every time Jacob's shot somehow met its mark, provided, of course, that the mark was situated on another man's body.

"Chuck the hickories! They're the hardest. That'll get 'em," yelled Jacob, encouraging Morgan to step up the fight. Morgan rose above the protection of the wall and fired hickory nuts at his friends, but was careful to miss. Jacob was not so careful, and he launched an effective counter offensive with the sling shot.

"Chuck the bombs, Morgan! Chuck the bombs! You can't hit nothin' with those hickories."

"Which ones are the bombs?"

"You know, the bombs. Those things!" He pointed to the large green balls of the Osage orange.

"Oh, yeah, the bombs."

Morgan began grabbing the big orbs and tossing them like grenades, sight unseen over the wall of the tree house. He threw them extra high and far, in hopes that their intended trajectory would both impress his brother and spare his friends. They landed without consequence on the soft ground.

"The bombs aren't workin' either, Morgan. You can't hit nothin' like that!"

Jacob seemed desperate. His army, his brother, was failing him. The invaders were pressing forward without casualty or deterrent. He dropped his slingshot and whipped handfuls of acorns and hickory nuts against the foe.

"Help me, Morgan! We'll chuck the grape shot. That'll stop 'em for sure at this close range. Keep chuckin'!"

Morgan laughed. "Chucking. Jake's learned a brand-new word, and he's certainly not afraid to use it," he thought. But he did as his brother instructed, and the boys began to dispense an effective indiscriminate spray against the onslaught of their attackers. It worked, at least for the moment. The invaders retreated against the steady hail of missiles and bullets.

Jacob peered cautiously through a knothole in a plank of the wall. All was quiet, much too quiet. He looked over at Morgan and whispered, "Are they gone?"

"I don't think so."

The boys listened closely, straining to detect any motion of the enemy. Jacob then pressed his ear to the wood, and suddenly lurched when the walls of the small fort again resounded with a slam and clatter.

"Here they come again! And they're comin' from all sides this time. Keep chuckin'!"

To his utter frustration, Jacob was rapidly discharging his munitions only to find them immediately thrown back against him. Nuts were flying everywhere, walnuts, hickory nuts, acorn nuts. The battle raged to perfection. The withering fire from both sides showed no sign of weakening as ammunition passed back and forth between the opposing armies.

"That does it!" cried Jacob. He knew his bombs would work, despite his brother's obvious ineptness. He gripped an osage orange in his two hands, lifted the large ball over his head and blindly hurled it from the fort. There came a scream and then, there was silence.

"Uh-oh," uttered Morgan.

I got me one!" Jacob boasted. "I think I got one."

"Uh-oh," muttered Lowe Yancy, now crouched beneath them in the relative safety of the fort's shadow.

"Damn!" Dewey grunted. He shouted for a truce. "Morgan, ya better take a look at this."

Morgan rose as best he could from the slippery floor of the tree house, and was horrified to find Cora standing on their battlefield, her hands loaded with the wet inky flesh of walnut husks. Her dress was randomly spotted and streaked with thick brown apple butter, still steaming from the fabric of her apron.

"Uh-oh," Morgan repeated himself, unable to find words. Cora pointed to the copper cauldron and the Osage orange that now floated at its surface.

"And just which of you children do I have to thank for this?" asked Cora, who seemed disturbingly calm. The men watched her hands clench tightly to the dripping bits of walnut. Jacob wisely hid in the corner of the fort.

"Come on, boys, which one of you did this?"

None of the men would respond, if in fact they even knew the answer, but Cora was intent on dealing justice. If no one would accept responsibility, she was about to punish the least gallant of the bunch. While Lowe, Black Jack and Morgan each offered their sincerest apologies, Dewey foolishly commented about apple butter and its positive effect on the appearance of young women. Within a second, his hat and shoulders were littered with the messy contents of her hands.

"Well, Mr. Dewey Baughman, two can play this game. I believe these walnuts actually go rather nicely with that shirt. Of course, anything is an improvement!"

"What ya go and do that for? I didn't throw it," Dewey whined.

Before Cora could formulate her answer, Annie returned from the house to check on the progress of her apple butter. She took one glance at Dewey and her daughter.

"Oh, my Lord! Just look at the two of you. What has been going on out here?" she questioned.

"Nothing much, Mama. We just had some extra spice added to our recipe, and I was showing my appreciation."

Annie looked at Dewey and simply shook her head. Then, she turned to the others.

"Mr. Clark, it's so good to see you up and around. It's been weeks. I was beginning to worry about you."

"You is very kind, Ms. Darrow. You and Ms. Baughman done a lot for me over de summer, and I's beholdin' to you for all yo prayers and good cookin'. My healin' be comin' along, except for dat scar dem fellas left me. Ma'am, dis here's my good friend, Lowe Yancy."

Annie cocked her head and took a long-awaited look at the man she had heard so much about. He had a robust appearance and was strikingly handsome, for a man of any age. No way disenchanted, she was pleased he had met her expectations. She curtsied.

"Mr. Yancy."

Lowe nodded in respect. "Mrs. Darrow." He stared, almost to the point of rudeness, and then, dropped his eyes and blushed.

"Where have you been hiding, Mr. Yancy? I've been told so many good things about you, but was beginning to wonder if you actually existed. I had hoped you would have visited before now."

"Yes, ma'am. Summer's a busy time."

Annie understood. At least, she thought she did. She walked the short distance between them and offered her hands in welcome. She could feel the calluses on his own as he squeezed her palms.

"Well, you are here now. Between Mr. Clark and the boys, I'm not sure who tells the most Lowe Yancy stories, but you've become legendary on this small piece of the mountain. After all this time, I feel I know you."

"Perhaps from another life, Mrs. Darrow."

Lowe loosened his grip, but she hesitated before withdrawing her hands. "Quite so. We've all lived those other lives," she replied.

The Osage orange was still afloat in the cauldron, and Annie politely excused herself to pick up a ladle and dip it out. She let it cool before touching it.

"Lowe Yancy, I have a small question."

"Yes, ma'am."

"We are now all friends gathered here, are we not?"

"I would hope so."

"Good. Because, as a friend, I have to say that I'm somewhat disappointed in you."

"Me, ma'am?"

"Yes, you. What kind of example do you set? You are a grown man. I would think you should know better than to conduct yourself in some childish affair like throwing nuts at my boys."

"Uh, yes, ma'am."

Lowe did not know how else to respond in his sudden embarrassment, and he dropped his head in subservience while the woman rebuked him. As a result, he did not see the turning of her smile, nor did he see the large green ball now covered in apple butter and spinning with dead-on accuracy through the air.

"We had just enough spices, Mr. Yancy. Thank you very much!"

Those were the last words Lowe heard before the massive fruit smacked hard upon his forehead, spotting his hat and face with apple butter.

"Oww!" he cried. "That thing hits like a cannon ball!"

"Wage a battle, take some casualties!" Annie yelled in response. "But remember, we are all friends."

Before he could seek a rightful explanation, the sky was again lively with the tools of Jacob's war. This time Annie led the charge and Cora followed, scooping and whooping and throwing nuts in a joyful fury. Black Jack, more than happy to change his loyalties, joined Jacob and Morgan in cheering the women as they chased the demon army from the field.

Jacob marveled, "Get 'em, Mama!" He had never seen his mother run so fast, throw so hard, laugh so loud, or live so well.

Morgan saw, too. "Way to go, Ma," he muttered. "You know, Jake, the best miracles are usually performed by mothers, and I think we just witnessed one. Let's go honor the victor."

The boys found their way down the rickety ladder of the tree house and ran over to hug their mother, and their sister, in a fitting accolade. Then, as usual, Jacob's fancy drifted as fast as the gray smoke of battle could dissipate from his mind, and he scampered again across the nut-covered yard on some new mission, known only to his imagination.

Annie's long hair had unraveled from her bun, and her dress was soiled by an assortment of nuts she had hastily gathered in the course of her attack. She was not accustomed to being so disheveled and vainly attempted to put herself back in order before the others could assemble. But her satisfaction and pride were still evident when she greeted Lowe and Dewey, who, now wounded and defeated, marched slowly out of step on their way to the cottage porch. Here the combatants pledged their peace, and here, they gladly communed on walnut brownies, hot and fresh, full of flavor and free of shells. Annie had won more than a war.

She pulled a damp cloth from her apron and pressed it to Lowe's head. "Mr. Yancy, I hope I did not seriously hurt you. It appears I put quite a lump on this poor noggin." Her touch was gentle and soothing. Her voice spoke softly and sent a warm, light breath across his cheek.

"On the contrary, ma'am, it's been far too long since I ever felt this good."

Jacob was nowhere to be found when it came time for his face washing. His mother, armed with soap and towel, searched every corner of the house and yard for her son, and would have soon given up the effort had she not heard the strange cricket scratching loudly in the shed. At age six Jacob was already a fair mimic of wildlife, mostly songbirds, but his midday cricket imitation seemed somewhat out of place. She opened the door widely and was surprised to find no one there. Another cricket sound from the rafters above her head gave away his position.

"Here I am, Mama. Couldn't you find me?"

"I found me a big cricket. Jacob, why don't you come when I call you? Now get down from there, and let's get you cleaned up."

The boy swung down from his perch and reluctantly accompanied his mother to the wellhead. She pumped the long handle until a flow of clear water gurgled from its spout.

"Okay, son, put your head under there, and let's just see if we can't get some of that dirt off your face." The water was cold and the boy jerked back to prevent it from dripping down his back. "I will never understand how you can get so grimy in so short a time," Annie said, wiping the excess wetness from his neck and hair.

The dirt vanished with the first stroke of the towel, but Jacob's face remained as brown as river mud. She scrubbed harder and harder until the boy hollered in discomfort.

"Mama, that hurts! I won't have no more skin!"

Annie examined the boy's splotchy face and ran her hand over the dark discoloration. She licked her fingers and rubbed them against the spots, as if her own water might carry some magic solvent not found in the well. She laughed aloud.

"Dear Lord, that beautiful pink skin has all turned to brown. I think my little boy is becoming a Negro. How in the world did you get that stain on your face?"

The child was stunned by what he heard and looked at his mother with overwhelming dismay. "I don't wanna be a Negro, Mama. I wanna be Jake, just like I was."

"Oh, honey, you will always be my Jake, and I'd love you even if you did start changing colors. I'm just teasing you because your face is so stained by the walnuts that I can't wipe it off. You'll be fine. It wears away in time."

He felt reassured by the squeeze of her arms and the small kiss she placed on his forehead, and he ran to the porch to share his exciting news with the others. He was quick to show his hands. A new olive brown tint covered them from fingertip to wrist.

"Look, Morgan. Look, Mr. Yancy. Look, Dewey. Look here, Mr. Black Jack, I'm a Negro!"

He seemed to derive some pleasure in the notion of different skin, in the thought that this might be an adventure he had never before envisioned. He pushed through the small group of men and cuddled next to Black Jack.

"I'm a Negro, just like you."

Black Jack humored him, "Well, Master Jake, let me be da first to welcome you to de race. I be most proud to show you around. We black folk has us a rich heritage, goin' back thousands o' years, and we is a strong and upstandin' people. God made lots o' good Christians out o' colored skin, you know. Is you a good Christian, Master Jake"?

"Yes, sir. I'm a very good Christian."

"Well, den, you looks to be a right fine Negro at dat."

Jacob drew up even closer, and for a while, did not have much more to say. He was contemplating the advantages and possibilities of being a boy of color, and the change, in his mind, was not without merit. How fortunate he was to have such a friend to show him the way.

Of course, Annie was mortified. In his innocence, Jacob had crossed the unexplained line of propriety and left his mother to deal with the uncomfortable truth. John Lewis Clark was a black man, a Negro, but still, it need not be said. Speaking of it only served to bolster a prejudice that prevailed in her society, a bias that she, herself, had held in times of a not so distant past. Black Jack was but a man, and she liked that man. In fact, black or white, there were few men she respected more. He was self-made and competent, unpretentious and caring. Despite the criticism he suffered from many in the mountains, he never knew bitterness. He never passed judgment. He was a friend to all who would have him.

To Annie, this one man was living proof that a person's skin counted as neither strength nor frailty, and reaching into her own faith, she found that skin, whatever the color, was just the wrapping God placed on another of his special gifts to the world. Black Jack's friendship had been such a gift, especially to Morgan, and it was now being offered to Jacob.

In another time, she could not have understood these things. She had come to know Black Jack through the hearts of her sons and from others like Dewey Baughman and Lowe Yancy. Until now... until now when she was forced to remember how she once so lowly regarded the persons of his race, Annie had completely forgotten that the man was black.

"I'm so sorry, Mr. Clark. Jacob just says what comes to mind and doesn't mean to offend," she said.

"Why, Ms. Darrow, dere ain't no call for dat, no need for apologizin'. De boy honors me. Me and him gonna be great friends. Dat's for sure."

Annie took Black Jack by his forearm. “You are a good man to be so understanding.”

“To be truthful, ma’am, I’s pleased as punch to have a few more o’ my kind in dese parts. All you white folk seems to be changin’ yo color today. Look at yo hands. Look dere at Mr. Yancy’s hands. Yes, indeedy, I’s havin’ me a day.” The man grinned.

Everyone gazed at the olive brown tinge of their palms, like fortune tellers reading their own lines of life and love. One by one they ambled to the water pump to scrub what they knew would not rub off. Black Jack and his new friend, Jacob, stayed behind, content to be right where they were, next to each other and the walnut brownies.

Lowe dried his hands on the back of his britches. “Annie. Uh, Mrs. Darrow, with all this good fun, I nearly forgot why I came to visit. I’m sorry to keep you from your work.”

Annie moved the light brown hair that dangled between her eye and temple. “I am very glad you came. I haven’t been in a battle like that since I was a little girl. I don’t know what I was thinking though, throwing that big old nut, or fruit, or whatever it was. I could have killed you. I hope you’ll recover.”

“I fully expect to, at least until our next little skirmish. You’ve fixed me up real proper like, and I don’t feel a thing. But I do know which army I’ll be joining in the future. With that throwing arm of yours, you ought to take up baseball.”

“That’s just what the team needs, a woman pitcher. Yes, that’ll be the day.”

“Someone always has to be the first, you know.”

“True enough, but it won’t be me. Tell me, Lowe, why did you come to visit?”

“There’s a matter I need to take up with Lawson regarding young Morgan. I stopped by the mill this morning, and no one had seen him. They thought maybe he was resting at home today. A number of the boys over there are down with a fever. Lawson’s not ill, is he?”

“He may be, but I wouldn’t know.” Annie dropped her head

and covered her mouth with a hand. She seemed ashamed. "Lowe, there are some things I would not want others to hear, but perhaps you, as Lawson's long-time friend, should be made aware of them. This may not come as a surprise, but I haven't seen my husband since Thursday. He's been gone two nights without even a word."

Lowe was honestly troubled by what he heard. "A fight with the devil's a tough one to win," he said. "I knew Lawson was drinking a lot, but had no idea the problem was this bad. When we were boys back on the Gauley, he binged every time he could sneak a bottle. He never got caught. I actually thought he would give all that up, having you and a family."

"He did for a while. Now he drinks hard, so hard that he sometimes forgets himself for days on end. We were supposed to go to the social tonight, but I doubt he'll have any desire to do that, even if he does make it home. Mr. Yancy...."

"I liked the way you called me 'Lowe.' I haven't heard that name from a woman's lips in a long, long time." His face reddened at his own impertinence. "I promise to be discreet. I can find your husband. Let me bring him home to you."

Annie was grateful. She was relieved to know that she had a friend, one willing to listen, one able to help. Still, she shook her head.

"No, we have been through this before. My family has learned to wait. Lawson will return only when and if he wants to, and bringing him home will not bring him back to his senses. It was kind of you though."

"Well, just the same, I'll keep an eye out for him. I've seen how alcohol can affect the man, and I suspect he's up on Jasper Creek bumming as much of it as he can from Silas Monk. Quite a few folk head up that way for the same reason, and it's not unusual for many of them to stay the night. Lawson is likely on his way back home, as we speak."

"Thank you for caring. It means a lot. Anyway, you did not climb that long hill to hear about my troubles. What exactly was your concern with Morgan?"

"I need him. I need him to finish running that survey line in the Big Timber. I figured Lawson would have some reservations, considering the boy's schooling and all the problems at our last outing."

"Well, with my husband gone, I don't see why you should have to wait on a decision. Unfortunately, you are right about Morgan's education. It must come first. To be honest, I wish he could work with you again. He grew up more as a man, and he learned more about real life during those days with you on the mountain than we could ever teach him here at home."

"That's kind, but so untrue, ma'am. He came to me extremely well prepared, and he handled himself accordingly." Lowe hesitated, being a little discomfited by what he must say next. "You have a right to know, Mrs. Darrow, that I've taken a rather improper liberty. I talked to Arthur Tutwiler about the matter of Morgan's studies. He's the principal at Devlin School."

"Yes, I know very well who he is."

"It seems a lot of the children have to be taken out of school from time to time to help out around the home or farm, and with a little extra work, some additional studies and reading, they manage. Mr. Tutwiler is quite confident in Morgan as a student, and says he's one of the best he ever had. He thought Morgan would be fine missing a week or so, just as long as he tended to some of the school work while he was away. I can see to that." Lowe hesitated again, still embarrassed. "Uh, Mrs. Darrow, I truly apologize for doing this without your permission, but I thought it best to check the situation before discussing the matter with you or Lawson."

"So, the teacher has already given his blessing."

"Yes, ma'am."

"And if I permit my son to go with you to this Big Timber place, you will allow sufficient time for Morgan to work on his studies?"

"Of course, ma'am."

"It will be colder up there, you know. You could hit snow. I expect you'll bring adequate provisions."

"Yes, ma'am. We'll have everything he needs."

"And will the others be going as well? I mean Mr. Clark, Silas Monk, Dewey?"

"At this point, ma'am, I'm not too sure about Dewey. The teacher didn't have quite the same praise for Dewey's academics as he did for Morgan's." Lowe tittered as he went on to explain, "What Mr. Tutwiler actually said was that Dewey tends to sleep through class, that he couldn't get any further behind in his studies if he missed a full decade, and that a trip into the real world might be just what the boy needs to wake him up. I talked to the Baughmans this morning. They were a little dubious of him going, but agreed to give me their answer later today."

"Lowe, you would have to promise that Morgan will come back unharmed this time. No more fights. No more bears. And right now, I'm not too pleased with the thought of Silas Monk and his whiskey being around my son."

"You know I cannot make guarantees and would certainly never deceive you. Things happen. People get hurt. And as for Silas, he's a rough old buzzard, but he minds himself around the boys. I need him as well. But I'll do my best to keep Morgan safe, just like I would for any of my men. Mrs. Darrow, I really need his help. He knows the business now, and he has the strength and energy I only wish I could find again. Surveying is good work. It pays a man well and, compared to other jobs in these parts, it's healthy. Someday, Morgan may want to take up the trade where I leave off."

Annie thought only for a moment, while she secretly studied the face of Lowe Yancy. He had aged well. His was a rugged face, buffeted by the years of harsh winds and hostile suns. His leathery skin held tight against the square of his jaw, but could not prevent the deepening of two dimples that surfaced at the very hint of his smile. He was rough, but he was gentle. He was strong, yet vulnerable. She could see that in him. She could look right through his iron frame to the soft heart of the man and know that he was to be trusted. His allure was of something deep and indefinable, and against this, Annie's will dissolved into nothing. Her son would do well to know this man, and she could not find reason to deny him.

"Okay, then, you have my consent. I'll inform his father when he returns, but you tell Morgan. I'm sure he is anxious about my answer."

"I'm obliged, ma'am."

"Lowe, how long does a man have to know a woman before he calls her by her rightful name? I am 'Annie,' or don't you remember? In any case, I think we're beyond the formality of 'ma'am,' especially considering today's events."

"Yes, ma'am," he replied.

Annie rolled her eyes at the response. She had never met a man who could listen. She continued, "And I think that you and Mr. Clark should join us at the pie social this evening. I'll be bringing plenty of dessert for everyone and could sure use more mouths to help eat it all. Please come, Lowe. The children would love it."

"Thank you, but we'll have to see. Black Jack wouldn't feel right, and I don't reckon I'll come without him. But I appreciate the offer just the same. I couldn't help but smell what's been baking in your kitchen. So, who knows? My stomach is likely to change my mind. It does that on occasion."

"Please, think about it. We'd love to see you."

The invitation was tempting, perhaps more so than Lowe could resist. He felt such contentment in the presence of this family and was stirred by the growing affection he had for each of them. But an inner voice reminded him of what intimacy might bring. He feared stepping on ground owned by another man, and most of all, he feared what he saw in the beauty of Annie Darrow. He had been there before.

The burial ground of First Methodist Church spread across the knoll without pattern. In some places graves almost hugged the walled foundation of the church, but for the most part, memorials were spaced seemingly at random over the wide lawn and under the generous cover of aging elms. There were no gates with arches, no angular walls of stone or black iron fences. There was no expensive statuary, only 60 or so markers scattered like grazing sheep on a distant hillside. Some were obelisks, tall and ornately scribed, but most were common tablets of sandstone, flat and simple and etched with little more than a name and two dates. A few were just faceless rocks that marked the final beds of some poor or unremembered souls. In the gray light of dusk, they all rose up from the earth like a gathering of ancestral saints, each waiting with eternal patience for the call to vespers.

Sadie Buck hurried when she approached the burial grounds. It was not that she was afraid of what might lurk in the dim shadows. She had never believed in ghosts, but was genuinely concerned for the safety of two pies now balanced in her hands. They might cool. They may fall before others could fully appreciate the perfection of her culinary handiwork. Still, as she was about to enter the door of the fellowship hall, she stopped to look across the cemetery and gazed at a large, pointed column that partially disappeared into the crown of a nearby tree. It was dark there, just beyond the reach of the walkway lamp, and she could barely differentiate the straight lines of the stone from the curves of the trunk. The night would yet blacken to pitch with a moonless sky, until even ghosts would stay clear of the place for fear of tripping. It was utterly private. Her luck had ensured her purpose.

Sadie was ready. When the young man opened the door behind her, she instantly spun around and disappeared inside.

"Why, Mr. Darrow, what a pleasure to find you here tonight," Sadie said, hoping he had no idea of the truth. It seemed strange that he, of all people, would be the one to greet her at the door, but she was happy to accept his presence as a sign, a good sign of things to come. Sadie knew that Morgan would be at the social. She expected him. She had talked to his sister on two separate occasions just to be certain of his attendance. And, of course, he was the very reason for the pies.

"Hi, Sadie, can I help you with these?" Morgan took the pie from her left hand, removed its cover and held the plate to eye level. He was pleasantly surprised as he turned it slowly. "Mmmm, Jeff Davis, isn't it? I haven't tasted any of this in centuries. It used to be my favorite, and, gosh, it's still warm. If it's half as good as it looks and smells...hey, maybe we should sample a piece now before I accidentally drop it."

"You better not drop my pie, Morgan, after I've baked it for two hours and toted it up this hill. If you want some, you'll just have to win it like anyone else. You did bring money for the cake walk, didn't you?"

"There wouldn't be much point in coming tonight if I didn't. But mmmm, I sure hate to leave something that looks so good up to chance. How about just a tiny little sliver?" He knew full well the futility of the question, but nothing so honors a cook as hands that reach for a coveted taste. Both the pie and the girl had earned his flattery.

"No, absolutely not," she replied.

"Just a fingertip?" He dabbed his index finger lightly into the sweet topping.

"You keep your hands out of that pie, Morgan Darrow! It's for the cake walk. You're going to spoil it."

Sadie was ecstatic, not angry. His response had been predictable and perfect. After talking with Cora, she knew that Morgan was partial to this one dessert, with its rich center and light meringue. It was not easy to bake, and she had no idea what she would do if Morgan showed disinterest. Cora had told her that her brother ate very little in the way of sweets, but for some reason, he could never quite resist his mother's Jeff Davis pie. There was considerable risk in competing with a mother's cooking, especially Annie Darrow's, whose baking was renowned around Devlin. Nevertheless, Sadie persuaded her friend to steal the recipe. She was intent on winning Morgan's favor. All of her talents, all of her guile, would be dedicated to the effort.

The girl moved some cakes already positioned at the center of the table. She placed one pie in the opened space and motioned to Morgan to bring the other.

"Now, put that right here. You know, a sweet word and a little begging might just get you anything you want. If you don't get your taste tonight, I could be persuaded to bake you another. Maybe. It all depends on you."

"I'm willing to do a lot of begging."

"Good. You keep that thought."

Sadie Buck was an attractive young woman, much like her older sister. A little round in the face, she was also rounded in other places, which added to her appeal. Her striking red hair was the most obvious feature, but in short order, the attention of men almost always drifted to the fullness of her lower curves. She did not mind. She pretended not to notice how men became silent when she walked away from them, or how their eyes scanned her body when they thought she was unaware. She thrived on their interest, and at 16, any attention seemed nice. She reveled in her achievement as man after man would debase himself in such a way. Sadie wore her weight well, and despite her youth, she could mercilessly wield it to her advantage. There was always a man or a boy ready to take her hand and do her bidding.

As children, the two tended to ignore each other. She was just a friend of Morgan's younger sister and he was just another bashful boy. But unlike the reticence of his childhood, which made him appear to her as dull and slow-witted, the quiet confidence of the man proved him most desirable. He was a true gentleman in a world where mountains and hard living often brought out the bestial sensuality of men. He was different from the others. His consistent disregard of her, of her body, despite her often unseemly advances, had consumed her since she was old enough to care. She was of age now. She wanted his hidden passion. She wanted to know the strength that only his touch could reveal.

Sadie recalled her hot June afternoon swim in the Charity River, when Morgan so gallantly leapt from the cliff at the mere sound of her cries. She was foolish to have shouted him away in that hideous show of false modesty. To be certain, she would have won him that very day, but Morgan turned from her nude body, as any gentleman would, only to find Sarah Dabney innocently wading in the shallows.

Sarah was the problem. While Sadie's wiles had seemingly

captured Morgan's interest, her mind was acutely aware of the threat of competition. It was not a particular observation, but mere intuition, that disclosed Morgan's fondness for the girl. And Sarah, herself, had never divulged any real attraction for Morgan. Still, Sadie had staked a claim, and she would fight family, foe or friend to keep it.

Sarah, the friend, would never deserve Morgan Darrow because she had done nothing to earn him. Yet, unknown to Sadie, Sarah had already taken to her heart the essence of the man, his thoughts and yearnings, his devotion. Sadie wanted that devotion. Now, more intently than ever, she pledged that she would have it, that she would have all of him, if for no other purpose than to show she could. Sarah be damned. Her friendship be damned. Morgan would come to love only her.

Over 70 people stood up when Sam Blackman yelled, "What do you say? Let's have us a cake walk!" He started picking at the strings of his banjo, and a fiddler followed his lead into a lively tune.

"Come on folks, let's form a circle. We've got us a lot of goodies up here to give out and a lot of money to make. Big circle now. Plenty of room for everyone!" The music continued as he spurred the crowd into action. "You know the rules. You see the numbers on the floor. Keep walkin' round until the music stops, and if we draw your number, you get your pick of pie or cake or cookies or brownies. Any questions? No? What else we got up there, Annie?"

Standing next to the table, Annie was surprised by the sudden announcement of her name, and she stuttered finding her answer. Sam was quick to rescue her.

"Besides all this baking, I know we have a lot of canned goods and candies for sale. Please tell me, Annie, that some of your famous apple butter is up there again this year."

"I brought a few pints for the occasion, and there's a quart jar with your name already on it, Sam. But, of course, it will set you back a whole dollar."

"Anything for the cause," Blackman replied. He laughed, as he pulled a silver dollar from his vest and slapped it on the table. "I was ready for you. Here's your dollar, lady. I'll be eating good come morning."

His eyes squinted to discern the contents of the other jars, while he rummaged through his pockets for a bent pair of spectacles. The wire rim glasses tilted awkwardly on the bridge of his wide nose, but served their purpose.

"Goodness gracious! Look here, folks, we not only got some of Mrs. Darrow's outstanding apple butter, but there's a whole host of preserves and jams, some canned pears and peaches, and it looks like a couple types of fudge and other candies. Lots of good stuff for sale here tonight. So, open up your wallets, and let's start this circle moving!"

The music picked up pace as a base fiddle joined the sound, and listeners clapped and tapped to the sprightly tempo. They spontaneously grasped hands and began to orbit the room. A few stayed in their seats along the wall, happy to savor the local entertainment, and some saved themselves for the country dancing that would inevitably follow later during the course of the evening. The band would have no rest. As one player might leave to join the revelry, another usually slipped unnoticed into his place.

It was a nickel for the cake walk, which generally continued until the food or the walkers or the band played out. For children, it was a penny. Any offering pretty much guaranteed some type of treat, since everyone would bring at least one dessert and most brought more. Anything left over was sold for a fair price, and all the receipts were donated in support of the local relief fund.

Hand to hand or in single file, the ring of dancers sped up and slowed down all to the rhythm of the music, until the strings suddenly fell silent and the circle froze in its place. Sam Blackman pulled a number from his upturned hat. He pointed his finger, and the winner stepped out to proudly make his selection from the table.

"Our first winner, ladies and gentlemen, Mr. Dewey Baughman!" The crowd cheered. "And what did you choose, Dewey? Hold it up for us."

Dewey lifted a plate and looked at the name on the card beneath it. He had to speak over the commotion of the room. "I'm lookin' at one scrumptious rhubarb pie, made by Mrs. Lydia Steinmueller. Don't bother askin'. I ain't gonna share. Tonight, it's every hungry man for himself."

The crowd cheered again. Dewey rushed to set his prize on the closest sill and scooted back across the floor to rejoin the moving circle. The music stopped almost before it started.

"No, no, no, no!" cried Blackman. He looked at Dewey with a wide grin that lifted his round, rosy cheeks. "Dewey, I have to watch you like a hawk, or you'll be eating everything on that table. You know the rule. Sorry to say it, but you've got to ante up or sit this one out."

"Come on, Sam, I'm only in it for the dancin'. If ya happen to pick my number, just draw again, or you can always give me one of them silver dollars from your vest. I sure wouldn't mind winnin' a few more of these desserts."

"Uh-huh, you just dance."

The man pulled his banjo against his big tummy and strummed a couple chords, tuning as he did so. The fiddler waited. Then, he drew out one tediously long note with a slow pull of his bow, and like a deep breath finally vented, his lively melody suddenly erupted across the room. Sam Blackman joined in, and their feet bounced while their music played on.

And so it went. The music played and stopped, played and stopped, until the table was half clear of its countless desserts. When it ceased again, Sam Blackman looked over at the small boy who was jumping with joy and racing up and down the length of the long table.

"Now, who is this young fellow?"

Jacob calmed for the moment. "I'm Jake."

"Oh, yes, Mr. Jacob Darrow. I didn't recognize you, son. It looks like you've already found some pie. Must have been blueberry, judging by that color on your face."

"No. Walnut. I was chuckin' walnuts by my fort, and then Mama said I looked like a neg...."

Annie's hand reacted faster than ever before, thanks to her

nervous anticipation of what her son might say if given the wrong opportunity. She cupped his mouth in the nick of time.

"Just find what you want, honey, and I'll read the name of the person who made it. Okay?"

"Sure, Mama." Jacob began to inspect each delicacy and questioned his mother about every plate. It was important that he make the right choice.

"Come on, Jacob, you have to pick something. Folks are waiting," Annie pleaded.

"I want this one."

He handed his mother a tin of fudge, and she read the hand printed label. "It's peanut butter fudge, made by Sarah Dabney." She winked at Jacob. "It looks way too good for a little boy to eat."

Jacob grabbed the tin from his mother, just in case she was not teasing, and scampered away to sample his prize in peace.

Morgan's eyes darted across the room in search of Sarah. He wondered why he had not seen her earlier, especially since he had stayed so close to the door on the chance that she might enter. Sadie Buck saw him looking.

"She's not here, Morgan."

"Who's not here?"

"Sarah isn't coming tonight. I believe she's having dinner with her father and the Devlins."

"Oh?"

"Isn't she lucky? She's dining with the owner of the company and, of course, with his son, Austin. There could be others, but I'm not sure. It's quite an honor, don't you think, being invited to such an occasion? Austin Devlin is the catch of the century, and it looks like Sarah has tossed in all of her hooks. The man is smitten. Come on, Morgan, let's rejoin the circle."

Sadie waited for the next lull in the music to whisper her request to Sam Blackman. He nodded, then, pulled on his suspenders to raise his pants. His large body jiggled with the beat of a new medley, and in seconds, the trousers slipped back to their place below his belly.

After several revolutions, the circle finally halted, this time leaving Morgan the winner. He politely pretended to want every dessert remaining on the table, but knew there was only one real choice. He lifted the last Jeff Davis pie, acknowledged the baker and, like his brother, moved away for an undisturbed taste. Sadie caught him by the arm and ushered him toward the door.

"Come with me. Come outside for a few minutes and I'll slice it for you. This way you won't have to share. Come on."

She took the pie from his hands and giggled with satisfaction as he followed her like a puppy to a bowl of milk. She led him past a dozen gravestones, beyond the light to the dark place beneath the elm.

"This is crazy, Sadie. It's a cemetery and it's cold out here. I really don't mind sharing."

"Sh-sh-sh. Just try this." With her bare hand, she put a thin sliver of the pie to the edge of his mouth. "Open up. Taste it."

Morgan did as she instructed, and she rewarded him by slowly slipping the entire piece against his tongue. Her fingers dragged lightly against his lips.

"It's good, isn't it?"

Morgan mumbled as he swallowed, "Very good."

"Would you like more?"

"Yeah, you bet. This is great. I'll try some more."

"More of what, Morgan?"

Before he could even think of an answer or realize what was happening, Sadie was nestled against him. She raised herself on her toes until she could move her mouth freely against his. Her tongue swept across his upper lip. Her body squeezed tightly against him until the fullness of her bosom pressed warm upon his ribs. He fell back against the column.

"My God, Sadie, please stop this. It's not right. We're in a cemetery, a church. There are a hundred people, and besides, I'm...."

It was useless resistance. She pulled him away from the stone and squeezed him tighter as they now rocked against the tree. Her kisses were firm and long.

"Is that better?"

"Sadie, we have to stop." His words lacked resolve. "Really, we can't go on."

He returned her kisses, all the while protesting in the faintest of whispers, half hoping she would not hear. The girl responded with more passion and ran her hands down the small of his back and across his legs.

"Morgan, quit fighting me. I want this. I want you!"

Morgan had never known such feeling, such weakness. He quaked in her arms. His breath shivered, not against the cold of the night, but from the heat of temptation. He was on fire, and he finally found his strength as he smothered her writhing body with his own. Sadie moaned with delight. She wanted more.

It was all too awkward and much too wrong. When the door opened at the fellowship hall, both Morgan and Sadie broke their embrace. A shrill voice intruded into the night.

"Morgan! Morgan! Where are you? It's time to go home. Morgan! Mama wants you!" Not seeing anything except a shadowy movement among the graves, Jacob quickly closed the door.

"I'm sorry, Sadie. I forgot myself. This just isn't right."

It was all he could say. He could barely see the girl who stood before him in the darkness, and for that he was thankful. It would be hard enough to hide his guilt. He loved Sarah Dabney. He walked slowly back into the light, tortured with the shame of his betrayal.

It was not a long drive home. The evening air was cool, but the warmth of a wool shawl was sufficient for Annie, who waited in the passenger seat of the motor car. Morgan cranked the engine and began to drive slowly in the loose procession that ambled away from the First Methodist Church. A buggy pulled closely alongside, and he could not help but see Dewey Baughman with his big arm draped over the shoulder of Auralee Buck. Sadie sat quietly next to her sister, her face turned toward the young driver of the automobile. She waved secretly, knowingly.

"Brother-in-law!" Dewey heckled. He snapped a whip over the rump of his horse, and the buggy pulled ahead. Morgan could still hear his friend's laughter as he wheeled out of sight.

“Ma, what did you do, select your own brownies?” Morgan asked. He hoped the idle conversation might push Sadie from his mind and conscience.

“No, I brought these with me to give to Mr. Yancy and Mr. Clark. I thought they might make it tonight. “

“Lowe’s a bit of a loner, Ma. I don’t think he takes much to big parties. He’s good with people, but prefers them one at a time. And Black Jack, he just wouldn’t be comfortable.”

“I understand, son, but a gathering of friends may just be what those men need, being gone so long and so far from any civilized life. I wish they had come, for their sake.”

“Yeah, me, too.”

The car moved slowly down the bumpy road without the sound of further conversation. Jacob slept, his small mouth open, his nose pressed against the brown leather of the seat. On his lap, cradled between his tiny hands, was the tin of Sarah Dabney’s peanut butter fudge. Another adventure had ended. Come morning, he would be searching for more.

# CHAPTER 10

Dewey slumped in the comfort of the old maple rocker and lifted his leg to the porch rail. He pushed and the chair creaked sharply as it teetered back. When he released, there was not so much as a chirp from the rocker, but instead, a long, sustained groan from the floor planks bearing his shifting weight. He pushed and released again, this time more slowly, noting the exact place and moment that each sound occurred. Back and forth, creaking and groaning, the chair swayed with a varied cadence as he studied the sounds. It was the simplest of intrigues.

"Hey, Morgan, come listen to this."

He pushed again to generate the noise, as Morgan closed the cabin door and took a seat on the top porch step. Morgan heard the squeaks, but found nothing of particular interest.

"Yeah, I hear them. So?" He looked up with a fair expectation of Dewey disclosing some significant discovery, but his friend just kept rocking and listening, rocking and listening, rocking and listening.

"Ya hear it? The chair squeaks goin' one way and the floor squeaks goin' the other. Curious, ain't it?" Dewey finally said.

"Dewey, when I asked you to kill some time while I finished up my chores, I had no idea you could do it so well. Thanks to you, there is now irrefutable evidence that wood joints creak. Amazing! Did you figure this out on your own?"

Dewey had thought his observation was rather clever, but now realized how silly the whole experiment appeared. He searched hopelessly for a saving response.

"Well, yeah!" There was no time to prepare. Two tiny words

were all that came to mind, and they were certainly not the ones that would save him.

The response diminished him all the more. Morgan's friend could be very insightful when he was not absorbed in some type of amusement. Unfortunately, there always seemed to be things that could capture his fancy and ultimately deliver him from the boredom of more serious contemplation. But he was who he was, and there was no merit in trying to belittle him. Still, Morgan could not resist so obvious an opportunity.

"There's bound to have been some studies," Morgan said.

"Of what?"

"Of wood noise. It must be a science somewhere."

"A science, huh. Ya really think so?"

Dewey was not stupid, but his continued interest in the matter made him seem so. Morgan looked at him with incredulity.

"Are you kidding me?" He was suddenly returned to the brink of sarcasm, but forced himself to manage his words. "Of course, it's a science. Dewey, it has to be. A sound can say a lot about the properties of wood. The government or some college somewhere probably has volumes on the topic already."

"Ya don't say."

"I do say. I read an article on this very subject."

"About squeaks?"

"Yes, indeed. Wood squeaks."

"Well, I'll be. A science. I wonder why?"

"Because creaks tell a lot about the quality of wood. That's why. And because wood is used in so many, many areas of our lives... houses, wagons, paper...you know."

Dewey had already made two mistakes that branded him a fool. He refused to make his third by believing such an outlandish explanation. If Morgan was intent on rambling through a lie, he certainly should be free to get lost in it. Dewey let the story unravel.

"It's all rather simple really." Morgan spoke with confidence, which was, of course, just feigned, but a few right words made his presentation convincing enough. "The wood's density, the length of the fibers, the moisture, the straightness of the grain, these are the properties that affect the sound of wood when it creaks. Every board has a different quality, and every joint and every pin or nail you put in the board can cause a different noise when there's movement."

"Really?"

"That's right. Dry woods tend to make the most cracking sounds, because they tend to split a lot. Hard woods, like chestnut and oak and hickory, they don't make much noise at all, unless you join them, and nails as fasteners make just about everything creak. Of course, anyone will tell you that if you drive a good wooden peg instead of a nail, you'll never hear a thing. Lumber holds real tight with pegs. Special properties, they make all the difference as far as sound goes."

Morgan went on and on, never realizing Dewey's utter disinterest. When he was through, he found his friend stone-faced and ready for reprisal.

"An entire herd of Holsteins couldn't drop a bigger pile of shit. Do ya know that?" asked Dewey.

"What do you mean?"

"I mean that ya spread it wide and deep, when ya have a mind to. If manure made sound, my ears would need boots."

"I've offended you."

"Hell, yes, ya offended me. There may be two half-wits standin' here, but only one of 'em is listenin' to his own twaddle."

"You didn't like my explanation?"

"I don't care for that damned arrogance of yours. I ain't no dolt. Sometimes ya treat me like one."

Dewey's comments had teeth, and they left deep marks on Morgan's pride. In friendship, no man is the better, no thought is the least. Morgan had forgotten.

"I'm very sorry, Dewey."

"Don't be. It ain't worth 'sorry.'"

"Nevertheless, I am. I apologize."

The two shook hands. It was a telling moment in their friendship, when Dewey was bright enough to teach humility and Morgan was man enough to welcome it. Both boys would remember the lesson, but, of course, would discount it often when faced with the perfect taunt or tease.

Morgan left his seat on the porch and disappeared momentarily into the house, only to return with a hammer firmly in his grip. With three strategic blows, he silenced both the floor planking and his discussion with Dewey Baughman.

"Now, what was it you really wanted to see me about?" Morgan asked.

"Oh, I just came by for the details."

"Details about what?"

"You know what. I heard 'bout last night."

"I have no idea what you're trying to say."

"Sure ya do. Last night...the cake walk, the pie, the girl, the cemetery." Dewey now had Morgan's attention. "I heard ya was makin' love with Miss Sadie outside the church."

"What! Where do you come up with these things?"

"This one came direct from the horse's mouth."

"Sadie told you that!"

"Well, not exactly, but I did get the word from the horse's sister. Sounds to me like things are movin' purdy fast with you two. I know a lot of fellas who'd like to be in your place right now. I hear she's one part wildcat and the other part kitten. And in my way of thinkin', ya can't go wrong with neither one."

Morgan was dumbfounded, embarrassed, and the more he tried to speak, the worse he fumbled with the words.

"Dewey, you...I...I...she...we...."

"That's well put, Morgan. I understand she has that same effect on all them fellas. She's turned my head more than a few times, I have to admit."

Morgan held his breath as he tried to salvage his wit. He would have strangled his best friend in that very moment had he not already acknowledged that any disgrace related to Sadie was of his own doing. Finally, the words flowed.

"Listen, Dewey, I'm not now and never will be one of those fellows. All we did was kiss, and I regret having done that more than you'll ever know."

"Ya regret it? Ya regret makin' love to Sadie Buck, the liveliest little firecracker in all of Devlin? Next to Auralee, o' course."

Morgan raised his voice in temper. "We didn't make love! I don't love her, and I don't want her!"

"Then, why did ya kiss her?"

"Enough!" Morgan crashed his fist down on the floor planks, and Dewey felt the tremor radiate through his chair. The rocker froze in position. There was an awkward silence as each boy feared the next utterance.

Morgan cupped his hand over his forehead and gathered his thoughts. He waited for Dewey to speak his mind, but when the quiet seemed unending, he knew that the first comment must be his own. He spoke softly.

"I've got no better friend than you. And if I can't talk to you about such things, then who will listen? I know how Sadie feels about me, and I suspect those feelings will end the very day she wins me. She's that way with men. I think she's beautiful, and it's near impossible to resist her. But I'm trying. It drives me, body and soul, to insanity, but I am trying. I guess none of this makes a lick of sense."

Dewey lifted himself from the rocking chair and moved next to Morgan on the porch step. "I don't always think with my britches, Morgan. Sometimes, I use my brain, sometimes my heart. If ya got somethin' to say, I want to be the one to hear it."

"Trust me, Dewey, I want to tell you. Sadie is a decent enough girl, a bit fickle, but I think that comes with youth. She'll change. We all change. Despite what she says, she doesn't need me or anyone else taking advantage of her. God forgive me for not keeping my distance."

"Is that what's botherin' ya? Conscience is one big pain in the ass, ain't it?"

"I just wish...well, I wish I could say it's that simple. And maybe it should be. My conscience is only a part of the problem."

Morgan showed worry in his eyes, a new and dark expression that Dewey found troubling. Life was not meant to be serious, but it proved increasingly so. It seemed that childhood, with all its laughter and carefree adventure, had slipped away at some point without even a warning. The boys were now suddenly thrust into a world of concern, a world where everything mattered, where every move made its mark. When did this happen? How could they not be prepared?

Dewey stared at a cobweb formed at the corner of the step. A moth squirmed in the hold of the filaments as the spider crept across the wood to close for the kill. With an almost instinctive slap of his right hand he smashed the spider, and with a gentle sweep of his left, he destroyed the web and pulled the moth to safety. He wanted to do no less for Morgan.

His friend continued, "Not so many weeks ago, I would have begged for Sadie's attention. No one else seemed interested, and I had no sense of what I really wanted in a woman. Then, there was that day last June when you and I went...."

"Wait just a minute! Hold on there! It's that yellow haired girl. You've fallen for that Sarah at the swimmin' hole. Well, I'll be damned. Ya ain't after Sadie Buck at all!"

"It sure doesn't take you long to hit the heart of the matter."

"Long enough. The whole problem's been written across your face for three months. I am a dolt. Only a fool couldn't see it was Sarah."

"I've been trying to hide it, Dewey, both from myself and everyone else. The real fool is the fellow who falls for the one girl he can never have. He knows that such a want will only lead him to misery, and yet, he commits to it because he'd rather be miserable than empty. And I am so miserable. I've thought of nothing except Sarah since that day in the river, but she still doesn't know me enough to even form an opinion. Just as well, I doubt there is much about me that would please a girl like her. Sarah is of a different world, that's for sure, and I have no chance of being there with her. You're lucky, Dewey. It was different for you and Auralee."

"That's true, I reckon, but then again, I let the woman I love know exactly how I felt, and I only gave her one choice.

"What choice?"

"Me, of course. Morgan, how can ya just go 'bout your day feelin' the way ya do, without at least tellin' Sarah your thoughts? The worst that can happen is that she laughs at ya and sends ya packin'."

"The worst that can happen is that she end up with that Austin Devlin, and I can't compete with the likes of him."

"Horse apples! Big stinkin' horse apples! Ya may not win, but you sure as hell can compete. Morgan, you've always known when to back away or when to fight. This is your fightin' time, if ever I saw one."

Morgan listened. His friend was making sense, but there was a great risk in opening up the heart. If Sarah rejected him, it would be forever. In his silence, there was at least hope.

"Well, thanks for hearing me out. I've been dwelling on this all summer. I can't shake her. I can't even make myself want to shake her."

"Yup, that's a tough one. You're in a mess all right."

Morgan stretched his long legs and squirmed to reposition on the step. The plank was a hard and unforgiving seat, and it creaked as he shifted. He instantly leered at Dewey.

"Don't even start again," he said. "We'll have no more experiments."

Dewey smiled. "Nope, done with that. Hey, I haven't told you the bad news."

"Oh, yeah, and what's that?"

"I ain't goin' with ya to the Big Timber, on account of a serious matter at home."

"Not going? But I was planning on you."

Dewey's expression did not validate his concern. He was still smiling, and Morgan knew to simply wait for an explanation.

"Yeah, my folks are of an opinion that my book learnin' has become a particular *serious matter*. Ma mumbled somethin' 'bout not havin' to feed me the rest of my life, 'bout school pavin' a road to better things. You know mothers, always the worriers, always the prophets of doom and gloom. Anyway, she weren't angry, but she sure was clear. I ain't goin' to the Big Timber, not while there's school."

"But Mr. Yancy said we'd only be gone six or seven days."

"Yeah, that's exactly what he told my Ma. But I think her reply was that six days from school was two months too many, at least for me. So, I expect you're headin' on without Mr. Dewey Baughman. Just as well, the weather's turnin' nowadays, and I don't cotton to cold any better than summer heat."

"It won't be much fun without you," Morgan lamented.

"I swear, Morgan, ya got yourself some strange notions. What work is ever fun?"

The crisp autumn air was laced with musky wafts of fallen leaves. A soft light angled through the limbs of the trees, and there was a distant chatter of squirrels and birds and people, all tending to the final details of their harvest. A woodpecker tapped against a looming poplar, then flew, and a wood chuck, its jowls packed full, raised his furry head from a hole at the corner of the fence.

But the boys were oblivious, and their discourse somehow rambled through the lazy afternoon until the woes of their world were rated and resolved, one by one.

The gray slicker seemed dark and shiny in the cold steady drizzle, but turned coal black when the mill finally shut down its boilers. The whole town went black, as well, with the exception of the gas-lighted Market Street, and it remained so for several long seconds until the oil lamps were fired in a scattering of windows.

The stranger shivered, and he hunched to make the most of his thin undercoat. His rain slicker could stop the wet but not the damp chill that permeated from head to foot. With a brief glance at its face, he shut the cover of his time piece and slipped it back into his pocket. It was 10 o'clock. The mill was never late in closing.

Like a phantom lurking in the night, the man had sinister form.

He watched the faces, as best he could see, and listened to the voices, as best he could hear against the splatter of the rain. He crept ever closer, as a short and steady stream of members left the Lodge and hurried on their way under wide umbrellas. The door lock finally clicked, and before long, only one pitiful soul still stood before him.

Lawson Darrow used the brick wall to keep his balance as he pulled a cigarette from his jacket and attempted to strike a match. The match stick broke, as did several others, before he threw his smoke to the ground in frustration. He looked up the slope of Briar Mountain toward his home, but with little hesitation, whirled away toward the river and the other side of the tracks. He staggered recklessly, but with the help of every post and pole and wall along his way, he managed to find the saloon. It was alive with music and thriving on iniquity.

He paused to gather himself, having sobered little in his walk through the rain. He adjusted his clothes and ran a hand through his hair, then opened the door that led to a lavish parlor. The stranger in the slicker still watched and waited.

Lawson did not really know the woman that greeted him, but everything about her was allure, and he warmed instantly to her obvious charms and advances.

"First time in, honey? I'm so glad you came by tonight. You know, I've seen you around town on occasion. It's about time we became acquainted. So, why don't we sit down and have us a drink, and then...who knows?"

"I'm ready for that drink, but, lady, I'm not sure about the rest."

"We can just talk, if that's what makes you comfortable. They call me Alice. What's your name?"

"Whatever you'd like it to be. Otherwise, Lawson will do. I don't know what I want, other than a long, full glass of really decent liquor. No rot-gut, no watered-down turpentine. Just give me your best."

"Then, we'll start with that. The bar only carries the finest brands, nothing local. You stay close to me, and I'll fix you up like a gentleman deserves."

The woman was professional. Like a vixen pouncing on an unwary brood, she moved stealthily from man to man, draining them of both money and soul until little of either were left. Lawson was the easiest quarry, too inebriated to reason and too drunk to protest anything that she might propose. He had come for wine and women, and in short order, she offered him both. She took his hand and led him toward the bar in the back of the room.

"I'll have champagne," she said to the bartender, who winked at her.

"Coming up. You want the bottle?"

"Of course, we want the bottle. Does my friend here look like the type of man who doesn't treat a lady right?" She smiled at Lawson, and he nodded his approval, though he much preferred a double whiskey. The woman commanded the evening, and he was willingly hers to lead.

"You'll need to pay for the champagne now," she said, as the bartender popped the cork and filled two crystal glasses from the bottle. It was a rather cheap crystal, but a very expensive wine.

Lawson pulled his wallet from the breast pocket of his coat and asked what he owed. It was a voice from behind that responded, "Did you drink it?"

"Huh...no...no, I just got it," Lawson answered, without looking for the source of the question.

"Good. Then, don't. And don't pay for it either. Sorry, miss, but my friend here just made a wrong turn tonight. I'll see he finds his way home. I hope he hasn't been a bother to you."

The man in the slicker gripped Lawson's collar and led him forcefully across the room.

"Hey, who do you think you are? You can't just bust in here and disturb our friends like this. Let him go!" the woman screamed. Her voice quieted the saloon, and everyone stopped their pursuits to listen, except the two men now grappling by the door. She yelled all the louder, "Mister! Who's paying for this champagne?"

"I'd say you are! You ordered it. You're drinking it."

Those were the final words in the matter, and Lawson was

dragged from the premises, like an errant schoolboy being led to the woodshed for his punishment.

The two men struggled against one another for almost a block before Lawson finally twisted free of the man's iron grip. But a second hold proved even more powerful, and Lawson Darrow soon found himself pinned hard and helpless against an alley wall.

"This won't do. I'm telling you, Lawson, it just won't do." The man pointed, almost pressing his finger into Lawson's eye.

"What do you want? Money? I can give you money." Lawson offered his bribe, hoping his assailant would simply take it and flee. But the man again held him by the collar and this time shook him violently.

"Don't be a fool! You have a family, a wife and three fine children, and you're not going to ruin them, no matter how intent you are on destroying yourself. Damnation, man, just look at you!"

A cold, heavy rain and the weak ambient light of the alley were hindrance enough to his senses, but the alcohol had thoroughly muddled his vision and thinking. Lawson became even more confused when every reach for his wallet was met by a hand that forced it back into his pocket.

"Take the money!" he insisted.

"This isn't a robbery. Believe me, I'm here to help."

Lawson closed his eyes tightly as he tried to muster some control of his faculties. It took time, but he eventually came to recognize the voice of Lowell Yancy.

"Yancy, why are you doing this?"

"I just told you why. You have a family, and I'm taking you home where you belong."

"Leave me be. There's no law against a man having a couple drinks."

"You were in for a lot more than drinks, whether you know it or not."

"So what! I found me a little friendly company. Anyway, what business is it of yours? I'm still not breaking the law."

Lowe released his grip. He was suddenly thrust to the other side of an argument he had defended for years. "For what you were about to do, I'd say the law is rather certain. Check with Silas Monk, if you don't believe me. He's got some pretty compelling points on the subject of adultery. Check with John Clark and his 'Good Book.' It's all there. Now, let's get you home to your wife."

He reached again for Lawson's arm, but this time Lawson pushed hard, sending Lowe to the ground. He yelled, "First, you stalk me through half the town. Then, you slip up behind me and start knocking me around. You got no call for doing that."

"Your family is worried about you."

"My family is my affair. I'm not going home just yet. You can run on back and tell my wife, if you want, or you can both go straight to hell. I really don't care. And if Annie resents my being out, she ought to come down here and say so herself. I don't need some would-be Pinkerton tailing my every move."

Lowe lifted himself from the ground. He was angry. "Your wife doesn't even know I'm out here, and she's never to know. Do you understand?"

"Just who the hell are you to say that to me? She's my wife. I'll say what I want to say, and if she sasses me, I'll up and bust her lip. Damn you, Lowe! I thought we were friends."

"Not tonight. Tonight, I'm Annie's friend. And if you ever threaten her again, if you ever harm her or any of those beautiful children, you'll answer to a side of me that a grizzly should fear. Hear me clear on this, Lawson. So help me, you are going to give up your drunken ways and become a respectable man for that family of yours. I don't know how you manage to keep a job under the curse of whiskey, but you won't keep a wife acting like you do."

"And just who's going to take her from me, you? I thought there was somebody else, and I should've known. It's been you and my Annie all along. That bitch!"

Lowe's arm shot so fast that his fist barely had time to close before it rocked against Lawson's cheekbone. The man reeled through the alley and back into the street, where he crumbled instantly in a sopping heap.

Lowe stood over him, ready and more than willing to deliver

a second lesson, if necessary. "No woman deserves that word, especially your Annie. You had best hear that real clear, as well."

Then, he bent down and grunted as he strained to lift Lawson's limp body to his shoulder. Wobbling under the extra weight, he began to make his way toward the railroad tracks. It was a loud Irish brogue that halted his slow progress up the hill.

"Hold right where ya are, mister! I feel obliged to ask some questions, seein' that long sack o' potatoes you been haulin' up ma street."

"And who are you?" Lowe asked.

"Shawn Hannigan. I'm with the local constabulary." The policeman displayed a silver badge.

"Well, you certainly have the right. Let me just set this 'sack o' potatoes' down, and I'll give you some answers."

"No, sir, ya just hold on to those potatoes. I wouldn't want them, or you, to run off quite yet."

Constable Hannigan walked up to Lowe and spun him around to better examine Lawson's face. "Now, what have we here? You haven't killed the poor bugger, have ya?"

"He's a friend," said Lowe.

"A friend, ya say. Well, I'll be. Some o' you boys sure have a strange way with those ya claim as close. I saw that fist ya laid upon the man, and it seemed none too friendly to me."

Hannigan lifted Lawson's eyelid and attempted to smell his breath. "Whew-wee! If he be a dead one, it would not be so from some common blow to the head. Ya no doubt poisoned this poor man. He smells more o' varnish than good whiskey, and that's a bloody shame. If nothin' else, I have in mind to arrest ya both for an extremely bad taste in spirits." The policeman walked in a tight circle around the two men, sizing them up with every step. "And your name is what?"

"Yancy, Lowe Yancy."

"And your sack o' potatoes?"

"Lawson Darrow."

"What's your business in these parts, Mr. Yancy?"

"I do survey work."

"For the Watoga Company, I assume. Right here in Devlin?"

"Yes, we are both employed by the mill. I work on contract and take jobs where I find them, which can be anywhere in this part of the state."

"And do ya expect to work tomorrow, Mr. Yancy?"

"Maybe, if I ever get home," Lowe complained.

"Now there's no need to sharpen your tongue. Have ya been drinkin' with your so-called friend here?"

"Nary a drop. I'm as sober as you are."

"Mr. Yancy, I am an Irishman. The alcohol runs with me blood. You can be twice as sober as the likes o' Hannigan, and still be a vagrant and a drunk and a menace on the public avenues. Our fair city may have to accommodate you and this sack o' potatoes for the remainder o' the evenin'. You can appeal, o' course, to his Highness, the magistrate, but with so busy a docket, I'd expect we'll enjoy your company through the jail's noon supper."

"Use his name, will you? Darrow is a decent man who's a bit down on his luck, and I intend to take him straight home, to that side of the tracks." Lowe was tired and defiant. He pointed to Briar Mountain. "He's got a wife and children up there, and they expect him back tonight. I refuse to let them down."

Hannigan approached, pushed his face up to Lowe's, and drew a deep breath. "Oh, ya do, do you? Ya refuse? Maybe the law will have somethin' to say about that." He took another breath.

"I already told you. I haven't been drinking," Lowe said firmly.

The policeman nodded in agreement. "You're clean, Mr. Yancy, just as ya say, and that is a rare occurrence for this little street. All right then, get on with you, sir. Deliver your package straight away and don't let me see you, or Mr. Lawson Darrow, for the rest o' this cold and rainy night." He added an afterthought, "And don't drop the poor lad. He's suffered enough. If his bride is anythin' like mine, he'll have bruises aplenty come mornin'!"

"I'm obliged," Lowe said. He grunted again as he looked up the long road through town and at the steep slope beyond.

Lawson had already begun to recover before Lowe reached the base of the mountain. It was a good thing, at least for the man who carried him, and Lowe was more than relieved when he finally heard the words, “Put me down!”

Still, leading a drunk to the very place he wants not to be proved an equally strenuous ordeal, and Lowe reconsidered the idea of just carrying the load. But Lawson protested vehemently, and Lowe, instead, continued to rely on his iron hand and a fierce persistence as he forced the man toward home. Finally, they were there, standing at the foot of the steps. The small house was quiet, and if not for the single lamp burning in the window, would have appeared vacant. Lowe wondered if it was.

He braced Lawson, then, cautiously backed away. The man teetered on the spot, but had regained just enough of his coordination to counter what looked to be a certain fall.

“That’s good,” said Lowe. “Now, fix your sorry self up. We don’t want to worry the woman unduly.”

Lawson continued to sway, and Lowe steadied him. In a soft voice, he finished what he had to say, “Look here, Lawson, don’t make more of this than there is. I waited for you at the Lodge only to get permission to hire your son for another trip into the mountains. Annie already agreed, but I wanted to offer the courtesy owed you. You won’t remember tomorrow, and frankly, I don’t care.” As before, he carefully backed away.

“Take him. Take them all,” Lawson mumbled a reply, much to Lowe’s surprise. He placed two hands on the stair rail and began to pull himself upward. The floor creaked, the door squeaked and, in a moment later, he was safely home.

Lowe again was alone in the drizzle. He watched through a window as another lamp began to glow from across the room and as Annie appeared before her husband. He saw her chestnut hair, tousled and curled across the shoulders of her gown. He saw the yellow light that warmed the pale rose of her cheeks. She was quite beautiful, even in the late of night, when all appearance unavoidably falls unguarded or forsaken.

Annie came to Lawson and held him close. They never spoke. Lowe turned slowly and went his way.

# CHAPTER 11

Lusuci was worth more, far more, than four bottles of low-grade hooch, and she deserved much better than just a farewell slap on the rump. But, for some, the want of whiskey burned like a killing fever, one where men might trade their very souls for the remedy. In light of this, Luci was but a small price to pay for relief. The pleasure she brought to men could not measure against their more iniquitous pursuits, and she was easily and often forsaken by those she had come to trust.

Luci had lived her whole life as chattel, being passed from one brute to another. Her only possession was an ungenerous fate which often denied her the next meal or a sheltered bed. However, this time seemed different. This time, her intuition sent her willingly and warmly into the hands of the old gentleman, who just wanted something to love.

Silas squatted to take a better look, and Luci stood obediently still. He massaged her floppy ears, felt for ticks and then pulled on her long upper lip to inspect her teeth. His hand was instantly covered with saliva, but he took no notice as he went on to stroke her head and neck. Her tail wagged approvingly.

She was in fine shape, lean and fiery, and was no doubt a hunter. Almost purebred, she showed the lines of her bloodhound sire, but whatever else was in the mix would remain a mystery. Her lineage made little difference to Silas.

“So, ya got yer whiskey. Anythin’ else ya be wantin’?” he asked the man, almost rudely. Silas had little regard for anyone who could not appreciate such a magnificent animal.

“Maybe it ain’t enough,” the man replied, seeing the immediate attachment between Silas and the dog.

"Oh, it's 'nough. Ya got the deal ya made. Best ya move on before the night sets in."

The man was prepared to renege and placed the bottles down on the ground. "She'll cost you double, and that's still a bargain." He commanded Luci, "Come here, Lucifer! Come!" He was stern and threatening. "Come, Luci!" He slapped his hands loudly and the dog winced. Luci froze for a moment, then, paced nervously in a tight circle around Silas.

"I said, 'Come'!" the man again commanded. Luci trembled with confusion. She cowered, but moved no closer to her previous master.

"Lucifer?" Silas questioned. "What the hell kind o' name is that fer a sweet girl like this'n? I hope ya bit the bastard that saddled ya with such a sorry handle." He again rubbed the dog behind her ears, and she settled by his side. "Like I said, mister, ya best be movin' on." He pointed to the whiskey. "And take all that with ya when ya go, so ya cain't be tellin' folks I cheated ya."

"But you are a cheat, old man. Now give me back my dog!" The man was determined to have his way and took a dangerous step toward the aging woodsman. Silas held his ground with an almost cocky defiance, as if to encourage a scuffle, and the man faltered in surprise. Then, he dared a second and third step.

Too old for a real fight, Silas reached for the axe on his chopping block, and without hesitation, he heaved it 40 feet, end over end, past the ear of his assailant and into the dead center of a half-hewn log. The blade buried in the wood with a thud, and the hickory handle rang like a tuning fork.

"Wanna see it again?" Silas goaded, as two hands lifted a broad axe used for squaring timbers. "I rarely miss. Been throwin' tools all my life. It seems like I was born petulant and ne'er grew out o' it. Temper and tools, I throw one and the other goes a flyin' as well."

The man took one look at the acute, hand-filed edge on the big axe and another at the person holding it. He decided it best to respect them both. He yanked up his bottles, and when he was beyond the range of Silas' arm, he cursed loudly until he was long out of sight. Silas beamed with satisfaction.

"Ya know, girl, I didn't cotton to that feller from the first. I'm glad I filled them jugs from a sour batch. He won't know what hit 'im. Well, let's jist rustle up some grub, and then I'll show ya around the place."

The two walked side by side to the cabin, Luci's tail wagging at the mere sound of the old man's voice.

The dog was a welcomed addition to the small survey party as it loaded on the train and headed into the mountains toward Camp 7. She had spirit, the kind that was contagious, and everyone was more alive just being in her presence. She must have known this, because she dispensed her affections evenly, passing from Silas to Morgan to Black Jack to Lowe and then back again to Silas. A kind word and a soothing scratch was her customary reward, which she gratefully collected at every opportunity.

The pack animals felt otherwise. While Blu was indifferent to the newcomer, Noggin came to understand why she was named Lucifer. She would track him when he wandered and prod him when he stalled. She could bark as loud as Silas Monk, but unlike the old man, her bite was real. She would nip just hard enough to push Noggin to compliance. If he kicked, she leapt away. If he ran, she raced faster. If he hid...well, he could not hide from the devil, especially one with bloodhound senses. To Noggin, Luci was Lucifer. To Silas and the other men, she was the best a companion could be.

Luci let her tongue trail in the air as the flat car clanked slowly up the grade. She tottered with every sway and jerk, while the others huddled against the coolness of the autumn. By the time they reached the camp, they were nearly numb. They unloaded their gear and scrambled to the mess hall, where Cookie's hot lunch and the pot belly stoves would work to restore their warmth. Then they moved on, with a half day's light still left to burn.

It was a long walk, but much less difficult than what they expected. They had passed that way only weeks earlier, but the fall climate proved much more merciful than the heat of August. And the rail line had been extended, which made the passage easier, with or without a train. The men were again greeted by the fellers and haulers and diggers they happened to meet, and they marveled at the rapid efficiency of their work. The forest had slipped farther and farther away under a relentless pace to harvest wood. The wilderness was shrinking to oblivion.

It could be a threatening sight to those not directly involved with the business, and the surveyors were comforted but little when they finally reached a thick, untouched stand of trees. They moved steadily through the forest, hoping to leave the ugly effects of logging as far from their feet and minds as possible.

Morgan was troubled by the devastation which dominated the once green landscape, but the rutted slopes, laden by a sea of mangled branches and limbless logs, were just another reality of his world. He was more disturbed by what he had left behind in Devlin and was pleased to be away, far away from school drudgery and family squabbles, far from Sadie's smothering affection and even far from Sarah, who somehow remained blind to the obvious truth of his steadfast adoration. He vowed not to ponder these things and found work to be an effective distraction. He sensed his kindred place among the men and animals, who, just months earlier, were complete strangers to him. Their camaraderie and banter were a panacea for his ills, and he cherished every moment of the journey.

"Say, did I e'er tell you fellers 'bout the time I marched with ol' Armistead across the plains o' hell?" Silas asked, breaking a trance that had settled as they hiked the miles without break.

"You mean Gettysburg?" Lowe tried to clarify.

"Yup."

"Back in '63?"

"Yup, it were '63 and a time to recollect. The cream o' all Virginia flowed that day, like a wave, right smack dab into the face o' them Yankee devils."

"You were cream?" Lowe mocked.

"Yup, I was. I was thar amongst 'em."

Black Jack interjected, "Who is dis Armistead?"

"The general."

"I thought de name o' dat fella were Pickett. Least wise, dat be his name each time you tells us de same old tale. Just which o' dem generals was it?"

Silas was indignant. "Both, ya blamed fool. An army has more'n one general. Now, you folks wanna hear my story or don't ya?"

The answer came in unison, "No!"

"Hmmph! The hell ya say!" Silas grunted at their disrespect, and then looked to Morgan for reassurance. "How 'bout you, son? I know how you school boys enjoy yer history."

Morgan was quiet, which was the exact invitation Silas had sought. He went on with his story.

"It were an ugly fight, fierce and hateful mean. Them cannon got so hot they was glowin', but our boys kept lobbin' metal into them heathen lines, hopin' to break 'em before we got thar. But, wouldn't ya know...."

Morgan finally spoke up. "Actually, Mr. Monk, I do recall hearing this the last time we were out." The old man frowned, and Morgan immediately changed his tack. "But, a great tale like Gettysburg can't be heard too often, can it? Do go on. Please."

And Silas did. He went on and on and on, while Lowe and Black Jack stepped lively with a mule, a horse and a dog, all marching close in quick retreat.

Black Jack was anxious to make the meadow before dusk, and once there, he slipped away from the camp chores to fish the beaver pond. The tents went up without him, and by the time a good fire was raging, he had returned with 10 fat brook trout. No one accused him of shirking.

The men gathered close to the flames as the night grew cold and damp. There was a starless sky and dead air as a winter front edged toward the east.

"What we gonna do if dis storm hits, Mr. Yancy?" Black Jack queried, not really concerned.

"It wouldn't be our first. It's never too bad this early in the season. We can ride it out right here if we have to. Frankly, I'd rather have the snow. Fall rains are so damned cold."

"Dey cuts right through you, sure enough. Weather willin', where we settin' up in de mornin'? Seems like we finished surveyin' de ground around dese parts. You ain't never said."

Lowe pointed to the mountaintop, which was now consumed by a total darkness. "Yonder. The contract indicates a property just over the ridge. It's 300 acres, more or less. We'll take everything with us and make the climb in the morning."

"You was just up dat way, wasn't you?" Black Jack asked with a hint of suspicion.

"Yeah, somewhere up there." Lowe rose to his feet to avoid further questions that might lead to speculation. He walked over to the animals and began to secure them for the night.

When Morgan offered to assist, Black Jack excused him, "No, boy, you and Mr. Monk head on to de sack. It be gettin' cooler by de minute, and we got us a steep walk in de mornin'. I'll help Mr. Yancy. We be along directly."

Black Jack grabbed some oats and passed a handful each to Blu and Noggin. Lowe set the tethers.

"Now, what dis all about, Lowe?"

Lowe looked up blankly, and Black Jack continued to press him, "I know dere ain't no contract, so what dis all about? We ain't here freezin' in dese woods for nothin'."

Lowe stood close to his friend. "You're right. We don't have a contract, but this one's going to be on me. It won't cost you a dime. You'll understand everything tomorrow, and that much I promise. But the others are not to know. Can I trust you to keep this quiet? Will you trust me?"

Black Jack was somewhat shaken. His concern was never about the money, but it was all about the trust. Lowe should have known that. Never before had Lowell Yancy concealed his business affairs from his partner, and never before had he questioned their utter confidence in one another. If not intentional, it was still a hurtful lapse in judgment.

Black Jack replied, "Yes, if after all dis time, you requires an answer."

"Good. I should have confided sooner, but there were reasons. You'll understand before too long."

"No more needs be said, Mr. Yancy."

Lowe thought before he spoke further, uncertain as to how much should be disclosed. He again pointed into the blackness. "There's a hill right there, buried in the night, and hidden beyond is nothing less than paradise, a wonderment beyond all comprehension. Yes, Jack, just trust me."

Black Jack was instantly intrigued by Lowe's cryptic way and suddenly reborn with a new excitement and curiosity. However, he would not probe further. Lowe had revealed little, but it was enough.

Luci paced along the base of the cliff, sniffing as she went. At times she stretched her forelegs high against the wall and scratched, as though trying to climb. She barked and then paced some more.

"She's on the scent o' some varmint!" Silas exclaimed. "I knew that girl was a hunter."

The group rested where they were and watched as the dog repeated her motions. She was frustrated by the granite barrier and by the continued slow progress of the others. She beckoned them to come. There was much to explore.

"Yessa, she on de trail o' somethin'. I never seen such jitter in a dog. Look at her go. For sure, she smells a critter up in dem rocks." Black Jack was amazed.

Lowe walked over to Luci and tried to quiet her, but the dog was far too agitated. He scanned the cracks along the cliff, but nothing stirred. He shrugged. "With her nose, whatever it is could be miles from here."

The dust beneath the wall was embossed with animal tracks, the area below the escarpment being a natural corridor for wildlife. Most of the prints were Luci's. Some were of deer that passed the previous evening on their way down to the valley, and others were from a solitary raccoon just foraging the hillside.

It was Lowe's nature to spot animal sign. He had done so all his life, and the tracks at his feet were recognizable with only a glance. Luci had nearly obliterated the rest, but still, Lowe checked the ground for whatever he could find. He walked only a few short steps further along the wall, and then stopped and stooped.

There before him was an unusual print, similar to the hound's but devoid of claw marks. Canines show distinctive claw marks. Lowe placed his hand next to the print. It was bigger - much, much bigger. He was compelled by disbelief to measure again. He even examined the breadth of Luci's paw, just for the comparison. She was no small dog.

Lowe paled in the instant. While he had never encountered such an animal, he knew beyond doubt what had pressed the large indentation into the soft, dry dirt, and he knew full well what to expect if it chose to abandon its concealment to strike an unwary prey. He looked at his men, at the pack animals and at the curious creature that was still barking and busy pursuing the scent. They could be quarry. They all could be quarry to what may be crouching silently among the rocks.

Lowe cried an immediate warning, "Ready your weapons, boys! Luci's found us a cat."

"Ya mean a bobcat?" Silas shouted back.

"No, I mean a mountain lion!"

"Holy Sweet Jesus!" Silas exclaimed and moved closer to see the prints for himself. Black Jack and Morgan went fumbling through the packs for guns and scrambled to join the others.

"No wonder she's been so antsy," said Morgan, observing the fresh lion track. "She's probably never seen anything like this. Neither have I, for that matter."

"And neither have I," responded Lowe. "There can't be many big cats around these parts, and those that are must stay pretty much in the backwoods. I guess that's exactly where we are, the backwoods." He and the others looked nervously at the rock ledge above them. The cat could be long gone or, just as likely, held up on some hidden shelf planning its next move.

Silas reached into his memory. "I seen a few back in the ol' days, most already shot and skinned. By God, I thought they was all gone. I'd sure love to see this'n." The old trapper was warmed by his wistful sentiment. Man and lion, they were both remnants of a bygone age.

"Well, Silas, you're probably the only one. I'm not easy about this at all. We need to stay on our guard. Watch Noggin and Blu. Keep that dog close." Lowe opened the cylinder of his pistol and checked for bullets. He handed the gun to Morgan. "This won't help much, I'm afraid. I doubt that cougar will show itself, but if it does, he's up to no good. You know how to shoot, don't you?

"Yes, sir."

"Good. Aim for its shoulders. Try to slow it down." He then checked the rifle as well. "I'll keep this one handy, just in case."

Lowe took some time to really examine the cliffs and the trees. He followed the tracks until they disappeared at a break in the wall. He then noticed the pack animals. They were calm. Even Luci had lost her interest in the scent, searching more for the attention of the men gathered about her. The alarm was over.

"Rest easy. I think the cat's moved on, at least for now," Lowe concluded. "Why don't we do the same? We can climb the cliff here."

Morgan grasped the rock for support as he took the lead up the narrow trail that ascended the crag. His palm turned black from the touch, and he paused only a moment to determine the cause. Portions of the cliff had been painted with soot, and many of the larger trees were scarred from fire. Fire was an uncommon occurrence, but a natural one that would periodically sweep the steep slopes of their litter. He cleaned his hand against his britches and, without further thought, took long strides to mount the escarpment. Lowe was not far behind.

"So, this is what it's like," Lowe mumbled to himself.

"What's that?" asked Morgan.

"Oh, the last time I saw this place, it was covered in fog." He looked across the narrow plateau for landmarks. There were the gnarly trees, left deformed and dwarfed by a constant wind, and the boulders erect like statuary. There were the vast granite floors, devoid of soil and pocked with basins of rainwater, and the thin grassy plains that laced the open ridge. Yes, it was all there, exactly as he imagined it to be, strangely beautiful, yet inexplicably foreboding. Like a boy alone in a burial ground, he sensed an indefinable spirit watching and waiting and warning. Lowe tried, but could not distinguish it.

"This place is kind of barren," said Morgan, "and eerie."

"That it is, but give it time. We have lots to see." Lowe strode to the edge of the cliff and looked for Silas and Black Jack. They were not there. The climb was difficult, and for different reasons, both men had been forced to stop and catch their breath. Black Jack held his side where the wounds were not yet healed.

"You fellows okay down there?" Lowe called to them, still unable to see either man as they leaned against the rocks.

"Yup, we'll be right along," shouted Silas in response. "But ya best watch out fer that mule!"

Suddenly, a huge animal rushed up the trail, and Lowe dove to avoid disaster. He rolled across the ground and without stopping, sprung back to his feet, bringing his rifle to bear. His horse rumbled up behind and both halted at the urging of a screaming dog.

"I nearly shot the poor mule, thinking of that lion!" Lowe cursed. Luci was barking a litany of commands, and Noggin, already turned and restless, kicked dirt in her face.

Seconds later, Silas appeared with a sheepish grin. "Sorry 'bout that, boys. Ol' Noggin gave me the slip and Blu took up after 'im. We tried lockin' on to their tails, lookin' fer some help up that steep path, but the ornery beasts wanted no part of it. They shot up one way, and we fell back the other. I reckon ya knows the rest."

"No damage done," replied Lowe. "Luci seems to have things under control, even if you don't." Lowe gave Luci a deserved pat. "You're a good dog, girl."

Daylight was in short supply that season of the year, and the crew had little time to accomplish more than making camp. It was a good site with grass and water for the stock and wide flats for the pitching of tents. When the sun dropped, the men again migrated to the fire. Lowe began the conversation.

"I don't hold much with the stories you hear sometimes. Legends have a way of growing until there's nothing even reminiscent of truth. But, sometimes, when I'm out here in the woods, especially these woods, I can't help but think of that Indian boy lost in the fire. I find myself in his place, and I wonder. What if it was me? What would I have done?"

Everyone thought for a moment, reviewing in silence the ancient tale of the Shawnee warrior. It had been carried on the lips of the generations, and over the span of time, it remained unaltered like the mountains themselves. The men knew every detail to the word. It was their story to present like a gift, as their parents and their parents' parents had passed it on before. It was local and relevant to a hard life in the hills, and many would ponder its validity as they gazed along the high ridges that darkened with the closing of the day.

Lowe continued, "It's hard to imagine a fire you can't outrun, but you hear of them. The flames ride the wind right through the tree tops, and when that happens, a man can only hope to hide. What was it again that trapped that Indian boy?"

Silas ventured an answer, "The mountain. He ran clear up the hillside chokin' smoke with that fire singein' the hairs off 'is ass. Them Injun boys could run, but it weren't 'nough to save 'im."

"Yes, I guess that was it. He couldn't quite get up the mountain."

"No, dere were more to dat struggle dan just mountain," Black Jack was quick to correct the others. "He climb dat big hill all right, but dem pines toward de top got to burnin' so fast dat he plum run out o' juice to go on further."

"But he did go further, didn't he? Think about it. There was something else."

"A cliff?" Morgan responded this time, already taking interest in where Lowe was leading.

"Yeah, I think there was a cliff, the Shawnee Scarp. And if I recollect clearly, it was a pretty sheer wall that supposedly blocked his way while the fire closed in. So... where did he go?"

The group was again quiet, contemplating both the story and Lowe's unusual interest in such a child's tale. Time passed without response.

Lowe asked again, "So, where did he go?"

"Why the hell do ya even care? This here yarn's 'bout as lame as most city folk. Git on with yer point, if ya got one to make." Silas was as impatient as he was curious and confused.

"I'm making my point. And some would agree with you, Silas, about the legend. There may not be a lick of truth to any of this."

"I don't agree!" exclaimed Morgan. His eyes widened suddenly as his mind uncovered the treasure. "I think I know just where he went. He climbed that cliff to the rocks at the top. He found the pools of water, where the flames couldn't burn him. That's it! And then, he went out among the giant trees to be healed."

"Healed? Thar weren't no healin' in the story. That Injun cashed it all in right thar on the rock. You young fellers are always lookin' fer a happy endin'," Silas countered gruffly. "That ain't the way o' life."

"I reckon we've heard it told both ways, haven't we?" Lowe tried to mollify both sides before a real argument could ensue.

Morgan had no intention to debate. He was enthralled. "Why, I've seen signs of fire all over this place! And look -- look at this rock! The whole place is just one big rock, and there are little pools everywhere. Are you saying we found it?"

Lowe chose to not respond. He just looked Morgan in the eye and winked.

"This is it, the place. This is the Shawnee Scarp!" Morgan rose to his feet and spun in all directions, squinting past the fire glow and into the screen of darkness. "But where are the trees? There has to be big trees!"

Silas was the skeptic. "Scarp, hell! Son, it jist ain't prudent to believe everythin' ya hear. It were all a long, long time ago, if it e'er did happen. If this be the place o' such tales, which I ain't sayin' it is, them trees is bound to be dust by now." He looked straight faced at Lowe and shook his head. "Now look what ya started with yer fool notions."

Morgan settled momentarily to reconsider. "You're probably right, but still, this could be the place, couldn't it?"

"Maybe is. Maybe ain't. How ya e'er gonna know such things fer certain? Mr. Yancy ought not fill ya with such cock and bull nonsense."

Lowe refused to defend himself and listened while the discussion unraveled.

Black Jack smiled, remembering well what his friend had told him about paradise. "I reckon you gonna be wrong dis time, Mr. Monk. Come de risin' sun, I 'spect we'll find us dose trees. Praise de Lord! I think dey out dere." He looked to Lowe for affirmation, but the man still would not respond.

Morgan could hardly contain his enthusiasm and pulled back from the light in the hope of seeing his trees. But the night was not revealing any secrets.

"I'll be back after a while," he said, and started out into the darkness.

"Whoa, now! Where are you going?" Lowe asked, with a sense of alarm.

"Just to look around."

The three older men laughed. Patience was not a virtue of youth, nor was good judgment.

"Come on back here, son. Have yerself a seat," said Silas. He patted a spot on the log beside him, and Morgan reluctantly returned. The old man raised a hand. "Now, o'er here we got us a cliff jist awaitin' to break yer neck. And out thar's a beast prowlin' and droolin' gallons fer a good long chew on some boy's juicy innards. And o'er yonder is a black hole we ain't even seen as yet. So, tell us again where yer headed."

Morgan got the point. "To bed?"

"That's a sound direction, and take that pistol along with ya when ya go. It'll add some comfort on a night like this'n." Silas slapped Morgan on the back. "I'll be headin' fer the mat myself, so keep to yer own side o' the tent."

Lowe cautioned the old man, "Before you go, you might want

to tie up that dog. If the lion's still in these parts, Luci may take out after it. I've got some rope over in the packs."

"Thank ya anyway, Lowe, but I leashed my last dog years ago. I once had me a big mutt that chased after stars, and I liked to ne'er git 'im back when he'd run. One night I had me a bright idee to give 'im some lead and cinch 'im to my leg, thinkin' o'course that the rope would keep 'im put."

"Yeah, what happened to him?"

"Well, I'll jist tell ya what happened. That fool animal caught scent of a polecat down the hill and dragged me to kingdom come before he and the skunk went at it. The skunk won. Me and the dog suffered fer days. No, I don't use the leash no more. Luci'll jist have to show some common sense when it comes to mountain lions."

"Suit yourself. I hope she does," Lowe responded. He was much too tired to argue. "I'm turning in, too. It's been a good day, boys. I'll see you tomorrow."

Black Jack yawned. "I reckon tomorrow be even better dan today. De Lord been busy in dese woods, and I, for one, is ready to see dem big trees he planted." He pulled the collar of his heavy coat close around his neck, and then, slipped away from the fire to have a closer talk with God. He went into the darkness alone.

The roar of a caged lion will shake the nerves of even the most intrepid. Greater then is the horror at the cry of the cougar, free and wary, prowling through the black of night for a kill.

Needless to say, Morgan could not sleep. At first it was the legend. His mind raced a mile a minute thinking about the discovery. If the story was true and Lowe was correct about the place, there would be incredible finds come morning. He had dreamed of some monolithic forest, where enormous trees were anchored deep in the fragile, fertile earth. Unseen and untrodden, the woods would have incomparable balance and beauty.

From the banks of the mill pond, he had often witnessed the unloading of giant timbers only to be told of better ones, most of which remained concealed in remote pockets high in the Big Timber.

Magnificent logs, he was captivated by every one of them, but the larger the cut the more he wished he could have stood in the shade of the living tree. Perhaps tomorrow might grant that wish.

The men buried their faces as they nestled into the warm bedrolls, and not so much as a breath could be heard. In the dead quiet, Morgan's thoughts wandered through the sides of his tent to the hidden lair of the mountain lion. Where was that cougar? Was it gone, or was it waiting in the cover of the night for the first man who would dare show himself? Sooner or later nature would call, and someone would have to venture to the privacy of the bushes. The cat could pounce and drag a body over that cliff before the others could even doff their blankets. It was an unsettling feeling, and he was thankful for the seeming security of the thin canvas walls.

In reality the tent provided no refuge, and the revolver beneath his makeshift pillow gave little more. Encouragement came from his sleeping comrades, who knew well the creatures of the forest. Their peace was his comfort, and if that was not adequate, Luci and the pack animals would certainly give the necessary alarm. Nonetheless, while others rested, Morgan kept his vigil.

The minutes passed like hours, as Morgan strained to hear anything that moved. He lay upon his back with the intention of keeping both ears uncovered, but despite the poking lumps and bumps from beneath his bedroll, his eyelids still were much too heavy to bear. He dozed, only to reawaken time and again from the crack of twigs beneath the feet of the animals or from the rustles and snorts of the men in their slumber.

Then he heard it, a near indiscernible growl just to the outside of his tent and mere inches from the head of Silas Monk. He froze with fear. Like a rabbit hiding in the open grass as the red fox neared, he dared not move until his stalker moved, lest he reveal his vulnerability. He froze with an instinct to become invisible. Maybe the cougar would lose its interest and travel on.

But it did not. It sniffed and purred and grunted and growled again and again, and it lingered over Silas like a ghoul. Without adjusting his head, Morgan looked for the hound that was warmly curled at the base of his feet. How could she not hear this? And the horse and mule, how could they not fear what he now feared? The stealth of the lion was much greater than he ever imagined. And now, now that it was so close, Morgan prayed that even the animals would continue sleeping. A startling response from any in the camp could mean death for others.

Again, there was a sound, an almost guttural groan that brought chills and sweat in the same moment. Morgan's hands tensed by his side, nowhere near the loaded weapon. He wanted to warn the old man of the danger, but could not bring himself to break the silence. His every sense was acute as he focused on the intruder. The lion would not move, and Morgan knew, that at some point, he would have to.

His heart pounded so hard that he was sure the beast would detect it. He slowly drew his hand along his chest and over his shoulder until he finally found the pistol. His thumb cocked the hammer with a click. The growling stopped.

"What ya doin', boy? Put that thing away," Silas mumbled, without changing his position.

Morgan tried to listen for any movement outside the tent, but everything had become still. "I thought I heard something."

"Yeah, somethin' worth killin'?" muttered the old man.

Still trying to be invisible, Morgan wanted to shush him. "I thought it was the mountain lion. It was right there above your head."

Silas rolled without opening his eyes. "Then I'm sure glad ya didn't shoot. Ya might've missed." He squirmed trying to remold his body to the hard ground, and when comfortably situated, he fell quickly back to sleep.

Morgan sat up. He was dumbfounded by the old man's lack of concern. He heard what he heard, and what he heard was extremely dangerous. He waited and listened and all the while searched his tired mind for an explanation, but neither sounds nor reasoning were forthcoming. Strangely, the threat seemed over. The cougar, or ghoul, or whatever it was had vanished. Even the dog still slept. He needed to do the same.

Silas sniffled once and his mouth fell open as his slumber deepened. Then, he twitched and grunted and snored and purred, and all the growls resumed. Morgan laid the gun at his feet and settled into the softness of his bedding. He was now red-eyed, red-faced, and ready to sleep. He looked at the old man comfortably curled on the ground. Come morning, Silas might well have forgotten their brief conversation. The boy could only hope.

The sky may have been a gloomy gray, but the ground was white. A couple inches of snow had collected on everything not made of rock, and Lowe awakened shortly after dawn to a view of wonderland. The snowflakes, wet and wide, landed like tiny doilies on a tea table and melted against the still warm stone beneath his feet. It was the first snow, always the best, always the most magical.

The air was pure and clean and welcoming, and Lowe drew a deep, satisfying breath. His vapors tumbled on the cold as he exhaled. The squall would not last long, he thought, but while it did, the mountain would be transformed. He was eager to experience it. He hurriedly placed some sticks on the few remaining embers of the camp fire and set out to be awed by the winter and the wild.

Black Jack and Silas smartly stayed in their tents until the fire was raging. They, too, were surprised by the snow when they threw open the flaps, but went on quietly about their chores as though they were starting a new spring day. They had fed the animals and heated the water for coffee before either uttered a word.

"Lordy, what a mornin'," said Black Jack softly.

"What ya whisperin' fer?" Silas replied.

"Young Morgan. Looks to me he still be restin'."

"Yup, out colder than a match in a mire. I reckon the boy stayed up half the night listenin' fer that big cat."

"I heard me some noises off and on, but none so loud as to rouse dis achy body from its peace. Could you hear dat lion yo self?" Black Jack asked, wondering if he missed something.

"What's that ya say?"

"Dat mountain lion...did you hear it?"

"Nah, the evenin' passed right quiet like. I napped like a sucklin' lamb jist off the teat. Didn't hear a blame thing and wouldn't cared if I did. Ain't that right, Luci?" The hound was up and raring to go, her nose already white from a romp in the snow. She nipped at the flakes as they drifted down.

"Well, dere ain't much in de way o' sign around here. A cat would sure enough leave its mark in dis snow."

"That don't mean nothin'. Could be a critter or two passed through before this blizzard even commenced. O' course, if they did, my Luci would've taken 'er notice."

"I been told dem lions move like ghosts," said Black Jack.

"More like air, I'd say. Trust me. That cat's a fer piece down the hill by now, or this girl would've been yelpin' on the hunt of 'er life."

Accolades were not enough to hold Luci's attention, and since breakfast did not seem forthcoming, she left the camp to follow the only prints she saw. They were boot prints, and before long she was with Lowe, sitting on a large root of a white oak tree.

Black Jack wasted little time in following the hound. He knew what might be ahead of him and was more than anxious to catch up to his partner. As he disappeared into the curtain of snow, Silas called out.

"Hold on. Hold on! These ol' legs ain't what they used to be, and damn my eyes, I cain't see nothin' in all this brightness."

Black Jack waited and the two made their way toward Lowe together.

"Good Lord o' mercy!" Silas exclaimed when he came upon the magnificent tree. "Ain't this'n a beauty to behold." He walked to the massive trunk and put his hands on the rough bark. He looked small and insignificant against the girth of the tree.

"Amen," replied Black Jack. "Amen." He reached down to an enormous limb that skirted the ground and raked back the snow. Then, he sat and marveled as he tried in vain to absorb the miracle before him. Through the depth of time, there could never have been a more perfect trophy of creation. He was forced to squint to barely discern even the middle of the huge sprawling crown, the top branches being hidden behind the glare of snow.

"So, dis be yo paradise, eh, Mr. Yancy? Dis what you brought us here to see?" Black Jack asked, knowing in his heart there could be nothing finer in all of nature. "It takes de Master to craft de mighty oak. All along de Lord's been hidin' dis here tree for dis here mornin'. And why? So we be de ones to first see and sing his praise. We's honored, Lord. We's humbled, and we thank you for dis precious gift."

"I'll send up a big 'hallelujah' to that," said Silas.

"Yeah, there's a divine hand at work here," Lowe agreed. "She's an old one, but she's got to be the most beautiful lady that ever graced a woodland."

Luci had no time for homage. She raced around the tree and under the branches at such speeds that her legs slipped at almost every turn and left her rolling with pleasure. She shook to rid her coat of the whiteness, but with every tumble, she came up frostier than before. Unlike the men, she sought nothing but the freshness of the snow.

It was the silence of the camp that finally woke Morgan, and while groggy at first, he was soon filled with new energy and anticipation. He immediately saw the tracks that led across the dome and started in pursuit of his friends, pausing for only one second to note the absence of cougar signs around his tent. He paused again as he came upon the vague silhouette of a giant tree, clouded by the driven snow and towering high above the open ridge. He could see very little and could hear even less. Everything was absolutely still, everything except a steady downward drift of delicate wintery motes.

He cried out, "Mr. Yancy!"

The response was immediate, "We're here, Morgan! Over here."

Morgan looked upon the silhouette and felt the tiny crystals melt against his face and hands. He moved slowly, watching the tree gain sharper form and color, watching for whatever else might lay hidden beyond the wall of white. Like the others, he was captured by the wonder of it all.

The blizzard kept the men at camp for most of the day, spending their time preparing better shelter against the elements. The tents were cleared of the weighty snow, and a large tarp was erected by the fire as a common area. They swept the ground as best they could and brought in logs as seats. They even lashed limbs together for a makeshift table and constructed a stone stove for cooking and extra heat, using the coals of the larger, outer campfire. From a preponderance of nearby rocks, they built a short length of wall, and spruce boughs were cut and snow mounds were molded to serve as additional windbreaks. It was rustic innovation at its best, and when they felt protected against the wet and cold, they turned to checkers and Gin rummy to pass the hours. They ate and talked and worked and played continuously, content to be at peace with the unrelenting storm.

Lowe was wrong about the squall. By the time the clouds began to break, it was the edge of night and there were eight inches of snow across the mountaintop. The falling flakes were faint and few, but it was too late, too dark to venture over uncertain ground. The men turned in early, hopeful that the morrow would be one of even greater discovery. They would not have to wait for morning.

Luci heard it first. Her ears perked and her eyes widened at the one sound that could not be silenced by the blanket of snow. She growled, and before Silas could free himself from his twisted bedroll, she bolted from the tent and bounded toward the distant bawling of the lion. Her yelps were piercing as she darted with determination among the rocks above the cliff, but in the short time it took for the astonished men to gather, the baying had become almost indiscernible.

"Stop 'er! That pup's out to git 'erself flayed, if she gits away!" Silas cried out.

"Gets away? She gone, Mr. Monk. Dere aint nothin' gonna stop dat hound from runnin'." Black Jack stated the obvious.

Silas cursed as he struggled to jam his foot into a cold boot, "Damn these ol' shoes!" He pulled hard and the boot finally slipped over his tattered sock. "And damn me fer not puttin' a rope on my Luci! You was right, Lowe. I should've kept 'er tied."

"Don't blame yourself for that, Silas. You can't cage a dog forever, like a lot of folk do. You either run them or you break their spirit. Luci was sure to take out on her own come one chance or another."

"Well, she's gone now, and I reckon I got no choice but to try and fetch 'er. That cat's fightin' on 'is home ground and my Luci ain't got a prayer o' bestin' it."

"She's got better odds against that lion than you've got traipsing across this ridge when it's dark and icy," Lowe cautioned the old man.

"I got fresh tracks, and they'll show plenty good in this snow. I don't need no daylight."

"Silas, I know you can find her, but she's a half mile away already. And the cat's gone twice that distance, no doubt. It'll keep running unless Luci corners it, and I reckon it takes more than one lone hound dog to corner a wildcat. She'll head back to us when she tires."

"When she tires, that cat'll take 'er. If the wind kicks up a good blow tonight, I'll lose both them tracks and a right fine animal."

"Maybe so, but what happens when those tracks carry you over the cliff, or when some wounded mountain lion suddenly lunges at you? What will you do then? Listen, your Luci's far more fit for this detail than any of us. If you head out there, someone's getting hurt."

"I weren't born jist yesterday, Lowe, and I learned me a thing or two 'bout these woods. Hand me my rifle. I'm goin'."

Lowe knew he was right to discourage Silas, but he also knew that Silas could never be dissuaded from retrieving his dog. He may have entered his elder years, but he showed a heart and gumption and conviction that younger men only pretended to have. To hold him back, even for his own protection, would be like caging the hound. Lowe would never break his spirit.

"Well, then, if I can't convince you, we'll both go." Lowe checked his weapons and grabbed a knapsack with a few provisions and water. "Black Jack, can you do something to calm those animals?"

The pack animals were clearly agitated. They had slipped the horse blankets Morgan had placed over them and were now threatening to pull free of the tie line. In their state of fear, there was no telling how they might react once free of the tethers. It could be a deadly consequence considering the weather and the nearby escarpments.

"I's aimin' to go with you, Mr. Yancy. Three's a might safer dan two."

"But someone needs to stay with the stock. I'd feel more comfortable with one of us being here."

"You right about dat. I'll stay, but you take Morgan along in case somethin' happen."

The three men traded the comfort of camp for the perils of night without further hesitation or faintness of resolve. It was a fool's mission to save the dog. Luci had set out to do exactly what she was bred and trained to do. She was more adept at the chase and the fight than all of her rescuers, and nature alone would determine her fate against the lion. But, nevertheless, the burden of the search was now theirs. They stepped cautiously along a line of tracks that drew them closer and closer to the treacherous brink.

There was little hope of finding Luci, unless Luci found them first. They knew that, to a man, but also knew that a friend was in danger. To Silas, Luci may well be the last true companion of his life. She had come to him from nowhere, and he would not have her return there without at least trying to bring her back. As Silas loved his dog, so was he loved by Lowell Yancy, who had come to think of him as a father, and by Morgan Darrow, who was completely enthralled by the color of his stories and the richness of his unbridled life. They were concerned for the dog, of course, but their truer purpose in crossing that ridge was to see the old man safely home.

Luci's stride was long and direct as she sprinted toward the cry of the cougar, and her prints clearly showed that she never faltered. Her path led the men a quarter mile over rocks and logs, through thickets and pools, before they saw signs of the cat. Here, both sets of tracks zigged and zagged along the edge of the cliff as the lion crept deeper into its haven and the dog unwittingly followed. The men followed as well.

Silas called out, “Luci girl! Luci!” Hearing nothing, the men walked another 50 paces and called again, but the snow deadened the sound of everything except the old man’s heaving breath.

“You doing all right, Mr. Monk?” Morgan asked, worried.

“Yes, boy. My ol’ lungs are ‘bout as bad as my legs. Nothin’ stretches like it used to, ‘specially in this cold night air. I’ll catch me some new wind here in a minute, if you fellers can hold fer a spell.”

Morgan called to the dog while Silas rested, but had the same disappointing result. “Why can’t we hear her? She’s not baying anymore.”

Lowe tried to supply an answer. “She may be too far ahead of us or just down in some hollow where the sound doesn’t carry. More likely, Morgan, she’s getting close to that cat, and she’s wary. She’s listening and taking her time working the scent, or....”

Silas interrupted, “Or she’s dead.”

“Yes, there’s always that possibility, but I seriously doubt it. You just keep listening. Any time now, we’ll hear those yelps again. She’s bound to be cutting more trail as she pushes the cougar down off this ridge. It’s sport, and when she tires of it, she’ll come on home.”

“I reckon that’ll be the case, Lowe, unless she pisses off that cat and ‘e turns. Ya mind much if I keep on lookin’?”

“We’ll track her all night if that’s what you want.”

“I’m obliged.”

The men continued slowly under the moonless sky. For the most part, the white ground was illumination enough and the sign at their feet seemed to go forever. They grew weary as they found themselves pulled farther and farther from camp. The old man refused to acknowledge his own fatigue, but to Lowe, who watched over Silas, the dog had become a minor concern.

“Stop!” Morgan shouted, and gestured with an outreached hand. “Can you hear that?”

The bays of the hunting dog, faint but distinct, were a sweet song to the ears of the searchers. Luci sang it well, reviving the men and seducing them to carry on their quest. She was on the run again, but only God could know just where.

"Well, there you go," Lowe said, trying to comfort Silas. "She may be in another county by now, but at least she's very much alive."

The men listened intently as the baying went on and on, and it gradually became evident that the hound had actually reversed her direction.

"It sounds like she's coming to us!" exclaimed Morgan.

Lowe cupped his hands behind his ears. "Yeah, she's moving this way, and if she's coming to us, so is that cougar." He cocked his rifle, and a bullet dropped into the chamber.

Morgan never considered that he might actually encounter the lion. He had felt sure that Luci would have forced it clear into Kentucky by now. His feet were suddenly leaden, like in a recurring nightmare when the demons chased him and his legs were too heavy to run. He remembered the bear. He remembered Silas as its prey, being helplessly caught in the power of its grip, being tossed like a toy until it was broken. The bear gave the man up, but would a frightened, angry mountain lion be so merciful? Morgan knew the answer. The cougar must kill or be killed. The hound and the guns almost made that a certainty.

Weighted with fear, it became difficult for the boy to stand his ground and nearly impossible to push forward toward the sound of the charging animals. But he did. His pride and courage refused to let him do otherwise. With pistol in hand, he focused his attention on the noise growing louder and louder, just a hundred yards ahead.

"It's too dark for a good shot, and besides, we might hit Luci. Let's make some commotion! That cat might scare if it knows we're out here. I don't want to kill it unless we have to," instructed Lowe.

The men shouted as they moved steadily around and over and through the many obstacles of the ridge, careful to stay clear of the cliff and the chasms that sometimes cut into the steep rock face.

"What do we do if the lion doesn't run?" Morgan asked, half stumbling on a small boulder beneath the snow.

"It will run," Lowe assured, feeling somewhat short of breath himself. "But just in case, you hang back a little. I can't keep up with those long legs of yours."

Morgan was pleased to comply. He knew Lowe to be daring, but more importantly, he was a prudent and knowledgeable woodsman. Like Silas he could endure in a wilderness, and while mountain lions were somewhat of a new experience, Lowe showed an utmost confidence and a deep understanding of the ways of the cougar. Morgan trusted him.

The men were only 50 yards away when they heard the screaming roar and an almost simultaneous yelp of pain. There was horror in the sound, but greater horror in the silence that followed. When the two enemies finally engaged on a narrow precipice, the fight was brief. The men moved stealthily toward the scene, ever cautious and ever ready for what might lunge from the cover of night.

There was blood. There were signs of struggle where the snow compacted under the weight of rolling bodies. A small tuft of hair and flesh lay among a spatter of droplets, which would show red come the light of day. The cougar's prints and a wide rut led to the rim and disappeared together into the abyss below the cliff. Luci was gone. The stillness was cold and absolute, while each man eyed the long rut, a painful reminder of the swiftness of death and the agony of loss.

Silas slumped to the ground, biting his lip to keep it from trembling. Morgan sat beside him and placed a hand on his shoulder.

"Well, one of them sure took a hit from the looks of this blood," said Lowe. He peered over the escarpment for any indication of life below. "If there's something down there, I sure can't see it. We're a long ways up. Lordy, I doubt either animal would have survived the fall. There might be some ledges, but I can't tell for sure. Hey! There looks to be some tracks right here near the top."

"Stop it, Lowe. Thar ain't no hope fer Luci, so quit tryin' to spread it. I can see plain 'nough what's happened. That cat nailed 'er and dragged 'er on down with 'im. Mountain lions don't fall unless ya make 'em fall. Damn it! Damn my hide fer bein' too old and slow to even git a shot off."

"Silas, I know how you're feeling, but come over here and help me read this sign. The cougar got her all right, but the strike may not have been lethal. I really don't find all that much blood."

"Hell, Lowe, I can see from here how it dragged 'er to the cliff."

Lowe stooped down and closely examined the prints. Silas was right. There were no paw marks from the dog, only the trough in the snow where she had been hauled to the edge.

"Well, are you coming or not?"

"Not. Let's head on back to camp. We gave 'er our best."

"Wait! If a cat needed to drag a big animal like Luci, it would likely use its mouth and pull backwards, wouldn't it?"

"Ya know'd that before ya asked."

"Yeah, I did. But, regardless, you tell me which way the paws would face if it's pulling a carcass toward the cliff."

"I reckon most of 'em would be aimin' right at me."

"Not one is aimed at you." Lowe reinterpreted the scene. "I'll tell you, fellows, Luci may be over that ledge, but she wasn't dragged there by any lion."

"You don't say." Still mourning his loss, Silas was skeptical. He trudged through the snow to personally examine the tracks. With a tinge of a smile, he nodded.

"You see them, don't you?" asked Lowe.

"I see 'em... Luci tracks. It had 'er down fer a few feet, but by the look o' things, she broke away and rode that devil straight off the mountain. She was a fightin' dog to the bitter end. They's prob'ly both layin' in a heap somewheres thar at the bottom."

"Likely so, but I can see the cat's trail on this thin ledge just over the rim. There are some other marks farther down, but they're too distant for my poor eyes. Morgan, can you make them out?"

Morgan looked. "No, sir, it's just too dark."

"Well, I can't imagine Luci getting down this wall, but a hound's got four legs just like a cat. If we could get to the bottom, we'd have answers."

The men split up. At Lowe's insistence, Morgan and Silas headed back toward camp with instructions to search for a safe corridor through the escarpment. Lowe did the same, except he walked in the opposing direction another half hour up the ridge. They were to fire two signal shots if a suitable trail was discovered. It was a good plan that yielded no results. Lowe overtook his friends before they saw the light of campfires, and the three, sad and exhausted, slogged into camp together.

Black Jack was there to greet them in the wee hours of morning.

"I's about to come lookin' for you fellas. Dat dog's done kept you out way past yo bed time. I gots de coffee heated and de fire stoked in case you freezin'."

The others were sullen and sore. They went to the fire and with empty stares became lost in the flames. Finally, Lowe told the story.

"Looks like Luci didn't make it. The cat got her or she got the cat. Either way, she's likely at the bottom of the cliff a mile or so from here. Did everything stay quiet at camp?"

"Oh, yeah...yessa, it been real quiet for most de time...dat is, 'til dat ghost come to visit and spook old Noggin again."

"What ghost?" asked Morgan. He yawned.

"You be findin' dat out when you turns in for de night. Anyway, she out hauntin' de back o' yo tent, sleepin' like de dead been known to do. I patched up an ear, and she curled next to de fire for a spell. It were too hot, I reckon, and she moved on right quick to de tent. I ain't heard or seen her since."

"Huh? Are you talking about Luci? Luci's back?"

"She been back for some time."

"She's alive!" exclaimed Silas. He found it difficult to believe.

"Now I ain't so sure about dat, Mr. Monk. I 'spect she ain't no ghost at all, but dere's no tellin' by her wore out looks. Would've fired shots to let you know, but den, you might be thinkin' I's havin' me some serious troubles. And I would at dat point, seein' how skiddish dem pack animals been behavin'. I waited, figurin' on you strikin' back at any moment for de camp. You fellas was gone a long time."

Morgan scrambled to the tent with Silas and Lowe close on his heels. They pulled back the flap and found their friend huddled among the blankets, content against the cold. Silas stroked her gently, and the others smiled. Luci was safe. They were all safe.

The dog slept through the night, and no snoring man or ranging cougar could ever hope to awaken her. But come morning, she would again revel in the affection of her comrades as they petted and scratched and kissed her, and as they adorned her with a fine new collar. It was fashioned from a thick length of leather rein and fitted snugly to the short fur of her neck. If chasing cats was still her sport, Luci's play was now restricted to the lighted hours of the day, and the old man would carefully determine the other players in her game.

There was a job to be done, and the weather had already stolen too much of their time. But the men needed rest, and Black Jack would not deprive them. He tended to the morning chores and then unloaded and inspected each of the survey instruments. He had been tied to the camp for far too long and was anxious to see more of the paradise Lowe had promised him. The others could make their own breakfast. He was heading out.

It was a crisp, clear morning, and the sky had been cloudless and blue from the start. The snow was still cradled on every branch and blade, but Black Jack knew that the warm, rising sun would soon have its effect. First snows never last long.

With Bible in hand, he took a short hike to the great white oak and began his meditation. It was just him and his God in the quiet of the wild. Black Jack talked and God listened. He sang and God harmonized in the voice of a chickadee. He raised his head to the heavens, and God showered him with soothing beams of sunlight. This was his paradise. Black Jack would not close his eyes, even in the midst of prayer. His companion was his creator, and he could behold him in no better way than through the majesty of the mountains or in the purity of fresh fallen snow.

The temperature climbed with every passing minute, and the

tree began to release a steady drizzle of silver droplets, glistening as the warm rays shot through the tiny wet prisms. Morgan, Silas and Lowe finally approached, carrying with them only the essential tools of their trade. Lowe would send back for whatever might be needed, once he saw and evaluated the area of the survey.

The men realized from a distance that they were intruding on Black Jack's special time and backed away to ensure his solitude. They watched reverently, but could not avoid laughing aloud when the inevitable slab of snow slipped from its branch and lodged on their friend's uncovered head and neck. That was the end of meditation. There was no "Amen," no final word. Black Jack jumped from his seat on the low limb and pulled franticly at his shirt, while he wiggled and danced to rid himself of his cold discomfort. When he had settled, when it was clear even to him that he had concluded his worship, the others came forward. They were still laughing.

The dome was a solid floor of bedrock, an ancient volcanic intrusion that remained after the softer ground around it had long since eroded. Its soil, if any, was thin, and the plants that survived were generally sparse and spindly. There was no explaining the existence of the enormous white oak tree and its massive roots that pierced into the heart of the rock. It was unequalled in size and beauty, especially among the other trees of the dome, and it stood like a colossus at the mouth of a hidden passage. The men wanted to find that passage.

They moved across the dome toward the opposing escarpment, and wondered, as they toted their equipment, if this barrier would be as formidable as the one behind them. They came to its edge, and they braced each other as an unseen world opened up before their eyes. Breathless, speechless, they were suddenly gazing upon the miracle of Eden.

# CHAPTER 12

The train lurched with rhythmic jolts, but its load never shifted through the many bends and bumps. Brakes squealed and couplings creaked as the brakemen time and again cinched and released the heavy rolling cars. Speed meant disaster, and every crank of the brakeman's wheel was intuitively applied to keep the steel on the track. The run back to town was deliberately slow.

Morgan looked at the huge logs bundled and chained to the car ahead of him. He thought of them as once thriving trees, a small glen at the edge of a stream or a copse in the midst of a sprawling meadow. He could only imagine. He would never know for sure, but he passed the time trying to envision such things.

One log in particular surpassed all others. It was stout, straight and solid, and though sectioned, battered and shackled to the bottom of a rickety rail car, it somehow retained the noble eminence of what it once had been. He could picture it rising above the deep green canopy like a patriarch among the children. He could see it anchored in a deep loamy soil, standing confident against the wind and the brutal ways of nature. And then, he could see that it was gone. The land gave it up without whimper or fight.

At the very moment of its destruction, the forest began to heal itself and reestablish its lost grandeur. But the patriarchs, those trees that feed as much on time eternal as they do the nutrients of the earth, those would not return. It was a disheartening realization, but Morgan found it impossible to accept that generations of men might pass without having known such wonders. There were still trees. Perhaps, there was still hope.

Two things were noticeably absent in Devlin: snow and clean air.

The smoke of every industrial stack and cottage fireplace lingered low across the valley, and only the smell of fresh cut lumber could compete as the train, laden with logs, neared the yard and mill. When the engine eased to the side rail, four men rose awkwardly from the cold, hard deck of the flat car. They were almost sad to be back at home.

They had taken nothing from the woods but their vivid memories of fellowship and discovery. Yet, there would be no talk of the great white oak or any part of the strange wonderland beyond the high cliffs of the dome. They had promised Lowe, and they knew that any careless mention of the Big Timber would only lead to its more rapid demise. After all, Devlin was a logging town, and the Big Timber had always been the prize just beyond reach.

Lowe had the small crew wait while he disappeared on his way to Market Street, and they busied themselves completing their few final tasks. He returned shortly and handed each man an envelope.

"What's this?" Silas questioned.

"It's what I owe you. It's what you earned tromping and freezing all over that mountain."

"That's three times what ya owe me, Lowe, and frankly, I wouldn't feel right takin' a plug nickel from ya. I had me one hell of a time."

Black Jack agreed, "Dis weren't no business trip. You keep yo money."

"Now, boys, you're being ridiculous. I told Silas and Morgan when we started out that I was hiring you, and that's that."

"Yeah, that's that." Silas pulled on Lowe's right suspender and crammed the envelope down the breast pocket of his flannel shirt. Black Jack did the same.

Morgan opened his envelope and jingled the silver dollars. It was quite a reward, more than he had ever before received. He handed it back, as well.

"Thank you anyway, Mr. Yancy. I got my pay up on that mountain. If anything, I owe you."

Lowe refused the gestures. He insisted that Silas and Black Jack hold on to their envelopes, if for no other reason, to encourage Morgan to keep his. The men reluctantly consented, knowing all the while they would find some way to return the coin.

"I don't quite know how to say thanks for all you've done," Lowe told the men. "I put you through some tough times up there, considering the snow and the cliffs and that cougar. But you came through it just fine, like I knew you would." He looked at Morgan. "I'm proud of you, son. I never heard one single complaint from your lips. You're a hard worker and a brave soul. It's been a pleasure having you along. I expect we'll be doing this again, if you have a mind to join us."

"Just tell me when, Mr. Yancy. I'm raring to go." Morgan shook Lowe's hand. He felt rather homesick for the men he was about to leave, but dreaded a lengthy goodbye. He turned to Black Jack and again extended the hand of friendship.

"You finish up dat schoolin', boy, and den come lookin' for me and Mr. Yancy. By de time you finish yo book learnin', we be ready to teach you some things dat ain't never been written. A man gets too old to wander in dese parts without his strength o' mind and back, and we be right proud to have you with us, if you ever hanker for de trade." Black Jack pulled the boy to him and gave him a long, warm embrace. "We ain't never too old for a hug, is we, Mr. Monk?"

"I don't hug," Silas said gruffly, "but I sure shake the hand o' any man half as good as this young feller here." He gripped Morgan's hand so firmly that his knuckles ached. "Boy, hoof it up to my holler fer a visit, will ya do that? Yer fine company and Luci and I is gonna miss ya."

Morgan scratched Luci behind her bandaged ear, and she turned her head to lick his palm. Then, he lifted a canvas sack containing personal belongings and flipped it to his shoulder. With a single wave, he started the climb up Briar Mountain.

Lowe called to him, "Give our regards to Dewey when you see him... and to your Ma and the family."

"I will. Better yet, bring your message with you when you stop in for supper some evening. Ma would sure like that."

Lowe just smiled. The idea appealed to him.

Little more was to be said or done before each man went his own way, one to a bath and one to a beer, one to his hollow and one to his home. They would all remember the Big Timber and the time they spent together.

A week in the back country is just enough time for any civilized man to weigh the real comforts of his modern life against the true freedoms of his more primitive forbearers. He either sees new value in the warm, familiar spaces of home or comes to realize that no house will ever again be wide or wild enough to soothe his restless spirit. Of course, most men never make the choice. They never take the chance. They just accept the lot that someone else has cast for them. Better is he who sculpts his own destiny and is satisfied in the end.

Morgan wanted the freedoms. He never knew it before, but now he was sure. The woods were to be his life, and any hour away from them was just precious minutes squandered. He felt a need to run, and run fast, back to the Big Timber, but instead, he trudged up the hill toward the sound of the school bell.

As usual, Mr. Tutwiler was at the front door to greet him. While the other students doffed winter coats and scarves and slung them over the myriad wall pegs that lined the hallway, Morgan was asked to accompany his teacher directly to the large desk at the head of the classroom. He removed his hat and opened his heavy jacket as he walked.

Education was of singular importance, and Mr. Tutwiler would waste no time in presenting his pupil with a week's worth of past assignments. It was Morgan's first price to pay for choosing freedom over comfort. He looked at the stack of books and papers and missed his mountains all the more.

It was an odd sensation, coming back to the boredom of school after so rich an experience. He felt as though he had been away for months, or even longer, and that he had returned a stranger among the mates who began to take their seats around him. His friends moved chaotically as they tended to the last social details before their work would begin in earnest. Somehow, they overlooked Morgan in the midst of the commotion. He was left wondering if he had suddenly become unwelcome, or simply invisible.

Dewey was seated next to him, but never looked up as he scribbled a final love note to Auralee and raced to the front to deposit it on her lap. There was no time to await a response, and he hurried back to his place before the room settled at the command of the teacher.

Sadie flitted and flirted among the boys in the hall, but did not notice that Morgan was next door. Her red hair and cheeks flamed more than he could recall, probably accentuated by her pretty apple green dress and the frosty air of the morning. As usual her clothes did little to conceal her buxom form, and the boys were drawn like moths to her fire. Morgan felt the heat, as well, and there was a tinge of jealousy as he watched Sadie tempt and titillate the others.

But his desire for Sadie was of little consequence. She demanded such a reaction from men. She nurtured it with her every batted eye and deliberate pose of her body, and she pursued hardest that which she could not have. Morgan was forbidden fruit, so she picked him over the many others that appealed to her.

What Morgan felt for Sadie, if anything, was but a hedonistic yearning, a biological stirring, that pushed him to the very edge of his Christian bounds. He fought hard against his own lust and her unrelenting allure, while others clamored without conscience for just a moment of her affection. He had come close before, but would not cross that edge.

He watched the girl work her wiles in the hallway and was thankful she had not yet seen him. Her intentions for him were obvious, and her overtures were at times much too bold and embarrassing. As others filed through the classroom door, Sadie Buck surprisingly remained behind to help Horace Smith, who with a broken leg seemed to have difficulty maneuvering with his crutches. She slipped her shoulder under his own to give him support and then placed her arm firmly around his waist. It was a compassionate effort, a rare selfless offering, and Morgan realized in the instant that he may have misjudged her.

It had been callous to not recognize her kinder aspects, not to ever look beyond the physical assets she so confidently displayed. She was gentle in her care for Horace, a boy she and just about everyone else had grown to detest. He had always been a lanky, pock-faced ruffian who took his pleasure intimidating others, but in his time of need, Sadie was the one, the only one, who came forward to do what was right. Morgan was impressed.

The couple took only two short steps to where they were mostly hidden by the large interior door. Horace set his crutch against the wall, and Sadie whirled around to kiss him soundly. Apparently, it was not their first. She broke her embrace and briskly entered the classroom, passing by Morgan with complete indifference.

"I meant to tell ya, Morgan, that there's been some changes around here," Dewey said, having witnessed the same spectacle as his friend.

"I can tell."

"Yeah. Well, ya lost her and, frankly, it's your own damn fault. A man shouldn't up and leave a woman like ya did. Ya forced that poor girl into the arms of Horace Smith, of all people."

"I was only gone a week!"

"Ya know them Buck girls. A week is far too long for a woman of such passion." Dewey lowered his voice. "Ya just seen your girl in the arms of a lout, and all ya gotta say is, 'I was only gone a week'? One thing's for sure, you're none too broken from the shock."

Morgan thought it wise to quiet the conversation even more. He whispered, "First, I reckon I'll live, and second, she wasn't my girl."

"Oh, Morgan," groaned Dewey, feigning his frustration, "only a fool climbs the apple tree when the best fruit is layin' at his feet." They both looked at Sadie as she scooted across the bench of her desk. "Ummm... um! I can't believe ya passed all that up. Ya must've found some mighty fine pickin' higher up in the branches. I can only guess who."

Dewey had been leaning over from his desk, and at such a close range, he found it easy to unleash a barrage of light, friendly jabs against Morgan's arm. He was pleased to see his friend and quick to switch the subject.

"Well, it looks like ya lost a little weight out there, but I see ya made it back in one piece. I heard there was snow. It must've been a damn slow week."

"Not really. The time went by fast, much too fast for the amount of catch up work I have to do." Morgan showed Dewey the material given to him by their teacher. "It'll take two weeks just to make up the one I missed. But we had us some excitement, and, yes, a little snow. Eight to 10 inches, but not enough to shut us down. As you know, Mr. Yancy is determined when it comes to that surveying. They're a good group of men to work with."

"You're right 'bout that. How is Black Jack and Lowe, and ol' Silas? He went along, too, didn't he?"

"Yup, they were all there, and they're doing fine. They send their regards."

"I reckon Black Jack is purdy much healed by now, isn't he? Them bastards cut him awful deep the last time out."

Morgan put a finger to his lips. "Your language, Dewey, it sure hasn't improved any while I was gone. Black Jack's just about mended, a little weak from time to time, but he handled himself well."

"And Silas? I'll bet that ol' codger left ya in the dust climbin' up them hills. Has he shot the mule yet?"

"No. Noggin's still trying his patience at every turn, but Silas has a smart little dog now to keep him in line. It'll probably add another 20 years to the ol' man's life."

Dewey had missed something very special in the Big Timber. He could hear it in the voice of his friend. He could read it in the subtle movement of his eyes. Morgan seemed distant, still absorbed in the details of a fine adventure.

"Boy, I sure wish I'd gone with ya."

"Me, too." There was much to share, but faithful to his vow to Lowe Yancy, Morgan chose to say nothing more.

Dewey sat back, and Morgan began to watch his classmates scramble to their assigned places in anticipation of the morning roll call. He was still amused at the notion of being invisible. If he was, then only Dewey seemed capable of seeing him. Sadie Buck and the rest of his class certainly did nothing to show otherwise. Frankly, only one of them was of real importance anyway. She was the apple of his eye, the one still hidden in the high cover of the tree.

Sarah Dabney entered the room, and Morgan's heart sank with the weight of his ever-dwindling hope. With each passing day, she became more beautiful. With each passing minute, he loved her more deeply. Like the others, she moved quickly to her place without regard of the young man who watched her every step. Morgan longed for her attention, but expected none of it. Time and again, he was not disproved.

All eyes looked forward and all mouths fell silent the moment Mr. Tutwiler spoke. His lessons came with a fury, and soon nothing else seemed to matter to Morgan Darrow except the work before him. He was back to the routine of his civilized life.

At the morning break, the doors of the school house were thrown open with a crash, and children spilled out into the cold like a flood ripping through a levee. The two young teachers were frantically trying to hold back the horde, but it was too late for any semblance of order or quiet. They spent the entire recess matching tiny coats to little bodies, and by the time they bundled up the last of their charges, it was time to bring the children back inside.

The chaos was disruptive to the older students in the classroom across the hall, and it was clear Mr. Tutwiler was annoyed. But when he heard the hush and the tiptoes of young feet reentering the building, he offered a congratulatory smile to the flustered new teachers. He walked to his classroom door and summoned his assistants with a gesture.

"Ladies, children are like water. If you pull the stopper, they will be pouring out through the pipe and running all over the place."

One of the teachers responded apologetically, "We are so sorry for the interruption, Mr. Tutwiler. They became so excited, we lost control. It won't happen again."

"Sure, it will." Arthur Tutwiler rubbed his chin. "Children are made to run and play, not to sit for hours on end listening to us. We cannot change their human nature, nor can we corral their racing spirit. We are teachers, not tamers, and we just guide them as best we can. With this in mind, I might suggest putting on the coats while in the classroom, and then, having the little ones depart the building in a single file. It has worked for me over the years...ah...I should say most of the time. And remember, once you crack that door, they all are gone. Believe me. I have no complaint with you. We are all learning here, students, teachers and principals alike."

With that, he closed the door and addressed his own class, "I guess you have earned a short break as well. Take 20 minutes, and please, take it quietly in consideration of the children next door." He paused, peered over the rim of his spectacles, and then reiterated, "I said, 'quietly'. You are much too mature for single file."

His students laughed, and they rose calmly from their desks in support of the man they had long since come to respect.

It was that kind of day, like the first day after summer break when everything and everyone in school seemed strangely new and different, when concentration was feeble and body and mind both cried out for the habits of a more leisurely time. Morgan had changed somehow. He was out of place, like a grown man still donning his boyhood trousers. Though in good condition, the same pants simply no longer fit. The Big Timber seemed responsible somehow. He stepped outside where the fresh air and solitude might help him make some sense of it all.

Sarah followed. She passed through the doorway and stood alone at the top of the steps, waiting in silence for Morgan to face her. She shivered in the cold, gusty air and shook as she gathered her courage.

"Morgan?"

He finally turned. "Sarah, you'll catch your death of cold out here."

The girl's lips trembled, and despite a desire to say many things, she stayed voiceless and frozen to her place. The winter brought a light blush to her nose and cheeks, and she stood before him like a fragile china doll on the verge of falling and shattering into pieces.

"Sarah, what is it? What's the matter?"

She was not listening. She was watching. She was peering far into his eyes and soul, trying to find again what she had seen so clearly just months ago at Avery's pool. And it was there, just as she remembered, just as she hoped.

Sarah took a long, deep breath and descended the steps toward Morgan until their faces nearly touched. She said softly, "Will you walk with me, Morgan? I mean, after school, will you walk with me?"

"Yes, I'd like that." He responded without hesitation, and then fell immediately under the same spell that had bridled Sarah's speech. By the time other words came to mind, Sarah Dabney had rushed away, relieved to have finally asked her question. She would contemplate the answer until the ringing of the bell.

They were not reticent people, though the quiet walk down Briar Mountain would have them seem so. They were not timid people, but they knew to tread gently over this unknown and sensitive ground. These might well be the telling steps of their life, and they took them cautiously together.

Morgan looked down at Sarah as they ambled slowly, far behind the throng of students anxious to be home. He tried to read in her expression some hint of her intention, but was thwarted by the cute way she nestled her chin in the warm nap of her scarf. Her green crochet cap tipped to the side and gathered her long silken hair, except the few stray locks that curled about her ears. When he saw her this way, little else could matter. Her thoughts, his thoughts, nothing need be declared. It was enough to be in her presence.

Yet, there was much to share, and the opportunity would not lend itself forever. There was, after all, an end to the road they took. Sarah drew close where her slender fingers might fortuitously brush against his own, but the two hands never met. Morgan juggled words in his mind, but nervously dropped them all, preferring muteness to mistake. They walked, and they both waited for their perfect moment.

Sarah finally broke the silence, "I guess someone has to say something, and I suppose it should be me, since I pressed you into taking this walk. I hope you didn't mind. You didn't mind too awfully much, did you? If there is somewhere else you need to be, I'll understand." The girl stumbled from the start and wished she could begin again.

"A nice stroll is never a bother. It beats chores, and that's all I have to look forward to." Morgan stumbled, too. His answer did not come close to reflecting his true feelings. He tried to salvage his response. "I mean, well, what I really mean to say, Sarah, is that I enjoy the company...your company, that is. I've looked forward to our walk all afternoon."

"Me, too." She smiled. Her chin dropped into the warmth of the scarf.

The awkward silence dominated as they made their way much too quickly down the mountain road. It was clear to both of them that important things were to be said, but neither would be first to expose the concealed message of their hearts. They were well past Morgan's house and almost to the mill pond before Sarah stopped in her tracks. The place was noisy and muddy and clouded by smoke. She sighed deeply and looked around as though she had lost her way, or worse, that long-awaited moment.

"Oh, the road is gone."

Morgan did not understand. "It's in bad shape all right. We'll have to find us another route to get you home. It's not all that far."

Sarah lived in a large Victorian house, just a block from Market Street. It was not palatial, but it still loomed in the distance above the town's low skyline. She looked at it from where she stood and thought it much too near.

"Thank you, but what I actually wanted was more time." She was still struggling to find her words.

"More time for what?" asked Morgan.

"You know. Time to talk. Time to get to know one another."

"I'm in no hurry, Sarah, but if you are...."

She shook her head in frustration. "No. No! None of this has anything to do with time, not really. What I needed to say should have been said by now, but I was hoping for a big open tree in the field, or a brook through the glen, or some sunny overlook. I so wanted a spot that you would like. Not here. Not this place."

Sarah was disappointed in herself and could only imagine how badly Morgan must want to leave her and her incessant babbling. She had rehearsed for days, and her lines were to be passionate and convincing. They needed the proper backdrop for the scene to be effective.

"I like this particular place just fine," said Morgan.

"But the mill and that ugly pond, they're...oh, they're just ugly!"

Morgan sensed what she was feeling and what she might say if only given the opportunity she had envisioned, and his heart pounded so hard he began to breathe heavily. The vapor rolled from his mouth across the now still air. There was not a chance in all eternity that he would let this moment pass. He boldly took both of her hands in his and guided her to a nearby walnut tree, which stood leafless, large and lonely beside him.

"Well, we'll just have to make this do." He gently positioned her back against the far face of the broad trunk, then, spun around beside her.

"Now, tell me what you see," he said. "Do you see a mill? An ugly pond? The buildings of the town?"

"No, that's all behind us."

"Tell me, Sarah, what *do* you see?"

She took her time and looked closely over the landscape. "I see the river. It turns with the valley as they both narrow between the slopes of the mountains."

"Go on," said Morgan.

"Well, I see the rails disappearing through the shadows and the trees. There's a small farm on the hill just above the river's plain. It has cattle and a small red barn." She paused. "I so seldom look beyond the mill, and I don't know why. Somehow, I forgot about this wandering little river and those blue mountains. You must think me shallow."

Morgan lifted away from the walnut tree and positioned himself directly in front of Sarah. "I can show you miracles in those mountains. What else do you see?"

"I see you."

"Is there more?"

Sarah could not prevent the flow of emotion which brought tears to her eyes, and she would no longer hold back the words, be they babble or not.

"I don't want more, Morgan Darrow. I see you in my days when we're far apart. I see you in my nights and dreams. I see you in the faces of other people and in every single room or space we might ever have encountered one another. I am consumed by the slightest thought of you, and my thoughts of you are endless. My God, Morgan, I don't know if you even like me!"

Sarah tried to compose herself. She dabbed her eyes with her scarf and sniffled. She formed a smile, but lost it in the next wave of feelings. She had to clear her heart and soul of the truth now aching within her.

"I thought at first -- I mean the very first when I saw you at the river -- that you were as taken with me as I was with you. I just felt it, and I've tried to believe it ever since. But there was that time at the store and the dance, and now even at school. Why do you avoid me so? Is it Sadie? I know how you feel about her, and I can't blame you for choosing another, especially one so beautiful and popular. But what's wrong with me?"

She wanted to go on, but Morgan hushed her. His hands cupped her face, and with the tips of his thumbs, he erased the trails of her tears. He gulped. Now was his perfect moment, the time for perfect words. He whispered them as he pulled her close.

"I love you, Sarah. I don't even know you, and I love you. I've been a fool holding all this in, and now I see that I have hurt you because I was too proud to declare myself. I'm so sorry. For both of us, I'm so very sorry. I avoided you because I couldn't bear thinking of you with someone like Austin Devlin, or any man for that matter. It nearly broke me just knowing you had been dancing with another, and I asked the same questions. Why them? Why not me? Ever since I saw you at Avery's pool, I hoped for this day. Even if you change your heart tomorrow, I want you to know today that I love you. And I forever will."

It was all so honest and innocent, and Morgan never thought for an instant about any impropriety as two near strangers grasped at intimacy. His kiss lingered lightly against her lips, and he savored it as the fulfillment of his dream. Sarah melted against his chest.

"You love me," she uttered. She wanted to absorb the power of those words.

Sarah was content to stay in Morgan's arms even while the plunging cold nipped at their toes and ears. She wanted everything in the open, every detail of his life and every desire of his heart. She vowed to give the same.

"Austin Devlin and all his money were never my ambition," she said, in keeping with that vow, "and I've only danced with one man in my life, my father. But, if you recall, I once was promised a dance by another."

"I do recall. If you intend to hold me to that promise, I'll need some lessons."

"As will I. We can teach each other."

Morgan held Sarah's hand, and she cuddled against his arm all the way to the iron gate of the fine Victorian house. She reluctantly entered the yard alone and was soon safe in the comfort of her home.

A heavy door closed behind her, and Morgan was suddenly reduced to an empty stare. Ephemeral thoughts alighted and leaped away before he could really grasp at any of them. When most of these simply vanished from his consciousness, he was happy to dwell on the two that remained. Beyond the rocky heights of the Big Timber was, indeed, the miracle of ancient trees, but beyond that heavy door, that portal to her family and possessions and all things deemed dear, was Sarah Dabney herself. Morgan pondered the wonder of them both. The freedoms of the back country might be an easy trade, after all, for a civilized life with her. For the moment, it was true.

He ran. With soles but touching air, his shoes beat their own path across Briar Mountain. He ran and he ran and he ran. It made no difference where.

# CHAPTER 13

Sam Blackman approached stealthily, using the many racks of clothes and display cabinets to hide his movement. It was amazing that one his size could stalk so effectively, but he did, and the unwary visitor never detected as much as a swish from the big man's oversized britches. He was too focused on the bounty that lay unguarded by the cash register.

The clerk waited for the perfect moment to strike. He lifted his closest weapon, a wooden yard stick, high above his head and cautiously inched his way forward. When the time was just right, when one more step would be one step too close, he slapped it down hard against the broad surface of the oak counter. The thief tensed with surprise at the sound. His hands flailed, casting his spoils into the air.

"Lordy, Sam, ya 'bout scared me half to death! Now look what ya made me do," Dewey Baughman exclaimed. Five good sized jaw breakers had landed with a rattle and were rolling fast across the floor toward every dusty nook.

Sam Blackman nearly buckled with a hardy laugh. "Why, Dewey, I only did that to save you."

"Save me? From what?"

"From the man who runs this place for the company. He's been cracking down on you young fellows who sneak in here to pilfer his penny candies. If he saw what you were doing, he'd smack that hand of yours like you were a little toddler who didn't know better. Maybe worse. He's a tough old coot."

"But I thought you ran this store."

"Me?" Sam pretended to think for a moment. "Why, yes, now

that you mention it, I believe I do." The clerk smiled at Dewey and winked, and then tapped the boy's hand with the end of his yard stick. It was a light touch, but enough to sting. "I warned you that he was tough."

"Ow-w!" Dewey yelped. "Hey, I was gonna pay."

"Of course, you were. I just assumed you were helping yourself, like you've always done since the very first day you could reach above this counter."

"Huh, I never once thought ya noticed. Why didn't ya say somethin'?"

"Because you used to have little fingers and, back then, a handful generally meant just one. That's why. Now, if you were really planning on paying, I owe you a most sincere apology. But, either way, you owe me and the company about five cents."

"Five cents!"

"Well, just how many did you drop?"

Dewey reluctantly reached deep into his pocket and pulled out a buffalo nickel. Other than a couple of coppers, it was all the change he had. He laid it on the counter.

"I reckon five's 'bout right. Here's your money, Mr. Blackman." He stooped down and began to retrieve the jaw breakers.

"You can leave those be, son." The clerk raised the glass lid of the candy jar and offered the boy fresh pieces. "Take six. One's on the house for old time's sake."

"That's downright considerate of ya," replied Dewey. He took five new jaw breakers and stuffed them in the same pocket with the pennies. The sixth one went straight to his mouth. His teeth crushed down and the candy disintegrated.

Sam was astounded. "It's called a jaw breaker for a reason! You're not supposed to crunch it. You suck on it. How in the world do you bite something like that without breaking a tooth?"

"I'll show ya if ya want."

The boy began to reach again for the candy jar, but Sam raised his ruler. "Nice try, my friend."

The bell jingled as the front door opened and Morgan Darrow

stepped up to the threshold. He was hardly recognizable, and Sam looked twice before speaking.

"Hello there, Mr. Darrow. Well, I'll be...just look at you. You are the quintessential look of masculine loveliness."

"What?"

"Never mind. You appear quite handsome in your fancy togs. If I'm not mistaken, someone's either 'goin' a courtin'' or heading out to a funeral. And I'm not aware of anyone dying."

"You were right with the first guess. Hello, Mr. Blackman."

Morgan was dressed in his finest suit, which showed some early signs of trouble against the challenge of his growth. His broad shoulders consumed every bit of available room, and his long legs defied the length of his trousers. But, still, he looked dapper. He was clean shaven and his neatly parted hair was wet with barber tonic. His shoes shined like new, and his stiffly starched, round collared shirt was impeccably pressed. He wore a red necktie gathered by a small gold pin, and in the pocket of his vest was the coveted gold watch of his grandfather. His black top coat draped across his arm and a matching brimmed hat rested in his hand. He was the near perfect picture of a gentleman. And he hated it.

Morgan addressed Dewey, "Any luck with the flowers and tobacco?"

"I ain't even asked him, yet."

"That's okay. I'll do it myself."

"Now, wait just a minute. I said I'd take care of ya, and that's exactly what I'm gonna do. Sam, I told Morgan I'd help him pick out a few things for his evenin' with Sarah Dabney. It's a big night... a *big* night. I've been tryin' to walk him around a bit. Ya know, he's new to this business of romance."

"Ha!" blurted Sam. "This ought to be interesting."

"Never ya mind that. I know full well what I'm doin'." Dewey was quick to defend himself. He was now the self-proclaimed maven of courtship and did not want Morgan to lose confidence in what he truly believed was sapient advice.

Sam shook his head and spoke directly to Morgan, "So it's Miss

Dabney, the fair-haired girl. I thought maybe you would be seeing that little red head you were with at the church social."

The young man blushed. "No, but that's a long story."

"Too bad. One rarely gets to hear the long story." Sam knew to move on. "All right, Mr. Baughman, what do you have in mind for your friend's 'big night'?"

"I've found that pretty flowers and good smokes make for right kindly gifts. You can't go wrong."

"True, true. Of course, December doesn't grow too much in the way of fresh flowers. If this is to be a present of sorts for the young lady, I might suggest imported chocolates. They can be somewhat pricey, coming from so far, but women absolutely love their sweets."

"Well, then, why don't we have us a sample? If we like 'em, we might just buy a couple boxes. Ya do offer some allowance for quantity, do ya not?" Dewey was serious.

So was Sam, who was still holding the yard stick. He patted his hand with it, and the young man realized that his suggestion, while seemingly appropriate, was in no way persuasive.

Mr. Blackman chuckled, "So I'm now supposed to dicker over candy, over two measly boxes of candy. Dewey, our rates are set by the company. You know that. The price you see is the price you pay."

"Well, if ya ask me, the management of this company don't know much 'bout business."

Sam cynically threw his hands over his chest to indicate the collective heartbreak of the C. O. Devlin Supply Company. "They'll be hurt, of course, but they think quite highly of you, so I'll be sure to pass your complaint along."

Dewey shook his finger. "Please, see that ya do this time. You never have before."

The repartee was customary. Sam Blackman had come to expect it, and Dewey Baughman was not one to disappoint. They both enjoyed pushing until patience wore thin.

The clerk pulled out a red decorative box, which contained a dozen Belgian chocolates, each individually wrapped in silver foil. "I recommend something like this, instead of the smokes. Most good women aren't too partial to the taste of fine tobacco." He waited for Dewey's response, sure that the boy would unwittingly react.

"We want the tobacco."

"Why? Chocolates are much better suited for the occasion."

"But we still want them."

"What for!"

"I just told you what for. For Morgan's evenin' with Sarah."

"And I just told you that ladies don't care for tobacco. That's the whole point of the chocolates."

"Believe me, the tobacco is not for any lady!"

"Excuse me? Miss Sarah Dabney certainly is a lady."

"Well, I know that, Sam."

"Then why defame her fine reputation by saying that she's not? I am rather surprised, Mr. Baughman, that Morgan puts up with your vulgar opinion of such a lovely and proper woman. If she were my girl, you and I would be heading out to the alley."

"I ain't goin' out to some alley on account of no lady!"

"No lady?"

Dewey was flustered. "For cryin' out loud, just stop it! Of course, Sarah is a lady. She's one of the finest of ladies, maybe the best, finest, properest lady in all of Devlin. In all of the state. Oh, hell, in all of the world, for that matter! But it just don't matter. The girl can be any damn thing she wants to be, but she ain't gettin' tobacco from me."

"I know. Mr. Darrow will be the one giving it to her."

"Yeah, that's right. No, it's not right! No one's givin' the girl tobacco."

"Frankly, Dewey, I'm confused."

Dewey pulled a jaw breaker from his pocket and jammed it past his lips. He crunched loudly, while he gathered his frayed wits. Then, he spoke slowly.

"Once and for all, the chocolate is for Sarah. She will not be gettin' tobacco, at no time and from nobody."

"Then why buy it?"

Dewey rolled his eyes. He looked to Morgan for help, but Morgan simply smiled.

"The tobacco's for her Pa. Did ya hear me, Sam? It's for Sarah's Pa."

Dewey was actually beyond flustered, and Sam and Morgan could not be more delighted. Sam wished that he could continue, but Dewey had been pushed far enough for one conversation.

"Well, why on earth didn't you say so? It's your decision, of course. You're the customer. You want some chew? Rolling tobacco? Perhaps some cigars."

Dewey groaned to express his frustration and then scratched the stubble on his cheek. "Hmmm, we'll take these chocolates, and I think the cigars are actually a good idea. Where are they from?"

"Cuba, I expect. Maybe from Central America. I'll check the box."

"No need. They'll do."

Blackman put the top back on the candy and pulled a sealed box of cigars from under the counter. Morgan noted the price and balked. Sam nodded understandingly and said, "I thought that might be a little steep for you. Take just two, one for you and one for the other fellow. He'll appreciate both the thought and the company. You want the chocolates, too?"

Dewey answered, "You bet. He'll take it all, chocolates and cigars."

Sam lifted the lid and drove his hand deep into the candy jar. He drew out an undetermined number of jawbreakers and dropped them in a bag. He handed it to Dewey.

"What's all this for?" asked the boy.

"Take it. You just earned it."

Armed with gifts and bolstered by Dewey's interminable tutelage, Morgan now faced a daunting 50 paces, which led across the yard from the low iron gate to a high pillared veranda. It was a grand Victorian home that stood before him, and even though his Sarah would be inside, he found every step closer to its door to be more laborious than the previous one. By the time he reached the base of the wide brick staircase, his legs were nearly locked with angst and his brow was damp, despite the cold December air. But he pressed on, and he lifted the brass knocker that would signal his arrival.

The door opened. The man on the other side bowed his head in a greeting to the guest, and Morgan nodded back, not sure what was customary for the likes of doormen and other household servants.

"I am here to visit Miss Sarah Dabney and her father. I believe they are expecting me."

"So they are. You must be Mr. Darrow. Please, come in. May I take your coat and hat?"

Morgan handed the items to the butler and watched as he carefully placed them on the ornately carved coat rack, one of several quality pieces in an already elegant vestibule. He was a middle-aged man, dressed casually in a green and red plaid vest. He wore no tie, not even an evening jacket, but despite his appearance, it was clear through his mannerism that he was a man of refinement.

"Why don't you come into the parlor and make yourself comfortable?" the servant said.

Morgan followed without response. He was led to a brown leather wingback chair, and he sat down immediately. The leather squeaked under his weight.

"Can I offer you something to drink, Mr. Darrow? Some tea, perhaps," the man asked.

"No, thank you."

"Would you mind if I poured myself a cup? I've been looking forward to a tea break all day."

Morgan was rather shocked by the question, and even more stunned when the butler took his own position on a settee not far across the room. The two stared at each other in a brief moment of awkward silence.

"Excuse me, but shouldn't you inform the Dabneys of my arrival?" Morgan inquired.

The man looked puzzled, and then, his eyes suddenly widened as he came to understand. "Oh, my goodness, lad! Please forgive my poor manners. I'm Irwin Dabney, Sarah's father." The man nearly jumped out of his seat to rectify the error. He thrust an open hand toward Morgan, an urgent gesture of both greeting and apology.

Morgan stuttered, "I...I...I thought you...you...oh, I thought you were...."

"You thought I was the hired help?" asked Dabney. He smiled. It was a warm, welcoming smile. "We don't have any servants at our home, except the cleaning lady who kindly drops in a couple days a week. Sometimes she helps with the cooking when Sarah isn't up to preparing the meal. I, myself, am a lost cause in the kitchen. How about you?"

"Hopelessly lost, sir. I can't even cook water."

"Aptly put. Yes, very aptly put. It's the same with me. If I tried, I'd be sure to burn it every single time."

"I'm sorry to have presumed that you could in any way be a common servant. It was very rude and *unperspicacious* of me." Morgan was embarrassed. His hands sweated and trembled, and he had no idea where to place them so as to hide his discomfort.

"All work is noble work, Mr. Darrow. It doesn't matter if you are the street sweep or the president. Any man who does his best has earned his accolades. Wouldn't you agree?"

"Yes, sir, I do agree."

"After all, we are all really just servants to each other, are we not?"

"We certainly should be, sir."

"Well said. Yes, I like your style."

The sweat dampened his collar. His ears felt hot and his mouth was dry, and Morgan wished that Sarah would, in the next second, come sauntering into the room. He was at ease with her. He was strong and confident with her. But he also knew she would not be coming, at least for a while. This was the time reserved for inquisition, the time where the father coolly sits in judgment while the lover melts in the fire of his living hell. Irwin Dabney was nothing less than a congenial and gracious man, but he was still Sarah's father. Morgan feared him. He revered him, by virtue of that fact alone.

Dabney knew full well how his presence chiseled the nerves of the young man before him. He had been seated in that chair many years ago and remembered the painful details of his own insecurities and blunders as though they were yesterday. He liked what little he knew about Morgan Darrow, and he truly regretted the tension he was causing.

"You know, Mr. Darrow, I have every confidence in my daughter. She has a sharp mind and is diligent in her pursuits. She has told me how deeply she feels for you, and I think I see in you a similar emotion. Her life is just that, her life, and whatever she decides to do with it will have my blessing. She has never let me down. A friend of hers is a friend of mine. It's that simple."

Morgan was only partly relieved, but fully appreciative of Irwin Dabney's understanding. "Thank you for that assurance, Mr. Dabney. And I can assure you, Sarah is everything to me. I won't let you down either." He paused, thinking there might be something more to say, and reached into his pocket for the two cigars. "Would you care to smoke while we wait for Sarah?"

It was to be their symbol of accord, like the pen that is passed at the signing of a treaty, like the ceremonial pipe in the lodge of a Shawnee king. Morgan offered it and Irwin Dabney accepted it as a token of their peace. Dabney struck a match.

"Sir, aren't we supposed to snip the taper before we light up?" Morgan hesitated to ask.

"I really can't say. I've never tried one of these before today. How do you normally do it?"

Morgan examined the cigar closely. There was no saving himself from the truth. "I don't, I'm afraid. Forgive me for saying so, but I've never really liked the smell of a burning cigar. Frankly, my knowledge of any tobacco is rather limited."

"Good. That makes two of us. We'll be ignorant together." Mr. Dabney extinguished the match and held his cigar in the light of the lamp. "It looks like a quality smoke to me. I appreciate the thought, but let's just keep these as souvenirs. What do you say?"

The men were suddenly at ease with each other, and they found themselves talking about everything, everything except Sarah Dabney. An hour passed, along with Morgan's dinner reservations. Finally, there was the rustling of a dress and a woman's soft voice on the hidden landing above the stairs.

"Father, are you done? I'm starving."

"Yes, dear, I suppose I've occupied Morgan quite long enough. You should come now and save him."

As his daughter descended the stairs, Irwin Dabney rose to his feet to excuse himself. "Well, son, we neither cook nor smoke. So, there are at least three things we have in common. That's a good beginning to a friendship, I think."

"I agree, sir, but what is the third thing?"

"Sarah, of course. Enjoy your time together. If the hotel won't seat you, try Whitman's Restaurant. Sarah loves their broiled trout."

It was the next morning, and despite staying out well into the wee hours, Morgan awakened more bright than a noon sun. He and Sarah never tasted the broiled trout, since both the hotel dining room and Whitman's Restaurant had been filled to capacity. But they spent their time together strolling aimlessly through the tiny town, seeing it as though for the first time. They finally dined by candlelight on cold sandwiches and hot cocoa, all lovingly prepared by Sarah in the warmth of her own kitchen. Of course, Morgan helped. It was the best meal he could ever recall.

Only on rare occasions did he ever find himself up and out of the house before Jacob would even stir, but on this day, he had pressing questions and wanted answers before the start of school. His brother did not hear a sound as he washed and threw on his clothes. Forgoing breakfast, Morgan raced to the mill in search of his father.

The thick wooden steps that led to the saw filer's room were steep, but Morgan just glided up them, lifted by the magic of recent revelations. Over the past few days, he and Sarah had walked and talked at every available opportunity, disclosing their histories, discovering their qualities and laying down their aspirations and affections for one another. In so short a time, he came to understand why his love for her never waned from their very first moment. He somehow knew her well in the instant, but still, he reveled as they continued to unwrap the gift of their friendship.

His once mundane life had suddenly become an amalgam of discovery and emotion. In but a half a year's time, he had beheld both the perfect woman and the perfect place, his Sarah and the wondrous woods beyond the great white oak. He had faced bullies and bears and bats and mountain lions. He lost much of his father to the poison of alcohol and nearly drowned in the murky waters of the mill pond. There were new friends and new enemies and new, uncertain days ahead. Morgan was overwhelmed. He now needed someone to point a direction.

Lawson Darrow was not the best of fathers. He was never warm to his children and only rarely displayed any real love for his wife. When he was not moody, he was mean. He seldom showed that sensitive side of himself, the one Annie had cherished in the early days of their relationship. Maybe the alcohol possessed him, maybe not, but whatever kindness he originally had now seemed to be pickled and shelved. From all appearances, Morgan's mother never ceased trusting that her husband could and someday would reform with the help of those who loved him. He would someday emerge from the brine as fresh as the day she met him. Whether or not Annie really believed it, Morgan did not know. But to his way of thinking, there would be no recovery. It was clear that his father preferred whiskey over family. Time and again he made that choice, and he soured more with every wrong decision.

Morgan took much for granted. The comfortable life, the life among civilized people where there would always be a warm home, nice clothes and a table abounding with favorite foods, that life emerged from the sweat and toil of Lawson Darrow. Morgan did nothing to earn his place, except to be born to it. And, yet, he found fault in the accomplishment of his father. Money is but a cold treasure when a warm embrace is sought, and Lawson's hugs had been hurtfully missing for far too long. Morgan once yearned for them, as his mother and sister and brother still did, but he became hardened to his father's absence of tenderness. Ample love and playfulness, thoughtful discipline and mentoring, these were the true and necessary offerings that Lawson had unconsciously withheld. Morgan found it hard to forgive him.

It was not simply out of respect for Annie that Morgan went to see his father. Lawson was pragmatic and financially successful, and his advice, at least concerning the material aspects of life, was valuable. A sot by night, he seemed to gather his faculties at will, and he always willed his sobriety in time for the saw mill's morning whistle. Whatever else might be said of him, he was a respected saw filer and a decent provider for his family.

The filing room was in the highest loft of the mill, situated above the sawyer's platform and a movable carriage that positioned the logs and delivered them into the teeth of the spinning band saw. The saw itself was a 35-foot ribbon of steel, belted tightly around two nine-foot iron wheels. It was 15 inches wide with two-inch dragon-like teeth projecting on one side along the entire length. The filer could directly access the band by means of a low door, and with a little time and effort, he could install one of the three spares that hung from his ceiling. If the saws were broken, the mill was broken. Lawson kept them dagger sharp and ready, and he was paid accordingly.

"What do you want? You can see I'm busy," Lawson grunted as he adjusted his equipment.

"Anything I can do to help?" Morgan offered.

"No. What I need is fewer interruptions. You can stand there for another five minutes or come back later when I'm done with this. Your choice."

Morgan chose to wait. He backed down the stairs to where he could watch a fat 16-foot log being hauled up the jack slip from the mill pond. The conveyer seemed to hesitate under the strain, but the chain held and the log was soon seated and dogged on the carriage. The sawyer examined the piece quickly and gave his signal. Minutes later, the large, round timber was reduced to 33 rectangular planks, already forwarded to the planers for trimming and finishing. Another log was systematically loaded, and the carriage again moved against the wheezing saw. It was an efficient, continuous operation. Morgan never tired from observing, and he marveled at the ease in which a properly maintained saw would dissect even the densest of woods. His father executed his trade with utter precision.

"Damn those stupid wood hicks! I'd like to have someone's head for this," Lawson cursed loudly. "These teeth must have caught on another nail or wire, the way they're all bent up. It's the second time this week! All I've got to say is that when Devlin has to take in old farm timber, this mill must be hurting for wood. Tell me, what the hell am I supposed to do with this?" Lawson was clearly aggravated. The once razor edges of the metal band were now dog-eared, blunted and chipped.

"Are you sure I can't help out? You taught me a thing or two about filing."

Lawson set his wrench against a nut and began to tighten it. "I don't need your help," he said. He foolishly looked up at his son while applying the torque. The wrench slipped, and Lawson's hand grazed against the jagged teeth. His blood flowed instantly. "I don't need any of your help. This is what happens when I'm distracted. Why don't you get on out of here? We can talk when I get home."

Morgan came close to examine his father's wound. It appeared to be more serious than it actually was, and Lawson's first reaction was to merely stop the bleeding by applying a filthy oil rag from the back pocket of his overalls.

"Pa, you're going to need to do better than that. You might need a doctor."

"It's a scratch. Does your Ma send you to the doctor for every little scratch? There's a box over on that shelf." Lawson pointed to an obscure weathered crate almost lost amongst the disheveled collection of old parts, dark shadows and cobwebs. "Get me some iodine and gauze, will you? Looks like you finally got my attention."

Morgan retrieved the supplies and watched as his father splashed the iodine against the cut and rolled the gauze tightly around his palm and wrist. "I guess you're right, Pa. I should talk to you later," he said.

Lawson knew he had to wait for the bleeding to stop, and consequently, it became as good a time as any to give his son the requested audience. While he waited, he calmed. "No, boy, just get on with it. What's on your mind?"

Morgan was not sure where to start. "Well, I've been thinking a lot about jobs. I'll be finishing up school soon enough, and I know that I'm going to need to settle."

"Amen to that! You already took four years more for schooling than a man should ever need." Lawson's cynicism was annoying, but Morgan was accustomed to it. "As far as jobs are concerned, that's easy. You're going to find a good mill somewhere and take up saw filing. I didn't show you this work for you to go out and do otherwise."

"It's a good trade, Pa, no doubt. But haven't you tired of the same walls working here day in and day out? Don't the constant noise and dust and dim light start to bother you?"

"Sometimes that's the case, but a man endures his hardship and a smart man follows the payroll. There's decent money in this work. I want the money. What's this nonsense all about?"

Morgan did not want to answer. His father's reaction would be predictable. "Well, I've been offered an opportunity to take up surveying. I enjoy the work and I like the people."

"Surveying, huh?" Lawson gave the matter only brief consideration. "It's not for a family man. Surveying is no career. There are no roots to it, at least in these parts. You'll either walk yourself to death or starve yourself to death. Either way, it's a poor arrangement. A man needs work that guarantees a living."

"Lowell Yancy seems to make a good going of it."

"A good going? The man has nothing, son! He's got no house,

no wife, no family, no foundation, no future. I doubt he even has friends."

"He's got friends." Morgan tried to counter, but his father was not through with his tirade.

"Yancy's business is what he can carry on his back and legs, and someday they'll play out and leave him a broke and broken old man. Is that what you're looking for? You're young now. You need to look ahead. Stop listening to morons and start thinking for yourself and your future."

"But, Pa...."

"No 'buts', Morgan. It's not for you. Open your eyes! Look around. We may not be rich, but we'll always be comfortable. You have good clothes and a closet full of them. You live in a fine house, not some company cracker box but a substantial home, one that is already bought and paid for. You stay in school when other boys have to work just to afford a meal. You drive a modern car when other boys ride mules. You've got life easy. Why? Because of me. Because of this job! And I'll tell you something else. Someday, you'll meet a girl and the devil will push you to marry. Women like nice things. Women like men who can give them nice things. This trade can get it all for you."

It was impossible to argue with his father's reasoning. Morgan just stood with his mouth agape while he awaited the words of his own protest. Nothing came, because Lawson was right. There was now Sarah to consider, and in every decision he should be thinking of her.

"Actually, Pa, I have met a girl, and I reckon it's become serious."

"Oh, yeah? Just how serious?"

"Well, I'd marry her tomorrow if she'd have me."

"Marriage? You may be old enough, but you're a long ways from ready. I'm glad you're meeting some ladies, son, but I don't need to hear talk about any marriage. There isn't time for what I got to say on that subject."

Lawson finally stopped talking and looked at Morgan as if to say, "It's your turn," but the boy would not comment. He had sought direction, and in response, his father had just mapped out the way. It may have been his own way, but, right or wrong, he had put it plainly.

In the brief and awkward lull that followed, Lawson's face went flush with a sudden pulse of anger. "Lowell Yancy," he spoke the name with contempt. "Lowell Yancy. Is that the son of a bitch who's put you up to this?"

"Sir?"

"Is Yancy the one who's going to give you a job?"

"No, sir, Mr. Clark made the offer."

"You mean, Black Jack Clark!" Lawson glowered. His bandaged fist slammed hard against the table. "Boy, I'll tell you straight up. No son of mine will ever work for a colored! You take that as gospel."

# CHAPTER 14

Lowe was again in the mill conference room, standing before the wide mural of the Watoga Lumber Company. But this time he was alone, and he took a few uninterrupted minutes to really absorb the work, as fine art requires and justly deserves. The soft rays through the window so enriched the water colors and deepened the contrasts that the mural took on an almost photographic sharpness, unusual for such a medium. Lowe examined it with a novice eye, and he appreciated it as though it were a DaVinci hanging at the Louvre on just the right wall, under just the right measure of light.

It was a fine representation of the mill and a genuine tribute to the men who labored there. The artist must have known such men. He may well have been one of them, with dusty hair and calloused hands, with hidden untried talents and secret aspirations. The painter may have found his way just far enough from the mundane to discover a richer, fairer part of his self. To Lowe, it must have been so, for the work captured the very essence of a people and of an industry thrust into the belly of the wilderness. Such empathy required more than feeling. It took knowledge.

As much as he hated to admit it, the mural also honored the man, Charles A. Devlin, who built his company from the tall, broad trees of this once secluded valley. It was a good likeness, much too good for one who would discount the artist's effort as a mere "caricature."

"You horse's ass," Lowe said aloud, looking into the painted eyes of Devlin. The door opened in the same instant without warning, and Lowe stepped back, red faced with surprise.

"I'm sorry. Did you say something, Mr. Yancy?"

Lowe gulped. "Uh, no, not really. I am again taken by this painting. The man shows true understanding."

"Who, the artist or Mr. Devlin?"

"I was referring to the artist."

Irwin Dabney walked closer to the wall. "I agree with you. I often stop to look at this, and I always see more than just a mill. He knows the people and the land. He cares about his subject. It's good work. Speaking of good work, I want to thank you for all your efforts on these surveys. You and Mr. Clark have been in some hard country on my account, and your reports are most accurate."

"Thank you. It is what we do, and we try to give our best wherever we go. I appreciate your confidence in us, and, of course, the contracts. Mr. Clark gets the credit for our reports. I'll be sure to pass the compliment."

Both men turned their attention back to the mural, but continued with their conversation as they observed the detail in the art. Dabney spoke to the point, never offering a seat to his visitor.

"Lowe, there will be more contracts. You can count on it. But I called you here today to offer a different opportunity, if you want it. In about 15 minutes, this room will be filled with teams hired to check out our options in and around the Big Timber country. I know you know that area. Mr. Devlin is pushing hard and is willing to buy untold amounts of land, or the wood on that land, if it's high grade material. Our teams have been authorized to enter private properties and evaluate the stands. No surveying, mind you, just some timber cruising. If you are interested, I can find a place for you and Mr. Clark."

"When does the work commence?" asked Lowe.

"Right away, unfortunately. We can't wait for spring. Devlin wants a jump on this part of the state, and he's taking no chances concerning our competitors."

Lowe thought for a moment. It was a kind offer from a man who owed him nothing, and he was reluctant to reject it. But there was other work that would keep him closer to town through the upcoming winter months, and he knew any decision could not be made without Black Jack's concurrence. Irwin Dabney saw that he was conflicted.

"It's quite all right to say 'no.' Your answer will have no bearing on future projects, and there are plenty of other fellows looking for this kind of work. I just wanted to offer you the chance, in appreciation of your past contributions to the company."

"I enjoy working for you, Mr. Dabney, and am grateful for these kinds of opportunities. But, if it won't compromise my standing with you, I suppose it's best that I pass. My partner is still recovering from some summer injuries, and I've got a few previous commitments at this time. I hope you understand."

"I most certainly do. Don't give it another thought. I'll be back in touch with you come springtime and the results of these preliminary tallies. I expect we'll need to run a few surveys at that point." The men shook hands as Irwin Dabney ushered Lowe to the door of the conference room.

There were other men already assembling in the hallway, and Lowe gave a courteous nod as he weaved across the small room toward his exit. His final obstacle was a large man who moved almost willfully to block his way.

"Pardon me," said Lowe, attempting to squeeze through a narrow parting of the crowd.

The man grunted some inaudible remark and held his ground, ignoring Lowe Yancy altogether. Lowe was about to repeat himself when another person pulled at the big man's arm and prompted him to move aside. He did so reluctantly. He knew well what he was doing and to whom.

Lowe had spotted Farley Ochs down the length of the hallway, and despite the presence of side and back doors, he moved deliberately toward the front and the inevitable confrontation. Lowe could sense the man, like the dog had sensed the mountain lion, but in this case, the man was too fat, too red, too brutish and much too vociferous to be lurking. He stood obvious in that hall, like a high, unstable wall ready to tumble upon the innocent and unsuspecting. He had always preyed on the unfortunate who might step in the black of his large shadow, and he thrived on exposing their cowardice. Lowe Yancy was no coward, however, and Ochs had much to prove by breaking him. Their fates were now entwined, and lethal.

Lowe pretended to not recognize the menacing figure as he brushed against him, but he was too close. He could smell the contempt on the man's sweat and breath, and his own loathing became all too familiar and personal. There was an undeniable justification for his feelings, but this was not the place to reveal them. Out of respect for Mr. Dabney and his future relations with the company, Lowe knew better than to provoke Farley Ochs. Nevertheless, his judgment yielded to the power of his hate.

"Stay out of my way, Ochs. Stay out of my sight." He murmured so only the man could hear, and then, he disappeared through the doorway.

The wooden sidewalk was 10 feet wide along the face of the building, only four short strides, and yet, Lowe's shoes did not touch gravel before he heard the creaking of the planks behind him.

"Well, Miss Sally, just where are ya runnin' off to?" Farley hurled his insult. Blocking Lowe at the door may have had no effect, but challenging his manliness was a sure way to force a fight. It took all of Lowe's self-restraint to prove him wrong. Still, he stopped dead in his tracks and turned.

"I meant what I said in there."

"I heard ya. I guess you don't believe in lettin' bygones be bygones. That's good. Myself? I hold more with 'an eye for an eye.'"

"Funny, I would never have taken you for a religious man," Lowe said flippantly.

"Oh, yeah, I'm a regular evangelist. I've sent plenty of sinners back to their maker. If you're interested, I'd like to oblige you the same way."

"Another time, perhaps." Lowe grinned at the audacity of the man. His words were just winds on an empty sea, threatening but to no one.

"Tell me, how's that darkie of yours? I understand we cut him real good."

"My 'darkie?' Oh, you mean John Clark. He's doing just fine. It takes a lot more than some scrawny oaf with a little pig sticker to put down a real man like that. Now, as I recollect, you were pretty much unconscious by the time that knife showed itself. It was my 'darkie' who took care of that." Lowe enjoyed mocking the man. "Yeah, he's healed up right nicely. Mr. Clark's all muscle and mettle, and he's damn near indestructible."

"I'm glad to hear that. He and I have some unfinished business, I believe. You tell him, will you? You tell him that I've been lookin' for him."

Farley put his hands on his hips and puffed up his chest in a vain attempt to be intimidating. His wide girth rendered the effort ridiculous, and a series of coughs, resulting from an over inflation of his lungs, caused Lowe to laugh almost in his face. Ochs seethed but was not sure how to vent his surging rage. He was not prepared for Lowe's cockiness. Such bold resistance left him dubious of the tactics that had served him well in the past.

Lowe answered, "You can tell him yourself. I expect him here at any time, and I'm sure he'll be just pleased as punch to meet up with you again. He, too, is quite religious. And you know how those 'darkies' are, mean and tough as nails."

It was a calculated lie. Black Jack was across town at the pool room, happily engaged with a beer and a cue stick. But, of course, Farley had no way of knowing, and he had learned to respect the force that accompanied Black Jack's anger. His stout neck contorted as he looked up and down the walk for his wiry adversary. He was relieved that Black Jack was nowhere in sight.

"No. Like ya said, 'maybe another time.' I've gotta get on to my meetin'. Sorry ya won't be goin' with us to the Big Timber. One never knows what can happen in them far off places. But I'll be seein' ya. There's no doubt about that."

Lowe was left standing on the edge of the walkway, wondering if the time was approaching when he or Black Jack would again do battle against this Goliath of a man. He was not quite as confident as his words made him seem, and the thought of another brutal fight was unnerving. But fear had never been a sign of cowardice. It was running, running away, and Lowe knew in his heart that he would never turn from the taunts of a bully.

It was approaching noon. Market Street seemed rather empty of traffic, but it must have been busy enough in the early morning hours. Horses had left their sign everywhere, and the town's honey wagon was woefully behind in its collection. The two men that worked it seemed close to exhaustion, and neither showed an ounce of enthusiasm for the work. Of course, no one nearby was surprised.

One man stopped to rest against his shovel, and in three seconds, he had reevaluated his entire life. He whined, "Twenty-two years and this is what I hold to show fer it. Bobby Lee, the next time them Irish policemen tell ya to move on, please do it! Please, keep yer mouth shut and jist walk yer ass on up the road. That judge says, 'Two days o' hard labor or five dollars fine.' Next time we pay, ya hear me? We pay! I don't cotton to hard labor."

"I hear ya, brother, but thar won't be no next time. Things are gonna change fer now on. After today, I ain't touchin' no booze, I ain't backsassin' no lawman, and I certainly ain't ridin' behind no horse. Ya might as well throw in smokin' and gamblin' and floozies. I ain't doin' none o' it. Nothin's worth this kind o' punishment. Amen?"

"Amen!"

Lowe could not overhear the conversation, but as he neared the wagon, he felt genuine sympathy for the hapless wretches who filled it.

"Keep up the good work, boys," he said, trying to be gracious.

"Right, bub. It's bad enough we gotta pick up shit, but I guess now we gotta hear it, too. Thar's a shovel right here, if ya care to take yer turn. Otherwise, shut yer trap!"

It was testy remark, but Lowe understood. "I prefer to shut my trap. I meant no offense."

The one named Bobby Lee responded, "Ah, none taken, mister. Eddie's jist pissed at me, and he's throwin' his complaint on everyone else. Toil o' any sort makes us a bit cranky. Ya can jist imagine how we take to this here shovelin'."

"I can't blame him. It's nasty work, a real tough job. Well, I hope the day turns out better for the both of you."

"It cain't git no worse now, can it? Ya watch where ya step."

Lowe did just that. As he crossed the road, his eyes were so pinned to the ground that he nearly knocked over a woman just leaving the H. H. Castle Store. Two cans rolled from the top of the box she carried, and Lowe danced a quick jig to avoid crushing them. He was mortified by his lack of attention and good manners, but without even acknowledging the woman, he dropped to his knees and fumbled for the cans.

"Ma'am, please forgive my utter clumsiness. It's been one of those days."

"One of which days, Mr. Yancy?"

Lowe did not expect to hear his name, and he glanced up awkwardly from his crouched position. Holding one of the cans high in his hand, he looked like a beggar pleading for alms. He reached low for the other and suddenly resembled a knight kneeling before his queen. When Annie Darrow held out her hand, he was not sure whether to kiss it as royalty or use it like a rope to pull himself up. He smartly chose the latter.

"Oh, thank you, ma'am," he said, finally making it to his feet.

"I thought we were over that. My name is Annie. Surely you remember."

"Yes, my memory seems cursed at times, but you...I will always remember. Annie. Annie Darrow. Lordy, I'm sure glad that I ran into you."

"Why? Were you aiming for me, or do you just hate knocking down strangers?" Annie giggled.

Lowe found it difficult to look her in the eye. He again faced the ground, suddenly overcome with childlike bashfulness. For some reason, he was easily shaken by Annie Darrow. It was an inexplicable feeling.

She repeated herself, "I asked a question. Why? Were you aiming for me, or do you just like knocking down strangers?" Annie felt cheated. It was a rather witty riposte, especially from a woman who rarely felt sufficiently at ease to quip with a man.

"Why no, ma'am, I was just crossing...."

"Now, Lowe, a joke's no good if you have to tell it twice or explain it. Lord knows how difficult it is for me to say something funny. The least you could do would be to pretend some laughter." She looked stern at first, and then grinned widely to make her point. Her eyes twinkled, and Lowe finally chuckled.

"I warned you, Mrs. Darrow. It's one of those days. My poor noggin hasn't even a clue whose neck it's on. I just meant that I would rather bump into a friend than a perfect stranger."

"I know what you meant, and I'm relieved that you've come to think of me as your friend. You've kept your distance. I've wondered why."

Lowe finally faced her. "I do think of you that way, Annie, as a friend. I hope that's all right. I would not want you to think me improper."

"Of course not. We certainly are friends, dear friends. I'd be hurt if you thought otherwise."

Annie took the cans and returned them to their place in the box, already heavy with groceries. When she lifted it, she winced.

"Well, I must be going. It's a bit of a walk from here," she said.

"You're walking? In this weather? Carrying so much? I thought Castles had delivery."

"They do, but not when all the boys are in school. A little exercise never hurts a body, but frankly, I really didn't intend to buy everything in the store. I usually send Morgan and Cora to shop when there's so much."

Lowe was more than willing to assist a person in need. It was in his nature to be courteous and helpful, but it was also a learned trait from many a paternal lesson. His father painstakingly trained him to put others first, and while it was a long time ago, he still vividly remembered one particular time when he failed to heed a warning about jumping in puddles.

Of course, Lowe Yancy, the boy, ignored the directive in his typically independent way and managed to splash a steady, muddy spray on the dress of a passing young lady. The woman dropped her bundle as she attempted to whisk her clothes from the ruinous deluge, and she nearly tripped over the excited urchin, who darted from puddle to puddle, back and forth across her path. Lowe's father steadied her in the nick of time, but not before the dress bore the marks of a child unchecked.

The lady's astonishment would have been lesson enough, but a month of chores was required to pay for the cleaning of her dress, and Lowe was further expected to walk a long mile like a true gentleman, toting her bundle and escorting her safely home. He was only seven but not too young to learn. His father said afterwards, while he hauled his son on his shoulders over that same long mile back, "Have your fun, boy, but never ever at another's expense."

Lowe smiled at Annie. "I'll carry that for you. I can drop it off later if you prefer, or I'll just take it up now if you're planning on more shopping."

"No, I'm done with shopping. It's awful heavy though. I hate to burden you."

"It would be my pleasure."

"Well, sir, all things considered, I gladly accept your kind offer. But I'll just walk along beside you, if you don't mind."

Lowe did not mind. He rather liked the idea, but with some reservation. Devlin was a small town where there was no such thing as a secret. Truths and untruths alike were passed like germs in a school room, and rumor gained acceptance faster than fact. In Devlin gossip was a dangerous practice, but a popular one, nonetheless. He thought of Annie's reputation.

"Are you sure? Folks might get the wrong idea."

Annie laughed. At her age, it was rather flattering to hear someone worry about her honor. Other than her husband's conduct, her life of late had yielded little fodder for rumor. She would love to hear what people might say about this handsome man, who but carried her groceries.

"I'll risk the scandal," she said.

They took their time. They walked and talked. When the box became heavy, Lowe set it down and they talked more, well beyond the point of rest.

"And how are the children?" Lowe asked.

"They are wonderful, loaded with all the good and bad that God can squeeze in a human body." Annie thought for a moment. She was not sure how much to tell since the stories could go on endlessly.

"Well, my Cora has a new beau. At least, I think she does. She's been very quiet of late, which means she's up to something. She's become quite meticulous about her clothes and hair, which is a sure sign there's a boy looming. I was the same way at her age. She'll tell me what I need to hear or ask me what she needs to know, in her own good time. And Jacob..." Annie groaned. "O-oh, that Jacob! I thought he had killed himself last week. I stepped out to call him in for supper and heard him holler from the treetops. He must've been 30 feet up and probably would've gone higher if there was so much as another twig above him. About the time he was half way down, the branch broke and my boy dropped like a hammer."

"Is he all right?"

"He got up and didn't even brush himself off. Now, he's decided to make the tree his next fort. You know, it's higher with a much better view of his *enemies*. Trust me. There will be no such fort, if I have to tie him to the ground just to keep him from climbing."

Lowe listened intently to her many accounts of the children. It was clear how deeply she loved them and how happy she was sharing that part of her life with a willing listener. He liked being that listener.

"Tell me about Morgan, Annie."

"Yes, I saved him until last for a reason. Morgan worships the ground you walk on, Lowe, and what you have shown him this year will be his treasure of a lifetime. You know, he doesn't even discuss his experiences in any detail, but I see how they affected him, how they've rounded him into a complete man. He's become enlivened with special goals and desires and a new resourcefulness to fulfill them. You gave him that, like you gave him back life at that miserable mill pond."

"No, ma'am, Morgan is who he is because of his mother and father. What he found out there in the wilderness was nothing more than what was inside his heart all the time. Morgan is like me. The woods bring it all together. They sift out the meaningless burdens we place on ourselves and sort out the things we should value in this life. I only showed him a place. He found the rest on his own."

Annie set a hand to her breast and felt the beat accelerate as Lowe continued to speak. She knew his words to be true, and she was moved by the way the man had come to understand her son. Despite her closeness as a mother, she envied Lowe's growing bond with Morgan. They were two of a kind, separated by age but not by character, by experience but not by dreams. In one she could see the other, and in neither could she find a flaw. Perhaps within her was an even greater envy, one being suppressed by the weight of propriety. It was the friendship her Morgan found in such a man.

"You have humility, Mr. Yancy. I was quite worried about Morgan over the past few months. He seemed so disoriented, sad one minute and happy the next. I prayed he would work things out eventually, but wasn't ready to watch him fall time and again back into his misery. He was never that way as a boy. He was always vibrant and thirsty for life. I don't know what you did, but Morgan rediscovered his former self in that...what do you call it, the Big Timber country?"

"That's the place. So, he's better now?"

"Yes. He is better, and he's in love." Annie watched to see Lowe's reaction. He just smiled, being not at all surprised. He knew the boy was smitten when he first saw him pining for that pretty yellow haired girl, who was walking away down the far side of Market Street.

"Let me guess. Sarah Dabney?"

"Why, yes, but how did you know?"

"Let's just say I know a broken heart when I see one, and the first time Morgan and I crossed paths, he was hurting something fierce watching Miss Dabney on the arm of another. It's a long story, but I told him then that things would work out. I couldn't be happier for the two of them."

"I just hope it lasts. She's a very sweet girl, but feelings do change. Time can tarnish a relationship. People fall out of love for a lot of reasons."

"True, but not all people. Morgan's the type that only loves once, and he'll make certain his feelings for this girl will endure to his final breath. That much I know."

"How do you know?"

"I just know."

Annie was suddenly full of questions, personal questions, but she kept them to herself. Propriety again dictated a comfortable distance, even in conversation. She would have to be content to simply wonder.

Christmas was only a week away, and Annie Darrow, like every other woman in Devlin, was busy with preparation. The season of giving, it was really a time when mothers and wives offered all of their labors and love to create a more tender world for those in their care. A time of red bows on green boughs, of sugar cookies and cinnamon laced cider, of caroling and fiddling and dancing, of reflection and worship, Christmas was because women made it so. All the presents of others, neatly boxed, paper wrapped and ribboned, were insignificant against this gift. Too often, only God seemed to understand and truly appreciate them, but the women, including Annie, worked tirelessly without expectation to bring enchantment and joy to those they loved.

"What are your plans, Lowe, for the holiday?" Annie inquired.

"I don't do much, as a rule. Me and Black Jack like our breakfast, so we make that the meal of the day. Sometimes we fish, if it's not too cold. Sometimes we just walk around. I like to get him a gift of sorts, but it usually isn't anything to write home about. And Black Jack tries to go to church, if there's a black congregation in town. Christmas? I don't know. We don't do much."

"Don't you ever want to get home to see your family?"

"I don't have any family left that I know of, and Black Jack's folks are spread from Savannah to Chicago. The closest thing to kin for either of us is old Silas, and he generally likes to keep to himself out on Jasper Creek."

"Surely there are friends from earlier days. An old chum perhaps?"

"I wouldn't know about that. At my age friends have either moved on or you just plain can't remember them."

"At your age! For goodness sake, Lowell Yancy, you are still a young man." Annie's rebuke was more like flattery. In truth, he was no older than she, and she was far from ready to concede anything to the greedy hands of time.

"I reckon you're right, ma'am. On some days you just feel older. When you're out there in those woods with every muscle aching, eyes going bad, and there's nothing but your thoughts for entertainment, you can't help believing that the days are fast overtaking you."

"It seems like a hard life to me," said Annie.

"It can be. But there's nothing like being awakened in the pit of night by the brilliance of a rising moon or being warmed by a late autumn sun after the rain and cold have seeped through your bones. And there's nothing quite like an April frost forming on your beard or the smell of air after a lightning strike. Yes, it can be a hard life, but I can't imagine a better one."

Lowe somehow made it sound so right. Beyond every agony was a healing gift, like the birth of a child, like a rainbow. Never having been there, Annie could now imagine the beauty of his world, and she began to understand for the first time the lure that drew him, and her son, to the far reaches of the wilderness. Still, Lowe's answers concerned her deeply. Whether they would admit it or not, Lowe and Black Jack needed more. They needed people. They needed the fellowship of a community. They needed to belong to someone and some place. They needed a home.

Their life was not necessarily a matter of choice. It was, in part, the misfortune of their work that carried them across remote regions and into a host of hamlets still struggling for a permanent spot on the map. But to a much greater degree, it was the consequence of a great friendship that dared span the racial bounds of an intolerant generation. Neither was welcomed in the other's world, so they created their own in the few places they could stand as equals, in the hidden green valleys and the rolling blue mountains.

There would be another world for them soon, one carefully prepared by the hands and heart of Mrs. Annie Darrow. These men needed their Christmas, and Annie resolved that they would have it.

"What the devil has come over you, woman? You've either lost your mind altogether or you're just looking for trouble. Well, you'll sure enough find it if I hear any more of this." Lawson thought that was the end of the argument, but Annie was determined to have her say.

"But I thought the two of you were friends."

"Whatever gave you that idea? I knew the man a long time ago."

"They have no one, Lawson, and we have so much. Is it too hard to share just one evening of the year with people in need?"

"What need, Annie?" Lawson raised his voice. "What could they possibly need? They're free to go or do anything they want, so let them do it. Stop interfering in the lives of strangers."

"It was no stranger that pulled our Morgan from that pond. It was no stranger that stood up to an angry bear or faced a hateful bunch of brawlers in the lumber camp. Men who risk so much for others can never be strangers. They have shown that they care about Morgan, and Morgan naturally wants them here. They are a new and important part of his life, his friends, and they need...."

"Again, Annie, what need?"

Annie took a deep breath. Her mind should have been clear on that question, but it was not. There were many right responses, and she was satisfied to finally settle on just one. "They need Christmas. Everybody needs Christmas."

Lawson slammed the kitchen table with a tight fist. He scuffed across the room and was so perplexed that he came close to tearing the door off a cabinet that concealed his half-full pint of scotch. He reached blindly on a high shelf for the bottle, and in doing so, carelessly dislodged Annie's porcelain tureen. The bowl shattered upon the floor. Without apology, he lifted the bottle to his lips and drained it of its contents. Annie watched, as she had so many times before.

"That's never the answer. You can break every plate in the house if you want, but we are going to talk this through."

"The talking's done. My decision is final. Lowell Yancy can partake of Christmas anywhere he wants, anywhere except here. Not at my house. Not that man."

"So, it's Mr. Yancy that bothers you," Annie said, starting to hear what sounded like jealousy. She wondered if she was in some way deserving of her husband's distrust.

"He's a meddler. I don't like meddlers. But it's not just Yancy. Old man Monk is content to stay a hermit, so why not let him be? And Clark? He's a colored. There'll be no black man sitting at my table, not in the presence of my children and wife. It's not right. Now let's just drop the subject." He lifted the bottle again, forgetting that it was empty.

Annie was disappointed. For some reason, she had thought that Lawson would understand this time. He knew these men. He knew what they had done for his son. He knew that they had lived alone too long and had forgotten the many blessings of a family and home. She hoped that Lawson's lost sense of compassion might be restored by the spirit of the season and the company of friends. But he rejected it all. In doing so, he rejected her.

Annie held back both tears and rage as she made ready the last word. Strangely, she selected a new topic, which confused Lawson and convinced him all the more that she had lost her sanity.

"Morgan will cut the tree, and I'll help the children decorate it. Even Jacob will join in while we clean up the parlor and adorn it with the candles and greenery. Cora likes to wrap the presents, so

I'll sneak her a little money for the effort. She and I will probably bake for an entire day and then, on Christmas Eve, we'll cook the pork roast. Between supper and sweets, I suspect we'll fill our gullets as we do every year, and then groan while I play the piano and the children sing their favorite carols. Morgan and Cora will read passages from the family Bible, and then, we will all open our gifts in front of the warm fire and pass along our hugs and kisses. In the end, I'll offer a prayer about 'peace on earth and good will to men.'"

Annie looked coldly at her husband. She had outlined the events as she had always remembered them. "Where are you in all of this, Lawson? When did you cease to be a member of this family, only to become its tyrant?"

"I'm there."

"Sure. You're there for the dinner, and you are there for the Christmas toddies that I make you. The children are left wondering why you don't sing or how you can just sit in your chair when they are so excited they could burst. How can you look into those faces and not want to be involved in their lives? You do nothing to support our Christmas and little more the rest of the year."

"Well, isn't that gratitude? Just who do you think pays for this family, not just for their Christmas, but for their dinners and clothes and school books and everything else they require? I work solely for your contentment, and as long as I do, I have a right to expect some measure of obedience from my wife and children. Damn it, woman, who do you think you are?"

Nothing else Lawson could say would sting like the word, "obedience." Annie was not a subject, but a spouse. She was not a servant, but a partner. Many in Devlin may have felt as Lawson, that marriage was an autocracy where the man's whim was law. She could endure such thinking when her husband ruled with understanding and benevolence, but he was different now and had long since forgotten that his proper place was beside his wife, not above her. Her trust in him was to be earned and his power over her to be granted. Lawson had no right to either.

"I have forgotten who I am," Annie replied. "Listen to me, Lawson. I intend to enjoy Christmas Eve, the same way we have done each and every year since the birth of our first child, and just like in the past, I plan to take the children to holy services the following morning. I wish you would join us. I wish you would again be involved in our traditions, for the sake of the children. But at four o'clock on Christmas Day, things may seem different, because all of us are going to welcome these three deserving people, who I say are in need of what we have to offer this precious time of year. Some decisions are simply not yours to make. This is one of them."

"Annie, I will not abide your incessant rebellion! Try to go through with this, and I swear you will go it alone."

"Don't you hear me? I always go it alone. I'm tired. I'm tired of your sour attitude, your temper and your alcohol, and God forgive me, I've grown tired of you. Do what you want. The children and I will manage."

Annie stared at the porcelain fragments strewn across the floor. The tureen was once her mother's, and now they both were gone. Her tears began to flow silently down her cheeks as she stood defiant against a barrage of vulgar threats and gestures. She had given enough of herself. She had lost too much of what had been dear to her and now clung tightly to what little was left of her shattered pride. Sad but determined, she stood until the man was there no more.

The Farmers' Almanac had been quite clear about the week's precipitation, but it was Thursday already and the valley had thus far experienced only a few scattered showers. The drizzle was more of a heavy mist than rain, and the metal roof above the school house was quiet, except for a sporadic patter of drops blown from the trees. It was a bleak, sleepy day.

The students were disappointed. A drop in temperature might have cured the contagion of yawns that had overcome them. It might have provided relief from the ever-deepening gloom and the insufferable monotone of Mr. Tutwiler's lecture. They had expected snow, and they wanted lots of it.

Of course, there was rarely a lasting benefit with snow, unless it reached blizzard proportions and could be measured in yards. The children walked to school in any weather, and only the worst of storms could excuse them from their studies. Still, a good tramp through a snow bank was more romp than burden. Even when but a frosting, the white of winter was the one color that would stir their interest, warm their hearts and leave them begging for the out of doors.

The dreariness had been overbearing, and Mr. Tutwiler felt no insult when every eye began to watch intently through the windows panes. Only the portraits of George Washington and Abraham Lincoln seemed to give him any attention, and he could swear that even they would occasionally glance at the small flurries drifting by the glass. By the time of their dismissal, three inches of clean white carpet stretched from the school to the steps of their homes, and every student tromped gleefully upon it.

"Are we still goin' on Saturday?" Dewey asked. The brim of his brown hat held a quarter inch of snow.

Morgan looked into the sky as best he could. "I think we should ask the girls. A lot depends on this weather."

"Ah, but the more snow the better."

"Sure, just as long as we can get there. It's a long way to Avery's farm. You can't trust the Ford in this mess, even if Pa were to let me use it. And he won't. Besides, there are some steep hills out that way. I'd have to run the car backwards to keep gas in the engine, and there's absolutely no traction going backwards."

"We ain't gonna need your motor car," Dewey said emphatically. "And I gotta tell ya, that contraption's more finicky and more demandin' of attention than a birthday party princess. It don't do hills. It don't do snow or mud. It's a horseless carriage, all right, one that just sits there until ya hook it up to the team. Why'd your Pa get the damn thing anyway? It ain't like we got roads in these parts."

"That's a fair question. I guess some folks just have to have what's new."

"Well, as far as I'm concerned, all this new-fangled machinery is a sure path to ruination. Mark my words. The day's comin' when a man won't even know how to calculate 10, unless some machine counts his toes for him. There ain't gonna be no such thing as farmers and loggers, just a bunch of folks who fancy themselves as *thinkers*. You watch. The damn machines will prob'ly be doin' that, too."

Dewey had forgotten what he really wanted to say and rattled on about the future of man and machine until his original thought returned. "Oh, yeah, set yer mind at ease 'bout gettin' to Avery's. I got us other means," he said assuringly.

Morgan had his doubts. "If this storm keeps up, a team of oxen couldn't tow a hundred-pound buggy."

Dewey slipped the hat off his head and flicked the layer of snow with his fingers. "You just worry 'bout Miss Dabney. I'll take care of the rest."

The snow was rather fickle for the remainder of the week, alternating between occasional flakes and blinding windswept walls of white. By the time Saturday morning arrived, there was two feet of powder shrouding the landscape.

Dewey knocked hard against the wooden door and waited. He was about to knock again when it finally opened, and Annie was there to give him her best 'good mornin' smile. A light breeze played against her hair, and the freshness of the day rushed across her skin.

"Why, hello, Mrs. Darrow!" Dewey almost shouted in his excitement. He took a deep bow, and as he rose up, he let his arm sweep around until it pointed to something special. "Would ya care to come a courtin' on this fine wintry day?"

Annie looked across the yard to find a shiny red sleigh parked before her gate and a bay gelding patiently waiting for his lark in the country.

"Why, Mr. Baughman, I do declare, you know just how to treat a girl. I would be honored to accompany you. Just give me a minute to grab my cloak and to ask my fiercely jealous husband about his thoughts on the matter."

"Ah, husband? Perhaps we should postpone this little outing until Morgan and I bring back the trees."

Annie feigned her heartbreak, "Alas, I am wounded, sir. But if you must."

Morgan had heard the knocking, and he wasted no time racing down the stairs and across the room toward the kitchen and back door. He hollered in his haste, "Ma, we won't be back for several hours, so don't worry about us! And I'm taking the gray horse blanket and your old quilt. Goodbye!"

He was gone before she could respond, but Annie knew he needed more than just wraps. He was headed for the shed. With axe and saw in hand, he would reappear at any moment, sliding through the snow like a youngster who should know better. She lingered at the door to have her say.

"I'll not worry as long as you stop running with those sharp tools!" she yelled into the cold. "Have you boys got everything?"

Morgan looked to Dewey, who nodded, but with some uncertainty.

"I could put together a food basket for you," Annie offered.

"Thank ya kindly, but I got it all. We're loaded up and hurtin' for nothin'."

Morgan hurriedly jumped onto the front seat of the sleigh. Dewey snapped the reins and the horse set out.

"Now don't forget the girls in all this rush and remember that you are gentlemen!" Annie cautioned, but the sleigh glided faster than her voice.

The breeze from their movement gave the chill extra bite, and Morgan was quick to tighten his scarf around his neck. His eyes watered from the air.

"Go on and hunker down under them blankets, if ya want. That's why ya brought 'em," Dewey suggested, speeding the horse along. "I suppose ya been wonderin' 'bout the rig."

Before Morgan could respond, the sleigh was jostled by a hidden bump, rendering the boys air borne for a long, risky second. They bounced hard on the return. Morgan wiped the tears from his eyes and firmly gripped the rail of the seat.

"Is that the best you can do?" he cried, exhilarated by the ride. Dewey prodded the bay for more.

"Oliver P. Buck, that's who," said Dewey, in response to his own comment about the rig.

"Who what?"

"That's who provided this sleigh, Oliver P. Buck. Auralee's ol' man had it under cover in the back of his garage. It must've belonged to someone else at some point, 'cause he told me he's never ever once hitched the thing up. Some folks think of snow and hibernate like them bears. That's Olie for ya. Others get themselves a proper conveyance, like this here sleigh, and hit the winter head on. Mr. Buck said to clean her up and take her for a run, so that's just what we're doin'. What ya think?"

"I think we owe him. This is great!"

"Nah, he don't want nothin'. He likes me. He thinks I'm gonna take one of them girls off his hands, and I might just up and do it. Let's stop off for Auralee and then cut over through town for Sarah. Will that suit ya?"

"Hey, I'm just following the horse."

The passage to Avery's farm went by too fast, with Auralee snuggling to make the most of Dewey's warmth and with Morgan and Sarah huddled in the back like nestling doves. The scenery was breathtaking, as was the winter air. White mountains melded with the clouds and the vales, and only the dark trunks rising in scattered groves provided contrast. The couples nuzzled in the privacy of their wraps but emerged often to behold the stark beauty of the frozen, frosty land.

The snowflakes were fewer but larger now and could be felt tickling and trickling when they met their mark. Sarah wiped the wetness from her cheek, only to catch another flake with the very tip of her nose. She buried her face on Morgan's chest, and he pulled the blanket high.

It was convenient that farmer Avery was a distant relative of the Baughmans'. Dewey had no idea just how distant or from which limb of the family tree he would hang. Of course, the details were of no real importance, since the same could be said for almost anyone living within wagon's reach of Devlin. Every man seemed to be kin to every other man, and it became too confusing to remember whether he was a cousin or uncle, brother or friend. What was important was that Mr. Avery was a kind soul, who welcomed young visitors to his small piece of the river and to the cleared rustic plains that comprised the family farm. Of course, there were trees on the farm, a small copse here and a high grove there, a scattering of field oaks and a young stand of spruces and firs that fringed the entire length of his northern boundary. These, too, were important. The evergreens were low and full and pointed, just perfect for a Yuletide parlor.

Dewey hitched the horse to a limb and tossed a blanket over its bare back. Then, he and Auralee took off on the run.

"He'll be back," Morgan said to Sarah. "He'll be out of breath within 50 yards and will suddenly remember the saw. I'll bet you a bear hug that he'll be back."

"Of course, he'll be back. They'll need the saw. But I'll take that bet. I can't lose."

Sarah watched the couple disappear into the trees, and she laughed when Auralee quickly came scampering back to the sleigh.

"Can't cut trees without a saw," Auralee said sheepishly.

"Where's Dewey?"

"Back there. Breathing." She rolled her eyes, grabbed the saw and hurried back to join her man.

Sarah held her arms out and waited. "Mister, I'll collect that hug now, if you don't mind. You were close, but Dewey never returned. So, pay up!"

Sarah looked cold standing in the deep snow, yet said nothing to indicate her discomfort. But when a brief gust of wind came blowing across the knolls, it sent a strong shiver racing across her slender body. Her reaction was noticeable, and Morgan quickly retrieved the quilt from the sleigh and delicately wrapped it around her. Then he held her tight until she cooed with pleasure in his warmth.

"We should start looking before our feet get too cold," he said. "You may want to keep this around you."

The girl nodded her appreciation, and the two walked slowly from the edge of the field into the open stand of young spruce trees. They separated as they began to inspect each and every candidate for height and shape and fullness, and in the snow, their tracks looped and weaved a pattern across the miniature forest.

It was just a matter of time before Morgan approached, displaying his own sheepish look. "Guess who forgot the axe?" he said, laughing at himself. "You wouldn't want to run back and get it for me, would you?"

Sarah was willing, but she shook her head out of principle. "Unless you are out of breath, I wouldn't want to start a bad precedent. I'll find the tree. You get the axe."

One went one way and the other went back, but it was not long before Morgan returned to the area, only to find that Sarah was gone. It would not be hard to find her. A single line of prints branched away from the many rings already pressed in the snow. Morgan followed her, like a fox on the scent.

He must have run a hundred yards curling in and around the trees, expecting to see her at any point along the way. The woods became dense with rounder, older saplings, but he plunged right through, still close to Sarah's conspicuous trail. The snow laden branches bent easily with the passing of his powerful frame and flung their powder high to drift again with the winter breeze. He stopped to listen but could hear nothing. He could see nothing, except the wall of trees and the tiny boot prints that disappeared beneath them. He almost called out, but like the fox, he preferred the chase to be stealthy and silent. He moved another 30 or 40 yards before he cleared the stand of spruce, and then he found himself beneath the tall hardwoods that lined the banks of the Charity River. He had been there before. So had Sarah.

Avery's pool was a lovely place in any season, but not near so inviting in the winter. The water was blue with cold, and the once vibrant growth of summer now looked foreboding and bare. Icicles skirted the cliffs, and thick silver columns stood in the sluggish flow of the seeps and falls. The river was higher, both in the still waters and across the breaks that formed a natural dam. While snow enhanced the river's beauty, it left it unfriendly, frozen and wild.

Morgan could see none of it from his perch above the precipice, except the shimmering of a mist being tossed up by the breaks. He now worried about his Sarah. Her tracks led down. He knew well the treachery of the cliffs, where any misstep, even in dry weather, could send one plummeting toward death. Nothing, except Sarah, could have drawn him further into this danger. He followed ever so carefully to the first ledge and peered over into the void.

His mind suddenly saw what his eyes could not, and his muscles flagged with the shock of disbelief and fear. It was not Sarah, but another, who had lured him to the threatening heights.

Perhaps a ruse of the glistening white that encircled him, his vision of an old woman was ghastly real for but a fragment of a second. Still, she existed. He could plainly see her there, standing statuesque and precariously poised on that thin, icy shelf. Her head and body were draped in a tattered woolen mantle, the features of her face subdued in shadow. She was of a distant time and a forgotten world, deserted by her own and left to perish by the will of nature. Frozen near death, she was more spirit than flesh, and her toes, numb and aching in the worn-out fur of her moccasins, edged toward the rim of the slippery crag. Her heart and mind had long since been abandoned to some faint recollection of her past, and her agony, her loneliness, her mourning for a loved one lost, would soon cease on the jagged rocks or chilling waters below.

Hers was a piteous fate, and Morgan was helpless to alter it. "Don't!" he yelled, in a desperate attempt to save the woman, but when he blinked, she vanished. Once a young and black-haired girl, now old and scraggly gray, she had finally found her way to the arms of her long-departed warrior.

Morgan rubbed his eyes and cursed his horrid imagination. It had conjured a living being out of nothing more than the frigid air, then, placed her in peril. Worse, it left her suffering. He had seen her breath and heard her moans as though she were beside him. No ghost was ever so tangible, no other vision so acute.

He was stunned. Maybe she was a ghost. Or maybe, she was simply the end of the ancient tale, an answer to some question rekindled high in the Big Timber. Why he had seen her at that particular place and moment was beyond his reason, but she was much too perceptible, much too frail to dismiss.

He suddenly refocused on the tracks set deep in the snow banks along the rim. "My God, Sarah!"

Morgan literally leapt to the second ledge below, and with such power that he nearly overshot the landing and slid perilously to the brink. He took more time getting to the third, and once there he fell prostrate, clenching the ground for anchor. He had to force himself to search beyond. In the depths or among the boulders of Avery's pool, there might be a girl in a patchwork quilt. He was afraid to look.

"Hey, down there! You taking a nap?"

Morgan rolled over in the snow and looked up into the face of Sarah. She was all smile and radiant with discovery.

"Come on," she urged, "I found just the right one!"

It was nearly impossible to loosen the terror that had gripped him, but Sarah's voice, so lively and innocent, gave instant relief. Morgan took another moment to collect his wits, but before he arose, he again checked the deadly space below. Anything could be imagined, he thought. But he had to be sure.

There was a scramble of prints on the narrow path that led from the ledge to the top of the cliff. Morgan had overlooked them at first, but he now followed them back to Sarah. He lifted the scarf that concealed her face and looked intently into her wide, blue eyes.

"What?" Sarah asked.

"You're alive. That's what, and you certainly have no fear of heights."

"They never have been much of a concern, but I suppose it wasn't very smart to move down to that rock. I just wanted to see our pool. The cliff seems much higher from above. I can't imagine what made you jump from here last summer."

"I reckon you'll remember." He put an arm around her. "I sure wouldn't want to have to do it again. From up here, someone could easily fall to their death."

"Someone like me?"

"Yes, someone like you."

Of all the trees on Avery's farm, Sarah selected the one growing closest to the pool. Perhaps it was a sentimental choice, or perhaps she had exhausted the search and decided the last one would have to do. But in any case, the tree was perfect in Morgan's eyes.

"So, this is the one." He grabbed at the leader branch.

"Yup."

"Are you sure?"

"Yup."

"So I can start chopping."

"Yup."

"Would you like to chop it?"

"Nope. That's a pleasure reserved for you. It's to be your tree, so you should take it down."

Morgan looked at the cold, wet snow amassed at the base of the sapling. "Miss, you are ever so considerate," he said facetiously, as he dropped to his knees. He was already damp from head to toe, so a little more of the same was really no deterrent. With his arm he raked the snow from around the trunk to allow for the cutting. Then he shook the tree, and the frosting of a thousand needles coated him even further.

Sarah laughed. She moved close and brushed the white from his hat and coat. "I love being with you," she said. "I love being here in this place."

Morgan smiled in agreement. He hesitated for a moment, as though he had forgotten something, and Sarah handed him the axe.

"No, that's not it," he said, almost to himself. "I think a lot lately about you, about our memories here and about things to come that may bring new memories."

His heart was trying to speak, and he understood that it was useless to hush it. Still on his knees, he removed her gloves so he could cradle her hands in his. He marveled at how soft and small and delicate they were. His own calloused hands showed the marks of a different kind of life, and he wondered if he had any right to the words that would follow.

"I never will be rich, Sarah, and I'm a long way from knowing just what I can do to find a living in these hills. I may be young, but not so young that I can't see what hardships could be ahead, if you and I, well, if we ever...."

Sarah began to melt. Her own knees settled in the deep, white snow before Morgan could find his message. She faced him and listened.

"Don't you see?" he pleaded, recalling his vision. "Life is not a gift. It's a loan. I could lose you in the blink of an eye. I could turn around one day and you might be gone. Sarah, I truly believe I have nowhere to go if it's not with you."

Morgan's lips quivered. He was ashamed of being vulnerable. He had moved to that dangerous edge and was afraid Sarah would somehow let him fall.

She heard the words, but his eyes were what gave them meaning. She comprehended fully what was being asked of her, and it was more than she had expected in so short a courtship. Morgan's virility was fraught with honesty and tenderness, and even if he was reluctant, he could always articulate the things of his heart. She owed him the same clarity, regardless of her answer. There was no deliberation, no hesitation.

"Nowhere to go? Then, come along with me."

Morgan's hold tightened against her palms. "Do you know what you're saying?"

"I think so."

"But I have no job, no money."

"We can wait until you find one. I can work, as well."

"And what about school?"

"Yes, I think we should graduate."

"And your father? I'll have to ask his permission."

Sarah smiled. She understood. Morgan had no second thoughts, though one at his age, by all accounts, should. He could hardly anticipate his tomorrows. She knew that he posed such questions not for her answers, but for her own consideration of the consequences.

"No, the two of us should tell him. Daddy will respect that. Morgan, if our plan is to make it through a lifetime together, I suggest taking shorter steps so I can keep up with you. We have the time. I'll not love you one bit less whether it's a month or a decade to the day we wed."

Morgan was dazed by a spectrum of emotion, but not in any way deterred. Relief and worry, jitters and joy, they were the chisels that helped him craft his way. Each cut differently, but together they shaped what was to be his will. And his will was to take those steps with Sarah, wherever they led and for as long as she and fate would allow.

"Tell me this. You could have anything, go any place and win over any man in the entire world. Why do you settle for so little?"

He was either modest or too much in love, both good traits to Sarah's way of thinking. That might have been the answer in itself.

"I never settle, Morgan. I choose, and I chose you the very first day, down beneath this cliff in the middle of that river."

He had run out of obstacles. One by one, she removed them all. She convinced him that she would never let him fall. Morgan pulled her hands against his chest and rose up on one knee. He swallowed hard, took a deep breath and asked his question plainly.

"Sarah Dabney, will you marry me?"

"Yes, Morgan Darrow, I will."

"Are you sure?"

"Oh, yes, just as sure as my toes are cold."

The tree was set in the corner to the left of the hearth, and it looked quite beautiful, despite being crooked and undecorated. The redolence of needles permeated the room and masked the smell of a year's worth of wood smoke, generated by an open fireplace and Annie's kitchen stove.

"A little to the left," Cora said. Morgan pulled the branches toward him. "Whoa! Whoa! Too much. Push it back some."

He did as he was instructed. "How's that? Is it straight?"

"Yeah. No. I don't know. Why don't you get up and take a look for yourself?"

"Because, Cora, I'm the one holding the tree!"

"All right, then, I guess it's straight."

Morgan drove some shims around his makeshift stand and backed away gingerly. For a split second, the tree was true, but then it listed toward the wall for a fifth and final time. He lifted the tree, stand and all, and slammed it back to the floor.

"Enough of this! Where's that axe? I'm going to make kindling out of this stupid thing!" He actually meant it, but only for the brief time it took to blurt his threat. Morgan rarely was one to show temper, but, on occasion, a simple task gone awry would push him past the point of restraint. The annual raising of the tree was often that occasion.

Cora calmed her brother, "Now, Morgan, we don't need to mangle the poor thing. You have already killed it. Let's try again. You're doing good. We can make this work."

"Yeah, there's the *we*," Morgan groused. "That word sure gets tossed about, especially when I'm the one providing all the labor."

It was all part of the tradition, the leaning tree, the ire, the encouragement. Cora was right. They would make it work, just like they had done each and every year.

Jacob was pretending to do his lessons when he smelled the balsamic fragrance of a fresh cut spruce, and with anticipation of good things to come, he bolted down the stairs to do his part.

"Wow!" he shouted, witnessing the season's first bit of magic. He knew there would be more.

"It's for you, Jake. It's one of those new indoor climbers," Morgan kidded.

The boy looked intently at the spruce. He was hopeful, but realized quickly that it was far too short and prickly for his purposes.

"No, it's not. It's a Christmas tree." He ran over to Morgan and tackled him on the spot. The commotion brought everyone, except Lawson, into the room.

"Oh, my," said Annie, "isn't this a lovely one? We should have Sarah select our trees every year. Will she be joining us for the trimming?"

"Maybe next year. She's with her father tonight."

Annie heard something in the reply and wondered if her son had left a hint of sorts. Morgan and Sarah had become close, and to her way of thinking, it was just a matter of time before he proposed. That was the natural course of life, and she prayed that her son had the good sense to follow it. She might never know for sure. All that he left her was hints.

Even if he had been particularly mute on the subject, Morgan's changing moods and erratic behaviors had already revealed his deep feelings for the girl. Annie honestly believed that a sudden love could prove just as abiding, unwavering and real as any long-developed relationship, though young hearts were often impulsive and cruelly inconstant. Morgan and Sarah had forged their bond in a mere tick of time, and still, it seemed instantly selfless and strong. It was a rare blessing, a mother's hope and woman's romantic vision of a pure and perfect love. In every possible hint, Annie sought a glimpse of their plans for the future. But Morgan guarded his secrets well.

"Maybe next year?" she pried. "Hmm, a lot can happen in a year, son."

"Not necessarily. At this rate, it could take a whole year just to decorate one tree." Morgan refused to fall into her trap.

It was time for trimming, and the family became busy with their usual assignments. Annie gave the orders, and her children gladly marched along. While she and Jacob popped the corn for stringing, Cora wired white pine cuttings for garlands and Morgan secured his crooked tree. It would be a collective offering befitting the spirit of Christmas before they were through, and nothing better would ever adorn its place in the parlor.

Spiraling from tip to base was the garland, woven with

intermittent strands of red ribbon and pointed with bright red bows. Sprigs of cedar laden with clusters of round blue berries rested on the branches, and red balls of papier-mâché were hung from the limbs like apples. White paper angels and stars twisted or fluttered with every movement in the room, and Jacob's endless chains of popcorn draped neatly up and around the Christmas green. And on the very top was a lone golden candle, their star of Bethlehem, to be lit only on the eve of the holy day.

"What a mess!" Lawson complained, when he entered the room. "You've got this whole house so tore up I can hardly get through."

Annie looked at him sternly. The moment called for praise, not criticism. "Now, Lawson, an artist's studio is always splattered with a little paint," she said, minimizing his remark for the sake of the children. "How do you like our masterpiece?"

Lawson stopped just long enough to glance at the handiwork of his family. He found a smile for them and patted Jacob on the head. "Well, now, that's right nice." Then, without further observation or comment, he moved on to the kitchen.

Annie tidied the room and prepared a light supper for everyone before they reassembled in the parlor to officially commence the season. The children were excited as she jotted five numbers on separate tags of paper and placed them in the large pocket of her apron. In accordance with tradition, each child was asked to select one. Then, she drew a slip for herself. The last paper was for Lawson.

Jacob scowled when he saw a five. It was the worst of numbers. It was the worst of luck. Five meant he was last, and come time to take his turn, every decent limb of the tree would be filled with the adornments of others. He crawled across the room where he could cuddle with his mother, and at the same time, surreptitiously switch his tag for the one still tucked against the bottom seam of her pocket. He rummaged secretly until he found it. No one was fooled, and no one cared.

"All right," Annie said. "Let's remember our positions and go get our ornaments. Cora, tell your father it's time and ask him if he'll join us."

The children dispersed and minutes later came trickling back into the room, holding close the ornaments of their choosing. Every person would select two, a memory of the past and a sign of the present. Each decoration would have some personal significance and, by tradition, would need no explanation or justification to assume a rightful place on the tree. The only requirement was a small and hangable size. Still, a good deal of thought and reflection was necessary.

Lawson was not there. Annie waited. She waited while the children sang their carols. She waited while Morgan opened up the Scripture and began to read from the Book of Luke. Annie waited while Cora offered up a prayer for peace and protection across the world, and she waited while Jacob jumped with excitement at the calling of "number one." Lawson was not there. Annie waited, but he did not come.

The mantle clock ushered Christmas with a midnight chime, but only Annie Darrow heard it. The others slept. The home was dark, and she could smell the spruce through the walls of her bedroom. Her eyelids were heavy, much like her heart.

On the tree were eight special ornaments, a bracelet from grandmother and a dried red rose, a golden pocket watch and a sealed envelope with a handwritten poem, a lead toy soldier and a dried-up walnut, an old family tintype, and next to it, a wrinkled fragment of paper showing only the number five.

# CHAPTER 15

Silas's iron cauldron had been used for just about everything. It was a vat for soaking corn into whiskey mash, a pot to condense maple sap into sugar, a water trough for the mule, and a wash tub for clothes too foul and offensive to be tolerated yet another month. But the fire under it was now roaring to a higher purpose. The flames topped the rim, and the water within began to bulge and pop with bubbles. All was ready, except the old man who would just as soon wait for a summer splash in the river.

He may not have liked it, but Silas understood the necessity for this winter bath. Still, he paced about gruff and grumbly, barking commands to his valets who humored him with compliance. Black Jack broke the thick slab of ice that capped a large rain barrel, and Lowe transferred the contents by bucket to the half empty cauldron.

"Why all dis fuss? Dere be plenty o' good clean water in de barrel just de way it is. When you boils up dis soft pure rainwater, it turns all hard and milky with mineral. It stiffen de hair. It wrinkle de skin. Dat ain't no bath for a fine gentleman like yo self," Black Jack goaded Silas, who was already stripped down to his faded red skivvies and starting to shiver.

"Yup, well, ice purdy much has the same effect on an ol' man's body, but it ain't near so satisfyin' as steam. Keep movin' them buckets."

"Dat be my other point, we's emptyin' dis barrel just to fill it back up. Seems to me, you might save us a mess o' time and trouble if you was to jump right on in dere and scrub up fast. What you say to dat, Mr. Monk?"

"I say yer damn lazy. I cain't remember my last good washin', but I'm right sure it took some real soakin' before I sparkled. This may be Lowell Yancy's idea, but it's Silas Monk's skin we been talkin' 'bout. I'll be pickin' my own time and temperature, thank ya very much, and I can tell ya right now that I like it hot. So, boy, you keep on dippin'."

"I fully agree with Silas," commented Lowe. "Cold water will never do. It's important that the water be sufficiently scalding to kill all the vermin farming the dirt on his back." He lifted an old half-used bar of soap. "This is so crusty and discolored from lying around that I thought it was a brick. My senses are telling me that we're going to need a heap of lather for this nasty job." He held his nose until he was sure Silas had seen him.

"Quit flappin' yer damn tongues and jist git to heatin' that water," cried Silas. "I'm freezin' my willies out here. I'll be in the cabin until yer ready, and don't you call me before then. Ya hear?"

Black Jack nodded. "Yessa, but you best check dis first. By now, it likely be warm enough."

Silas stepped off the porch into the snow and walked briskly to the barrel. He sunk his arm, sleeve and all, to the middle. "I like it hot, real hot! It needs a couple more o' them pails, and then, mix it all up and add in the rest. Feels like ice down thar on the bottom. Hell, don't you black fellers e'er take ya a bath? It has to be hot! Now, like I done told ya, I'm headin' back inside and don't want no bother until ya get it right."

The large oak hogshead was refilling rapidly as Lowe and Black Jack added one steaming bucket of water after another. Before long, it was filled to the brim and emitting a heavy plume of fog into the late morning air. Black Jack stirred the contents slowly like a simmering pot of soup, and this time, he made sure the temperature was warm throughout.

"Dat'll do, Mr. Yancy. Dis should heat dem sorry old bones. Mr. Monk, you come runnin'! Yo tub's hot, but coolin' fast."

The door creaked open and a white haired, naked old man flew out on a bee line for the steam. Amazingly fast but stunningly scrawny, he looked like a skinned rabbit racing to its own stew pot.

Lowe and Black Jack laughed, but neither was ready for the sight of Silas Monk, sinewy and bent, scrambling through the snow and rolling awkwardly over the edge of the barrel.

"Eeeooow!" Silas hollered, as he slid up to his chin into the makeshift bath. The displacement flushed like a geyser.

"What, too hot?" asked Lowe, while hurrying to find a bucket of cold water.

"Does fish ass git wet! O' course, it's too hot."

Lowe began to pour.

"Now hold yer horses, son! Give 'er another second until I know what's what." Silas waited until his body acclimated to the temperature. "Aaaah, that ain't so bad actually. You boys do good work when ya have a mind to. Yup, this is nice. Oooo, real, real nice."

"Here's your soap, Silas. We're not in any hurry, so make the best of it. I'll bring you more hot water whenever you want."

Silas Monk was like a nine-year-old boy, who always hated the thought of bathing until he settled in the tub. He just stood there for the longest time, head deep in water, his nose barely above the surface. He was warm from chin to toe, an infrequent pleasure that he intended to relish. The others left him in peace and moved over to the fire to find their own relief against the cold and cloudy day.

"What you hear, Lowe, about dat property?" Black Jack inquired.

"Nothing, yet. I met with an agent. The fellow who owns the land lives out in the Arizona desert. He's got 2,500 acres or so up around the Big Timber, and he wants to sell it all. Unfortunately, he's looking for one buyer."

"Dat means some large timber company gonna grab it. Mr. Devlin gonna get his way. He got de cash."

"Well, I've got a chance. The agent said he might take back an offer for 10 percent of the holding, but nothing less than 250 acres. He's asking a reasonable price."

"You gots dat kind o' money? I might add a little somethin' to help you."

Lowe had heard that offer many times before and often

wondered just how much savings his partner really had. Black Jack was a most generous man, especially with his friends and those of lesser fortune. It seemed the more he gave, the more he had available to give. It was a curious circumstance, one with religious implication. After all, it was God's money, and there was no end to the supply.

"Thanks, but you hold on to what you have. You'll need it later, if not for you, then for one of your many causes."

"You knows my feelin' on money. It ain't mine and it ain't yo's to fret about. If you needs it, Lowe, you go on and take it."

"In all my days, I never knew a less selfish man. I believe you'd forfeit your seat on a buggy ride to heaven if it meant another could go in your place. I'll be all right. My folks did right good by me when they passed on, and over the years, I've been able to put aside a modest bit myself. It's really just a matter of whether the man will sell."

"He crazy to even think on sellin'. Dat land be special, sure enough. Any soul trusted with such wonders as de Lord set down on dat place, he got no cause for lettin' it go."

"But he doesn't know that, and neither does his agent. Except for us, no one alive has ever been on that mountain. The property is just a small circle on a big map to them, and the original recorded boundary was rough at best."

"Still, to me, tradin' off yo riches seem senseless, even sinful, when you don't make de effort to ever know what dey is."

Lowe nodded to show that he agreed. Black Jack was as wise as he was charitable.

"Apparently, the man inherited the entire tract after he moved west. He's a lunger and isn't coming back to the East on account of his health. I think, maybe, he needs the money for medical bills. I don't know."

"Did you tell dat agent about dem big trees?"

"No. If I did, I imagine the price would jump well beyond my reach. As far as they're concerned, the site is too inaccessible to draw full value, but then again, they haven't had the pleasure of talking to Devlin's people. The mills, mines and railroads have been changing just about everything of late, and the price of land is moving with them. I hope to get a little piece of this ground before they own it all or take it all down around me. And those big trees? Well, I want them. I want them on my ground, safe from the axe and pure as the day they sprouted."

"If you don't mind, I be prayin' for dat, Mr. Yancy."

"Sure, if you think it would help."

"You knows my response to dat."

Silas suddenly felt the sweat stream down his forehead and into the corner of one eye. It stung and blurred his already impaired vision. He rubbed his eye with his fingers and wiped his brow with a dripping forearm, which seemed only to exasperate his condition. Beads reformed across his temple, and another trickle flowed through his sideburn to the cup of his ear. He slapped the side of his head to clear it and then cursed his discomfort. Silas had had enough. He signaled to his friends.

"What you need dere, Mr. Monk? Lookin' for more o' dat heat?" asked Black Jack.

Lowe scooped another bucket of hot water from the cauldron, and without waiting for Silas's response, he began to add it to the barrel.

Silas hollered, "That's hot!"

"Yup. Just the way you like it," replied Lowe, as he walked away with the emptied bucket.

"Aaaaa! Too hot! Too hot!" He splashed out as much of the water as he could. "That was before, ya dadblamed fool! I'm already cooked. The meat's fallen off my bones, and yer jist addin' more juice fer the gravy. I been in hot springs from time to time, but I ain't ne'er brewed a sweat like this'n. Git me out o' this infernal thing!"

Jumping in the barrel was certainly easier than climbing out. Silas was not strong enough to pull himself up and over the rim, and Lowe and Black Jack were situated too low to lift him. There was only one solution, and Silas yelled his disapproval when the barrel began to rock back and forth. Finally, the weight of the water took over, and the two men were helpless to further guide the barrel's fall. The contents, including a pink and wrinkly old man, went gushing across the snow and down a short open hill.

Even Silas laughed. The snow felt good against his hot skin, and the slide was an amusement only surpassed by the stunts of his childhood. But he did not dally in the cold. He jogged toward the cabin door, wiping the slush as best he could from his bare backside. His body steamed like a fresh mound of sawdust.

"Come on in, boys!" he called out. "We'll have us a snort whilst I git all gussied up fer the party. Ya come on in."

Shaved and combed, clean and well attired in a loose brown suit, he was suddenly a different man. He was winsome and composed, younger in heart if not in appearance. While Silas struggled to attach a suspender, Lowe balanced the loops of the old man's tie and tugged to tighten the knot. Black Jack lifted the brown coat and waited for Silas to don it.

"Not yet," Silas said. He walked across the room to an old chest of drawers and removed a woolen vest, butternut colored and adorned with four tarnished buttons. He handed it to Lowe. "What ya think?"

"Very nice."

"Ma Emma made it. She cut it from what was left o' my tunic. She said thar weren't 'nough material around them bullet holes to make nothin' else." Silas rubbed his hands lightly across the fabric and rolled one of the buttons between his fingers. "I always loved this here vest. She took a rag and made somethin' fine out o' it. Emma could do that with jist 'bout anythin'. I reckon the last time I wore this was the day I had to bury 'er. And that were a good long while ago."

Silas became a little choked as memories and emotions took their hold. Lowe looked closely at the brass buttons and noted the worn relief that made them significant. Each had a single 'R' at its center. They were a simple reflection of the man who wore them proudly.

"What does this letter represent?" asked Lowe.

"I was infantry durin' the Cause. 'R' stands fer *Rifleman*. I could pop the stinger off a hornet at 200 yards. Emma insisted I keep them buttons. She knew how I liked 'em."

"You miss her, don't you?"

"Yessir, she were a good ol' girl most o' the time, and she was mighty kind to me. I do miss 'er. I miss my Emma."

Silas finally accepted the assistance with his vest and coat, and then led his friends to the three saddled mounts hitched to the top rail of a fence. They rode out together in a close, single file along a path that skirted the icy falls and snow laden banks of Jasper Creek.

There was little being said. It was a time for thoughts, for fond remembrances of the better days and of the dear people who had made them so. Soon, the men would gather once again at a Christmas table to feast on homespun joy. Emma Monk would likely be with them, alive again in the grace and spirit of Mrs. Annie Darrow.

Jacob was tortured by boredom, but found his escape when a sudden call of nature lured him from the house. On his return from the privy, he noticed that the door to the shed was strangely ajar. It was a perfect enticement.

The boy became excited as he rummaged. He had no idea what he was looking for and even less a notion where to find it. But the shed was loaded with possibilities, and the search in itself was satisfying.

The place was quite disorganized, at least upon first impression. It was a relatively large structure, part shed, part garage and part workshop, but available space was never a justification for such haphazard storage. That was his young opinion, anyway. He was not sure why it mattered.

The open floor was reserved for the motor car, which was spattered with mud and entirely too large for the minimal space allotted. There was scarcely room to walk and no area whatsoever for play. But then again, if the car was not there, some wagon would be, and that might prove even more intrusive. It might come with a horse. Jacob brushed against the side as he moved past the vehicle, and his trousers cleared some bits of dirt.

At the rear was a long, narrow work bench with a heavy vice bolted to the top and implements scattered carelessly about, having never been returned to their proper place. An old chest of drawers supported one side of the bench and was filled with hand tools, assortments of fasteners and glues, used hardware, old fixtures, everything small and anything little that had even the slightest potential for future use. The rest was tacked to walls or thrust into corners.

Each inch of space seemed occupied by dusty tools, flimsy bulging boxes and unused scraps of every material known to man. Rags and ropes, broken chairs and empty frames, chains and old leather harnesses, they were all hung from the studs on protruding nails, and a score of paint and solvent cans warped a thin shelf set on blocks below the window sill. On the floor were large bottles of kerosene and gasoline and between the overhead rafters were the planks, pipes and longer pieces of earlier projects. A spinning wheel, waiting years for its repair, was lost behind the curtain of clutter.

The room was gritty and grimy and grossly overstocked, and to Jacob's way of thinking, wonderfully so. It was equipped with every curiosity, from sickles to sawblades, and the boy handled them all in his attempt to find that special one. He would know it when he held it.

Suddenly, there it was, in the corner by the bench, just waiting for a good man to come turn a good day's work. Jacob had seen it used before and wasted no time climbing onto the wooden seat and starting to pedal. The grind stone rotated slowly at first, but with every stroke of the boy's leg, it turned faster and faster until it seemed to spin on its own. He took a screwdriver from the work bench and pressed it against the wheel. Sparks flew like fireworks. He grabbed a chisel and more sparks shot from the end of the metal, some of them raining upon his hand and arm. He marveled at the painless spray of fire.

It was the same for a hammer and a shovel, for a broken saw blade, a steel hinge, and a bent section of angle iron. Of course, nothing sharp was made sharper and nothing dull more blunt, but many a functional piece was transformed into junk before he uncovered his greatest find, a hatchet resting on an upturned pail.

It was already razor sharp. Its bevel shined silvery in contrast to the weathered iron gray. He lifted it and waived it high above his head. He chopped it like a tomahawk in the midst of battle, and then, he examined it ever more closely. The curved handle felt good in his grip. The weight on the end was just right, easy to wield and easy to throw. He looked at the evenness of the blade, but mistakenly tested the cutting edge by running his thumb down the length of it. A thin, stinging line of blood appeared in an instant, but without concern, he pressed the thumb against a sheet of newsprint, leaving a series of similar red images across the page. The hatchet was a worthy weapon, indeed, and was in no way in need of the grinding wheel's service. He left the shed to see what such a weapon could do in the adept hands of a Shawnee warrior.

Morgan's chopping block did not have a chance, though the first throw missed it altogether. By the 10th throw, Jacob made it stick, and he let out a war whoop that echoed across the valley. Tomahawks were not so easy to master, and he learned quickly, that with every deflection and every miss, he had to trudge through the wetness to find his weapon buried in the snow.

Then he saw the wood pile with a stack of short logs just waiting to be split for use in Annie's stove. It was usually Morgan's job to make kitchen wood, but that was bound to change at some point or another. Jacob thought the time was at hand. He picked out a nice round piece and balanced it on its end atop the large block. He raised his hatchet and brought it down forcefully. The log flipped one way and the hatchet veered the other, both ending up in the snow.

Jacob prepared for another try, but the log would not stand. He held it while he initiated a second blow, but just before impact, he released his grip, and the log toppled before the blade could catch its mark. He would try yet again, but on this attempt, he would not let go. He took his time. He laid the sharpened edge against the center of the log to visualize where the chop should land. Then, he squeezed the handle tightly, closed his eyes, and raised his arm to strike.

"What are you doing!" Morgan intercepted the handle before the hatchet started downward. "Are you crazy, Jake? You would've cut your hand off doing it that way."

"Huh?" The boy was startled. "That's how *you* do it."

"I most certainly do not."

"Well, then, show me."

"I will not. Maybe on another day, little brother. Another day and about five more years from now. And if you even think about touching an axe before then, I won't wait for Pa. I'll tan your hide myself. Do you understand?"

Jacob did not like being rebuked, especially by Morgan. For some reason, strong words from his brother seemed to hurt worse and last longer. Morgan never made mistakes, and he seemed to know just about everything that could be considered important. Believing this, Jacob would often gauge the severity of his misdeeds by the strength and tone of his brother's voice. As reprimands rushed from Morgan's mouth, tears rolled from the young boy's eyes.

"I'm sorry, Morgan. I wanted to split some stove wood. I wanted to help you."

"You wanted to play, and you wanted to play with something that you knew darn well was dangerous. I mean it. Don't you ever touch that hatchet again." Morgan squatted down so Jacob could see just how serious he really was. "Now wipe your face and go inside. Ma sent me out to tell you to get a coat on, and she'll be wondering where we are. Go on now."

Jacob walked slowly to the back porch of the house. Though he was pouting, he truly understood what Morgan meant about the danger. His thumb had begun to bleed again, but now it was throbbing and making him wish he had never discovered the deadly tomahawk. The ointment his mother would soon apply was sure to hurt him all the more.

The young boy took one last look at his brother before entering, anticipating what was about to happen. Morgan arched his back as he lifted the hatchet high over his shoulder, and with a quick whip of his elbow and wrist, he sent the tool flying across the yard toward the side of the chopping block. It settled firm and deep in the stiff flesh of the wood.

Luci was not invited to dinner, and it was just as well, since Silas had always refused to take her on his forays into Devlin. There was no animal on Earth sweeter than Lucifer, no company more pleasant, but bringing a half wild hound to a busy town had more potential for disaster than gulping a tonic before a long, long trip. Silas Monk was smart enough to know better, and he wanted no part of calamity.

He also wanted no part in breaking Luci's free spirit and roving tendency. Leashes and cages were for city pets, not companions. The man left his dog a meaty ham bone, telling her it was hers to either horde or share with the critters. Once she finished it, she would be on her own to hunt or scrounge for her next couple meals. Luci was gnawing contently when the men rode off and showed no interest in following.

Of course, with the dog at home, Silas was unfortunately alone when it came to managing his mule, and he was more than a little wary as the long passage through the hollow went without incident. It was inexplainable, considering the past behaviors of both man and animal.

Noggin must have sensed the same spirit of Christmas that had been settling over his master. He never balked, bucked or brayed on their entire journey, and he was sure-footed over the icy rocks and roots buried beneath the snow. Perhaps it was more aptly due to the current disposition of the man, who was talking softly and riding gently, and for a change, treating the mule with the respect owed such an old friend.

When the three men turned their mounts onto the far end of Market Street, they gave little notice to the two adolescents huddled on the corner curb. But as they passed slowly by, the boys cowered to avoid recognition, making it clear they were up to some sort of mischief. The men could hear the flare of matches and knew full well what was happening.

Lowe laughed at the predictable way every generation reinvents the same old vices. He had sat on similar curbs in his time, testing the limits prescribed by his elders, straining the vigilance of those who would protect him. Children are rebels, he thought, with a natural yearning to learn things the hard way. Regarding tobacco, there was more delight in defiance than in taste, and many a child would sample the forbidden just for the thrill of risking detection.

Lowe felt obliged to expose their folly, but knew the boys would not be listening. They would learn best without the meddling of strangers, and in the meantime, the taste of a little smoke was not the worse trouble they could find. Still, the temptation to teach old lessons was overwhelming. Each of the three men had something to say.

Silas rode past. "Howdy, young fellers. If yer gonna light up, ya need to go 'bout it proper like. Suck down some smoke. Savor it. Don't jist lip the dadburn things."

Black Jack was next. "Boys, dem bad habits be hard to break when you gets older."

And then came Lowe. "I've seen better places to hide. Good luck when your daddy finds you. Sooner or later, he will."

The animals maintained their gait, leaving little opportunity for response, and the children never offered one as they continued to conceal their faces. But as Blu trotted by, they broke from their mysterious huddle and tossed their lit tobacco with a hot string of firecrackers far out into the slushy street. Without waiting even a second to witness the impending bedlam, they raced for the back alleys of Devlin, screaming loudly with the joy of victory.

Nothing happened at first, and it seemed the trick was more on the boys than the riders. But, all at once, the rattle of the firecrackers ripped through the calm, and the two horses instantly kicked at the air and whorled around in utter hysteria. They bucked wildly. They jumped high. They did everything their instinct bid them do to avoid the bewildering white flashes and menacing loud snaps. Noggin just turned his stout neck and watched.

The riders held on for their very lives, clinging to stirrups and reins and horns and manes to keep from being thrown. Lowe gripped Blu with strong legs and rocked back and forth and up and down like a wrangler breaking a mustang. Then, he lost the reins altogether and was forced to grasp for the pommel of his western style saddle. The horse repeatedly tossed him high, and then, slammed him unmercifully against the hard leather seat. Near breathless, shaken, and sore, he was still in the saddle when the animal finally quieted.

Black Jack was jolted forward almost instantly, but somehow landed on the poor horse's neck. He tried to scoot back, but the saddle horn proved too formidable an obstacle. His hands went for the animal's ears, and his legs flailed once free of the stirrups. The horse tried in earnest to shake him loose, but like a wrestler hopelessly pinned, it acquiesced after the last firecracker was spent. Its head drooped low to the ground, and its forelegs spread wide for balance. The horse held its ungainly position until Black Jack finally rolled off into the snow.

Noggin was stolid. When the commotion subsided, he moved nonchalantly and without further coaxing toward the double doors of the livery. It was a show of arrogance, a way of extolling the steadiness of his kind over the skittishness of horses, if, in fact, mules were even capable of such narcissism. Noggin, with Silas still mounted, waited by the doors while Lowe and Black Jack approached on foot, leading their frightened animals behind them.

"If ma Luci were here, we'd have us some fun rootin' out them li'l hellions. But to tell ya the truth, boys, I enjoyed the show," Silas said, while expressing his gratitude to Noggin with a scratch along the withers.

"Yeah, they got us but good," replied Lowe. "I thought those squibs they were lighting were just some rolled smokes. Didn't you, Jack?"

"Dey was. I seen dem smokes, but I's surely fooled by de rest. When dey dropped dat string o' crackers and it start to poppin', dese animals wasn't de only ones dancin' de jig. My heart stepped right lively, too, and it still be poundin' at a double time. I 'spect, now dat it's all gone, dem boys gonna regret wastin' deir precious supply on de three of us."

"I seriously doubt that. They'll be laughing at us for at least another year."

Silas joined the argument, "Hell, them boys ne'er saw nothin' to laugh at. They was headin' fer cover before they even lit the fuse. I reckon, by now, they's more interested in startin' a blaze in some feller's wood shed than thinkin' on how silly two growed men looked with their horses squirtin' out from under 'em. And, brothers, it were quite a sight."

It was sheer coincidence that the mill whistle suddenly sounded the alarm. Before the men could enter the stable, a fire brigade had assembled and the pump wagon raced right past them toward the homes on Briar Mountain. This time Noggin was moved to action, and he gave a hurried chase like a lone fireman who missed the call.

Nothing would stop the mule, except the mule himself, and Silas had no choice but to take the ride that was given him. Fully aware of that, the old man resorted to the one thing he always did well. He cursed the beast beneath him.

Morgan yelled as he stuck his head back through the doorway, "Ma! I'll be back in an hour or so. I'm heading down the hill. You need anything?"

Annie stepped out of the kitchen. Her hands, face and apron were covered in flour. "Yes, you could help me tidy up a bit before company comes, and I'm going to need you to cut some kindling for this oven. I've been cooking all morning, and it can't continue without that wood. I don't think I can wait another hour."

"But Sarah said she was putting something on her veranda for us. She was afraid to leave it out long and told me to be there by three. I left you plenty of cooking wood by the shed, some good dry locust I split a couple days ago."

"Well, that should do. Can you bring some up to the back porch?"

Morgan wavered. He wanted to help, but felt an urgent need to reach Sarah's in time. "Ah, Ma, I'm in a huge hurry to get there. I'll clean up around here when I get back. I promise. I'll have the time. Can't we ask Jake to fetch the wood?"

Morgan was shaken when he heard his father call out from the back room. He was not even aware that the man was home, but knew immediately that he was in trouble. His father had little tolerance for disobedient children and even less for whining young men. To Lawson, Morgan had suddenly become both, and he acted quickly to remedy the problem.

"Have you gone deaf, boy? Your mother told you to get the wood and to start tidying up around here. Is there any part of that message you didn't hear?"

Morgan may have been startled by the sound of his father's voice, but not by his tone. He had become accustomed to it. He had not seen the man for two days, but still, there was no surprise when his father's first words were used to berate him.

"I heard her, Pa. I meant no disrespect."

"You're too old to have to be told to get your chores done before you run off and play."

Morgan was insulted. "Yes, sir, I am, but this is not play."

Lawson became angered. "You know, boy, I'm up to here with your constant impudence. Of course, it's play! Your mother works all day preparing a feast for your friends, and you head out the first chance you get to that girly girl of yours...to play."

Morgan's patience was thin, but it held for a while longer. "I told you, it's not play. Sarah asked me to pick up something, something for our Christmas dinner, I suppose. I said that I would do it, and it may spoil if I don't get down there soon."

"Nothing spoils in this weather. Try another one. I'm feeling stupid." His father refused to listen to reason. Their conversation was about control, not communication, and he was intent to have Morgan's total compliance on his terms. "You can go when I say you can go. Right now, I'm telling you to come back in here to clean up this mess and fetch that kindling, or you can tell your little honey to just stay home tonight."

Morgan came back into the house and walked defiantly past his father toward the kitchen. He asked his mother, "Is there anything you need while I'm out?" He spoke loudly to make certain Lawson could hear him. "I'm leaving now, Ma. Right now. Jake's in the yard. I'll ask him to bring in the wood."

Annie knew that neither of her men would yield to the other and that only she could prevent another family catastrophe. She thought hard, and in the split of a second, she had developed her plan.

"I need some flour," Annie said. "If Sarah's home, ask if I can borrow a pound of flour." She watched Lawson's eyes as she constructed her lie. It was clear that he was skeptical. "And I need some tea. Hurry now. I don't want Cora to have to do all the clean-up. Tell Sarah how much I look forward to seeing her."

Annie was always prepared, especially in the kitchen, and she had every ingredient necessary to create her special dinner. Lawson and Morgan should have known that, but for some reason, they were blind to her guile as they exchanged final taunts.

Lawson grabbed Morgan's arm before he reached the door. "Boy, if you're not back in 60 minutes, we'll continue this right where I left off."

Morgan nodded, but he was much too strong and, in terms of experience, had lived far too long to feel threatened by such words. "I hope we do continue, Pa, and you think on this while I'm gone. Her name is Sarah. Don't you ever degrade that name again."

Morgan stomped out of the house without witnessing the cold expression on his father's face. Lawson was seething, but strangely unable to react to the implied threat. He was not ready for so strong a response, and while furious and frustrated by his son's flagrant insubordination, he knew deep within his conscience that Morgan had just cause. His demeaning references to Sarah Dabney were intentionally derisive and rude, and any man with a nickel's worth of character would have to stand in the girl's defense. Morgan took that stand, and in a way, Lawson respected his vehemence.

"I swear I don't know what's come over you of late," Annie said, once Morgan was gone. The softness of her voice showed the depth of her concern. She wanted Lawson to listen. "You've been pressing the boy ever since he came back from his trip into the mountains. I don't think he understands, and frankly, neither do I."

She walked over to her husband and started to massage the tense muscles of his neck with the heel of her hand. "What's wrong? What has happened to build such a wall between you two?"

He pushed her hand away. "I'll tell you what's wrong! He's grown too big for his britches around here, and if he keeps it up, he'll be looking for a new home before the snow melts."

"Trust me, Lawson. That time will come soon enough."

"Well, he's of age. He's old enough for steady work and a place of his own. I'll not have anyone living under my roof that won't abide by my rules."

"Have you talked to him about this?" Annie knew the answer before she asked the question. "We can both speak to him if you want."

"What good is talk for someone who doesn't mind you? That boy's ungrateful and doesn't have an ounce of respect for authority. You coddle too much, Annie, and Morgan's the worse for it. He needs to learn the hard way, and that means moving out where the world's not so friendly."

There was irony in the accusations, and Annie wanted to place the blame where it really belonged. But she understood the hidden frailty of her husband, and he was much too weak a man to accept the criticism and responsibility. She was careful to not force his anger.

"You certainly see a different boy than I do," she explained calmly. "Morgan does a lot to help out around this home. He's good to his brother and sister and me, and he's picked up jobs here and there ever since he was 10. He's a very hard worker and a caring young man."

"Aah! I fully expected you to take up for him. He's Momma's boy, all right. You may be the only thing around here he does value, except, of course, that girl."

Annie may not have liked what she was hearing, but it was the first time in a long time that Lawson made any effort to discuss his feelings. He had at some point declared himself dictator in the home, and from then on, his feelings were well guarded, as though they might be dangerous to his continued reign. The drinking made him mean, but something darker and more debilitating made him drink. Annie knew what that something was, and she was determined that Morgan not be sacrificed in payment for her debts.

"Now that's unfair and you know it. If I've coddled my child, it's only because his father gives him too little attention. Morgan wants to please you, but after 18 years, he still doesn't know how. He has tried all his life to earn your affection and acceptance, when all the while they should have been given freely. We've talked about this before. He's your child, not some thief breaking into your heart. He wants nothing more from you than some love and respect, and you owe him at least that much. It's his birthright. Our Morgan has become a man, and you're running out of chances to put things right with him. Please, Lawson, try. Please don't force our son to run from us."

"*Our* son?" Lawson was pierced by the two short words. They drove deep to the heart of the matter.

Annie's mouth gaped. "Oh, so it's come to that again. I thought that might be behind all this. Didn't we agree to let the past lie where it fell? When you came back, I made my choice. You pleaded for it. You accepted it. You made me believe in you, and since then, we have lived a whole new life together. Why resurrect the dead now?"

"Because maybe the past never really died. I think it's here in Devlin, very much alive, and I think you've seen it."

Annie knew what Lawson meant, and she regretted the truth. Perhaps the past was immortal after all. She had relived it often enough, in her quiet moments of the day and in her sleepless dreams of the night. There was but one story she would never share with the man she married, the mystery of a time when he coldly left her to struggle on her own. She held a complete volume of secrets from those days, the best and worst days of her life, but she never once recited a word. For years, Lawson longed to know the real cost of his indiscretion, but it was the one thing Annie would not divulge.

The truth was that she loved her husband, but could never retrieve that special part of herself, once willingly offered to another. While Lawson wanted all of what he so callously discarded, Annie could only present back to him that which was still hers to give. It was not enough, and the disappointment poisoned his spirit.

"You left *me*. Remember?" she replied. "I never asked why you had to go, or where you went, or who you were with. There was no value in knowing, just more pain. Once we vowed to try again, I buried those questions like I buried that entire period in my life. Forgive and forget."

"So there was no other man? You must think me simple."

"No. You are a husband and a father and anything but simple. You've made your mistakes, but refuse to put them behind you. What else can I do to make things right?"

"You can tell what really happened, for a start. You can tell me what I already know about Morgan."

"I made a choice a long, long time ago," she explained. "I have lived faithfully by it and by you. Why continue to punish the boy for what may have happened years ago? It's just so wrong, Lawson."

"You're right. The sins of his parents were not of his doing, and I should try to remember that. But, woman, they were of your doing, and I'm finding it damned hard to forgive and forget."

Annie's world had been melting beneath her, one mean look, one bitter word and one drop of whiskey at a time. She now gazed at Lawson with incredulity. There were sins, sure enough, and she would acknowledge her share of them before God, but not to this man who arrogantly found no fault of his own. After 18 years of skinned knees and stomach aches, of hunting trips and fishing holes, of training at the mill and ball field, Morgan was clearly his son, regardless of the past. Annie would not validate his doubts with an answer.

"I made my choice, and for me, that was the end of it."

Lawson would have to find contentment in that.

The hour went by and Morgan was yet to return home, but it made little difference since Lawson himself had slipped away to some corner saloon on the other side of the tracks. He needed a drink or two to sort through a jumble of thoughts.

Jacob had already hauled in a large supply of kitchen wood, but Cora was having little success getting it to light. Despite repeated lessons on how to start the stove, the girl consistently ignored the essential requisite of combining good fuel with adequate air flow. She generally allowed for neither, and the match was more often than not the only thing with any real likelihood of burning.

Annie strained to open a canning jar of string beans. She gripped it tightly with a damp cloth and twisted. The only thing to budge was the cloth. She tapped the edges with a wooden stir spoon and tried again. It was a very obstinate jar. Taxed by this, the simplest of kitchen procedures, she was determined to keep her patience. She bit down on her lip and quietly counted to 10.

Cora was frustrated by her own problems. When Annie glanced over to find her daughter still struggling with the fire, she was not altogether sympathetic, considering her many efforts to teach the girl. There would have to be yet another lesson, one that would wait for another day. Annie put down the jar, took a moment to straighten her tired back, and she yawned. It was time for some fresh air.

"Let's take a short walk, Cora. We're ahead of schedule and could both stand a break."

"I'd like to, Mama, but I just cleaned out this firebox and can't get the kindling to hold a flame." She struck her ninth match and watched it extinguish when she placed it against the wood.

"That can wait. We'll get it when we come back. By then, Morgan or your father should be home, and they can deal with it."

"What about Jacob?"

The boy was sprawled on the parlor rug near the base of the Christmas tree, issuing orders and making gun sounds as a serious battle of miniature lead soldiers unfolded.

"He's in another world with his toys. We won't be gone long. He'll be all right." Annie addressed her son, "Jacob, your sister and I are taking a short stroll. Do you want to go?"

"No!" He was too rapt in the art of war to be bothered with strolls.

"Well, you holler loud if you need us. We shouldn't be too far away. And, if Morgan gets back ahead of us, would you ask him to fire the stove for me?"

The boy nodded his head while an airy roar of cannon fire emanated from his mouth. Annie and Cora donned their boots and cloaks and went outside to be greeted by the beauty of another gentle snowfall.

The war was not over, but the battle had been decisively won by one side or the other, and Jacob now realized that he was home alone. It was an opportunity seldom found, and he ambled through the house looking for something that might peak his interest. Christmas cookies were a good start, but he had to be careful not to over-indulge lest his mother notice the voids on the platter. He carefully reorganized what was left and forced himself to step away.

He was tempted to bring in more wood. It was a man's job, and he rather liked being asked to take on such tasks. But the pile on the porch was virtually untouched, and he did not fancy the frustration of putting on his snow boots. He saw the open firebox beneath the burners of the stove and leaned over to analyze the problem.

The wood seemed dry enough. Perhaps it was cut too thick to burn. He went back to porch and sifted through the stack for every tiny chip and sliver he could find. It was what Morgan would have done, and Jacob was pleased to amass a modest little pile of very fine kindling. He placed it in the firebox. He looked for the matches.

They were right there in front of him, right where Cora left them, right next to the stove.

Morgan had always boasted of using a single match when starting his fires. He believed the secret was in the proper selection and use of the kindling and that more than one matchstick was just a careless waste of the forest. Jacob again would follow his example. When he slid open the matchbox cover, the boy was careful to remove only one piece and quickly closed the box back up. Then, he fluffed the tiny pile into a loose cone and struck his match. He was ecstatic when it flared and even more excited when the kindling flamed. But he watched it too long and forgot about the need to stoke a new fire with increasingly larger sticks. In just moments, the pile was reduced to little more than smoke.

He was determined to try again. This time he rolled newspapers into tight balls and laid them across the base of the firebox. He covered the papers with as many cuttings as the box would hold and struck a second match. The paper burned with a fury, but the packed wood, starved for air, only singed before the fire was gone. The boy took another cookie and pondered his next move.

The answer to the problem was resting on the floor of the shed. Jacob had seen it work well on similar applications and was sure about its success with the kitchen wood. He wiggled and twisted and tugged on his boots, but even after a series of strenuous pulls and grunts, his feet still would not properly seat. So, with boots halfway on, he awkwardly dragged and tiptoed his way across the backyard to the shed.

The gasoline and coal oil were exactly where he remembered them to be. He studied the large bottles for a moment, trying his best to read the words on the worn paper tags that were wired to the necks. Neither label made any real sense to him, so he selected the bottle with the least content. He then pushed the gasoline back against the shed wall and toddled back to the house with the lighter load.

In his own mind, he was being very careful. Jacob knew he did not need an entire gallon to accomplish his purpose. He unscrewed the nozzle cap and splashed some fuel over the wood, but most of it caught the metal door and cascaded down to the floor. He splashed some more, and this time, he accidently coated the top of the stove. Of course, his mother would never tolerate such a mess, and he felt obliged to find an old towel or rag to clean up the spills.

The boy inadvertently knelt down in his own puddles, and he dragged his shirt against the oily surface as he attempted to swab the floor and wipe the stove. When he was finished, he was quite pleased with the clean luster he had created.

But there still remained the problem of treating the wood. Jacob took the coal oil and laid the bottle on its side. He tilted the back and let a measured amount fill the cup of his hand. Then, he carefully lowered his hand to the firebox and tossed the fluid upon the kindling. It worked well, but the smallness of his hands dictated that he repeat the process three or four times. Finally, he was ready. The stove looked clean, the floor looked clean, and the wood was adequately doused with fuel. He wiped his hands on the oil-soaked cloth and reached for the matches.

The black firebox turned orange with the light of new flame. There was no explosion, but the bright glow spread rapidly over the rough pieces of wood and the smooth plates of metal until the entire box was engulfed. It was a finer success than even Jacob could imagine, at least for the moment.

Thick smoke began to billow through the open iron door, and the boy wisely reached over to slam it shut. But the door struck much too hard, and it rebounded with a loud clang, pulling with it enough flame to ignite, at first, the outer face of the stove, and then seconds later, the top and the floor. It was a low blue flame that steadily crept over each exposed surface, like a heavy cloud moving up the valley. It may have burned itself out had Jacob left it alone. But his panic and instinct misdirected him, and he began to frantically beat the fire with his oily towel.

He screamed for help, “Mama, come quick! There’s a fire!” No one could hear him. He screamed louder, “Mama! Morgan! Please, come quick! There’s a fire!” Still, there would be no response.

The boy yelled as he struck down the flames, but the fanning of the towel pushed the fire further from the stove toward the kitchen walls. When the fabric itself began to burn, he abandoned the cloth to the stove top where it suddenly burst into high flames. He ran to the porch for the sand bucket, which had been placed there for just such a purpose, but the sand proved too heavy to lift.

Jacob then remembered the sink. It was a bit high to reach, but with his best stretch, he managed it. He turned the handle until water spewed through the spigot, and then shoveled it toward the stove with a frying pan. There was no effect. He was simply too little and too late to make a difference. An entire corner of the kitchen became blackened in just minutes.

Jacob never felt the flames that somehow attached to his boots and pressed up the side of his trousers, but he saw them. In horror, he swatted wildly at his burning clothes, as he ran for the front door and screamed again for his mother. His boots, still not fitted to his feet, slowed him considerably, and when he came to the brink of the porch steps, his tiny ankle buckled and he plummeted hard onto the white lawn below. His small body rolled another 10 feet across the yard toward the open gate. Limp and lifeless, he smoldered in the wet of the snow.

Lowe Yancy could look up the mountainside and see people scurrying about, but it was not until he drew closer that he realized the Darrow home was aflame. He kicked Blu hard to make the most of his speed and never looked back to see if Black Jack was following. The horse was still running as he dismounted, and Lowe raced through the small contingent of firemen and into the smoky house. There was no time to panic, and he knew he must be thorough.

Lowe vaulted up the stairs and threw open every door. He cried out for Morgan and Annie as he swiftly moved from room to room. He checked under beds and in the two small closets, shouting in vain for Jake and Cora and Lawson. The smoke was thick enough to gag him, but he kept moving, staying low to the floor and taking shallow breaths. He tried to cover his mouth and nose with a kerchief, but choked violently while calling out the names. It became clear the family had escaped, and he was anxious to do the same.

By the time Lowe reached the kitchen, Black Jack had already found the fire bucket and was using the sand to smother the flames rising from the floor. Others were on the scene, as well, scurrying ineffectively to form a bucket line. But there were too few vessels, and what little water could be brought to bear against the flames did nothing more than create steam and confusion. Finally, the trained fire brigade was ready with their equipment. They leveled their hose, and a loud order was issued for the four firemen outside to begin working the pump handles. A long, strategic spray of water spewed from the nozzle, and in short order, it quickly ended the remaining threat. As a precaution, the firemen took their axes and hacked the plaster from the ceiling and walls, making sure the blaze had not found its way into the laths and framework. By miracle, the house was saved, and by luck, only the kitchen really suffered. The rest could be restored with a week of hard scrubbing and a season's worth of fresh air.

Lowe and Black Jack both coughed as they moved onto the front porch and into a light, clean breeze. They were astonished to see a gathering crowd. Tragedy always had a disquieting way of pulling town people together, but in their haste up the mountain, the men failed to notice the countless others who were also scrambling to the scene.

One of the firemen called out a general announcement, "It's all over, people. Fire's out. Some damage done to Mrs. Darrow's kitchen, but things will be okay." He was not aware of the small casualty only thirty feet away, now cradled in his bewildered mother's arms.

A voice sounded from the crowd, "Is anyone here a doctor? We need a doctor!"

Another voice replied, "Doc Brown's down at the hospital."

"For God's sake, someone fetch Doc Brown! The boy's been hurt. Quick!"

Without question or hesitation, a half a dozen men took to horse or foot to summon the help.

Lowe's eyes stung. His vision remained blurred from the smoke, and he strained to make out faces across the yard. The snow kept falling and falling, and everyone stood somber and white around the crèche-like pose of Annie and her son. Finally, he saw them.

"Dear God," he uttered, not even aware that the words had slipped from his mouth. He made his way through the murmuring crowd. An older man moved ahead of him.

"Yer grazin' like a dad-blasted herd o' sheep! Either help the poor woman or git out o' my way so I can."

Silas pressed through the onlookers like a hot knife through butter. Those who did not yield to him were summarily shoved aside. There was no time for etiquette. He knelt down in the snow next to Annie.

"Let loose o' the boy, missy. I ain't no doctor, but I been around this sort o' thing a time or two. Let go, so I can git to work."

Annie grabbed her son even tighter, as if she thought Silas might steal him away, and she began to rock young Jacob to the cadence of some unsung lullaby.

"Please, ma'am, I gotta see."

She kept rocking and rocking, deaf to the old man's pleas, until Silas finally tried to wrest the boy from her clutch. His age had taken some of his strength, and when Annie resisted, he shook his head as a sign of quiet resignation. The frosty air became even colder, and it carried a hush of lost hope into every waiting heart. The boy was likely dead.

Lowe slumped to the ground and put his arms around the trembling woman and her son. He lifted Annie's soft brown hair from around her ear and whispered reassuringly, "I think if we need a miracle, old Silas is the one to find it. Annie, you have to let Jake go."

The faint voice was somehow more compelling than the chaotic commands of her shocked and addled emotions. She was soothed by it, and she emerged willingly from her stupor to find comfort in the face of Lowe Yancy. It was a strong face, with chiseled lines that showed the years of a hard but self-reliant life. And it was an honest face, with the look of a man who could be trusted with the greatest of treasures. At his urging, Annie released her treasure to the safekeeping of the stranger. She handed over her son, and then, broke into tears as she sensed the worst. Lowe held her ever closer, his warm face now against the cold of her ruddy cheek.

Silas immediately leaned over and tore open Jacob's soot covered shirt. He listened, but heard no sound of a heartbeat. There was no rise and fall of a breathing chest and no movement whatsoever from the small body that had always before been in perpetual motion. He reached for the child's thin neck and felt for a pulse. And he watched his mouth, waiting for that small puff of warm air to cloud as it passed his lips. There was not one visible sign of life.

He lifted the boy's eyelids and observed the black, dilated pupils, and he reached around the back of his head to feel for bumps and blood. Silas found nothing. Then, he opened his Barlow knife and carefully cut away the scorched, tattered shreds of the trousers. Jacob's skin pulled with it, leaving the raw meat of his calf and ankle exposed and oozing with a thin, pink fluid. The stench of burnt flesh turned many who watched, but Silas diligently pursued his purpose.

The old man was actually more determined than confident, though the tick of every critical second made him less of both. In the growing doom and despair, he looked to the crowd for anyone who might take his burden and save the child. After all, he was not a healer. He was simply a man from the mountains who had learned a few tricks of survival, and who, on occasion, had the pleasure of denying the grim reaper its rightful collection. But those were the battles of his own life. The innocent boy before him deserved much better than to be defended by backwoods remedies and luck. In truth, Jacob had no prayer with Silas Monk.

And that was the answer. Silas was certain of it when his eyes locked onto Black Jack, now standing alone on the porch, his hands folded and his head lifted to the snowy heavens.

"Git on down here where ya can do some good!" he called out to his friend.

Black Jack hurried to his side. “How can I help, Mr. Monk?”

“Finish up. I ain’t no religious man, but I reckon you are, sure ‘nough. Jist talk to that Jesus and conjure up some sort a miracle. I got nothin’ to give this boy. Maybe some’n else does. Pray yer best. That’s what ya can do.”

“I already been tendin’ ta dat.”

Black Jack placed his hands over Jacob’s grotesquely disfigured leg, and he bowed his head. When others saw him, they bowed as well, and they each pleaded with their God for mercy. Silas could not fully understand their magic, but he was grateful for it. Never accomplished in prayer himself, he had long since come to know the bleak situations that required it. It often proved to be the only cure, and this looked to be one of those times.

He waited. With trust in a divine power he never understood or pretended to need, with a new modicum of hope and patience, he waited for Black Jack’s conjury to work. His calloused fingers, numb from the cold, had little chance of detecting a pulse, but his half blind eyes could still discern one critical sign. His stare locked on the boy’s thin, parted lips.

Jacob’s white breath tumbled onto the frigid air, but so vaguely that Silas disregarded it as wishful thinking. It seemed forever before any real sign of respiration could be detected, but it was finally evident, the air clouding more and more distinctly with every shallow pant.

Silas threw his hands up high and yelled, “Yes, by God, I knew it!”

Despite an unbalanced array of missing teeth, the old man’s beam was the most beautiful Annie had ever seen, and she understood at once its significance. Her Jacob lived. She instantly drew close to her son to feel the warmth of his breath for herself. She again cradled him in her arms and struggled to shelter his pale, soft face from the falling snow. To Silas Monk, Annie’s own grateful smile would surpass all others.

But there was more to be done, and Silas was not selective as he snapped a series of commands to those around him. “Y’all run into that house and find us some blankets to put around this l'il feller. And git us a stretcher from that thar fire wagon. We're gonna need to move 'im, and I ain't too sure 'bout 'is back or neck. If thar ain't no stretcher, find somethin' sturdylike. Thar might be some planks in that shed around the side. Now git the lead out! We ain't got time to waste. Black Jack, start packin' snow around them burns." The old man looked up to those who still watched. "The rest o' ya? Well, jist keep up yer prayin'. We ain't out o' this yet."

Silas grumbled to himself, "Doctors, hell! All that schoolin' in science, all them books 'bout medicines, and they still ain't worth a single drop a gnat's spit if they ain't where ya need 'em."

The old man was exhausted, but never more alive. He squeezed Jacob's tiny hand as the boy eked out another breath, and he felt the cruel irony that would grant an aging devil his vitality while leaving a blameless angel faltering in his existence. Battles for life should be waged by the elderly, not the young, he thought. Looking down upon Jacob's still and decimated form, Silas had his doubts about victory.

# CHAPTER 16

The infirmary was an unimpressive building, even for a town the size of Devlin, but it was a contribution of the lumber company and few citizens found cause to complain. Its basic design, modest quarters and simple frame construction indicated a temporary status, and much consideration had already been given to a more substantial structure, assuming the continued prosperity of the town. Of course, good fortune had its limits.

Like the stone bank and fancy hotel, like the well-equipped firehouse and moving picture theater, like the fine railroad station, the sidewalks, gas street lamps and a school that offered 12 grades, the hospital was to be yet another public asset that turned an ephemeral little village into a thriving community. In time, it would require major improvement to keep pace with Devlin's robust development.

But the green forest, or the black coal veins beneath it, would have to surrender much to insure the town's vigor and viability. Stumps and tunnels were but indications of past profits. It was the stout trees and mineral rich ores that marked the future, and these were not in endless supply. Devlin, like any other logging or mining boom, existed on the ample giving of the earth, and at some point, even nature would become destitute. Perhaps the infirmary would remain as it always had been, until time and weather brought it to the brink of ruin. That was the way of such towns. The life of anything, or anyone, was always in question.

Jacob was carried to the hospital before Doctor Brown could be found, but the alarm whistle had carried far and clear and the good doctor responded at once to the crisis. Before long, his horse and buggy were at full trot on the outskirts of town, the hooves and wheels flipping up so much of the wintry mix that the driver finally arrived more like a snowman than a physician. The humor of it was understandably lost on those who waited. With his medical bag at hand, he rushed through the bystanders and into the building.

There was no time for his customary social grace, and he spoke with a cold authority that stunned those who had known only his gentleness. Still, a more forceful demeanor was somewhat reassuring in times like this. It showed decisiveness. It proved confidence. If there was any hope at all, it rested in the abilities of this extraordinary man, and no one questioned his means and manners.

"You two men there, help me move the boy into better light. Everyone else, out!"

As one nurse assisted with the transfer, another began to usher the people from the infirmary's only ward. Annie resisted as Cora attempted to guide her away from Jacob's bedside.

The doctor repeated his command, "Nurse, I said 'everyone' and I meant it. Clear the room!"

"But, Doctor, these are the boy's mother and sister."

"I don't care if they're Florence Nightingale and Clara Barton. I need everyone out of here!"

It was a rather rude reaction, uncharacteristic of such a professional, but the stress of finding the tortured form of a seven-year-old boy and the fatigue from two sleepless nights of viruses and fractures, lacerations and births, stomach disorders and pulled muscles left the doctor but a sparse reserve of forbearance and wit. And he would need all of that reserve for even a chance at saving the child. Nevertheless, he drew together his unraveling faculties and attempted his apology.

"Ma'am, forgive me. I wish you could stay, but it's best for everyone involved that you don't. Wait in the other room, and I'll send you word the minute I have something to report. I promise."

He had a softer tone, but refused to face Annie as he began in earnest to examine her son. It was a common deficiency of his practice that he found most difficult to overcome. Strangers were easier to treat, in cases like this, because strangers were easier to lose than friends, and his first glance at the young patient offered him no encouragement. Cecil Brown had always been a country physician, and his long career in Devlin left few faces around town that did not invoke some name or special memory. Far too many of those memories had been sad, and he understood full well that this day was likely to be among them. He had grown fond of the Darrow family. They were not strangers, and he simply could not look up lest Annie see in his eyes the hopelessness of his efforts.

"I'll be on the other side of that door until you open it, Cecil. You come tell me that my boy is fine," Annie demanded. More so, she pleaded. "No matter how long it takes, you tell me that he is all right."

Pity engulfed the man. Not so long ago, he had joyfully announced the boy's arrival when he delivered Jacob into the world. He dreaded the imminent task of declaring his death.

"Mrs. Darrow?"

"Yes."

"Annie Darrow, you keep your faith. I'll do everything in my power to help little Jake."

"I know you will." The nurse escorted her slowly from the room.

The crowd dispersed quickly once the fire wagon rolled away. Many followed the transport that carried Jacob to the hospital, hoping for a chance to somehow assist or give comfort. Annie never tallied her friendships, but on this day, it was apparent that she and her family had made their mark on Devlin.

Only two remained behind, and they stood wondering what to do next. From outside the house, they could smell the reek of scorched timber and horse hair plaster as the delicate white flurries replenished the trodden snow. It would have seemed right, if only the timbers had been Yule logs and not a home. But it was not Christmas anymore, not for them, and certainly not for those who just minutes earlier looked to the house as their haven. Their senses, their emotions, their resolves were all in conflict, and the men waited in dazed silence for some clarity beyond the thick cloud of confusion.

"What dat poor fam'ly gonna do now, Mr. Yancy?" Black Jack asked, speaking mostly to himself. He was numb, not from the outside cold, but from the chilling realization of the horror that must have overcome young Jacob and of the living nightmare the boy's mother now would face. Black Jack expected no answer to the question of why, so he posed the only other thought weighing on his mind. "What? Just what dey gonna do?"

"Survive, I suppose. There aren't many options in times like these, so they'll just endure. I think they're going to need a great deal of help."

"Yessa, I 'spect you right."

Lowe watched a lone figure move hurriedly up the street, and he saw him stumble several times as his feet slipped upon the packed snow and ice. He arose quickly after every fall and, without hesitation, continued toward the house.

"Who's up there?" the man cried out, not stopping for a reply.

"It's Lowe Yancy. Is that you, Morgan?"

Lowe recognized the long, rapid gait as Morgan crossed the yard. With a wave, Morgan acknowledged the familiar husky voice that called to him from the porch. Still, he stopped, disoriented and fearful. The pillowy white ground he crossed just a hundred minutes earlier was now reduced to a flattened sheet of tracks, muddy ruts and scattered bits of charred debris. Morgan looked about for anything familiar, just to be certain he was home.

"Dear God, so it's all true? I heard the whistle, but thought it was some mill accident. I was heading down that way when a fellow in town said I should get home. He had heard there was a fire on this street."

Lowe was not sure what to say. "Unfortunately, Morgan, the man was right. Your Ma's kitchen is pretty much gone, but the fire was contained without substantial other damage. Still, you'll be cleaning up the place for a while."

"That's good news, all things considered. Worse can happen.

I always thought this whole town would go up in blazes, bearing in mind the amount of wood used to build these houses. Ma's probably beside herself with worry, this being so close to Christmas and all. She's been slaving away getting ready for you fellows. And Pa? I don't even want to guess what he's thinking right now. I'd best go in and check on them."

Morgan climbed the steps and disappeared into the cottage before Lowe could warn him. He passed right to the kitchen, but stopped short at the threshold. The floor was gone. The ceiling and walls were ripped from the studs, and the only visible thing not utterly destroyed was the stove itself. He looked over the scene with disbelief. He had to force his lungs to breathe, and the damp, sooty air almost turned his stomach.

"Whoa! I sure didn't expect this," Morgan said, hearing Lowe and Black Jack behind him. He leaned over and picked up a steel pot. The wooden handle had been burnt away. "What happened?"

"I don't suppose anyone knows just yet," Lowe answered.

"Where are my folks? I can't imagine Ma and Pa walking out with a mess like this behind them."

Lowe looked to Black Jack for a ready response. When he did not have one, they both dropped their heads to hide their inadequacy.

"What's going on here? Where's my family?" Morgan asked again, this time with a commanding tone. He read dismay from the lines on their faces.

At a time in his life when so many dreams had finally become fulfilled, Morgan was now to be dashed against a harsh, unyielding wall of reality. The truth, if they even knew the truth, would surely crush him, but the men understood full well that they could not be his shield. Life turns and men react. This time it turned on Morgan Darrow. The pain and the fear were his to bear, and his friends were helpless to do more than stand beside him.

Lowe pulled the hat from his head and rubbed a hand through his graying hair. "Morgan, your brother's been hurt. Cora and your Ma are with him at the hospital. You take Blu and get on down there. They'll be looking for you. We'll see to things here."

"Jake? What's happened to Jake? And where's Pa?"

"Go on, boy. You'll get better answers from your folks, and I'll find your Pa."

Morgan's eyes were misty, but he held back tears. It was not the time for them. It was not the time for any show of weakness or surrender. Whatever tragedy might have broken upon him and his family, he was determined to make things whole. He ran past Lowe's horse and down the mountain. Nothing, except his racing mind, could have moved faster.

Lowe and Black Jack scavenged some lumber and nails to secure the house from the elements. All the while, they expected Lawson to suddenly appear, but when he failed to arrive, they quickly finished sealing the back door and a couple broken windows and headed toward town. Lowe voiced an opinion as to why Lawson had not yet returned, and Black Jack promptly rebuked him.

"Now, Lowe, you don't know dat to be true. De man may be down at dat hospital dis very minute tendin' to his fam'ly. Ain't dat so?"

"Possible, but not real likely."

"Well, den I be more dan willin' to stay back and keep fixin' up de place, at least 'til Mr. Darrow shows his self."

"I wouldn't do that. People in these parts may misjudge your intentions if you're up here alone. However, you might head to the hospital to make sure Lawson isn't there, just in case I'm wrong about him. Besides, Morgan might need a little encouragement right about now. There are four or five places I can expect to find Lawson. I'll join up with you after a while."

"Mr. Yancy, out o' respect for de man, you check de mill first. He may be workin' de job and far from dem -saloons. You do dat for Morgan's Pap. You do dat for me."

"It's Christmas Day, Jack. He's not there. No one is."

"From what I seen, de stack is still smokin', and dat means dey's doin' some kind o' business."

"You know as well as I do that they're generating minimum power, just enough to keep the lights on around here. That's a skeleton crew down there, and Lawson has no reason to be with them."

"You check it, Lowe. If Mr. Darrow ain't at de hospital, he be in dat filin' room catchin' up his work. Da mill's de place to find him."

"I wouldn't wager on that, but I hope you're right, Mr. Clark. In any case, tell Annie and Morgan not to worry. We'll be along soon."

It was dark when they departed, but the street lamps and the snow worked well together to illuminate their way. Lowe went straight to the mill, and while a boiler was still pushing smoke through a stack and the electric lights were still shining high in the lofts, the last shift had ended a couple hours earlier and most of the lumber men were now at ease in their homes.

The mill's sawyer was anxious to join them, but laid aside his winter jacket when he heard Lowe approaching up the steep stairway toward the saw filer's shop.

"Oh, I thought maybe you were Lawson," said the tall, thin man. It was not much of a greeting. He shook the top of his denim overalls, and the saw dust fell through the legs like an avalanche. "Nice trick, don't you think?" he mused, knowing how absurd he must have looked.

"Yeah, I guess you get a lot of practice in your line of work."

"Every single day, except Sundays and a half a day on Christmas and the Fourth of July. These britches have been known to collect a good deal more, but the mill closed early this evening. Working next to that band saw, you don't only wear the dust, you learn to eat it. Now, how can I help you?"

"I'm rather surprised to find anyone here. I figured everyone was cozy at home by now."

"Well, I sure as heck would be, were it not for my glasses. I thought I lost them at the house, but they were here all along setting on that carriage. I've got grandchildren back home to see, and believe you me, there's no Christmas supper without the spectacles."

"I'm glad you found them. Actually, I've lost something myself... Lawson Darrow. Is there any chance you've seen him this evening?"

"Well, sir, I'm not sure I should say. You the law or some sort a bill collector?"

"No, not hardly. The man's son has been hurt, and Lawson's needed right away at the infirmary."

The sawyer sized Lowe up in an instant and deemed him sincere. "Darrow comes and goes at his own discretion around here, especially lately. But he did stop by about 20 minutes ago. He didn't stay long."

"Did he say where he was headed?"

The look on the man's face would have been answer enough, but he pulled out his watch and held it up to Lowe. "It's after six, isn't it? We all know the routine."

"The Lodge?" Lowe queried, just to be sure.

"If it's open. Yes, sir, that would be my first place to look. He was with a couple other fellows."

"Thanks, and Merry Christmas to you and your family."

"And to you. God speed with your search."

Lowe started back down the stairs, but stopped when the man called to him, "Say! Does this have anything to do with the alarm whistle?"

"Yeah."

"Oh, dear Lord, it must be serious. I hope the little boy's all right." The sound of the alarm was always serious, and it was far too frequent. The man waited for details to follow, but Lowe's only response was the creak of wooden steps as he hurried on his way.

It was still snowing, but the planks of the loading dock were almost black with creosote, and the icy flakes melted the moment they touched the warm deck. Lowe could see three men at the far end of the dock, but when he hailed them, they merely glanced in his direction and then disappeared far into the lumber yard. He picked up his pace in pursuit, only to find in time that Lawson was not among them.

"I'm sorry, gentlemen," he said. "From the distance, I thought you might be someone else."

"No, I don't think so," answered a skinny young man, who was clearly enjoying the effects of one too many toddies. “I’m just me, purdy much the same fool I was both yesterday and this mornin’.” The man swallowed hard, and his large Adam’s apple seemed to jump in his throat. He was prepared to say more.

Lowe winced. He had neither the time nor disposition for chat. “I’m a bit pressed looking for somebody. Frankly, I was pleased to find you men still on the job.”

“We ain’t workin’ actually. I’m just showin’ my cousins the mill. They’re up visitin’ from Ohio, and we just stuffed ourselves to the gills. We do it every single year and never seem to learn. A good walk after dinner makes just enough room for dessert. Ya know what I mean? Mister, I hate to brag, but our girls can cook!”

“I suppose that’s the way it ought to be at Christmas.”

“I don’t know how it ought to be, but that’s sure the way it is.”

“Well, again, I’m sorry to bother you boys,” said Lowe.

“Don’t be silly. Nothin’ could bother the three of us after that big meal. Who ya lookin’ for, anyway?”

“Lawson Darrow.”

“Hmmm. Name’s familiar, but I can’t rightly say I know the man. Does he work here abouts?”

“Yeah, he’s your saw filer.”

“Oh, you don’t say. He’s one of them experts, a big money man. I work the other end of the line, right here in the yard. I’m a racker and a stacker. These stacks of boards you see were laid in just yesterday, most of them by me. I don’t reckon I know any of the fellows up in the mill tower. Lawson Darrow, huh. No, I don’t recall him. But I wish you luck with your search.”

Lowe was disappointed that Lawson had not gone to work as Black Jack had predicted, not for his own sake, but for the benefit of the missing man and his family. It also would have been good for his partner, who, with steadfast optimism, held to the notion that Lawson Darrow would be found both sober and right. Black Jack’s constant faith in others certainly deserved some proof that it was not misplaced, and Lowe was sorry that this instance would provide no gratification.

Over the years he had grown to respect Black Jack's way, and he often wished he could be more like the man. Black Jack could find good in the vilest soul. He would seek it, knowing it was there. He could find hope in a dying breath. He would uncover it, never daunted by disappointment, never surprised by miracles. Lowe might wish, but knew full well he would never attain the depth of character and caring that was the essence of John Lewis Clark. While his sympathies often flowed, they ran much too shallow.

His opinion of Lawson Darrow was a good example. From Lowe's point of view, men created their own demons, and they were obliged as men to fight them off or live with the hellish consequences. Lawson gave no fight. He surrendered everything dear and was forced to seek his peace either in the distraction of work or the destruction of a half empty bottle. He was far more than just missing. He was irretrievably lost. While Lowe did not respect him, he felt at least some measure of compassion and grief for what seemed to be a wasted life.

Lowe's search led him unsuccessfully to the Lodge and the pool room, and then, one by one, to every other drinking establishment as he moved beyond the tracks. A description of the other two men might have helped, but in the rush to find Lawson, he neglected to ask the essential questions. Nevertheless, it was just a matter of time. Lawson was too predictable and the town too small to hide him.

Lowe flicked his collar to dislodge the white frosting that had gathered too close to his neck. He brushed the shoulders of his heavy wool coat, and the snow fell like glitter to the saloon floor. Before it landed, he knew his search was over.

There were three men sitting around a small table with one unlabeled bottle and three smudged glasses, all of them empty. A waiter brought over a second bottle from the bar and set it down without comment. As he moved away, Lowe edged closer, using the heavy, gray smoke of the bar room as his shroud. His focus locked on the figures at the table.

Lawson's back was toward him, but the red hair and big, round head of Farley Ochs and the shrill, cackling laugh of Leon Hopper were immediately distinguishable. The thought of Lawson Darrow sharing such company was preposterous, and Lowe stepped forward into their view trying to be sure.

"Now ain't this somethin'! You turn up in the strangest of places, don't ya, Yancy?" blurted Farley Ochs.

"I might say the same about you."

Lawson glanced over his shoulder at Lowe, but said nothing, as though trying to be obscure. Farley continued to taunt.

"Looks like we're gonna fix you but good this time. Better yet, it looks like you've done it to yourself. Dabney sure won't be happy, and Devlin's likely to bury you and that blackie of yours when they hear what you've been hidin'. I can't wait to spread the news."

Lowe was careful not to fall into Farley's trap and kept his focus on the mission. He chose to speak only to Lawson.

"What's this all about?" he asked, looking straight into Lawson's face.

It was Leon who replied, "Ya tell him, Mr. Darrow. Tell him about the Big Timber and how yer boy found it right on the very ground surveyed by Lowe Yancy here. Ya tell him about all that wood he's stolen for himself." Leon stood up and addressed Lowe directly, "Yeah, Devlin's been chompin' at the bit for that timber, and you were all this time holdin' it back for yerself. Folks around here ain't gonna feel too kindly once the word gets out."

"Shut up, Leon!" growled Farley Ochs.

Lowe looked down at Lawson, and a sense of betrayal must have shown through his eyes. Lawson responded to the look.

"That's right, I told him. Morgan told me and I told these men."

Farley interjected his support, "And it's good you did so, Mr. Darrow. Those trees will mean a lot to this company and this town. I'll negotiate some arrangement, and you and I will settle once Devlin coughs up some 'thank you' money."

Lowe kept staring at Lawson, totally ignoring the others. Lawson's nerves began to unravel, and he stuttered as he tried to explain his actions. "Lowe, you brought this on yourself. Your report apparently wasn't honest, or those trees would have shown in the descriptions. Sooner or later…."

"Have you seen my report, Lawson?"

"No."

"Did you look over my maps or read my contract?"

"No, but Ochs here was telling me…."

"You've said more than enough. Get on your feet and let's go. I've come to tell you that there was an accident at the house. Your son's been injured."

"Which son?"

Lowe was astonished. "Does that really make a difference to you?"

Lawson drew a deep breath while he considered his answer. "No, I guess not."

"It's Jake. We need to go now."

"Jake? Are you sure? That boy is indestructible."

Lawson picked up the bottle and attempted to pour himself a final shot, but Lowe's hand whisked his glass from the table. It shattered at the base of the bar.

"I said now! That *indestructible* little boy is in a fight for his life."

The truth shocked like ice water, and Lawson sobered as though at will. Lowe yanked the chair with one hand and pulled Lawson to his feet with the other. The man offered no resistance.

Farley Ochs closed the conversation, "Oh, that's too bad, Mr. Darrow. I trust that your boy will be just fine. You head on and don't worry about a thing. We'll handle this business from our end and settle up later."

A piercing glance showed how little Lawson now cared about the *business*. He led the way as the two men moved quickly toward the door of the saloon.

The hospital was modest but modern, and it had the latest conveniences in plumbing and electricity, such as steam heating, indoor toilet and bathing facilities, and overhead lighting and fans. There was one ward of six beds and two individual patient rooms, for those who could afford the privacy or required medical isolation. There was also a small operating room, a surgical prep room that doubled as space for simple checkups, an office, and a rather Spartan waiting area with bench seats and a coat rack.

Whatever it may have lacked in technology, the infirmary gained in the dedication of its staff. Doctor Cecil Brown and three nurses provided the only professional care for miles around. Of course, there were midwives and a host of home remedy practitioners. Other trained physicians were called on from time to time, when epidemics or disasters or even a preponderance of house calls dictated a need, but for the most part, Doctor Brown and his infirmary were the only true source of care. Appearance aside, the small building adequately served its purpose, and when it could not, there was always the railroad and its link to better medicine in the cities.

Morgan crashed through the door that led to the waiting room. “Ma, what has happened?” He ran to his mother and smothered her with an embrace.

“We don’t know yet, son.” She wept as she spoke. “Your brother looked so puny, so utterly helpless and puny.”

“I need to see him!”

“No. Let the doctor do what he can. I gave my word.”

“Is it that bad?”

Annie’s tears dropped heavily from her cheek, and she held tightly to her daughter’s hand. Cora had to answer for her.

“It’s bad, Morgan. Dear Lord, I can’t bear to think of little Jake lying in there, so ashen and still. He was burned, but worse, he doesn’t move so much as a twitch. He won’t respond to anything or anybody. No one knows the reason why, but he just won’t wake up.”

“Someone knows. I’ll get some answers.” Morgan was desperate to see his brother. He motioned toward the inner door, but a firm hand suddenly grabbed at his shoulder.

Black Jack’s voice was immediately calming, “What you gonna do, Morgan, dat won’t best be done by dat doctor in dere. Give de man his space, and we’ll just trust he and de Lord knows deir work.”

"I can't simply sit here and do nothing, Mr. Clark."

"It ain't easy, son, but doin' nothin' is a heap more helpful dan bein' under foot. It ain't yo time to help just yet, but dat moment is comin'. You make yo self ready and strong."

"But Jake's...."

"Dat child be sleepin' peaceful and prob'ly don't feel a thing. He breathin', and burnt legs ain't likely to keep a boy like him from carryin' on."

"Black Jack, I need to know that Jake will be all right."

"Well, I ain't gonna pretend to have an answer. Yo brother gots him a nasty burn along his leg, but I seen worse. It look like he took to flyin' off dat porch and suffered a real bad landin'. Dat's what sets me to worryin'. A bad fall can cause damage you ain't never gonna see. But you and me, Morgan, we ain't no men o' medicine, and worryin' sure ain't de cure for nothin'. Doctor Brown seem to know his business, and he gonna give us de good word after bit."

"But how could something like this happen?"

"I can't rightly say. But I's sure o' one thing, we needs to stay strong for de sake o' dem two sweet ladies." He pointed to Annie and Cora. "You stay by yo Mama. In due time, we'll have us a clearer sight of de future. And remember, dere's no sense in frettin', unless dem folks on de other side o' dat door say we need to."

Morgan nodded. He looked at his mother. She was pale, and as never before, she seemed feeble and frail.

A vigil began without prompting, and the silence of it became deafening for Morgan Darrow. People, many from the First Methodist Church, paced quietly about him, and some prayed openly for him and his family. He hated the attention and begged under his breath for God to send them away so he could deal with his feelings in private. But God was not listening. If he had been, Morgan's world would not have turned so suddenly dismal and wanting. At a time when faith would serve him well, he had abandoned it to bitterness. God was to blame until he would know otherwise. For everything gone wrong, God was to blame.

It became an unbearable test of patience. Morgan longed to

be anywhere or anyone else during the ordeal, but understood full well that his rightful place now was either on the arm of his grieving mother or at the tortured side of his little brother. He would not leave them even for a second, knowing if he did that Jacob might call for him or might even pass to another world without a proper goodbye. Morgan trembled. He had never considered the possibility of that goodbye. The imminence of death loomed heavy and cold, and he was not prepared to say farewell to one he loved so dearly. For that, he would never be prepared.

Each rattle of a door handle brought both fearful gasps and hopeful sighs, as all waited for a sign from Doctor Brown. But it was always the wrong door that opened, and the quiet was broken often as friend after friend came in to show their concern. The fresh winter air that entered with them offered welcomed relief from the stale, medicinal scent of the room. One would come and another would go, but it never took long for the anxious watch to resume in earnest.

The sound of carols was faint from a small chorus singing on a distant corner of town, and harness bells jingled when a sleigh moved up the street. Morgan had all but forgotten about Christmas, and the bells were a reminder of what was supposed to be a very special evening. In the crisis, he had not given a single thought about the holiday supper, or about his new friends who had come so far to feast and celebrate with him. He had even forgotten about Sarah, who was probably alone in her parlor, dressed in fine fashion and left wondering why her beau had kept her waiting. But now he thought of them, and he was reassured just knowing they would be with him through this tribulation. Lowe, Black Jack and Silas, they were strong and seemingly unassailable men. They knew how to deal with tragedy. And in her own way, Sarah was just as strong. A year ago, these people were not even names to him, but now, on this stormy, forlorn night, Morgan sought his shelter in the depth of their friendships.

The handle rattled again, and the outside door cracked open just enough to allow an oversized head to peer inside. The flaps of a homemade muskrat hat were pulled below the ears and a long, woolen scarf was wrapped high about the chin, but there was no disguising the face of Dewey Baughman. The boy took one look around the room and quickly shut the door. He was afraid of entering, afraid of seeing his best friend in this ordeal, afraid of saying the wrong thing at the wrong time to this family he had known and admired all the days of his life. For 17 years, he had been spared any real calamity, and now, with it striking so close and so hard, he was not prepared to take that important walk across the room. It was only seconds later when the door reopened, and Auralee Buck came through it, leading Dewey by the hand.

She escorted him first to Annie, where he was supposed to simply express his concern, offer support and move aside so that others might do the same. But upon witnessing Annie's distress, Dewey ignored Auralee's prompting and threw his arms around the older woman. Auralee tugged on his shoulder, but the boy refused to let go.

"Oh, Mrs. Darrow!" he cried, almost smothering Annie with a long, powerful bear hug.

"It's all right, Dewey," she said, squirming against his grip.

Dewey finally backed away. His eyes were red and his nose was running unchecked like a toddler with sniffles. He turned to Cora.

"Oh, poor little Cora!" he moaned, overwhelmed with sorrow.

The girl had never seen Dewey, or for that matter any man, so dejected and pitiful, and she was not sure what to make of his behavior. He had always been a child of surprises, and most everyone had long since learned it was best not to predict what Dewey Baughman might do or say. When she saw him approach with outreached arms, natural impulse caused her to cower. A big wall behind her and a big man before her, she braced for the worst.

Dewey squeezed Cora's tiny frame until she thought she would break. Her face was so engulfed by his large body and heavy winter parka that her pleas for him to loosen his hold were muffled beyond recognition. In his own time he released her, and then, he blubbered inconsolably.

"Poor little Cora," he repeated, slowly shaking his head from side to side in grave concern.

"Oh, for goodness sake, we are all going to be fine." Cora started to laugh at his pathetic expression but thought better of it. Instead, she returned his hug, reached her arms around him as best she could and said, "You're an old cry baby, Dewey Baughman, and we love you for it." The boy's misery was almost comical, and the girl realized, like many others in the room, that he was the one person who brought the smiles back to their faces.

It was quite difficult for him, but Dewey finally turned to Morgan. The two were accustomed to much better times, and he wondered what it was that Morgan most needed to hear. Awkwardly wiping his tears with a parka sleeve, he tried to speak but was sobbing again before the first sound passed his lips.

"Dewey, you're a mess," Morgan said, hoping to put his friend at ease.

"Yeah, I know I am. I'm just a big ol' girl when I'm sad."

"That's a picture I wish you hadn't painted. Stop being so sad. Cora is right. Things will work out. I'm awfully glad you've come."

"Well, I'm right pleased to be here." Dewey rolled his eyes at the stupidity of his own reply, and finally, after his eyes were dry and his sleeves soaked with tears, he asked, "How's the half pint? What ya hear 'bout Jake?"

"We don't have any news, but at least it isn't bad news. So far, Doc Brown's left us in the cold."

"In the cold?" The phrase jostled Dewey's memory. "Oh, damn, you ain't all bein' left out in the cold. I forgot she was still holdin' the horse!"

The boy bolted for the door and swung it wide as he raced outside. Moments later, Sarah stood upon the open threshold, shaking the snow from her fur-lined hood. Her cheeks were rosy red, and against the back light of the street lamps, her yellow hair radiated.

This time Morgan wept. His brittle emotions close to shattering, he saw his Sarah standing there in beauty and confidence, and for a split second, he was strangely compelled to lower his guard and allow her to glimpse his frailty. As much as he loved Sarah Dabney, in that short moment, he knew that he needed her even more. Two tears squeezed from the corners of his eyes and trailed silently down the sides of his face. Sarah moved straight for him. She embraced him, and the tears were gone.

It was half past nine, almost two hours later, and much of the crowd had departed before Lawson came through the door. He fully understood the seriousness of the accident, but still entered the room more angry than concerned. He brushed coldly past Morgan and Sarah. He ignored Cora who grasped lovingly at his elbow. Then, he turned his wrath on the woman he judged responsible for the harm and agony now befalling his family.

"How is he?" Lawson demanded.

"We don't know yet."

"What? You haven't asked? Your child's dying for all you know, and you won't even ask?"

"They're doing all they can for him. We were told to wait. It's best we don't interrupt."

"The hell with that! That's my son in there, and no one is going to stop me from seeing him."

Lawson tugged in vain at the door knob, which the nurse had locked. He ground his teeth, as he faced the blank white door and resisted an overwhelming urge to knock it down. There was little he could do but press his hands and head against it while he searched for composure.

Others were watching, and Lawson sensed their eyes upon him as he considered his options. He needed a whiskey and repeatedly swept his fingers across his chapped, dry lips. There was no feeling of shame, just the anger. He sidled close to Annie and spoke privately.

"Answer me this, will you? What kind of mother could ever allow something like this to happen to a seven-year-old boy? I work. You watch the children. Remember?"

Annie did not respond. They were cruel and hateful words, meant to inflict the same pain that her actions had once caused him. But if she even heard the words, Annie was not about to allow their intended effect, not this time. She looked past the man as he continued to mislay his blame and contempt.

"Woman, I'll tell you one thing. If you've killed my boy...." Lawson left the sentence unfinished. He had made his point.

"Thank you," she said softly.

"Huh?" Lawson was astonished. In confusion, he jerked his head backward to better see her expression. A warm smile adorned her face, and it was suddenly clear that it was not for him.

Annie reached with both arms for Lowe Yancy's hand. "Thank you for finding him, and thank you, Lowe, for coming to be with us. It means more than you might ever know."

Lowe nodded, and not wanting to intrude, he backed away to give Lawson and Annie their time. But he would not go far. Something in her touch told him stay, and he knew without doubt, her greater trials would be ahead.

The white door finally opened, and a disheveled, disheartened Doctor Brown stood in the void. With bleary eyes, he peered at the many frozen faces staring back from throughout the room. There was somber silence. There was sadness.

"Annie. Lawson. I need to see you alone."

# CHAPTER 17

The New River was rushing with spring melts, and the surrounding hills showed ever so faintly the pale greens and yellows of the emerging season. Mallards and herons waded in the shallow backwaters as a whitetail stripped swollen buds from a nearby sapling birch. Neither the drone of steam whistles nor the advancing rumble of railcars could draw the animals' attention as the long train pursued its path through the river's gorge.

Annie was no less indifferent. As much as she loved all things of nature, she looked toward the creatures through a smudged window of the passenger car and saw nothing. The C&O Railroad was carrying her closer and closer to Charleston, farther and farther from home, but in that moment, she knew not where or who or why she was. It was a brief but needed respite from her reality.

The train slowed to a crawl when it passed the whistle stop on the east end of Thurmond, a young and bustling railroad town. Situated in the middle of the New River gorge, the natural corridor through the high Alleghenies, it was an essential station for the Chesapeake and Ohio Railroad, which channeled a ceaseless stream of goods and materials through the town to distant places east and west. The river wide and the tracks too many, there was no room for a large street in Thurmond. Instead, there were only the rails, with a long row of buildings and businesses supporting the industry that rolled across them. Every train traversing the mountains eventually shook the very center of town. All of them slowed to a crawl.

Annie failed to notice when the train actually stopped, and she hardly observed the conductor as he quickly entered the car to announce an unexpected delay. A replacement engine was to be added to the front and a string of freight cars to the rear. Passengers were encouraged to disembark for a short meal, a breath of fresh air or just a good stretch of the legs.

Many took advantage of the situation and crowded into the narrow aisle while waiting to depart. Annie's bench was banged and bumped repeatedly, but she continued to peer blindly through her window as the boisterous line filed toward the station platform. Suddenly, all was calm, and it was the silence itself that became too loud for her peace of mind. She yawned and rubbed her eyes.

The conversation from outside her window was partially muffled. "Did you say 'an hour?'" a man asked. "That's an unusually long delay."

"That it is, sir," the conductor replied. "We've experienced some engine trouble, and the time we expect to lose while switching out apparently complicates some of the routing up track. They've asked us to hold here in Thurmond."

"Then I guess it's time for a quick tour of the town."

"Thank you for understanding, sir. We regret the inconvenience to you passengers. I was told 60 minutes, or there abouts, and that should do it. Listen for the whistle. You'll have 15 minutes to re-board after you hear it."

"It might just prove to be a nice break, if you could offer a recommendation for a fast bite. Maybe a coffee and dessert?"

"Right smart of you to ask, sir. The hotel generally keeps a good selection of fancy cakes and such, but my tastes lean more toward whatever Otie Tibbet is baking on any given day. Try the Tibbet Inn behind the bank. And I might warn you. You'll only have time for one piece of her pie. Otie's a generous woman."

"Thanks. That sounds just right. I'm indebted to you."

The mention of food, especially dessert, seemed to stir Annie. The ride had become monotonous and cold, and a little refreshment would go a long way to make the trip more comfortable. She gathered her coat and small handbag and hurried off the coach.

It was a brisk walk to the Tibbet Inn, and her exertion in the cool, spring air seemed to have restorative powers. Annie glowed with enthusiasm when she first knocked on the door of the quaint boarding house, but when no one answered, she moaned with genuine disappointment. She knocked again and waited patiently, until the slam of train couplings reminded her that time was limited. She looked around, knocked yet again, then twisted the brass handle and passed like a thief through the doorway.

"Hello?" she said meekly. "Hello?"

There still was no reply. The room's air was rich with the smell of fresh butter and dough, and a sudden waft of cinnamon lured her toward the kitchen.

"Hello?" She repeated herself as she made her way down a darkened hallway and a short flight of steps.

A tiny woman with thin white hair and a long blue apron was tending to her oven, and on hearing footsteps, she turned to greet her latest guest. One of her teeth was missing, but her smile was welcoming. Her body was hale, despite her shrinking frame and a back humped from 80 or more years of bending for chores.

"Well, howdy," the woman said, with clear enthusiasm. "I was sure hopin' there'd be others. I'm glad ya didn't disappoint me. Honey, ya just come on in and set yerself down. I don't get much chance to chat with other girls."

"I'm so sorry to barge in like this. I knocked," Annie apologized, but Otie Tibbet dismissed it with a flip of her hand.

"Think nothin' of it. My door's always open. I don't hear so well these days, so it's best that friends just make themselves to home." She took a tea towel and with asbestos-like hands, pulled a hot pie from the oven. Annie cringed.

"Don't ya worry none, missy," the woman reassured. "Don't ya fret about these old hands. I've been yankin' pies from this here oven longer than trains been runnin' with the river." She leaned over to smell her handiwork, then waved some of the aroma toward Annie.

"Mmmm. Now don't that look good?"

"Yes, ma'am, better than good," Annie agreed.

Otie scurried across the room with surprising agility and placed her creation in a pie safe for cooling. Then she hurriedly moved back to formally greet Annie with a short hug, which required no explanation. To the likes of Otie Tibbet, everyone was family.

"Well, I know why yer here. Those railroader boys always send me a few needy souls. I'll cut the pie if you pour the tea. Best grab an extra cup for that young fellow out in the root cellar. He's fetchin' me more apples." Otie winked and grinned. "The man came by just a few minutes ago, afflicted with an acute case of the sweet tooth, so I set him to work with a promise that I'd find him the cure. I reckon he'll take his with a spot of cream and just an extra pinch of sugar." She thought for a moment, trying to recall any missing details. "Let's see. Water's steamin' on the stove right here. Cream's in the ice box yonder. Sugar's on the table. And the tea's in a blue tin on the second shelf of that cupboard. That should be everythin'. You help yerself. Oh, yes, ya might prefer some cheese with yer apple pie. Some folks do. The cheddar's in the ice box."

"None for me, thanks."

Otie Tibbet took a broad spatula and quartered a second pie that had been cooling for a few minutes. She carefully lifted each large piece and set them on oversized sheets of wax paper before transferring them to plates. She was accustomed to using the paper. Visitors often had more appetite than time, and the waxy sheets allowed for some quick packaging of the leftovers. She scooted one plate in front of Annie.

"There ya go. You be my tester. Here's a fork if ya prefer, but I generally find pie just a little sweeter when it comes off my hands. Go on now, try it. What ya think?"

Annie lifted the huge slice as best she could and raised it past her lips to the tip of her nose. She took a deep breath and smiled at the old woman. Then, gazing at the piece, she strategically positioned it for the perfect first bite. The drooping corner barely made it to her mouth before it broke off, and she groaned with delight before she swallowed.

"O-o-o-h! That is delicious." Annie mumbled with a mouth full of pie, but Otie understood. She nodded with pleasure and picked up one of the sections for herself.

The women ate with a sense of purpose, like judges in a juried contest. There was little opportunity for discourse. Words were unnecessary, as the two strangers devoured every flake of crust and every dripping morsel of apple filling. Finally, they talked, grateful for some brief minutes of companionship.

Annie's fingers were caked with the remnants of her treat, and she licked them one by one, following Otie's example. Her thumb was still pressed deep between her lips, when the back door opened and a man came stumbling through. He donned a pink apron, bordered with twists of blue and yellow flowers. It was gathered high around a bulky load of apples, some of which were about to spill out. Concerned with his own condition, he had no regard for Annie's thumb. Still, she blushed with embarrassment. The apron may have been a thin disguise, but it was effective. Annie was completely unsuspecting when Lowe Yancy called her name.

"Why, Mrs. Darrow, I'd swear you were a daffodil if I didn't know better. You pop up in the strangest of places, but you are always a lovely sight to see." Lowe was rather verbose for a shy man, especially one so astounded to find a familiar face. His world was shrinking and meeting Annie Darrow in this small back room of this quiet back street inn was absolute proof of it.

"Lowe?" Annie grabbed up a cloth napkin and properly wiped her fingers. "Well, I'll be. I never expected to know anyone way out here."

"Me, neither. Are you staying with Mrs. Tibbet?"

"No, but that certainly would be nice." She smiled graciously at her host. "I'll be taking the train in another fifteen minutes or so."

"Me, too. I'm heading to the capital on some business."

"I'll be in Charleston, as well."

Lowe assumed as much. He was aware of the situation that pulled her so far from Devlin.

"I thought that might be the case. I suppose you're weary from your travels back and forth."

"Yes, but it has to be done."

"Certainly, it does. Listen, Annie, I'll only be in town for a day or so. Maybe, if you find you have the time, we could meet for coffee one morning before I return. That is, of course, if Lawson would not have objection. Mr. Clark and I have stayed rather busy over the winter, and I'd sure like to catch up on how your family is doing. I've heard little Jake is faring badly."

Annie nodded. She reached for a ready cup of hot tea, added the cream and sugar, and passed it to him. "Lawson's not here to ask, but I know I would very much appreciate your company."

Lowe was pleased. The woman warmed his soul, and the anticipation of seeing her again reminded him of feelings long since withheld. He should have seen them as a warning, but his own feelings were the few signs of nature Lowe never learned to read. He was blind to their meaning, and he innocently, and readily, took the next step that might lead him toward the forbidden. Neither he nor Annie recognized the danger as the bond of friendship pulled them closer and closer together. They should have.

"You look fine, Annie. Are you holding up all right?"

"I thank God for his strength, because I certainly have so little, but yes, I'm doing well. We are all doing well, considering." Her voice was not convincing, but Lowe thought it wise to probe no further.

"I'm relieved to hear that. If there is anything you need or I can.... He stopped abruptly, puzzled by the woman's untimely grin. "What, have I said something wrong?"

"No, not at all." Annie contained the grin as best she could. She pointed, and Lowe dropped his head to rediscover the apron.

"It's just not a fitting look for you," she said. She laughed as Lowe rapidly rolled the apples onto the table and floundered in his attempts to pull the apron off.

"For heaven's sake! I forgot I even had this on," he grumbled, fumbling with the ties behind him. "Mrs. Tibbet insisted I wear it while I fetched the apples."

Otie spoke to his defense, "There was no sense in gettin' a nice suit like yers soiled in that filthy root cellar."

Annie snatched up her napkin to again wipe her face and hands. "Oh, I completely understand. This is the same woman who just taught me how to eat pie with my fingers. You were right, Mrs. Tibbet. It does make it all the sweeter."

"Oh, honey, at my age I just assume I'm right. Smart folks know better than to argue with an old lady, and fools have no inklin' about the truth, whether they hear it or not. So, I am always right. I like it that way."

Otie began folding the wax paper around the two remaining slices of pie and reminded her guests that it was time to depart. She asked them for their promise to return, and after handing both pieces to Lowe, she made him vow to give one to the conductor.

"I sure enjoyed my visit with you young folks," she said. "Say, which of them rail riders was it that sent ya over to visit with me? I'm beholdin' to him."

Lowe answered, "I'm not sure, ma'am. He was a rather portly fellow."

"I thought so. That would be Little Joe Delano. He's my favorite of them all. My cookin's what made him so fat in the first place, and that's somethin' an old woman can be proud of. Give him my love, and you two have yerselves a real safe trip. Be good and be sure to stop by anytime." With that, she ushered them past her door and waved as the two hurried toward the tracks.

Lowe returned to his original seat on the forward passenger coach, which was separate from that of Annie's, and he wondered why he never asked the woman if they might share the remainder of the journey. Perhaps it was that same sense of propriety that had directed him on other occasions, or maybe, it was simply his pride that preferred she offer him her invitation. He took his seat and, like Annie before him, stared blankly through the glass.

The train rolled slowly, but before long it was passing the mouth of the Gauley, leaving the higher mountains and the gorge to the east. Lowe knew this country. The memories of his family rested among the thousand hills that guarded the river, and the one romance he had permitted himself bloomed in the shade of the sycamores that lined its banks. It hurt to look at bygone years, but it was not to be avoided. Lowe slipped deep into his past and longed for those who were once his life. It was Annie who brought him back.

"May I join you, Lowe?" The words went unheard. She tapped the man on his shoulder, and Lowe jerked his head to break the grip of his thoughts. He was dazed, even when he looked up to find Annie teetering to and fro with the sway of the car.

"Oh, please do," he replied. He stood and motioned to a place beside him on the bench.

Annie took her seat quickly but said nothing for a few unsettling moments. It was obvious she was pondering something important. Hers was a troubled heart, and while Lowe was more than curious about her thoughts, he waited.

The woman drew a weak and wavering breath. "Lawson left me."

"What?"

"He left me. The children, our friends, our home, he's abandoned it all."

"Annie, I don't understand. You mean he just walked out?"

"Yes." Annie's voice quivered as the cord that harnessed her strength began to unravel. "It was a week ago. He wrote a note. He said he was headed for Minnesota or Oregon or anyplace away from Devlin that might offer mill work. He said he was taking half of the money and that I should keep the house. He said…." She laid her face between her hands, then pulled a handkerchief from her sleeve and dabbed her eyes. Her body trembled. "He told me that he once loved me, but in light of things, he now was no longer sure."

She paused to better gather her thoughts. "I'm so sorry, Lowe. It's not right to put this on you, or anyone, for that matter. Today, for some reason, it just all came crashing down. When I needed a friend the most, you were the one who walked through Otie Tibbet's back door."

Lowe clutched the woman's wrist, as if to show that his own strength could carry her burden. "I'm listening, Annie."

"That was about it. It was a short note." Annie took another breath and impassively held her head high, reclaiming her composure. Lowe recognized the pretense.

"Did he not give you his reason?"

"No, but it wasn't necessary. We've been struggling for years. He's not a forgiving man, and he let the past sour until it became a poison. I have to acknowledge that I haven't been faultless through all of this, but I at least stayed committed to him, hoping for change. It hasn't been easy. I gave up a lot. Now he blames me, and rightfully so, for what happened to Jacob. Lawson never could deal with sorrow. He has no religion, except his whiskey, and whiskey offers a very weak kind of solace."

Lowe was speechless, and he was cautious. He thought he knew Annie's past, and privy to that knowledge, he recognized the importance in not saying something that could cause more pain. The real issue at hand may not be Lawson, or the fire, or even Jacob. Lowe listened, hoping to better understand what might bring her comfort.

"It's all inexplicably sad," Annie continued. "The man can't face the loss of one son, and yet, he's done everything in his power to drive the other from our lives. Morgan deserves better from a father. Our family deserves better than to be trampled by guilt and anger."

She stopped and looked at her friend. In the awkwardness of the quiet, Lowe finally felt obliged to speak. "We all make our mistakes, and we all live with the consequences. Some folks are better at moving on than others, and I suppose Lawson isn't one of them. But, Annie, that fire was not your fault. There is no fault. You must believe that, even if Lawson cannot."

"I wish that I could. My prayers for forgiveness go unanswered. My prayers for healing go unheard. If Jesus is talking, I can't hear him. It hurts to lose a husband. It's unbearable to lose a God. Where is he, Lowe? That fire *must* have been my fault."

Lowe Yancy had asked the same question every day for a score of years. He wandered through time like a man searching for light in the depths of a vast, uncharted cavern. Certain it was not there, he was compelled, nevertheless, to look for it. It was different with Annie. She knew beyond a doubt that the light existed, but now questioned why she was suddenly blind to it. Her faith, tested and weakened, was still faith, and she waited impatiently for her God to act. Lowe had witnessed it clearly in the life of John Clark, and he expected to see the very same in Annie Darrow. People of faith always seem to find their answers. He envied them.

Lowe tried to respond, letting nature make his point. It was the only piece of life he thought he understood. "Sunlight chases rain clouds. In my experience, it always has, and it's my full expectation that it always will, though at times we have to wait a little longer for the storm to clear. Black Jack likes to say 'God is here and there, everywhere and always'. Hasn't that been your belief, Annie? Don't forsake what has worked for you all these years. You have to bear this out."

Annie shook her head as if to argue. "Some storms are deadly, Lowe. My Jacob is dying in a hospital far from home."

"But you are his home, Annie, and he is still alive. And hope is alive with him. Black Jack told me something else, 'God's hands have a soft touch, and whether you feel it or not, you're still blessed.' Maybe, just maybe, there's some good to come of this yet."

"I just can't see how, Lowe. Have you talked to Morgan?"

"No, not for weeks."

"He blames himself for everything, the accident, for Lawson's leaving, for their strained relations. He's ended his engagement with Sarah and absolutely refuses to see her. He says he's responsible for the family now, and that Sarah deserves her own life and her own home with a man who can devote himself to his wife. It hurts him to be reminded of what might have been, so he avoids the girl altogether. Her heart is broken, poor dear. His spirit is shattered. Lowe, we need much, much more than a soft touch."

Lowe was stretched beyond his ability. He found himself defending that which he had often battled. If there was blame for the tragedy of this family, it did not lie in the heavens, or in Annie Darrow, or in young Morgan. It rested squarely with Lawson, beginning 20 years earlier, the first time he abandoned those who needed him.

"What of your husband? Won't he return once he calms and becomes rational?" Lowe asked.

"I think...I think that he will not come back this time, and, God help me, I don't want him back. Too much has happened. Too much has passed us by. There are probably more, but right now I only have three concerns, my two sons and my daughter. Cora has been a rock through all of this, and Jacob's fate is in the hands of doctors and the will of the Lord. But, Lowe, I have great fear for Morgan. There is no one to heal his hurt. I cannot bear to think of his dreams burning away in that fire. He came so close."

Lowe was moved. He cared deeply for Morgan, perhaps too deeply, since the mere mention of the boy's sorrow stirred within him a fierce, yet undirected anger. It was his instinct to fight for those downtrodden, even against an unknown foe. It was his nature to shelter and soothe those wounded and weary, especially one he had come to love as a son. Lowe's anger served a single purpose: to steel his resolve and make things right for Morgan Darrow.

The train lurched, tossing Lowe and Annie ever closer together. For a long second, the two were but inches apart, her weeping eyes so near to his own that Lowe could not distinguish her detail. His promise passed through his lips before he thought just how he might keep it.

"Morgan will live his dreams. I will see to that, and I expect little Jake will be chasing after him before too long. It may be a dim light, but I think it's starting to glow, and before long, we'll see a path leading out of this darkness."

"We, Lowe?"

"You have friends, Annie. Where I come from, friends walk together."

Farley Ochs leaned smugly against the hitching post and drew a smile that was no less devilish than his soul. He was basking in the victory of his vengeance, satisfied with the thought of having destroyed Lowe Yancy. Of course, he had wanted much worse for the man, but ruining his reputation and life's work was more than an adequate compromise. In any moment, Yancy would be turning the corner toward the mill office, wondering and worrying about the purpose of his meeting with Irwin Dabney. He would know soon enough. It was a glorious day for Farley Ochs, one worthy of his patience.

Lowe wanted to be early, but as usual, he found himself racing against time. If he even noticed Farley on the way, he gave no indication, and the big man scowled with disappointment. Still, Farley waited the better part of an hour just to witness the shame and anger that would surely accompany Lowe's departure. When the door opened, he lifted himself away from the post and squared to face his adversary.

"Yancy, you were sure in there a long enough. Been meetin' with the man?" Farley already knew the answer. "Long meetings are pure hell. I can't stand them myself. Those big shot company men sure like to talk, don't they? It's just plain brutal to have to sit there and listen while they go on and on pumpin' themselves up. Of course, I guess this particular meetin' wasn't about them."

Lowe had no interest in the conversation. He attempted to step past the big man, but Farley moved with him, maintaining his block. He pressed him further.

"So, I understand you and the nigger boy finally felt the sting of old Devlin's boot. He's kicked you clear out of the business and right onto your ass. That's the word, anyway. Oowee! How I hate that kind of meetin'."

Lowe looked through the man, as though he was invisible. "It was a rather good meeting, actually." He said as little as possible, hoping to discourage any additional discourse, and began to walk a wide loop around Farley's position.

"A good meeting, that's it? No details? No fiery retort? Why, Yancy, you disappoint me!"

Lowe stopped. "Come to think of it, there was one significant detail I should convey. Mr. Dabney mentioned that he intended to catch up to you. You might want to stop in and save him the trouble of looking."

"Well, I might just do that. He owes me. I expect me and your pal, Darrow, have a little something comin' to us."

"You got that right. Something's coming."

Farley, still smug, ambled back to the mill office and boldly pushed the large door open without so much as a knock. Lowe tilted his hat back from his brow and headed quickly to the livery for his horse. Blu was rested. They would soon be moving on.

The company store was busy as people readied for spring, with garden seeds being the more popular items. Pole and butter beans, radishes, squash and cucumbers, collards and kale, even potatoes were selling fast now that the ground had finally softened for planting. It was all very predictable. Once May brought its warmth to the mountains, everyone took to the out of doors and their crops.

Sam Blackman had just finished filling a long list of supplies. He was suspicious of the last item, "tobacky plugs," written in a childlike scribble. Still, he tossed the entire order into a box, smacked his hand on the counter and smiled at his customers.

"What else can I get you fellows?"

"Dat should do it," Black Jack replied.

"Hold on thar! Did ya git my tobacky?"

"Yes, sir, Mr. Monk, it's all right here in this box."

"Well, I ne'er got to see it, much less git me a good sniff. How can I judge quality from the bottom o' that box? Go on, Sam, pull it on out o' thar fer a quick inspection."

Sam did as he was instructed and started to pass the tobacco over the counter to Silas when Black Jack intercepted it.

"What's dis?" Black Jack questioned. "Mr. Blackman, does ya mind me takin' another look at Lowe's list?" Sam handed him the wrinkled sheet of paper. "Uh-huh. Silas Monk, you is one shifty old rascal! What you doin' gettin' Mr. Yancy to pay for yo sinful ways? You know how he hates all dat spittin' when he's up on de mountain."

"I know no such a thing, and that's a fact. Me and Lowe Yancy has indulged with plenty a good chew from time to time."

"If dat be true, yo time to time was a long time ago. I think we best leave dese particular items right where dey was."

Silas leaned over and snatched the tobacco from Black Jack's hand. He slowly inhaled the distinct aroma. "Think all ya want, but these li'l beauties are gonna be travelin' to the Big Timber. I cain't eat beans every mornin'. This here is my nourishment. Tobacky's a vetchtable, don't ya know. Didn't yer Mama e'er teach ya 'bout yer vetchtables? We're gonna need vetchtables, or, by God, we'll ne'er raise that cabin Lowe wants."

Black Jack looked up at Sam Blackman. "Put dem 'vetchtables' back in de box. I'll let de old man do his own explainin' to Mr. Yancy."

"Anything special for you, Mr. Clark?"

"No, dat be de list and den some."

"Okay, then, that about does it. Will you be paying with company scrip, cash or credit?" Sam asked. It was his customary phrase at the end of a transaction.

"Dat be cash today, sir." Black Jack reached into his pocket and withdrew a wad of bills, most of them dollars.

"I heard about your find in the Big Timber. Are you boys planning to log it?" Sam inquired.

"Mr. Blackman, we just plans on lovin' it. It be a fine patch o' woods, the likes of which ain't never been seen before."

"That's nice to hear. Rumor said otherwise. I fear the great forests are disappearing far too fast."

Sam held the door as the two men began to carry out their supplies. His big belly almost blocked their way, and Silas could not resist the opportunity to pause and pat the man's wide, round center.

"Lordy, Sam, what ya hidin' in thar? Ya come on up to the hills with us, and I'll show ya how to whittle down some o' that sizable girth."

"No, thank you. I've tried just about everything to lose this belly, cakes and candy, gravies, cream sauces, cracklings, dumplings. You name it. Nothing seems to work. Of course, I haven't sampled your particular strain of 'vetchtable,' but I believe I'll pass on that, if it's all the same to you." Sam laughed hardily, as he shifted his position to allow Silas to pass.

"It's yer decision. To each 'is own, I say!" Silas shouted to the air. He never looked back.

"And to each a safe journey," Sam replied.

The men planned to meet at their usual place by the tracks near the mill pond. Silas and Black Jack had the gear tightly packed for transit, and Noggin, already behaving badly, was tethered by a short lead. Before long, Lowe appeared at the far side of the yard with an unsaddled Blu in tow.

"Here he is, boys! I believe Blu is as antsy as I am to clear out of here," Lowe called to his friends, wishing he could join them.

Silas responded, "Cain't say the same for this damn mule. He's tried twice to sneak back home to the holler. He's lazier than a rat snake under a Sunday sun."

"Oh, Noggin will come through for you. He always does. Did you get everything you're going to need?"

"Yup," answered Silas.

"And den some," added Black Jack. The rail cars shifted loudly when the Shay engine coupled with the train.

"Good. Well, I guess it's time to load, so I reckon we'll meet up again in 10 days or so. Silas, you find me a little knoll by a cool spring, will you? But stay clear of the big trees. Watch for the roots. We don't want to damage anything by setting a building too close. Most of all, mind your backs. You're not as young as you once were. Let the animals do your hauling and lifting."

"Are ya quite finished?" Silas complained. "Next thing ya know, you be tellin' us how to change our britches! If yer so blamed worried 'bout things, come on with us. Otherwise, hush up and help us git this load movin'."

Everyone laughed, except Silas, and the three men proceeded to stow the gear and secure the animals, as they had done so many times together. The only difference on this occasion was that Lowe would not be with them when the train whistle sounded and the iron wheels rolled.

"I wish I was taking this trip. I promised Morgan that I'd see him graduate, and that's a vow I intend to keep. Ten days. Be watching for me. Be watching for us. Morgan doesn't know it, but he's coming along."

The train slipped through the shadow of the mill, and Lowe gave his friends a brief wave before they disappeared around the first bend. He had no other plan for the day, so he stepped across the tracks and a rutted, muddy street on his way to a cool beer and a friendly game of pool. It had been a while since he had enjoyed either.

Seeing Leon Hopper in the pool room should have been an omen. Whenever Leon stood before you, Farley Ochs was sure to be lurking at your back. Lowe was well aware of this, but he was denied even an instant to react. As he peered across the table's green felt, lining up the nine ball with the far-right pocket, he recognized the skinny little man with his slick hair and skewed, wicked grin. A second later, he felt the sharp sting of a cue stick cracking across his back.

"You son of a bitch! You cockroach! What did you say to Dabney? He sacked me. He sacked Leon, and he would've sacked Darrow if that drunken fool hadn't already quit. I'll kill you for this!"

Farley threw the splintered stick across the room and bared the hands that would carry out his threat. He pushed Lowe to the edge of the table and wrapped his fat fingers around his neck. The grip was locked, but Lowe countered with his own strength, pressing his fingers deep into the tendons of Farley's wrists. The big man's hands began to weaken, and with a burst of power, Lowe pushed him up and away until both men stood upright, face to face.

"Do you really want to do this, Ochs?" Lowe asked calmly, as if nothing had yet happened. "Your problems are not of my doing, but I can add to them if you want to press further."

Farley's face turned redder than his hair, and his sweat streamed down it in large, rolling drops. With one violent move, he broke free of Lowe's hold and cocked his right arm for a single, deadly strike. His fist fell like a hammer through the air, and it landed on its mark against the left jaw as Lowe twisted to evade. Lowe's body did not falter. His lip bled as he stood his ground and prepared for another shot, but Farley chose wisely to back away, rub the salty water from his eyes, and simply look on in disbelief.

"I've had enough, if you have," Lowe again said calmly, hoping to end the battle before it went further. Both his back and face throbbed, but he refused to react to the pain. Instead, he set his hands upon his waist and struck a cocky pose that may have overstated his confidence.

Farley yielded to the bluff. Lowe Yancy had taken one blow already and may very well absorb the next. No man had done that before. There were others in the room that watched and waited for Ochs to fight. He would not. He could not chance the humiliation.

"Yeah, I'm done," he said, "for the time bein'."

# CHAPTER 18

The graduation ceremony went as expected, with the exception of Dewey Baughman, who actually did pass his final year to the surprise of many. There were eight graduates in total and six other students, who would receive certificates showing they had completed their eighth and last attempt at formal education. Principal Tutwiler felt a sense of accomplishment in that ratio. In the past, far too many of his students had abandoned their studies, generally for reasons beyond their control. He encouraged every child to persevere through the extra years, but for most, the ability to simply read and write was sufficient for the greater education that life itself would proffer.

Each of the seniors stepped forward as they were called by Mr. Tutwiler, and each was invited to address the families and supporters that filled the room from wall to wall. They all praised their principal and their teachers. They all thanked their parents, and most expressed their faith and enthusiasm for what was thought to be a clear pathway through the future.

Morgan and Sarah spoke of the same, but neither really believed it. Doubt clouded their eyes, the very eyes that once sparkled with a discovery of new love, and loss overshadowed their destinies. Lowe could feel it from his seat far at the back of the room. Annie could see it from her place near the front. But for others watching and listening to the words of the honorees, the two seemed as ready as any for their upcoming walk in the world.

Only one speech stood out as memorable, and it drew a sustained ovation. Dewey accepted his diploma and proudly stepped to the podium.

"Uh...uh...," he started, while eyeing the diploma. "Hey, Mr. Tutwiler! What does this word here mean?"

The audience erupted in laughter, and Dewey bowed like an actor at the fall of the curtain. Exhilarated by applause, he had nothing else to say. It was his best performance.

Lowe Yancy watched Morgan with a feeling of pride and could only imagine the thoughts that passed through Annie's mind as she witnessed the proceedings. It was the first time in months that her son had ventured a smile, and while he did not keep it long, he would hold forever the satisfaction of having achieved at least this one particular dream. When the ceremony concluded, Morgan went straight to his mother and sister and hugged them warmly.

Lowe remained at the back of the room for a while and continued to observe. He could not help but notice the searching glances that Morgan cast at Sarah Dabney. She did the same, careful to avoid detection, but on occasion their eyes would meet and instantly look away. If actions speak volumes, eyes speak truth. Lowe saw what was in their hearts, and he knew that it was right.

Another man was intently watching, as well. He was younger and fashionably trimmed in a light cotton suit. His clothes were freshly pressed and adorned with a diamond tack in the center of his blue silk tie and with a bright red rose pinned to his lapel. The flower was one of two dozen he had specially shipped from Pittsburgh, all of them for the girl he intended to pursue in earnest. His jet hair was cropped with expert precision, and his aspect revealed the thoroughness of his social training. Just standing, just watching, the man wore the scent of success. He was a person of considerable means, and he projected an unseemly haughtiness in the midst of more humble people. Lowe was unsettled by his presence.

Austin Devlin was a cad when Lowe first encountered him in conference with Irwin Dabney, and there was nothing to change that opinion. Lowe cared little for the man at that initial meeting. He disliked him all the more in what was to be their second.

Devlin slipped the boutonniere from the button hole of his coat and walked toward Sarah. Pressing through the crowd, he brushed by Lowe, and when he did, Lowe seized an opportunity. He grabbed Austin by the sleeve and held fast.

"Pardon me. You must be Mr. Devlin."

"I am, but if this is business, take it up with my father. This milling operation is his little lark, not mine." Devlin smirked. He looked for wrinkles on the sleeve when Lowe released his grip.

"I'm Yancy, Lowe Yancy."

"Yes? And?"

"Well, perhaps you don't remember me." Lowe identified himself, knowing full well that Austin Devlin would rather not be bothered. "We met some time ago with Irwin Dabney at the mill office. I'm the surveyor."

"Oh, of course, the surveyor. Father is still angry with you for stealing his forest. It wasn't just the money, you know. He has a strange obsession about really large trees. It's actually quite embarrassing at times. Frankly, Mr. Yancy, I'm not quite sure how I feel about you myself."

Lowe could not have cared less, and the whole idea of befriending someone like Austin Devlin, even for a moment, was repugnant to him. Nevertheless, any time spent talking was well spent, if it deprived the man of his audience with Sarah Dabney. It was the least he could do for Morgan.

Austin looked impatiently in the direction of Sarah and attempted to end the conversation. "Well, this has been nice, but beauty calls. Good day, Yancy."

Lowe again grabbed his sleeve. "I'll say one thing for you. You have exquisite taste in women, if your interest is Miss Dabney. Sarah certainly is an upstanding and beautiful girl. I hear tell she's about to marry one of our local boys."

"You hear wrong, sir. Rumors are dangerous, and I would think better of you if you did not spread them regarding the young lady. She's an elegant woman, hardly the type that could long abide these mountain people. No offense meant, of course."

"Oh, but of course. Yet, she chose to finish her schooling in this little mountain village."

"Merely a matter of convenience, I assure you. Her father has been situated in town just for the time being, and despite his urging otherwise, she preferred to be by his side instead of at some boarding school. I understand her feelings completely, the man being a widower and all, but I hope she hasn't compromised her education."

"I see," said Lowe.

Devlin again attempted to break away for Sarah, and Lowe, again, grabbed on to the sleeve. He enjoyed being an annoyance and had every intention of protecting Morgan's future.

"Oblige me for just a moment more, Mr. Devlin, if you would be so kind. Watch Sarah's eyes. She has lovely blue eyes, don't you think? Did you notice how they sweep across the room while she accompanies her father? I believe she's looking for someone. Maybe it's you."

"Most likely so. I told her I'd be here." Devlin waved as Sarah's head turned in his direction, but she looked past him without any sign of recognition. He was incredulous.

Lowe went on to make his point, "Well, it doesn't seem to be you after all, does it?"

"She must not have seen me through all of this crowd."

"Perhaps not, but she does see that other fellow, one of these *mountain people*, the young man right over there."

Lowe pointed to Morgan Darrow. Sarah's attention was unmistakably fixed on Morgan's every move and expression. Her eyes danced as she followed him, and it was evident to all who would witness that Morgan was the real object of her search and affection.

"I'm sorry, Mr. Devlin. As you now plainly see, it is no rumor. I thought it only fair to warn you."

"And what is all of this to you?"

"I suppose I'm just a common meddler. A tree thief and a meddler. And I am someone who strongly believes in Morgan Darrow and Sarah Dabney. That being said, I'll be glad to give Miss Dabney and her father your regards, if you're suddenly ill or your busy schedule is about to take you elsewhere."

"Perhaps it would be more accurate if you simply express my regrets. And, Yancy, I've finally decided something."

"What is that, Mr. Devlin?"

"I don't like you any better than Father does."

Austin dropped his rose onto the wooden floor and mashed it with the sole of his polished black shoe. Sarah did not see him that day or ever again, and it was clear, very clear, she did not care.

Lowe Yancy's left knee ached, his right ankle clicked with every step along the trail, and to his deepening dismay, his feet and shoulders were not faring any better. Lowe was accustomed to walking great distances, but the addition of a 60-pound pack seemed to be the difference. Luckily, Dewey Baughman had asked to come along, and Dewey was in far worse condition.

Lowe tried to set a reasonable pace, but at 15 yards apart, he could still hear Dewey sucking air even on relatively flat terrain. The boy tried to conceal his fatigue, and he intentionally stopped every half mile to pose some question or to observe some aspect of nature that would require a break in the journey. Lowe certainly did not mind. They both could use the rest.

Morgan was with them, but one would not have known by simply listening. He had little to say and moved with the quiet ease and muffled footsteps of an Indian hunter. The men walked miles before the boy put forth more than two sentences of conversation.

"I should have gone with her, you know," he said, finally. "Ma shouldn't be traveling alone back to Charleston. She's just absolutely worn out."

"But I think she wanted you to be here, son. Your Ma saw this trip as a chance for you to sort things out," Lowe replied, "and I agree with her."

"I'm not sure there's anything left of my plans to sort. Everything's changed so fast."

"I know. There's a lot to consider."

The two kept hiking, and the thin path began to climb and twist through a dense, unyielding stand of mountain laurel. The bushes jutted across their way and grabbed relentlessly at the men's trousers and packs, leaving them weary, scratched and frustrated. When they cleared the laurel, Lowe motioned for a halt.

"Whew! That makes for a tough obstacle, even with a trail running right through it," Lowe muttered. He pulled a kerchief from his pocket and wiped the moisture from his neck. "Say, where's Dewey?"

"Back a good ways, I'd guess."

"Reckon we should hold up?" Lowe asked.

"If we expect him to catch us, we should. As long as I've known Dewey Baughman, which is all my life, he's only had one speed - slow."

The two looked down the trail and saw nothing of their companion. It was a good opportunity for Morgan to finish his thought.

"Mr. Yancy, I don't mean to question how nice it is to be out here. I appreciate your company and concern. Ordinarily, I'd be jumping at the chance to be in these mountains, but frankly, if the woods aren't offering big wages to people traveling through, I belong back at that mill begging for a job. Ma's having a tough time making ends meet, and it's time I did my part. You know I'm right."

"Morgan, that's one of those things that has to be worked out. But for the next few days, it might help if you let loose of your troubles until you regain your sense of direction. That's what your Ma really wants. Seeing you happy, that's what she really needs. We've got a lot to do up in the Big Timber, and there's nothing like hard work to set a mind in order. Will you give it a chance?"

Morgan was slow to answer. He pondered the question as he impatiently watched the thicket for some sign of his friend. Finally, he replied, "Of course, I will."

Dewey broke through the laurel like a hungry bear, and he growled just as loud. By the time he reached his companions, they were pushing to resume their journey. Soaked in his own sweat and breathing heavily, he was indignant and not afraid to say so.

"Damn yer hides! I catch up, you head on. How 'bout some

rest for ol' Dewey? My blood's on fire, and the water now pumpin' through this skin ain't doin' a blasted thing to quell it. Ya just keep up this pace of yours, and I reckon I'll sizzle until my fat all turns to cracklin'. I could just die out here. I think I will."

Morgan spun around in place and pointed a finger. "Don't!" he exclaimed. "Don't you ever say that! Never, never ever joke about dying. It can happen, you know. Your heart could quit on the very next step."

Dewey lowered his head in shame. "Lordy, Morgan, I wasn't thinkin'. With all ya been goin' through, I, well...."

"It's all right. I know you didn't mean any harm."

"No, I didn't, but just the same, it was a cruel remark seein' how little Jake is in the fix he's in. I'm a sorry excuse for a friend."

"You're a good friend, Dewey, the best. I shouldn't have snapped like that. Right now, I just can't imagine losing someone else, especially you. I'll hang back, and you and I can take our time. Does that suit you, Lowe?"

"Sure, I've been pushing us a bit. There's a storm brewing, and I wanted to get as much territory behind us as we could. Let's all take it a little slower."

The sky roiled with the threat of spring rains, and the stirring breezes were a welcome relief. Still, Dewey felt compelled to complain with every uphill stride. He could hardly breathe. He could barely talk, though he tried.

"Where's your horse, Mr. Yancy?"

"Blu's up on the mountain with Black Jack and Mr. Monk."

"What's he doin' there?"

"Hauling."

"Haulin'? Well, what happened to the mule?"

"Noggin's up there, too."

"But what's a mule for if the horse is doin' all the haulin'?"

"More hauling, I guess."

"Ya mean to tell me they got both them animals up on the mountain haulin'?"

"It would seem so," replied Lowe.

"Well, that don't make a lick of sense. Could ya just tell me why?

"Why what, Dewey?"

"Why they got both the mule and the horse haulin' up there, and we ain't got nothin' down here." Dewey stopped for a second and placed his hands on his knees. The burden of the heavy pack was eased from his shoulders, and he drew a long, desperate breath. "They could've at least left us the horse."

"What on earth for?"

"To help me get up this damn hill, for one thing!"

"Listen to me, son, Blu wouldn't be any help to you in any case. You'd still be walking. They need the muscle power a lot more than we do, and besides, they carried most of the gear for us."

"Well, hell's afire! If they already took my gear, what's all this weighin' down my back?"

"Extra food mostly."

"Oh, why didn't you say so?" Dewey walked on, all the while losing ground against Lowe's steady pace. A minute later, the discourse renewed with a shout, "Hey! Why couldn't your horse carry the food, too? Ain't that what God intended for dumb beasts?"

Tired of the questions, Lowe responded curtly, "Yes, Dewey, that's exactly what he intended, and you're doing just fine!"

The blackened sky now became their issue, as winds began to whip the forest into a frenzy of swaying trees and dislodged leaves. Twigs and branches dropped like rain, and the squall was upon the three men before they could seek shelter. Small stones of hail bounced on the brims of their hats and stung with every strike against their uncovered hands. They ran up the grade as best they could under the weight of the packs, looking for a safer place that might anchor them against the gusts.

Lowe led the way; the boys faithfully followed. Despite Dewey's pleas for rest, he refused to let them stop. He raced on until he reached a narrow swath of open land, a small grassy glade strangely misplaced in the midst of a sylvan sea. Trees moaned and cracked all around. Lowe wasted no time getting clear.

He shouted to Morgan, but was hardly audible above the roar

of the storm, "Get out in that field, drop your pack and lay down next to it!"

"What's that?"

"We need to get out from under these trees and lay down in that grass until this blows over!"

"What about lightning?"

"Forget lightning! The woods are coming down on us. Guard against the wind! Cover yourself with your pack. Go on!"

"But where's Dewey?"

It had not taken long for Dewey to disappear in the swirling chaos behind them. Lowe immediately dropped his pack at the meadow's edge and turned back to find him. "Go now!" he cried to Morgan. "I'll get Dewey."

Lowe showed amazing speed and agility running down the hill, until a sudden burst of air buffeted his side and sent him rolling into the brush that lined his path. He lifted himself up without hesitation and continued his search for Dewey. He found the boy over a hundred yards away, clinging tightly to the base of a young hickory tree. His face was buried in the fleshy crease of his elbow, and he felt abandoned to the will of the storm.

"Come on, son. You can't stay here," Lowe said, in a comforting tone.

Dewey was relieved to hear the familiar voice. He had attempted to flee the raging winds, just like Lowe and Morgan, but, as his legs played out, he falsely concluded that the safest spot was exactly where he was standing. He would not release his hold on the tree.

"Come on, Dewey. It's not much farther," Lowe repeated. A large limb snapped from its trunk and crashed with a thud on the ground next to them. "I've got your gear. You head up that path until you find Morgan. Lay low in the grass. I'll be right behind you!"

Free of the burden of his pack, pressed by his own fears, Dewey was out of sight before Lowe could square the pack on his shoulders. And by the time Lowe reached the tiny meadow, it was all over. The wind had ceased. The black sky was speeding to the east.

"What in the world was that?" Dewey asked in awe. "Just look at this place."

Leaves littered the earth like large confetti, some still drifting from the tree tops. Broken limbs dangled from their trunks, and whole trees, with roots upturned and bark shattered, now leaned against their stronger neighbors. A single poplar was twisted and cracked beneath its canopy, like a wash towel wrung of its water. A large oak was laid low across the ground.

"Just look at this," he said again.

"I can't believe it," responded Morgan. "We were right in the middle of it, whatever it was. Not a drop of rain, not a flash of lightning. Just that wind. I never felt anything like it. What do you think, Mr. Yancy?"

Lowe was trying to recall something from his past. "I weep, my friend, when green leaves fall.... Such nature whims and takes us all."

"Huh?"

"It's a poem, one that's just found some relevancy after a good number of years. I'd say, boys, we were nearly nailed by a fair-sized whirlwind. That weather front was moving fast, and it likely spun out a lot of storms like this."

"Say, 'bout that poem, you don't really like poetry, do ya?" Dewey sounded worried.

"Not one bit, but I have to hand it to Mrs. Mabel Yokum. She made me memorize this one, and it stuck with me over time. She was the toughest teacher I ever faced, and looking back, she was by far the best. I think she had us memorize, because she knew darn well we would never read verse again once we left her. Unfortunately, she was right."

"We know that kind of teacher all too well. Don't we, Morgan?"

"Yeah, Mr. Tutwiler. Can you still recite it, Mr. Yancy?"

"I think so." Lowe tried to remember the entire poem, and after several false starts, he managed to piece the lines in their proper order.

*"I weep, my friend, when green leaves fall,*
*As nature plucks them one by one*
*Whilst still they sip her sun and air.*
*I weep for foliage brown and done*
*Before its time, for arbors fair*
*Left void, for shaded glades now lost.*
*I weep when tender blades are cast*
*To howling winds, and know great cost*
*May yet be borne, when here at last*
*Such nature whims and takes us all."*

"Do you know its meaning?" Morgan asked.

"I didn't back then, but I suppose I do now. It tells me that fate does not discriminate. The force that blows a young spring leaf can also topple the tallest tree. Just look at these broken woods around us. Whether it's an innocent child full of joy and promise or a gruff old man who let his dreams fade somewhere along the way, it doesn't matter. Nature strikes as it wills, and we're fools to assume blame or to hope we might pass through this life unscathed."

"That was a gloomy poem for a young boy to have to recite."

"It sure was, but I chose it myself. It was penned by a Yankee soldier awaiting battle at the Wilderness. He had already seen the effects of war, how it mowed down men and trees with the same indifference and ferocity. He anticipated his death, and sadly, he found it there in the smoke and fires that overcame so many of the wounded. Tragedy like that tends to grab hold of a school boy's interest."

Lowe looked squarely at Morgan and continued, "Bad things do happen to the innocent, son. There's no blame to be placed, and sometimes, there's nothing humanly possible that can be done to set things right."

"Are you talking about Jake?"

"Yes, and I'm talking about you."

The familiar sight of the long escarpment brought exhilaration to the three very tired men. They were charged with anticipation at this moment of rediscovery, and new energy seemed to propel them on their steep ascent of the cliff. When they reached the openness of the dome, they were disappointed to find that the sun had already set on the near horizon. But in the gloaming, there was yet light to find their way and glow enough in the west to profile that wondrous giant oak, rising from the rock and resting high in the starlit sky.

They were welcome there. They could feel it, and while darkness seemed to envelop them, they rested on the long, low limbs of the tree, each to his own thoughts.

Lowe was the first to move. "It's best we get going, fellows. Black Jack and Silas are waiting somewhere at the bottom of that next cliff. The sooner we get there, the sooner we eat and get off of these worn-out feet of ours."

The boys were too weary to comment, and they followed their leader in silence to the head of a precipice. The yellow glow of campfire radiated against the blackness of the woods below and partially illuminated the immensity of the nearby trees. Lowe was captivated by its grandeur, even in the dark of night, and his heart and mind were overloaded with emotions at the realization that he now owned such wonder.

But they were fleeting emotions. He knew all too well that one could never really own such land. His deed was just a paper, handed back and forth between men who had no real right of possession. The land would survive them all. It would outlive the generations. Still, it was Lowe's turn to hold that paper, and as long as he did, he would marvel at what others said was his and would cherish that forest as though it were Eden itself.

"How do we find our way down from up here, Mr. Yancy? I don't see nothin' but air between us and that campfire," Dewey asked.

"You're right. It's too dark and dangerous to be probing around this cliff."

Lowe drew his revolver and held it to the sky. He fired two shots and waited. Almost like an echo, two more shots rang from the distance, and the men heard barking and the almost indiscernible calls of their fellows.

"Wait thar!" shouted Silas. "I'm sendin' Black Jack out ta guide ya down them rocks. Don't ya shoot 'im thinkin' he's that ol' wildcat we been hearin' at night! He don't show up so well in the dark, and I damned near dropped 'im twice o'er the last week. And don't kill ma dog neither! She'll be comin' with 'im."

"Could you hear what he said?" Lowe asked the others.

"All I could understand was that Black Jack's coming. The rest was garbled," answered Morgan, "but I could sure hear Luci plain enough."

Lowe rested on a warm slab of rock and rubbed hard against his throbbing knee. His other pains would have to wait in turn, and even then, there would be no immediate relief. Experience had taught him all too well that only a good night's sleep would soothe the pangs of an ever aching and aging body.

"Well, I guess we wait for the next signal. It won't be long now, boys, and thank God."

It was the splendor of the morning that woke them. Birds flitted with great enthusiasm for the new day and alighted on every possible perch with cheerful songs of reveille. The rumble and swish of a nearby brook played its recurrent melody, and the few clinging leaves of an autumn long since passed quaked and rattled in the breeze. The men arose to the sound of that symphony. Then they gasped with delight at the wondrous sight of the sylvan stage around them.

Here was the Big Timber. Here was the heart of a wilderness, the secret of the ages, the marvelous, mystical source of legend and lore. Here, they stood with heads cocked toward the heavens and toward the great wooden web of limbs spun high above. The men's eyes drifted down and about to the huge, living columns of the forest. Yellow poplar, white oak, chestnut, sugar maple, ash and hickory, trees of many sorts, they all had their roots in the lee of the mountain. They lifted heavily out of the soft, deep soil and reached 40 yards to the azure sky.

These were not mere trees. They were testaments, and any soul just touched by their shadows was humbled, even to the point of reverence.

Morgan walked among them like a pilgrim in the temple. He moved slowly, careful to avoid the tender ferns at his feet, and he touched every tree as he passed. Never in his life had he imagined such a miracle of nature, and for the first time in too long a time, he transcended the woes that had preyed on his spirit.

There was boundless magnificence, both high and low. The boles of the trees measured three to five feet, often eight, and sometimes 12 to 13 feet across. They tapered little toward the crown, and the massive limbs that radiated from their tops were larger than many a whole timber taken at the mill. Some were taller, some were smaller, but all of the trees were immense and wonderfully out of place.

Creation takes time, and this hidden hollow in the Allegheny Mountains had counted eons long before the living grove took form. These seemingly indomitable trees had somehow withstood the trampling march of years, 300 or more, but long composted mounds upon the ground attested to their forbearers' same endurance. It was all a slow unfolding of God's creation, perfect at every stage yet forever transforming.

Along the deep, narrow brook and up the slope to the base of the cliffs, dense thickets of rhododendron swept across the basin like planted hedges. Blossoms scented the air, and the petals of dogwood glided on the morning zephyrs. Red trilliums and white may apples topped blankets of blue violets, and lingering clusters of spring beauties, with their pale hues, appeared in the distance as remnant patches of snow. Orange trout lilies dotted the ground where Christmas ferns did not yet grow.  And toward the drier reaches of the escarpment, bleeding hearts and lady slippers displayed their showy pinks. The Big Timber was more, much more, than any name could suggest. It was paradise, even in the midst of Eden, and to these men of the mountains, it was a treasure more dearly prized than wide, pure veins of precious metal and gems. They were grateful for its creation and satisfied just to look.

"Come on, boys! Quit yer lollygaggin', and let's git on with the makin' o' this here cabin. Breakfast's on the fire. Come and git it!"

Four men came straggling back to camp, each still gazing at the sights around them.

"What's for breakfast, Mr. Monk? I could eat me a bear," asked Dewey, hoping for a stack of pancakes high enough to rival the nearby forest.

"Bear, huh. Too bad. Yer plumb out o' luck on that'n. We got squirrel though. Fried eggs and squirrel and a cold side o' beans. Now that's eatin'!"

"Ooo, yuk! Squirrel? Why squirrel?"

"'Cause they been easy to come by, that's why. I flushed two of 'em this mornin', and both run right up that monster tree o'er yonder. Jist seconds later, they was layin' limp as boiled spinach right next to the toe o' my boot."

"Really? I must've been sleepin', 'cause I sure never heard the shots."

"Yup, you was out deeper than a lake bottom catfish, but I didn't need no gun. Them squirrels climbed so high up that tree that they managed to hit thin air, got all dizzy like and fell right on down to where I was waitin'. Around these parts, I reckon ya can git squirrel any time ya have a hankerin'"

"I never had me much of a hankerin' for squirrel meat, Mr. Monk."

"That's good to hear, 'cause I ain't got no eggs to go with 'em, no how. Sit yerself down. Eat some flapjacks."

Silas and Black Jack had made a good effort on the new cabin. They chose a small flat close to the base of the cliff and far enough from the large trees to prevent their damage. It was a fine site, sheltered from winds and surrounded by trees of lesser, more workable dimensions. A few yards away, spring water bubbled generously from the earth and meandered down to its confluence with the brook. Lowe was pleased with their selection.

He was also pleased with their progress. Black Jack had already begun the stone foundation, completing one length of it and collecting sufficient boulders to finish the rest. He would have done more had he not been worried about Silas, who, in the course of felling trees, suddenly dropped to his knees and clinched at his side in anguish. The old man claimed later that the pain was a spasm, nothing more, and that he deserved it for having become so sedentary. Black Jack was not so sure.

Nevertheless, they carried on and managed to cut enough timber to fully wall the structure. It was a far simpler task for Blu and Noggin to drag the poles to the site than it was for the men who would have to square them. Little had been accomplished regarding the hewing, but in this endeavor, Silas was an expert. He relished the opportunity to hone his craft, and even more, he looked forward to teaching his new apprentices the finer points of cabin building.

With breakfast over, the crew went to work. Black Jack and Lowe continued on the foundation, carefully selecting and placing each rock so as to lock them down, one against the other. They laid the stones with measured precision, making sure the wall was straight and tight and even, and most of all, strong enough to bear the heavy burden of a mountain home. And when they were done, they would gather yet more boulders to begin on the chimney.

Silas stood at the end of a log and lifted a spud, a shovel-like chisel designed to remove bark. Then, he leaned over and picked up an adze. Made for shaving and shaping wood, the adze worked like a garden hoe and cut like an axe. Silas said nothing. He simply held the two pieces in his hands and waited for his young assistants to get the hint. The boys were familiar with such tools, and they now knew the task before them. They walked over to Silas and accepted their assignment.

"We gotta do this two logs at a time. Yer gonna strip off that bark, best ya can, and then, I'm gonna show how to trim that timber into square beams."

Silas displayed his broad axe. "I reckon ya know what this is?" he asked.

"Of course, we do."

"Ya know how to use it?"

"Certainly," said Dewey, almost indignantly. Morgan glared at him and he corrected his answer. "No, actually. I've seen 'em though."

"Ya seen 'em. Well, today, ya'll see 'em in real action, first hand. Ya got yer gloves?"

"Yes, sir."

"Well, put 'em on! Ya'll be masters at this in a couple days, if I ain't called upon to patch yer sore and bleedin' hands."

The boys donned their gloves, and Silas commenced the next phase of their higher education. "The blade's wide and heavy and sharp. Keep it sharp. Don't ne'er bury it in the dirt, and when ya ain't usin' it, sink it in the soft face o' some log or stump. It ain't a fellin' axe, so don't even think 'bout slammin' it against some tree. And don't ya e'er abandon this here piece to the weeds or foul weather. Ya take good care o' yer tools, and they'll serve ya better than any dotin', starry-eyed woman."

The old man walked stiffly to a fresh stump and wiggled the handle of a felling axe until it dislodged. He presented it for comparison. "See the difference. This the smaller, that one the bigger. And look here at these other things. Ya gotta match the right tool to the right job. Ya hear?

"We hear."

"Ya ready?"

"We're ready."

The boys worked hard clearing the outer bark from the two logs, and time to time, Silas would borrow back their tools to demonstrate his technique. It gave his helpers a needed rest and the old man his chance to feel young and useful once again.

With the logs clean, he squatted at the end and scratched in a perfect eight-inch square against the butt. He did the same at the opposite end. Then, using the corners of the squares, he set four straight lines down the full length of the timber. He took the felling axe in his hand, stood upon the beam and began to vertically score the sides with a series of consistently deep cuts along the line. He worked fast and effectively, and the boys wondered if the job might not be done more expediently if Silas actually sent them elsewhere. It may have been true, but their teacher would never give consideration to such a notion.

It was time for the broad axe.

"I'll lay odds one o' ya limps home without 'is leg after this. Pay attention to me, close attention, so ya don't make cripples of each other."

Silas stood adjacent to the log, his calves brushing against the bare wood. He lifted the axe with both hands and brought it down along the line and against the previous cuts. Chips flew from the edge of his blade. Then, he backed up and struck again and again and again until the log had a flattened face and was ready to be turned.

"Yer time to shine, Morgan." Silas handed over the broad axe.

"You make it all look easy."

"It will be, after a spell."

"Can I try this standing on top of the log? I've seen it done that way. It seems safer."

"Sure. Yer decision. O' course, that ain't no more than a three foot handle yer grippin'. Ya can stand on top and lop off yer foot, or do it my way and split wide yer shin. It's a matter o' personal preference fer most folk." Silas grinned. "No, Morgan, I reckon we'll do 'er like I showed ya. Swing easy until ya git the hang o' it."

Morgan and Dewey did well with their first attempts, and before long, the three men were an effective team, with Silas scoring and the others hewing one log after another.

The fire light was soft on sleepy eyes, and Dewey turned in early. He could not remember a time when work was so satisfying. Silas ended his day, as well, and Lowe saw the evening lull as his opportunity to slip away for a long, pensive walk through the hollow. Black Jack and Morgan took turns poking sticks into the fire, fidgeting and figuring as thoughts rattled in their heads.

"Morgan, tell me, how dat little boy comin' along? I been prayin' for him."

"No change that I know of."

"Mmm, dat's a shame. What dem doctors have to say?"

"Not much. They can't figure him out. Everyone's waiting. He can go either way at this point."

"Mmm, mm. Sometimes I struggle against de Lord's will. We ain't to see what all he sees, but if we had such vision, we might just show him a little more patience. But I's disappointed. I thought for sure dat boy be up and kickin' by now."

"Yeah. Me, too."

Morgan rose from his makeshift seat and walked to the wood pile. He took an armful of large, dry sticks and dropped every one of them onto the flames. The fire erupted into sparks, and the light flared high and hot. Black Jack scooted back toward the cool of the darkness.

"I guess dat's yo way o' sayin' you don't want to talk. I respect dat."

"No, sir, I need to talk about this, but I don't know how. I'm so angry and worried."

"Angry at who, son?"

"Myself, I guess. I'm the one who taught Jake about that coal oil, and I sure didn't pay him much mind in the months before the accident. The way things had been with Pa, Jake needed his big brother all the more to keep him straight. I completely let him down."

"Yessa, we humans do dat from time to time. We makes mistakes faster dan God can clean up de mess. Still, life seem to go on despite us."

"Not this time. I think Jake's gone. You're a religious man, Mr. Clark, what kind of god steals a little boy? Can you answer me that?"

"I don't rightly know all I wants to know, and I reckon I won't 'til I walk dose hills o' Heaven myself. But dis much I do know. God don't start no kitchen fires, and he don't bring harm to his people. He ain't like dat. If it yo brother's time to go, de Lord will be right dere to welcome him home, and he ain't gonna feel bad at all watchin' dat youngster come a runnin' through dem gates. Dey both be happy, 'cause dey together again. Death ain't no problem for God, Morgan, and for dat matter, it really ain't nothin' to us either. He got him a good plan, and we all a part of it. Whether down here or high in de heavens, dat little boy lives."

"He didn't have much time with us, did he?"

"Well, he ain't gone yet. In de face o' all eternity, none o' us have much time to fumble around dis earth. I gets a century, you gets a year, another man counts his days somewhere between. If you think on it, a lifetime be but a blink o' de Lord's eye. Time ain't nothin' special when dere's no end to it. Praise de Lord, he made it so."

"You mean God doesn't care if we get sick and die."

"I ain't sayin' dat. He care. He care 'cause someone he love be feelin' poorly. He hurt when we hurt. He cry when we cry. But death ain't a cryin' situation when you de Lord. He rejoices just to have you near again."

Black Jack pulled his log seat closer to the fire and to Morgan. The men sat for a while watching the flames, looking deep into the quivering orange glow of the coals. They had much to contemplate, and further discussion served no purpose.

"Well, Mr. Clark, I guess I should get some sleep," Morgan finally said, as he stood up to take a long, sprawling stretch. "I'm beyond weary." He looked down where the soft light of the flame bounced from the leathery black face of his friend. "Your words have been helpful."

Black Jack smiled. "Good night, Mr. Darrow."

Lowe returned to the camp a few minutes later and was surprised to find anyone up and awake.

"You have yo self a good walk, Mr. Yancy?"

"I most certainly did. Every step is a wonderment out there, even in the night."

"Dat it is."

"Have you been meeting with Morgan?"

"Yessa, we had us a good talk."

"And did you tell him?"

"No, I thought it best he hears it from you, and I figures you might have some more to say while you at it."

"You're right. I reckon I should speak with him tomorrow."

The woods screamed with the sound of insects, while the two men planned the tasks of the coming day. Eventually, they would have to build scaffolds for ripping boards from whole logs. The timber would be raised between the scaffolds, and with one man above and one below, they would cut the entire length into as many planks as the piece would yield. The boards were needed for door and window frames, and if time and energy allowed, more would be cut for flooring. It was a dirty, difficult job.

Lowe inquired, "Just where in the world did we come by a pit saw? I saw it leaning against the tree."

"Mr. Monk, he brung it. He told me it was his granddaddy's. Ain't it funny how de old man kept dat blade in condition all dese years? You wanna start dis work tomorrow or wait 'til we ready for dem boards?"

"Let's build it. Let's at least start the cutting so we'll have a few planks when we need them."

"Now I gots to ask you, Mr. Yancy, you figure to stick me down on de bottom with all dat dust flyin' about?"

Lowe wished that he could. "Well, let me ask you, Mr. Clark, are you going to stick me on top where I have to do all the lifting?"

Black Jack paused to consider the challenge of both jobs. "Dat's a good point. When you is tired, we switch. Same for me."

"All right, then, and we'll make darn sure those boys stand ready to relieve us. My arms get weak just thinking about this. We've got us a tough day ahead."

Luci was comfortably settled in a leafy depression. She had not moved for a full hour and had dozed through the tedium of a dozen evening conversations. Suddenly, her body tensed. Her head perked. Every sense of her being became engaged.

"What is it, girl! What's out there?" Lowe exclaimed, startled by her movement.

The dog dropped her head back down against her paws, but her eyes and ears remained widely alert. Then, she jerked up again, only to return once more to her previous position. On the third time, she rose to her feet and growled.

"Easy girl," Lowe said. He strained to detect what Luci sensed in the darkness. There was nothing.

"Lowe, dis what happen every night. She smellin' dat cat. We heard it hollerin' a couple nights back, and it set me and Silas to cowerin' by de fire like a couple baby girls. Dat were a devil's cry, and it brung chills to my spine."

"You think it's the same cougar we ran across before?"

"I do, if it even be a cougar. Whatever out dere, it don't come to camp, though I seen tracks only 30 yards shy o' dis here fire pit. De animals don't spook no more. And Luci, she lost her bark or her will to fight, one or de other. It's like dey all come to some agreement, dat cat and dese animals. It gets a might unsettlin', knowin' dis to be goin' on. It can fray a nerve or two, but so far, dat lion ain't harmed or threatened nothin'. I reckon he out dere right now just watchin' us."

"Did you see it?"

"No, but we took shots in de dark, mostly to run it off. Lately, I'm like Luci. I let de cat be."

Lowe could feel it. Something was there, just beyond the light. It was watching him, judging him, determining if the man was worthy of the ancient ground on which he stood.

"I don't like this," said Lowe quietly, as if the mountain lion might somehow understand. "At dawn, I'll take the rifle and track it."

"Dat won't do no good."

"And why's that?"

"First, you ain't gonna find it. Second, you can't stop de breath of a wanderin' ghost, Mr. Yancy. Just ask de old man. Silas been convinced from de start dat, cat or no cat, what walks dese woods has Shawnee blood runnin' cold through its veins. It won't be killed no more."

The walls and roof trusses went up easily with some critical assistance from the work animals and a couple of stout hemp ropes. The cutting of the doorway and two windows proved simpler yet, using a two-man crosscut saw.

It was the same with the construction of a chimney, which might have been challenging even for experts more practiced in the work. But like the best of masons, Black Jack was limited to setting one stone at a time, and consequently, his progress was deliberately slow and free of mishaps.

Of course, the roofing and the chinking between the wall beams and stonework still had to be addressed, but there was nothing about those procedures that would tax the talents and stamina of the crew. Silas had already started splitting the wood shingles, and there was plenty of mud nearby to mix into a thick wattle for filling cracks. Lowe and Morgan managed to rip a few boards from a maple log, but the saw dragged against the green wood and the heavy dust choked their lungs. It was a grueling chore, and they produced only what was necessary to complete the window frames, shutters and door. The floor could wait for another day, or perhaps for another trip to the Big Timber.

The cabin rose from the surface of the woodland without incident or delay, far exceeding expectation. The men understandably gloated at their handiwork, but safe and steady as it was, the continued success of the project should have been recognized as more than just their personal achievement. There was a certain amount of luck involved, and deprived of due credit, that luck was sure to sour.

Lowe refused to rise when the morning light began to cascade through the tall trees, and the dawn had come and gone before he emerged from his bedroll. His shoulder, back and neck all ached in painful unison without the slightest movement. His thigh muscles burned when he stood. His arms, sore and powerless, dangled like rubber straps at his side, and his ribs felt stabbing pains with each twist of his torso. His hands tingled. His foot was bruised and his ankles swollen. And worst of all, his head throbbed from the inhalation of a tree's worth of saw dust. He was crippled with pangs, and his body seized in the chaos.

"Good mornin', Mr. Yancy. Sleep well?" asked Silas, as he struck his maul against the fro and popped another panel of shingle wood from the block.

"Ugh! Don't ask. I hurt too much to even lie about it. Every inch of this body is screaming, except that bad knee of mine. Go figure."

"Well, what ya expect? Cuttin' them planks weren't meant to be no contest. I heared ya crowin' after winnin' yer challenge against Black Jack and Morgan, but now ya gotta pay. You ain't the rooster ya used to be."

"Dewey and I really whooped them, didn't we?"

"Sure, but yer side took on a heap more casualties. Yer young partner ain't even seen the daylight yet, and it's likely to be this time tomorrow before he's up to turnin' a lick o' work. That boy was whinin' and wailin' the better part o' the night."

"I heard him, too. He must've had some cramps. I'm not surprised."

"Cramps? I thought fer sure he was 'bout to deliver triplets at one point. Ya darn near killed 'im. Jist might be so, by the sound o' things now."

It was a quiet morning, dead quiet, but whatever the cause, Lowe was grateful for the peace. He looked around, careful to not further strain his body. He saw a neat stack of floor planks ready for installation and was again pleased with the results of the contest. Somehow, his agony diminished with the realization that most of the hard work was already done. He became anxious to resume his labors.

"We've still got work to do. Where are the others?" Lowe wondered aloud.

"They quit."

"Huh?"

"Yup, they up and quit, and just as well. They ain't neither one fit fer duty. But if yer aimin' to fetch 'em back, ya could try that big oak above the cliff. They had a mind to sit this particular mornin' out and thought ya jist might want to join 'em. I'll tend to things down here."

There was no real trail through the cliffs, just a few scuffs and tracks over a rising jumble of boulders. The walk to the base of the rocks was difficult enough for Lowe, considering his worn condition, but the steeper climb to the dome stole his breath and accentuated every piercing, throbbing pain. Strangely, he felt rejuvenated when he reached the top, and he headed almost spryly for the white oak tree. Black Jack and Morgan were waiting.

Lowe hailed them, "Hey, what is this, some sort of labor strike? You union men are never happy."

"I reckon it be more like an epidemic, Mr. Yancy," responded Black Jack. "De boy and I am quarantined on dis here limb, and de sickness may very well last dis whole day long."

"You feeling feverish, are you?" Lowe went along with the fun. He placed his hand on Black Jack's forehead.

"Yessa, we's achin' all over."

Lowe picked his spot on the limb. "Well, slide over, Morgan. Make room for another patient. This sounds a lot like the muscle sickness, and we won't be healing any too soon."

It was good sitting in the shade of the oak, witnessing the vivacity of springtime in every aspect of the view. Breezes across the open dome tipped the tall grasses, and the crystal clarity of the sky brought distant mountains near. Everyone was pointing and wondering. Everything was alive.

"Devlin must be over that rise, don't you think?" Morgan pointed to a faded hill at the horizon. "Where is it, Mr. Clark?"

"All I can say is dat I is here in de midst o' some mighty fine country with some mighty good friends. I don't know where nothin' is, except dese two tired feet and de body dey toted to dis here place. I'm a thankful man." Black Jack pointed to the heavens.

"How about you, Mr. Yancy? Do you know where Devlin is?"

"Well, I could find it in a day or so, but from here, I'd say it's yonder." Lowe's aching arms lifted, and he did just as the others. He pointed, but in two very different directions. "Take your pick. It's either way, depending on how far you want to walk. That's the beauty of the wilderness. Towns don't know where you are. You don't care where they are."

Morgan never received his answer, but he was content to wonder. A silence enveloped them as the three men were again absorbed by the absolute grandeur of the white oak tree. They stared into the wide space before them and down into the deep hollow that cradled the virgin forest. It was a secret they guarded for one another, and while others might someday know about the Big Timber, on this day they were the privileged few. Their knowledge made them brothers.

"It's a whole different place in the daytime," said Morgan. His mind wandered and was quick to recall the unsettling sounds from the pitch of night. "A friendlier place, I'd say. I heard it. Did you? The shriek of that lion could terrorize the dead."

"I heard it, too," said Lowe. "It was loud enough to make a statue jump."

Black Jack laughed at the imagery. "I used to jump, when me and Silas first come to camp. But I don't do it no more, and I can't say why. I gots me a feelin' about dat cat. It keeps a guard on dese woods, and he been checkin' to make sure we ain't fixin' to take dem trees. Dis his home, and he and de timber ain't leavin' here for nothin'. Dat's what he sayin', when he calls out in de night."

Morgan remembered some earlier remarks from Silas Monk. They stunned him at the time, but he was now beginning to understand. Since Silas was not with them, he shared the comments with his companions.

"You know, Mr. Monk refused to believe the legend, at least at first, but he conceded yesterday that the mountain lion might just be that Shawnee warrior, like some kind of ghost or reincarnation. He told me that all his days spent in the wilderness never prepared him for what he senses right here in the night. He's never seen or heard the likes of it before. It is possible he's right. Isn't it, Mr. Clark?"

"I ain't one to hold with such things, but I reckon dem Indians dat come here long before us felt some truth in dat. Dere may be no cat at all, but somethin's sure been watchin' what we do, listenin' to what we say. I feels it starin' at me both day and night. It sizes me up, all of us, and I figures it ain't too sure what to do about strangers in de Big Timber."

"It's a mystical place, strange and beautiful," said Morgan. "I love it, but I'd have a hard time enduring these nights alone. That cougar's got me spooked."

Lowe was listening and did not know what to believe. He had been there alone, and the fears of that long ago night flooded momentarily back upon him. But he now owned these woods. He possessed this great white oak that so freely offered its comfort. Papers proved that it was so. Here was a garden like no other, and it was his garden. He would not allow fear to keep him away.

"It's a welcoming place," he uttered. "There is nothing to fear here, not from the night or from any other time. Maybe that's what Luci and the other animals have each come to find. They are at peace in that hollow. We should be, too." He looked into the faces of his companions. Each of them was deep in thought.

Eventually, Black Jack ended the trance. "Well, Lowe, dis be a good time for me and Dewey to take another turn on dat pit saw. Sittin' don't get it done. I aims to put Mr. Baughman in such fine shape, dat when he gets home to dat pretty Miss Auralee, she won't even recognize him. You fellas come break us in a spell. Knowin' dat boy, we ain't gonna be at it for too long."

Lowe had deliberately delayed his discussion with Morgan. The boy was immersed in the details of the project, and his hard work coupled with the magnificence of the forest and the fellowship of friends did much to restore his spirit. Lowe was hesitant to suggest anything that might break that spirit. But the cabin was nearing completion, and what needed to be said had to be spoken now.

"Morgan, how are you feeling after that effort we made yesterday?"

"Are you asking me about my broken body or my broken pride? I'll never live down that loss to Dewey."

"Your body, actually."

"Well, as Dewey often says, 'I'm a hurtin' puppy'."

"Me, too. Though I may have won the contest, I expect I was the worst for it. You mend. At my age, I gather aches like a squirrel forages for winter. So, what do you think of all this?" Lowe spread his arms to encompass the entire scene before him.

"I think you know the answer to that. All the trees in the world, including those giants they say are growing in California, don't measure up to what lies beyond that cliff. And what's beyond the cliff pales against the glory of this one white oak. To say this is a special place is to say too little and do it dishonor."

Lowe was pleased with the answer. "I don't know if you heard, but I finally got the papers on it. It's mine now."

"I did hear, and I'm as envious as I am happy for you."

"The thing is, I can't keep it. I'm thinking about selling this land when the time is right and giving Silas a good home in the city. The day's coming when he'll need to leave Jasper Hollow."

"Sell the Big Timber? Mr. Yancy, you can't just walk away from something you love so much. This place is a treasure. If you sell it, you destroy it. There has to be another way."

"Well, maybe, but it would require considerable sacrifice."

"The really important things are worth the effort. Don't you agree? I've seen you. I've heard you. The wood and the wind and the water, they are the blood in your veins. You can't live without them."

"I suspect you're right, son. It would be difficult, but there is always another way around a problem. Like you said, 'You can't just walk away from something you love'. That brings me to my point."

"Sir?"

"To my point. To you and Sarah Dabney."

"I don't understand."

"I think you do. You just explained it to me. You can't anymore walk away from that girl than I can abandon this forest. Now, what are you going to do about it?"

"What can I do? I've got Ma and my family to think about now. I've got a seven-year-old brother struggling for his life in a cold medical ward way too far from home. I can't give Sarah what she wants and needs. She deserves much more than what I'm able to provide."

"So, you really do believe that. I'm sorry for you, Morgan. After all the misery you went through trying to win her love, you never really found it."

"No, sir, I found it all right. We even made plans."

"Then, boy, you're walking away from *your* treasure. That's a mistake you'll regret for the rest of your life. Someone else will be rich, but not you. The really sad part is what you are stealing from Sarah. You're taking away the one thing she really does need and want. That's you."

Morgan had no arguments to present, but he had no solutions either. He stood up and took a long walk around the white oak tree. Lowe waited for his return.

"I have an offer I'd like you to consider. I was climbing through the rocks on my way up here this morning, and realized that, in more ways than are countable, I'm a broken man. I've lost my strength and energy for what must be done tomorrow. For what I should have done long ago, I lost my opportunity. I have no children, no family, and all I do have is sitting right on this mountain with me, my friends and a little piece of this green earth. I've built up a pretty good business, me and Mr. Clark, but we're both getting to that point in life when you plan ahead because you have to. We need your help, Morgan. We need your strength to see us over these mountains. We want you as a partner."

Morgan was shocked. He was hearing the answer to a prayer, and it was an awful long time in coming. Lowe had more to say.

"Surveying is a fine enterprise, and with a little hard work, it's more than sufficient to feed a family. Think about this before you answer. It may not be what you want to do in this life. You have options. You can work the mill, file the saws like your daddy does. You can be anything you wish to be, go anywhere you want to go, do anything you want to do. So think on it. Let me know."

"I don't need to think, Mr. Yancy. I'll start today if you want me."

Lowe smiled with relief. "Well, son, we're not earning money today. Why don't we make it official over a nice dinner back in Devlin? We'll take the whole family."

"And Sarah?"

"Well, that depends. Is she family?"

Morgan's eyes widened with new revelation. "She will be. By God, if I'm not too late, she will be."

# CHAPTER 19

Anticipation has a way of stretching miles and minutes, and Morgan's journey from the Big Timber back to Devlin seemed twice as long as he remembered. He pushed himself hard and fast, keeping well ahead of his small party of friends. Sarah Dabney was the reason for that. Nothing, but nothing, was more important than seeing Sarah again and begging her forgiveness for a man's foolish notions.

Morgan reached Camp 7 just in time to catch the return run of the log train, which placed him in town a full day before the others. He headed straight to Sarah's, only to face the disappointment of finding no one at home. He plopped down in a wicker chair and waited a full hour in the shade of her veranda. When Sarah did not come, Morgan paced the deck with growing desperation. He hated that feeling, and when he had enough of his own pity, he departed, all the more determined to make life right.

The long, steep walk toward home was the final leg of a grand adventure, and he thought it particularly strange that these last few steps, ones he had taken a thousand times before, would be so challenging. An unforeseen wave of fatigue splashed over him, and he felt weighted down like wet boots slogging in marsh mud. It reminded him of Lowe Yancy, a man who, with half a life yet to claim, often lamented his many aches and pains and the constant ebb of his endurance. Morgan's trudge, more pronounced with every sluggish stride, made him wonder if that ebb came earlier for some.

There was no surprise that his own house was empty. Morgan's mother and sister were in Charleston, dutifully watching at the side of his brother. His father could be anywhere, except in the place he should have been. Over the months, Morgan had trained himself not to care.

He opened the locked door and passed to a room familiar with the trappings of home. It was as his mother had left it, clean and notably tidy, unlike the young man staring back from Annie's full-length looking glass. Morgan's clothes were coated in a week's supply of sweat and dust. His face was lost to a thin, dark scraggly beard, his hair still powdered with wood chips from the teeth of Silas' saw. Without delay he dragged out the wash tub, peeled off his boots and shirt, but before he drew even a drop of water, he curled like a baby and napped soundly on the braided parlor rug.

Another hour was gone before his tired body felt the hardness of the floor, but by then, Morgan had already awakened to the stir of cool air circulating through the room. He struggled to his feet and continued the quest for a shave and a bath. Time being short and the kitchen spigot being weak in flow, he opted for the cold water he could quickly bucket from a shallow front yard well. Consequently, he never saw the empty crock left sideways on the kitchen counter or the broken lid in pieces on the floor. And he never noticed the kitchen door, which was ajar and shifting ever so slightly with the passing drafts.

It was a very short and frigid bath, not a unique experience for one who just spent a week isolated in the mountains. A spring brook was never colder, but there was neither the time to fire the stove nor a desire to boil water. Morgan had to find his Sarah. He had to make her understand that what was once good between them could and would be again.

He reached for a clean shirt and could still smell the freshness of the country air that dried it. Shrinkage confounded every effort to button, but Morgan's long fingers persevered, twisting and pressing until the wooden fasteners were finally forced into place. Between the grunts and the grumbles, he rehearsed his urgent message to Sarah, until it became evident that perfect appearance and a well-practiced speech were of no real value to any honest expression of love and truth.

He stood before his mother's mirror and peered at the reflection of his own eyes. He wanted to see in them what Sarah would see. She would need to study those eyes to know how much he had missed her. It was always that way with Sarah, and now, if the eyes were no longer an acceptable measure, if his presence alone did not invoke some sign of her lasting affection, he would know without words that the girl was gone.

Morgan was not averse to begging, if in the end, Sarah would come back to him. It was not the way of most men, but it was the way of determined men, who recognized the essentials of their life and set about to making them happen. But he did have his pride and just one absolute condition. On this night, she would give him an answer. She would accept him fully or cast him free altogether. She either loved him or she did not. He would not cling to any false hope of re-winning her heart.

It was easy to be homesick for the Big Timber. The smells and sounds and the lights of town were more invasive than Morgan could recall. Street lamps masked the moonlit sky. A blended waft of gasoline and horse floated from the hard-packed dirt of the road. The noise was constant, though more subdued with the onset of darkness. Morgan knew that he would adjust in time, but still, there was a certain longing for the peace and purity of the wilderness.

In his haste, he raced past 30 people without so much as a nod. The oversight might have been an insult to many, who customarily waved to just about any friend or stranger. He was not aware of his rudeness, but an unlikely acquaintance was more than pleased to point it out to him. As Morgan sought his short cut down the alley, Farley Ochs stepped innocently into his path. The men collided blindly, and Morgan offered a quick apology as he widened his gait to make up the lost second of time.

"Hey, hold on there! Where's your greetin' for an old friend?" Farley Ochs' voice was loud and coarse.

Morgan halted, then spun around. He was surprised to see Ochs. "I wasn't aware we ever were friends."

"Sure we are. Just 'cause we tangled once doesn't mean the

fight's still on. It ain't healthy to let bad blood stand too long, and I'd really like to bury the hatchet."

"I'm sure you would, right in the middle of my back," Morgan replied.

"That was uncalled for. I stand before ya bearin' an olive branch. You could at least help me put all this hard feelin' behind us."

"I'd be willing if you really meant it."

Farley laughed at the boy's naivety. "Look here, sonny, I dropped by your place the other evenin' and couldn't find a soul. Where's your old man, anyway? I've been lookin' for him."

"Oh, yeah? What does someone like you need from a man like my father?" Morgan glared.

"Now, boy, there is really no need to get so ugly about this. I swear you're just like your friend Yancy. I simply want to catch up to your daddy. He and I have become pals, so I couldn't help but notice he's been a might scarce of late. I worry about him."

"You do, huh. Pa wouldn't have any dealings with the likes of you."

"You're wrong about that. We're partners. At least we were until we lost the Watoga business."

"Partners in what?"

"I'm surprised he didn't discuss this matter with ya. We started a little survey group of our own...you know, some honest competition for that land cheater you've been hangin' with."

"But you're not licensed."

"We were gonna be. I know some people, and I had me a bona fide surveyor ready to join up with us. With your daddy's money and a little know-how on my part, we expected to put a good deal of hurtin' on Yancy and that black boy of his."

"Those men are my friends, and I'll thank you not to...."

"Yeah, yeah, I understand, but lucky for me they ain't been so chummy with all you Darrows. Anyway, I know one in your family that downright hates the mention of Lowe Yancy. Where is your father, boy? He owes me."

"In Oregon, the last I heard."

"The hell you say. Oregon? When did all this take place?"

"Back in January. Listen, I have to go."

Farley laughed again. "That don't hardly seem possible. Say, how do ya know he's in Oregon?"

"Letters. Ma gets his letters. I'm in a hurry to meet someone, Ochs. I really have to cut this short."

"Hold on for a second! There's no sense always bein' in such a rush. Did you see the letters?"

"No, they weren't meant for me."

"Well, that drunken, connivin' old weasel! Looks like he's run out on the whole lot of us. That's it all right. The bastard's run out and left me in the lurch. So much for plans."

Morgan held his anger. He knew Farley's tack. He knew he was being baited, but was too smart to bite. A fight would prove no match, and besides, there were more important tasks at hand. But Farley not only pressed him to the limit, he pushed him well beyond.

"Say, with daddy on the lam, I reckon that means your pretty mama is free for the courtin'. You tell her that Farley Ochs may be stoppin' by. I'll bring her flowers."

Morgan's restraint shattered. "You stay clear of my house and my family, Ochs! That's a warning, my only warning, and you'd better heed it."

Farley had maneuvered Morgan perfectly. He wittingly squeezed him into a corner, and if Morgan was any kind of man at all, he would have to fight his way out to save his honor.

"That's no warnin', fella. It's a threat, and I don't take kindly to threats!"

Farley's large arms shot from his side with amazing speed and violently shoved against the boy's chest. Morgan reeled, but ultimately kept his balance, and to Och's utter astonishment, he recoiled with a solid punch to the center of the big man's belly.

Farley hardly felt it. He responded with a strike of his own, an upward jab of his good hand that caught Morgan on a cheek bone and drove him backwards through the air. Morgan hit the ground hard and tumbled in the dust. Blood dripped from his torn face.

It took a few moments to gather his senses, but Morgan understood the importance of getting back to his feet. It was a matter of pride if nothing else. He crawled at first, and then, abruptly rose up with a heave of his strong legs.

Morgan looked with disdain at Farley. He slapped the dirt from his trousers and jacket, and through the rising cloud of dust, he noticed a figure, alone and safely anonymous beyond the edge of the shadows.

“I see you over there, Leon. He won’t need you this time. I know when to walk.” Morgan dabbed the run of blood that trickled down his cheek. Then, he drew dangerously close to Farley Ochs in a foolish display of mettle. His knees nearly buckled from the weight of his fear. “Just remember what I said. You stay clear of my family.”

Farley laughed for a third time. Then he let the boy walk away.

“What’s the matter with people?” Ochs asked, looking to the man in the shadows. “First, Yancy, and now, this stupid kid. I can’t even drum up a good fight in this town.”

The doorbell rang repeatedly, but every call went unanswered. Morgan sat on the top step of the large veranda, wondering what to do, wondering if he had lost the best thing that would ever touch his life.

It was a warm spring night, and flower gardens sweetened the air with a medley of natural scents. The porch swing swayed with a faint breath of wind, and the moon, full and unobstructed, bathed the valley in black and white contrast. Sarah was likely on the arm of another by now, strolling slowly down the lane toward home. Morgan decided, in the best interest of all, that he should be gone, perhaps forever.

The blood still dripped from his wound. It caked in three branching lines across the left side of his face and neck. His collar was soaked red. Morgan struggled to stand and was forced to pull himself hand over hand up the white porch column. His legs had weakened, his vision had blurred, and his cheek bone throbbed rhythmically with shooting pain. He lost his grip on the column and dropped in a heap to his place on the step.

He saw and felt nothing in the passing hour. When he did awaken, one eye opened narrowly to find Doctor Brown examining the other. The light was piercing, and he felt involuntary tears streaming from his swollen lids.

"Oh, Mr. Darrow, you are back with us," said Cecil Brown, with little emotion. He anticipated the recovery.

"Doctor Brown, is that you? What's happened?"

"You tell us."

Morgan was still very weak and groggy, but he used his one good eye to scan across the room. He saw tall windows with frilly curtains. A white and gold armoire stood high against the wall. There was a lacy canopy draping the bed and a small bouquet of fresh flowers centered on a side table. A painted doll, complete with pale blue petticoats and a matching blue sun bonnet, sat staring from the corner of a small settee.

"But where am I?"

"You're at the Dabney home. We've moved you to Sarah's room."

"Sarah. Is she here?"

"I'm right here, Morgan." She took his hand in hers and caressed it.

"Sarah, I need to tell you something."

Doctor Brown interrupted, "You need to stay quiet, young man. You've got a nasty gash there. I've stitched you up, but you've lost a lot of blood. You rest now. Talk can come later."

Doctor Brown moved from the bedside and waited at the door until Sarah and her father had also left the room.

"I'll be back," he said to Irwin, while he put an arm through the sleeve of his coat. "The cut bears watching, but he'll be fine. By the look of it, someone caught him with a really big ring or a set of brass knuckles. He's always been a good, upstanding boy. I can't imagine who would want to take him down like that. Was it a robbery?"

"There's no evidence of one. Maybe he just fell," replied Dabney.

"Well, perhaps, but in my professional opinion, I don't think so. This is a rather typical Saturday night wound. I see it too often."

"Well, Cecil, thanks for coming so quickly. We'll get the word out to his family, and in the meantime, this will be his home."

"That's good of you, Irwin. Like I said, he needs his rest."

The front door had barely closed behind the doctor when Sarah raced back up the stairway and returned to Morgan's side. She cradled his hand between hers and kissed his fingers, then, laid her head softly upon his shoulder. He slept and she waited, wondering and hoping about what he longed to tell.

It was dawn before Sarah's father peaked into the room. He whispered, "How is he?"

"Still sleeping. He was out the entire night."

"No, I'm awake now. What happened?" Morgan stirred. His first words were slurred, and he lay motionless as he tried to reclaim some degree of awareness.

"We don't know, Morgan," Sarah explained. "You were collapsed on the front porch when we got home. I think you've been fighting. You have stitches over your cheek, and you lost a good deal of blood."

Morgan had to strain to recall the events of the night, and when he did, he grimaced. "It sure wasn't much of a fight. I broke like porcelain."

Irwin became angry. He had his own suspicions about the assailant, and he wanted justice. "Who did this to you, Morgan? I think I should contact the authorities."

"I'd rather you not, sir. It was just a disagreement that got out of hand."

"Well, it's none of my business, but I'd sure like to know. It was one thing to beat you so, but yet another to leave you alone while you bled to death."

"That's not exactly what happened."

"Still, someone is responsible, and a crime like this should be reported. I wish you would tell me."

"I'm afraid if I told you, Mr. Dabney, that you might make it your personal business. That could be dangerous. It's all over now and best to leave it that way."

"Very well. That's your decision, son. You'll be staying with us for a while. Let us know what you need and try to get some rest. Sarah, you see to it."

"I will, Daddy."

Sarah was again alone with Morgan, and the two spent precious moments looking at each other.

"You said you wanted to tell me something," said the girl.

Morgan struggled to sit up, and it was apparent that the sudden move restored the pain and dizziness. Sarah reached out and gently guided him back to his pillows.

She said sternly, "There's no need to move. Just say what you want to say."

"I wanted to tell you that I'm sorry." He paused, then, continued to speak from the heart. "I love you. I've made huge mistakes, Sarah, but I have always loved you. I was on my way here to prove just that when I ran into trouble."

"And how were you to prove it?"

"I don't know. I thought that, if I could just make it to your door, the right words would come to me. I have missed you."

"And I've missed you, Morgan. You don't know how many times I've answered that door bell, hoping you'd be standing on the other side. Of course, I didn't expect this."

Morgan lifted his hand to the side of his face. "I must be a horror to look at, a gash on my face, my eye swollen shut."

Sarah placed a fingertip lightly upon his swollen eye. "Right now, you are the most beautiful thing I have ever seen."

Her own eyes twinkled as she gazed at the broken man before her. In their shimmering blue, he found his solace.

"Sarah, please. Take me back, and I'll pledge you the rest of my days."

She cuddled warmly at his side. "Oh, Morgan, don't you see? I never let you go."

Morgan healed quickly, too quickly for one who had so enjoyed Sarah's constant attention and hospitality. He was anxious to be up and around only one day after his injury, but Sarah insisted that he remain in bed. While there was little nursing to be done, a great deal of pampering seemed to be required. Sarah intended to serve him, and Morgan was more than happy to oblige her. He remained an invalid for as long as his conscience could bear it, and she glowed as she cared for him tenderly.

In that single day, Morgan sampled her cooking four times, including breakfast, dinner and supper, followed by a midnight candlelight snack that he discovered when awakened from a deep and restful sleep. She prepared them all, and to him, all were feasts. She massaged his hands and rinsed his feet. She read him stories and poetry. She beat him soundly in a tournament of checkers and taught him the basics of stud poker. Of course, Morgan lost that game as well, but he never questioned the source of her expertise. Sarah tucked in blankets, fluffed up pillows and bleached the blood stains from his shirt. She wiped his brow a dozen times and kissed him tenfold more. She was sad when he dressed to leave.

"I can't be a burden any longer," he said. "I must confess that I've enjoyed taking advantage of your good nature, and I'm quite tempted to brawl again if it means you'll be caring for me."

"Oh, I'll care for you, but only if you promise to avoid those brawls."

"I guess I can make that promise. I only hope the other fellow has agreed to a similar one."

Morgan suddenly became pensive. Sarah was radiant with a spring morning's light, and her slender face glowed like the ghost from his now forgotten dream. He slid his hand across her rosy cheek to be certain she was real. His fingers twirled her flowing hair, and he leaned over and kissed her.

"Thank you," he said.

"For what?"

"For second chances, mostly."

Morgan Darrow was indebted to another, as well. He was unaware of the vow Lowe Yancy once made to his mother, but he naturally felt gratitude as he gazed adoringly at Sarah. When Morgan tossed his dreams away, it was Lowe who fetched them back.

Morgan could, without a doubt, draft a lengthy list of caring friends, but in some enigmatic way, Lowe's name did not belong among them. He was more a keeper, who delivered him from danger, or a guide, who taught him prudent ways and proper thoughts at a time when young men often stray too far and forever lose their bearing. Lowe knew Morgan better than Morgan knew himself, and with that knowledge, he steered his young protégé on a positive course. He came seemingly out of nowhere, and in their short time together, Morgan grew to rely upon this self-appointed guardian, not so much as a friend, but as a father.

Without warning, his mood brightened, and Morgan threw his arms around Sarah's waist. He lifted her off of her feet and whirled her until they both were giddy.

"I love you!" he cried out. He was shouting to the world. "Sarah Dabney, I love you." Then he left her, while she was still giggling and staggering from the spin.

"Be mindful of your wounds. You're still weak, Morgan!" she responded.

She smiled as she watched her future, with a black eye and stitched cheek, racing down the street. He stopped at the corner and turned for one last look. Sarah was still there. She waved, and as Morgan disappeared from view, she heard her name heralded above the eclectic din of Devlin.

The crock must have been empty. That seemed to be the case more often than not, and the absence of a little cash or coin did not necessarily indicate trouble. The money Lawson shared with his wife never lasted long, and it stayed in the jar on the shelf only until the next shirt was torn, or the next cough needed treatment, or the next meal required some special cut of beef. Annie Darrow had no intention of hiding her money. Everyone had a "cookie jar," and most kept as little treasure in it as did Annie. The crock was more for the training of her children, who learned that temptation and easy access was no excuse for thievery. Of course, if everyone had one, then everyone knew just where to look when their intention was plunder.

Morgan shut the kitchen door and looked down at the broken shards of the lid. He picked up the three larger pieces and tossed them in an old ash can reserved for such refuse. There was no chance of repair.

He had no idea how long the door had been open, and he recalled the time when a squirrel once burgled the house. Curtains were torn. Bits and pieces of nuts and apples were strewn across the furniture and floor, and malodorous patches of yellow and other telltale signs were left on the counters and carpets in the centers and corners of every accessible room.

Morgan remembered the words of his mother that day, "A crook's take wouldn't amount to as much as what this furry-tailed robber just stole from us." The clean-up took days, much had to be discarded, and the burglar never came to justice. Morgan remembered something else. The rodent broke nothing as it tip-toed among Annie's fragile curios. One thing was certain this time. Whatever it might have been, the intruder was most definitely not a squirrel.

Morgan slid open a kitchen drawer and searched for the largest, sharpest weapon he could find. He picked up the carving knife. He had to be prepared, even though he sensed no remaining threat. What occurred must have happened during his absence in the Big Timber. However, Farley Ochs did mention that he had stopped by, and there was little reason to assume he would not be back. Morgan searched cautiously, room by room, but saw nothing out of place. He was baffled, and he was relieved until he heard muffled voices from the front of the house.

He moved to the top of the stairs and listened again. The talking suddenly stopped. He descended in silence and made his way to the parlor. Morgan pressed his ear to the front door. Still, there were no voices, just the scuffling of feet, and at one point, a long, loud, solitary breath. Someone was there. He reached boldly for the handle.

"Mr. Yancy, I reckon de boy ain't home. We best get on with de day."

Morgan instantly recognized the voice. "Hold on, Black Jack! I'm here!" He turned the handle and threw open the door.

The first thing Black Jack saw was the knife. "Whoa, now!" he exclaimed. "I ain't de one! Mr. Yancy done it." Black Jack pointed to Lowe.

"Done what?"

"Whatever call for quick justice with dat knife."

Morgan lowered the blade. "Oh, I'm sorry about that. Someone's broken into the place. I just finished checking to see what was stolen."

"You all right? Dere been quite a struggle by de looks o' dat face."

"I'm fine. This face is another story."

Lowe walked into the house without formal invitation. He stared at Morgan's eye and stitches, but his concern for them would wait.

"Did you check the upstairs?" he asked.

"Yeah, everywhere."

"And nothing's missing?"

"Best I can tell. They may have gotten a little cash, but not much to speak of."

"How about jewelry or firearms? I know your father has guns."

"He sold them all, not so long ago. Hey, wait a minute!" Morgan bolted up the stairs. His footsteps could be heard as he rummaged through his room. He returned more slowly than he left. "It's my Winchester. They've stolen my rifle and shells."

"The new one?"

"Yeah."

"I was afraid of that. In these parts, a gun is a better trade than cash. It may not help recover your property, but I suggest we inform the police. There needs to be a report. You can never tell, they might know something we don't know, and that gun could turn up yet."

"Dat de truth," Black Jack added. "And dis same thief may soon get busy with other folks' homes. We needs to stop him if we can, before someone gets hurt."

"All right, I'll head down and make the report."

"Why don't we all go down?" said Lowe. "I'll spring for dinner at Whitman's, and Jack and I can fill you in on the details of our upcoming boundary survey. You are still with us, aren't you, son?"

"All the way, Mr. Yancy."

"Good. The first order of business will be titles. We're partners now. Call me what you like, but don't feel obligated to formality. 'Lowe' has been a good handle for me. You're welcome to use it."

"And I answers to 'Black Jack,' or 'John,' or 'Jack,' or whatever else suits yo fancy." Black Jack thrust his right hand forward. "I be proud, Mr. Darrow, to be workin' with you."

Morgan took the hand. "I guess I respond best to 'Morgan.' I can't thank you enough for this opportunity and only hope I won't let you down."

"Don't let dat be yo worry. We gonna show you up from down, forward to sideways, and before you knows it, you be de one teachin' us a thing or two. Let's grab us dat dinner, Mr. Darrow, in case Mr. Yancy come to forget dat he made de kindly offer."

The three men conducted another inventory of the house, and everything, including Annie's gold wedding broach and a necklace, appeared undisturbed. The one exception was the rifle.

The police station was a four-room annex at the rear of the town hall. One room served as a lobby and processing area, two were offices and the fourth, considerably larger than the others, comprised the jail with three very austere confinement cells. There were two prisoners awaiting arraignment on disorderly conduct charges, but otherwise, the station was surprisingly still.

Morgan approached the uniformed man behind the counter. "You don't seem too busy today."

"What day is it?"

"Tuesday."

"Well, that explains it. We make our living at the end of the week. What can I do for you, young fellow?"

"I want to report a burglary."

The constable pulled a form from an open stack of trays near the counter. "Go ahead, but talk real slow. I'm writing all this down."

For five minutes, Morgan answered questions and provided the required information. The constable finally looked up from his report and reached over to pick up yet another form from the stack.

"Now, how about your warrant for assault? Whoever did that to your face, man or woman, needs some quiet time to see the error of their ways. Seeing how it's only Tuesday, I'm sure I can accommodate him. What's the name? Where do we find him?"

"Never mind. It was an accident."

The policeman looked more closely at Morgan's wounds. "Accident, my granny's big bunioned toe! If you happened on that by accident, you best take up a desk job and sit out the day. Moving for some is just too dangerous." Then, he spotted Lowe and Black Jack. "You boys know anything about this?"

"Not yet," replied Lowe.

"Well, Mr. Darrow, I'll be right here for another three hours, if you change your mind. We'll keep a lookout for the rifle."

"Thank you, sir."

Lowe had little to say on the way to the café, but Black Jack had a fair idea of what he was thinking. They sat down at a small wooden table that was whittled and hacked by the pen knives of a thousand woodsmen. The café had once tried to end the destructive practice. It even ordered new tables at one point, but the whittling continued until it was part of the simple charm of the place. The woodsmen wanted the food and the café needed the woodsmen. The tables soon ceased to be an issue.

Morgan read off names and dates and singled out a few of the better carvings. He was interrupted by a round-faced, full-bodied woman, who set three unordered coffees around the table.

"Well, I reckon I know what Lowe and Black Jack will have, but, honey, you're a mystery. How 'bout me giving you the specials of the day, and we'll take it from there?"

She somehow always knew the particular appetites of her customers, sometimes before they could make their own determination. Lowe and Black Jack were regulars, two of her favorites, and she was a long-time waitress in a town of few restaurants. She was talking only to Morgan when she orally recited the menu.

"So, sweetie, what will it be? Or, maybe you need a little more time," she said, careful not to rush his decision.

When Morgan looked up to respond, she was startled by his piteous young face. "Oh, my! You poor darlin'. You go with the meatloaf, and Miss Ruby will make sure you get extra portions. Someone 'round here needs to take better care of you." She scowled at Lowe, as though he were the reason for Morgan's predicament.

"Are you Ruby?" Morgan inquired.

"I sure am, honey."

"It's a kind offer. I think I will have the meatloaf."

The others did not rate the same arrangement, but they were content. The café never scrimped on a meal. Sometimes the gravy alone could fill a man to the top of his gullet, but portion size aside, the food was tasty. And for bachelor men, like Lowe Yancy and Black Jack Clark, Whitman's offered the closest thing to home-cooked cuisine.

Ruby left, and Lowe was quick to guide the conversation. "All right, new partner, let's start talking about that face of yours, and I don't want to hear a story about some accident."

"There's nothing to tell. Me and another fellow just had a disagreement. He managed to throw a little more persuasion my way than what I put to him."

"And?"

"There is no 'and.'"

"Sure there is, Morgan. I've got to know you pretty good by now. You're not a fighter, unless you're provoked. And compared to anyone else around here, Black Jack excluded, you're not easily moved to any sort of violence. I can think of only two or three people who might take that kind of shot at you, and I'd rather not guess."

Morgan did not want to say more, but he understood too well that Lowe would not let loose of the matter until it was resolved.

"It's just not right to tell. I fought. I lost. It's all over, and I'd like to leave it that way."

Lowe just stared, sending his message through cold eyes. Morgan finally relented, "If I tell you, will you promise to keep it to yourselves? Will you swear that no more will come of this?"

"No promises. However, if what you say has nothing to do with me, I'll keep my nose out of your business." Morgan hesitated, and Lowe continued, "But I believe you're going to tell me that Farley Ochs gave you that black eye. And that has everything to do with me."

"No, it doesn't. Not this time."

"So, it was Ochs."

"I didn't say that."

"I think you did."

Morgan finally gave the details of his altercation with Farley Ochs, and he tried to reiterate that the matter was settled. But Lowe would not hear of it. His anger was a force to fear, and his expression deeply troubled his two friends.

"This foul business with Farley Ochs has to end. He pushes until he breaks something. This time it was you, Morgan. Next time? Well, who knows? I'll find him, and then we'll end this."

"No, you won't, Mr. Yancy! This was my fight. I won't allow another man to fight my battles."

Lowe smiled. "And you shouldn't, Morgan. But this most certainly was not your fight. Ochs wants me, and he's happy to hurt others to get to me. Don't you see, son, you were fighting my battle all along, and I can't abide that any more than you would."

Morgan was torn with emotion. He understood Lowe Yancy. He could not fault the man, and yet, he wanted this episode of his life to disappear before someone he loved was harmed. Ochs recognized no bounds in his pursuit of vengeance, and his vehement hatred of Lowe could only lead to destruction. Two things were further evident. Farley Ochs would never stop his attack on Lowe, and Lowe Yancy would never run.

Farley Ochs stopped to enjoy a peaceful picnic on the east bank of the Charity River. Lowe might have laughed at the sight of it, if he were not so consumed by rage. He charged through underbrush, but still, his crashing movement would have been undetected, except that Black Jack wanted their presence known. He worried that his friend was intent on going too far, and that this time of reckoning would hold a deadly consequence.

"Now, dis ain't right, Lowe. You is just givin' yo self up to meanness, and somebody bound to come away hurt," Black Jack rebuked him loudly.

Lowe moved swiftly and undeterred. By the time he reached Farley Ochs, the big man was prepared. He knew why Lowe Yancy was there, and if diplomacy failed him, he would be ready. He slid brass knuckles over his fingers.

"Well, Yancy, come for a picnic? It's a nice little spot, if you can put up with the usual intrusions," he mumbled. A half of sandwich was stuffed in his mouth, and bits of food sprayed as he talked. He shook ants from his pant leg and boot, and he smashed others with his hand.

"No, I don't particularly like the way you treat your company at picnics."

Farley knocked away a few more ants, then wiped his mouth with a sleeve.

"Look, if you're here about my new survey team, I'll be glad to discuss it. I wasn't tryin' to steal your work. There's plenty to go around. Besides, a little competition is good to keep ya honest."

"Are you saying I'm not honest?"

"It's just a figure of speech, Yancy. Of course, you did fix it so old man Devlin won't hire us, but there are other jobs to be had, if not here then somewhere else. No hard feelings, right?" Farley held up an empty bottle of Coca Cola. "You ever try this stuff? It's a little sweet and fizzy, but it's good. I've got a couple more for you fellas."

He hurled the empty to the center of the river. Then, he rolled over on his knees and awkwardly rose to his feet. He extended his right hand to Lowe. His left hand, armed with the brass knuckles, was concealed by a pocket.

"Seriously, no hard feelin's," Farley repeated himself.

Lowe took a few seconds to better size the situation. There was nothing about the man he could trust and even less to like.

"Ochs, why don't you jump in the river and get that bottle out of there?"

The diplomacy had failed, and the big man readied himself for the offensive. He started his fight with words. "No. I don't cotton much to swimmin'. Maybe Black Jack here will fetch it for ya. Niggers and dogs are good at that kind of work."

Farley pulled his hand from the pocket, but Lowe was much too fast with his attack. He hit him hard and square against the jaw, and Farley tumbled like a boulder down the bank and into the shallows of the river. He floundered trying to find his footing.

Black Jack was disgusted. "Lowe Yancy, dat ain't de way. Dere been a demon in you beggin' to come out, and you just now cut it loose. God help you." Black Jack scrambled down the bank, stepped waist deep into the water and offered Farley his hand.

The big man pushed him away. "Don't you ever touch me, boy! And Yancy, you're a dead man."

Lowe smiled with satisfaction. "You can't very well back that up lying in a stream like a sweating sow, can you? Come up! We'll settle this now."

Farley Ochs was hiding in the water, issuing threats that might never be kept. He knew that he was alone in this fight, and when he saw Lowe's chestnut eyes turn black with fury, he realized there would be no quarter. He reached into his bleeding mouth and felt a loosened tooth. He spit blood, then, massaged his swelling jaw.

Lowe was almost disappointed. "I didn't think so. Bullies are cowards. You're a coward, Ochs! The only fight you want is the one you know you will win. You can hurt a boy like Morgan Darrow, but you can't take me. I don't care what business you're in, who you run with or where you go. I don't care about our quarrels of the past, but if you ever hurt another friend of mine, I'll end this stupid feud of ours real fast and permanent. If your mouth hurts, just consider it payment in full for your treatment of Morgan. We're even now. Never bother him or me again."

Black Jack grabbed Lowe by the arm and led him away. "You made yo point, Mr. Yancy. You done yo damage, and now be de time to let go o' dat anger." He turned back to Farley Ochs and pleaded, "Mr. Ochs, we's goin' our own way. Please, you find yo's. It for de best dat we don't meet up again."

# CHAPTER 20

Morgan felt a little uneasy about crossing Market Street, and he wisely waited until Farley Ochs and Leon Hopper had moved away from the opposing store front. There was no sense in stirring up more trouble for himself or Lowe Yancy, and he had made a promise to Sarah that he would avoid fighting. Any chance meeting with Farley had a potential for violence. He had learned that much. He walked down an extra block and then another, solely for the purpose of keeping his pledge.

The train whistle sounded as the locomotive passed the one-mile whistle stop, and Morgan knew he would have to pick up his pace if he was to meet his mother and Cora at the Devlin Station. Ordinarily, he would have driven his father's motor car, but that was the first luxury to be liquidated when Lawson chose to abandon his home. The cost of fuel and upkeep had become too prohibitive for Annie's limited means. It was just as well, considering the deplorable condition of the local roads. The vehicle was certainly an entertaining contraption, but had little practical application in a land of steep hills and deep, muddy ruts. In wet weather, it was always stuck. On the more extreme inclines, it would choke for lack of fuel until the car was turned and forced to take the hill backwards. It was a good decision to sell it, and with just part of the money, Annie was able to purchase a small blue buckboard and a sweet-tempered mare, both of them showing their few years of gentle wear.

Morgan actually preferred the buckboard, but, of course, just when he needed it the most, the wagon proved vulnerable to an unseen pot hole, which delivered a jolt sufficient to crack a spring board and nearly toss the driver into the street. Both carriage and horse were summarily entrusted to the care of Johannson's Livery, and Morgan resumed his jaunt to the station on foot. He was running short of time.

The detour led him past the lumber mill, which was in full production, evidenced by a steady stream of round logs climbing the jack-slip at the near end of the massive building. On the far end, a constant commotion of men and carts moved neatly planed boards to cure in the warm, wood-scented air of the yard. The four towering stacks spewed parallel columns of translucent white smoke, and roars and clangs of machinery rode heavily on a stagnant summer air.

No one actually noticed, except Morgan, and yet, his vision was more toward the past than the present. The mill had for so long been the center of his life, of everyone's life in Devlin. He looked at the frothy, black water of the pond and painfully recalled the foolish dare that almost took that life. When the railcar rolled its load of giant logs into the water, he could almost size each piece by the horrendous splash. Even then, he knew those timbers paled in comparison to the great trees beyond the dome. Morgan watched the bull chain haul the logs closer and closer to the razor teeth of the band saw, and he could not help but think of his father witnessing the same sight day after day, year after year. The mill brought much to mind.

As he walked, Morgan naturally wondered what became of Lawson Darrow. It was good that his father went away, far away to Oregon, both for the sake of his family and himself. His behavior toward Morgan's mother had become intolerable. His decision to flee his parental responsibility was even worse. It was cruel and unforgivable, especially in light of Jacob's failing condition. The alcohol that robbed him of his family likely cost him his job, as well, and re-employment as a saw filer would be very difficult anywhere in the surrounding area. Rumor was the only thing that traveled fast across the mountains, and to Lawson's misfortune, reputations spread far. It was only right that he was gone. Nevertheless, the man was Morgan's father, and from time to time, there were good memories. Morgan tried to recall them.

The train was unusually slow in its final approach to the depot, and the delay gave Morgan the extra time he needed to make himself presentable. When it came to the appearance of her children, Annie was particularly adept at finding those out-of-place buttons, hairs, smudges and tears that others would never detect. Morgan was convinced it was one of those lifetime missions of motherhood, and he dared not show himself unkempt after so long a separation. He examined his reflection in the station window and made last minute adjustments to a crooked tie and a loosely tucked shirt. He dusted off his jacket and hat, ran a hand through his thick, dark hair and waited.

Devlin Station hugged the tracks like any other rural depot. Twice as long as the average boxcar, the building had a wide, wrap-around platform, sparsely occupied by an empty hand truck and a long, weathered bench. There was a small freight room on one end with a double-door entry. On the other end was a passenger lobby, with two back-to-back pews in the middle of the floor and an artless array of wall maps and schedules situated around a big circular clock. The clock kept perfect time, even if the train did not. In between the larger rooms, a cramped ticket office was strategically cluttered with all things railroad.

The station was an attractive structure, built of stout planks with board and batten siding, all sharply dressed in a mustard color trimmed with white. An over-extension of the pitched metal roof provided shade and shelter to people and materials alike, and centered on the gables were two signs with bold block letters that simply read, 'Devlin.'

Morgan paced impatiently across the platform as the train crept forward, and he checked the hour on his final pass of the lobby door. Exactly on schedule, the train stopped, and a porter stepped down from the coach to assist those passengers ready to disembark. There were not many. Cora first came into Morgan's view, and he watched her peering from the door in search of a familiar face. He waved his welcome.

"Watch your step, miss," the porter said, as she descended the steep, narrow stairs. He took her by the forearm and guided her safely down. "Any luggage?"

"Yes, but it's taken care of. Thank you." Cora touched the ground running and jumped into the arms of her older brother. "It's so good to be home," she sighed.

"It's good to have you home, Cora," Morgan replied. "With you and Ma gone, the place has been a little lonely. Did you have a comfortable trip?"

"Not too restful, but quite enjoyable. But that's enough about me, Morgan. What in the world has happened to you?" Cora examined the stitches on his cheek. The eye was still blackened but no longer swollen.

"Oh, it's a long story. I'm much better now." Morgan looked across Cora's shoulder toward the empty coach door. "Where's Ma?" he inquired, with some concern.

"She's coming. There was some disagreement as to who would carry the luggage. I finally gave up and came on out."

"What! Ma shouldn't have to carry those bags. Listen, I'll get the luggage, and Ma and I will meet you at the cab."

Morgan pointed to a covered carriage by the corner of the station. It was one of only three such conveyances that operated in the town. The hack tipped his hat in recognition.

"Just wait. Believe me, Morgan, Mama has more help than she knows what to do with," replied Cora.

The porter re-entered the coach, only to step off again just seconds later. A large valise immediately rolled down behind him.

"That's all right, but there's no need to throw them. I can take them from here," the porter said. He sounded almost frustrated. "You're doing a fine job, but that's what the railroad pays me for. Just drop the other one there, and I'll grab it. Ma'am, pardon me while I move these bags to the platform. I'll be right back to assist you with the stairs."

Morgan moved to the sound of the commotion and relieved the porter of the two bags. "Too much luggage?" he asked.

"No, sir, too much help. But I think we're managing."

Morgan looked up to see a third bag emerging from the doorway. Half scooted and half lifted, it seemed to catch on every obstacle. Finally, a small, boyish foot kicked hard into its side, and the valise tumbled to the base of the stairs.

"There, Mama! I told you I could get it."

Jacob Darrow was home. He stood in the opening of the rail coach and scanned the town and the green mountains beyond. It was the only real world he had ever known, and in a glance, he could see that everything was in its proper place. He had worried about that on the long journey back from Charleston. The boy took a deep breath of air and grinned. There was nothing sweeter than the very first homecoming, and Jacob vowed, when his foot touched down on the Devlin dirt, that he would never have need for another.

The shock depleted Morgan. He did not anticipate the moment. He never held true hope for the life of his brother, and the sight of Jacob standing bright-eyed in the summer light made him tremble with joy. Jacob came at him like a dart.

"I'm back! Morgan, I'm back! You wanna see my scar?" Jacob lifted his pant leg to show the pinkish, wrinkly skin.

Morgan stooped down to take an obligatory look. "Yup, that's a real humdinger of a scar, Jake. Beats anything I ever got."

Jacob saw the stitches. "It looks you'll have a new one soon, a good one, but it won't be as big as mine."

"No, not a chance."

Morgan lifted his brother high in the air. He was light, as he always had been. The boy's hair was longer and more disheveled than Morgan could recall, but the look was fitting considering the untamed spirit of the child. Jacob was pale and no doubt weakened by months of inactivity, but his energy and outlook had suffered nothing during his ordeal. Morgan hugged him long and tightly.

"I sure have missed you, little brother," he said, trying without success to hold back tears.

Jacob made it easier for him. "Hey, where's our new horse? Mama said you got rid of the Ford and bought me a horse."

"I sure did. She's at the stable."

"Will I like her? 'Cause I sure liked havin' that motor car."

"I hope you will. I like her. She's very gentle, and I think the two of you will be fast friends."

"Well, then, let's get goin'. What's her name?" Jacob grabbed firmly to Morgan's hand and tried to lead him away.

"Hold on. What about your mother and sister?"

"I've seen them. I want to meet my horse." He tugged again on Morgan's hand.

"Give me just one minute, Jake, and if Ma agrees, I'll take you to Gretel."

"Where?"

"To Gretel. To the horse."

"Gretel's her name?"

"Yes, Jake."

"Where'd she get that name?"

"Not from me. I guess she was born with it."

"Can we change it to somethin' else if I don't like her?"

"Only if we can change *your* name if she doesn't care much for *you*."

"Oh. Well, I'm sure we'll get along."

"Yeah, like I said."

Annie made her way off the train and met Morgan at the side of the cab. She hugged him. "Well, how do you like my little present?"

"I like it very much, Ma. I can't tell you how much."

"I know. I feel the same way. It was a miracle. Four days ago, he awoke from his coma as though it was just another time for breakfast. He wanted food. His burns were well on their way to healing, and after a couple days of observation, the doctors couldn't find any reason to keep him. I'm not sure they could hold him even if they wanted to. He's very proud of those scars."

"Oh, yeah, so I've seen."

"My goodness! What's happened to your face, son?"

"Nothing really, Ma. I took a tumble."

Annie looked closely at the wound. "Oh, that must've been

some tumble. I keep telling you that you need to slow down and be more careful. Did this have anything to do with our missing horse and buckboard?"

Morgan smiled. "You noticed, huh. But, no, I had to leave them both at the livery on the way down here. The carriage has a cracked spring. It'll be fixed by tomorrow."

Annie lifted up on tiptoes and placed a kiss on Morgan's cheek. "Well, we're all home and one family again. Thank the Lord. I love you, son." With Morgan's assistance, she took her seat in the carriage.

"Ma, everything is in order at the house. You and Cora go on. Jake and I would like to walk home. We have to visit a horse along the way."

"Your brother has been talking about that horse for close to a hundred miles, but he's weak, Morgan, even though he doesn't show it. I'm not sure he can take these hills."

"We'll walk slowly. I promise. And when the time comes, I can carry him. Jake eventually looks for a ride, even when he isn't weary, and I've rather missed that of late. You go on. He'll be fine."

Annie smiled her approval. Morgan nodded to the driver, and the carriage rolled with a snap of the whip.

For Jacob Darrow, life was far too exciting to squander on recuperation. To him, the accident was an obscure piece of history with nothing but scars as relics. It happened ages ago. He would have raced all the way up the mountain if it was not for his brother's restraint, and he constantly urged Morgan to hurry.

"You're slower than a three-legged box turtle, Morgan."

"Where did you get that one?"

"Dewey. I used to think he was a turtle, but he's a bullet compared to you."

"A bullet, huh." Morgan laughed at the image of Dewey flying with invisible speed. "Insults will not make me move any faster, and it's too hot for you to run. You've been laid up for a long time. You need to take it easy. Besides, I promised Ma."

Jacob kept pulling at his brother's hand, but even at the slower pace, he quickly grew weak and winded. He stopped suddenly and puffed.

"You got any money?"

"I have enough. Why?"

"I'm thinking of ice cream. How about you?"

"Hmmm. That sounds good, but only if you agree to slow down."

"I'll slow down. Let's go." Jacob grabbed Morgan's hand again and set out on a course through town.

"But the ice cream is that way, Jake. Don't you remember? We have to go by way of the mill to get to Whitman's."

"I don't want to go to the mill. We should go on this way."

"But that's completely in the wrong direction. Besides, another log train's just come in, and they're dumping the load. Don't you want to see the big splashes like we used to?"

"No, I don't!" Jacob's lower lip began to quiver. His eyes teared.

"What's the matter?" Morgan asked, mystified by the sudden change in emotion.

"I don't like that mill, and I really don't like that pond. Mama says it's dangerous."

"We sure found that out, didn't we?"

"That's what I mean, Morgan. We should stay away from there."

Morgan tried to understand. "Look, Jake, there's nothing dangerous about the pond, if we just use good sense and stay back from the edge. What happened last year was no one's fault but my own. I still like to watch when the trains come in."

"Well, not me!"

The fears of the child were not difficult to comprehend. The incident at the mill pond cut a deep mark on Morgan's memory and forever strengthened his respect for the frailty of life. The experience was certainly all the more traumatic for Jacob, who helplessly watched as his brother vanished in the murky depths.

"Okay, if that's what you want. But someday, I'll expect you to come back with me so we can see the logs again. Is that a deal?"

"I guess, but let's go this way for the ice cream."

Jacob got his way and proceeded to take Morgan on a convoluted route through every street and back alley of town. Lost, but too proud to admit it, he eventually found both the horse and the ice cream and was well over half the distance to home when he finally yielded to fatigue.

"Can I ride on your shoulders, Morgan? I'm a little sleepy."

"Sure, you can. Do you want some help hopping up?"

"No, but you need to get lower."

Morgan squatted down. "How's this?"

"Lower."

"I can't, Jake. My body doesn't fold but so far."

"Then this is good."

The boy knew the routine well. He scrambled up his brother's back, slinging one leg at a time over the shoulders and sticking one hand in Morgan's eye while the other yanked a lock of hair. When Jacob yelled that he was ready, Morgan clamped down on his ankles, reared up like a bucking mustang, and then, froze in his place.

"Come on!" urged Jacob.

"I won't do it."

"Why? Let's get going."

"You know why. What did I always tell you about driving a blind horse?"

"Oh, yeah."

Jacob's tiny arms took a new position around Morgan's forehead. When Jacob moved his hands, Morgan moved his feet, but as was their tradition, the dialogue bore repeating every 30 or 40 steps.

The cadence of Morgan's stride had a restful effect on the tired boy. Jacob's head bobbed to the even rhythm, and he began to daydream. He imagined himself on a great bull elephant, crossing the thick jungles of Africa and issuing orders to a mile-long entourage of carriers and guides. He spied snakes and panthers and other deadly beasts that could not reach him on his high perch, and while he lumbered through the tropics of another continent, he saw nothing of the streets of Devlin. Morgan broke the dream when they turned the last corner toward home.

"Welcome back, little brother. There it is."

Jacob awoke, initially startled and disoriented. He studied the building from his seat on Morgan's shoulders and was pleased to find both house and yard intact.

"I didn't burn it down?" he asked, with a genuine sound of relief.

"Not even close. In fact, Jake, if not for you, Ma would never have gotten her brand new kitchen."

"I did that?"

"You sure did. Do you want down?"

Jacob was still looking wistfully at the house. Before replying, he strained his neck to glance back at the mill beyond the town.

"Morgan?"

"What?"

"That was a long, long way from down there."

"For shorter legs, maybe."

"Daddy wouldn't carry me so far. He never once did, and he didn't come to see me at the train."

The comment struck like a boulder against Morgan's heart. "I guess he couldn't."

"Why, 'cause he went to *Organ*?"

"Where did you hear that?"

"I wasn't sleepin' on the train, not all the time."

"Yeah, Pa did go to Oregon. It's another state way on the other side of the country. He went to find his new job there."

"Why didn't he take us with him?"

"Oh, maybe he knew it was best we didn't go. Our friends are here. Our house is here. Would you like to leave Devlin and head all the way out to Oregon?"

"No, I like it here at home. Will Daddy come back after his job?"

"To be honest, Jake, I don't know. But if he doesn't make it back, how will you feel about it?"

Jacob thought long and hard about the question. Lawson Darrow had put little time and effort toward the raising of his children. He never recognized the value of play or the importance of silly words and strong, warm hugs. He never helped with school work, or sang songs or attended family picnics. He never went to church, and he rarely laughed. Even an infant could sense coldness from a father who remained so distant, and any child stung repeatedly by a swarm of personal affronts, mean acts and broken pledges would naturally retreat. Lawson left a void where a father's joy should have been, but Jacob knew no better. It was simply the way it was. He loved the man that he inherited.

"He's our daddy," Jacob said, as they reached the steps of home.

"Yes, he is, and he always will be."

The boy continued to think about the question, as Morgan wheeled around and let him dismount onto the porch. It was a query he was not prepared to answer. He was much too young, and perhaps, only time would tell.

"Morgan?"

"Yeah, Jake."

"Will you be here?"

"You bet I will."

Jacob smiled, and he dashed away to rediscover the marvelous world that again was his. The screen door slammed hard behind him.

No one, but no one, was surprised when Morgan and Sarah announced their engagement. They were as natural a combination as songbirds and springtime, and just as fresh and hopeful. Their love was private and true, never shallow or showy like the fleeting affections of so many young romances. For them, there was no infatuation. From the moment they met, their souls were coupled, like mourning doves paired in flight. They were inseparable, and to those watching, a rare and enviable match.

The engagement would be a short one, if they were to have their way. October was four weeks to the day, and neither Morgan nor Sarah relished a winter wedding. But Devlin was already buzzing with the news, even without a firm date, and everyone who knew them anticipated being a part of the celebration. After all, Morgan was their native son, and Sarah was beloved the moment she first stepped onto the rail station platform.

For Morgan, the sudden notoriety was more plight than pleasure. Friends and strangers alike loaded him with sage advice at every turn, and there was always someone's spouse ready to counter with a long diatribe on the failings of their own marriage. The message became so mixed and disheartening that he ceased listening altogether.

Everyone offered good wishes, and all were inquisitive about his and Sarah's plans for family. There was no chance for privacy and even less opportunity for a quiet pursuit of his own agenda. Morgan Darrow and Sarah Dabney were the talk of the town, and Devlin was a very small town where personal circumstance became fodder for gossip. Morgan may have understood this, but he certainly did not like it.

While Sarah busied herself with a host of preparations, Morgan flirted more and more with the notion of elopement. It was a well-guarded thought, however, and remained suppressed through the tedium of endless wedding detail. He struggled to be supportive, but he longed for some semblance of the ordinary. Lowe Yancy finally supplied it.

"We've picked up some local work, Morgan. Black Jack and I checked out the site yesterday, and we're ready to run the survey tomorrow. Six o'clock. We'll meet at the bridge."

"I'll be there. How many nights do we pack for?" Morgan was anxious for the solitude of the backwoods.

"None, actually. We're setting property lines on some plots here at the edge of town. Sorry to get your hopes up."

"Yeah, I could've used the break."

"Wedding woes?"

"More or less. I never see Sarah, with all her involvement, and, frankly, Ma's been running around just as much. They want everything perfect. I want everything over."

Black Jack's grin showed that he understood. He spoke from personal experience. "Dis happens all de time. Yessa, de groom's feet, dey bound to get chilly come marryin' time, and dere's good reason for it. Remember, yo feet ain't movin' so fast as Miss Sarah's.

De weddin's de woman's thing. She scamperin' about, all de time plannin' and shoppin' and partyin', while you's just sittin' dere wonderin' what be goin' on. Sometimes dem ladies get so busy with de show dey completely forget what dey really after. But, Mr. Darrow, when yo bride takes dat ring and looks on yo smilin' face, you be all she sees, all she wants and all she needs. Yo heart gonna pump nigh on to burstin', and yo blood gonna race 'til you dizzy and weak. And den, dat's when dem feet start to warm back up."

"I know," said Morgan. "Others have told me the same thing, but still...."

"Are you having second thoughts, Morgan?" Lowe asked.

"No, not a one. Not about Sarah, anyway. I simply want my girl back. Lately, she hasn't been the same."

Black Jack chuckled. "Dat's just de way o' things 'tween a man and a woman. Been so since Adam first admired Eve, and it ain't likely to change now with yo frettin'."

"I suppose you're right, Black Jack. Maybe work will take my mind off of this marriage business."

"I guarantee it," said Lowe. He handed Morgan a brown paper package, a soft bundle bound by twine.

"What's this?" Morgan inquired.

"Call it an early wedding present, or my apology, whatever."

"An apology for what?"

"For what we intend to put you through in the morning. I hate to start you out this way, but a job's a job."

Morgan pulled out a pen knife and cut the twine. He rolled back the paper just enough to catch a glimpse. "Buckskins?"

"Yeah, for tomorrow."

Morgan uncovered the leather shirt and pants. They were surprisingly heavy and darkly soiled with a half decade worth of sweat and dirt. He held them up to check the fit.

"Sorry," Lowe said, "I never did get around to cleaning them. They were a tad long for me, so they ought to do the trick."

Morgan was baffled. He tried to read the truth from Lowe's stony expression but detected nothing that might indicate a prank.

This was their first project as partners, and a man with any savvy at all might rightly anticipate some hazing.

"And I suppose, Mr. Yancy, you're not going to tell me the real purpose of this frontier outfit."

"Sure, I'll tell you. I'm keeping my word. Sarah made it quite clear that, if I put one more scratch on your body before the big day, she and your Ma would have my head. Isn't that right, Jack? There are some forces I'm not fool enough to mess with. Sarah Dabney and Annie Darrow are two of them."

Morgan laughed. "Whew! So, this is a joke. I really don't have to wear these awful things."

"Yessa, I reckon you do," replied Black Jack. "Dis be for yo own good. You'll see come mornin'."

"But I'll look like some bumpkin walking through town. I'm getting married, you know. I have my reputation to think of." Morgan was not particularly serious, even though he dreaded being seen in such garb.

"You have that flesh on your bones to think of, as well, and if you decide you want to keep it, I suggest you wear those leathers."

There were six acres to be evenly subdivided, all of them within a stone's throw of the official limits of Devlin. Not so many years prior, the ground was cleared for feed crops and grazing, but it sat idle just long enough to collect every bramble and weed known to botany. For the most part, the land was flood plain, but a gentle rise a short distance from the Charity River provided good, dry sites for construction. The owner intended to build houses.

It would have been a rather routine day for the survey crew, but the greenbrier along the low waterfront and the wild rose and blackberry vines that invaded the higher ground covered the property like a crop themselves. They formed an impenetrable thicket of prickles and thorns, and there was no skirting such an obstacle. The growth had to be cleared as the bearings dictated.

The men met at the bridge according to their plan, and still unsure as to why, Morgan arrived fashioned in buckskin. He was a curious sight in such modern times, even in the mountains, and he had jogged every back alley and trail through town just to avoid recognition and the need to explain his appearance. He grabbed his knees and drew a deep breath.

"Well, if it ain't Mr. Dan'el Boone, his self. Dose Indians still chasin' you?" Black Jack did not mean to goad.

Lowe was wearing a pair of western chaps and Black Jack had on his own suit of leathers. Both donned wide, straw hats for protection from the hot sun, and Lowe had a pistol holstered against his waist, which he sometimes carried against the common threat of rattlesnakes. Their look was conspicuously out of place, and Morgan could not hold back a loud guffaw when he first greeted them. The others joined him in the laugh.

"Boone only wished he looked this good," Morgan said. "Let me see. You must be Hickok and Cody. I heard of you hombres."

"Yup, partner, but de folks here abouts just calls us Bill," Black Jack quipped with a bad Texas accent.

Lowe heaved the transit and tripod over his shoulder, while the others grabbed the chain and pins. They followed the road for several hundred yards, until they reached the long edge of the briar patch.

"Unfortunately, fellows, I'll be taking the readings, which means one of you will be out front taming that jungle as we go." Lowe handed out machetes.

"Dat be me. I does de tamin' on dis crew," Black Jack stated.

Morgan argued, "I beg your pardon, Jack, but you know the rod and chain a lot better than I do. Let me do the clearing. And, besides, I've got some frustration to work out, remember?"

"I sure likes dis boy," Black Jack said to Lowe. "He ain't at all like you, always tryin' to give up de dirty work."

"A lie is not a good start to a day, Mr. Clark. Tell him how it really is." Lowe took a quick look through the transit across the overgrown field. He began to plumb his tripod.

"A point well taken. Morgan, we trades off from time to time. I do de chain, you do de clearin'. I do de clearin', you do de chain. Soon enough, you knows everythin' you needs know about de survey. Den, Mr. Yancy won't have to do no work at all, and he can lay in de cool shade and be all sassy and old. Dat's what he really after." He winked at Morgan. Lowe scowled.

It was slow and sometimes painful labor, but straight, narrow corridors began to show from the river to the road. The men left markers at the corners and mid-way in between, then pivoted to run another course through the thicket. Both Lowe and Black Jack took their turns with the machetes, while Morgan practiced the art of the survey. They were a good team, and they were so pleased with their progress that no one thought of dinner when the noon sun slipped into position.

"Lordy, boys!" Black Jack exclaimed. "It nearly one o'clock. What you tryin' to do, Lowe, starve dis poor lad before de weddin'?"

Lowe reached into his pocket and pulled out his watch. "Well, marriage makes a lot of men fat and lazy, so maybe I'd be doing Sarah a favor if we forego a few meals."

"Don't stop on account of me. I can keep going if we need to," said Morgan.

"That's the spirit, but old men need nourishment to keep pace with you youngsters. Leave the equipment. Grab your lunch pails and let's head down to the water. It's cooler there. I saw some good size rocks on the sand bar, and it's probably the only decent place to sit away from these weeds."

The river was beautiful. The summer had stolen a third of its flow without any diminishing effect. The ripples now jumped across the shallow rocks, and the water followed the meander of a channel that shifted back and forth between the banks. The leaves were already thinning, though the autumn drop had not yet begun, and early reds of the dogwood and Virginia creeper splashed vibrantly across the vista.

Lowe and Black Jack looked on in disbelief as Morgan laid out the contents of his pail. Two meatloaf sandwiches were topped with lettuce and huge slabs of ripe, red tomato. A handful of peeled carrots and a crisp yellow apple were placed beside them. Then, he reached into a separate gunny and retrieved two cookie tins.

Lowe wrestled with a bite of beef jerky while he watched with envy. He slapped a thick chunk of cheese on his only biscuit and jammed half of it into his mouth. “My goodness, Morgan,” he mumbled, “if the way to a man’s heart is through his stomach, that girl’s taking no chances of losing you.”

Morgan opened the first tin. “The chicken’s for you.”

Lowe’s eyes widened when he saw the crisp, golden brown of the fried chicken. He instinctively spit out the biscuit to make room. “For us?”

“Yeah, and that isn’t all.” He opened the second tin filled with a dozen rectangular slices of banana bread.

“Holy smokes!” Lowe took a deep bite of the chicken leg. “Oh, I just might have to kiss that Sarah myself.”

“Save it for Ma. This food comes with the compliments of Annie Darrow. I think her words were, ‘A man needs to eat, and those two haven’t had a decent meal in a month.’”

“Well, I’ll be.” Lowe blushed with the thought of the kiss.

Dinner took much longer than any of the three anticipated, but none of them pressed their return to the briars. It was a banquet, and they felt no compunction when the last morsels passed their lips. The result was predictable. Black Jack stretched comfortably across the long, flat boulder and moaned his sign of contentment. The others did the same.

Lowe listened to the river rattling through the rocks and let his hand dip into the cool, steady flow. His eyelids grew heavy, and he pulled the brim of his hat to the bridge of his nose.

“Marry that girl tomorrow. If they get away, they’re gone,” he said, still thinking about the chicken, still remembering his past.

“You are reading my mind,” responded Morgan from his own corner of the rock. He pulled a dry stalk of grass from a small crevasse and put it to his mouth. “I’d grab her and run right now, if she was willing.”

“I’m convinced that’s the better way. Steal the preacher, too, if you have to, but go and be happy. Don’t plan it. Just do it.”

“You mean elope.”

"I mean live, before your only chance is lost." Lowe repositioned on the stone and locked his hands behind his head. He thought for a moment about what he had just said.

Morgan was thinking, too. For some reason, he had never imagined men of Lowe's age and station being so affected by love. Romance, after all, was for youthful, hopeful hearts. It was for people with idyllic expectations, not those in their waning years whose minds and futures were already shaped, perhaps tainted by personal experience. In this he had been clearly naïve, but was now ready to admit that love was both indiscriminate and timeless. Lowe Yancy's unfaltering passion, in every aspect of his life, taught him that much.

Over a year had passed since the campfire argument between Lowe and Silas Monk. Morgan had had no right to listen that night and no reason to recall it as often as he did. Having heard the man's secrets, having seen his anguish, he felt he knew that woman from Lowe's past. She was exceptional. She had to be for so long a sacrifice. As much as he loved his Sarah, Morgan marveled at the enduring breadth of Lowe Yancy's fidelity.

He had to ask, "Tell me something, Mr. Yancy. Why didn't you ever marry?" The question met with silence. "Mr. Yancy?"

"I heard you." The long pause that followed seemed to end the discussion. Lowe's eyes were closed, and his breathing became audibly deep. "I'll tell you this much, Morgan. I would have liked to have been married. I just never found me the right woman."

"Never?"

"Don't waste yo time," Black Jack interjected. "Dat man *is stubborn* when it come to talkin' about such things. I been tryin' to find him out for years."

Morgan continued to probe, "Surely, there was at least one girl you favored."

"I favored a lot of girls."

"Yeah, and?"

"You've become a nosy little cuss. I didn't know that about you."

"I didn't know you were so sensitive to the subject. We talk about me and Sarah all the time. But it's your life. Keep it to yourself if you want to."

Morgan had made his point, and for some reason, Lowe felt compelled to offer more. "I favored a lot of girls, but I guess I only wanted the one. There were complications. She needed to go her separate way, and I let her. It's that simple."

"Did you ever try to see her again?"

"I was afraid to."

"Afraid of what?"

"Myself, mostly. I was afraid of stirring up emotions I needed to suppress, afraid of destroying her happy life, afraid of discovering that I'd been forgotten. I left home afraid, and that was one very awful feeling. I was determined not to look back."

"So you never returned."

"Sometimes it's best to just walk away."

"And you never looked back?"

"Oh, I looked back all right. I've seen her night and day, every day, just the way I left her, but looking back is not quite the same as *going* back.

"But you did want to be with her again, didn't you? You must've yearned for more than mere memories."

"Of course."

"I don't quite understand, Lowe."

"Well, it was all a very long time ago."

Lowe wished that he had never answered the boy in the first place. His sentiments suffused at the mere thought of this woman. His recollections of her were forever recent and real, much like the heartbreak they evoked. He might have done things differently, if life could yet start again, but there was no returning to another day. Knowing that, he settled for what the years would afford him, a few fond thoughts and a poignant sense of regret.

"I will never marry," he said bluntly. "I'm sure of it. There cannot possibly be another like her. Her last three words to me were simple and sincere, intentionally so that I might never forget them. 'I love you,' she said. She meant it. It can never be better than that."

"But, Mr. Yancy...."
"Son, it can never be better than that."

There was little left of Annie's garden, except some pole beans and tomatoes, a few cabbages and peppers, and a tangle of persistent runners bearing squash, pumpkins or melons. What did remain was decimated by the drier weather and the appetites of two chubby cottontails. Annie struggled all summer to defend her plot with a steady barrage of home-style repellants, and she was willing to try anything in her desperation. Egg shells, ammonia, black pepper, dried milk, fencing, scarecrows and even a neighbor's cat were brought to bear against the pilferage, but nothing deterred the brash little thieves. At the peak of frustration, Morgan was asked to rid her of the problem, although discreetly for the sake of Jacob and Cora. But before he could act, Annie relented. The rabbits were just too cute.

It was not the first time that she had lost the battle for her garden, nor would it be the last. In the year prior, something was smashing her prize watermelons, one each day for the better part of a week. Every morning, rinds were found at the base of the picket fence. It appeared to be the work of vandals, or more likely, the playful destruction of one Jacob Darrow, but Morgan had other suspicions. He set a snare in the cover of the vines, just in case the culprit had four legs, not two, and was relieved to trap a fat and very contentious raccoon.

Somehow, the animal knew to push against the melons until they broke free of their vines and rolled down the hill to crack against the fence. It was ingenious larceny, and Morgan regretted having to destroy such a cunning beast. He carried it all the way to Avery's Farm for a covert execution, only to be later castigated by his family for his cruel ways. The raccoon returned in three days, very much alive, but no one apologized to its would-be killer.

It was an annual routine with similar losses from year to year, and while Annie pretended to fight for her garden, she actually became complacent with a realization that there was plenty to share. She picked and pickled what she could and had more than enough to fill a pantry with a long winter supply. Canning was tedious joy, and there was rarely disappointment with an early season frost.

Annie Darrow laid down her paring knife and whirled around in place. She looked at Sarah. "You know what? I'm really tired of peeling tomatoes and snapping beans. Why don't we sit down and talk this problem through? Maybe it will help."

Cora took the comment as a hint and tried to excuse herself. "There are still a lot of beans out in the garden. I think I'll gather what I can, and we can finish later."

"Please stay," said Sarah. "I have something to ask you, as well."

Cora took a seat next to her friend. It wobbled on uneven legs, and she unconsciously moved to another. It was a habit from childhood, when she and Morgan always raced for the better chair. Annie sat with the wobble.

"Would you girls like some tea? Sarah? Cora?"

"No, thank you. Maybe later," they chorused.

"Some cake?"

"No, ma'am."

Annie had been hearing distress in Sarah's voice and sensed that the girl needed a woman's attention. She had become attuned to such emotions, learning well from Cora as she passed through her teenage years, and she knew that the girl would never volunteer the source of her troubles.

"So, tell me, Sarah, what has Morgan been doing to make you feel that way?"

"Nothing specifically. I'm afraid he's changing his mind about the marriage, or maybe, he's just not interested in having a wedding. Morgan keeps quiet when I suggest ideas. There's so much to be decided, but he doesn't seem to care anymore."

"Did he actually say that he doesn't care?"

"Well, yes, in so many words. He said we should do it my way and that the details just didn't matter to him. Mrs. Darrow, I want everything between us to matter. Everything."

Sarah's eyes became misty. She had been alone in this, her

greatest decision, and she needed assurance that her heart would not be broken. Her mother had been dead for more than a decade, and while her father had always showered her with affection, he was simply unequipped by nature to fully understand her fears. She felt the need for a mother's strength, for embracing arms and listening ears, for soft words of comfort.

Annie's own eyes were wet when she rose up from her seat and cuddled Sarah by the table. "Now, you listen to me, Sarah Dabney. Someday, you will realize fully what I'm about to say. No one knows a son like a mother, not even the son himself. Morgan needs you more than the air he breathes. He loves you more than life. Men don't care much about weddings. They may not even care about marriage itself. They just want to be close to the people and things they love. Do you hear me?"

"I think so." Annie ran her fingers through Sarah's shining hair and straightened the few strands that were out of place. She hugged the girl.

"Mrs. Darrow, there is more. We received an invitation yesterday from Charles Devlin to hold our reception at his estate in Pittsburgh. Daddy has a lot of friends in the city, and the two men have worked together for a very long time. Mr. Devlin also offered his summer cottage at the shore for our honeymoon."

"My goodness! That's so wonderful and very generous."

"Mr. Devlin has always liked my father, and he wants to do something special. But, well, would you, or anyone for that matter, consider coming all the way to Pittsburgh for a wedding?"

Annie smiled. "Sarah, you are about to marry my first child. You will soon become my second daughter. I'll go anywhere you ask me to go. It's the same with me as it is with Morgan. We love you. We want you to be happy."

"It really is a generous offer, isn't it? It would be a beautiful wedding, a truly formal affair. I always dreamed of such a day. And Cora, I already picked a gown for you. It's my gift to my Maid of Honor, if you'll accept the role."

Cora was as delighted as she was surprised. She threw her

arms around her friend. “Me? Sarah, of course, I’ll accept! I’m so happy for you and Morgan that I don’t know what to say. So much is running through my mind. I always wanted a sister, and I’m glad it’s you.”

The three women spent an hour at the table conceiving their perfect event. From veils to vows, from cake to candlelight, from toasts with crystal glasses to rings with golden glows, from a slow procession up the floral aisle to a sandy walk beside the sea, they planned to the limit of their fancy. Every detail was considered, except the one that suddenly came stomping through the door with a groan and a grunt and a suit of buckskin leathers.

Annie was astounded. “Morgan Darrow, you are a sight in those filthy deer skins! Where on earth....”

“From Lowe Yancy. That’s where.”

“But why?”

“We worked all day in a briar patch, and I’ve never been so glad to wear leather, whether it’s hideous-looking or not. If you think I’m a sight, you should see the others.”

The skins were crisscrossed with scrapes and scratches suffered from the thorns, and two short blood trails marked the side of Morgan’s neck. Sarah noticed them instantly.

“Oh, Morgan, you’re bleeding. Just look at your poor neck.”

“It’s nothing. I generally do worse with a morning shave. So, please, don’t give Lowe and Black Jack a difficult time. They try so hard to keep me safe that they’re afraid to even work me. I hope that changes after the wedding.”

“Don’t worry. We’ll be nice,” Sarah promised. “Your mother and I were only teasing. Those two men are so cute. They always take us seriously.” She added, “Boys are sure easy to fool.”

Morgan crossed the room and leaned over to kiss her. “I wouldn’t be so sure about that,” he cautioned. Then, he gave his mother a peck on her cheek, and the chair wobbled as he followed with a hug. He glared at Cora. “So, you stuck Ma with the bad one, huh?”

“Of course,” replied Cora.

"You, young lady, are downright despicable."

"Me? You do it all the time."

"That's different. I do it to you. Besides, I'm Ma's favorite. She doesn't expect me to sit there."

"Hmph!" grunted the girl.

Morgan vowed to fix the chair, as he often had before, and stretched across the corner of the table to kiss his sister on the forehead. "You don't deserve this, but I wouldn't want you to feel left out."

Cora grinned. "Thank you, brother. It's nice to finally get something from you besides sass."

Morgan saw the empty canning jars steaming in a large pot on the stove. Bits and pieces of vegetables were scattered about the table, counter and floor.

"Are you just getting started?" he asked.

"Lordy, no," answered Annie. She pointed to the full shelves in the small pantry.

"I'm quite impressed. You must've had some fine help from these two. Just what in the world were you talking about all this time?"

"You know the answer to that. Yes, we did discuss the wedding," replied Sarah, "and we came up with some truly wonderful ideas."

"So did I, believe it or not. I was giving this wedding business some serious thought and figured out the absolute best place for us to be married."

"Really," said Cora sarcastically. "And here I was betting you would try to elope."

It was playful sparring, but this time Morgan could muster no retort. For a split second, he thought that his secret had been compromised, and he watched Sarah's face for a reaction. When she smiled, he knew no harm was done.

"Sarah, let's just pick up the entire wedding and move it from Devlin to somewhere else. That's what I'm thinking."

The women froze with wide-eyed stares. Their mouths went agape. Morgan's timing was just too coincidental, too perfect.

“Move it? You mean, like to Pittsburgh?” The devil had a hold on Cora’s tongue, and she drew out the name of the city as an obvious clue. Her friend waved her back to silence, but not before Morgan caught the signal.

“Why? Are you thinking about Pittsburgh, Sarah?”

No one dared answer, and Sarah wisely diffused the sudden tension. “I’m still waiting to hear about the absolute best place to be married.”

“Well, to tell you the truth, you won’t like it so much. I was thinking about the Big Timber. I want you to see it. I want all of you to see it. It’s magnificent.”

“You mean to have your wedding way out in a wilderness?” Annie asked, incredulously.

“Ma, if you could only imagine the place. The wonders of those woods defy description. It’s a hallowed garden, for sure, and you’d know it just to stand there under those great tall trees, with spears of light plunging through their canopies and mountain blossoms all bunched between their roots. It’s more than mere wilderness. You just have to see it. You have to come feel it for yourself.”

“It does sound wonderful, son, but a woman wants a church altar and a grand reception hall, not a forest. The woods are not practical or proper for a Christian wedding. How would we even get there?”

“I am talking about a Christian wedding. No cathedral could be more holy. No palace could ever seem so rich, and no place on God’s green earth could make for a better start to a marriage. But you’re right, of course. The Big Timber is far, much too far. I was foolish to even mention it.”

“Don’t say that. I think it’s a very romantic notion. Isn’t it, Sarah?”

“Very.” The girl was moved by Morgan’s thoughtfulness.

“Well, I’ll be pleased with anything Sarah wants,” said Morgan. “We could even hold the ceremony right in the front yard here. As long as I have my bride, a few good friends and my family with me, Cora’s company excluded, I’ll be happy.”

His sister noted the exception. She was not offended. “Then

you're bound to be unhappy, brother, because this is one wedding I refuse to miss."

"Good. I didn't really mean it." Morgan winked at Sarah. "You know, it never crossed my mind until now that home might just be a good place to start a new life together. Don't you think? Like I said, Sarah, whatever you want is what I want. Anyway, I'd better change out of these skins before Cora acts up again. I'm sorry to have interrupted your planning."

"Yes, leave us," commanded Cora, still acting the imp. She dismissed her brother like a queen at court.

Sarah watched Morgan disappear from sight, then, gradually returned her attention to her companions. Annie was wistful. Cora was excited, and she grasped wildly at Sarah's hands.

"Well, it looks like we're heading to Pittsburgh for a wedding!" Cora exclaimed. "Morgan seems agreeable, and all that's left to do is pull the pieces together. We'll have the grandest of times! It will be a dream wedding, Sarah, an absolute dream wedding."

"But what do you think about all of this, Mrs. Darrow?"

Annie gazed at the golden-haired girl and nodded approvingly. "I think you should call me "Annie." And I hope that one day you will come to think of me as your mother, because I'm so very proud of you right now. You've already made your decision, whether you know it or not. It requires no endorsement from me. And it's a good decision, one that will bless you for the rest of your life. This *will* be a dream wedding. I can promise you that."

Sarah stood and threw her arms tightly around Annie's neck. She whispered, "Thank you...Mother."

Cora could not contain her enthusiasm. "My, we have so much to do! Is there a ballroom at the estate? There must be. Will there be dancing with an orchestra? There just has to be, along with servants to pour the champagne. How will we get there? I suppose we'll take the trains. Oh, and what in the world do we do about flowers? It's the fall. Sarah, this could all cost a fortune!"

"Daddy said he would expect a large bill, but champagne and orchestras don't seem so important right now."

"What are you talking about?"

Sarah paused. Her father once told her that loving a husband would be a lifelong lesson in selflessness and compromise. It was a disheartening, even frightening, thought for a young girl who found romance in every corner of her imagination. The message had been resonating through her consciousness all these many years, but she now understood for the first time what he really meant. Giving is both the planting seed and the harvested fruit of marriage. It is both the work and the reward. She hated to disappoint Cora, but her friend would have to learn that same lesson for herself, and in her own good time.

Cora pleaded, "Just think about it. A big stone church where choir voices echo from the vaulted ceilings, a manor house with formal gardens and gazebos and a lawn party filled with the all the right people, a secluded cottage on a white sandy beach. It's perfect, and it's all yours if you want it. Champagne and orchestras? Of course, they're important. What could be more so on such an occasion?"

"Loving the man more than the moment, that's what. I'm not a princess, Cora, and I don't want castles. What I do want is only what I need, and what I need is Morgan Darrow. How could I have forgotten?"

Sarah looked over at Annie and marveled. She wondered how the woman knew just what her answer would be. Then she tried as best she could to better explain.

"You see, Cora, home *is* the proper place to start our life together. Home, or in that secret garden way up in those mountains. They may have named it the Big Timber, but Morgan calls it paradise. Well, Mr. Darrow, I expect your paradise will be well worth the walk. Maybe we'll try it your way."

# CHAPTER 21

"Tell me just once more, who are we supposed to meet?" Lowe asked, as he and Black Jack entered the back lot of the wagon house.

"Yo head, sure enough, never followed yo body out o' bed today. If it did, it done run off again." Black Jack was becoming annoyed. "Higgleby. For de fifth time, Lowe, de man's name be Jonas Higgleby. He de stable manager for de mill."

"Right. Jonas Higgleby. Stable manager." Lowe had trouble concentrating. He was sure he had met the man at some point, but strained his memory to recall the occasion. When a short-framed, older gentleman stepped from a side door of the wagon house, he offered a casual two-fingered salute and an answer to the puzzle.

"Howdy! You Yancy?"

"That would be me, and you must be Mr. Higgleby."

"Yes, sir, it's good to meet you, Mr. Yancy."

"And this is my partner, John Clark."

"Mr. Clark."

The men shook hands warmly, while Lowe, still searching for a connection, studied Higgleby's rough, gaunt face. "You look familiar to me, Mr. Higgleby. Have we met?" Lowe questioned.

"Not that I know of, and I'm usually fairly good with faces." He studied Lowe for a second. "And yours is one I'd certainly remember."

It was a strange comment, and Lowe was not quite sure what the man meant by it. He unconsciously stroked his cheek, as though expecting to feel some protrusion or creeping rash on his skin.

Jonas Higgleby continued, "I've got me a theory about faces. The good Lord only made so many of them, and after 30 years or so, we've purdy much seen them all. I swear, at my age, every face is a familiar one."

If their paths had not crossed previously, they should have. Jonas Higgleby had made Devlin his home for the past six years, and in such a small town, it was unfathomable that the two would not have had at least some dealings with each other. Lowe asked him why.

"Oh, I reckon I don't get out so much these days. I work the wagons and stock the whole day long, and when I'm through for the evening, I don't much tarry on the road back to home."

Lowe looked into the large corral and counted close to 18 mules browsing the remnants of a hay bale. "Are those the ones you handle? That's quite a number."

"Well, sir, that isn't all of them by a long shot. We've got that many and more skidding timber up on the cut. Mules don't demand much, just a little feed and some occasional shoe fitting. The skinners give them all the rubbing they need, and I handle the ferrier work."

"No horses? No oxen?"

"No oxen. We work a few horses, but the mule's a good, dependable animal out there on the mountain. They have littler feet and tougher hooves, and that makes them a bit more stable, considering all the rocks we got in these parts."

"Dere no argument with dat," replied Black Jack, almost under his breath.

"Of course, their days are numbered," Higgleby added. "Steam engines and tractors can go just about anywhere a mule can go, and it won't be long before the whole business turns to machines. Aww, I reckon it isn't so bad. Oil-driven equipment is a heap easier to feed and is bound to make things a whole lot cleaner around here." He took a deep whiff of rank stable air and pointed to his manure-caked boots. "But I will tell you, men, this country races toward change like a skeeter drawn to blood. I never thought I'd see the day of telephones and flying machines and automobiles and the like. It's a little unsettling for us old fellows. There's got to be an end to it all sometime, and machines might just get us to the finish long before we're ready to quit."

Both Lowe and Black Jack were nodding their heads in agreement. Lowe responded, "Things do move fast nowadays, too fast to adjust. I guess there's some good in all that change, but I'm having real trouble seeing it. Did you say you maintain the wagons, as well?"

"Yes, sir, mules are the easy part. We've got us a fleet of freighters and flatbeds, and when a wagon's down, I'm the one sent running. My pappy was a wainwright, and I paid him a good deal of attention growing up. Learning early sure makes a difference when you're talking livelihoods."

"I reckon that's true. My father taught me his trade, as well. I learned most of his ways just by tagging along as a boy. Pa made sure I had a great start on life."

"And just what is it that you do, may I ask?"

"Surveyor. Mostly for mill and mine properties."

"That's real good work for a man. I used to fancy the idea of doing that myself. There's nothing like healthy, outdoor labor to fortify the body, mind and soul. Are you your own boss?"

"Yeah, it's just me and my partner, Mr. Clark here, and we recently recruited the young fellow who's fixing to marry Ms. Dabney. All that 'healthy, outdoor labor' you mentioned starts taking its toll after a while, and we felt we needed a dose of youth to keep things going."

"Aww, you are yet a couple of pups compared to me, certainly too young to feel played out. But it sounds like you're happy with your lot, and Mr. Yancy, I sure hope you got around to thanking your father for it."

"Every single day. He's passed on now, but I thank him still."

"Good. Good. Sometime, when you're free, you two come by and we'll jaw some more. I can just imagine some of the stories in your line."

Small talk was not a waste of time, but a common courtesy, especially when served in limited portions. Never one to hurry his conversations, Jonas Higgleby knew just how and when to finish them, and whether friend or stranger, no one was ever made to regret his acquaintance due to a long-winded discourse.

"Now, Mr. Dabney said I was to take good care of you fellows. What do you need exactly?"

"We're hauling tables and chairs for his daughter's wedding."

"How many?"

"I can't say. Whatever the mill can spare, I guess."

"That's a lot! I've seen a mess of folding chairs and just about as many tables over in storage. The superintendent uses them for his meetings and socials."

The man thought for a moment, trying to picture Irwin Dabney's daughter. "You know, I believe I saw that girl once. She's a pretty little thing. Did she find her a good man?"

"Yup, she sure did. The best."

"That's fine, real fine. The Dabneys are nice folk. I wish the couple a long and happy marriage, as has been my good fortune. You boys have wives?"

"No, sir, neither one of us."

"That's a real shame. A woman can be a blessing, if you don't tally every little failing and foible. But you're still young with a little of the hunt left in you. If you decide to pursue it, I can vouch for married living."

The man slapped Lowe on his shoulder and then walked away toward the stable.

"Can we help you with a team?" Lowe asked.

"Nope, you stay put and I'll be right back. Your wagon will be that big one on the left. Just wait and see what's coming up next."

The old man was gone for 10 minutes, and Lowe and Black Jack became curious when he never showed in the paddock. Finally, the big twin doors of the stable opened wide, and two magnificent Belgian draft horses were led out, side by side.

"Well, what do you think of these beauties?" Higgleby proudly inquired. "They're a matched set."

"Lordy," responded Black Jack. He drew near and examined the pair more closely. "Talk about yo machines. Dese here be de real tractors, and dey ain't gonna seize up with orange rust whilst settin' out in some field." He rubbed the top of a foreleg. "Dat muscle as hard as granite rock. How old dese hosses, three, maybe four years?"

"Three. They're the trophies of the Devlin Mill and, by far, the finest team I ever worked. Where the Shay can't go, what the mule can't pull, these here horses live for the challenge. They're yours for the day, boys, with the compliments of Irwin Dabney, Charles A. Devlin, and Jonas G. Higgleby."

Higgleby backed the team to the tongue of the wagon and set the harnesses. The animals knew what was expected of them, and the only prompting they received was a click or two from the old man's mouth before they stepped backward in unison to their intended position. The Belgians were both sleek and hulking, with their bulk being little else but the sinew bred into them. Their huge feet and thick legs, their broad, muscular shoulders and iron necks revealed an obvious purpose of being. There was power, even in their standing still, and immeasurable might in their movement.

"I don't know what to say, Mr. Higgleby. A couple mules would've worked just fine. We won't have that much of a load."

"I know, but the boys need their exercise. They're gentle giants. You won't have any trouble. Attila's on the right, Genghis on the left. Genghis only has three boots, if you somehow get them mixed up." He pointed to the white hair above the horse's feet.

"Attila? And you say they're gentle?"

"Aww, what's in a name? Yeah, they're as gentle as lambs and love being with people. By the way, if you have to separate them for some reason, just be sure to team them back the same way. They know their place and get confused if you reverse their positions. Best of luck with the wedding."

Lowe and Black Jack climbed up onto the wagon, eager for new experience. Both the vehicle and the animals that pulled it were much larger than anything they had driven, and there was an understandable degree of nervousness as Black Jack held the reins and kicked the brake free with his right foot. They were ready to roll, and when Higgleby clicked his mouth again, they did just that. Their harness bells jingled with a rhythm.

The draft horses drew attention like a band on parade, and after they stopped to collect the chairs, Lowe and Black Jack took the long way through town just to prolong the show. A small crowd followed, and by the time the wagon neared the Dabney house, there were many young hands raring to assist with its cargo.

Annie Darrow heard the clopping of the hooves. She heard the loud "Haw!", as Black Jack coaxed the team to a left and final turn. She had anticipated their arrival for hours, and the sounds, though common to the streets of Devlin, sparked a childlike response that sent her springing across the yard toward the iron gate. While the horses made their slow approach up the shaded lane, she busied herself hiding the cosmetic effects of a long morning's labor. Her loose blouse had pulled free from the top of her skirt, while her rolled sleeves unraveled from her elbows. Her hands were soiled, and her chestnut hair trailed wildly across the corner of her eyes. It was clear that her work was hard, but even more evident that she was well accustomed to it.

The wedding was tomorrow, and come that time, Annie would sparkle with the elegance of a young and polished debutante. But on this day, she was hardly the model of gentility, as she worked like a servant readying for the royal ball. She had no way of knowing that her appearance, disheveled as it was, would prove all the more alluring for one man who had already come to respect her womanly strength and self-reliance. As others crowded for a closer look at the massive Belgian horses, she slipped through the gate to better see that man.

Annie beamed at Lowe Yancy. The radiance of her smile and reddened cheeks, flushed by the heat of the rising sun, hid any flaws left uncorrected. He smiled back, and she knew in the instant that, at least to him, she was beautiful.

"You ask for chairs, ma'am, you get chairs. Where do we put them?" Lowe inquired. He tipped his hat.

Annie curtsied in response. “On this side of the trellis, if you would be so kind. Morgan and Dewey have been busy as honey bees setting things up. They’ll be happy to see you brought so much help with you.”

At least a dozen of the neighborhood children gathered at the back of the wagon for their chance to carry a chair or help with a table. There was hope for reward. Perhaps a ride might be offered in payment for their services. Maybe more.

Jacob Darrow sensed opportunity. He climbed up the spokes of a giant wheel to assure the onlookers that there would, in fact, be compensation for those who earned it. He organized a single line and prohibited anyone, including those children twice his age and size, from scaling the sides of the wagon unless he had otherwise granted his permission. Such permission would not be forthcoming until the last of the furniture had been neatly placed in its row on the lawn. Jacob was inflated with the air of authority. That, coupled with the fact that the teamsters both called him by name, made him the indisputable leader of the small work force. There were no complaints.

“He’s quite the organizer,” Lowe said, laughing in amazement at a seven-year-old’s power of persuasion.

“Yes, he’s my little union man. Lord help the company,” replied Annie.

“Well, he certainly has control of this situation.”

“He does, but you watch. Before this day is over, he’ll somehow wangle that control into profit. He’s smart, Lowe, and he just emptied your wagon for you. Be careful he doesn’t empty your pockets looking for his reward.”

“Why, Annie Darrow, is that any way for a mother to talk?”

“You’ll see.”

Lowe helped where he was needed and found himself involved in tasks generally unsuited to a mountain man. His hands were clumsy as he tied bows of white ribbon. Annie held the knots so he could tighten them. He had no eye for color or space, as he wove garden flowers through the vines of wisteria that covered a long wooden trellis. One after another, Annie made them right, until the long arch was full and rich with autumn color. He cut stems and set bouquets. He polished silver ewers, wiped windows and beat the carpets clean. He aligned and realigned the chairs and banquet tables. He even chopped vegetables for the relish and pared fruit for the punch, all under Annie Darrow's watchful eye. Where the woman led, the man gladly followed.

"Well, I guess that's about all we can do," said Annie. "I can't thank you enough. The ladies from church already decorated the sanctuary, and they'll be here in the morning to add some finishing touches. Mr. Dabney has hired cooks and servers for the reception. Really, I just can't thank you and Black Jack enough for all your hard work."

"Oh, I reckon I was more in your way than helpful."

Annie laughed. To some extent, it was true. "I suppose you wish you had taken that long wagon ride with Jacob and the children."

"No, ma'am, I enjoyed my time here, and besides, you were right about Jake. Black Jack had to fork out for 11 ice creams, two scoops each, as I understood it."

"That's my little boy." Annie looked across the yard and spotted Morgan stealing a kiss from Sarah. There was no attempt at secrecy. "And that's my other little boy with his soon-to-be new wife. They seem so inseparable. I envy them. Don't you?"

"I suppose I do."

Annie lifted one of the chairs from its row and turned it toward Lowe. She sat and sighed as her pride overtook her. She was weary, but more so, she was enraptured by that particular moment of her life when every feeling was warm and every aspect of her future was hopeful. She rested in the contentment. "I can't believe all this. We've seen some hard times, but today that's all behind us. I thank the Lord."

"Good things should come to good people, and from where I stand, Annie, I see a woman whose reward has been too long overdue. I'm very happy for you and your family."

Annie looked up with tired eyes. "And from where I sit, Lowe

Yancy, I see a sweet man who somehow makes those good things happen. I do not look back at my mistakes, but I do look forward with hope in my heart. You put it there, and I will not lose it again. You may not know it, but you are my very dear friend."

"I am, Annie. I am."

Lowe walked quickly across the yard toward the lane where Black Jack stood with the Belgian team. The wagon creaked as he climbed aboard.

"Are you coming?"

Black Jack combed his hands through the horses' long, identical manes, then finally made his way to his seat. A voice called from behind them.

"Hey, you there, wait up! Is this the Dabney residence?" A stocky boy in a uniform cap jogged to catch the wagon before it departed. He was almost breathless.

"Take yo time, son. Get some air. We ain't in dat big a hurry," responded Black Jack.

"Thanks, I've been looking for the Dabney house."

"You found it."

"I have a telegram intended for a Mrs. Lawson Darrow. Her neighbor said she might be at this address."

Lowe pointed to Annie, still sitting and resting. "She's the pretty woman, right over there."

"Much obliged, mister."

Black Jack clicked his mouth twice, and the draft team lunged in unison with their first step. It would be an easy walk, all downhill to the stable.

"I gots to have me one o' dese, Mr. Yancy. De Lord can sure build him a hoss."

"It seems he's made a lot of things right," Lowe responded, looking over his shoulder to see Annie one more time. She was reading her telegram.

"Now you catchin' on! I believe dat God's good grace flow from some bottomless well. I keep dippin', and it fills right back up 'til it bubbles over de side and splashes on just about everythin'. Take dis here weddin'. I pray for a happy marriage, and he not only bring de two young folk back together, he give de man a job, he fix de little boy's head and leg, and he put de smile back on Mrs. Annie's face. And I reckon he have a little somethin' in mind for Lawson Darrow, too, if de poor man ain't already blessed. Dat said, I think it a cryin' shame dat a father shirk his fam'ly callin' at such a prideful time as dis."

"I would agree, though it's selfish and cowardly anytime a man leaves his woman and children."

Black Jack switched the subject, "You know, Mr. Yancy, it been a long time since I's asked to a weddin', especially one for white folk. It be an honor, don't you think? It give me hope for dis old world. Dat Morgan and Miss Sarah, dey like de line 'tween ocean and sky. Dey so right when dey's together you can't see nothin' but de blue. I like bein' part o' dat. It make me want to settle again. Yessa, it make me want to find another lovin' woman and build a proper home. I wonder what my Hettie thinks on dat. And you, Lowe, when you ever gonna allow yo self somethin' more dan memories? I heard yo words to Morgan out on de river, and it saddens me thinkin' you give up like dat. Jonas Higgleby right, you know. You is young. Dere still much life to live."

Lowe had nothing to say. As his friend talked, he sat stone-faced, knowing all too well that what often started as harmless natter might soon evolve into a sermon on the ills of his personal life or habits. He sensed that Black Jack would eventually turn the discussion against him, and experience told him to simply not participate.

It was neither the first time nor the last for such one-sided discourse. It had become their routine, a common pitfall of a long-time companionship. Lowe hated to be lectured, but he was at least honest enough with himself to acknowledge, and even value, some of Black Jack's insights. Spitefully mute, he still listened and never let on that he even cared.

Black Jack could not be fooled or dissuaded by such treatment.

By his way of thinking, what should be said must be said, and he had waited much too long already to not speak his mind now. He tugged hard on the reins and brought the wagon to a stop.

"Lowe, you needs to listen, 'cause I needs to talk. I figure on trampin' dese woods de rest o' my days, and I hopes to do it with you. But I can't abide another second watchin' you torment yo self over some woman dat likely don't even recall yo face. Mind you, it ain't for me to judge de rights and wrongs o' yo life, but as yo friend, I intends to weigh in on yo happiness. Dat woman set her mark deep on yo heart, and you wears it like a scar. Both time and me bear witness dat you been true to her, even now she been gone some 20 years. Dat be too long a while, Lowe, if not for you, den for dat lady of yo dreams.

"'Dis here my point. Dat young woman you been holdin' so tight, she gone. If she even alive to dis day, she taken a new home or a new man dat brings her contentment. She ain't waitin' for Lowe Yancy to come callin', and she wouldn't even know de man now if he did. She gone, Lowe. One way or another, she gone, and you has to move on with yo life, too. Someone needs you, and you needs to find dat someone. You needs to let her into dat big old heart of yo's, and when you do, I thinks you'll see dat dere be more dan enough love for both yo memory and yo life."

Black Jack saw a soul mired in regret. The past might be a mere puddle, but Lowe Yancy was unable to navigate his way around or through it. He stayed stranded at the edge, ruing and reflecting. It blocked any passage to real relationships, and while he desperately wanted more than memories, he had too little resolve to wade beyond where he might again find a right and lasting love. Lowe stared blankly at the road ahead, weighted by the haunting disappointment of that past.

And there was more. There was Annie. While she had been tossed back to the world by her fool of a husband, she was neither available nor ready to consider another. She was, after all, still a married woman. Lowe had no right to the feelings that were churning within him, and he had no desire to resist them. He would not confide this to his friend or anyone, especially Annie. To do so might bring his shame on her.

Black Jack did understand one thing well. Lowe needed someone who needed him. He pressed the point, "You needs a fam'ly, Lowe. You needs folks dat can care for you when you old and people dat depend on you while you young. I ain't yo fam'ly, and while I's right fond o' you, I ain't quite up to de task at hand. Dat all I'm sayin'. Dere be a whole lot o' good back dere to remember, but a whole lot more ahead to come to know. I'd like to find what I been missin'. Wouldn't you?"

Lowe still said nothing, and Black Jack, unsurprised, snapped the reins and clicked his mouth. He was content to speak any further thoughts to the fine horses that were pulling slowly back to the heart of town.

Annie gripped the small wad of white paper in an angry fist and was swept up the hill by an unprecedented surge of Irish rage. She had always been slow to anger, but Lawson Darrow had become adept at pushing her to the brink of self-control. This time he went too far. He was waiting for her, only a block from the house he once called home.

"Hey, darlin', I'm over here," he said rather quietly, as he stepped suddenly from the concealment of a high wall. Annie froze with fear at first, but was more than ready to defend herself when she saw the bearded face of her husband.

"Oh, Annie, how I've missed you!" Lawson moved toward his wife and held out his arms for an expected embrace.

She dropped the paper and slapped him hard upon the cheek. "What were you thinking?" she shouted. "I'm not the fool you obviously think I am. You left, remember? You walked away for good, remember? You abandoned your wife and your children when we needed you most. Don't you remember, Lawson? What are you doing here!"

"I've come home to make things right."

Annie massaged her hand, which was still tingling from the slap. Lawson reached to hold it, and she pulled it fast away.

"I'm sorry I struck you," she said in atonement. "I never meant to treat you so."

Misunderstanding her softened tone, he edged closer to her and tried again for the embrace. She would have no part of it.

"It's all right. I no doubt deserve your coldness. But I'm here to say I've changed, and I'm back for good if you'll have me. I need you, and it wouldn't be right to wait another second to say how much I love you. That's why I'm here."

Annie spread her hands in front of her to ward off yet another advance. Unaccustomed to her own outrage, she bit her lip to avoid cursing and silently summoned a greater strength. It was slow coming.

"But you left," she said again. "We were forced to start a new life, one without a husband or a father. Now you show up without warning and want us to welcome you to the family you've forsaken? It's a bitter pill you offer."

"I sent you the telegram. Wasn't that warning? My son is getting married and I want to see it. My wife is alone and I long to be with her. I miss my children and my world."

"You miss us, do you? Did you even know that Jacob recovered? Did you notice that Cora now welcomes the attentions of young men? Do you even care that Morgan has a job and will soon begin a family of his own?"

"Of course, I care."

"Then where have you been, Lawson? How can any man stay away when so many good things finally come to his children?"

"I couldn't. That's the whole point. I've never been so distant that I couldn't see what was happening. I went to Virginia for a while, filling in as a filer at a small mill close to Bristol, but for the most part, I've been near."

Annie laughed at the irony. "I told everyone you were in Oregon. I was beginning to believe it myself. I was happy knowing you were far away. There's no room in my heart for you, Lawson, and I worry for your sake how the children might feel. I'm afraid you've burnt your bridges with Morgan."

"I'll make it up to them, just like I intend to make it up to you. I've given up the drink. I haven't touched a drop in a month. Whiskey's always been my devil, you know that, and now I've beaten it."

"No, Lawson, there were far more problems than just whiskey. I have forgiven you for them, and I ask that you forgive me and let me move on in peace."

Lawson had difficulty understanding Annie's attitude. If she intended to be forgiving, truly forgiving, she would have opened her heart to him, just as she had always done before. He knew there would be obstacles. He knew how badly he had hurt her and how she could rightfully resist his return after so long an absence. Annie's resolve in the past always seemed to wither at the words "I love you," but this time, she was standing firm against him. Perhaps he had miscalculated the consequence of his bad behavior, or perhaps, one obstacle held greater influence than he anticipated.

"It's Yancy, isn't it? I was never enough for you, and now you look to him."

"You were once enough."

"So, it is Yancy. Has it gone that far? Have you betrayed me, Annie?"

Lawson's questions were undeserving of an answer. If she had feelings for another, they were properly placed. She would neither surrender herself, body or soul, to any man other than the one she loved, nor stay wedded to one who abused and dishonored her. Her silence incensed him.

"Damn it, Annie! Why do you act this way? I will have you back, you know that. We will be a family again. You'll see."

Annie shook her head defiantly. "I cannot walk this road again with you. It leads to nowhere. I believe we should divorce."

She paused, stunned by the word. As harmful as their relationship had become, as distant as she felt from the man who was her husband, she had never fully conceded, until now, that their marriage was finished. Her mind would not let her consider such a desperate conclusion, even though her vision of their future together had long since been lost. Divorce meant failure, and Annie found it difficult to acknowledge it as the final solution.

"You don't mean that, Annie. You're just mad."

"I…I am sorry, Lawson, but I do. There is no other way to bring peace to this family. I'm very sorry. Listen, we can talk again after the wedding. I have too much to do and too much on my mind to continue this now."

"I plan to be there tomorrow, and I'd like to sit with you."

"Whether you come is between you and your son. But you talk to him first, Lawson. Don't surprise him on his wedding day. If he wants you there, maybe it is best that you sit with me, at least for appearance sake. But do not…just do not read anything into that. What we once had is now gone."

Annie was overwrought with emotion and lifted the hem of her long skirt to allow her legs to speed to the refuge of home. She could hear Lawson following at a short distance, and she abruptly turned. With cold eyes, she pleaded that he stop.

"You'll regret your decision," he said threateningly. "I belong here. I belong right here with you. You have both my name and my children, and I don't intend to give you up."

# CHAPTER 22

Morgan showed little expression when Annie informed him of his father's return. Her son was young, but still, he was an adult about to embark on the most serious journey of his life. He could handle the truth. Ever mindful of her own bias, she was careful to not disgrace Lawson in the eyes of his child.

"It is your decision, Morgan. He means well, I think, and I know he loves you, even if he has a hard time showing it."

"Ma, I don't fault you for your feelings. I've watched him mistreat you for so many years. I've seen him run back to you with his tail between his legs every time he gets sober and suddenly misses his home. It's been an endless cycle of ups and down for us, and I understand why it has to stop. I don't much like my father, to tell you the truth, but I do love him. If there's any chance he means what he says, then I want to keep him in my life. People do change for the good, and Pa could be one of them. I think I want him at the wedding."

"Then, son, you tell him just that. It will mean a lot to him."

The evening was a long way from over, and Annie had departed on yet another errand when Dewey and the other boys stepped up on the porch and banged heavily on the door.

"Morgan Darrow! Get yerself out here right now, or I'll come in there to fetch ya. I'm countin' to 10!" Dewey yelled loudly and started his count.

Morgan hollered back from his small room on the second floor, while he adjusted his suspenders and threw a jacket over one shoulder. The thin walls of the house could not muffle his response.

"That's a real laugh, I'd say. Dewey, you wouldn't know how to count to 10 if you spent another 12 years in school! Come on in. The door's open."

Dewey heard, but he waited. He snickered and then turned to the small group of men crowded on the porch steps. "Hell, he don't know nothin'. I could learn my numbers up to '10' in half that time." When they laughed, he put his finger to his mouth to quiet them. Their presence was a surprise for Morgan Darrow.

Morgan scrambled down the stairs, grumbling all the way. "Lordy, Dewey, you're worse than a spoiled lap cat. You know, you could've let yourself in and saved me some effort. That door never stopped you before." He swung open the door and pushed back the screen. "So, what's this all about?"

"I'd say it's all 'bout you." Dewey backed away to reveal five of Morgan's closest school friends, all astir with their anticipation for mischief.

"Well, I'll be. Hey, boys, what brings you out?"

Dewey responded for the group, "We just came by for a visit. Thought ya might be lonely, this bein' your last night and all. We got us an idea."

Morgan was aware of tradition. "Well, I'm not particularly lonely, but I'm all ears concerning any idea the six of you could agree on."

"It's your weddin' day tomorrow. We were all just sayin' how we was gonna miss ya, and we decided to drop in to tell ya so."

"That's mighty kind of you, but I'm not really going anywhere."

"Oh, that's for darn sure," one of the boys was quick to say. Certain of its relevancy, he was anxious to share a family secret. "You ain't goin' nowheres. Yer name's not the only thing Sarah's 'bout to steal from ya. She'll have yer time and money, too, b'fore ya know it. I learned that much from my cousin who got himself hitched jist one short year ago. He feels saddled and rode hard and is already havin' second thoughts 'bout the whole marriage thing."

Another boy chimed in, "Yeah, that's just the way I hear it. You can kiss your freedom goodbye. No more hangin' with your pals, no more spoonin' with the ladies, no nippin' at the jug, no swimmin' in the river, no baseball, no ...."

"Yeah, yeah, I get the picture. I've heard it all before."

A third boy, a couple years older than the rest, finished the thought, "And, o' course, there'll be no more crossin' to the other side o'the tracks for those particular indulgents."

"Well, now you have me worried," said Morgan. He was playing along with the ruse. "The wedding is off. There are some things I just won't abide giving up. But I really don't sample much in the way of whiskey and haven't yet crossed those tracks for what you're talking about. Have you? Have any of you?"

Every eye scanned the rest of the group to see who would dare reply. No one was prepared to be so honest, and they mumbled and grunted until, one by one, they lied.

"Sure, I've been over there," said one.

"You bet. Lots o' times," replied another.

"Sure 'nough, I been sneakin' cross town for years," added a third.

Dewey topped them all. "Hell, them painted ladies know me by name. In fact, they've even given me some sweet little handles."

"Which are what exactly?" questioned Morgan, who was highly skeptical about every one of the claims.

"They like to call me either 'Sweet-kiss' or 'Big Boy', but I ain't at liberty to tell ya just why, on account of my bein' such a gentleman. One should not brag 'bout personal endowments, ya know."

The others chuckled at Dewey's racy boldness. Morgan beamed.

"You are by far the biggest and worst liars I have ever seen. So, where are we going? And I better not hear 'to the other side of the tracks.'"

"Avery's. Where else?"

It was as though the decade had never passed. They were once again seven boys bent on their own destruction, hopelessly engrossed in a steady volley of reminiscence. They traveled the long, gravel road wrestling and running. They pushed and they tackled until every knee or elbow boasted a bruise or scrape. They mourned lost sweethearts, only to realize it was often the same young girl who had stolen each other's affections, and they poked fun, especially at Dewey, who had unselfishly provided them with a lifetime of anecdote and humor. All was just as it used to be. No one mentioned weddings. No one talked of jobs. No one recalled a single hope that lay founded in the future. They were there only for the past, and before they realized it, they were standing at the cliffs of Avery's pool.

Morgan asked, "Did the rest of you fellows know we were coming all the way out here?"

"O' course."

"It's been a great walk, but I can't help but wonder why we didn't hook up a wagon. Dewey, a wagon would have been a whole lot easier."

"Well, I tried to find suitable transportation, but no one would oblige me on account of this being your last get-together with ol' friends. I reckon everyone expects the worst on such occasions."

"And they sure weren't wrong, were they, Dewey?" one of the boys asserted. He giggled like a girl, and his friends berated him for conduct unbecoming a man.

"Hush up, Ernie! It ain't that time, yet. Let's all set for a while. We can jaw 'bout Morgan Darrow some more, since he's the one who's fixin' to leave us."

The tales went on for a half hour before everyone realized that any story about Morgan would ultimately implicate Dewey Baughman. It was not long before Dewey's misdeeds were the real focus of conversation, and at that point, Dewey decided it was time for the mischief. He pulled a round, brown jug from a knapsack and set it on the boulder in front of his companions.

"I thought we weren't going to do whiskey," Morgan reminded Dewey.

"Wrong. We agreed to nothin', except stayin' clear of the other side of the tracks."

Morgan rolled his eyes. "I suppose I can be thankful for that much."

Dewey held up the heavy ceramic with two hands. "Gentlemen, I propose a toast. To Morgan Darrow, the best and smartest of us all, a man with a solid future and all the good luck his Irish blood can muster. Take one swig and pass it on."

Dewey took the first swallow and watched as the jug made its way around the circle of young men. Each in turn gasped and choked from the burn of the alcohol, then declared the beverage smooth and sweet, like a flow of tupelo honey. Morgan refused to drink.

Dewey offered a second toast, "Someday, we'll all be old and bald and decrepit. We'll be hitched up to elderly fat women with bosoms down to their knees and calves the size of mill logs. And worse, yet, we'll be surrounded by a dozen ugly, screamin', messy-butt grandbabies, all of them wantin' their place on the lap. Yup, that's the way of married folk, and Morgan's only the first to follow the course. When that day is upon us, let us each remember good friends and these good ol' times we had together. To Morgan Darrow and the good ol' times!"

Again, the jug was passed around.

"Dewey, why not just 'To old friends'? We can drink a whole lot more if you talk a little bit less." Ernie Zimmer intentionally shortened the toast.

"I'll drink to that, too, if that's what floats your boat."

Morgan again refused to drink, but continued to circulate the jug as he listened to his friends propose one inane toast after another. Dewey became perplexed. "Ain't ya gonna join in, Morgan? This is your night."

"Yes, it is, and tomorrow's my day. You are not going to get me to do something I might regret in the morning. I'm having my fun just being with you fellows. You all go on and have yours."

"Fair enough. I've one last thing to say, and then, we'll end this here ceremony and just have us a time."

Dewey had thought about this particular toast, and what he was to say was most heartfelt. It was the very reason he had gathered the friends. He looked Morgan directly in the eye and found it surprisingly less difficult than he thought as he began to deliver his message.

"I reckon I'll just have to miss ya, Morgan. We've been the best of friends for as long as I remember. From time to time, ya pulled me from some real scrapes and rescued my dignity from my own foolishness. You always laughed with me, not at me. You walked with a slow, clumsy, chubby boy when any other fella, who could run like you, would rather race the wind. Don't think I didn't notice, and don't ya think for a minute I didn't appreciate, the way ya stepped down from your rightful place in this life to spend time with a poor soul of half your quality and ability. Just knowin' ya has raised me to heights I could never climb on my own."

Morgan tried to interrupt, but Dewey silenced him with the raise of a hand. Then, he continued, "I'd only allow one person to ever step in the middle of this here friendship, and that's 'cause only one person could care more for you than I do. It ain't easy for me to admit, especially after all these years of hecklin' and play. Your Sarah Dabney was bound to take my place all along. Call it fate, if ya will. Chalk it up to the heavens where good marriages are arranged. Marriage is actually the best of friendship, isn't it? It's the way of things when a man and woman are right together, and I never before seen a more right couple. That girl is the prize. She's the prettiest gal I ever did behold. Only the beauty of her heart and mind surpass those big blue eyes and soft, golden hair. We've all seen her, we all admire her and we all envy that ya finally caught your rainbow. You treat her good, just like ya did me, and nothin' will come to set ya apart."

Dewey stood as best he could after sitting so long and imbibing so much. The evening had suddenly become too honest and emotional for him. He lifted the jug once more.

"Gentlemen, this time we drink to the honor of Mrs. Morgan Darrow, our beloved Sarah, the golden treasure at the end of the rainbow." His toast ended with a hiccup and a long, deep belch. "Oh, pardon me," he apologized, with uncharacteristic sincerity. "Like I said, 'To Sarah!'"

"To Sarah!" The cry issued from every mouth before the lips touched the bottle. One by one, they rose in respect, including Morgan, who took hold of the great jug, rested it high on the fold of his elbow, and gulped his share before the burn could close his throat.

"Whew! Where did you get that stuff?" Morgan asked, hardly able to speak.

Dewey spun the bottle in his hands until he found the initials etched in the glaze, 'SM'. He showed it to his friend.

"Compliments of Silas Monk. Of course, he meant it all for you, but I knew ya'd prefer to share."

Ernie made his way down to a lower ledge of the cliff. The daylight had begun to wane and the deepening shadows along the Charity River made it difficult to detect anything along the bottom land.

"Shush!" he exclaimed, as his fellows continued with their revelry. "Quiet down! I think they're here."

The young men calmed and strained to hear some telltale sound. It came from a distance.

"Dewey? Boys?" It was the voice of Auralee Buck. "Dewey? Where are you?"

Dewey stood extra tall from his perch on the cliff and began to wave his hat. "Up here! You girls come on up!"

"No, you boys come down. We can't cross over and we're not dressed for any climbing."

"Then, wait for us. Don't go anywhere. We'll be right there."

The men, all but Dewey and Morgan, rushed to their descent along a circuitous path that safely led below. The remaining two watched them until they abruptly stopped at the water's edge. The women, huddled on the opposing bank, lured them like sirens.

"Now what?" questioned Morgan, as he wisely stepped back from the rim and returned to a seat on the hard but stable ground. The woods had begun to spin around him.

"Now, they'll dive right in like hardy men or just stand there lookin' like the numskulls they really are. It could go either way at this point. It's been a warm day. We ain't likely to have such a day again until next summer. We thought the girls might like to have a final swim. Come on, Morgan! It'll be good for ya."

Dewey dropped his suspenders and pulled off his shirt without loosening more than the top two buttons. His white belly jiggled in the process.

Morgan's jaw dropped with disbelief. "Are you out of your mind? If the river's not cold enough to do it, you'll freeze to death in this night air. I'm afraid to ask what you intend to wear."

"That depends entirely on the girls. One can only hope."

The two friends could hear splashing and a flurry of giggles from the base of the cliff.

"It appears they braved the water," said Morgan.

"Yup, it sure does." Dewey was anxious to join in the fun. He started on his way. "And it's likely them girls shamed 'em into it. Come on, Morgan. It's your last shot at true freedom."

"Tell me something, exactly who is it that's down there?"

"I don't know. I reckon just Auralee, Sadie, Cora, Sarah and some of their friends."

"Sarah's with them? And my sister! Those boys had better have kept some trousers on or I'll be skinning them alive. Dewey, I swear! You're a challenge to the bitter end."

Dewey recognized the changing tone of his companion's voice, and it certainly was not the first time he had invoked Morgan's anger. He took another swig from the jug and passed it. "Here. Think of this as medicine for that temper of yers. Ya don't want to set yourself to worryin' this near to the weddin'."

"I'll set myself to murdering, if I find my bride and sister skinny dipping down at that swimming hole!"

"Well, uh, wait just a minute." Dewey cupped his hands to his mouth and shouted, "Hey, Auralee! Honey? Are Sarah and Cora with ya?"

"No, they said they were too busy with the wedding and all. Hurry down! I'm not getting in until you get in, and everyone else is already freezing cold."

"I'm on my way!" Dewey looked over at Morgan and smirked intentionally. He had been falsely accused and now awaited the apology that was due him. He did not receive it.

"There ya go, my friend, no harm done and no need to worry. Why don't ya change your mind and join us? We won't be long, and Auralee brought that wagon ya was talkin' 'bout. We'll all ride back to town together, snugglin' and singin' songs like on a Fourth of July hayride."

Dewey was at least consistent. One could certainly count on his easy nature, his giving heart and his unfettered knack for antics. Morgan smiled.

"No, I really can't. I believe I'll head on home. I could use some time alone, and a long walk will do me some good. Thanks, Dewey, for your kind words. I feel pretty much the same." Morgan took the jug from Dewey's hand and lifted it to his mouth. "Here's to you, my best friend. You will always be that to me."

The two men coughed in natural response to the fire of the whiskey, but continued to indulge themselves with a few more hefty swallows. Then they went their separate ways.

Morgan disappeared with his usual quick and even pace, and before he reached the nearby field, he heard the splash and squeal of Dewey Baughman testing the depths of the Charity River.

"Damn! Oh, damn it, that's cold!" The words thundered across the valley.

Morgan laughed in recollection of such times, of so many times at Avery's pool. And he thought about the coming day, about his future with Sarah and about the one thing that likely destroyed his parents' marriage. Gulping as much cool evening air as his lungs would hold, he vowed to never again partake of liquor. A burning chest, a spinning head, a queasy stomach, not to mention his disapproving mother and soon-to-be wife, they each stood out as sound reasons for sobriety. He coughed again. This pledge, like the one tomorrow, would be an easy one to keep.

The sunset hid behind the nearest mountain, and the last of

the light of day was extinguished without glory. It was dark before Morgan could put the first mile behind him.

His brisk walk was doing wonders to subdue the effects of the alcohol, and Morgan figured that the Charity River likely caused the same, if not a more immediate, result on his friends. Dewey and the others must have been freezing. While he wanted no part of that, he did regret not staying with them at least a little longer.

He could not remember the last time he had taken this particular hike without Dewey Baughman, who generally lagged behind, disparaging the inflated values of daily exercise and fresh air. Morgan missed the complaining, and he wondered what would become of their friendship over time. Dewey had always been the best of companions, and it seemed wrong that they were not together on the eve of the wedding. But the sparkling heavens and a wandering mind made for fair enough company, and before long, Morgan was absorbed by the promise of his future. He stepped lively, anxious to get there.

Each of a thousand stars had a thousand more beyond, and the narrow country lane shone distinctly, even without benefit of a moon. Morgan's mind became locked on Sarah, and the more he pondered a life with her, the faster he moved to shorten the distance between them. But the brightness of the road and the darkness of the trees that lined it would play their customary tricks, and it was just a matter of time before Morgan was seeing more through his imagination than his eyes. His focus shifted as he detected movement in the high weeds that lined his course. He stopped, and a heavy rustle of dry branches ceased as well. It could be anything, he thought.

He gave the matter little notice, having grown up surrounded by fields and forests, but the persistence of that singular night noise, that faint, ever nearing rustle, made him pause to reconsider. He strained to see, but there was nothing of the unusual, only the inky outlines of rose hedge and juniper. He strained to hear, but again, there was nothing. The cicadas and crickets, once loudly lamenting the end of their season, now hushed, and their sound dissipated like an ocean wave retreating across the sand. The sudden quiet was curious, if not unnerving. Something was out there.

Morgan gathered his grit and moved on, much slower and more vigilant than before. The rustling, almost indiscernible over the crunch of the gravel beneath his leather shoes, seemed to move with him, paralleling his progress, stalking his every step.

"What's out there?" he queried, now wary of the unknown presence. He did not have to speak loudly. The night air carried his voice with clarity. "Who's out there?"

Morgan picked up a rock and waited for the sound to repeat itself. He now could almost hear the shallow breathing of whatever stood just a few yards away. He struggled to see more, to hear more, but to no avail as he unconsciously rolled the rock in his hand to better select the perfect grip. He cocked his arm and steeled himself against a growing fear.

"Dewey, if that's you and the boys, come out now before someone gets hurt. This has gone far enough. I've got a rock and am liable to pop one of you right between the eyes."

There was no surprise in the lack of response. The threat was feigned, of course, a show of open defiance just to prove his mettle, if only to himself. The girls and the whiskey, neither of which had been previously experienced to any high degree of tolerance, had certainly captured the attention of his young friends. They were of no mind or condition for any concealed pursuit.

Morgan stooped down to gather a handful of pebbles and tossed them blindly into the weeds. They landed with no effect. He held his rock even tighter. It was all he could do to not throw it, too, and then run frantically for safety. The boy had fleet, long legs, and no man within 50 miles of Devlin had the quickness or endurance to overtake him. But the stealth of what lay hidden before him seemed beyond any human capability. Perhaps the speed was, too. He drew courage from the lessons of life, which were now reminding him that running from danger was not always the best way to avoid it. He steadied himself, resolving to be bold regardless of the consequence.

Those same lessons had taught him to perceive, especially when nature masked her details in darkness. So Morgan listened, smelled and strained to see, as he recalled the many quirks and traits of the forest denizens he had studied or encountered, all the while resisting that strong temptation to run.

He considered wild dogs or foxes. They were inquisitive, and more so, they were wily. He thought about smaller mammals or deer, which never would have followed in the first place. A night bird should have flushed from its cover the very moment he stopped to confront it, and a black bear, by now, would have committed its assault or retreated with indifference to the nearest grove.

Maybe it was wishful thinking, but he soon conceded that his pursuer was nothing but some small, insignificant creature or a harmless swarm of his own night jitters. Anything or nothing, whatever it was, it was certainly not worth his concern. But all was surmise, and Morgan became more frustrated than fearful when his knowledge of the forest failed to provide the answers.

There was one remaining option, inexplicably lost among the other considerations. Morgan's blood turned cold as he acknowledged the remote chance of it. The rock gave no defense, yet, he gripped it tightly. His legs offered no escape. Still, he stretched them in preparation for the sprint of his life. He backed away cautiously.

Morgan thought he heard a deep murmur, but only one, and in the ensuing quiet, he could not be certain whether it was actual or imagined. He edged away, one step at a time, pausing after each short stride to listen and better discern.

If it even existed, the animal was not advancing, and with every step backward, Morgan began to feel much more reassured. Another prank of the night had come and gone, he thought. He felt both foolish and relieved.

The lights of Devlin were a welcomed sight, and they emboldened Morgan. He turned one last time to look down the abandoned road, expecting either a noisy wagon full of old friends rolling his way or some wild creature skulking in the gloom. It was the latter that surprised him. The sleek form of a giant, long tailed cat eased across the lane and melted into the dark. Morgan rubbed the illusion from his eyes and hurried toward the sanctuary of the lights. He never suspected the greater peril ahead.

The mill was ghostly quiet, and its lumber yard, shrouded with blackness, loomed like a Cajun cemetery crammed with high, square crypts and eroding sandstone monuments. The train cars and engines sat heavy in their place along the siding, and the mill pond, filled to capacity, was choked dead with enormous logs. A few incandescent bulbs spilled dim light and cast ominous shapes across the scene. The stillness was all the more eerie in a place noted for bustle.

Morgan paused to collect his nerve. He could hear an occasional clang, probably from the distant machine shop, but there were no other sounds, neither man's nor nature's. Ignoring the trespass signs, he chose the straightest path toward home and set out across the expansive yard through the thin corridors lined with walls of lumber and shadow.

He did not see the small freight wagon parked at the other side until the brief glow of a match revealed three huddled faces. Morgan smelled an immediate waft of cigars, and as he neared the wagon, he observed that the men were so closely bunched on their seat that any one of them might fall upon the stirring of the others. The horses, like the men, seemed bored from their wait. Morgan passed without words.

"That was him, wasn't it?" The first voice was familiar.

"Hell, I don't know!" Morgan recognized the second, as well.

"Leon, you're a blind fool. Pay some attention for God's sake! We sit here waitin' the better part of an hour, and ya let him drift by like dust on air."

"Why pick on me, Farley? He's Darrow's kid. Don't Lawson even know his own boy when he sees him? And besides, what's wrong with yer eyes?"

Farley Ochs refused to argue. Arguments were exchanges between equals, and Farley had respect for no man. With a single hand, he grabbed Leon by the nape and lifted him from the center of the seat. Leon twisted and wiggled, and when finally free, he scrambled to the back of the wagon where he moped and cowered like a flailed puppy. The third man watched his companions with his usual feeling of contempt.

Farley turned his attention to Lawson Darrow. "Well, was that your boy, or not?"

Lawson stuttered, "I...I...I don't think so."

"Oh, come on! You know damn well it was. Who else would be comin' through here at this hour?"

Lawson found some courage. "No, it couldn't have been Morgan."

He knew better. Annie had told him where to find her son, anywhere between Avery's farm and Devlin, and she also mentioned how he tended to shortcut through the mill yard. She never expected that her husband would share the information, especially with the likes of Farley Ochs.

It was to be a meeting between a father and his child, a badly needed chance to forgive and forget, but Farley somehow imposed by offering to drive Lawson in search of the boy. He had a sinister motivation, of course, to have both his vengeance against Lowe Yancy and a lucrative role in the eventual harvest of the Big Timber. It seemed that Morgan Darrow was his only means to both, and it did not matter in the least that the boy was to be married the following day. With a little strategic pressure, a threat to his family or a light bruise or two against his ribs, Morgan would react like every other man Farley had confronted. But Lawson was finally sober, if only for a brief while, and for the first time, he saw clearly into the black soul of his associate. Even if it meant their partnership was forfeited, he would not betray his son.

"I don't know, but it isn't Morgan. Morgan knows better than to be on this property after dark. Besides, he was out with all of his friends. It just wasn't him. I'd expect him along the road over there, if he's coming at all. I told you, Farley, we should have waited farther up the way toward Avery's. We've probably missed Morgan altogether sitting around here."

Farley yelled back to Leon, "Get out and go see who that was."

"Don't bother," countered Lawson. "I'll jump off here, and if it is Morgan, I'll just walk back with him. Thanks for the ride."

"Get your ass back in this wagon! I've got my own business with the boy, and ya ain't gonna scare him off 'til he and I have our talk."

"Your business can wait for another couple days." Lawson lifted from his seat, and Farley forced him back down with a violent pull on his shoulder.

"Lawson Darrow, you're a sorry excuse for a man. Ya know that? You're a drunk, a liar, and now, I come to find out you're even a damn poor actor. Don't ya think I know what's goin' on? You're playin' me for a fool. I ain't gonna waste another second here. Instead, I think we'll head on up the hill and wait with your pretty wife until her son does get home. I expect she's honest and far too smart to ignore the consequence of bein' otherwise. But blast my memory, Lawson! I almost forgot. Annie ain't even your woman no more! Well, I guess that'll make it easy."

Farley waited and watched the anger envelop Lawson, but the smaller man was too slow reacting to the prod. Before Lawson could respond, Farley launched across the wooden seat and threw the great mass of his body into his side. Lawson tumbled through the air to the hard ground below.

The big man took his time. He reached beneath the seat and retrieved his coiled bull whip. "Yeah, I changed my mind. You do get off here. Our partnership is hereby dissolved. I can't abide disloyalty, and I absolutely despise the sot and snivelin' coward you turned out to be."

He cracked the whip above Lawson's head. "That boy of yours will sure enough lead me to what I want, and you and Lowe Yancy and everyone else can go straight to hell. Now, get out of my way!"

The next crack tore through Lawson's britches and left a bloody line across his calf. Lawson tried to stand, but another strike of the whip slashed across his arms as he raised them to guard his face. He fell back into the dirt. Farley lifted up with the reins in one hand and the whip in the other. He cracked it again and again as Lawson, rolling and crawling, inched his way closer to the wheel of the wagon. The man would not retreat.

"Farley, behind you! It's that boy!" Leon shouted out his warning, then settled low in the bed of the wagon to avoid the coming conflict.

Farley watched Lawson curl tightly in anticipation of another lash, then turned slowly to find Morgan Darrow only a few feet away.

"I thought that just might get your attention," said Farley, without emotion. "We have business."

Morgan leaned forward, his feet quite stable on the ground. His left fist was tense and locked at his side, while his right hand again maneuvered his jagged rock until it rested comfortably between his fingertips. He stood with cold confidence. His rage freed him from the hindrance of any rational consideration. His body, his future, his reputation, even his life was now irrelevant. Only the rage mattered, and he focused it, all of it, on Farley Ochs.

"You think so? Come down from there and let's get to it!"

Ochs reveled in the challenge. He threw back his arm, and the long braided whip trailed out behind him. With a powerful flick of the wrist, the leather popped dangerously close to Morgan's ear, but missed its mark altogether as the boy dove headlong beneath the wagon box. Morgan resurfaced almost instantly on the other side, while Farley, limited by his crippled hand, scrambled to gather the weapon for a more effective assault.

"He's over here!" cried Leon.

Farley's huge legs were crammed into the confined space at the front of the wagon, and it was all he could do to keep his balance. A reflexive reach for the high back of the seat failed to brace him, and he teetered but for a brief moment. Morgan seized the opportunity and with all his might, catapulted the rock toward the rump of Farley's lead horse. The wagon lunged, and the big man tumbled over and over, backward and downward, until he lay still in a drifting cloud of dust. Leon screamed for mercy as the spooked team carried him deeper and deeper into the dark.

Morgan wasted no time finishing the fight. He knew that once he stunned the viper, he had to kill it or wait to be poisoned. He leapt on his assailant's chest, and grabbing the thick lapel of Farley's coat, he lifted him up just to send him back into the dirt. His fist landed hard against Farley's jaw. His hands gripped tightly to Farley's red hair and ears, as he violently shook the man's oversized head.

"Morgan!" Lawson was crossing the ground on his knees. "Morgan, the man is done. Let it go."

Morgan hesitated, but rose up forcefully and unexpectedly. With unbridled strength, he drove both fists into the hulk beneath him, and then he simply crumbled upon the body of his foe.

"I've killed him," he said. "My Lord! I have killed this man."

"Are you okay, son?"

"Pa, did you not hear me? I have killed Farley Ochs."

"Oh, I seriously doubt that. You can't kill the devil, but even if you did, not one soul within a thousand miles of here would fault you."

Morgan took an extra deep breath and pulled away from Farley. When he did, the big man moaned unconsciously.

"Well, thank you, God," uttered the boy. "I thought for a moment that he was…."

"I know, son. We'll just be grateful he's alive, whether he deserves to be or not."

Morgan rose to his feet and offered a hand to his father. They clenched wrists, and he pulled him up.

"And you, Pa, how are you?"

"In some ways, never better. Ochs would have whipped me to pieces if not for you."

Morgan noted a difference in the person before him. His father had somehow lost his anger. There was now warmth in his face and softness in his tone. Morgan remembered such a man from childhood, and that brief, fond memory now sweetened the bitter years that followed. Forgiveness came easy.

"It's good to have you home."

"That means everything to me right now. I've messed things pretty good."

"Past is past," Morgan said, reassuringly. "Right now, we've got Ochs to worry about. He may be breathing, but his back could be broken for all we know. I'd best fetch Doc Brown."

"Wait. He'll tell us soon enough what he wants."

Lawson was right. Farley Ochs groaned. He was contorted, almost mangled on the hard-packed ground, but never attempted as much as a twitch until he had silently evaluated the extent of his injury. He grunted and moaned some more and eventually opened his eyes. He slowly rolled over and struggled unsuccessfully to lift himself from the ground. It was not his wounds but his weight that burdened him. With blurred vision, he saw the two men standing and staring.

"You're dead. You are both dead," he said coldly, assuming full control of their fate. He was beaten and bruised, but the viper still had potent venom. It would strike again, next time without warning.

"Are you all right, Ochs?" Lawson asked.

"Get the hell out of here!"

Farley made it difficult to feel compassion, and Lawson would not force the issue. "Seems like sound advice to me. Let's go, Morgan. Let him lie there in the filth all night, if he wants to. It's a proper place for snakes."

"What do we do about Leon?"

"What do you want to do? I say we let nature or Farley deal with him, but I don't rightly care."

Morgan wondered about the mountain lion. He was still not sure what his eyes had seen. He cautioned Farley, who was now sitting upright, swatting the dust from his clothes. "You had best find your friend. That road out there can be a dangerous place."

Farley scowled. "I'll see to my own. Don't you worry none about that. Just remember to watch your back, boy, 'cause that's where I plan to be the very minute ya forget."

Morgan took his father by the arm and steadied him, as Lawson limped away from the mill. It was a slow walk, intentionally slow, and it offered them precious time to be as they needed to be, a father with a son, a man to a man.

"Pa, would you mind telling me something? What in the world are you doing with the likes of those two?"

Lawson had anticipated the question. "We were in business together."

"So I heard, a survey business, but there's got to be a lot more to it than that. You don't know a single thing about surveying, and using Farley Ochs as an example, you apparently know even less about the quality of men."

"I don't blame you for your opinion. I had my reasons."

"I wouldn't mind hearing them."

"Well, with all that's happened lately, I believe you're entitled. I know how you feel about your work with Yancy and Clark. I was disappointed when you didn't take to my trade, so I thought I'd take to yours. Partly, I wanted to share in your new life, but to be more honest, I wanted to take something back from Lowe Yancy. I've been searching my soul and am finding it hard to admit all of this. I see how close those men have grown to you and your Ma, and frankly, whether it's justified or not, it makes me despise Yancy."

"You despise him?"

"Yeah, I do. I've come to understand him more clearly now that I've given up the drink, but in some ways, I dislike and fear him all the more. He's a better man than I am, Morgan. That's the plain truth of it, and I'm ashamed. He's able to take from me without the slightest intention or malice, and I've grown to hate him for what has really never been his fault. And my business with Farley Ochs? It was just pure vengeance. I'm a man of poor character, son, but I still have enough to want to set things right. I sure hope that, in time, you can understand this."

"I can try, Pa. I will try, but right now, I need to get you over to Doc Brown's." The blood had soaked through Lawson's torn shirt and britches.

"Don't bother. Your Ma can fix me up just fine."

"Yeah? That's assuming she's willing. Have you had time to patch things with her?"

"Not enough, but I'm working on it. I've been sober for weeks, and I think she knows that the whiskey was the only real problem between us. Your mother is an understanding woman. She'll soon trust that I've changed."

"But you changed before, Pa, time and again. We all know what the alcohol does to you, and we've felt the pain you brought to this family."

"You speak your mind. I'll say that for you. Those days are over, Morgan. They're behind us. I ask you to forgive me and let me prove myself."

"It's not just Ma and me, you know. You have a lot to make up for with Cora and Jake."

"I know that, especially Jake. It'll take some time, but I'll make it all good if it takes the rest of my life."

"Well, you will always be my father. No matter what might come between us, I'll try to respect you for that. But I don't speak for Ma. You've hurt her deeply, and she's finally found her a life that again brings her joy."

"She's found another man. Is that what you're telling me?"

"No, I'm telling you that she's learning to live contently without her man."

Lawson's face reddened. "There is someone else. I understand that, and I think we both know who he is. She's cutting me out to make room for another."

"Like I said, I don't speak for Ma, and I won't speak about her, other than to say she's deserving of her happiness."

Lawson was broken with jealousy, but even more so, he was determined to win back Annie's favor. It would require the untested power of his will, a level of calm and self-restraint that he had never before sustained. He wanted Morgan's blessing. He needed all of his children's love and support. They were to be the intermediaries in his quest for the heart of his wife.

"Pa, I assume you've got a room here in town. It's best I take you there. I'll tend to your leg if you won't see the doctor. You have to understand, it's not my place to bring you back into the home. Ma has to do that in her own time."

"I suppose you're right. I have to be patient. I owe her that."

The men continued toward a boarding house at the far side of town, and they talked honestly, rebuilding the bond that Lawson had recklessly broken. Morgan welcomed the return of his father, even if Lawson could not keep the promises he so earnestly vowed to fulfill. But Morgan seriously doubted that there was any hope for a reconciliation of his parents. There was no healing, only a numbness to their pain. Annie would not be as welcoming as her son.

"I'd like to be at your wedding, Morgan. It's a new start at life for both of us. I'd hate to miss it. Your mother said I should ask."

"She didn't care?"

"She said it was your decision to make."

Morgan thought for an instant. He was not sure how his family and friends would react, but he was quite certain that this one moment of trust was critical to the fragile relationship between him and his father.

"Sure, Pa, you come, but you leave the whiskey behind. That's all I ask."

"Son, I've been sober and I will be sober. God strike me dead if I'm not."

# CHAPTER 23

Jacob squirmed. The hard wooden seat and scratchy, stiff shirt were almost too much for a boy to bear. He pulled against the knot of his new tie and started thumping his feet against the back of the next pew. Annie calmed him instantly with a firm squeeze of his forearm, and he was forced to settle and simply endure his discomfort. But his mind would not rest, and Jacob took meager pleasure in realizing that no one, especially his mother, could actually subjugate his thoughts. His imagination was his own, and he was determined to let it run just as long as the woman remained so adamant on stifling his movement.

Jacob watched as the minister of First Methodist Church attended to one last detail before the ceremony. The man, dressed all in black except for the white of his cleric's collar, carried books to the lectern, and then passed to a side room without any acknowledgement of those gathering in the sanctuary.

The boy looked up at the altar and wondered what it would be like to become a preacher, a question that had crossed his mind on numerous occasions. It seemed to be the perfect job, more so than a host of other vocations he had recently considered, such as cavalryman, sailor, train engineer or Indian. They were each a worthy endeavor that, after some extensive role playing and analysis, somehow left him wanting for better opportunity. He was finally homing in on what was essential to him and felt he might well be ready to make a career decision after observing the pastor's upcoming performance at the wedding.

Jacob Darrow never delivered so much as a single sermon, or laid wet hands on a baby's head in the course of a baptism, or administered last rites to the nearly dead, not even in play. Preachers, from his limited perspective, dabbled in these on a regular basis, but did little else. Still, they seemed to enjoy an immense amount of prestige and power and wealth. Therein was the attraction.

Preachers were leaders. Whether the mayor or the doctor, whether the constable or his teacher, whether his mother or anyone else, everyone in authority over him seemed earnestly attentive to that man of the cloth. There were other benefits, of course. Preachers were allowed their special garb, and during communion, they drank amply from a fancy silver cup. They could walk freely beyond the long church altar rail, and they alone decided which hymns would be sung. No one else seemed so entitled. But it was the prestige and the power and the wealth that made all the difference to Jacob Darrow. On each and every Sunday, his minister was presented with four or five huge plates full of money, and if the pay was not sufficiently alluring, there was one advantage that surpassed all others. Preachers preached and people listened in fear of dire consequence. That was true power, a mighty inducement to Jacob's way of thinking. It was the perfect job, and the boy wondered why more men did not find it so.

The oak pew was cruelly ungiving, and Jacob had little natural padding to provide relief. It was bone upon board, or so it felt, and the aching now called for change. He squirmed and shifted again, simultaneously wrenching his neck to sneak a peek at the crowd forming silently behind him. There was another pulse of pressure applied to his arm, and his impatience began to boil his mind like a fever, until it bubbled over with a million inane questions. Some, he posed to his mother. Most, he kept to himself. All remained unanswered.

"Just where in the world is Morgan? He's supposed to be here. And when is this stupid weddin' stuff ever gonna start? We've been waitin' forever."

"Sh-sh-sh!" responded Annie. "And mind your language. It's only been a few minutes."

Jacob's small feet began to kick back and forth in place, as the tension intensified and more and more questions popped into his head.

"Who's that sittin' right behind me?" he thought. "I swear I know him. I can hear the man breathe, but I can't quite make him out. Why doesn't the fool say somethin'?" The boy started to twist around and see for himself, but Annie's stern look checked him.

"Why do I, of all people, have to sit up front in the second row with this woman? She's bein' so unreasonable. And, someone please tell me why the church even put in a first row, when no one, absolutely no one, tries to sit there. Oh, brother! Since today is Saturday, will Mama make me go through all of this again tomorrow?" The last question was especially disconcerting. "Mama?"

"Sh-sh-sh!"

"But, Mama, do we have to go to church again tomorrow?"

"Yes, and be thankful."

As if the pew was not punishment enough, the empty questions came relentlessly, one upon the other, and without answers, they consumed his precious, young mind with nothing more than anxiety. Jacob could not bear it.

"Mama," he whispered, this time nuzzling her ear. "I need to visit the necessary."

"Be still, Jacob."

"Mama, really, I need to go, bad!"

"You just went before we sat down. Now be still."

"But...." Jacob used the discussion as an excuse to wiggle and stand, and while pleading his case, he glanced across the beautiful white room and saw a hundred friendly faces. He waved to all of them.

"Sit down, Jacob," Annie commanded quietly, with a show of unwavering forbearance. "It won't be long now, I promise." She pulled on the back of his britches, and the boy fell into his proper place on the pew.

Seconds passed like hours. Jacob fidgeted. When three strangers stepped into view toting musical instruments, he arose, and he watched curiously as the men, all in matching morning coats, moved up the side aisle of the church and took their seats near the choir loft. There soon came a sound rarely heard in Jacob's valley, from large fiddles rarely seen. It was the harmonic blends of Pachelbel, the mellow moans of the viola, violin and cello, which ultimately quieted the boy. Jacob, like everyone who listened, surrendered to the entrancing notes of the string trio.

As if by miracle or some planned theatrical design, a ray of the sun's noon light suddenly reflected through the Tiffany window. It dabbed the colors of fine cut glass, reds, blues and golds, across the altar and around the large pine cross that adorned the facing wall. Jacob was dazzled. Nothing could be more beautiful, he thought. And then, he saw Sarah standing in the flickering glow of the wedding candles, holding tightly to the hand of his brother.

All went as expected: the vows, the teary eyes and the kiss. As Mr. and Mrs. Morgan Darrow raced down the steps of the First Methodist Church, they waved to a throng of well-wishers and headed straight for the personal limousine of Charles Devlin. The car was a gift for the day, which included a professional chauffeur, a chilled magnum of champagne and a dozen long stem roses selected from Devlin's own greenhouse. The couple sped happily away in style, barely noticing the old mule and cart that Dewey had arranged for the occasion.

It was a prank, of course. The cart had seen its better days. One wheel was warped and now wobbled with every quarter turn, and the other squeaked incessantly as it pivoted on an ungreased hub. Flakes of faded blue paint clung stubbornly to the sides of the wagon box, revealing the original color, while fresh white letters spelled out Dewey's messages of the day, "Morgan and Sarah, Hiched This Day" and "Best O' Luck, Mrs. Darrow." Twenty tin cans with labels intact and a pair of Dewey's old boots were strung from long cords at the rear, just beneath a rude sign that read "Stay Back, Shotgun Wedding in Progress."

Unfortunately, the mule that was to pull the cart, though

physically fit for service, was not inclined to provide it. Noggin stood head down and slumped, a reflection of his unconscionable and utter humiliation. A yellow sun bonnet, adorned with ribbon and strategically slit to accommodate his long, hairy ears, topped his oversized head. Pink and blue streamers decorated both his harness and bridle, and a shiny brass bell dangled from his neck. Past experiences with wagons had made an unfavorable impression on the animal, and while occasional work was to be tolerated, this particular mule held strong opinion about hauling people he thought too lazy to move themselves. It was a task beneath his dignity, and he was loath to be cooperative. Or so it would seem.

It was Principal Tutwiler who eventually asked the question of Dewey, "Mr. Baughman, is this cart of your doing?"

"Yes, sir, it is," responded Dewey.

"And the signs?"

"Yes, sir, they're mine. I did all of it."

"I see. Well, young man, I suppose I am ultimately responsible for the accuracy of your spelling. How is it that I neglected to teach you how to write the word 'hitched?'"

"What?"

"'Hitched,' as in 'I have *hitched* the mule to the cart,' or 'hitched,' as in 'Morgan and Sarah, *Hitched* This Day.'"

Dewey was stunned. He scrambled to the side of the cart.

"Lordy, Mr. Tutwiler, this here's a mistake, just a minor oversight. I know how to spell 'hitched.' Believe me, I just forgot the 'T' in the rush."

For that moment, Dewey was back in grade school begging for his mark. The principal reveled in the irony.

"I would hope so, but, nevertheless, I expect to see you first thing Monday morning. In cases like this, the law is very clear that we have to re-evaluate and possibly keep you for another whole year."

"What!"

Dewey's mouth dropped with both disappointment and disbelief, while Mr. Tutwiler struggled to maintain his typically sober expression. He was actually very proud of his mischief, rarely having a chance to display the trait. He knew that the opportunity for some friendly but just reprisal would not likely come again.

"Surely, you know that I am jesting," said Tutwiler, uncertain of the truth. "As I recall, you received a diploma certifying your ability to spell. I doubt the school board wants it, or you, back at this point. You are safe to write as you wish." The principal tipped his hat. "All in good fun, Mr. Baughman. All in good fun."

Dewey sighed in relief. "Good one, sir. For a second, ya had me."

"It was more than any second, according to my watch." The principal pulled out a tarnished gold pocket watch, one that Dewey had seen for so many years under the man's caring tutelage. The time piece often would rest on the desk, audibly ticking away the minutes that Dewey would serve in punishment on the stool of shame at the front corner of the classroom.

"Yes, sir, I know better than to argue with that watch."

"Good. I taught you something anyway, and lest I forget, that cart of yours...."

"The cart?"

"Yes, that cart. I think it is a nice piece of work."

Dewey was gratified. He suddenly realized how much he appreciated the old teacher.

"Thanks. Nothin's too good for Morgan and his bride, sir. A king's coronation calls for a chariot, don't ya think?"

"That it does, Mr. Baughman. Well said."

While onlookers were amused by the rickety wedding cart, no one, including Dewey, was really surprised when Morgan and Sarah passed it by. Morgan paused just long enough to acknowledge the effort.

"Good try! We'll take the motor car, if it's all the same to you."

"Smart idea. Have ya got extra room for me and Auralee?"

"Auralee can come along if she wants, but someone has to drive this 'chariot.' The mule is not about to lead himself to some place he's never been. We'll meet you at the reception. Don't be long."

Before Dewey could reply, Sarah had whisked her man away,

and the two disappeared in the rising dust of the road. Dewey reluctantly climbed up and onto the cart, and spotting Silas Monk in the crowd, he summoned the old man near.

Silas took one look at his mule and laughed. "I been seekin' a proper hat fer this here animal nigh on 10 years, but ne'er could find one he fancied. Jist lookin' at

'im, he ain't too thrilled with this'n neither. Good luck, boy! Noggin don't cotton much to wagons, and he downright hates the folks that drive 'em. Too bad ya ain't got one o' them apples with ya. That trick worked real fine down thar at the mill pond."

"Ya wanna ride, Mr. Monk?" Dewey asked, almost begging. He wanted help handling the mule.

"Nah, not a chance. I got me a party o'er yonder, and I believe I'll jist walk so's to actually git thar. I'll save ya some supper though." Silas began to walk away, but stopped with an afterthought, "Young fella, you can shoot that animal if ya git a hankerin'. No need to wait fer a reason. Noggin'll give ya one soon 'nough."

The wedding goers mounted their carriages or filed down wooden walks toward the Dabney house, while Dewey sat alone with Noggin. The mule was neither prone to forgive nor inclined to cooperate, and Dewey waited impatiently for a change in mood. His stomach rumbled all the while, and before too long, he wished he had a gun.

The sky was clear and the air warm for an October afternoon, a day that only autumn can offer. Sarah had been anxious about the weather and insisted that a long tent be erected in the yard for the reception. Between the large parlors of the house and the temporary arrangements on the grounds, everyone would at least have shelter if the heavens turned against her. As it was, the tent was an unnecessary expenditure, and Sarah regretted her extravagance. Her father assuaged her guilt with a strong hug and reminded her that he had the money. She was his only daughter, after all, and this was her day. Nothing should be spared to make it right.

In that regard, the string trio was a tasteful touch. Baroque played softly to the delight of many who were not familiar with such refinement in music, and after a generous country supper, complimented with enticing hors d'oeuvres and delicacies, the waltzes began. It was an unplanned change in program, and Sarah recognized the altered tempo immediately. She looked to the trio, but saw only couples rising from their seats and gathering at the edge of the open lawn. The guests waited and watched as Morgan rose from his chair and sheepishly stood before his bride.

"Sarah, a promise is a promise, and we never had that dance. I can't think of a better time than now, can you?" He held out his hand. "Hurry, girl, before I lose my nerve."

"But you don't know how...I mean...I mean you don't like to dance, so I didn't plan...."

"But I did plan, and this is just for you."

Sarah bounded from the table to the center of the lawn and beamed with joy as Morgan took her hand and waist. He moved her to the rhythm of the strings. Her gown was full, and as their feet tripped lightly over thick green grass, it lifted and alighted with the breeze of their motion. Morgan never missed a step, showing perfect finesse. Sarah marveled as she glided effortlessly in the strength of his arms.

Annie looked on with both satisfaction and envy. The very first dance - the enduring fantasy of it, the innocent beauty of it, the indelible power of it. It was the symbol of a new and honest love, and it was Annie's gift to Sarah. For days, she had drilled her awkward partner in the art of the waltz, until Morgan found his form and confidence. He added his own passion, and Sarah now melted in the moment. Just watching, Annie felt the same.

"They are certainly a lovely couple, Mrs. Lawson," Lowe said, having slipped unseen behind her.

"They are that, Lowe." Her misty eyes twinkled.

"Morgan once told me he couldn't dance a lick, but look at that boy now."

"Yes, he said the same to me. That was his mistake."

"Hardly a mistake, if those big smiles are any indication. It's evident Morgan had an excellent instructor."

"Why thank you, Mr. Yancy."

The waltz continued, and others began to join in. The two stood idly to the side, admiring the dancers and silently wishing to be among them, together. But neither would express that desire, nor break faith with the conventions that had kept them apart. It was a hopeless admission. They had missed their turn. For some, there could never be a first dance.

"And you, Lowe, do you like to dance?"

"Nothing so fancy as this, ma'am."

"I can remedy that, you know." She pointed to Morgan.

Lowe blushed. "Oh, Annie, I'd rather you not try, for your own sake."

"For my sake?"

"Trust me. *Clumsy* doesn't begin to describe me on a dance floor. A woman, as elegant and beautiful as you are today...." Intending no flattery, he became more embarrassed with every word of praise. "Well, I just mean that a fine lady deserves a whole lot better than a three-footed toad hopping all over her."

Annie laughed lightly. Her guests were watching, and while her heart encouraged otherwise, it was perhaps best that she avoid dancing with this particular man. She could not think clearly. She was conflicted with emotions - her pride in her children, her growing fondness for Lowe and her unyielding anger toward Lawson. Lawson was still her legal husband. He had his rights as such, at least for a while longer, and regardless of his behavior toward his family, the community still had their expectations of marriage. She gazed at Lowe's warm, weathered face, and in an instant, none of that seemed to matter.

What did matter was Lowe, himself. He was vulnerable. He was like a child lost and wounded in the woods, clinging to trees when he should be finding his way to refuge. Whoever would come to guide him, whoever would deliver him from his years of memory and pain, must be prepared for strong, enduring love. He was that kind of man. What little he cherished, he cherished deeply. To lead him, to save him, Annie would have to be that kind of woman, and through the cloud of her own failed relationship, she could not be certain. Lowe was smart to avoid her. A dance, clumsy or not, might take them too far from where they rightly should be.

"Oh, all right, I'll not press you," she said. "You are very kind, Mr. Yancy, and I doubt there would be much hopping about with the right woman in your arms."

Shocked by her own audacity but glad to finally divulge some small piece of her secret affection, she leaned over and kissed him quickly on the cheek. Lowe's face reddened with pleasure, and with boyish, bashful pride, he turned it away to hide his awkwardness. It was an endearing trait, even for a man his age.

The diverse ability of the string trio became even more evident when the violin turned fiddle and the cello and viola began to wail a familiar mountain harmony. The people cheered, and before the first song was ended, two other fiddles, a dulcimer and banjo, a mandolin and squeeze box, a harmonica and jug were all added to the band. Everyone seemed to play something, and in the real tradition of the mountains, they came to the party ready and raring.

"Looks like you've been saved, Lowe," said Annie. She swayed to the new rhythm.

"Yes, ma'am, for now anyway."

"So, do you play?"

"Play, like an instrument? Like the fiddle or banjo?" Lowe recalled the soulful sound produced by Lawson's fiddle and regretted that he could not offer a different answer. "Not a lick, Annie. I have absolutely no musical talent."

"Good!" she replied simply, choosing to provide no explanation.

Irwin Dabney interrupted their conversation, "All right, Annie Darrow, you've been hiding over here long enough. We can't let these children of ours completely show us up. I've ordered us a slower tune or two and would be honored if you would share a dance with me."

She looked at Lowe, and he nodded as though he had staked

some claim to her time. It was not intentional, but Dabney noted something in the gesture and qualified his request.

"That is, of course, if Mr. Yancy is willing to spare you."

"Certainly," responded Lowe.

"Wonderful! But, Yancy, I may not return her."

"I would expect not. This is your party. You two should enjoy it."

Lowe was gracious, but far from content being so. It had been a long, long time since he last felt envy. He did not like it then, and he hated it now. He slipped away to the quiet of the house and poured himself a drink.

Dewey reached the reception in time to offer a champagne toast, but nearly spit his sip back into the glass. The refined tastes of the gentry were questionable, he thought, if such stinky wine was indeed their pleasure. He did not venture another sip, and following the toast, he moved directly to the food. Morgan came to join him.

"Those were some fine sentiments, Dewey. They mean a lot to Sarah and me. I was beginning to wonder, but I'm glad you finally made your way from the church. Did you bring the cart?"

"Yeah, but no thanks to that damn mule. I guess I'm the last one here, huh?"

"Not the last. There's still one who hasn't shown."

Dewey understood the tone of Morgan's voice. "Your Pa?"

"Yeah."

"He might make it, yet."

"I don't think so. He missed the wedding, and that's the part a father should see."

"Well, he could be laid up. Even you said he was hurt purdy bad last night in that scuffle by the wagon."

"He's laid up all right, but not from any fight."

Dewey set down his fork and leaned toward his friend. "I'm real sorry, Morgan. I know what his bein' here would've meant to ya and to your family."

"I'm sorry, too. I was hoping today could be a new start for all of us, but I was wrong."

"And your Ma, Jake and Cora, how they takin' it?"

"Ma hasn't said a single word. The others were never led to expect him, so they at least haven't been disappointed. They think he's still out of town. For that matter, Ma knew the man wouldn't come in the first place, and I think she's just as content having him gone. It's over between the two of them, especially after today."

"Damn. Damn, I hate to hear that. Is she all right?"

"Best I can tell."

"And you?"

"Just look over there at my Sarah, and then ask me that same question again."

Dewey peered across the crowd of guests and caught a glimpse of the bride. Her smile and happiness warmed the air.

"Yeah, I reckon you'll survive. So, 'bout yer Pa, what ya think really happened?"

"This may sound cold, Dewey, but today I just won't care. Maybe tomorrow I'll let myself feel differently, but in the meantime, the man doesn't exist. It's best that way for all of us."

It was time to move to a new subject, and Dewey did so masterfully. "Hey, I went to a lot of effort. Are ya gonna ride that cart or not?"

Morgan answered with a look.

"I didn't think so," continued Dewey. "Mind ya, it don't bother me none. That stupid mule wouldn't take ya nowhere's if ya did ride, and I can't see Sarah, pretty as she is, climbin' on that rickety ol' seat."

"If it doesn't bother you, then why on earth did you go to so much trouble?" Morgan asked.

"My answer could be a long one."

"I'm all ears for about the next 60 seconds. Give me the short version."

"All right, since ya asked for it. Weddin's are just funerals without the bodies in a box, and to me, both tend to end up as a couple highfalutin parties where folks are too damn mindful of their manners. There's a lot of fancy dressin', a ton of fancy food and a good deal more of the fancy talk. Unfortunately, we gotta be either happy or sad, one or the other, and there ain't much tolerance for a display of different type feelin's on such occasions. I stand behind marriage, but a weddin' can be a bit stuffy with all that predictable behavior. Maybe the air is just too heavy with all them memories floatin' around, I don't know, but too many people end up cryin'. Think on it, Morgan. A proper buryin's got everythin' a hitchin's got: tasty food, strong drink, fine music and lively dancin'. It's got everythin', except after a funeral, some poor soul ain't goin' back home. It's all too serious for my taste."

"And the cart?"

"Oh, that's what's generally missin'. It's the one thing that doesn't fit with all the day's finery and misery, and it gives folks somethin' silly to think on for a spell. It's the laugh, or the reason to laugh, and if we don't laugh, it ain't really much of a party. Important as they are, weddin's and funerals should be the best of parties, don't ya think?"

Morgan was dumbfounded. His friend, a bit doltish to many, had somehow transformed a dilapidated old cart into the royal carriage, and with only his words. There was obviously more to the man than even his best friend had realized. In essence, Dewey was laughter itself, and Morgan suddenly questioned whether his way of levity and tomfoolery might to some extent be intentional. The cart certainly was. He wondered.

"When you put it that way, who could complain about a decorated old mule and broken-down wagon?"

"Well, they ain't much to look at."

"It's the thought that counts," Morgan said. "And you've apparently given this matter lots of thought. That cart's starting to grow on me, to tell you the truth. Sarah and I will surely remember it."

Dewey picked up his fork and began to eat again. For a few moments, the two friends were just sitting together, feasting on cake and watching the merriment of others. When his plate was cleared, Dewey asked his final question, "So, my friend, are ya gonna get around to tellin' me just where ya plan to honeymoon?"

He stared with hopeful eyes, waiting to be entrusted, while Morgan took his time formulating an answer.

The reply was emphatic. “Nope.”

Decorum, as best he understood it, told Silas to stop when he reached the threshold of the big parlor. He checked his shoes for dirt, a courtesy he had forgotten when he first entered the Dabney residence. He lifted his left leg to his right knee, then his right leg to his left knee, and examined the bottoms of both feet. It was an amazing show of balance for a man of his age, and he finished his routine by polishing the heels and toes against the fabric of his clean britches. Such an effort was never exerted, or even necessary, at his cabin in Jasper Hollow.

Silas found Lowe halfway across the parlor, standing by a large brick fireplace. There were two or three others in the room, but Lowe remained to himself, apparently perusing a collection of photographs and tintypes neatly assembled on the mantel. Next to him was a low sideboard, set with a punch bowl and glasses and a generous assortment of expensive liquors. Silas was curious about the liquors.

Lowe had helped himself to Irwin Dabney’s brandy, which he found to be sweet and not at all to his liking. When Silas pulled the glass from his hand and stole a sip, Lowe was actually relieved.

“Finish it,” Lowe said.

“Umm, I will,” Silas sounded his approval. “What is this?”

“French brandy.”

“French, huh. Good stuff, but it ain’t gonna win no contest against my own corn liquor.” He held up the glass to examine the color. “Tres bon, Monsieur Dabney. C’est merveilleux. La saveur est delicieux. Merci pour la liqueur.” He consumed the remainder of the brandy.

“What was that all about?” asked an astonished Lowe Yancy.

“Jist expressin’ my appreciation.”

“In French? At least I think that’s French. It’s a bit hard to tell while it slips off that hill country tongue of yours. But Silas, I am flat out astounded. Good Lord! Just when you think you know someone, he begins to speak another whole language. It's a tough one to figure."

"That thar was Canadian. Back in the war, I tented fer a spell with a feller from the Provinces. He and a few others was all that was left of a busted up Lou'siana brigade, and they talked that way back and forth all the time I's with 'em. One o' them boys could dice up a buzzard and convince ya that it were prime beef he put in yer stew. His kettle smelled o' sweet sausage and blended peppers every supper, and when yer only other choice gave off the stink o' smoke or boilin' flour, ya hustled up to grab yer place in line. Ya didn't ask 'bout the meat and ya didn't much care. He were that good a cook. Only problem was, supply was short and he was thar to serve them Frenchies. Real quick like, I learned me a few words from that boy in the tent."

"I'm rather surprised to hear of such a northern man joining the Confederate Army."

"Well, I reckon he come from the south side o' Quebec. He was kin to the Cajuns down in them Mississippi bayous, and jist like in Virginia, good families fight their meanest fights together. From what I heared at the time, none o' them Canadians could abide a Yankee any more than us Rebs could." Silas smelled the brandy from the rim of his empty glass. "This sure is one smooth swig and a swallow. Got more?"

Lowe pointed to the table.

"Great day in the mornin'!" exclaimed Silas. He began to lift each bottle to see the labels. "Which one's the one we jist had?"

"Try that crystal decanter."

Silas poured his own glass of brandy, and after a sustained sip, he smacked his lips and coughed. "Yeah, good." He sidled closer to the mantel and in dim light, began to study a portrait photograph of a young woman. "I s'pose this here is Miss Sarah," he said. His vision was not too clear. "She's a beauty."

"No, I expect that's Sarah's mother. I was admiring her, as well. You can sure see the similarity between the two, except Sarah's got that lovely yellow hair."

"Yessiree, they's both purdy as a couple o' high meadow daisies. And I'll show ya yet one other li'l gal that can turn some heads. That Annie Darrow's quite the spring breeze. If I were a younger man...."

"And she wasn't married," added Lowe.

"O' course! That need not be said. If I were a younger man and she weren't no married woman, I'd come a courtin' with the moon hitched high, a soft song in my heart and a passel o' promises, every single one to keep. That's what I'd be doin'."

"And what about Lawson Darrow?"

"Who?"

"The husband."

"Oh, I already said 'if she weren't married.' You know, I cain't fer the life o' me figure that sorry son of a sow man of 'ers. He seems like a decent 'nough feller, but he is either dumb as dirt or jist black hearted. The man has it all and wants none o' it. Why don't he let the poor woman be so she can git on with 'er life?"

"I suppose he loves her."

"Ha! That don't fit with my way o' lookin' at it."

"Nor mine, to tell you the truth."

Silas pondered for a second. "Ya know, I think Miss Annie takes a li'l shine to ya."

"You think?"

"Sure do. I reckon she'll be feelin' a bit lonely once this fancy soiree fizzles. A decent, solid kind o' feller could do 'er some real good."

Lowe shook his head. "I'll say it again, 'She's married'."

"She is indeed, but I ain't sure to what or fer how long. Bide yer time and cut lose that other gal ya been totin' around inside ya all these years."

"Silas, feelings are what they are, and they don't simply change because people want them to. You sound more and more like Black Jack."

"Yeah, I do, and Black Jack is a right smart feller. If ya ask me, yer soundin' like yer scared. One li'l woman beat ya up, and now yer afraid that others have in mind to do the same. But yer wrong 'bout that, and what's more, ya know yer wrong. I seen the peck she give ya. Annie Darrow's done stoked yer dyin' fire jist as sure as yer here denyin' it. If Lawson don't want 'er no more, ya might jist show 'er a proper life. She'd be right fer ya."

"Old man, is it just my business or do you sometimes tend to your own?"

"You are my business, boy, remember? Give some thought to Annie Darrow. I got me a feelin' 'bout the two o' ya."

Lowe was exasperated, but his friends were right. He was hopelessly locked to his past, while Annie seemed to be the only one who might hold a key. Whether or not she would share that key and whether or not he even wanted to find that lock, these were disquieting doubts.

Having said what he wanted to say, Silas tapped Lowe on the center of his chest. "You'll figure it. I reckon me and Noggin'll be headin' out soon. It's a long way up the hollow.

"It's still early."

"Yeah, I know, but these days I cain't seem to find my dancin' legs or my ridin' eyes. That trail gits treacherous after dark."

"Just hold onto the mule. Noggin can get you home."

"Could if he would, but thar's no tellin' what he's of a mind to do."

"If that's the case, why not stay over with me and Jack? I can get a cot."

"I'm obliged, Lowe, but Black Jack said he'd like to ride a ways with me, so we'd better git jumpin'. I reckon I can convince 'im to lay o'er at the cabin fer a night or two. What ya think?"

"I imagine so."

"So, yer on yer own. We've wished the boy and his bride our best, and it's time to git on. Ya got them two all set with supplies and maps?"

"Everything's together. I just have to load Blu and have him ready tomorrow morning."

"What time they settin' out?"

"There's a run at eleven. I expect they'll catch that one. It'll give them a little extra time to enjoy the morning." Silas snickered with a carnal thought, and Lowe rebuked him. "That's not at all what I was talking about."

"I know. Damn my mind. Half the time it don't work at all. The other half, it's jist plain wrong. But, hey, I can still remember that first mornin' when I woke to the sound o' Emma Lynn Pitzenbarger jist snorin' up a storm in my ear. She was Mrs. Emma Monk at that particular time, havin' jist undergone them weddin' vows. Lordy, that woman could make a noise, and to a feller brand spankin' new in marriage, it was a serious omen that come along too late to do 'im much good.

"But, Lowe, how's a man to know such things? That woman ne'er let so much as a breath touch 'er before she got my ring, and even then, she put me off fer another half day or so. She 'bout drove me mad holdin' out like that, but come mornin' after the weddin', all her snorin' stopped kind o'sudden like, and she commenced to learn this ol' boy a thing or two. Mind ya, son, I'd been to war. And I'd seen more red light than just the flash o' cannon fire, if ya git my meanin'. Whew! Emma, Emma. My mind ain't been the same since the day I married that gal."

Lowe listened intently. Silas' stories had a way of cheering the soul, and it made little difference if they were true.

"I tell ya, Lowe, she grew into a right tough ol' bird after that. Did I e'er share the story 'bout when she loaded the shotgun and run me out a my own bed? Dreamed I had me a whore, she did, right thar in the room. She pointed to 'er own deep dent in the straw o' the mattress, still warm, and swore she was gonna kill the hussy that left it thar. She weren't gonna abide no stranger sparkin' 'er man, 'specially not under that thar roof or 'neath them thar covers. Nosiree, she meant to lay a mortal consequence upon the whore. I thought on that a good deal since, and thar was many a time I wished she had jist gone on and shot the wench."

Lowe finally interrupted, "What happened to your need to get on the road?"

The old man paused momentarily to consider. "Yer right. Black Jack's been waitin' and I should git a goin'. We'll finish this o'er some campfire." He paused again for an afterthought. "Morgan'll need yer gun, ya know."

"I thought of that."

"Well, then, you think on this. Come up and visit an ol' man once in a while. I got a tub o' liquor and not a soul to even taste it."

"Are you going to stop nosing into my affairs?"

"Nah, I don't guess I e'er will."

Lowe took a deep breath and sighed. "I'll be there, Mr. Monk, just as soon as the young couple gets settled in."

Only a handful of people knew the plan, and Dewey was not one of them. Morgan and Sarah had registered at the hotel under the name of Adams, which the clerk permitted after a brief explanation and presentation of a marriage license. They knew that Dewey would be inquiring but felt their secret was safe. The second part of the honeymoon, the trek to the Big Timber, was thought to be even better guarded. They were wrong on both counts.

It was five in the morning when Morgan heard the knock on the door. He waited, hoping it to be nothing more than imagination. His bride was sleeping soundly, nestled warmly in the softness of the bedcover, when a second knock came more forcefully. Sarah moaned her disapproval. Morgan slipped quickly and quietly away from her, threw on his night shirt and stumbled to the door.

"Dewey!" he exclaimed in a very strong whisper. "What are you doing here? Get out of here!"

"Good mornin'."

"Good morning, my foot! It's barely five a.m."

"Lowe sent me. He said the only train goin' up to camp was leavin' at six. Ya gotta get movin' if you're gonna make it."

"At six? What happened to the other runs?"

"It's Sunday. They only make the one run."

"But...."

"No time for 'buts.' Grab your things and go."

"Oh, all right," Morgan whined. "Tell Lowe we'll meet him at the tracks. And thanks, Dewey."

"No need for that. I'm glad to do it."

It was too early and too dark, and Morgan was too sleepy to question why Dewey Baughman was the messenger. He woke Sarah in a panic, and the two were soon scrambling through the hotel lobby and down Market Street with bags in hand. When they reached the mill, the tracks were idle, the Shay engines were cold where they sat, and neither Lowe Yancy nor anyone else was astir.

Sarah cuddled against Morgan. "Did we miss it?"

"We missed something, but not our ride. That rascal! How did he do it?"

"What rascal?"

"Dewey. How did he know just where we were, and what kind of fool am I to fall for such a lame story?" Morgan shook his head in utter disgust at his own stupidity.

"You mean we got up for nothing?"

"It looks that way. I'm sorry."

Sarah lifted up on her tiptoes and gave Morgan a long kiss. "Don't be angry on this, our very first day. We should be up early. This is marvelous! What should we do?"

Morgan did not have to search for an answer. "Go back to bed," he said.

The sun's pale light found a slit in the morning clouds, and the dawn began to promise another warm, autumn day. But Devlin was slow to awaken to it, and the sound of a lone wagon with squeaky wheels and clopping hooves was the only sign of life. Morgan watched as an old cart wobbled around the corner and headed his way.

"Well, I'll be," he uttered. "Sarah, I believe we have transportation."

"On that?" She was happy and ready for anything, and she beamed.

"Exactly."

Dewey pulled the rig in close. "Need a ride, folks?" he asked.

"May I inquire, good driver, just where we are going?" Sarah replied, with a smile that left him weak.

"On such a day, ma'am, does it really matter?"

"Nope, not in the least." She hugged Morgan, and the two squeezed onto the seat beside their friend.

The ride was not so bad. Dewey had replaced the ill-tempered Noggin with Gretel, a horse of friendly deportment, and a generous application of axle grease seemed to muffle some of the screech of the rubbing wheel. The cart turned onto Walnut Street and rolled to a stop at a familiar iron gate. It was evident who broke the secret when Irwin Dabney answered his door. A contrite expression was locked to his face.

"Why Mr. and Mrs. Darrow, how good of you to come," he said, swinging wide the front door. "My home is yours." He squeezed his daughter long and firmly. "And I mean that, sweetheart. You and Morgan will always have a place here, just like in my heart."

"Oh, Daddy." A mist coated Sarah's eyes.

"Thank you, sir," said Morgan. "You have always made me feel at home." He kiddingly presented his hat to Irwin, and the older man instantly handed it back.

"Son, I gave up that butler job when you married my daughter. *You* are now her hired help, in case you didn't realize. Don't expect to get rich. Now, come in, all of you. We have a surprise."

The air was right with the scent of bacon and fresh ground coffee. The small group walked through the parlor to the paneled accordion doors that closed off the dining room, and Morgan knew that breakfast was to be something special. He was ready.

"Allow me," said Dewey, grabbing hold of the knobs. "I'm hungry, and you're movin' like an old married man."

Beyond the doors was a long table, with four chairs and the same number of place settings.

"Morgan, you sit there at the head," instructed Irwin. "Sarah, come right here beside him." He pulled the chair for his daughter. "They're prepared to serve whenever we are ready."

"We've been ready, Mr. Dabney," blurted Dewey. "I've been smellin' bacon since I was down by the tracks."

"Very well, let's eat." Irwin lifted a tiny bell and rang it for service.

Jacob came first with an oversized platter loaded with bacon, pork loin and sausage. He was extremely careful. Annie followed with a bowl of ripe, fresh fruit and Cora carried the coffee. Auralee was next. She was holding another large platter, this one slippery with fried eggs, cooked over-medium or sunny-side-up, and her sister was close behind with a plate stacked high with blueberry flapjacks. Horace Smith and Ernie Zimmer brought grits, white gravy and hot maple syrup, while two more of Sarah's friends delivered home fried potatoes, fried tomatoes, fried apples and fresh baked biscuits. Without a word, they placed the food upon the table, and like discreet servants, they returned to their station in the kitchen.

Sarah's excitement left her stammering. Words tumbled incoherently from her lips, until she finally gave up the attempt to speak. Her customary composure already abandoned, her mouth fell agape with the continuing surprise. Morgan saw opportunity, and without care of etiquette, snatched up a biscuit and planted it. Sarah's blue eyes bugged, and she giggled and scolded as she removed all but one bite of the bread.

"Morgan Darrow, you are an imp! Pardon his poor manners, Daddy. There hasn't been much time for training."

"I'm on his side with this, sweetheart. Your friends are all in the kitchen, if you need consolation."

Sarah jumped from her seat and raced to the kitchen door. "You come out here, every one of you!"

She hugged them all and only stopped when the boys started moving extra chairs and settings for the breakfast. Seeing everyone assembled, Irwin Dabney opened a bottle of champagne and combined it with the juice of fresh squeezed oranges, already poured into crystal glasses. He raised his own glass for a toast.

"To my wonderful daughter and son-in-law." He looked affectionately at the young couple. "And to my lovely new family." He smiled at Annie and her children. "And to my young friends gathered here today, you are always welcome." Irwin turned again to his daughter. "And you will always be loved."

Morgan added, "As will you, sir." The glasses pinged across the table in agreement, and everyone, except Jake and Dewey, sipped the sparkling wine.

The train to Camp 7 was, in fact, scheduled to depart at eleven, and Morgan and Sarah's accommodations, austere as they would be, were yet another gift by way of Irwin Dabney's high position with the lumbermill. Lowe would escort them to the end of the track. He would stay with them at the camp, but the two would then travel the next day in their own company to the deep seclusion of the Big Timber. They relished the adventure. It was a proper beginning for their life together.

Lowe Yancy waited quietly in the background, as friends and family hugged, kissed and cheered. The saddle packs were already stowed on the railcar, as was his horse, the gentle Blu, standing content and completely ready for whatever the task.

Lowe had considered every possible provision for their journey, from food and feed to blankets and cooking pans, tools and winter gloves. He even carefully stashed two bottles of imported wine, in place of Silas' large jug of prime corn liquor. And, of course, he remembered the rifle. It rested in an open leather saddle boot, fully loaded and accessible.

The steam of the Shay clouded the air like fog, and through its concealing veil, Lowe watched as Annie first embraced her new daughter and her son, and then as she placed her arms around Irwin Dabney. The emptiness rushed through his veins.

# CHAPTER 24

The small cabin was sturdy and well seated in the secluded hollow, much like the nearby trees that loomed high above it. It seemed so insignificant against the majesty of the grove, but still, it diminished the forest like a freshly cut stump squatting in the midst of a perfect landscape. Empty and idle, day after day, the structure was the foreboding mark of an intruder who would claim reverence for nature, but arrogantly rise to reshape the flawless handiwork of God.

The mountain lion agreed. It paced around the perimeter, eyeing the crude building with distrust. The stench of unknown beasts, of horse and mule, of dog and man, overwhelmed its acute senses. If the big cat was wary, it was rightfully so. The new sights and smells were alien, and the cougar had no choice but to watch cautiously from a distance and await the eventual return of those who dared enter his realm.

The mountain lion was king, but kings, like kingdoms, fall in the absence of vigil. As a predator with stealth, cunning and strength, it was accustomed to lording over the land with impunity, and the wilderness posed little threat to its regal power. But now there were interlopers, and more would surely follow. As it walked the wide loop around the cabin, the cougar left its own sign on the base of the trees and in the scratchings of the earth. The message was clear. Beware.

Morgan and Sarah were more than welcome at Camp 7. The woodsmen remembered Morgan for his indomitable pluck in that fateful confrontation with Farley Ochs. He was just a boy then, not so many months earlier, but he had handily dispatched the bullies who once struck fear into these strong, self-reliant men. They greeted him like a hero, and their tales of his exploit gave Sarah proud confidence in the man who would be taking her far into the wilderness.

Of course, Sarah charmed them with her own grace and beauty, and before the young couple could set out for the Big Timber, they were entertained by the endless recollections and hearty laughter of their tobacco-stained, wooly bearded hosts. Neither of them minded in the least.

Lowe Yancy, equally admired for his mettle and mastery in the fight, chose to stay to himself for the evening. It was Morgan's time to shine, and Sarah's place to be adored. Come morning, Lowe would feel comfortable sending the couple on their way, knowing that from thereon they would never see another stranger's face. Everyone on the mountain was now their friend.

The train left camp at nine the next morning, and as the locomotive pulled a new load of timber back to the mill, Lowe took turns with the fireman tossing wood to the firebox. It was his first ride on a Shay, and he insisted on doing his part for the privilege. The engineer lent him the controls from time to time, explaining the workings of the engine, but Lowe knew he could not be trusted with any real responsibility. There were dangers on the downhill run that even an experienced trainman might not anticipate.

As it was, the return trip to Devlin ended without incident, and Lowe climbed down from the big engine with soot on his face and smoke still wafting through his clothes. He lingered while the logs tumbled into the mill pond and wondered about what he should do next, other than finding a bath deep and hot enough to cut the oily grime. He favored several ideas, all of them calculated to bring him face to face with Annie Darrow, but yielding to his own better judgment, he went on to seek the bath.

Lowe finally found his nerve the following day. He would locate Annie and let providence determine what might happen next. He stopped by her home to tell her about Morgan and Sarah's start to the Big Timber, but she was not there. He went to the company store and to other shops along Market Street in hope that their paths might cross. Seeing wagons in front of the church, he even waited on the chance she might be attending a prayer meeting or Bible study. Annie often did that in the early part of the week. The woman was nowhere to be found. Lowe had exhausted both his ideas and his pride, and over half of the morning was gone. He felt foolish for having wasted it. Perhaps providence had intervened after all.

Dewey Baughman was en route to the mill when he spotted a dejected Lowe Yancy sitting on a bench. He was staring blankly down Market Street.

The boy yelled from the far side of the road, "Mr. Yancy! Hey, Mr. Yancy!" Lowe heard him and waved, while Dewey immediately crossed, zigzagging to avoid some of the faster moving traffic.

"Dewey, what's the matter with you? Are you trying to get yourself killed?"

"Aww, they saw me. I'm a big target. Hey, are ya busy for a while?"

"No, I guess not. I was just thinking about heading back to my room to prepare for our next survey. Why do you ask?"

"Well, I could use some help. Mr. Dabney's payin' me to move them weddin' tables and chairs, and frankly, I ain't sure I can handle them big horses. I was hopin' ya might manage the team, but if yer busy...."

"I'm not that busy. I've piddled away this work day, and I might as well finish it off the same way I started it. I'll be glad to help."

"Great! Mrs. Darrow's got some other jobs for me, but I can't get to 'em 'til I move the chairs."

"Is Annie at Dabney's place?"

"Yeah, and as far as I could tell, she's been there for most the mornin'."

Lowe did not want to find Annie Darrow if it meant seeing her at Irwin Dabney's house. He had come to suspect some relation between the two, and their recent closeness was especially troubling as he analyzed his own affections. Dabney was a fine man and much better suited for Annie than he could ever be. If Lawson was gone from her life, legally, physically and morally, she would never choose another who was anything less than Irwin Dabney's type. She would not want to chance the same mistakes she made with Lawson.

Irwin Dabney was a man of great character. He was successful, wealthy, refined and eligible. Lowe's own qualities could not favorably compare. He tried to resign himself, then and there, to the notion that he would never really win Annie, or anyone else for that matter. It was childish jealousy at play, and he pitied himself for the loss of something he never had in the first place. The ordeal left him all the more yearning for his past. Despite his fond feelings for her, Annie was too much the risk, too unattainable, too lovely and too perfect. It was far simpler for him to walk away, back to his memories, than to remain in pursuit of a life that could not be.

The chairs were almost loaded when a messenger from the saw mill rushed up the street and loudly called to Lowe from the gate. Sensing urgency, Lowe ran to meet him. Annie and Dewey were close behind.

"What in the world's going on?" he asked.

"Are you Mr. Yancy?"

"Yes, why?"

"Jonas Higgleby sent me up here after you. Some fellow named Cookie, who works out at the camp, passed a note by way of the engineer." The young man took a deep breath and pulled a crumpled piece of paper from his shirt pocket. "The engineer dropped it off at the main office, and as luck would have it, Mr. Higgleby just happened to be standing at the desk."

"Yeah, yeah, the note, man!" Lowe exclaimed impatiently.

"The train got in about an hour ago. Read this. It sounds important." The messenger presented his note. "Sorry, it's a bit tattered."

Annie and Dewey huddled to see for themselves, while Lowe silently read the words scratched hastily in pencil across the page.

*"Find Lowe Yancy. Trouble. Farley seen heading for Big Timber. Armed. Another man, likely Leon Hopper, following. Come quick."*

"What is it, Lowe?" Annie asked, seeing his bronze, leathery face turn pallid.

"Nothing, Annie. I'll take care of it."

"Is it the children?"

"No, they should be all right, but I do have to go."

Annie grabbed the note from Lowe's hands and read for herself. "Who is this Farley Ochs?" she asked.

Dewey provided the answer, "He's that ruffian that keeps tanglin' with us."

"The same one Morgan's been fighting with? The one from the lumber camp?"

"Yes, the same," said Lowe. He opened two of the folding chairs. "Sit down, Annie. I don't have much time. I'll be catching the next train back up the mountain."

"Lowe, what does this Ochs have to do with Morgan and Sarah?"

"Probably nothing. He's been searching for the Big Timber ever since I found it. This is certainly not his first trip out that way. I'm sure the timing is just a coincidence." Lowe wanted to, but did not believe his own words. Neither did Annie.

"Then, tell me this, what does a grown man like that have against a boy like Morgan?"

"Well, Morgan stood up to a bully. Bullies get even. That's a big part of it. But more importantly, Farley is after me, and he uses people like Morgan to get my attention. He won't rest until he has his day, and he expects that day to be coming soon. I'm sorry, Annie. I am very sorry that I've drawn your family into this."

"Can he hurt them?"

"He most likely won't even find them. But if he does, and if he means them harm, well, Morgan is armed and more man than Farley could ever hope to be."

"Farley Ochs and Leon Hopper, they were the ones with Lawson, weren't they? I seem to remember Morgan mentioning their names."

"That's all over now. Morgan saw to it. Wherever Lawson

went, it wasn't with Ochs. Now, I have to leave, and you have to do something for me."

"But I'm going with you."

"No, you're not!"

"I am going with you. He's my son, and for Sarah's sake, I have to go."

Lowe understood a mother's frustration at being forced to do less than her all, but for every reason, Annie needed to remain in Devlin.

"No, Annie, I'm moving fast and I'm going now. Send someone to Jasper Hollow for Black Jack and Silas. Tell them to come running to the Big Timber."

"I'll fetch them myself."

"It's too far. Please, send someone."

"Dewey will come with me. Won't you, Dewey? And Irwin, he'll help! Irwin can persuade the authorities to...."

"There is no authority up in those mountains, Annie, and if there was, there's been no crime committed to support its involvement. If Dabney wants to help, and I know he will, tell him to send word ahead to Camp 7. I'll need provisions, and I'll need a rifle."

"What 'bout a mule?" Dewey asked.

"I can move faster alone and on foot. Black Jack will have animals when he comes."

Lowe looked into Annie's worried eyes. "Morgan and Sarah will be fine, just fine, and I will deal with Farley Ochs. You have to trust me."

"I do," said Annie. "Completely."

Lowe arose from his chair, and without further discussion, he turned toward the iron gate.

"Lowe, wait!" She was running behind him.

"There's no time, Annie."

"Anything can happen out there. I know that. But you were never to blame, and you must know that. Farley Ochs might hurt Morgan, but I'm afraid he will kill you. Don't let that happen. Please, don't let that happen."

Annie threw her arms tightly around Lowe's neck, and she kissed him hard and long with more passion than she had felt in a score of years. It was intended as a message to his heart, meant to be clear and permanent, but for the most part, it would remain unread until his devilish deed was done. To finish his business with Farley Ochs, he would not need a heart.

Sarah led most of the way along an indistinct foot path. Morgan had to redirect her from time to time, but for the most part, she traced the secret trail like a skilled tracker. She enjoyed the challenge, and Morgan, with Blu in tow, was in no particular hurry as long as she was happy. He was with the one girl he wanted and in the very place he wanted to be. Nothing could justify his rushing from that.

It was all very different in the night, when the woods threatened with fearful distortions and haunting sounds. Sarah curled in the fire's glow, and she listened while Morgan told of the great white oak anchored to the floor of a solid granite dome and of the Big Timber trees sheltered beyond the high escarpments. She witnessed absolute wonder through his vivid description and longed to be there, never realizing that such a marvel was just a short day's climb from the valley where they camped.

"Sit with me, Morgan. Come close."

"Why? Are you getting cold?"

"I am a bit cold."

"And maybe a little afraid of things in the dark?"

"That, too." She laughed at her own faint heartedness. "Actually, it's not that cold just now, thanks to this nice fire of yours."

Morgan stretched out on the cool ground and rested his head on Sarah's thigh. Her fingers brushed through his hair. She listened for sounds beyond the gentle flowing of the stream, and she was almost at ease until a sudden 'thwack!' penetrated the peace.

"What was that?" she exclaimed, urging Morgan to get the rifle.

"That was just a beaver. There are lots of them in this little valley."

"Do beavers bite?"

"They bite trees. Would you like to try and see one?"

"No, let's stay right where we are. I like it here with you...and this fire."

Seeming to ignore her, Morgan lifted from the ground and moved toward the packs.

"Aww, don't leave. We were just getting so cozy," Sarah whined playfully.

"You told me to get the rifle, and I think it's a good idea. You never know when a herd of those beavers might come stampeding or stalking through the brush." He looked serious.

"Morgan Darrow, you are kidding, aren't you?"

"Of course, I am."

"Thank God. I'm already terrified about some bear or wolf coming to eat me. I don't need to hear another word about killer beavers."

Morgan chuckled. There were many dangers creeping in the forest, no-legged, four-legged and sometimes two-legged ones, which is why he pulled the rifle. He did not expect intruders, but nevertheless, thought it prudent to follow a few elementary precautions. He would keep the fire bright, hang their food high in a distant tree, scour their greasy cook kit of its scent and hope through the night that nothing troublesome would venture their way. But if it did, both Morgan and the gun would be ready.

Sarah cooed as she settled into the warmth and softness of her bedroll. She felt secure. Her body was more tired than she knew, and in the midst of watching Morgan complete the final tasks of a long day, she drifted to a deep and needed sleep.

Morgan checked his rifle and looked across the native lea now broken with moon shadow. He saw only Blu, calm and content and grazing the tawny meadow grass. That was enough of a sign for him. They were safely alone. His horse and weapon nearby, he kissed Sarah's cheek and, with another moment's passing, plunged into his own heavy slumber.

They awoke refreshed and anxious to scale the neighboring slope. Breakfast was light, with uneaten portions saved for the long walk ahead. This time Morgan set the pace, and as they climbed, he recounted the tales of the Shawnee warrior.

"So, that all happened right here?" Sarah would ask on numerous occasions, when they passed any remnant pine growth or sighted some faintly charred trunk.

The answer was always the same, "It may have, but just you wait. There's much more ahead."

Of course, Sarah could not wait. In her excitement, she questioned everything, until she finally scampered past Morgan and raced the rest of the way to the long, high cliff. There she halted.

"Which way?" she inquired. "It's a wall."

"You tell me," Morgan replied, sucking in the air after so fast an ascent. "You've performed quite respectably as a scout so far."

"Well, I just don't know. There's no indication of any traffic through here."

"Then, I guess you're down to gut feelings. Pick your way, right or left?"

"Aren't you even going to tell me?"

"Do you really want me to?"

"Yes!"

Morgan refused the request.

Sarah wanted to follow the cliff downward, since the route looked easier and the crag seemed to taper somewhat with the descending grade of the ridge. But Morgan winced, and she quietly took the reaction as a sign that she had made a bad choice. She skirted the base of the escarpment, looking for an entry, and began to wonder if even Morgan knew where he was. Eventually, she came across an old and undeniable indication of a horse or mule and proudly pointed it out to Morgan.

"Good eyes," he said. "The trail's not much more than a crack in all this rock. I reckon you'll see some more of those before you find it."

The woman moved on like a hound on a hunt. When Morgan, still leading Blu, finally reached the narrow entry point, she had already made the turn and found her way to the dome. The low, scraggly trees that spotted that vast rock surface were a disappointment to Sarah, who had a completely different picture painted on her mind. While she was thrilled to be standing on what seemed to be the top of the world, it was not the Garden of Eden that Morgan had promised.

She looked everywhere and at everything beneath the wide, blue sky, but saw nothing on those rolling hills that resembled her vision of the Big Timber. Sarah waited patiently with her disillusion until Morgan at long last mounted the cliff.

He sensed her feeling in an instant. It was predictable, and he smiled knowingly. "You're wondering right now if you ever should have trusted me, that perhaps the Big Timber is just some overstated figment of my imagination. Am I right?"

"Oh, no, you are so wrong. This is a wonderful place. I can see forever."

"But you can't see trees, can you?"

"I see trees."

"Not big ones, not the really big ones that I told you about."

"The trees are not all that important to me. I can see you, and that's what I really want to look at," Sarah said, flirting with her new husband.

Morgan walked over and kissed her quietly. "You deserve better after so long a hike, and I don't intend to disappoint you now. See if you can track your own way to edge of paradise." He pointed across the dome. "And be mindful of the cliffs! I'll be along shortly. There's a little grass up here, and I need to give Blu some time to feed."

"But what if we get separated?"

"Believe me, Sarah, if you head in that direction, I'll know exactly where to find you."

When Morgan reached the white oak, Sarah was cradled in a crook of its massive limbs, frozen with awe like the others who had come before her. Great was this tree, she thought. Greater yet was this joy in her life, and greatest of all, the God who made them so. Here, nature had done its best work, and Sarah felt humbled to merely sit in the breadth of its shade.

Morgan sat beside her, and with deliberate silence, he gazed beyond the dome to tops of the giants, still living after centuries, ever growing from the depths of the basin. Sarah could not detect them below the jagged edge of the crag, and she was not inclined to look further than the wonder of the oak. Morgan understood, and he loved her all the more.

One night in the wilderness was enough for Sarah Darrow to better appreciate the more civilized comfort of four walls and a roof. The cabin may have been roughly constructed, but it did afford some measure of protection from the savage world around her. She stayed close to those walls for the better part of the day.

By late afternoon, however, she was both bored and emboldened, and she wasted little time deciding her options. She walked slowly into the untamed splendor of the virgin wood, taking into her heart all that her senses could collect.

Sarah stopped to admire the vivid hues of autumn, splashed across the landscape as crimson saplings, yellow mosses and rusty red vines. Adrift from some broken twig of sweet birch, a whiff of wintergreen stirred her curiosity, and she moved farther into the darkened grove to discover yet other aromas, the lemony scent of the spicebush and the musk of fallen leaves left swirling in a brook. There were pockets of fragrance everywhere, and she drew deep breaths to capture their essence.

Most of all, she looked to the canopy. The high and mighty trees of the Big Timber, with their wide, straight boles and their fat, gray branches, were not specimens of particular beauty, but were to her the magnificent consequence of an unerring holy touch. Sarah could not comprehend such life, how it flourished or endured for so long, and as her thin white neck bent ever upwards, she felt smaller and smaller against the majesty of creation. She walked until she simply disappeared in the midst of a miracle, far from the safety of Morgan and the tiny cabin he had helped to build.

Sarah could not see the heavy clouds approaching quickly from the west, but she felt the wintry wind being pushed before them.

She pulled her arms close to her body and shivered. The sun, now trapped behind that front, shed a gloomy light at best, and Sarah felt a sudden urge to return. She tried to retrace her steps, only to find that the leaf-littered floor had hidden the clues. Time passed. The giant trees began to lose all detail, and the hollow grew vast in the coming dusk.

There were sounds now, snaps and thuds and squeaks, but only the wind was calling. She heard what she thought were footsteps but refused to yield to the taunting of her imagination. Of course, the movements followed steadily as she worked her way around the great trunks and over the small, mossy knolls. When she stopped, they stopped, but still, it was just the wind.

Sarah refused to panic. The growls and groans commanded her attention, but she would not let herself be swayed. She knew how trees would mimic and moan as they rubbed together, bark against bark.

A branch cracked loudly from a distant thicket. She heard a raspy cough, the flutter of wings, some far away whistles, but each and every one of them was nothing more than that cold, harassing wind. She bravely chose to ignore them all.

Then came the voice. It was muffled and low, but clear enough to be recognized for exactly what it was. She listened intently.

“Sarah, here I am. This way, come this way.” The wind tried to mute it, and the broken sound seemed queer as it filled her ears. Using the voice as her guide, she approached it as best she could, dodging obstacles hidden in the dusk.

“Sarah, Sarah.” The name was repeated time and again, but never boldly, as though a shout might offend the sensibility of this now strange and eerie grove.

“I will find you, Sarah. Come to my voice. Sarah, Sarah.”

Sarah knew that Morgan would be worried and that it was just a matter of time before he broke into view and crossed the field of high ferns that now separated them. But why would he not call out? She had no explanation. She braced herself against a creeping fear and cautiously edged closer to the sound of the voice.

"Sarah. Sarah, come this way."

A limb crashed down before her, and the young woman gasped in surprise. It was too much to bear, and she surrendered to fright with a scream.

"Sarah, I will find you. Come," repeated the unrelenting voice.

She now shuddered at what she heard. The voice did not seek her. It summoned her. It did not reassure her, but instead, shattered the very last of her resolve. Still, it had to be Morgan's voice, perhaps warped and twisted by the surging air. She found some comfort in the thought and steeled herself to go on.

Sarah yelled into the night, "Morgan! Here I am. I'm over here!"

A large shadow shot through the ferns before she could cry out again. Her eyes widened with horror, and she froze in place like prey resigned to its fate.

"Don't holler!" shouted the voice, this time forcefully. "If he comes, I will kill ya both."

Sarah had time for just one word. "Morgan!" She screamed it for her life.

It was difficult to know just how long she remained unconscious. Sarah's face stayed pressed into the mulch long after she began to recognize her plight. But her mind was faltering. While she sensed them both through the ground beneath her, she felt no threat from the chill or the prowling steps that seemed to encircle her dead-still body. She laid there hearing, but not assimilating, the vague footfalls on the dry leaves or the persistent purring that seemed to be revolving around her.

The movement was tactical, often drawing near, only to back away as it looped her position. Sarah felt watched, but in her stupor, could not react until both the steps and the deep guttural moans finally trailed off into nothing. The sounds now gone, she likely would not recall them again.

She struggled to her feet. Her head spun with a throbbing pain. In the distance was a beacon, a fiery glow that would lead her back to Morgan. She staggered and stumbled, but made her way.

The cabin raged with smoke and flame, and the surrounding land was charred as the wind whipped sparks with fury. It was no accident. Even in her injured state, Sarah knew the truth and understood the dangers. Careless of her assailant's whereabouts or her own diminished condition, she tripped forward toward the structure, but was thwarted by the blistering heat and blinding light. She was not deterred in her search for her husband. The inferno might turn her, but it would not stop her. She knew in her heart that Morgan lived.

Sarah rubbed her head in an attempt to clear her mind and vision, and then rummaged across the fallen ash to find Morgan. Fire was racing toward the cliffs and so would she. There was only one route to safety, and Morgan was sure to have taken it. In no time at all, she reached the wavy line of flame, and through its dense, smoky screen, recognized the crumpled mass just a few feet beyond. It was Morgan! Unable to leap, she walked through fire to save him.

His time was nearly gone. A long gash on Morgan's forehead was proof of a heinous assault, and the stench of coal oil on his clothes brought sheer terror. Morgan had been left to die, and his attacker, likely the same man who struck Sarah down, was vile enough to want him burned. He was a monster, and somewhere in the cover of darkness, he watched with pleasure as the woman searched desperately for an escape that was not there.

Sarah was weak, but what little energy she had left would be given for Morgan. She reached under his arms, and barely lifting his heavy torso, she pulled him back from death one inch at a time. She fell when the soil and rocks gave way under foot, but soon learned that, by planting her feet, her body could function like a lever. She could ratchet back and forth and scoot him across the ground to the base of the cliff. It was an exhausting effort. Inhaling the hot billowing smoke, she retched its sooty residues, then pulled even harder up the steepening hill. There was no time to clear her lungs, no time to fashion masks from her garments, no time to rest. She was losing ground to the advancing flames.

The escarpment was a natural break in the path of the fire, but an even greater barrier to the woman who was forced to scale it. Sarah left Morgan for only a few seconds to track their escape and luckily found a wide cleft that seemed to ascend the rock. But it twisted out of sight, perhaps to nowhere.

It would have to do. The flames raided into a cluster of young pines and rapidly gained a hotter, more vertical dimension. Their next victim would be the man soaked in coal oil. Sarah scrambled in the flickering light to Morgan's side and lifted him with her last reserve of power. Then, she let him fall to her back, like an oversized sack, and dragged him to the crevice.

She climbed. The smoke and perspiration stung her eyes like acid. Her soft hands were cut and abraded by the coarseness of the stone. But she carried her load upward to that twist in the cleft, and there, the trail and all hope ended. Sarah's spirit collapsed from the weight of her disappointment. Her legs buckled, and she and Morgan tumbled down through the crag to a heap beneath the pines.

She had no more to give and nowhere to go. With wounded hands, she pushed away what leaves and needles she could from the ground and pulled Morgan to the center of the dirt. Then, she stripped away his oil-soaked clothes and held him.

The cliff was at their back. The pines were in their face. Sarah prayed, but not for deliverance. There was simply no chance. She cradled her new husband in her arms and kissed him goodbye.

Lowe Yancy grabbed a quick hot meal before leaving Camp 7, and despite Cookie's urging that he wait until morning, he pressed on. Any hope of tracking Farley Ochs' movement was lost with that decision, and he came to regret the choice. A man like Ochs was bound to be encumbered in his passage through such a difficult wilderness. He would be careless in concealing his trail, and Lowe was counting on Farley's mistakes for his own edge. Maybe the daylight would tell him something useful, but in the night, Farley and Leon had the clear advantage. They could take him at will.

But, perhaps, a poorer choice was his rejection of Cookie's offer of a lantern. Lowe had learned as a young boy to depend on night vision, and when the sun was down, he rarely saw the glow of anything besides the moon and stars and coals of his campfire. Then again, he almost never journeyed beneath so dark a sky, and his eyes, now older and weaker, could not adjust. The lantern might have been cumbersome, but it would have been better than blindness.

As it was, Lowe lost valuable minutes, even hours, trying to recover from a series of wrong turns and countless collisions with the hidden trees and rocks. He was only two miles away from Camp 7 when a misstep wrenched his ankle, almost to the point of fracture. The pain was excruciating, and even after soaking it in the cold current of the stream, he found no relief. He bound it tightly with cloth and limped for another mile before succumbing to fatigue. For a few spectacular minutes, the moon peeked through a broken cloud, but Lowe was much too worn to look up and see the light.

The new morning brought only more pain. After three very guarded steps, Lowe would have readily discarded his hatred of Farley Ochs and headed for home, but his concern for Morgan and Sarah compelled him to continue. He reached the dale below the dome, just as the sun slipped behind the clouds and the winds began to howl.

A pink halo capped the mountain top, and from his position in the valley, Lowe had a fair idea of what it was. Evening had come quickly and was soon devoid of any glint of light, except that steady radiance now silhouetting the ridge. He knew that it was fire, and he knew that he would have to climb that mountain. In darkness, it would be difficult. In pain, it would be impossible. Those were his thoughts, and he set out at once to prove himself wrong.

Farley Ochs had unfathomable strength, and he needed every bit of it if he was to lift up Morgan Darrow with a single arm. The other arm was laden with a rather large bundle, including his rifle.

"Can ya walk?" he coldly asked Sarah.

She was not even startled. Her nerves were incapable of conveying fright.

"I think so."

"Well, do it or die. Suit yourself." He walked away, carrying his load to safety. He never looked back for Sarah, but she followed.

The three moved slowly along the bottom of the escarpment and eventually reached the trail that led up to the great white oak. Farley grunted and cursed, and then, dropped his entire burden to the stony ground. When Morgan moaned, Sarah rushed to nurse and to comfort him. His eyes were glazed, but for the first time, they were open.

"Girl, get the hell up from there!" exclaimed Farley. "Are ya comin' or not?"

"He needs help. I'll go where Morgan goes and no farther."

"We'll see. Give me any trouble, and that'll be it. Ya understand?"

"I understand." Sarah's contempt was evident.

"Then get your ass up that path. Wait! You take this." Farley pointed to the bundle, which was at least half Sarah's size. "I'll keep the rifle. Now, move!"

The massive tree was hardly visible, even as they neared within a few feet. Farley chose it as his fortress and wasted no time securing Morgan to a low limb. If that was to be their dungeon, Sarah was relieved. A thick stand of grass would ease some of their hardship, and the wide trunk could screen the breezes that buffeted the dome.

Farley opened the bundle and grabbed a woolen blanket. He threw it at Sarah.

"Put this over him. And, missy, if he somehow gets untied, I'll put a bullet in his brain. He only moves when I tell him to."

"What about me?"

Farley lifted a loose sweater and tossed it down. "There, that's all ya get!"

"I mean what if I need to move?"

Farley laughed. "I wished the hell you would. There's the trail! Why don't ya take it and head on?"

"I'm not leaving Morgan."

"No, I didn't think so. That's too bad for all of us."

Sarah did not know what Farley was implying, but she could guess. One thing was certain, they had to get away. If only she could nurse Morgan back to full consciousness, if he could gather strength, they might attempt a break. There was little else she could do without increasing their jeopardy.

"Why did you hit me like that?" asked Sarah.

"Huh?" Farley was surprised. "The question really is, 'why aren't you dead?' You screamed. I told ya not to."

"I don't even know your name," she said, thinking aloud.

Ochs did not respond. He was listening for more distant sounds and searching blindly across the dome to the nothingness beyond.

Sarah was intent on conversation. "You're waiting for someone, aren't you? I'll bet it's the law. Mister, if you're running, why not get on with it? Leave us alone and give yourself a chance."

"Lady, why don't ya just shut up?"

She did. Sarah was afraid to say more, at least at first, and she tended to Morgan's wound as best she could. All the while, Farley Ochs nervously fingered the trigger of his gun, his eyes crisscrossing the black space that surrounded him.

An hour came and went before she spoke again, "We're going to need some water, if you intend for us to stay here much longer."

"Oh, ya ain't goin' nowhere for a good while yet." Farley tossed a near empty canteen to the ground at Sarah's feet. Then, he asked her, "Exactly when were you two supposed to be headin' back?"

Sarah thought for a moment and realized she did not want to answer that question. She had quickly deduced the truth. If the man was fleeing the authorities, he would not have revealed his whereabouts by burning Lowe Yancy's cabin. He was anticipating someone, sure enough, but there was no need for hostages if that particular someone was considered by him to be friendly. That point, and only that point, was plain to her. She and Morgan were nothing more than lures, drawing their unknown, unsuspecting rescuer into a deadly trap.

She looked at her husband now resting in the tall grass and desperately wished to awaken him, if only for a few seconds. Morgan could make sense of all of this, and he would know just how to respond. Sarah took hold of his limp hand and knew that she alone would be fighting the fight.

The eyes of the big man were blacker than the night as he focused them on the wary young woman. He was anxious for her answer, and knowing this, she became all the more perplexed. No one at home would be missing them for days, and it would be well over a week before anyone could actually reach them in the Big Timber.

So, who was this unwitting soul to be wrongly taken at the edge of paradise? She guessed it was Lowe. It was his land, after all. The Big Timber, the white oak, the dome, they were his discovery and his treasure to lose or keep. She had heard, of course, of the huge, red-haired man who felt strongly otherwise, who launched his brutal attacks against Lowe Yancy, only to lose them all. For such a man, the bitterness of public defeat leaves a taste for private revenge. Yes, it had to be Lowe.

Another matter troubled her. Sarah knew too well her captor's proclivity for violence, and she now wondered how long he would remain content hiding behind the tree, nervously fidgeting with his gun. Their lives seemed only as sure as the big man's patience.

Angered by her silence, Farley repeated the question with force, "Woman, I asked ya a simple question. When were ya leavin'?"

She blurted out her answer, "Tomorrow!"

"Then we'll wait. Go on and get that water. Use the brook under them big trees. There sure ain't a drop to be had up here." Pointing down at Morgan, he warned her, "And don't ya get lost. You're the only doctor this boy's got."

Sarah hesitated at leaving Morgan's side, but she tucked the blanket warmly around him and collected the canteen. She could see her path only a step at a time until she entered the light of the still burning cabin. The forest fire was all but out.

She reached into the winding brook, and cupping its cool water in her sore hands, she took a long replenishing sip. Then, she rinsed her face of the sweat and grime and winced as her hand brushed the aching bruise on her head.

The canteen gurgled while it sank to the bed of the clear, rocky stream.

"Sarah, Sarah."

She heard the voice, and thinking it to be a cruel mutation of sound, yanked the canteen from its place in the brook.

"Sarah, I'm here."

A shadowy figure formed out of the darkness, and the chill of terror again swept through her.

"It's all right, Sarah. I'm here. Where is Morgan?"

She recognized the voice. "Mr. Yancy? Oh, dear God, Mr. Yancy!" She jumped across the brook and threw herself at her savior. "Mr. Yancy, I've never been so glad to see...."

"I know. But I'm with you now, and I won't let him hurt you again." Lowe cloaked her in his powerful arms, and she gradually calmed with the knowledge of his strength. "And Morgan?"

"He's with that awful man, and he's hurt."

"Can he move?"

"Not yet, but I think soon."

"Then it's best we wait. Sarah, are you okay going back to him?"

"Yes, of course, I have to. Morgan needs me."

"Good. I'll be near. Even though you won't see me, I'll be near. One last thing, do you think Ochs is expecting me?"

"I believe so, but I don't understand why he would be. We weren't supposed to leave until tomorrow. At least, that's what I told him. He's watching for someone, but he knows that no one would be coming this way unless they already anticipated some problems. As far as he's concerned, that should still be days."

"There was another man trailing behind him, his partner, though I would have thought Leon had made it up by now. Go back and tend to Morgan, and say little. It will be a trial, Sarah, but you must remain brave, knowing more help is already moving up that valley. In the meantime, just remember that I'll be near."

Lowe concealed his injury from Sarah. She had too many worries already, and it was important that she remain confident of their rescue. One thought was alarming. Why did Farley burn the cabin, if he did not expect anyone for days to come? It made no sense, unless he intended all along that Morgan and Sarah would die in the flames. The idea was unthinkable.

Lowe limped cautiously across the grove, and through the remaining cover of the darkness, he crawled up the crag to a protected position behind a low cairn. His rifle was loaded, and his target would be easy come the light of dawn. It could all be ended in the flash of muzzle, but an assassin would have to squeeze the trigger. Lowe was ready. He waited, and he watched.

# CHAPTER 25

Lowe Yancy found little comfort as he shifted his body time and again from one hard rock to another. While the stones felt warm against the chilly autumn air, they pressed mercilessly into his flesh until he had no choice but to squirm in pain. He lowered his rifle and twisted in place with a consuming sense of frustration. Every movement made a sound.

In this regard, the breezes served as an ally, kicking up new noises across the dome while concealing Lowe's in the midst of their din. But when the winds ceased abruptly in the early hours, every thump, snap or scratch could carry alarm to a leery and listening adversary. When Lowe's boot accidently hooked a branch of laurel, Ochs detected the distinct rustle and came searching. He stopped only a few yards from Lowe's position behind the cairn.

Sarah had heard the noise as well, and fearful that it might reveal her protector, she began to stir loudly around the base of the giant oak tree. Her sudden commotion confounded the big man, and he quickly returned to resume his watch. It was a near disaster for Lowe, who from then on would only move when Sarah walked, talked or sang songs to the ailing Morgan. She gave Lowe his cover, and he marveled at her ingenuity and bravery.

The night was agonizingly slow, and in some ways, the continued discomfort was a blessing to the exhausted Yancy. It kept him alert. He bided his time lamenting aches and weighing conflicted emotions, the warm affection he felt for Annie Darrow or the cold revenge he intended for Farley Ochs. His hatred prevailed for most of the night, but by daybreak, he had come to realize that he was no murderer and that the rescue of Morgan and Sarah would require more of him than what his rifle might deliver. He would have to disarm Farley somehow, and considering the injury to his ankle and the likelihood that Leon Hopper was lurking nearby, that task would prove formidable. He had no other plan but to wait and seize his chance when it happened.

His opportunity rode the back of a lean, bay quarter horse. With the fast-rising sun came a muffled clopping of hoof beats, churning heavily up the narrow path that climbed the escarpment. Lowe watched as Farley wheeled with panic and leveled his gun in the direction of the sound. They were both surprised when the horse trotted into view, riderless, fresh and totally unwary. It was Blu. The horse stopped at the first sight of Farley Ochs, and for a few seconds, it stared with black eyes shining.

"Well, things are lookin' up. That's Yancy's horse," said Farley. He cowered down behind the huge limb and looked all the more intensely across the dome. "I knew he'd come, and he's made good time."

For some reason, Morgan awoke with those words, and he looked up to find Sarah peering in the distance. "What is it?" he asked her. He appeared stronger. Sarah beamed as she stooped to his side and examined the head wound.

"Good morning. You certainly look better."

"I feel better. Can you untie me?"

Ochs interjected, "Leave it be!" He kept watching the horse.

"Please, mister," Sarah begged, "Morgan's been down on that ground all night."

"He can rot there, as far as I'm concerned," replied Farley. "And so can you. Now leave the ropes be."

"Please," she pleaded, and then disregarded the command. She unraveled the straps from Morgan's arms while Farley watched.

Morgan repositioned to catch a glimpse of his captor. He knew the voice all too well. "Mind him, Sarah, next time. This man is dangerous." He rubbed the swelling in his wrists. "What are you two looking at, anyway?"

Farley gave the answer, "A horse. It's Yancy's horse. That

bastard's out there all right. He don't know it, but he's mine the very second his head pops up from behind those scraggly trees. That's the way he'll come, just over that little rise, and he's got no clue at all that he's headin' right for the devil on a straight path to hell." Farley cocked his weapon, and a cartridge clicked sharply into the chamber.

"Well, you really are one back-shooting coward, aren't you? I never would have imagined," said Morgan, sarcastically. He was disappointed by a lack of response. "Listen to me, Ochs, Lowe Yancy isn't out there, and he never will be. We brought that horse with us from Devlin. It must've strayed in the night."

Farley laughed. "The hell you say!"

"But it's true. Blu's been with us for a couple days. I swear it."

"Boy, I've had my eyes wide open, and I sure don't recollect seein' no horse in them woods."

"Then you're as blind as you are ugly. I led him to the brook for water right before evening."

"Did ya leave him there all night?"

"No."

"So, where exactly did ya put him while I was torchin' that cabin?" Farley knew that the question would clinch the debate. "Nice try, boy. That's Lowe Yancy's horse, for sure, and if the horse is right here, Yancy can't be far away."

Morgan became momentarily confused. "You burned the cabin?"

"I did. Ya don't remember?"

"All I recall is your hideous face, right before you butted me with that rifle." Morgan touched his forehead. It was bandaged in Sarah's silk.

"Too bad ya had to miss it. From where I sat, the rest of the show was even more entertainin'. And if your woman hadn't been around, you might've made a nice little bonfire yourself."

"I'll bet." There was the undeniable reek of coal oil on the right shoulder of his undershirt. "I was wondering why I smell like kerosene."

Morgan was stunned by Farley's savagery, and his concern immediately shifted to Sarah. He noticed the bruise, darkening like a shadow across his young wife's cheek. Her ivory skin was so streaked with soot that he could not distinguish the damage from the dirt. He held her chin gently, and he turned her head to better inspect the injury. "Are you all right? Did he do this to you?"

"It's just a bump. Really, I'm fine."

Morgan glared at Farley. "You don't want to cut me lose. Right now, Ochs, just my thoughts are enough to kill you."

Farley felt unthreatened. He smirked. "No, I reckon I don't. For now, we'll keep them ties just where they are."

Sarah was growing increasingly troubled, fearful for Morgan and what might occur next if he continued to provoke his captor. "Morgan, don't upset him. You don't know what he's capable of."

"Actually, Sarah, I'm afraid I do know."

"Then, please, just stay quiet so he'll leave us both alone."

"He'll do what he wants to do, and nothing I say will make a bit of difference, one way or the other."

"Please, Morgan," she pleaded.

Morgan maintained his glare, but the redheaded man showed no interest. He was used to being hated and was otherwise occupied watching the slow ranging horse. It seemed to know where it wanted to go.

Morgan guessed what Farley was thinking, and he tried to encourage him. "Listen, Ochs, why don't you grab that horse and run? It's your best chance. Get out of here now, and I'll make sure the law doesn't get involved."

"All in due time, boy."

"But you may not have that time. Arson and assault are some serious charges."

"Yeah, and so is murder. If they get me after I take Yancy, it won't matter about the other complaints. But they won't catch up to me. Trust me. I've been through all this before."

Blu seemed content to graze on scant blades of grass, and as he ate, he migrated toward the rock cairn and Lowe. His course seemed deliberate, and Sarah's expression must have betrayed her concern. Luckily, only Morgan noticed.

"What is it, Sarah?" he asked.

"Oh, just Blu. Maybe I should fetch him before he wanders off again?"

"You do that," interrupted Farley. "Go nice and easy though. I don't want him spooked."

Sarah walked slowly toward the bay, hoping that her approach might move the horse in some other direction, but, of course, the animal stopped at the very back of the cairn. Blu was nuzzling Lowe when she finally took hold of the reins. She stroked his neck, and knowing Farley to be watching, only glanced down once to avoid suspicion.

"Leave the horse," Lowe whispered. "He bites." He reassured her with a smile and a wink. "Remember, he bites."

It was a puzzling remark, but Sarah readily complied. She returned empty handed and nervous, in expectation of Farley's reaction.

"I thought you were gettin' that horse! What happened?" Farley scowled.

She finally understood Lowe's whisper. "You get him. He bites! He bit me twice, and that's two times too many."

Farley cursed and shook the gun barrel in her face. Sarah backed away in fright.

"You stand right there," he said. "If ya take one step toward the boy, I'll shoot. Ya know I mean it."

Sarah just nodded. She froze in place while the big man lumbered across the dome. She calculated as his heavy steps brought him closer to the horse, and then, when Ochs was but a few feet from the cairn, she hollered loudly, "Hey!"

Farley spun around with amazing agility and aimed his weapon. The girl was exactly where he left her, her feet seemingly anchored to the ground. She gasped and her body clinched as it readied for his bullet, but the man hesitated. Before his finger could tighten on the trigger, he heard the click of a hammer and a calm, determined voice. The rocks behind him were suddenly speaking.

"Lower that rifle. Do it now."
"Yancy?"
"Do it now."

Lowe may have hobbled, but he never once dropped his guard while escorting Farley Ochs back to the tree. Even disarmed, the man was a greater threat now than ever before. Farley's life had carried him much too far from any real possibility of redemption, and all that remained for him was his own enmity and vengeance. He had no intention of serving time in some penitentiary, and it was just as well, since prison would only make him more malicious and ever more fervent in his desire to see Lowe Yancy dead. Farley would sooner die himself than yield this particular battle, and Lowe fully expected that he would have to accommodate him to bring the fighting to an end. He kept his gun aimed squarely at the big man's back.

"You sit right there," Lowe commanded. Farley squatted awkwardly. He sat on the very spot where Morgan had been tied. "Tell me this, Ochs. Will you ever let it rest, or is this a feud for life?" Lowe already knew the answer.

Farley looked over at Morgan. "I told ya to watch your back, boy. Me and Leon aren't ones to forget. I warned ya!" Then, he turned to Lowe. "And Yancy, I told you that you're a dead man. Nothin's changed."

"Well, sure it has."

Farley smirked again. He seemed overconfident for a man so closely guarded by two rifles. He grunted, and he muttered under his breath, "We'll just see."

Those words served as a good reminder to Lowe. He had rarely encountered Farley Ochs without Leon Hopper at least waiting in the shadows, and Cookie had warned him in the note that Leon had been seen heading for the Big Timber. Still, it made little sense that the two men would not have joined before now. The matter was doubtful, but worth checking.

"It looks to me like you've run out of friends. First, Lawson quits you, and it now appears that Leon's cut out."

"Why do ya say that?"

"Because they're not with you, and Leon, for one, is always with you."

"Oh, he's still with me. Ya can count on that. Maybe they both are."

Morgan entered the conversation, "You mean they're here at the Big Timber? You're a liar. Pa's done with you. That much I know."

"Figure it for yourself, boy. Ya didn't think I'd come all the way out here and not cover my ass."

Morgan called Sarah to his side, "Stay close to me, just in case he speaks the truth. There's no reason to be more of a target than necessary."

"He isn't speaking the truth," said Lowe. "He wouldn't know how. You are right about your father, and as far as Leon Hopper is concerned, he's afraid of his own shadow. He wouldn't spend one hour alone in this wilderness, much less two nights."

The words were reassuring, but a little caution was nevertheless prudent. Morgan knelt behind a low trailing limb and began scanning the terrain.

He offered a plan, "Perhaps we should look around. I could try to track him. There aren't but so many ways to get up that cliff."

"There's only one way from what I've found. No, son, you're not up to tracking anything, especially a man. Let's give that head of yours a chance to heal. Besides, I've got a little more experience around these parts. I'll go."

"But your ankle?"

"I'll take Blu. He's used to the woods."

The thought of venturing across the dome or beyond sat uneasy on Lowe's tired mind. He was crippled with fatigue and pain, but knew that Morgan was right. Soon, Black Jack and Silas would be coming, and they would be clear marks for someone hiding with a rifle. His friends had risked enough. He would not chance their lives.

For that matter, Lowe would be the simpler target, seated high on his mount, but there appeared to be no recourse. This was the time. This was his fight, and he knew his duty was to finish it, not to win it. It was a gamble, but he needed to be sure about Leon Hopper.

Lowe steadied Blu, and balancing on his good leg, he grabbed a handful of mane and whipped the other leg over the horse's powerful back. He winced as he settled.

"You're not in such great condition yourself. You need a saddle," Morgan said.

"Well, there isn't one. Blu's all I got, and he's always been enough in the past. We're used to bareback, and we'll take it nice and easy. Did you hear that, Blu? Go nice and easy."

Before prodding his horse forward, Lowe shot one last glance at Farley Ochs. The man was leaning comfortably against the bole of the tree. He was much too casual and far too brash for someone in his predicament, and Lowe suddenly had misgivings about leaving.

"Go on!" cried Morgan, "We'll be all right." He held up the rifle.

"That's the only way to stop him if he decides to move. We really should tie both his ankles and wrists."

"With what? There's not enough rope here to put a bow in Sarah's hair." Morgan displayed the frayed strands that had once bound him.

"Okay, then, but you keep your eyes on him, Morgan. And don't let him move, not for anything. Do you understand? If I hear a shot, I'll come running and expect to find this Mr. Ochs with a hole drilled right through him."

Morgan nodded, and Lowe rode away.

Farley Ochs now had his own opportunity. Lowe had misjudged him and could not have offered a better gift had he wrapped a pistol in paper and handed it to him. The devil was in his smile when he stood to face Morgan.

"Sit down!" demanded Morgan, brandishing the rifle. He was ignored.

"I don't think so, boy."

"What do you mean, 'you don't think so'?"

"I mean I won't be sittin' down."

Morgan's virtue and Farley's complete lack of it were equally essential to the big man's scheme. Ochs meant to kill Lowe Yancy, and Morgan would help by simply not killing Ochs. He studied Morgan's face, trying to gauge the boy's strength of character before testing his reluctance to shoot. His only chance for survival hinged on that singular aspect, the moral fiber of another man, the one now holding the rifle.

Farley was no fool. He knew that the young couple was devoted to each other and that they had a full life ahead of them. Morgan would not chance losing both his soul and future by murdering an unarmed man. Ochs, on the other hand, valued only the reckoning he had designed for Yancy. He needed that rifle. What he saw in Morgan's face told him he could have it.

"Boy, why don't ya tell your woman to fetch more water? We can all use some, and I don't want her here abouts as an excuse for ya to fire that weapon."

"I don't need more excuse than I already have. Now sit back down!"

"I think ya do, but whether or not ya believe it is the crux of my dilemma. Ya see, I'm countin' on ya bein' one of them good Christian brothers. You know, 'Thou shalt not kill'? As I figure it, your concern for this girl is the only cause that might provoke ya enough to prove me wrong."

Ochs reached into the pocket of his coat and pulled out the brass knuckles. He tossed them to the ground. Then, he crossed slowly under the shade of the massive tree, baring his open coat and hands. "Look, boy, I've no gun, no knife, no weapon at all. All I've got is my wits, and they're tellin' me that you are no killer. Send that girl away, put that rifle down and run just as fast as your legs can carry ya. That's the only way out of this. You and the girl can go in peace."

"And what about Yancy?"

"He'll find his peace when he's dead."

Morgan tightened his grip on the rifle and began to retreat slowly. "Sarah, get out of here! Head for Lowe and bring him back."

"I won't leave you with this man," she argued.

"And I won't have you stay! Go on now." The girl was reluctant, but she raced across the hard rock and into the scattered thickets of the dome.

Farley watched her disappear and then continued his advance toward Morgan. "Just put it down and follow her, boy. She's safe, and you'll both live to tell the story. Put that rifle down."

Farley Ochs was a huge man. Like the trees of the Big Timber, he was extraordinary in his girth, and his own limbs, all the way down to his fingers and toes, were stout yet surprisingly nimble. Truth be told, his mind and body were lightning fast, especially in a fight, and his fat was a cloak for the steel muscles beneath. Many a foe had fallen hard, mistaking Farley's great size for clumsiness. It was a mortal miscalculation for at least two unfortunate souls, but many more were broken by his swift, crushing strikes or the vice-like grip of his hands. Morgan rightfully feared the man, and he knew from experience to stay clear.

Farley's assault was to be slow and deliberate. He would move close and pounce with deceptive speed. Morgan backed away nervously as the big man steadily closed the space between them. His weapon may have been cocked and ready but did little to ease the tension. Ochs was right. Bound by character, the boy could never murder.

On the other hand, there was even less chance that he would hazard the life of a friend by freeing and arming his enemy. Punch for punch, Morgan was no match for Farley Ochs, but he was confident in his own strengths and would use them to his advantage. He aimed the rifle and fired one shot. Ochs stopped abruptly in his tracks, while the dust of the bullet plumed between his feet.

"You now know I can shoot if I need to. Here's the gun. If you want it, come and take it."

Farley lunged in anger across the short yardage between them, but Morgan deftly side stepped to avoid him and moved yet farther away. He was careful to never lose sight of his rival, but even more cautious about risking loss of the weapon. The action played like a game, and Farley cursed with what little breath he retained. He attacked repeatedly, only to be thwarted every time by Morgan's youth and agility. He threw rocks and sticks. He taunted and threatened, but Morgan kept his distance. Farley's opportunity had all but dissolved in the streams of sweat now pumping from his immense body. It was clear he did not like to lose.

The two men faced each other in stalemate and silence, and Morgan watched as the huge bully unraveled in hopelessness. He felt little satisfaction, but even less pity. Morgan could still smell the coal oil on his clothes. He visualized the bruise on Sarah's face. If mercy was his to grant, he offered no part of it. In the lull, Farley Ochs collected his remaining strength and pride and prepared for one final assault.

Morgan waited for the charge. His head throbbed. He grew dizzy in the sun.

Lowe scoured the edge of the precipice for signs, but found nothing. He rode Blu over a mile before concluding that Farley was alone. The exposed rock of the dome provided ample corridors to walk without leaving even the faintest of tracks, but if Leon Hopper had actually been there, he first would have had to find some reasonable passage up the steep cliffs. Lowe saw no break in the wall of stone. There was no evidence of a path from either man or beast.

He crossed to the other side, where he looked down on the Big Timber and scanned the open forest beneath him. The ground was gray with ash, and in some places, fallen logs still smoldered. The giant trees were merely singed across the tops of their huge jutting roots, but the burnt skeletal remains of young pines stood brittle and broken. There was nothing, absolutely nothing left of the cabin they had built, affirming the ease in which nature expunges the unwanted works of man. Lowe was not sorry for the irony. The Big Timber was again whole and pure, and by the first of spring, would abound in the pallid greens of both new and ancient life. It was all as it should be. He would not rebuild.

Somewhere in their searches, he and Sarah passed unnoticed. Unaware of Morgan's plight, Lowe returned to the one trail that he knew existed and braced himself for the difficult hike to the bottom of the cliff. Blu could not carry a rider, even Lowe, on such a radical, twisting grade, and the man reluctantly slid from the horse's back. To his dismay, his bad ankle absorbed much of the impact of his landing, and he buckled in agony.

Lowe lay upon the ground for minutes, massaging the injury and waiting in vain for the pain to subside. Finally, he focused on the task at hand and set out, half hopping, half sliding down the narrow trail. The horse followed, and once at the bottom, stood passively while Lowe rested his leg.

This time there were tracks. A quarter mile from the break in the wall, in a place previously untraveled, on a small uncovered patch of loam, were several distinct impressions. Three were boot prints, pressed sharply into the grainy soil. The others, more numerous and recent, were overlaid upon the markings of the boots. Lowe should not have been surprised, but he was. He had misgauged the courage of Leon Hopper, and he had somehow forgotten about the mountain lion that claimed the Shawnee Scarp as home.

Lowe hurried, as best he could, back toward the great white oak. He sent Blu up the bluff ahead of him, and before tackling the climb himself, he looked down the entire length of the high palisade. The dome had been anything but hospitable, beginning with this impenetrable face of cliffs. He wondered what would befall him next. With Ochs and Hopper and the big cat preying on his mind, he dragged himself to the top.

The sight of Luci springing from the thickets was enough to frighten any man, much less one so absorbed with an image of cougars. Lowe's heart beat like timpani, while the hound, her tail wagging with excitement, jumped up and demanded a proper greeting. The dog licked the man's fingers until they dripped, and Lowe, in turn, dried them in the soft fur behind her ears.

"Well, hey there, girl! You scare a man half to death and then expect him to give you lovin'. You're so presumptuous."

The tail wagged even faster, and as Lowe bent to pet her, Luci honored him with a couple quick kisses from her wet, slobbery tongue.

"You little hussy you. You'll just cuddle up to anyone, won't you? I'll bet you've been having yourself a time out here." Lowe looked over his shoulder toward the trail. "Where's that old man of yours?"

A voice bellowed from below, "Here I am, blast yer hide! I've damn near run all the way from Devlin jist to find ya lollygaggin' with my dog. Where's yer problem?"

Silas took the last few steps up the path and stood at the rim of the cliff. He tapped the grip of his pistol, holstered low at his side like some western gunman. A rifle was cradled in the other arm, and the wide brim of his hat tilted over one eye.

"Well, Mr. Monk, you certainly look ready."

"I am. Now where's this Farley Ochs. It's time we tend to the ugly side o' business."

"We have Ochs. It's Leon Hopper that concerns me now."

"Why? That scraggy cuss ain't nothin' more to us than another fly on an elephant's ass. The man jumps at 'is own shadow!"

"That's exactly what I told Morgan. But he's out here somewhere, and that means trouble. Where's Jack?"

"He and that Dewey boy is down tendin' to the animals. But that ain't all...."

Lowe heard footsteps laboring up the trail and was shocked when Annie Darrow eventually stepped into view. Her baggy denims, obviously borrowed, barely clung to her well-rounded hips, and splotches of dirt on the knees and thighs attested to the trials of her journey. The cuffs of the britches had unrolled below the backs of her muddy boots, and she pulled up on the pants in frustration, like she must have done a thousand times. In terms of filth, her face was certainly no worse than her hands, which seemed caked with all the soil a fertile earth could spare. She breathed heavily, and when she removed her wide straw garden hat to wipe the perspiration from her brow, her hair fell free, all tousled and knotted. She could not have cared less. Appearance was the last thing on her mind, and to Lowe, the sight of Annie Darrow at any place or in any condition was something to admire. She was beautiful, just for being there.

"The children. How are the children?" Annie asked immediately, having been distraught with worry. It was her first, but not her only concern.

Lowe found the term to be oddly inappropriate. Morgan and Sarah were now anything but children, in light of everything they had endured. He understood Annie's urgency, however, and even though he had many questions of his own, he withheld them all until she received his answer.

"They're just fine, all things considered. I left them up ahead." He turned to Silas to clarify his direction. "By the white oak tree," he said. The old man nodded.

"What exactly has happened?" Annie inquired further, thinking the ordeal must now be over.

"It's a long story, Annie, perhaps one you should hear from them. And I have to warn you, it may not have the ending even yet. Can you wait a while longer?"

Lowe's response, or perhaps his mere physical presence, had a restorative effect on the woman's dwindling strength and faltering spirit. She stood witnessing his utter exhaustion, but still, in those hollow eyes, she saw resolve and confidence. Though he was worn beyond capacity, there was more to be done for the safety of her children. Lowe had given his word, and nothing short of death would have him break it. Annie held fast to her faith in the man, and that was enough for now.

"Of course, I can wait, if you want me to," she responded. "Just as well, it might do Sarah some good to talk through all this when I see her."

Lowe smiled approvingly and attempted a few short strides to pick up his weapon. Annie noticed how he favored the leg, how he flinched in anguish with every step, and she scrambled at once to support him. For a few brief moments, she held him close. "And you, Mr. Yancy? How are you?"

"How am I? Well, ma'am, I can tell you this much, I'm a whole lot older than I was back there in Devlin, and that's too old to keep running these mountains." With Annie under one arm, he limped to the side of his horse.

The distant report of a rifle startled everyone, and Lowe rejuvenated in the instant. By the sound of the shot, it was sure to be Morgan's signal. Lowe vaulted onto Blu, and after instructing Silas to carefully watch for Leon Hopper, he galloped unwarily back to the thick of danger.

Pain was splitting his skull, and Morgan staggered from the effect. In that moment Farley charged like a bull. With head down and arms stretched out before him, he raced almost blindly toward the sound of shuffling feet and plunged heavily through the air toward Morgan's knees. He wanted to crush them. He wanted to cripple the boy's maddening ability to run.

Farley missed his mark. Morgan had regained his balance and leapt safely aside at the crucial second, leaving Ochs to tumble hard onto the rock. He gasped loudly as the sudden impact expelled the very last of his breath. His hands were gouged and the skin of one kneecap was shredded and rolled back to the top of his wide, white shin. He curled on his side and waited, his lungs sucking and wheezing, his pounding heart shooting blood through the breaks in his flesh.

"You son of a bitch!" Farley cursed. "Stand still and fight me or use that stupid gun of yours to end this. We've played long enough, and I'm startin' to get pissin' mad!" He looked at his injured hands. Grains of sand were lodged deeply in the wounds. Without the slightest show of discomfort, he summarily wiped them on the cloth of his jacket.

Morgan mocked him, "Now you're hurt. That anger of yours can only lead to more trouble and suffering. Why don't you sit back down under that tree?"

"You are sure a cocky one, aren't ya, boy? I'm an expert at cleanin' the smug off of faces like yours. You're about to learn the hard way."

"Well, we'll see. You can deal with my face when you get my rifle, but unfortunately, Mr. Ochs, that will involve time you no longer have."

Suddenly, the rifle seemed unimportant, at least for the time being. The struggle had ignited such an explosive rage that Farley stopped maneuvering for the gun and again drove his large body like a missile. He would not need the rifle to deal with Morgan Darrow. He would rather shatter his bones with the toe of his boot or squeeze his neck until it snapped from a powerful clutch of his hand. He wanted the wind and blood that kept the boy running and jumping and dodging, to watch his bulging eyes as death took away the very last of him.

First, he would have to catch Morgan. Time and again he attacked, only to be foiled by a younger man's agility. But Morgan grew faint with exertion, and in his weakness, he eventually stumbled over the uneven ground. Staggering to recover, he finally caught the full blow of Farley's flying weight, and both men tumbled as one to the foot of the tree. Farley grasped for Morgan's neck, but the boy's hands shifted up to block him. When a large, bloody knee crashed into his groin, Morgan heaved with empty gasps. His wind was gone. His blood was next. Ochs reached for the rifle and pressed its muzzle to Morgan's ear.

In the heat of the moment, neither heard the sound of hoof beats. Lowe pulled hard on the reins, but could not wait for Blu to stop. Swinging from the horse's shoulder, his body flipped as it touched down. He was a foot from Farley's back, and wasting no time to consider his own diminished condition, he reached up and yanked hard on the big man's collar. Farley fell sideways across Lowe's chest, and the two men continued the struggle wrestling over rock. Somewhere in the melee, their weapons were cast into the vast umbra of the tree.

Lowe was first to break free, and he moved toward the rifles with great difficulty. But Ochs was faster and could have passed him had he not preferred a more personal end to the vendetta. He tackled the man, and he again chose to take him with bare hands. His fist came down hard on Lowe's jaw, and for all appearances, Lowe was finished with a single blow. Farley arose with the pride of victory, and then tottered slowly toward the oak. Morgan would be next, and then, of course, Sarah. There could be no witnesses.

Morgan was still writhing with pain when his assailant attempted to lift him from the ground, but Ochs lacked the energy and let him be. His blood lust half satisfied, he changed his mind about the method to be used for the other half. He would end this particular grudge the easy way, with a gun, which he found rather quickly buried in the grass by a low hanging limb. He picked it up, cocked it and with tired, wobbly strides, he returned to Morgan.

"Sorry," he said. "I know ya had other plans, but, well, things just got out of hand, and now I've got to clean them up. You understand."

Morgan looked into the round barrel of the rifle. His mind thought of nothing worth saying. He anticipated the bullet.

Lowe's stirring proved an adequate distraction, and Farley paused to watch him crawl through the thin grass of the dome. Lowe's soul rested on his promise, and as he stood for the last time, he recalled his word to Annie. He had assured her that Morgan and Sarah would be all right. He limped noisily in search of a weapon, all the while holding the attention of his adversary and mustering his own meager reserves.

Both he and Farley could hear the approaching voices. They had to know that the fight was done, but Farley aimed the rifle back at the face of Morgan. Lowe, realizing that his body was now his only weapon, ran straight toward the man in broken steps and hopeless desperation.

Farley twisted slowly and reset the rifle's sight on this piteous new target. He might have laughed at Lowe's senseless waste of valor had he not heard the sudden thud and trailing reverberation of a gunshot. The bullet sent Lowe face down into the dirt.

"Leon? Well, damn my soul," uttered Farley, who accepted Lowe's fate with surprising indifference and who, once again, leveled his weapon against the hapless Morgan Darrow. In that very instant, another bullet ripped through the air and settled hard in the big man's brain. He fell dead before the hills could pass the echo.

Sarah heard the gunfire. The first shot was alarming. The second and third broke her heart. Someone she loved was likely dead.

She ran as fast as her tired legs could carry her, back toward the great white oak and to the side of her husband, but shock now muddled her senses. She knew neither where she was going nor where she had been, but thrashed through the thickets with a staunch determination to save Morgan. His battered face haunted every racing step.

Sarah was 700 yards from her destination when she thought she heard the voice again. It was forceful and near.

"Wait, girl! Wait! Come here."

She almost stopped, but now bewildered to the brink of insanity, she refused the summons and ran all the faster, her hands to her ears, her skirt tearing on the stiff branches of windswept trees.

"Sarah!"

She dared not see who cried her name. She ran from the voice. She was already white with terror, the utter dread of losing Morgan, and nothing, no sound or spirit or body or beast, could detain her. Then she saw the massive oak in the distance, and for one bittersweet moment, she paused. She feared even more what might be there.

The others were now gathered beneath the spreading crown. Farley Ochs was gone, and Lowe Yancy's breaths sounded shallow and numbered. Annie hugged and kissed her son, and seeing he was fine, she moved quickly to the man who saved him.

"Is he...?"

"He should be," answered Black Jack, "but I's afraid we be losin' him yet come sundown." With Dewey's help, he gently turned Lowe over and inspected the gaping wound. "Looks like de lead pass clean through him. I reckon' dat's good."

"That's only good if he ain't lost a gallon o' blood and an organ or two," corrected Silas. "Dewey, git my kit off that mule! We gotta stop this infernal bleedin'."

"Did dat bullet hit dem organs?"

"Hell, I don't know! I ain't no doctor, and I hate playin' this game o' bein' one." Silas laid his hand on Lowe's cheek. "Damn ya, boy, ya sure put me in some tough places. I ain't up to all this. Ya gotta hang on to somethin' more than this ol' man, or we ain't gonna see the mornin' together."

Black Jack rested his own hand on Lowe's chest and felt it rise as it gasped for air. He pleaded with his partner, "Stay stubborn, Mr. Yancy. Now ain't da time to give up yo fight."

Annie dropped to her knees, weak and worried. She turned her head to hide her tears, and while she did, she prayed. It was a wordless supplication, brief and unaffected, and she finished it with a kiss on the wrinkled corner of Lowe's eye. If their time was to be short, she would spend it with this man, not her Lord, and she trusted that God would know the purity of her heart and forgive. She now knew who and what she wanted for her life. In that moment, her most selfish moment, she realized both her love and her loss, and nothing else seemed to matter. Annie looked upon her champion's pale and broken body and wanted to be all that was left for him, his precious time, his final vision, his last fulfilled desire. She took the cloth from Silas' hand and tended to the wound herself.

Morgan was now standing and looked in panic across the dome for his wife. "Where is Sarah?" he asked. "I sent her out."

No one could answer. He knelt beside his fallen friend and spoke quietly, "Where is Sarah, Lowe? Did you see her? Did she find you?"

Lowe moaned at first, but felt relieved at the sound of Morgan's voice. His reply was mostly air, "Morgan, you're all right. Sarah? I don't know." He drifted out of consciousness.

Morgan grabbed his rifle and hurried in the direction he had last seen Sarah. It was he who had sent her away, and now, his feet seemed heavy with the burden of his guilt. He could not run fast enough. He could not see or hear above the sound of his own heartbeat. He yelled for her, but refused to stop even for a second to hear her distant reply.

"Ya best go with 'im, Jack," instructed Silas, as he and Annie continued to seal Lowe's wounds.

"Yessa, you right. Mrs. Darrow, take care o' dis good man 'til I get back."

"I will, with God's help."

Black Jack smiled understandingly, and then ran unarmed across the barren dome in pursuit of Morgan. He found him at the edge of the precipice, hopelessly looking to the wide wilderness beyond. It was Black Jack who spotted the girl. She was racing toward them.

"I sees her, Morgan!"

"Where?"

"Behind dem trees. She comin' to us." Black Jack pointed to a long stand of stunted spruce trees.

"Where?" Morgan asked again. He was anxious. "Where is she? I can't make her out."

Black Jack drew close and pointed again. "Right dere. She be right dere. You see?"

Morgan did see. He saw Sarah running and waving and calling to him, as lovely and alive as she had ever been. He was just setting out to meet her when another figure stepped from the cover of the trees. The man's rifle glistened in the sunlight.

Morgan shouted, "It's Leon Hopper!"

"I can't say for sure who dat is."

"That's him all right. It has to be. He's got a gun, and he's after Sarah!"

The man gradually slowed in his pursuit of the girl, and lifting his rifle high, he fired over her head as if to threaten or draw attention. Perhaps, he simply missed his mark as she bounded over the rocky way. Morgan was not certain which, but he would not chance a mistake. He aimed and discharged his weapon.

The bullet ricocheted across the hard ground. He readied to try again, but this time Black Jack intervened. "Don't!" the older man cried, and put his hand on top of the barrel to forcefully lower the gun.

"What are you doing? I have to stop him. Hopper's killed our friend, and I won't be giving him anyone else."

Black Jack noticed something in the obscure figure. It made him pause. "Morgan, dat man don't want yo Sarah."

Before Black Jack could explain further, another shot rang from the distance. The girl tripped suddenly, and both men, stunned by the consequence of their delay, were left floundering in a surging wave of horror. As a result, neither of them noticed Sarah rising unscathed and continuing her charge across the dome.

Morgan aimed again, and once again Black Jack was compelled to stop him. He pulled the rifle from Morgan's grip before the boy had a second chance to kill. "No! I say no, son. Dis here's one load you not to carry. I'll do what needs done."

Black Jack set the rifle to his shoulder. "Lord Jesus, forgive de sins o' dis yo wretched servant." He squeezed the trigger. The man fell to his knees, then, sluggish and slumped, he slipped forever from their view.

When Sarah appeared at the fringe of the clearing, Morgan beheld no less than a miracle, and he scrambled across the long rock and deep thicket to embrace her. Black Jack fell prostrate. He knew what he had just done, and he wept.

"It don't look good," said Silas.

"It doesn't feel good," replied Lowe. Blood trickled from his lips. His eyes would not open.

"We'll hold fer a spell, but we need to git ya down this mountain. Ya gotta have a doctor, son. I done all I can do." Silas loathed his incompetence. His hands could not heal, and his words were a worthless means to comfort. He was about to lose his only family and was powerless to prevent it. "Stay awake, boy. If ya drift now, I'll ne'er git ya back."

Lowe's eyelids were all but sewn shut. Yet, he listened well and tried his best to stay in the world he knew. When they finally did open, his first sight was of the people he loved. It was reassuring in a way, though their somber expressions might have portended his fate had he not already resigned himself to it.

His body called for quiet, but his friends awaited words. He spoke to give them some measure of peace, “Well, you sure are a fine bunch of souls. I guess this is it, huh? You wouldn’t look so long in the face otherwise.” He watched their smiles form one by one. “That’s better. It makes it easier.”

Black Jack reached for his friend’s calloused hand. It was bloodstained and weak. “Is you ready, Mr. Yancy?”

“You mean to die?” Lowe never knew Black Jack to mince words about religion.

“I prefers to think on it as headin’ home.”

“You would.” Lowe tried to chuckle, but he coughed. It left him breathless for a moment.

“I never been more serious. Never.” With a forefinger and thumb, the man swabbed the moisture from the corners of his eyes. He stared down at Lowe with stubborn patience while he awaited a more appropriate reply. Lowe understood.

“Jack, I am home. This tree above me and the rock beneath me are my home. You know that. They’re my heaven. Where shall I go?”

“To de Lord, if he be callin’.”

“As sure as I’m lying in the shade of a giant oak tree, the God who built it must be dwelling in the wonder. Don’t you think?”

“Yessa, he here, but is Jesus in yo heart, Lowe?”

“You should know. You’re the one who put him there. I’ve heard him every hour since the day I met you. When he calls, I expect his voice will sound quite familiar.”

“You mock me, Mr. Yancy.”

“No, Mr. Clark, I do not. A man has to believe in something greater than himself. It was easy to like your God, but much harder to need him. When the end comes, I guess we all do.”

“Thank you. Dere be a great comfort in just hearin’ dat. And you…I s’pose you found yo answer after all dis time.”

Lowe looked into the eyes of his companions. “I think I did.” His gaze locked on Annie, and he smiled. “Yes, I surely did.”

He did not want to leave them. He tried to memorize each face as his friends struggled with emotion. Even then, Lowe so disliked being the center of attention. Their silence and mournful stares were difficult to bear, and if he was going to die, he wished to get on with the journey. He was weary, and his slumber, whether eternal or not, would soon be unavoidable. It was the moment for goodbyes.

"I'm sorry for what's happened. I let Ochs go too far, and all of you have been hurt as a consequence."

Morgan argued, "Don't waste your breath, Mr. Yancy. Farley Ochs came after all of us at one point or another. The guilt lies with the dead."

"I've ruined your start in this new life together."

"Nonsense. We're the stronger for having endured," countered Morgan. Sarah cuddled close to her husband to better prove his point.

"Sarah Darrow. I like that name," said Lowe. "I've never known a braver soul than Sarah Darrow. Not one. You are soft and fresh like a mornin' meadow, brighter than the sun that warms the earth, bolder than the breeze that bends the grass. Did I get it right, Morgan?"

"That's how I see her."

"Well, Sarah, you take good care of this man. He finds more than his share of trouble. And Morgan...." Lowe's voice became strained, so he motioned for Morgan to draw near. "I reckon I'm heading down that road my father often talked about, but we'll wait and see. Either way, I want you to know now that I intend for you to have the Big Timber, the trees and the brooks, the Shawnee Scarp, this glorious oak, all of it. Do with it as you need. Cherish it if you can, like I know you cherish your wife." Lowe hesitated. He grunted in agony as he shifted ever slightly on the ground. "I never had a son, but I'd have been proud if he were half the man that you are today."

It was difficult praise. Lowe wanted to offer more to Morgan, but his feelings, even at that critical point in life, were much too personal to convey. He just nodded, and Morgan understood the rest.

Lowe moved through his circle of friends, offering each a token of his admiration. He tried not to, but coughed again. It was violent and painful. Annie and Black Jack repositioned him, and he began to breathe easier.

"Don't talk, boy, if it pains ya so," said Silas.

"I'll be resting soon enough. Let me just finish what needs said. You are a beautiful lot, being together like this." He patted Silas's arm. "Even you, you cantankerous old coot. I'd be wasting words trying to spell it out, but you know my feelings for you."

Silas tried to smile. His missing teeth always gave Lowe cause for laughter. "I'm right fond o' ya, son. Knowin' ya all these years has been my considerable pleasure."

"For me, as well, Mr. Monk. And you, Jack, it's pretty much the same. Words aren't adequate, are they?" The light glistened from the sweat on Black Jack's brow. "I never noticed the gold in all that brown skin until now. It must've just fallen from that halo of yours. Thanks, partner, for just about everything."

Black Jack squeezed his hand.

When his attention focused on Dewey, Lowe gently shook his head. "You, Mr. Baughman, are one amazing piece of work."

"Is that a good thing?" asked Dewey, a little afraid of the answer.

"I didn't think so at first, but you tend to grow on a man. Listen, son, why don't you marry that Auralee girl, instead of just talking about it? Have lots of children. You'll make a fine father, and I expect you'll enjoy every day of the job."

"I reckon I would at that." Dewey began to sob.

"That's about everyone, I guess, except for you, Annie."

The others looked at the woman now cradling their friend. Her fingertips caressed his unshaven jaw, and her hazel eyes peered down at his, searching the very depth of his soul. She found it weighted with sorrow.

"Maybe you could give us a few moments," said Lowe. His friends obliged him and drifted as a group to the far side of the tree.

"Annie, perhaps there isn't time to put together the right words, but I want to try. This year has been difficult. I've stayed my distance at times, and if I ever seemed cold or uncaring, it was simply out of respect for a mother and a wife. From afar, I have harbored much stronger feelings. I think you've known that.

"I spent over 20 years finding what I wanted and another 20 just throwing it away. I've only loved one woman, and I never could find the will or the power to break that bond. I never had the courage to say goodbye either, because I knew goodbye, like the love itself, would be forever. I chose the memory over the person, and I don't know why."

Annie's tears slid silently down her cheek. She knew all along what Lowe would say.

His voice was raspy and weak, but he insisted on continuing, "Still, I reckon I should have said something. To love so dearly and then simply walk away was the fault of a fool's pride, and I've lived to regret it, time upon time. Every recollection has been a spear to my heart. Every day has been a lie, as I've concealed the loss and the loneliness. It is important that you understand these things, that I held fast to the hope, that I never broke the faith, that I only loved once. Annie, forgive me for this, for hiding my heart and not standing by you as a friend. I loved you then. I love you now. I will love you...."

"Until the day you die? I'll not be cheated again, Lowe Yancy, not after waiting all these years." She kissed his lips. "Don't you dare say 'goodbye.'"

They had to gather the dead. There would be an inquest at some point, once they returned to Devlin, and the best of evidence might well be the bodies themselves. Black Jack, Morgan and Dewey set about the gruesome task, while Silas and Luci prepared to track Leon Hopper.

It would be an easy mission for the old man of the mountains. After so many years of practice, he could read the signs as well as any denizen of the forest. His vision had been steadily declining, but even a blind man could find Hopper's corpse. Of course, where the man might fail, the hound was certain to find the way.

Silas was almost fifty yards away before he turned back. He thought of something that had nagged him for years and realized that no one would complain if he now put the matter to rest.

"Mr. Monk, I thought ya left," said Dewey.

"I did. I'm back. Where'd ya put Lowe's bag?"

"On the other side of the tree. Why?"

"Ne'er ya mind, boy."

Silas rummaged through the loose pile of packs and packages until he found what he was seeking. He unbelted the flap of a saddle bag and reached in for a small leather satchel. He opened it to find the mysterious letter inside. It was aged like parchment, yellowed and folded, brittle and torn. He examined every sentence, as if they were ancient petroglyphs. Silas could not read, and consequently, he could not know what portion of his friend's heart and soul had been poured into the writing.

Annie had remained at the side of Lowe. She was lost in her thoughts and sorrow when the old man approached.

"Ma'am, I reckon ya wanna stay with 'im longer, but we'll need to move on soon. I ain't sure I got the right to hand this o'er, but I'm gonna do it anyhow. Lowe pondered this here paper on many an evenin', and I know it troubled 'im a might."

Annie looked up and was instantly warmed by Silas's caring expression. "What is it?" she questioned.

"The remains of 'is broken heart, I'm thinkin'. I'd have read the blasted thing years ago, if someone had only learned me my words, but you go on and read it to yerself. I know now that Lowe would want ya to. It should tell ya a li'l 'bout this man, maybe somethin' special that ya ne'er knowed before."

Annie accepted the letter, and finding it to be fragile, she unfolded it carefully and read.

*I have seen this day coming and feared it more than death itself. Life without you will seem like death, in a way. I love you so.*

*The past few months have been difficult. I have stood still, watching you place a distance between us and the promise of our life together. Like tricks that play upon a sleepless mind, the more I tried to hold you, the faster and farther you drifted until you no longer were there. I have been dying slowly with this vision, and now it is complete.*

*I know you love me. I think maybe you always will. I can never forget that not so long ago we were friends. No, much more than friends, we were lovers captivated by the vividness of our common dream. How I want you to tell me now that all these remain steadfast in your heart, that our future is not lost. I know you cannot.*

*I have little of me to give and nothing that will hold you close enough. So take my blessing, my last measure of devotion, and be a good wife and mother.*

*You touched my soul and upon it left the sweetest memory. And I will love you forever.*

Silas forced a smiled. "Miss Annie, I ne'er knew who that woman was, but I am total certain of 'is stronger feelin's fer you. Ya turned the boy's heart right around, and surely no other can make such a claim. I jist figured it fer myself, watchin' ya set with 'im, seein' the peace come o'er 'im while 'e rested in yer arms. Lowe loved that girl. Most nights I'd see 'im with this same ol' letter. I ain't got a clue why he ne'er sent it, except maybe he thought she'd be back some day. Thar's ne'er been a more loyal soul."

"I thank you, Mr. Monk. That means more than you could know."

Annie reread the letter. She was dwelling on each and every word and had nothing to say for a period of time. She knew that the old man was watching for reaction, that he might burst from his swelling curiosity. Without looking away from the tattered page, she finally asked, "Would you like me to read it to you, Mr. Monk?"

"No, ma'am, it's been private to Lowe all this time. I reckon it should stay that way. Thar's jist some things a man don't share with 'is fellers. And I understand it."

"You've been a good friend to him over the years."

"Well, the boy's meant a heap more than that to me." Silas tried to conceal his emotions, but they showed, nevertheless. "None o' this makes a damn bit o' sense, does it, Miss Annie? Not one damn bit o' sense."

"No, it does not." She was unable to bring him comfort. "God bless you, Mr. Monk."

Silas shook his head in denial. "It would sure be nice, but today, frankly speakin', God ain't off to an admirable start."

The old man walked away slowly, using his rifle, of all things, as a cane. He called to his dog, and with Luci in the lead, they filed out to find a trail of blood. They discovered a good deal of it within a half hour, and Silas concluded that the wound inflicted by Black Jack was indeed mortal. When the red splatters led him to the brink of the cliff, he was absolutely sure of it.

Luci began to pace the rim with new found interest. She yelped and pranced and dropped her head low to collect a scent, then repeated the process with increasing excitement.

Silas looked down to the base of the high escarpment and saw nothing. "Whatcha findin', girl?" he asked, expecting an answer of sorts.

Luci's floppy ears dangled when she cocked her head to one side, as if to admit she was not really certain. But the sniffing and yelping continued frantically, until Silas decided to finish the search at the foot of the rocky crag.

His age cost him time, but he took of it what was necessary to safely traverse the harsh terrain. All the while, Luci came and went as she applied her art of discovery. Silas was alone when he stumbled across the rifle, a .32 caliber, Winchester Model 1905. The walnut stock was cracked, and there was blood both on and around it. More significantly, there were tracks.

Silas stooped down and closely examined the signs. There was no question about a body having landed there. The soft earth beneath a thin layer of leaves bore the imprint, and from there, a narrow swath of turned-up litter cut the forest floor as far as he could see. Whatever stole the corpse dragged it, and whatever dragged it was both fearsome and powerful. It was a formidable player in a sylvan arena where strange and deadly forces continually competed for what was often a few mere seconds of life. Silas understood. Whatever it was that took Leon Hopper owned the wilderness around him, which included now the old trapper and his dog.

He knew what to look for, and he found fresh scratchings and prints in the sandy dirt beneath the wall. He was not afraid, but still, he made certain a round was properly chambered in his gun. Luci was nearly a quarter mile away, and Silas could choose to either follow her summons or pursue the newly broken trail down the mountain. It did not matter. They would lead him to the same revelation.

As Silas neared, he could see that his dog was facing off with a mountain lion. It was a mismatch of size, but not of tenacity, and both cat and hound held their ground amidst their feigning and fury. The lion bared its bloody teeth and jabbed it razor claws toward the dauntless canine. Luci may have barked, but she had the good sense to keep her distance. Neither animal would attack, nor would they give way, and Luci held her position until Silas could arrive and spur her on. When he saw the cougar, when he heard it scream its blood curdling defiance, he shuddered and called his dog back to his side.

The mountain lion glared with fiery eyes, and Silas marveled. He had decided then and there that he was too old to worry about dying. Death would come in its own good time, and if the beast was to be the means, so be it. What could be a finer tribute to his life in the mountains than for it to be taken by the natural course of the wilderness? Still, he held his rifle tightly.

The cat screamed again, but this time without effect. The man was studying its manner and features, absorbing all details of a once-lost species. He did not care who owned the forest, or who yelled the loudest, or who was the mightier. Silas only wanted to watch what he once thought he would never see, and his own stares, long and unflinching, eventually broke the fighting will of the great cat.

It moved away reluctantly, with slow strides at first and with its head turned warily toward the man and the dog. Then it bolted with deceptive speed back to its lair somewhere on the Shawnee Scarp.

Luci found the body, half buried beneath the leaves and mutilated almost beyond recognition. It was a ghastly duty, but Silas made himself look closely at the shattered and severely dismembered corpse. Only one side of the head bore any resemblance to a man he once knew, but that was sufficient to determine identity.

"Lordy, no," he uttered, averting his eyes to prevent any lasting impression on his memory. Only in war had he seen such butchery of human flesh. He forced the vision from his mind, as he had done so often across the bloodied battlefields. No one should witness such carnage, he thought, especially his weary, desolate friends who now faced the ordeal of a long, somber journey home.

Silas immediately began to cover the corpse with rocks. He laid them gently, one piece upon the other, one stone at a time, until the primitive grave was complete and inviolable. With a few chosen words, he petitioned Heaven on behalf of the dead, for the sake of a soul he had never come to like.

One ravaged body would not be returned to Devlin, and for a time, only Silas Monk would know of its shallow, mounded tomb.

# CHAPTER 26

The time of the wood thrush had come again, and Morgan listened intently for the trills. He rolled his porch rocker back to a point where it no longer squeaked, then strained once more to hear the dulcet tones. The chair was only part of the problem. The din of the mill and the constant clamor of his young brother had all but destroyed any chance for the evening songs of nature. With an early supper behind him, it was clear what he should do.

"Sarah, I'm taking a walk. Come with me."

"I can't right now. Don't you see we're finishing the dishes?"

Annie and Cora were scraping the plates, while Sarah was elbow deep in a wash pan cleaning them.

"All that can wait. The sun won't be up forever," Morgan reasoned.

His sister resented the argument. "Why don't you help us, and then, maybe all of us can go."

It was a fair request and one that might have been granted on some other occasion. However, this time Morgan chose to accept the barb as a friendly challenge.

"Alas, young love just isn't what it used to be. I would think, dear Cora, that a young woman with over half the boys in town begging to court her could appreciate my situation. I'm rather dismayed by your unsupportive attitude."

"Not near as dismayed as I am by yours, spouting that blarney while the women in the house do all the work.

"I thought you, of all people, would understand. I simply want to take a nice romantic stroll with my beloved bride. Isn't that what you ladies expect of your men?"

"Well, we sure don't expect any help in the kitchen!" complained his sister.

"That's good. Then it's all settled, and I'm pleased to have not disappointed you. Come on, Sarah!"

Annie agreed, "It's a beautiful evening, Sarah. Why don't you two go out and enjoy it while it lasts? Cora and I can handle this."

"But, Mama," Cora protested, "he never helps!"

"He does other things, and we couldn't get along around here without him. Morgan, you know how your sister is. Give her one of your big hugs to make her happy and scoot away before she changes her mind."

"Keep your old hugs to yourself!" cried the girl. She dipped her hand into Sarah's wash water and splashed her brother's face. Then, she scrambled to the far side of the table to elude his affection, only to find that Morgan was much too quick. He wrapped his arms around her and squeezed until she giggled with joy.

"Go!" she commanded. "Just get out of here so we don't have to look at you."

Morgan kissed the top of her head. "Thanks, Cora."

"Yeah, yeah, just go."

"I'm sorry to leave the two of you alone with this," said Sarah, with a feeling of genuine guilt.

Cora smiled. "It's not at all about the dishes. Mama and I are happy to do them. It's about brothers, the most shiftless of all earthly beings. Be glad you don't have one."

"Well, I did marry yours. Does that count?"

"Oh, yes, and may the Lord help you!"

Morgan took his wife's hand and led her out the door. They were halfway up Briar Mountain before she asked where they were going.

"To the park. You know, the little grove up by the school," he replied.

"Why there?"

"Frankly, Sarah, I just want to listen to the birds. We may live in these peaceful green mountains, but all I hear day in and day out is the chatter of little boy monkeys and the drone of great big machines. I want to be someplace where I can tell its springtime."

Sarah did not fully understand, but any invitation to be with her new husband was a welcomed one. His reason was immaterial. On the other hand, his frustration had been growing ever since the tragedy in the Big Timber. Bad memories seemed to haunt him, and he had no desire to return to his paradise. He sought the nature he loved in lesser woods, but found them uninspiring by comparison. Sarah knew that he must go back.

By the time they reached the empty school house, they were well beyond the loud intrusion of lumber mills and children at play, partly because both had finally settled for the day. Melodic rounds now penetrated the quiet, and Sarah closed her eyes to better concentrate.

"Are those your birds?" she asked softly. "They're wonderful. I've heard their sound before, but never knew what made it."

Morgan became thoughtful as he, too, focused his attention. He wrapped his arms around Sarah and listened before he replied, "I would think that's rather typical for creators of fine work, the musicians and composers, the artists and writers, the inventors, and now, of course, the thrushes."

"That's quite true. We may like what they do, but too often don't care who they really are."

"And, yet, they continue their effort despite such anonymity."

"Maybe that's the way it should be, Morgan. Inspiration is its own reward. I doubt the great masters created for the mere want of praise."

"I don't know about that." Morgan grinned. He had come there to wade in the gentle flow of the evening, not to wallow in the depth of some philosophical conversation. "Perhaps they did, perhaps they didn't," he said. "But answer me this one question."

"And what would that be?"

"What in Heaven's name brought us to this inane subject?"

Sarah thought for a moment. The discussion was, in fact, edging toward ridiculous. "Well, I can't exactly recall," she responded. "The thrushes, I guess."

"Ah, yes, the thrushes."

Sarah laid her head against Morgan's chest. The couple stood facing the grove, listening and hopelessly scanning the trees for a glimpse of the spotted, rusty brown songsters. When the warbles resounded across the high canopy, it warmed their hearts like an unexpected gift. A poem came to Sarah's mind. She knew it well.

*The gray mist of morning, the blue autumn skies,*
*The red cast of sunset, a moon on its rise,*
*These were my treasures 'til I looked in your eyes.*
*Maybe someday, perhaps somehow,*
*We might share them, my love.*

"Is that the verse I wrote?" asked Morgan, almost embarrassed to hear his lines recited.

"Yes, yet another creation."

"Oh, come on, Sarah. It was silly at best."

"I beg to differ. It was certainly beautiful to me, and I might add, to 10 or 12 other young ladies in the room. I will never forget so much as a single letter of it."

"You memorized it?"

"Of course."

"How?"

"Cora found a draft in your waste basket. She brought it to me. I read it over and over, pouting like an unloved puppy, wishing all the while that it was written for me."

"I must confess that it was actually written for Arthur Tutwiler, but every word, every sentiment, every ounce of passion -- it was all about you."

"About me? I swear I never knew. Until this very moment, I never knew."

"Well, it's true."

Sarah was moved by the revelation. "I was such a fool, I mean, all that time I thought you fancied Sadie. She swore that the poetry was for her. I became so jealous." Sarah began to recite the entire piece. It was her poem now, and the words fell smoothly from her lips.

The Devlin School seemed to shrink with every passing visit, and on this particular trip up the mountain, Morgan became curious of similar effects inside. While there still was sufficient light, he wandered to a window and peaked over the sill.

"Let's go in. Is the door locked?" he asked.

"No. Believe it or not, it's been left open." Sarah twisted the tarnished brass handle and stepped quickly into the long hallway. She was seated at her old desk in the classroom before Morgan even entered the building.

"Come find your place, Mr. Darrow," she ordered, like a school master confronting a tardy child.

"So you found your own desk. I wonder who sits there now."

"I don't know, but to tell you the truth, I hated this seat. I almost went crazy trying to find ways to turn around, just to see your face behind me."

"I rather liked mine for a similar reason, though it seems a bit more confining now."

Morgan tried to settle, but discovered, as did Sarah, that the furniture was smaller. In fact, everything was smaller, the blackboards and portraits, the windows and ceilings, even the teacher's heavy oak desk. In every other way, the school remained just as they had remembered it, but even after so short a time, it was evident that they did not fit. It was no longer their carefree world. Others had taken their place.

"Do you miss it, Sarah?"

"Not really, but I do remember it with fondness. Daddy once told me that we were just logs in the river of time, floating swiftly and forever away. Well, I believe I left those sweet days of innocence somewhere on the bank."

Morgan paused to reminisce, "For me, it was one particular bank."

"Where was that?" she asked.

Morgan slipped awkwardly off the bench and moved to the

head of the room. He pulled out Principal Tutwiler's chair and made himself comfortable.

"Now that's more like it," he said, and propped his leg on the corner of the desk.

"Tell me, Morgan, where did you lose the innocence of our school days?"

"At Avery's, of course. When I leapt from those rocks to the water below, I jumped out of my childhood and smack dab into life itself. It was all just games and dreams before then, before you."

"Fate has been wonderful to us, hasn't it? All things considered, we are blessed."

Morgan pondered the question. In regards to Sarah, he could ask no more of fate than was already offered. It had been generous. It provided just about everything he truly desired, his wife, his work, his family and friends, his place among the mountains. With the single exception of his father, they were all somehow molded to fit him perfectly. But life was not without its trials and losses, and fate had delivered those to him, as well.

"I can't complain. It gave me you."

Sarah blushed with a rush of passion. She adored the romantic aspect of her husband. He had shown her every admirable quality in a man, but it was his unguarded tenderness that earned him her heart.

"That was sweet," she said. She crossed to the front of the room and kissed him.

"It seems a little naughty doing that in here," remarked Morgan.

"Yes, it does." She kissed him again, this time with even more fervor. "But it's all right to be naughty. We've been wed."

"For some reason, when you kiss me like that, I don't feel so wed."

"Good! Occasional spice helps to season a marriage, don't you think?"

"I can't rightly say. I haven't had time to tire of the old taste, yet. I think now only of Arthur Tutwiler. While I'm all for that spice, I'd sure hate to be the ones caught sparking in his classroom."

"What! Do you really think you're the first?"

Morgan was shocked. "I'm not? Just how am I supposed to react to a comment like that?"

"I was talking about Sadie, not me, silly. Why? Are you jealous?"

"Absolutely not, but I am surprised. Some school boy must have been wearing a smile all that week, and I never once noticed. Sadie Buck is a great kisser!"

Sarah smacked her husband hard on the arm. "I warn you, Mr. Darrow, your wife does get jealous, even if you don't."

He rubbed his muscle. "Yes, ma'am, I expect I'll remember that."

The dusk was alive with the fluting of wood thrushes and some occasional peeps from a tree frog. Morgan stepped away to hear, and Sarah was glad to give him his moment.

"Just listen to this. I love the sounds of a late spring evening. You can't get this in town," he said, mostly to himself. He remained for another uninterrupted minute, and his face seemed to glow with pleasure. "We should take more time to get away. We ought to be camping on such a night. Where shall we go, Sarah? How about to Avery's pool?"

"It's too cold, too far and much too late."

"I don't mean to swim. We can set up on the bluff."

"No, not tonight." Sarah forced a smile in response to his enthusiasm, but she had become suddenly pensive. Morgan recognized the immediate change in mood.

"What in the world is wrong?" he asked out of concern.

Her answer surprised him, "Morgan, take me back to the Big Timber. We can camp on the dome right under the stars, or if you prefer, by the brook beneath the grove."

"Huh? Where did that come from?"

"We need to go back. What happened there was also part of our fate. The Big Timber really is an Eden, just as you told me, and it still exists for us, regardless of the fire or the nightmares that now keep us away."

"Please, Sarah, I'd go anywhere with you, anywhere except there. You know how I feel. I would just as soon cut those trees to the ground, especially that oak. I'll sell them all as lumber and give you the fortune, if you want. We could travel at will on the price they would bring.

"Is that why Lowe Yancy gave you his treasure? To have it plundered? I know you. Anyone but you could do such a thing. If we honor the Big Timber, we also honor Lowe. We owe him that, don't you think? Please, let's go back."

"I just left too much of me out there, Sarah."

"We can find the pieces. We'll search together for what is missing. It has to be there, still, and I wager it lies somewhere beneath those magnificent trees. Morgan, listen to me. It was God who painted that scene, not fate. He was the artist. He created the wonder, and he calls you to come and give the credit due him. That was your point, after all."

"But, Sarah…."

She finished her argument lightly, "And there are thrushes, my love, lots and lots of wood thrushes just waiting to be heard. Please? Pretty please?"

The girl beamed. Her blue eyes shimmered like on the day he first met her, when her face was drenched with river and mud and his heart was faint with desire. They were persuasive eyes, and she wielded them like a sword against Morgan's stubborn resistance.

"All right, we will go," he said, "but there had better be thrushes."

The events of the fall dropped a weighty toll on those involved, and any man or woman who had ever climbed the Shawnee Scarp was now either dead or left to sift through the unpleasant details. Each found it difficult to find any sense in the tragedy, and all were forced to cope as best they could through a seemingly endless winter of high snows and isolation. By late spring, when Sarah offered the invitation, they were ready to travel back to paradise, some as pilgrims to a spiritual glade, some as mourners seeking their peace. There would be strength in their fellowship and comfort in the ageless garden of the trees.

Morgan and Sarah set out a day earlier than the rest, being

anxious to recapture the magic that Farley Ochs had stolen from them. Their excitement grew stronger with every step toward the Big Timber. When they finally reached the dome, they were rewarded with a towering bank of orange clouds to the east and a round setting sun to the west, which they observed intently while both faded into the dark Gemini sky. The thrushes sang to them all the while, until the very brink of night.

"What a remarkable place. Are you glad we came?" asked Sarah. She cuddled to stay warm.

"I really am. I can't believe these stars. They're glorious! I'm sorry I put up such a fight."

"Remember that next time. The wife is always right."

"Well, I wouldn't go so far as to say that, but I have to admit your record is impeccable." Morgan wrapped her head in the bend of his arm and kissed her soft, yellow hair. For the longest time, they watched the twinkling in the evening sky and counted meteors one by one.

Sarah yawned. "I could sleep right here and now."

"Then why don't we? I'll unroll the bedding, and you can crawl right in. We don't really need a fire." He did not wait for a reply, but stood up slowly and unlashed the bedrolls. He spread them next to each other over a small patch of field grass that had grown thick in the lee of the great white oak. "I hope this will do," he said, out of concern for Sarah's comfort.

"It will have to. The only other choice is the cold, hard rock of this mountain." Sarah nestled and cooed like a baby when she finally settled between the covers. "Yes, this will do nicely. Aren't you coming?"

"I'll be along. Just let me find the canteen. I can't see much in this dark."

"And the rifle, Morgan. Don't lose the rifle."

"Oh, yeah, I forgot about your fear of beavers. Rest easy, they don't scale cliffs."

"There can be other things that prowl in the night, you know?"

Morgan understood the allusion. He, too, was anxious about

the possible presence of a cougar. "The bears won't bother us, and if you mean the mountain lion, you don't have to worry about that either. We only made up the story to impress folks."

"It was no story. I know full well what happened."

"And just how do you know?"

"Mostly from Silas Monk."

"Sarah, in his entire lifetime, Silas never stretched anything more than the truth. Yet, you still believe a tall tale like that one."

"I most certainly do."

"But why?"

"I don't know for sure. I guess it's just intuition."

"You must be horrified. I'm surprised you wanted to return to the Big Timber, having heard of the cat."

Sarah scolded, "Frankly, I am horrified, but it has to do more with my new husband lying to me. Why didn't *you* tell me?"

"I was wrong to hold back. I just wanted you to feel safe."

"I am safe." Sarah thought of her own encounter. Face down on the forest floor, exposed and helpless, she had sensed the animal moving around her. Though it lay vague in her memory, the incident was clear enough to be real.

"The cougar won't hurt us," she said. "It's a curious, shy creature, probably more afraid of people than we are of it."

"And I suppose Silas told you that, too?"

"No, he didn't, but I know it to be true."

Morgan was astounded by both her bravery and her careless lack of concern. The thought of a mountain lion being near was troubling to him, to say the least, and he was puzzled by his wife's reaction.

"You're probably right, and besides, it has likely moved into other country by now." Morgan reached to touch his rifle, then, pulled the heavy blanket over him. "In any case, we've no doubt seen the last of him. You sleep well."

Sarah continued to watch the heavens in the quiet that followed. She had almost succumbed to the drowsiness when yet another shooting star roused her attention.

"Did you see that one?" she asked in her astonishment.

"No, I guess I missed it, and I'm surprised you're still awake."

"Barely awake. Were you sleeping?"

"Just dozing. I've been thinking about Ma. I worry for her."

"Why? What is it?"

"She's taken all this very badly, you know. I wish I knew what to do."

"Your mother is a very strong lady, Morgan. Given time, she'll manage."

"I hope so. For some reason, she takes responsibility for Pa disappearing like he did. It's been that way as long as I can remember. She puts the guilt solely on herself, and that's simply not fair, considering all she's done to hold this family together."

Sarah thought for a moment. "There is much here we will never understand. We're not meant to have all the answers, and as much as we might want to, we cannot live other people's lives. Your mother will work this out."

"But she was so close to breaking free. You know, I actually had hopes for her and Mr. Yancy. That must sound strange coming from her son. I truly believe that if Pa had even the slightest contriteness and suddenly came crawling back to her, Ma would still embrace him out of that senseless feeling of guilt. And, then, nothing at all would have changed in her life. Mr. Yancy was so right for her."

"I suppose I agree, but it makes little difference now. What's done is done, and what happened here just seven months ago has certainly wounded her. It broke her spirit. She feels marked, like a punishment for some past wrongdoing."

"Ma's not capable of wrongdoing."

"We all make mistakes, Morgan. We all make bad decisions and pay a price for the error of our ways. Annie's a woman. Don't hold her to a higher standard and force her to disappoint you."

"You are right again, Sarah. I've been doing just exactly as you said." He rolled over to rest his head upon his young wife's breast and awaited more of her wisdom.

"We should encourage her to move on, but at this point in her life, it may prove difficult. She'll be toting some heavy baggage on what could be a long journey, and she might just prefer to stay right where she is at, at least for a while. We must be ready to accept that."

"I reckon I can, if it means her happiness. Still, I would rather her future be one she would share with a man who respects and adores her. I'd wish that for any woman. With Pa out of her life, good things could finally happen for her. They almost did."

"It is sad about Mr. Yancy, isn't it? They must have had deep feelings for each other, deeper than we might imagine. The two of them go back a ways, I suppose. Thinking about him and your father, I find it very difficult to see which life she mourns, the one she wanted or the one she had."

"So what do I do now, Sarah? How do you lead someone you love when you don't know where they should be?"

"You sleep. Your mother will find her own way in her own time."

Morgan tried to close his eyes, but the stars were bright and his soul was heavy. From time to time, he heard the stirring of the wilderness and wondered. There was no cry of the cougar, no patter of animals scurrying by, just the gentle murmur of a girl content. He drifted to the rhythm of her breathing.

Gray clouds draped like a pall over the Shawnee Scarp, quite appropriate to the somber moods and weary feet of those assembled in the valley below. They had come to honor their dead in the place of his final breath. Black Jack watched as a light rain swirled against the high jagged rocks, and he motioned to the small group to gather.

"It be misty on dat mountain. You gonna get wet if we head on up."

"Well, it ain't rainin' here. Why don't we hold fer a spell, fry up some dinner and see what all happens?" suggested Silas. "That sky ain't the kind to last so long."

The others concurred, especially young Jacob, who was thrilled to be immersed in his first camping adventure. He began to collect fallen wood for a cooking fire, while Annie and Cora unpacked the skillet and other necessities.

"What are we havin'?" cried the boy.

The answer came from the direction of the beaver pond, when a hook and weight plunged loudly into the water. 'Bloop'!

"Ahhh, that's the sound of fresh fried trout," replied his mother. It was the boy's favorite.

For some reason, Silas did not share Annie's faith in the fisherman and pulled a piece of dried beef from a sack. He jammed it between his jaws.

"I reckon I'll go on ahead," he mumbled, his mouth still full with food. "I ain't got my legs under me like I used to. Me and Luci'll move on now so's to not slow ya down later." The old man looked at Dewey. "Boy, bring Noggin' with ya when ya come."

"Uh, I'm feelin' a bit slow myself, Mr. Monk. Black Jack'll lead him for ya."

"Naw, that jist won't do. I ain't sure why, but Noggin cottons to ya. He thinks ya understand 'im, that ya got some real feelin's fer the plight o' them four-legged folk. Remember now, he's haulin' fragile cargo. Ya take good care of 'im fer me, ya hear?"

Silas did not wait for the anticipated rebuttal, but, instead, trailed up toward the Big Timber. He delayed calling back to Dewey until he was well under way, "Good luck with that mule, boy!" Everyone could swear they heard him laughing.

There was a much more noble reason for separating from his companions, and Silas Monk wasted no time tending to the matter. He climbed without rest to the base of the palisade, followed it past the narrow path to the dome, and then, slipped back over the hill to an unnatural pile of rocks. The mound was intact. The grave was yet undisturbed. With Luci sitting and patiently observing, he hastily placed more stones upon the site. He also scouted for tracks, but finding no sign of recent activity, he hurried to reach the Big Timber before the others might wonder where he and his dog had been.

The spring had been very kind to the basin. The fire from the previous autumn unleashed a new spurt of green from the ashy soil, and roots and bulbs beneath the dirt transformed the black earth into a snowy bed of blossoms. The lilies and may-apples, trilliums and spring beauties, all arose in their time, and it was the only occasion when the great trees played second to the splendor of the flowers.

The brooks were hedged with rosebay and laurel, which in many places grew dense and swallowed the shallow flows in the deep tangle of their roots. Their white, pink or purple hues at first bolstered the fading colors of April, that of the redbud and flowering dogwood, but by June they were the last and very best of the forest's showy bloom.

Such was the welcome to those who came to admire the beauty and bounty of the Big Timber, and there, by a sleepy brook and beyond the sooty effects of the burn, was the perfect ground for camping. They set tents on the soft, mossy floor, built their fire and talked through the early evening about people and things forever dear to them. It would be a restful night for all.

The morning sun was slow to reach the hollow, and only Black Jack and Silas attempted to move before seven. They stoked the fire and heated the coffee, then prepared for the business of the day. Black Jack pulled a hand sledge and chisel from the pack.

"What's all that fer?" asked Silas.

"To cut a fittin' inscription. I's plannin' to strike a few words on dat rock up dere by de oak tree."

"Well, I'll be dogged. Have ya done gone and lost yer mind? Look at this big ol' trunk. I could whittle the whole damn thing into a marker faster'n ya can chip out yer first letter with that thar hammer."

"You gots yo way, I has mine. Mine be more permanent."

"Huh! This million-year ol' tree ain't permanent? Besides, Jack, what ya think me and Noggin been packin' o'er these hills, river wash?"

"A good question, Mr. Monk. What is you packin'?"

"I declare. Where ya been, boy? I'm talkin' 'bout them markers Miss Sarah ordered fer this here occasion. Cut from real sandstone, they are. She aims to surprise young Morgan and Miss Annie."

"You don't say. Well, dats a right nice thing for de woman to do."

The men were not particularly quiet, and it was only a short time before others began to rise. Morgan was the first.

"Howdy, young feller," said Silas.

"Good morning, Mr. Monk. Good morning, Mr. Clark."

"How was yo sleep, Mr. Darrow?" asked Black Jack. "I know lots been weighin' on yo heart."

"I slept fine. This place has a knack for mending the troubled spirit."

"It surely do. I hopes yo mama come to feel de same way."

"So do I, but did you see her yesterday? Once she stood on that rim and looked down at this grove...well, she didn't speak for the longest time. I was hoping for some indication that she was feeling better about things, that she was ready to move on, but I'm not so certain it can happen. She took his death hard." Morgan noticed the tools. "Say, what's the chisel for?"

"To set down words on de face o' dat dome. You know, a memorial."

Silas interjected, "Or we can carve into one o' these here trees. It be a heap easier than bustin' up rock." He purposely did not mention the sandstone markers.

"That's mighty thoughtful of both of you, but I think I learned a lesson in all of this, a value I took from Mr. Yancy. Nature has what she wants. I'd rather not lay my mark upon this ground, unless it's one she can erase with little more than a gust of wind. Our cabin was a good example. Someday I'd like to erect a stone, maybe here, maybe back in Devlin, but for now, I'm content with my memory. How about you fellows?"

"Dat decision be yo's to make, son."

Annie left her tent unseen, and after bathing her face in the cool waters of the brook, she disappeared amidst the white blossoms and other wonders of the forest. She thought that no one would worry, that they would know exactly where and why she had gone.

Immersed in solitude, she was finally alone with her lingering grief. She had come to the Big Timber, to that primordial heart of the greenwood, just to be rid of it.

There was much to be reconciled. Perhaps it was the guilt, or the years of lost love, or the unfulfilled promises, but she was burdened beyond her strength and desperate for relief. Anxious to be free of her dispirited past, she had one thing left to do, to say goodbye. It had been far more difficult than she imagined.

The walk would give some solace. She was now alone in a grand arboreal cathedral, where massive boles rose as sculpted columns along a dark and boundless nave, where stout limbs of the high canopy crossed to form a vaulted ceiling, and long, mossy logs lined the ground like a matrix of countless, hand-carved pews. The sun cut the morning haze, and with bold, golden rays, it gilded the altars of a dozen woodland chapels. Annie knelt there in their warmth, and with tears streaming across her cheeks, she prayed. God was close. His answer came swiftly. His voice was clear.

Annie heard the footsteps approaching slowly through the leaves, the last one halting just feet away, but she ignored the intrusion, choosing instead to remain devout. Her hands were folded at her breast and her head stayed bowed. Strangely unafraid, she waited until God had said his piece, and then, with her eyes still tightly shut, she invited the words of another.

"I wasn't lost," she said.

"These woods can be dangerous."

"The Lord's been with me. I left to be alone, but I've found God in everything I see here. Still, I never intended to be gone from camp so long."

"It has not been so long, not from camp anyway, but from me, it's been seven cold, disheartening months. You once asked me to leave you. I think now I should have stayed away. It would have been easier for both of us. Ask me now, Annie, and I will go."

"I cannot."

"And I can no longer abide where I do not belong."

"It's not that. Even the children have welcomed you with open arms, with far more affection than I thought possible, but I...I remain torn by this relentless sorrow and regret."

"The children made it easy for me. I wish I could do the same for you."

"You are kind, but maybe it's just too late for the two of us. You deserve much better than what I now have to give."

"You owe me nothing."

"I owe you everything."

Her eyes were still closed. She was afraid to look at the man, lest he sway her wavering feelings. She wanted God to decide her destiny, whether to remain true to the memory or committed to the living. The last time she chose, she chose poorly.

"You need this time to yourself. I just wanted to tell you that I know how hard it is to let go. Even when the love seems gone, there's always enough left for sorrow."

"And for guilt?" she added. "In the end, he just wanted to be loved, to have a home and a family. He died with nothing. He died brutally, and he died lonely."

"But what more could you possibly have offered?"

"I don't know the answer. Perhaps, just a clear and fond 'farewell' some 20 years ago."

There was a lull in the quiet discourse, as both considered the consequences of Annie's choice. Somehow, they knew that they had reached the pivotal point between past and future. For their life together, this was the final chance.

"Much has occurred between us," he said. "I will understand if you choose a different life, but if you decide you again want me, if you come to need me...well, you know how much I love you."

Only her thoughts responded, "I love you, too."

He walked away. The woods were suddenly still, and she was again alone with her prayers.

"Lord, tell me the way, and I will go where you send me," she promised in a whisper, "but please, speak quickly. I'm about to follow my heart back into the arms of that man."

Annie paused for a miracle, a definitive answer from the Lord himself. It came in the form of continued silence. She arose suddenly and cried out before God could change his mind.

"Lowe, come back! I need you now."

The sandstone plates were heavy, so heavy that the men felt sorry for the poor beast that had to carry them. Noggin did not really mind the weight. He had hauled that much and more all the way from Devlin. Nevertheless, he stood rudely defiant until he won his usual concessions of an apple and a long rub with a stiff-bristled brush. After they remounted the pack frame, everyone met at the large oak on the dome to determine a proper placement for the memorials.

"Here," said Morgan. "I suspect it'll be tough digging, but I want them here. This is where it all unfolded from the day Mr. Yancy first brought us to the Big Timber. They may not be true graves, but I believe every cemetery needs a shade tree." His arms spread wide to indicate the height and breadth and majesty of the specimen before him. "And this oak, this great white oak, it is by far the grandest of shade trees. Here, we can sit beneath its sprawling shelter to consider our good fortune and remember the kindness of those who provided it. What do you think?"

There was no disagreement, except from the ground itself. A mere five inches beneath the turf, the shovel bottomed on the granite surface of the dome.

"I can drill dem holes with dis chisel and sledge," offered Black Jack. "It take some time, but dere's always enough o' dat to do a job right."

"Why not move down to that thar grove? The dirt's deep. The diggin' is easy," countered Silas.

"Dat be true. What you say, Mr. Darrow?"

"I guess that would make more sense, though they seem better suited to weather the ages beneath the oak. As special as the grove is, this lone tree anchored to stone seems a more meaningful site. But I don't care."

"I do," said Lowe. "This is the proper place." With a hand-fashioned cane in one hand, he knelt down stiffly and began to gather gravel with the other. "There's lots of this in these rock depressions. We can build up a low, wide pedestal with small boulders and level the top with sand and gravel. The tablets can rest flat and secure in the recess of the stones. Like the tree, itself, they'll still be standing long after we're gone. By then, maybe some young fellow will come along and straighten them. I say we set them here."

It was a fine plan, and the immediate abundance of material and working hands made the effort relatively simple. Within an hour, the pedestal was complete, and the sandstone tablets were set in their place, one at a time, side by side. Black Jack prayed, and they each in silence offered tribute to a childless Shawnee warrior and to a father, beloved still, who had somehow lost his way. There were tears, as Sarah read aloud the inscriptions:

*In Memory*
*The Warrior of the Shawnee Scarp*
*His Spirit Endures*

*In Memory*
*James Lawson Darrow*
*Born at Gauley Bridge, September 4, 1866*
*Died at Big Timber, October 20, 1910*
*He Walks in the Garden*

Some ambled back to the grove, others lingered in the cover of the oak, but at Annie's request, Silas led Morgan and his mother to a sepulcher of rocks obscured by the natural clutter of a wilderness. At some point, another marker might need to be placed. Morgan would attend to that. He would come frequently, and he would always remember both the grave and the man who rested there. Annie waited for the men to retire a fair distance up the hill before she made her peace. Standing alone by the crude, rocky tomb, she knew then that, unlike her son, she would never return.

Annie tried to picture her husband as he once was, before the whiskey broke him and the distrust drove him to near madness. She recalled only the best of him.

"There is no purpose in casting blame. The bullets are spent, and your reasons for sending them have died with you. Whether you were trying to destroy Lowe Yancy or rescue your son from the hands of Farley Ochs may remain a question for some, but I choose to believe in your love for Morgan. It has to be. You now know for certain, Lawson, what you always suspected. Morgan is not of your blood. In the wake of abandonment, I found my peace in another. It is true, but I have no regret about the boy who became our son. Even in your doubt, you loved him more than you could ever hate another man. You would not have killed except to save *your* child. I thank you for being there when he needed you most. I thank you for all that was once right between us, for our children, for my home. I thank you for the gentle times when the fiddle played softly and you, not the whiskey, came to kiss me goodnight. And I am sorry. I'm sorry that we could not keep what we should have cherished, but I shall always hold some love in my heart for you. I just wanted you to know that. God be with you. Goodbye, Lawson."

She hurried up the face of the mountain, and urging Silas and her son to move ahead, she climbed alone to the top of the precipice. Lowe stood patiently at the rim, bracing himself with the aid of his cane. He had come there for her, and now she for him, but nothing so revealed their truth as the broad smiles that now deepened the lines of their dirt-smudged faces. They were free to care. They were finally free to love. Both emotionally and physically exhausted, Annie threw herself into the arms of the man who had for so long waited for this moment.

"You once said the Big Timber was your home, Lowe. I'm afraid that Lawson has it now. He has your paradise, and you have me. Not much of a trade, I'd say."

Lowe smiled adoringly. "All I ever wanted was you, Annie. I've known that for over half my life. This may be Eden, but it was never paradise. Not for me."

Annie was surprised at his reply. The Big Timber had been his dream, and when he finally found his dream, it became his treasure. There was no hiding his ardor for the trees.

"I don't understand. What could you possibly value more?" she asked.

"I do love these green hills, this wilderness, this life. How could I not? But, lately, I've come to realize that paradise is not a place you can visit. It is more of a feeling that visits you, a spirit of peace that sweeps through and possesses the soul. Yes, I do experience it when I stand on this solid rock of a mountain, or sit on a branch of that timeless oak, or walk through that glen of towering trees. Anyone with half a heart would, but frankly, paradise for me is much more deeply rooted in the gentle touch of a loved one or the warmth of a happy home. I have lived too long without these things and now hope to find them again in you. Annie, my paradise has always been the very ground on which you walk. I want only to walk beside you."

Annie kissed his cheek and pulled away. "Come," she said, "we lost some time, but the days ahead have promise." She took the wooden cane from his calloused hand. "Lean on me, Lowe. We have a long, long way to go."

The mountain lion did not succumb, so it rightfully loathed the marks of conquest now being left upon its realm. It pawed at the strange mound of rocks, stacked high by an old man who had dared to trespass, but it only managed to turn a few. Determined, it tried time and again to dislodge the stones, but the effort had little consequence. Some signs of man were simply immovable. Some scars were set too deep.

The big cat could smell the tempest long before it slammed into the high wall of the Shawnee Scarp. From a sheltered ledge, it watched the forest shudder. The wind howled and green leaves fell like summer rain. The woodland heaved and moaned in protest of its plight, but the gusts still ripped mercilessly through its verdant coat and tossed tatters to the ground. When it was over, when the marauding air had finished its plunder, the mountain lion ventured from the lofty lair to see for itself what was taken.

The earth beneath its paws was wet and cool and soft, as the cougar trod slowly to the place of the mound. It sniffed the rich soil and paced wide circles in search of the hated mark. The sign of man was all but gone, almost buried beneath the branches, nearly covered by the storm-swept drifts of foliage.

With keen eyes, the lion saw a distant cluster twirl and plummet down. It looked to the trees for more, but these were the last green leaves to fall.

Lightning Source UK Ltd.
Milton Keynes UK
UKHW011119140620
364911UK00004B/890